MIGHTY JACK and ZITA THE SPACEGIRL

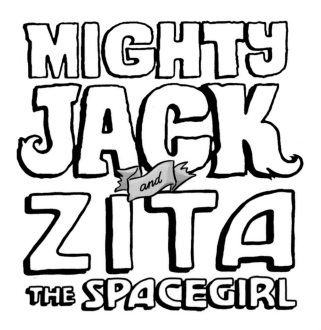

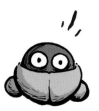

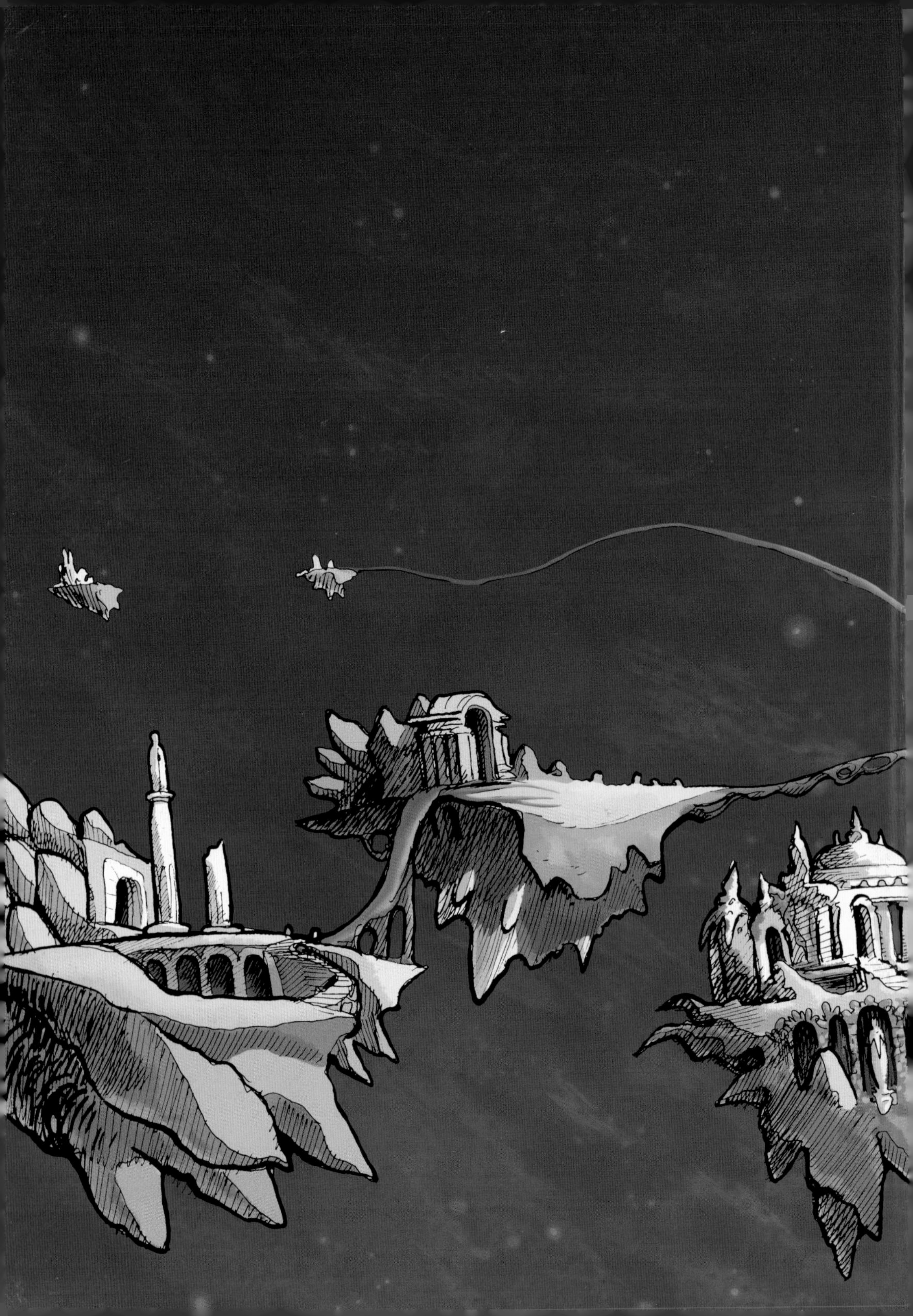

MIGHTY JACK and ZITA THE SPACEGIRL

BEN HATKE

Color by Alex Campbell
and Hilary Sycamore

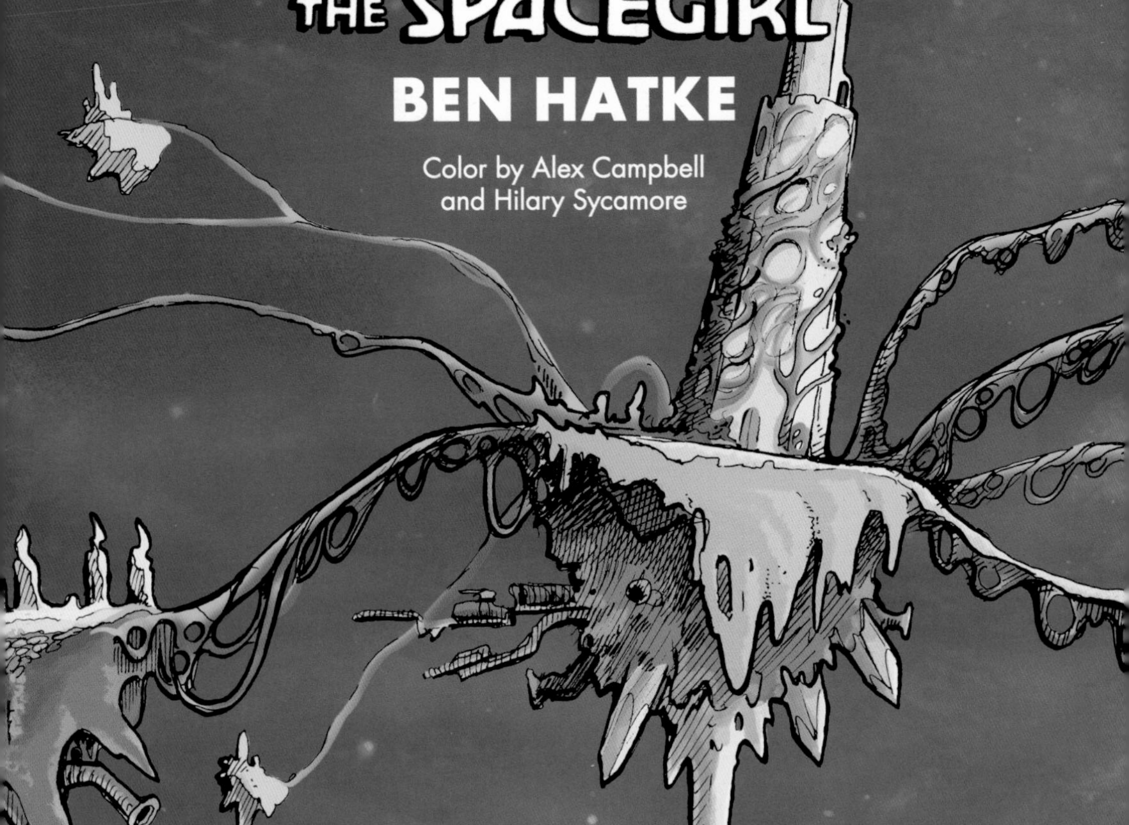

:01
First Second
New York

ZITA THE SPACEGIRL

The lives of Zita and her friend Joseph were changed forever the day they found a red button in a crater in the grassy hillside behind their houses. One press of the button and Zita was on her way to becoming an interplanetary adventurer. It's a life that has brought her both fame and infamy on worlds beyond Earth.

After overthrowing and destroying a corrupt prison planet, Zita and Joseph found themselves back on Earth. Joseph, now a mechanical expert with an alien cape, was content to resume his old life. But, unable to return to her interstellar adventures without a working jump crystal, Zita felt stranded on her home planet. At least she was joined by her friends—the roguish inventor Piper, the circus ring mistress Lady Madrigal, the giant mouse Pizzicato, the gentle Strong-Strong, and the robots One and Robot Randy. For two years they've stayed hidden in the everyday world.

But recently Piper and Madrigal, stirred by rumors of danger approaching Earth, have driven off in search of answers, and a way back to the stars…

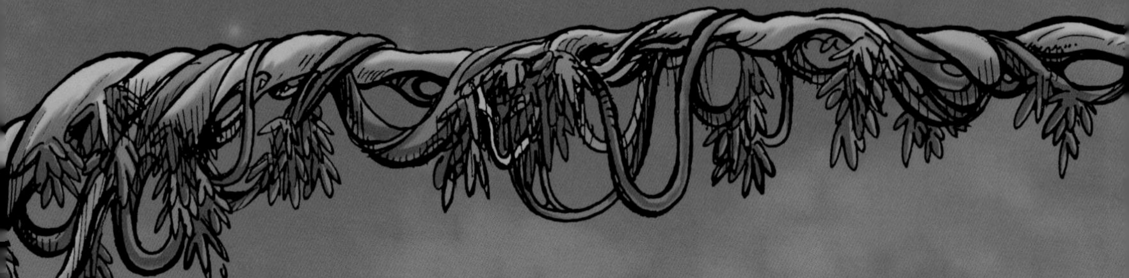

MIGHTY JACK

The lives of Jack and his sister, Maddy, turned upside down the day they took home a box of otherworldly seeds from the flea market near their rural home. The seeds they planted sprouted into a vast garden full of alien flora that brought danger and excitement into their backyard, along with new friends: Lilly, a precocious neighbor girl with a knack for swordsmanship, and Phelix, a dragon with whom Maddy developed a mysterious psychic connection.

But their adventures took a turn when Maddy was kidnapped by an ogre and dragged through a portal in the garden into a pocket dimension ruled by a trio of horrible giants. Jack and Lilly embarked on a desperate rescue mission to the Inbetween and returned forever altered—Jack imbued with powers from the garden's plants, and Lilly taking up the mantle of Goblin King and the ability to shift between human and goblin form. The three young heroes carried on with their lives, burdened with the knowledge that there are other, stranger worlds beyond their own.

And then, one autumn night, Jack and Lilly met Zita the Spacegirl and adventure called again...

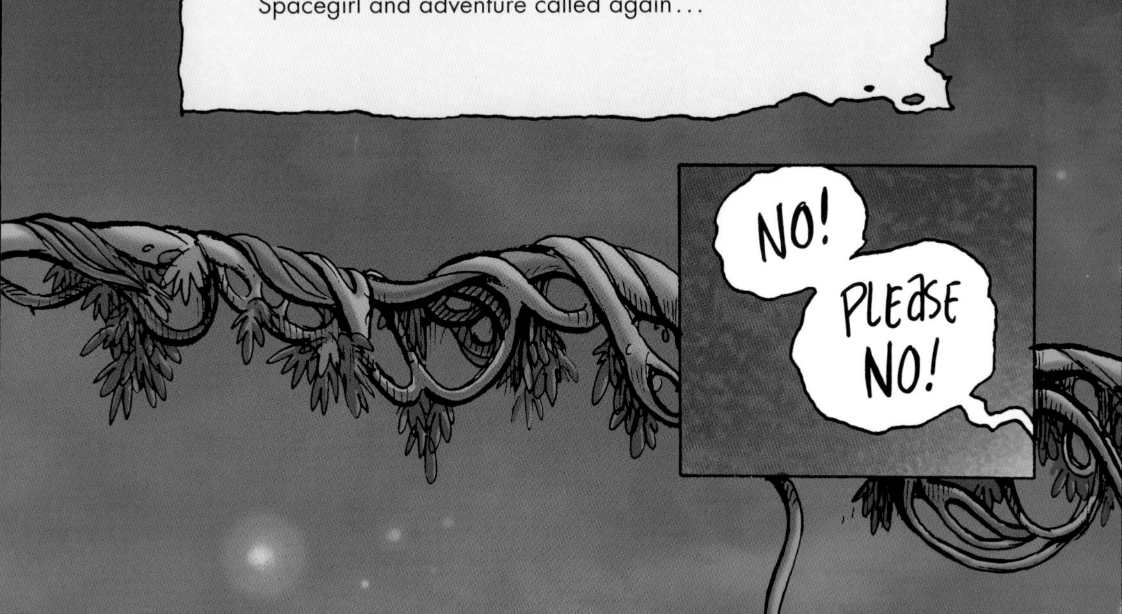
NO!
PLEASE NO!

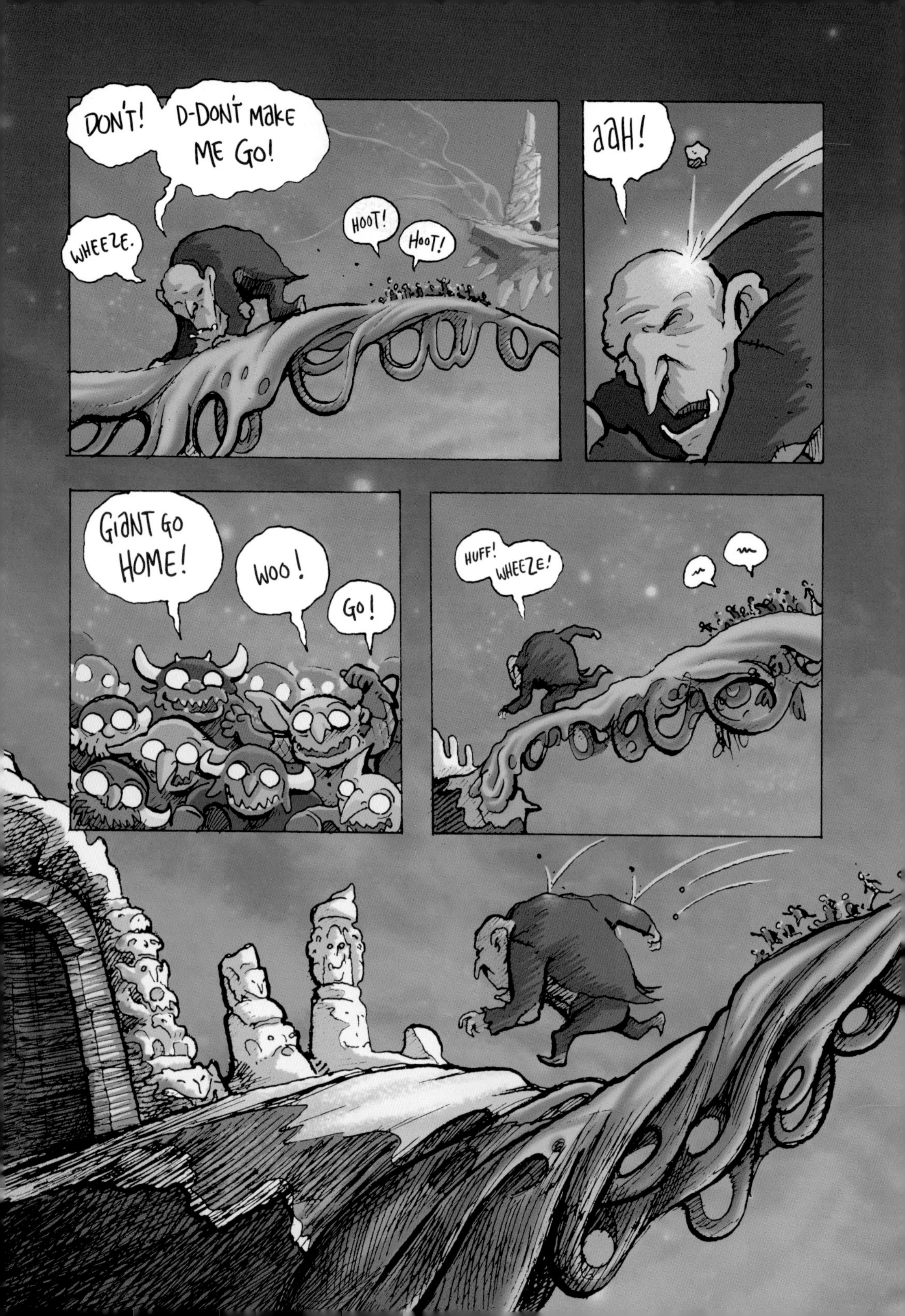
DON'T!
D-DON'T MAKE ME GO!
WHEEZE.
HOOT!
HOOT!
aaH!
GIANT GO HOME!
WOO!
GO!
HUFF! WHEEZE!

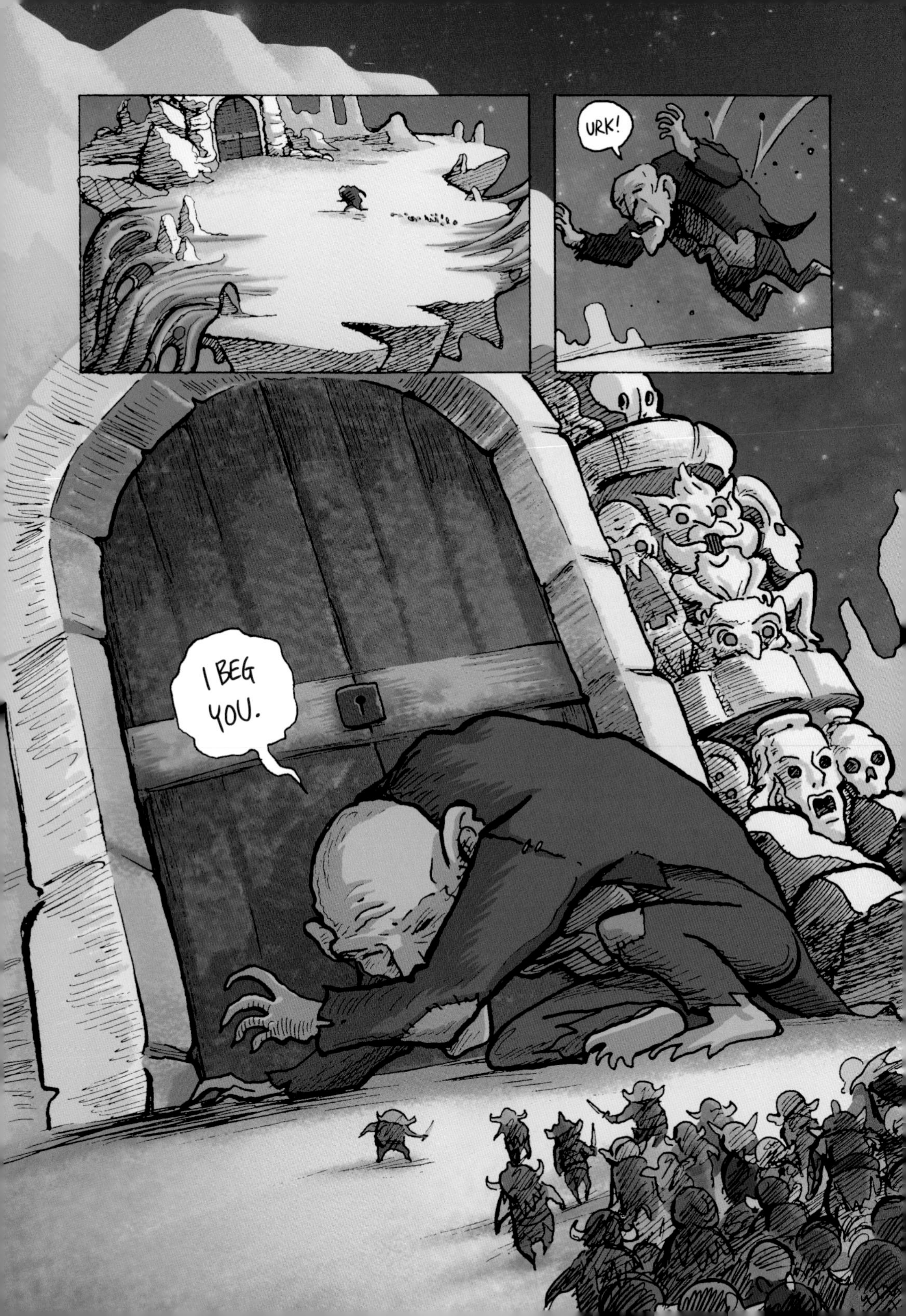
URK!
I BEG YOU.

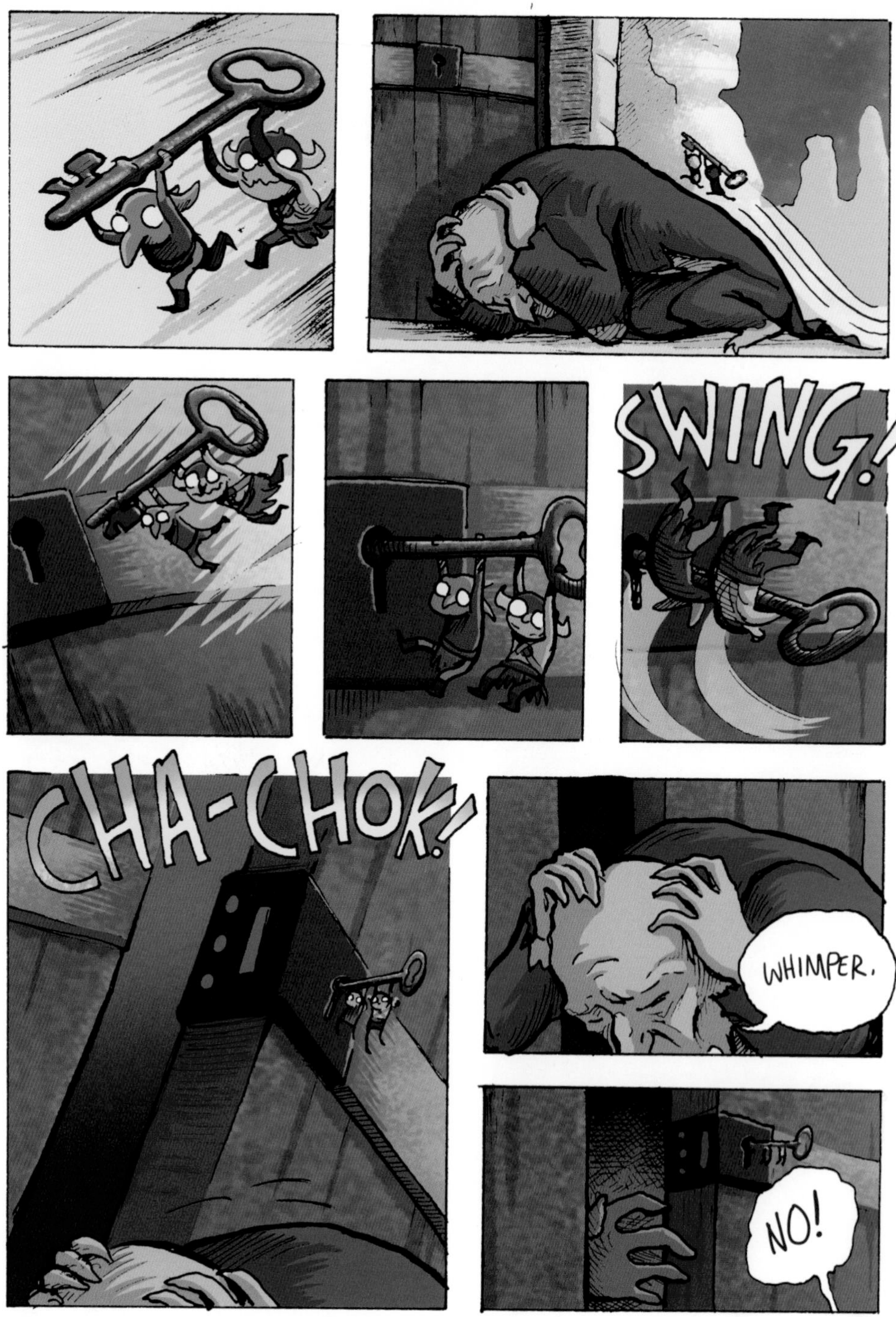
SWING!
CHA-CHOK!
WHIMPER.
NO!

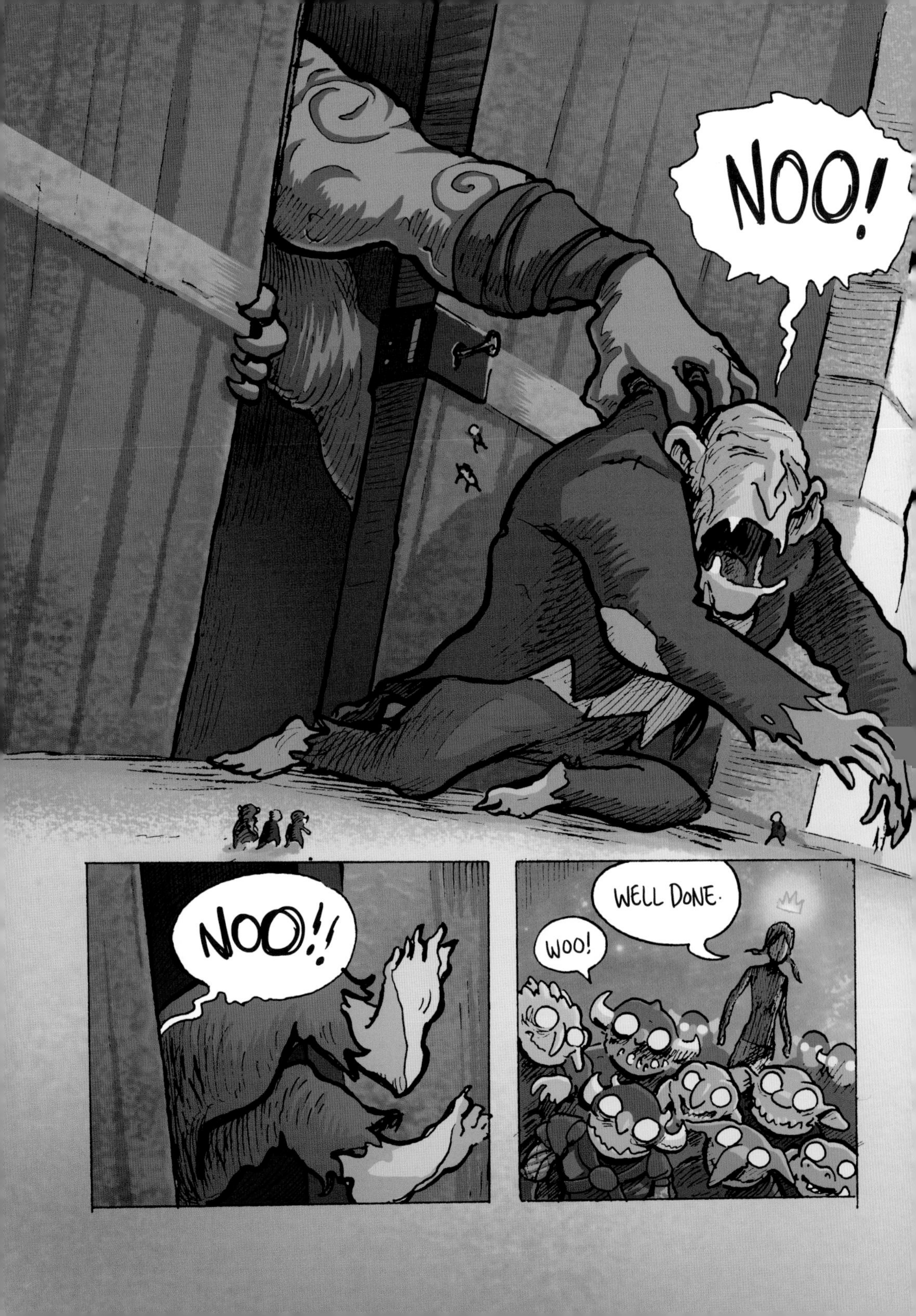
NOO!
NOO!!
WOO!
WELL DONE.

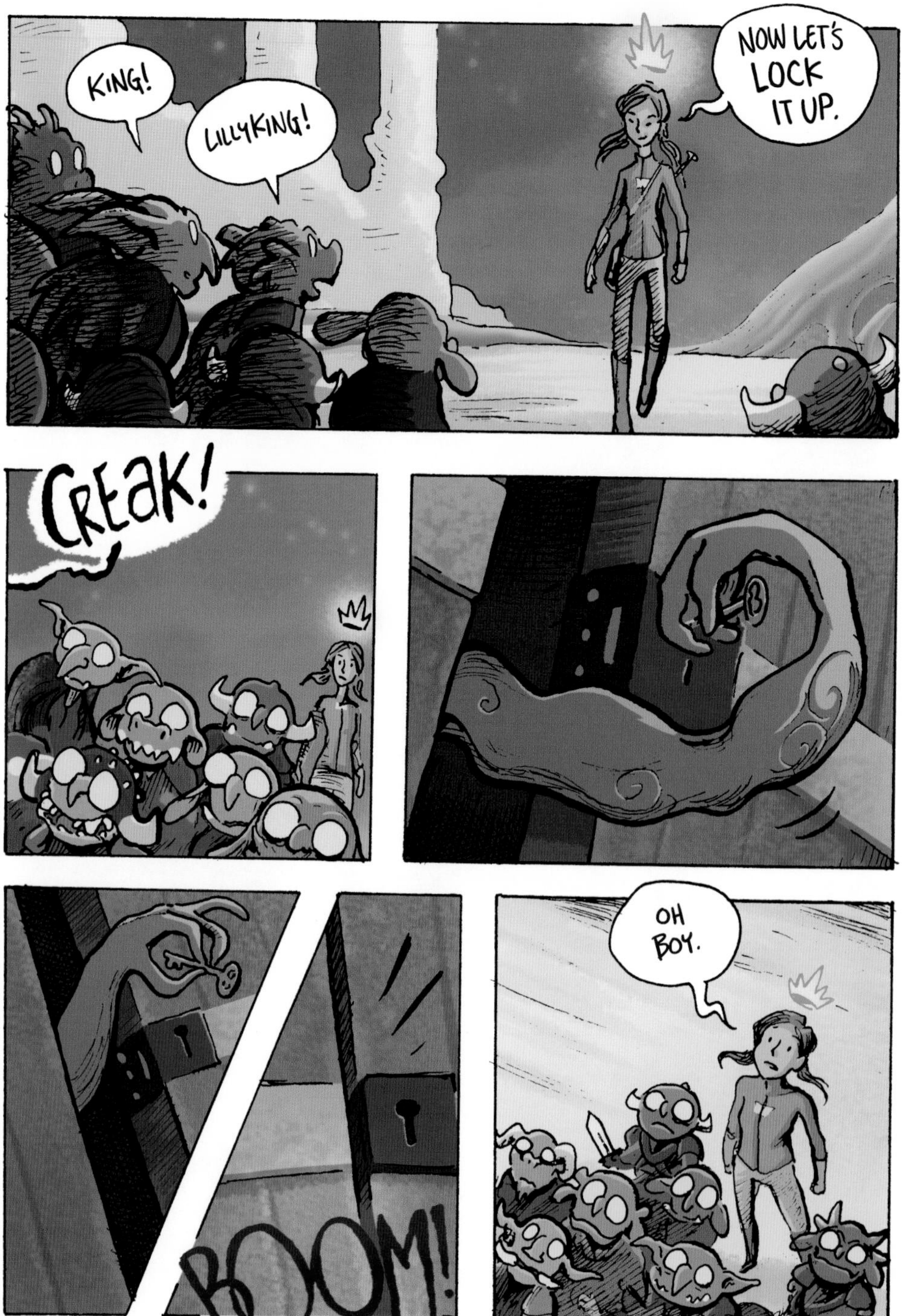
KING!
LILLYKING!
NOW LET'S LOCK IT UP.
CREAK!
BOOM!
OH BOY.

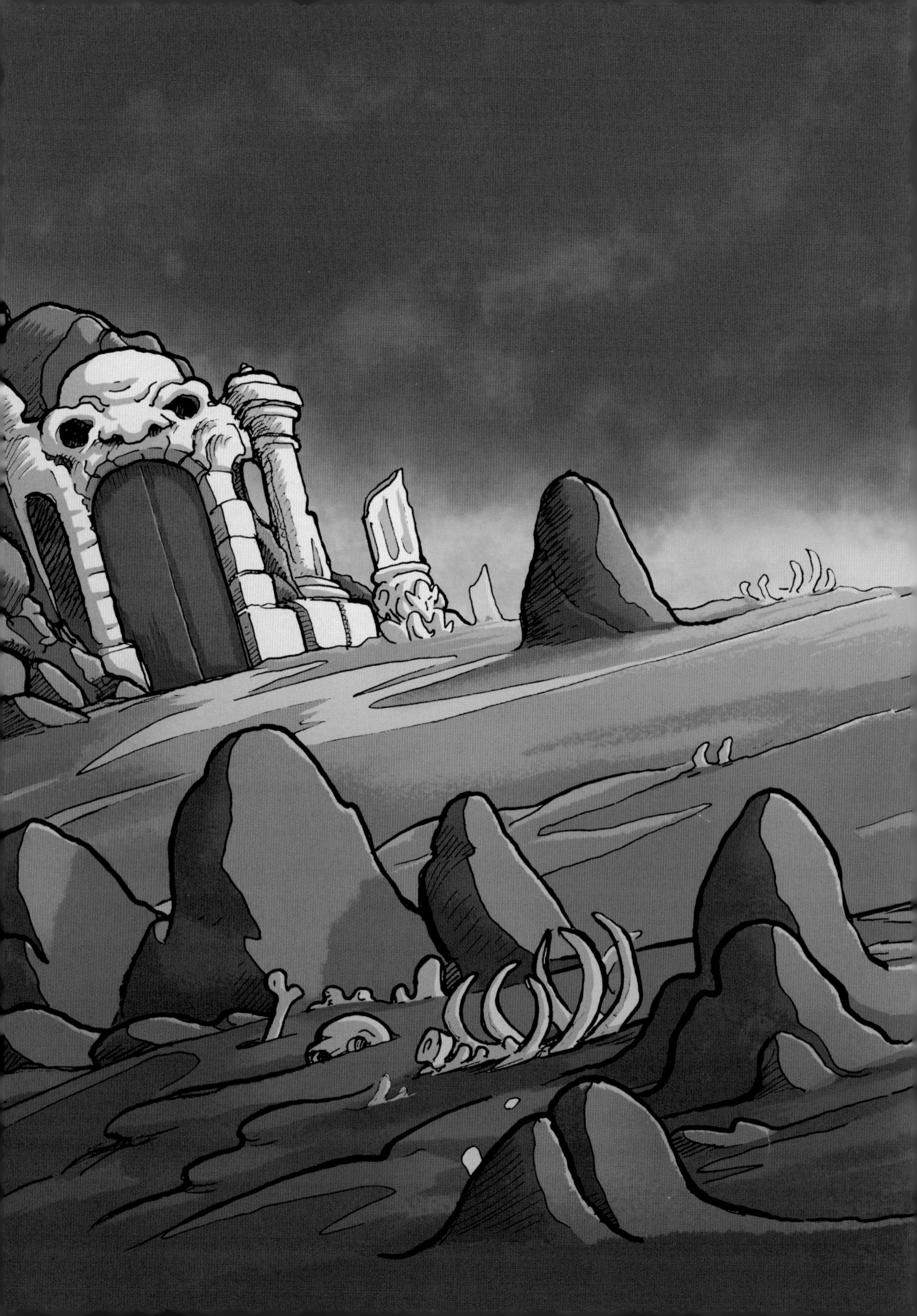

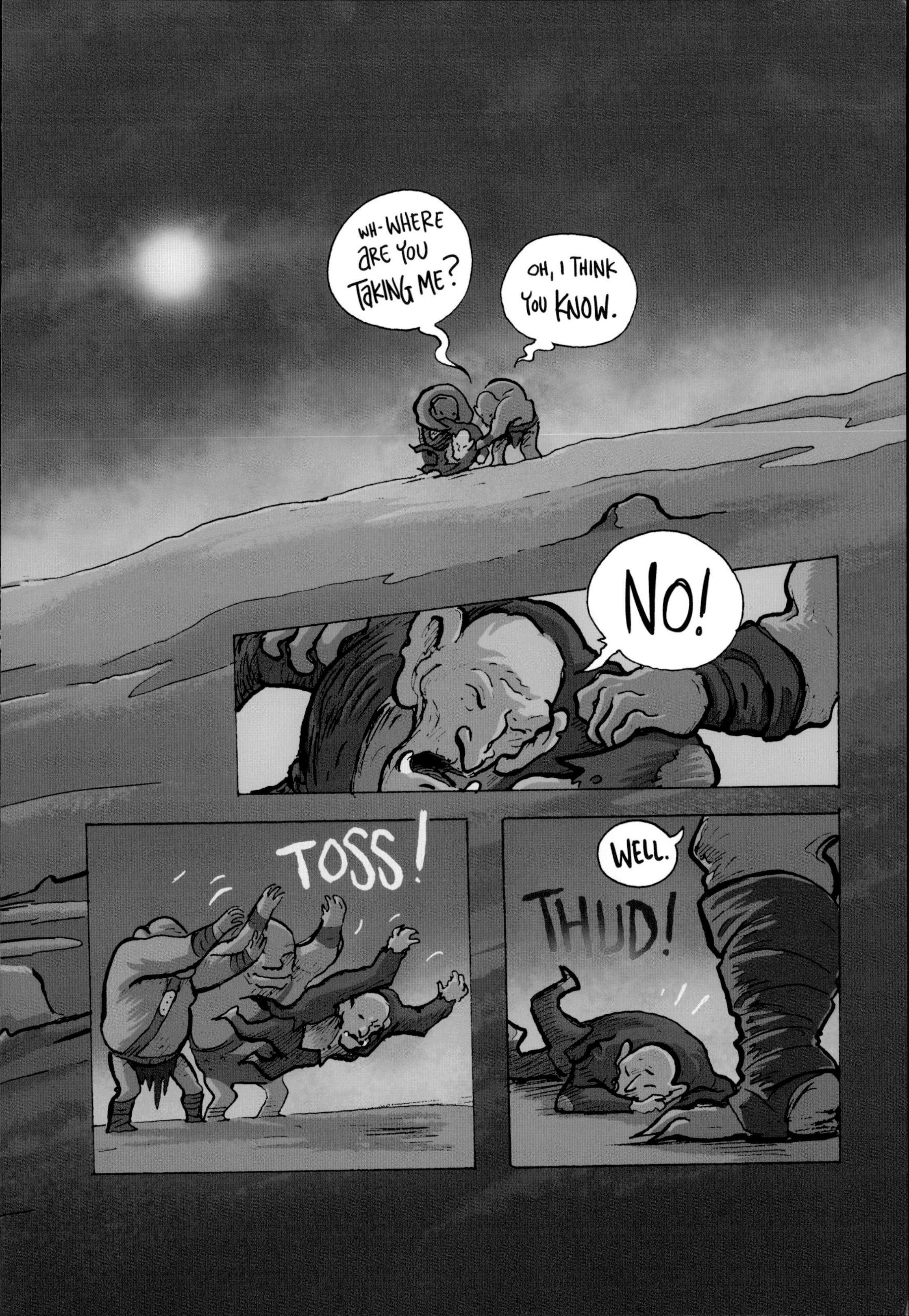
WH-WHERE ARE YOU TAKING ME?
OH, I THINK YOU KNOW.
NO!
TOSS!
WELL.
THUD!

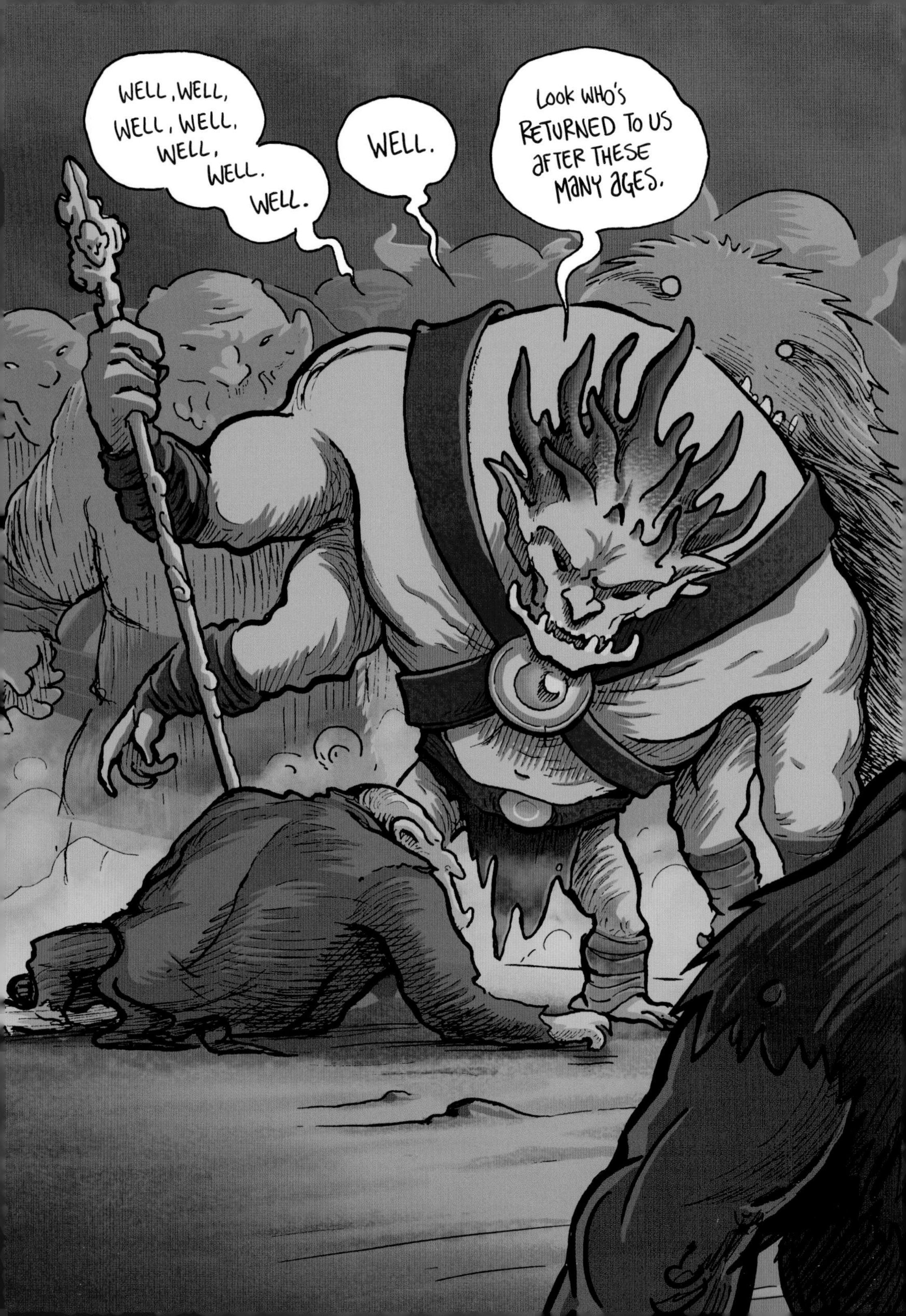
WELL, WELL, WELL, WELL, WELL, WELL. WELL.
WELL.
LOOK WHO'S RETURNED TO US AFTER THESE MANY AGES.

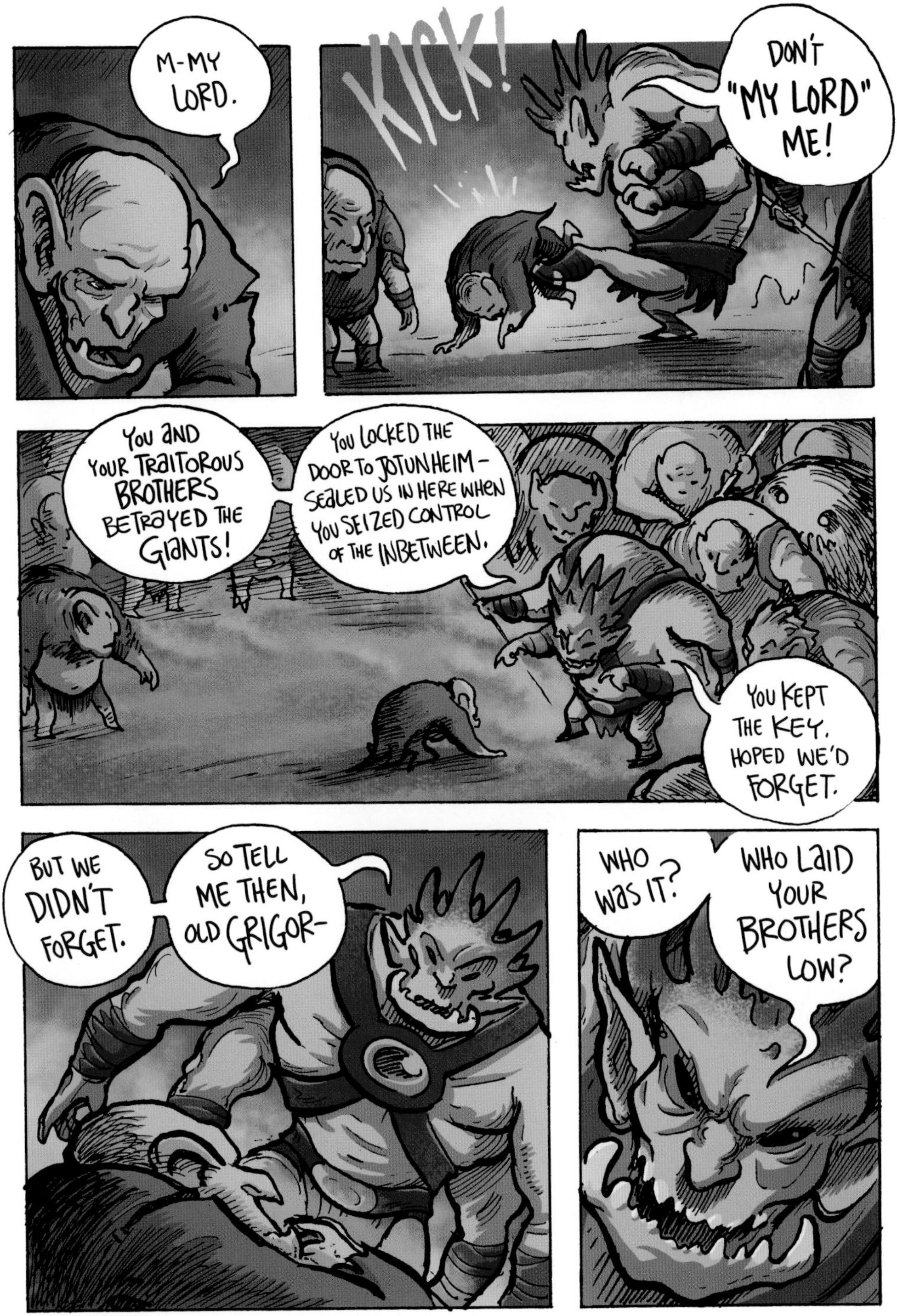
M-MY LORD.
KICK!
DON'T "MY LORD" ME!
YOU AND YOUR TRAITOROUS BROTHERS BETRAYED THE GIANTS!
YOU LOCKED THE DOOR TO JOTUNHEIM—SEALED US IN HERE WHEN YOU SEIZED CONTROL OF THE INBETWEEN.
YOU KEPT THE KEY. HOPED WE'D FORGET.
BUT WE DIDN'T FORGET.
SO TELL ME THEN, OLD GRIGOR-
WHO WAS IT?
WHO LAID YOUR BROTHERS LOW?

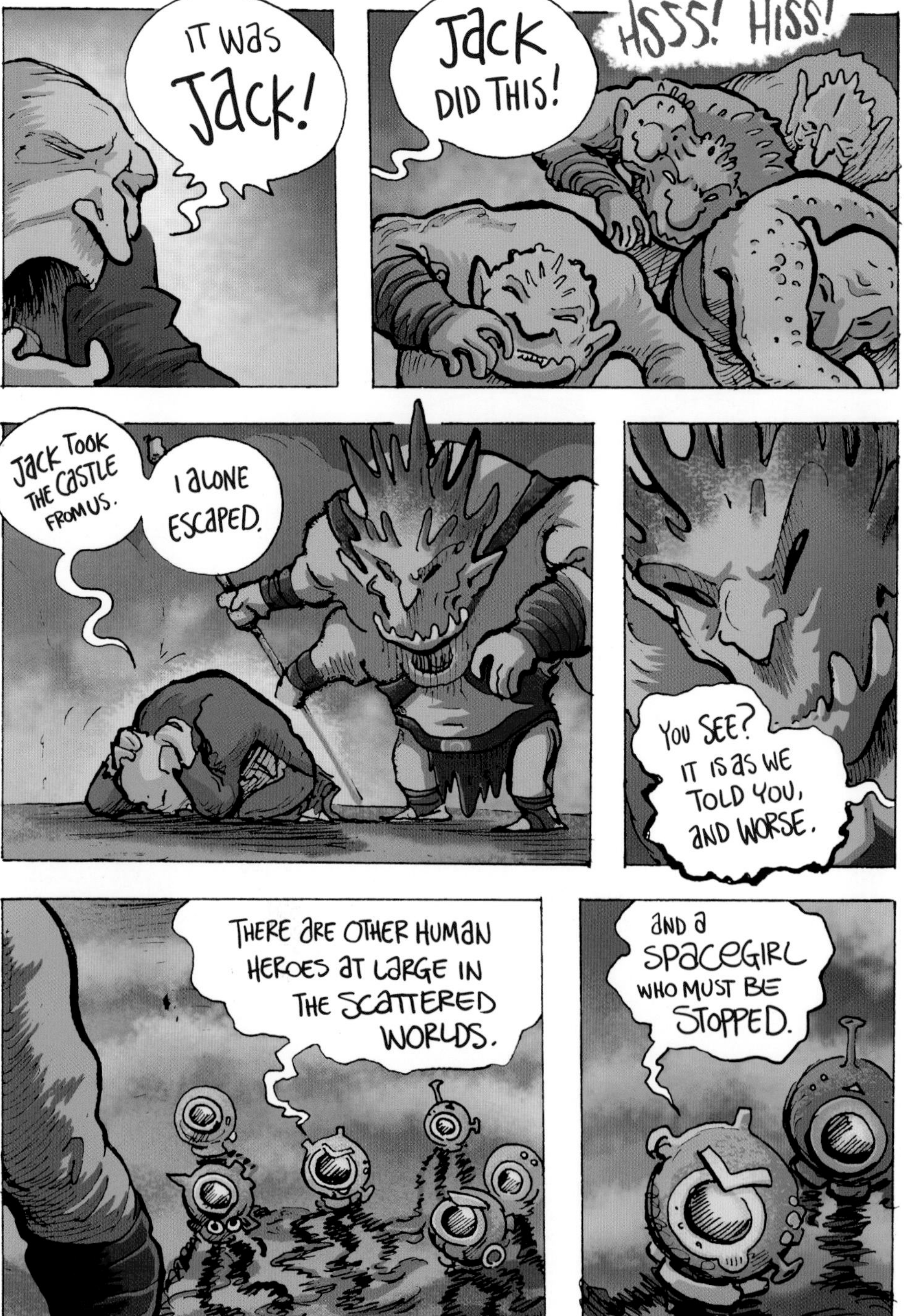
IT WAS JACK!
JACK DID THIS!
HSSS! HISS!
JACK TOOK THE CASTLE FROM US.
I ALONE ESCAPED.
YOU SEE? IT IS AS WE TOLD YOU, AND WORSE.
THERE ARE OTHER HUMAN HEROES AT LARGE IN THE SCATTERED WORLDS.
AND A SPACEGIRL WHO MUST BE STOPPED.

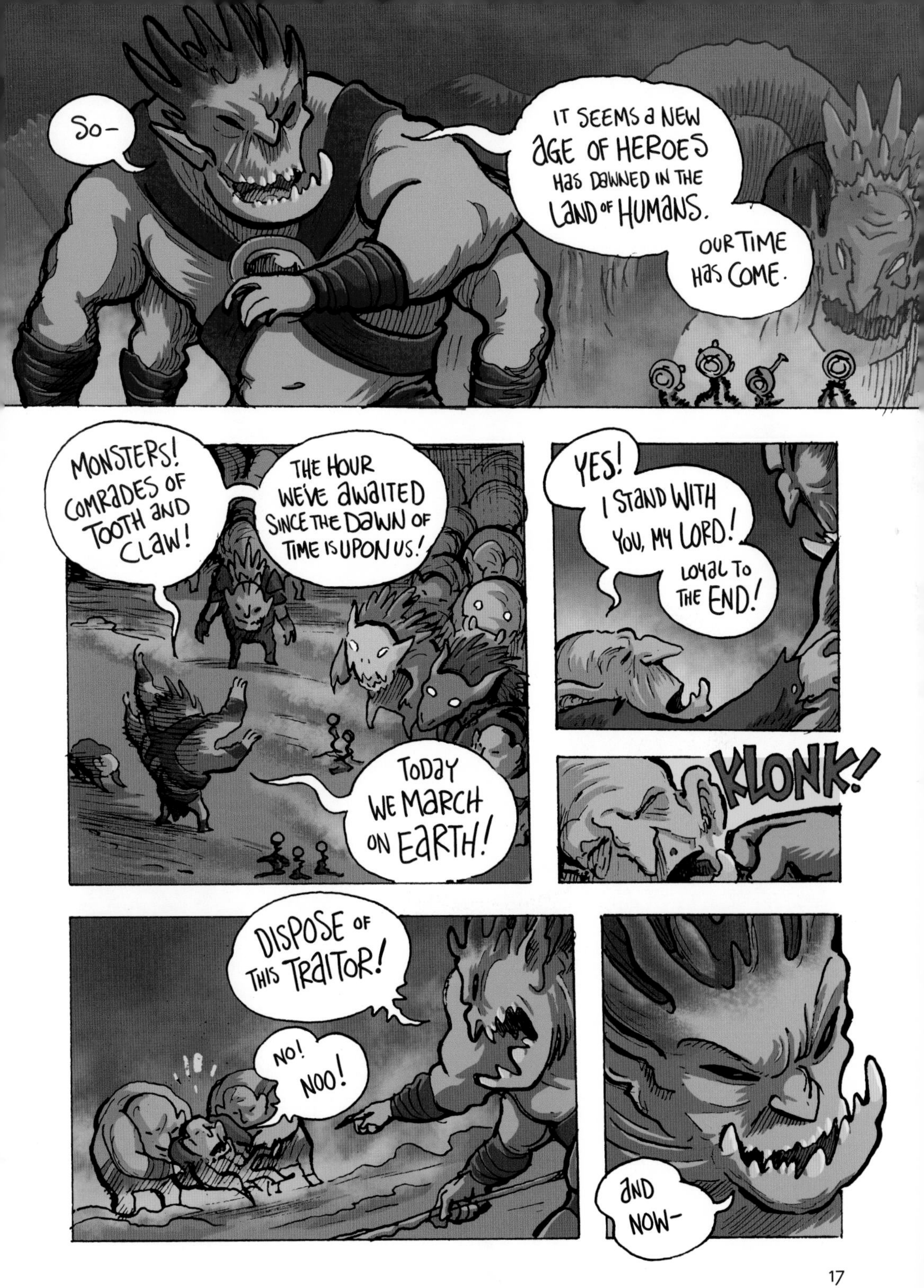
So-
IT SEEMS a NEW AGE OF HEROES HAS DAWNED IN THE LAND OF HUMANS.
OUR TIME HAS COME.
MONSTERS! COMRADES OF TOOTH AND CLAW!
THE HOUR WE'VE AWAITED SINCE THE DAWN OF TIME IS UPON US!
TODAY WE MARCH ON EARTH!
YES! I STAND WITH YOU, MY LORD!
LOYAL TO THE END!
KLONK!
DISPOSE OF THIS TRAITOR!
NO! NOO!
AND NOW-

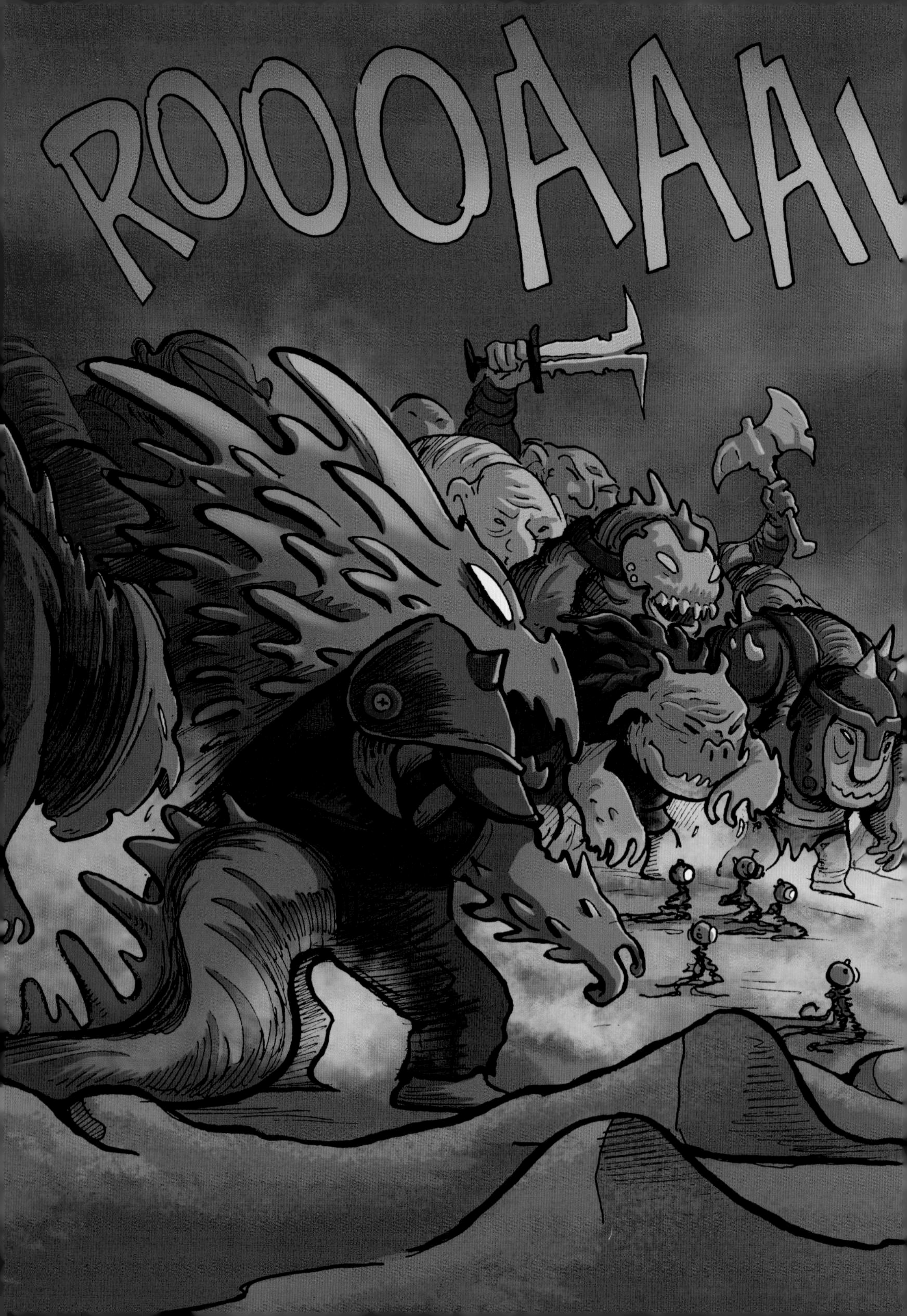
ROOOAAAR

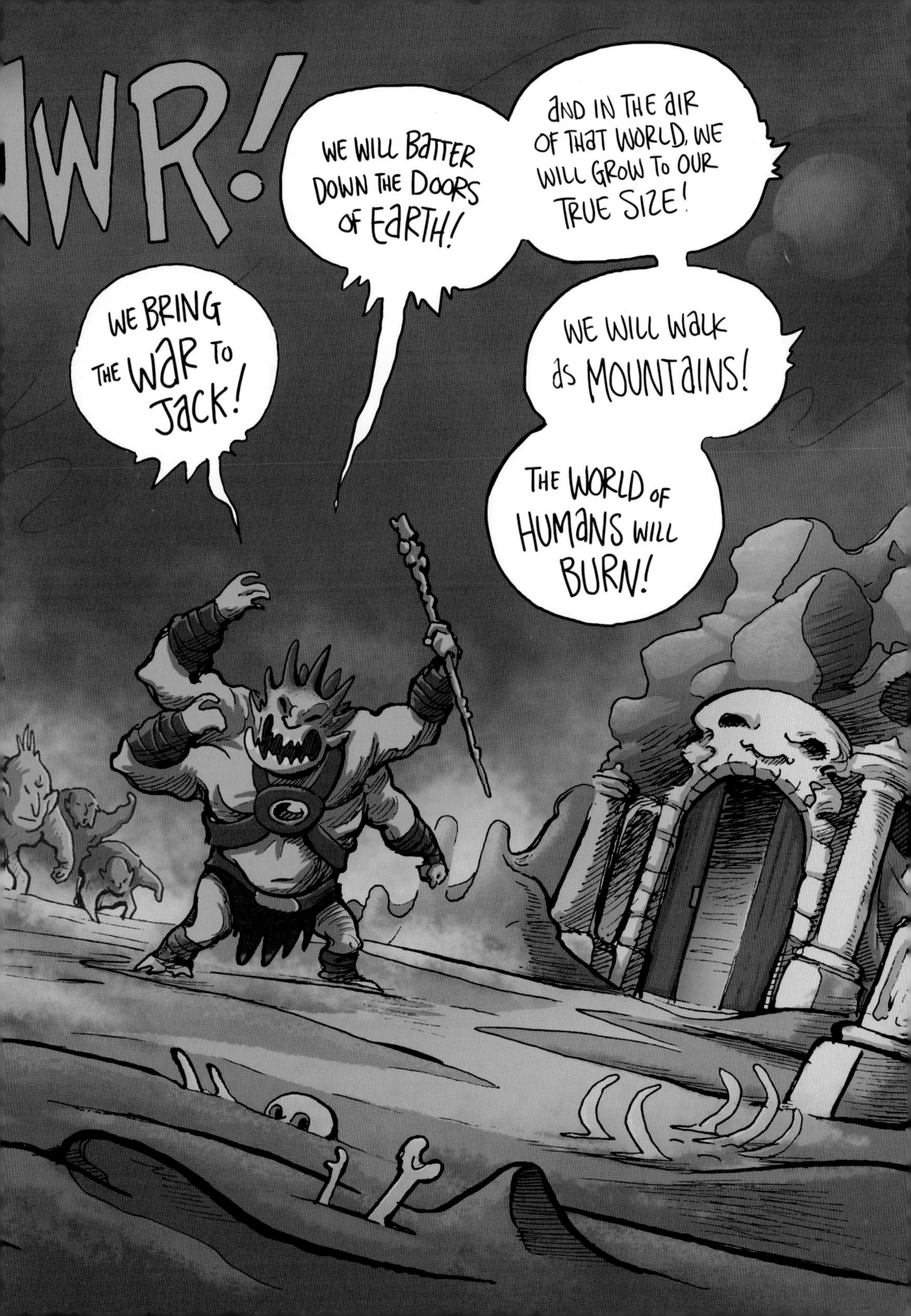
WR!
WE BRING THE WAR TO JACK!
WE WILL BATTER DOWN THE DOORS OF EARTH!
AND IN THE AIR OF THAT WORLD, WE WILL GROW TO OUR TRUE SIZE!
WE WILL WALK AS MOUNTAINS!
THE WORLD OF HUMANS WILL BURN!

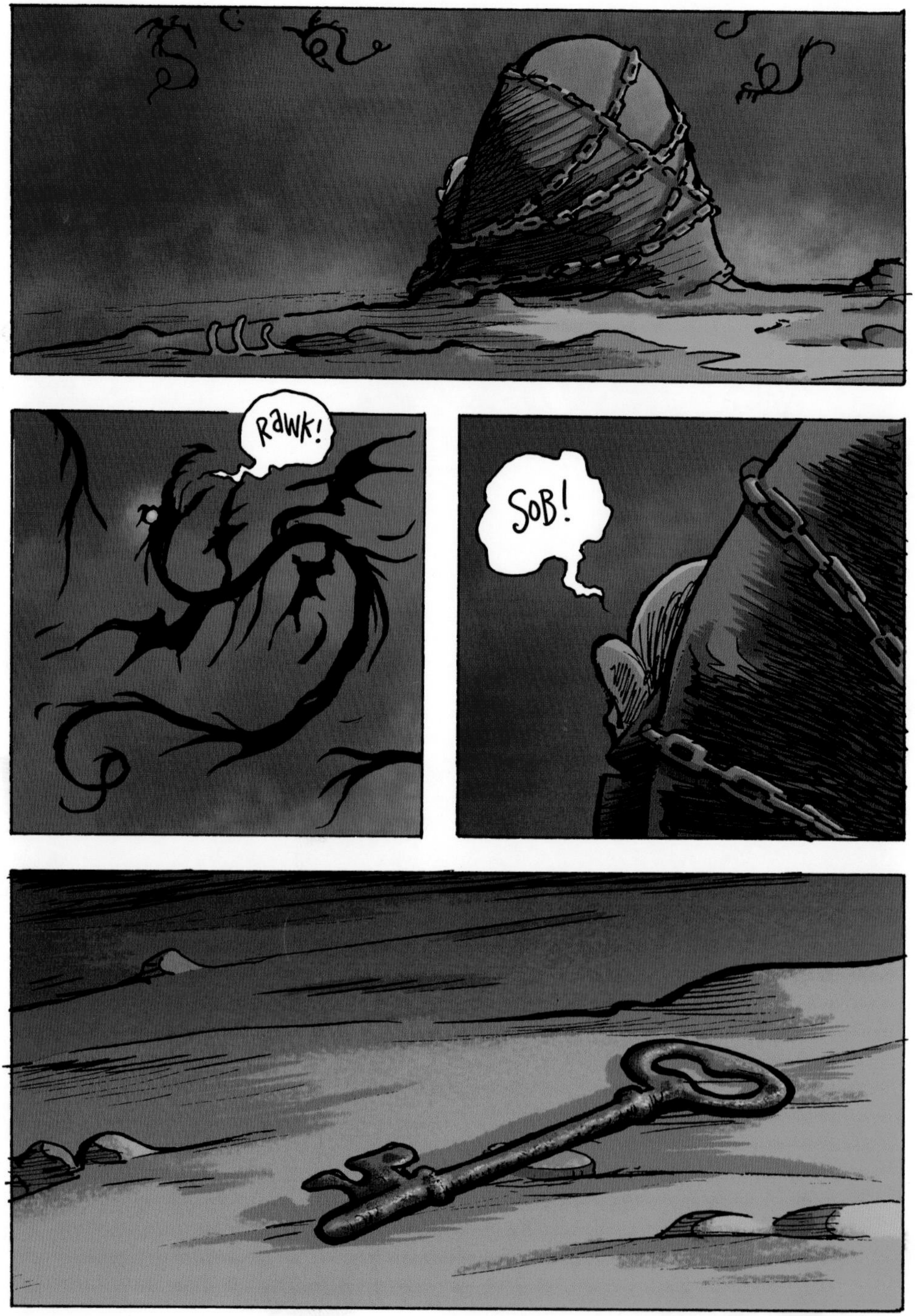
RAWK!
SOB!

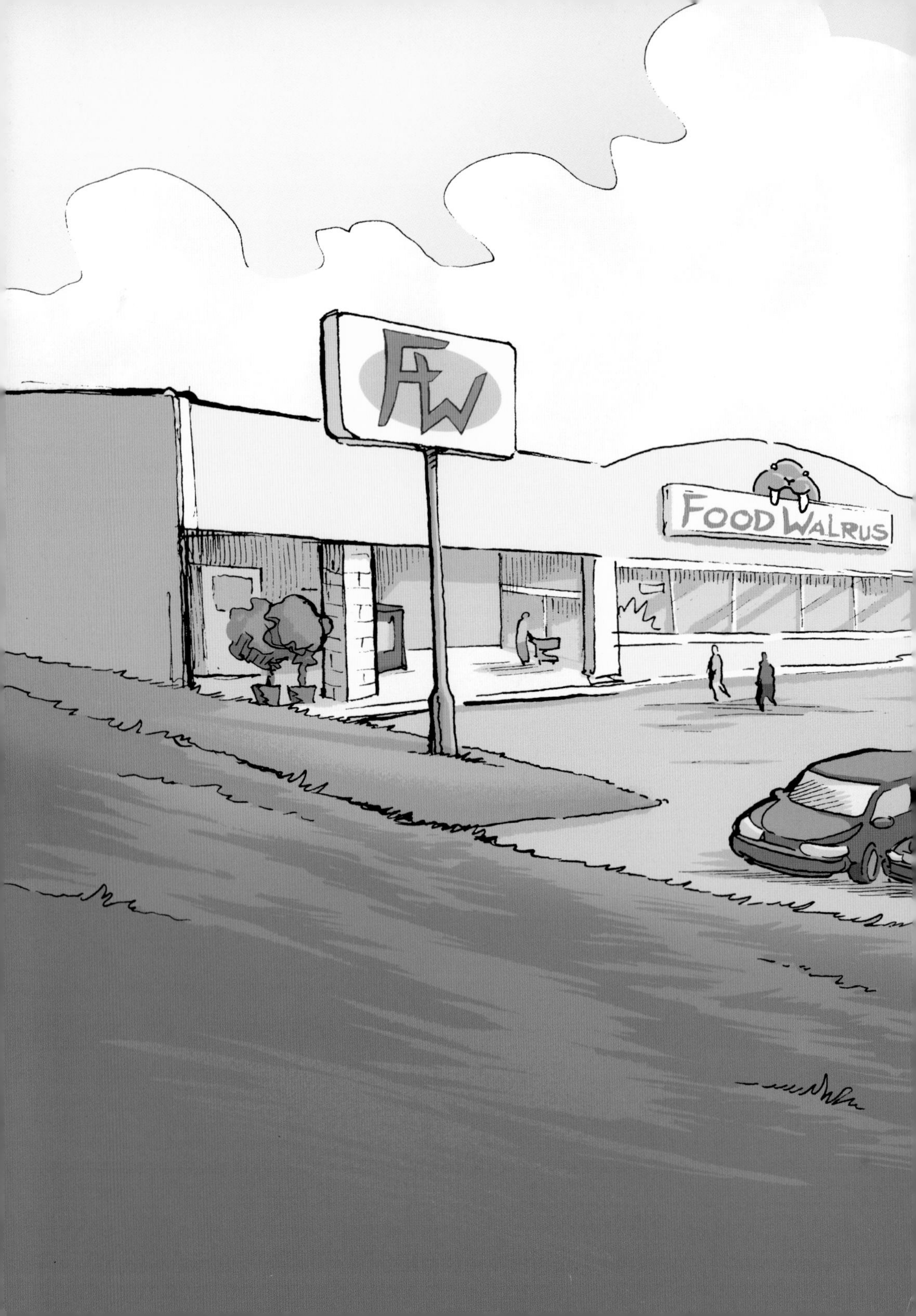
FW
FOOD WALRUS

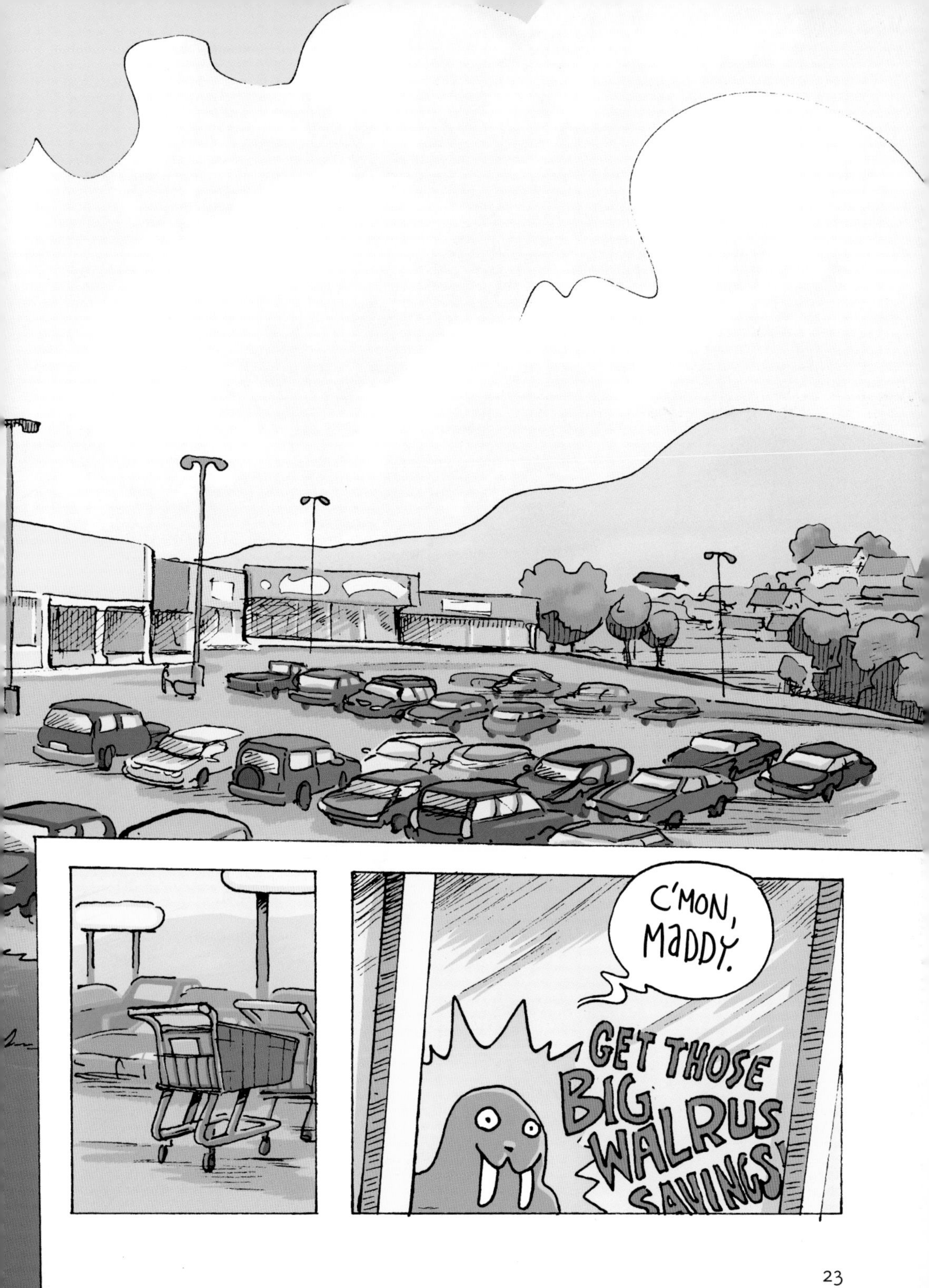
C'MON, MADDY.
GET THOSE BIG WALRUS SAVINGS

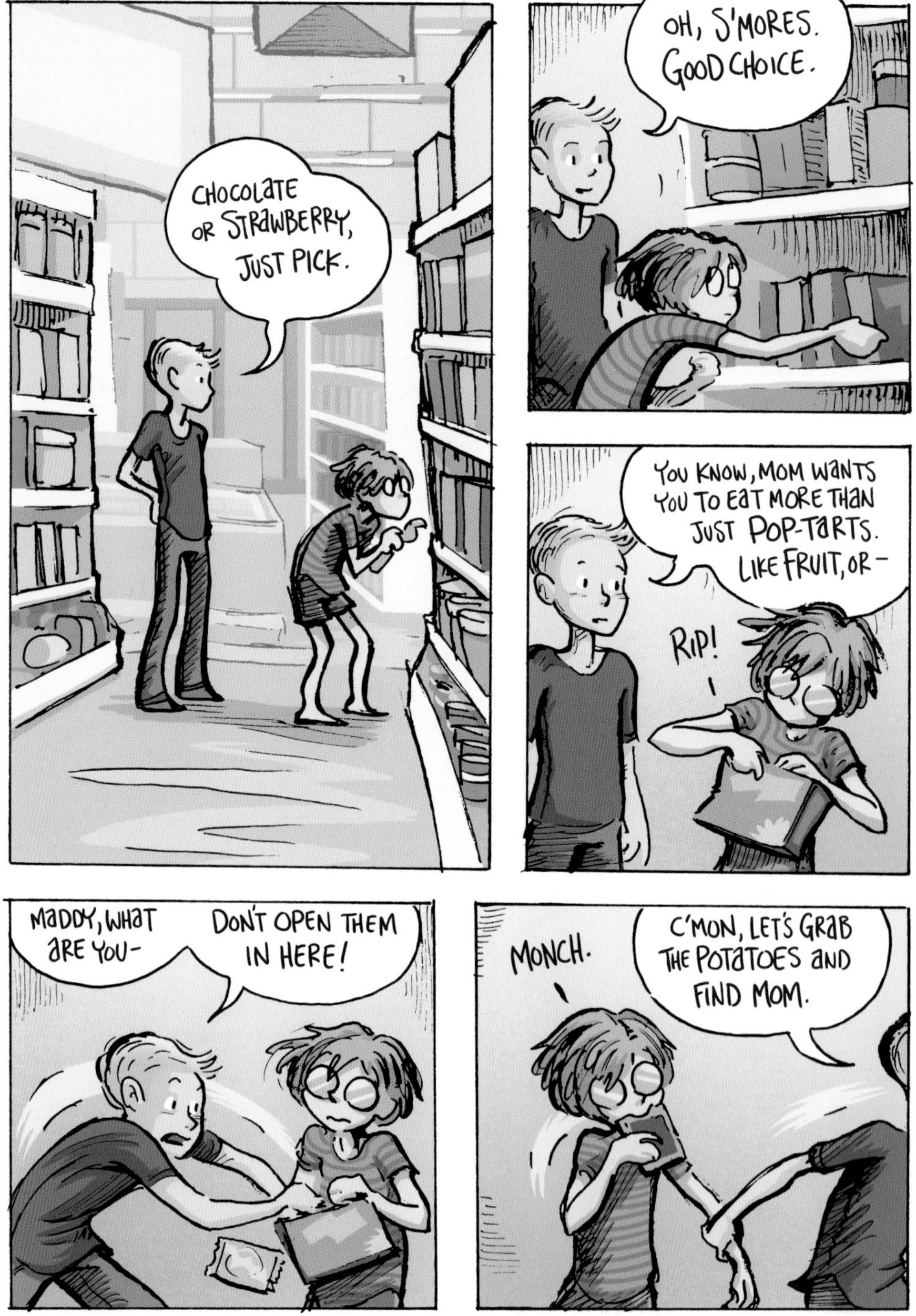

CHOCOLATE OR STRAWBERRY, JUST PICK.
OH, S'MORES. GOOD CHOICE.
YOU KNOW, MOM WANTS YOU TO EAT MORE THAN JUST POP-TARTS. LIKE FRUIT, OR—
RIP!
MADDY, WHAT ARE YOU-
DON'T OPEN THEM IN HERE!
MONCH.
C'MON, LET'S GRAB THE POTATOES AND FIND MOM.

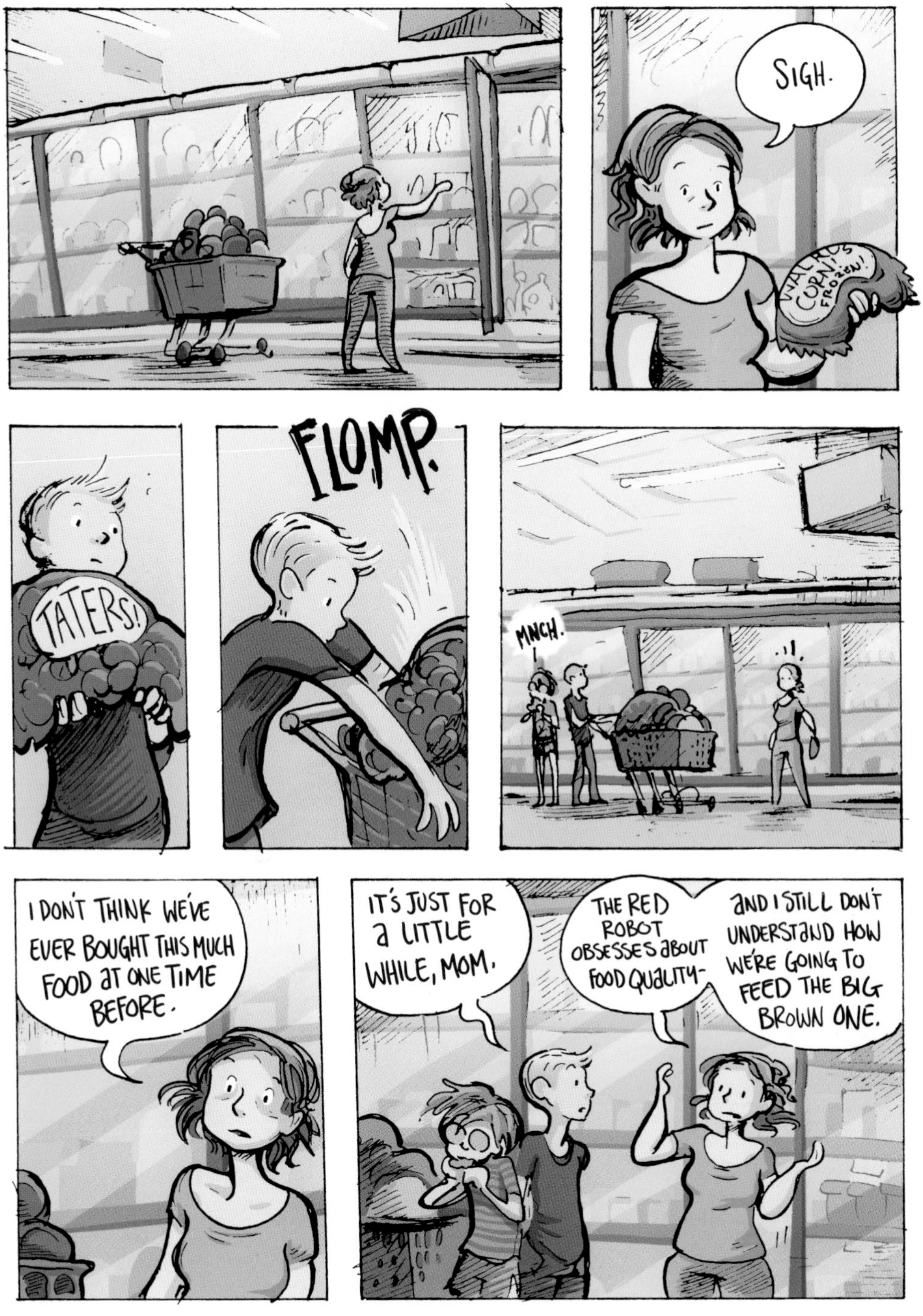
SIGH.
WALRUS CORN! FROZEN!
TATERS!
FLOMP.
MNCH.
I DON'T THINK WE'VE EVER BOUGHT THIS MUCH FOOD AT ONE TIME BEFORE.
IT'S JUST FOR A LITTLE WHILE, MOM.
THE RED ROBOT OBSESSES ABOUT FOOD QUALITY-
AND I STILL DON'T UNDERSTAND HOW WE'RE GOING TO FEED THE BIG BROWN ONE.

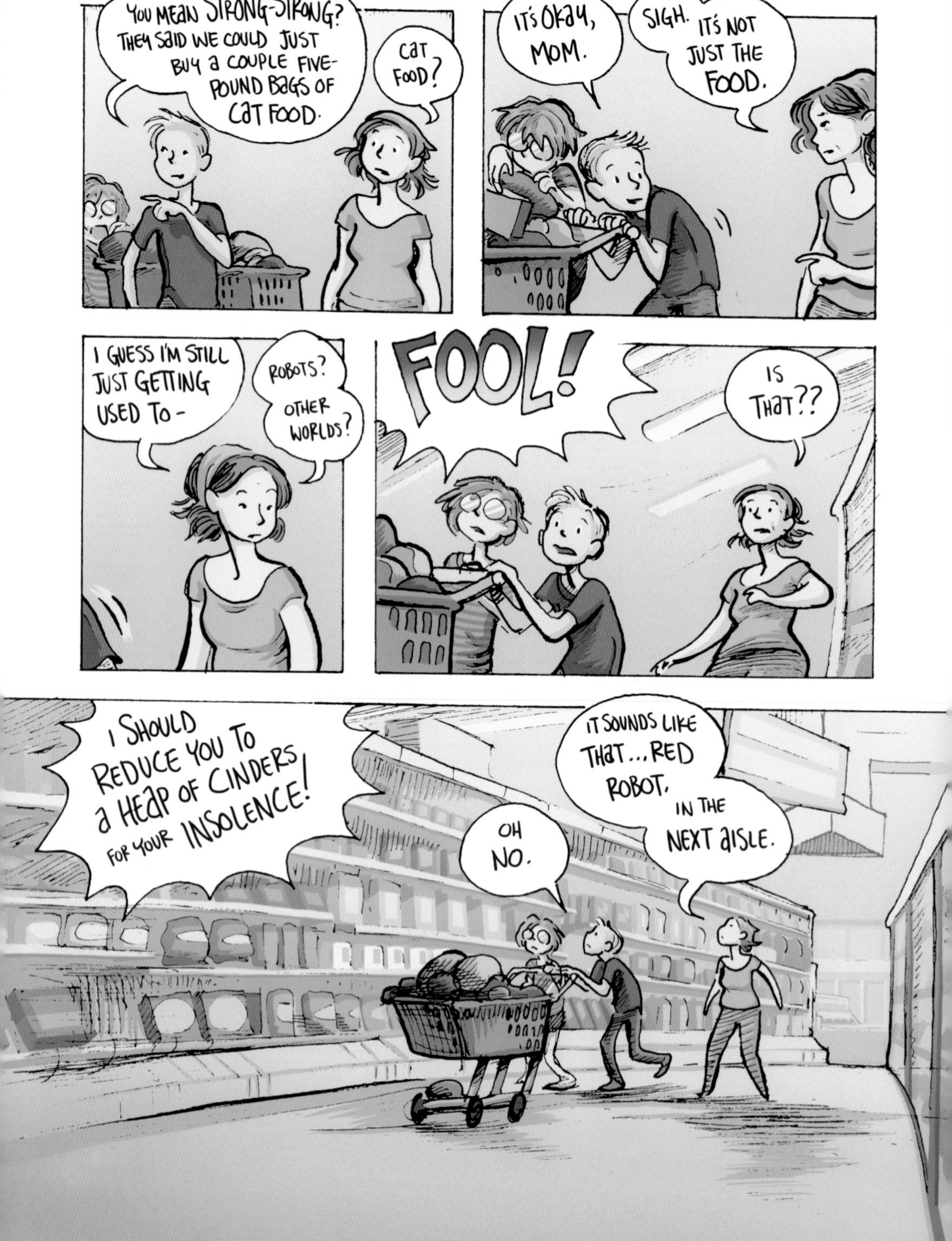

YOU MEAN STRONG-STRONG? THEY SAID WE COULD JUST BUY A COUPLE FIVE-POUND BAGS OF CAT FOOD.
CAT FOOD?
IT'S OKAY, MOM.
SIGH. IT'S NOT JUST THE FOOD.
I GUESS I'M STILL JUST GETTING USED TO -
ROBOTS?
OTHER WORLDS?
FOOL!
IS THAT??
I SHOULD REDUCE YOU TO A HEAP OF CINDERS FOR YOUR INSOLENCE!
OH NO.
IT SOUNDS LIKE THAT... RED ROBOT.
IN THE NEXT AISLE.

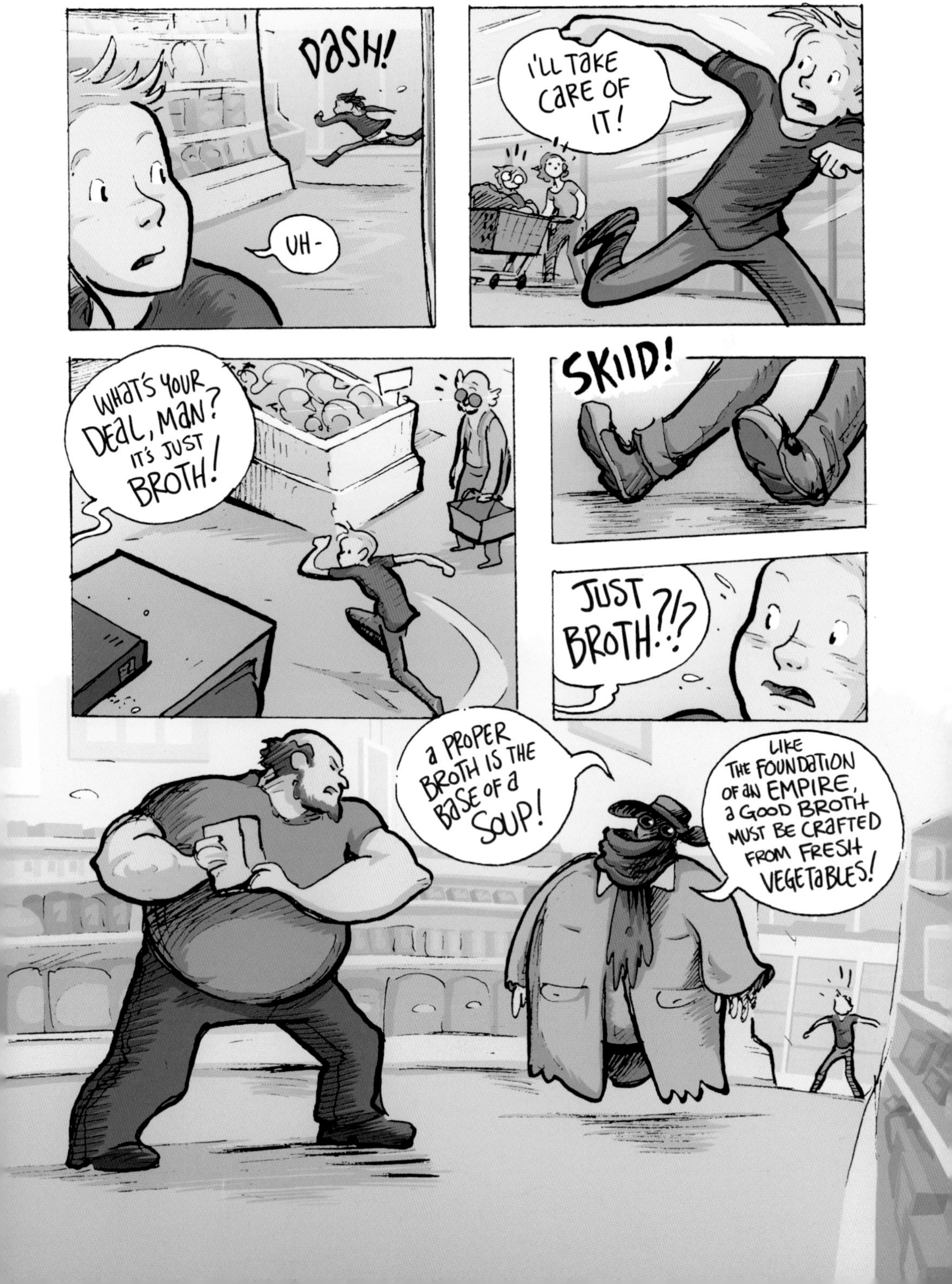
DASH!
UH-
I'LL TAKE CARE OF IT!
WHAT'S YOUR DEAL, MAN? IT'S JUST BROTH!
SKIID!
JUST BROTH?!?
A PROPER BROTH IS THE BASE OF A SOUP!
LIKE THE FOUNDATION OF AN EMPIRE, A GOOD BROTH MUST BE CRAFTED FROM FRESH VEGETABLES!

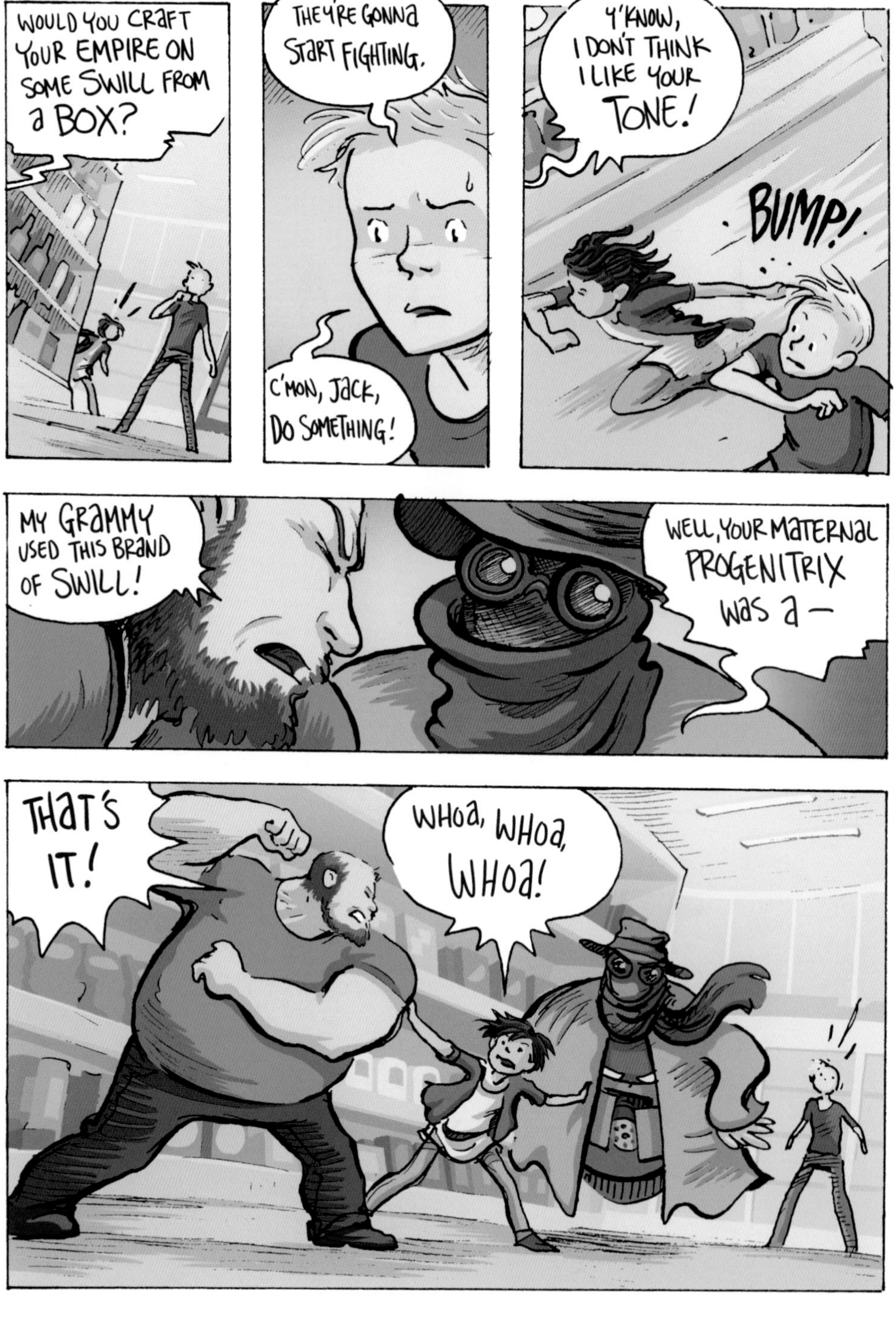
WOULD YOU CRAFT YOUR EMPIRE ON SOME SWILL FROM A BOX?
THEY'RE GONNA START FIGHTING.
C'MON, JACK, DO SOMETHING!
Y'KNOW, I DON'T THINK I LIKE YOUR TONE!
BUMP!
MY GRAMMY USED THIS BRAND OF SWILL!
WELL, YOUR MATERNAL PROGENITRIX WAS A—
THAT'S IT!
WHOA, WHOA, WHOA!

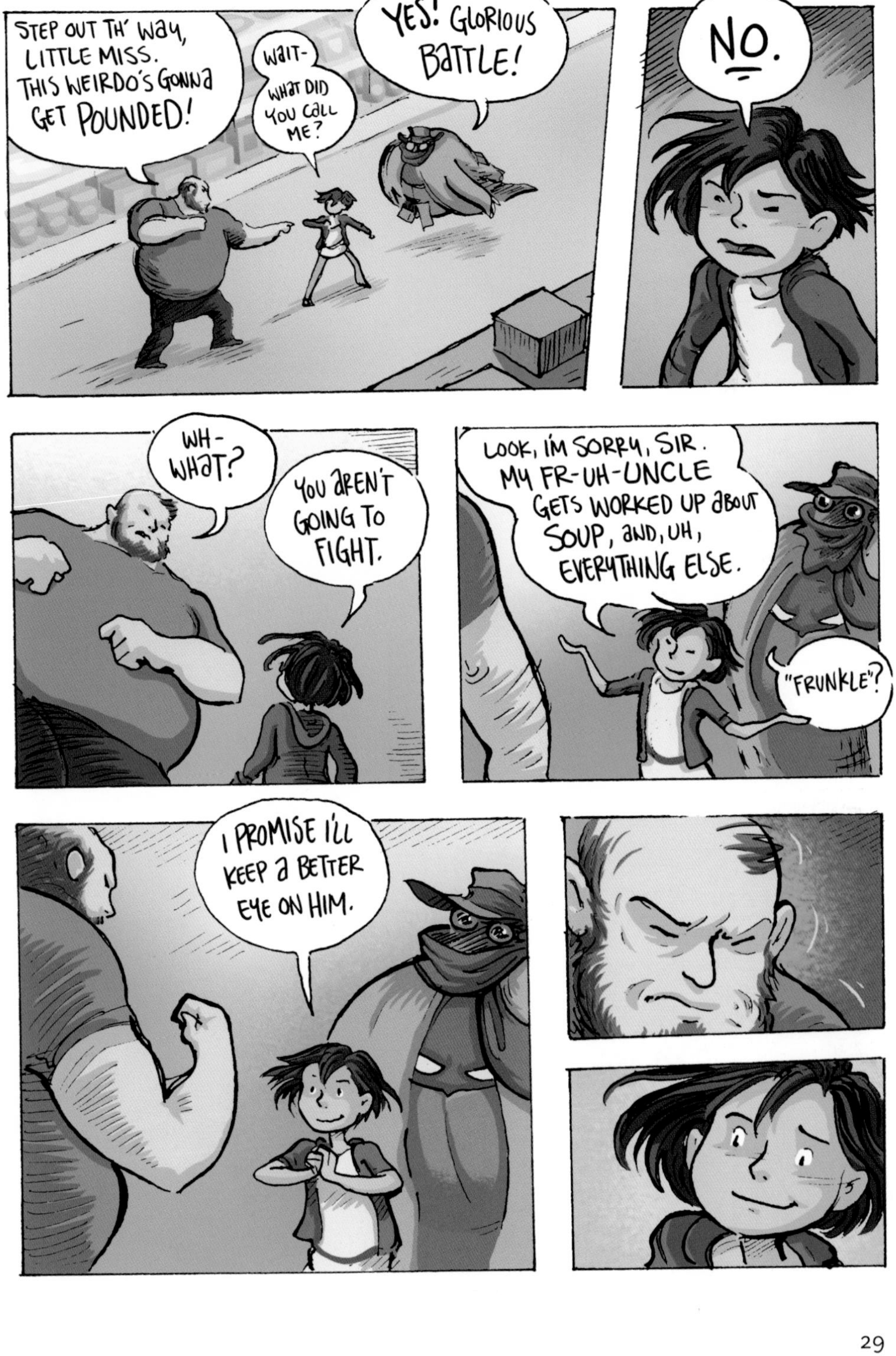

STEP OUT TH' WAY, LITTLE MISS. THIS WEIRDO'S GONNA GET POUNDED!
WAIT-
WHAT DID YOU CALL ME?
YES! GLORIOUS BATTLE!
NO.
WH- WHAT?
YOU AREN'T GOING TO FIGHT.
LOOK, I'M SORRY, SIR. MY FR-UH-UNCLE GETS WORKED UP ABOUT SOUP, AND, UH, EVERYTHING ELSE.
"FRUNKLE"?
I PROMISE I'LL KEEP A BETTER EYE ON HIM.

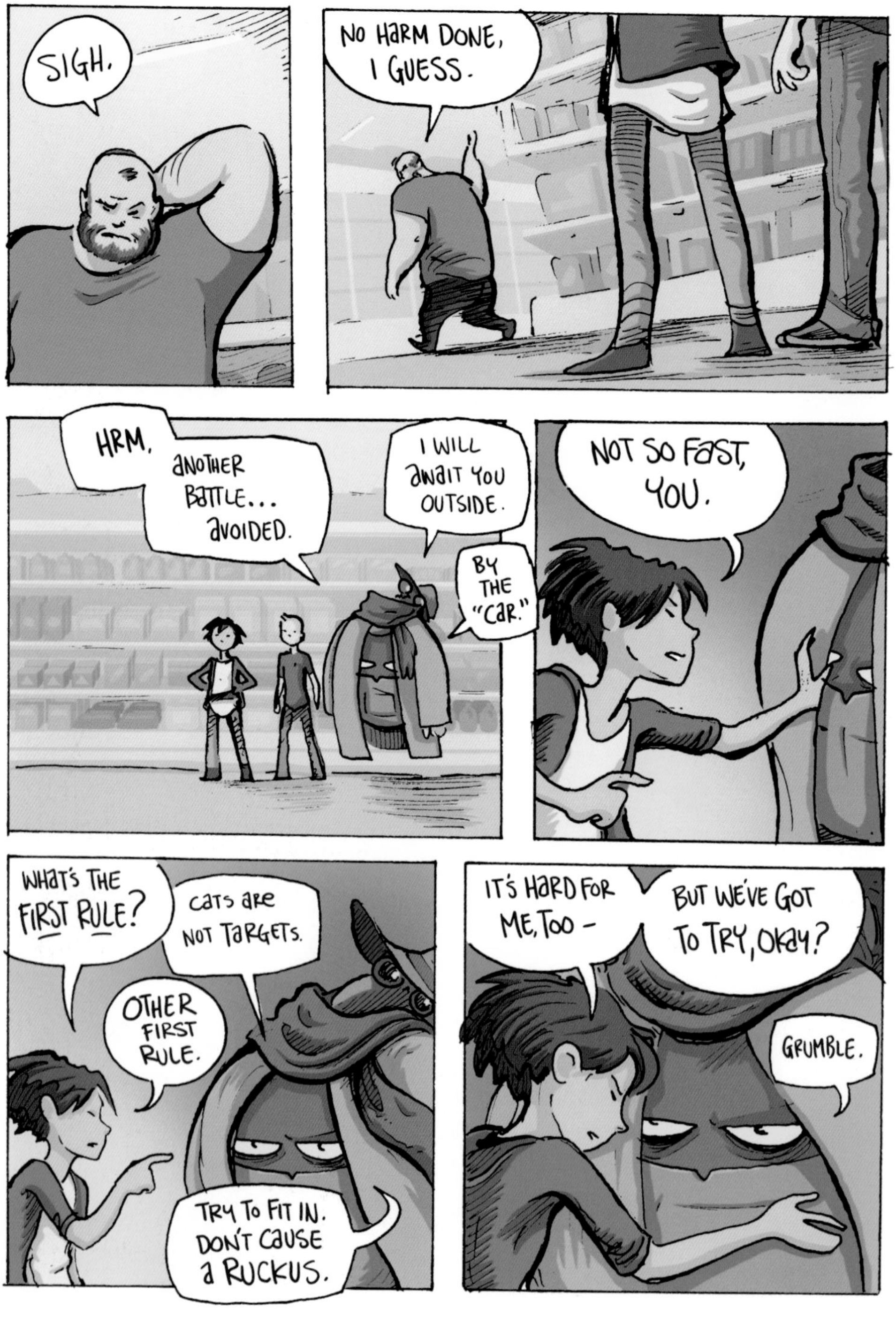
SIGH.
NO HARM DONE, I GUESS.
HRM.
ANOTHER BATTLE... AVOIDED.
I WILL AWAIT YOU OUTSIDE.
BY THE "CAR."
NOT SO FAST, YOU.
WHAT'S THE FIRST RULE?
CATS ARE NOT TARGETS.
OTHER FIRST RULE.
TRY TO FIT IN. DON'T CAUSE A RUCKUS.
IT'S HARD FOR ME, TOO -
BUT WE'VE GOT TO TRY, OKAY?
GRUMBLE.

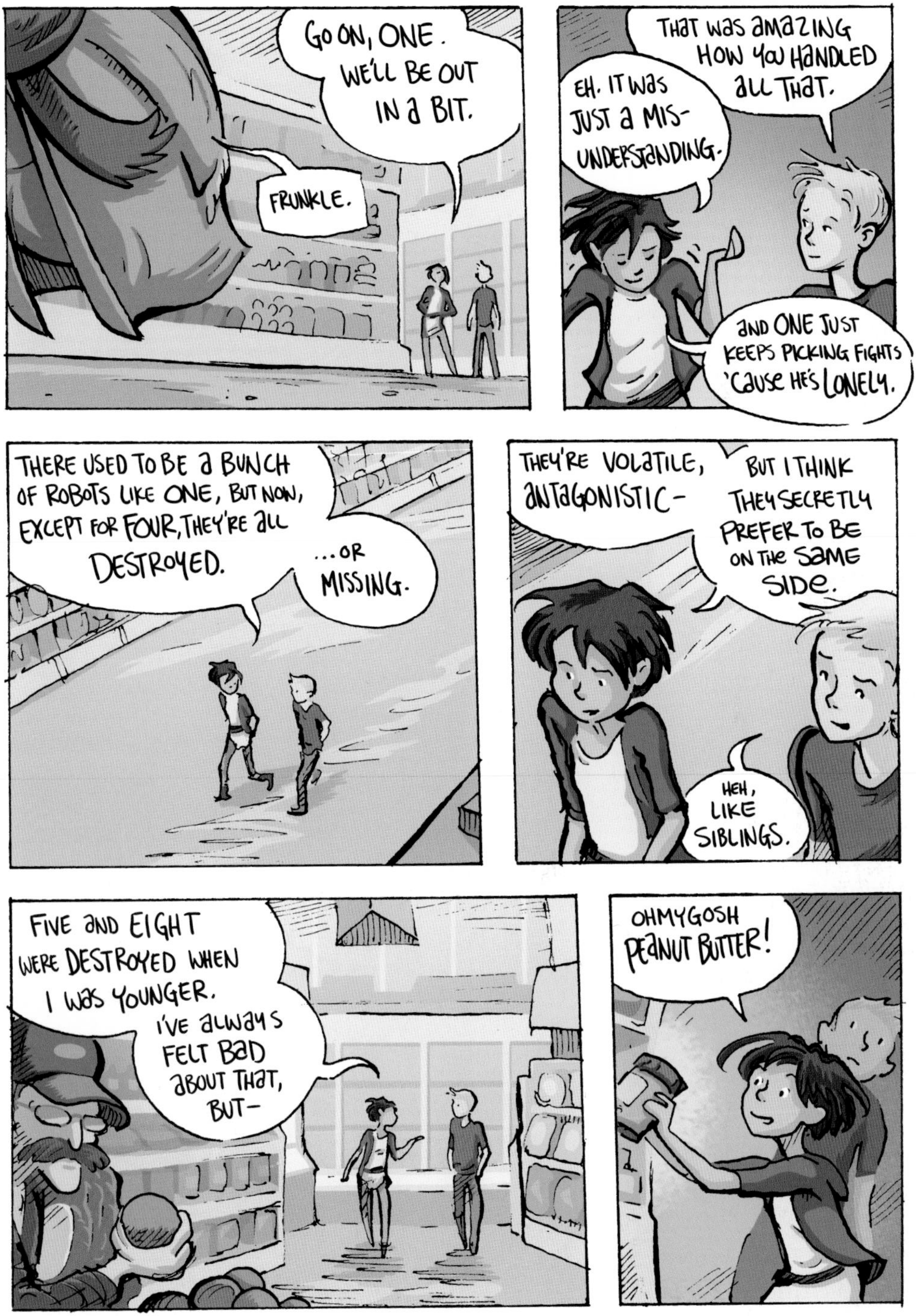
Go on, ONE. We'll be out in a bit.
Frunkle.
That was amazing how you handled all that.
Eh. It was just a mis-understanding.
And ONE just keeps picking fights 'cause he's lonely.
There used to be a bunch of robots like ONE, but now, except for FOUR, they're all destroyed.
...or missing.
They're volatile, antagonistic-
But I think they secretly prefer to be on the same side.
Heh, like siblings.
FIVE and EIGHT were destroyed when I was younger.
I've always felt bad about that, but-
Ohmygosh peanut butter!

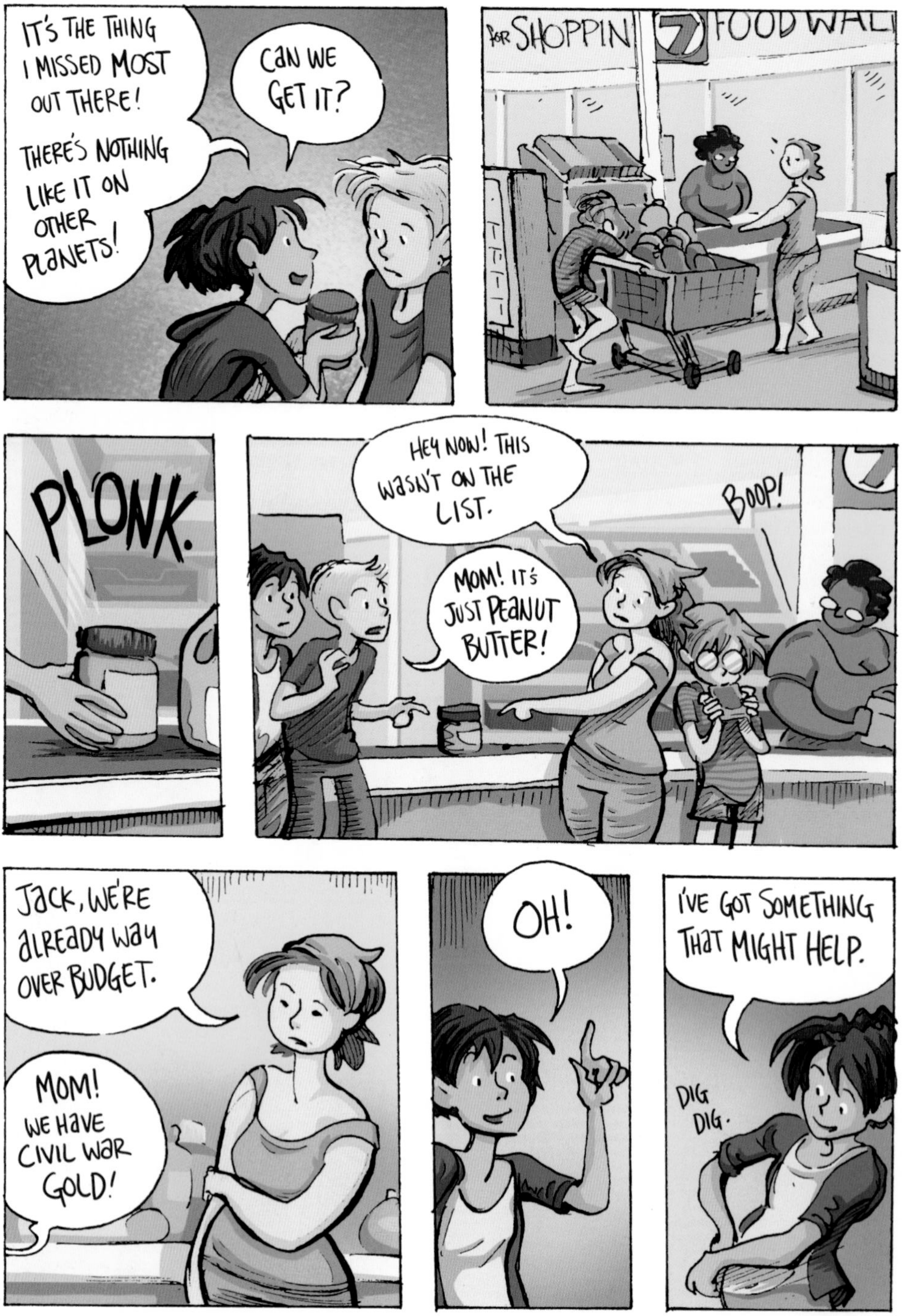
IT'S THE THING I MISSED MOST OUT THERE!
THERE'S NOTHING LIKE IT ON OTHER PLANETS!
CAN WE GET IT?
FOR SHOPPIN
FOOD WAL
PLONK.
HEY NOW! THIS WASN'T ON THE LIST.
BOOP!
MOM! IT'S JUST PEANUT BUTTER!
JACK, WE'RE ALREADY WAY OVER BUDGET.
MOM! WE HAVE CIVIL WAR GOLD!
OH!
I'VE GOT SOMETHING THAT MIGHT HELP.
DIG DIG.

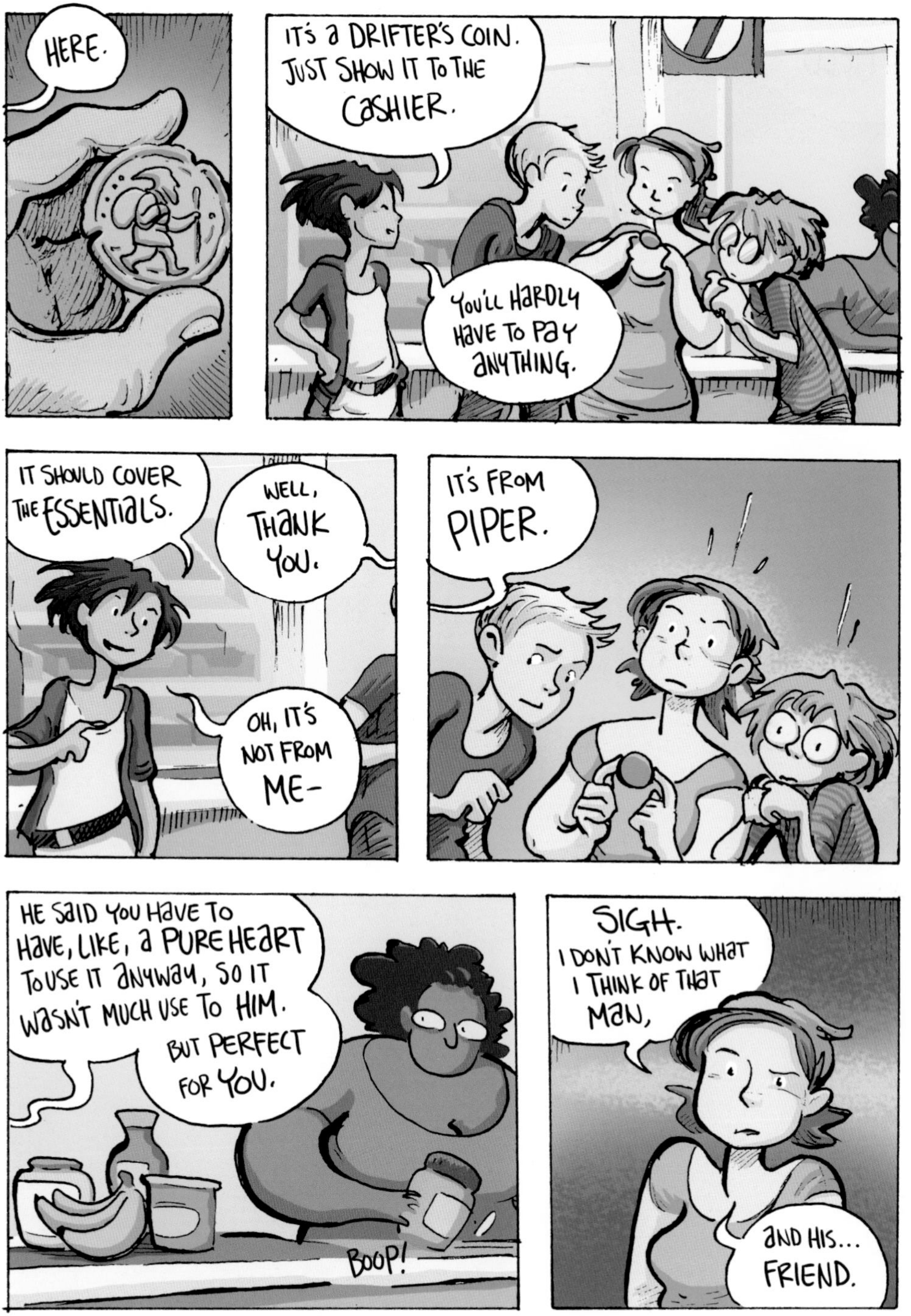
HERE.
IT'S A DRIFTER'S COIN. JUST SHOW IT TO THE CASHIER.
YOU'LL HARDLY HAVE TO PAY ANYTHING.
IT SHOULD COVER THE ESSENTIALS.
WELL, THANK YOU.
OH, IT'S NOT FROM ME-
IT'S FROM PIPER.
HE SAID YOU HAVE TO HAVE, LIKE, A PURE HEART TO USE IT ANYWAY, SO IT WASN'T MUCH USE TO HIM.
BUT PERFECT FOR YOU.
BOOP!
SIGH.
I DON'T KNOW WHAT I THINK OF THAT MAN,
AND HIS... FRIEND.

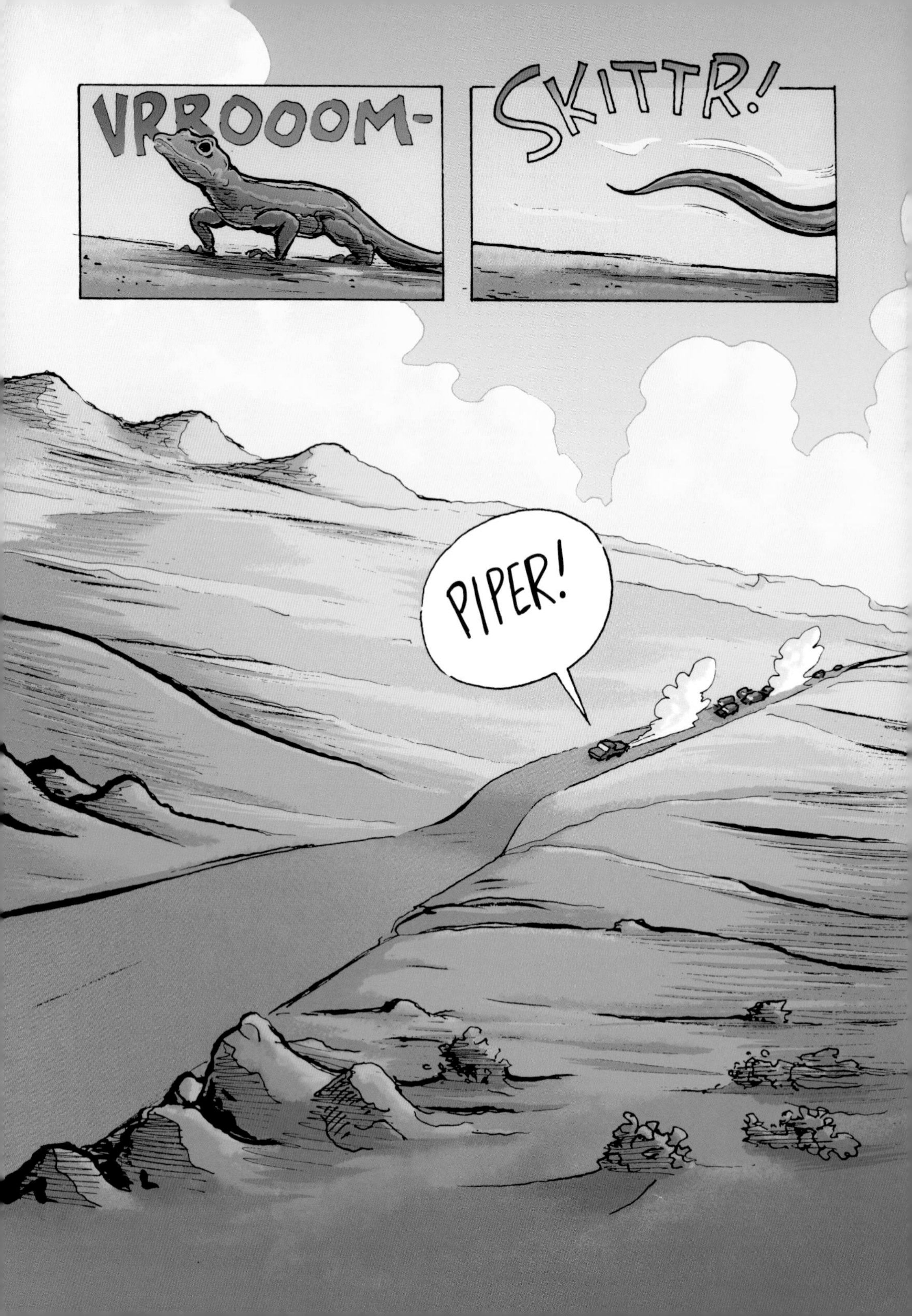
VRROOOM-
SKITTR!
PIPER!

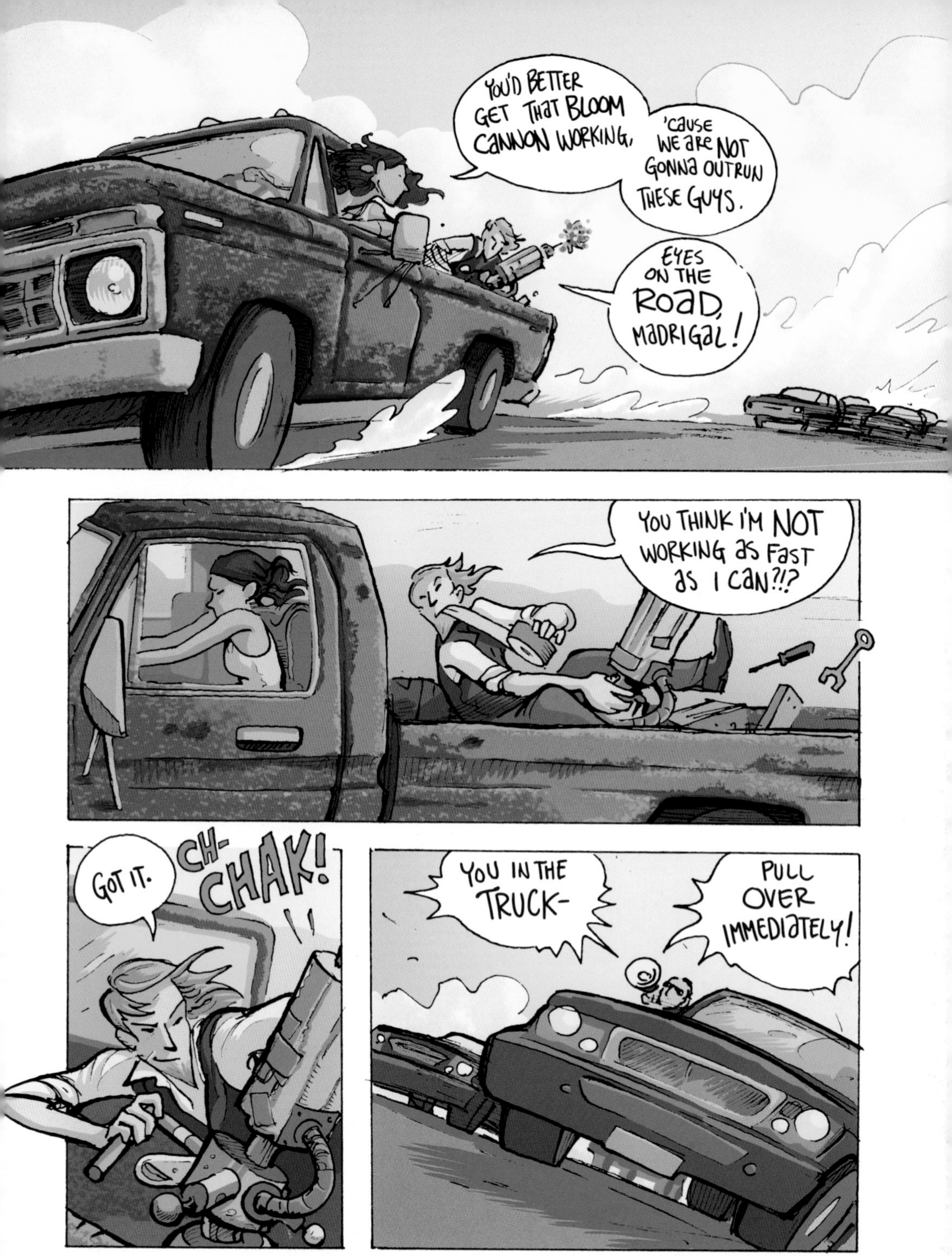
YOU'D BETTER GET THAT BLOOM CANNON WORKING,
'CAUSE WE ARE NOT GONNA OUTRUN THESE GUYS.
EYES ON THE ROAD, MADRIGAL!
YOU THINK I'M NOT WORKING AS FAST AS I CAN?!?
GOT IT.
CH-CHAK!
YOU IN THE TRUCK-
PULL OVER IMMEDIATELY!

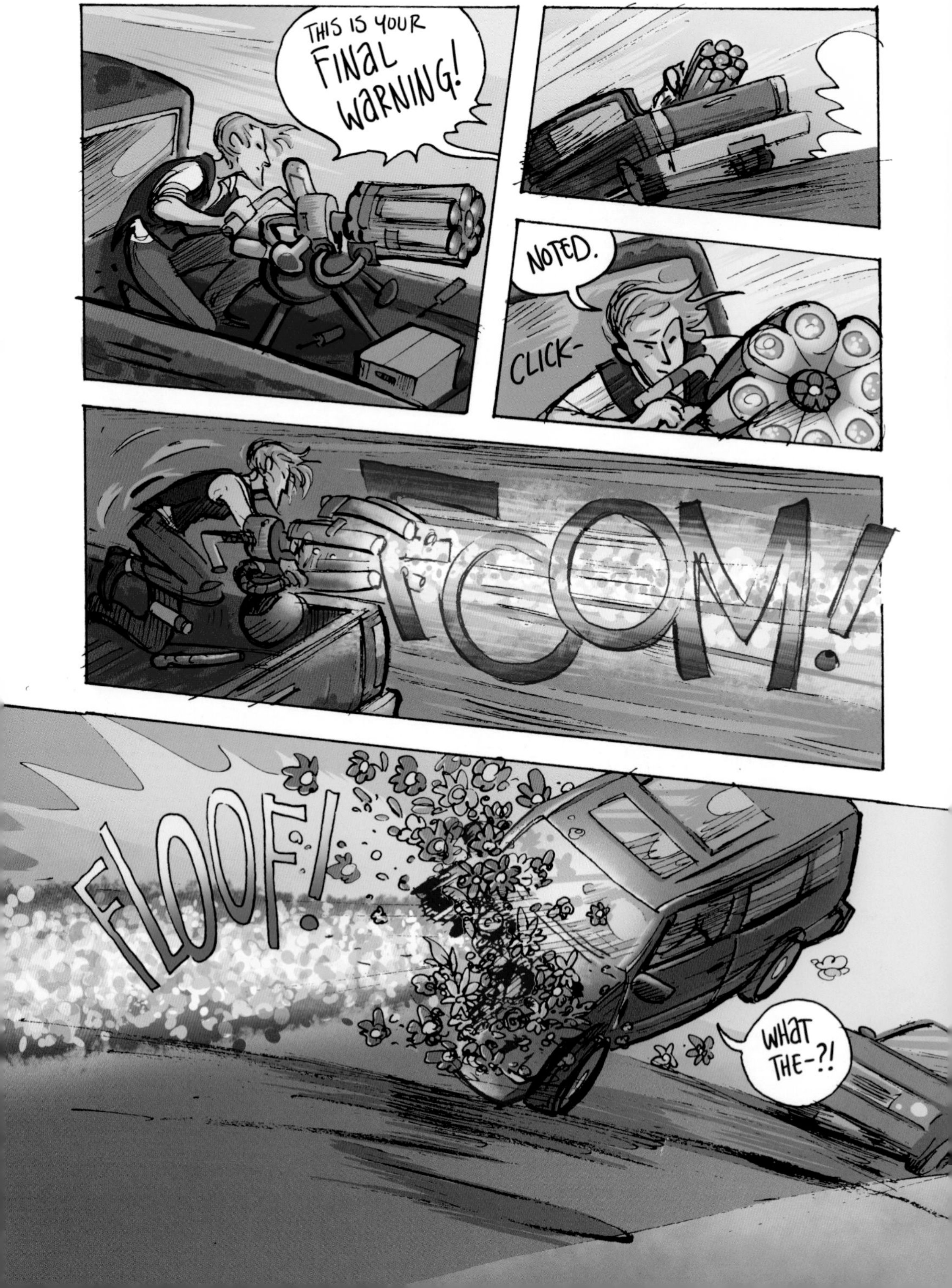
THIS IS YOUR FINAL WARNING!
NOTED.
CLICK-
BOOM!
FLOOF!
WHAT THE-?!

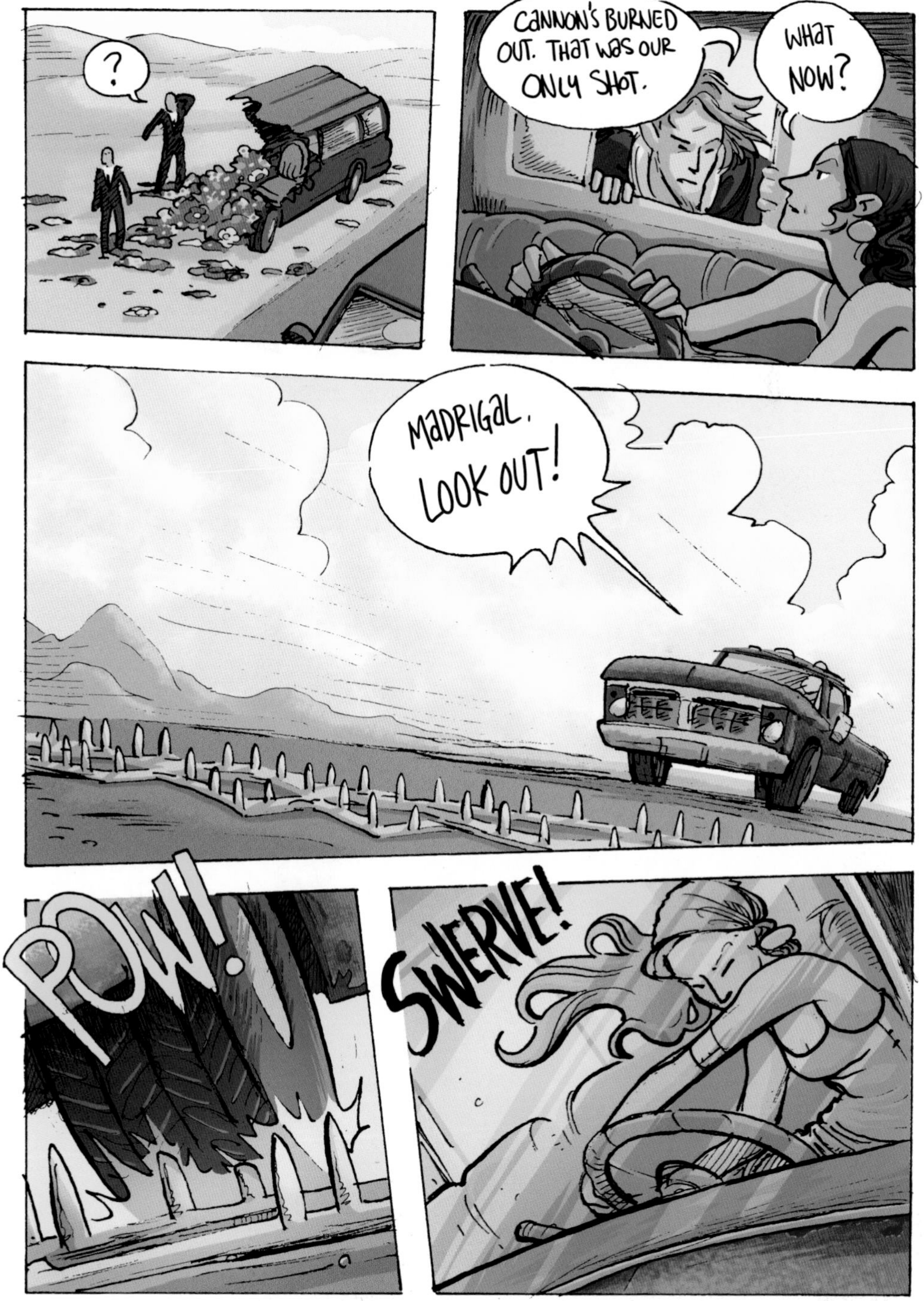
?
CANNON'S BURNED OUT. THAT WAS OUR ONLY SHOT.
WHAT NOW?
MADRIGAL, LOOK OUT!
POW!
SWERVE!

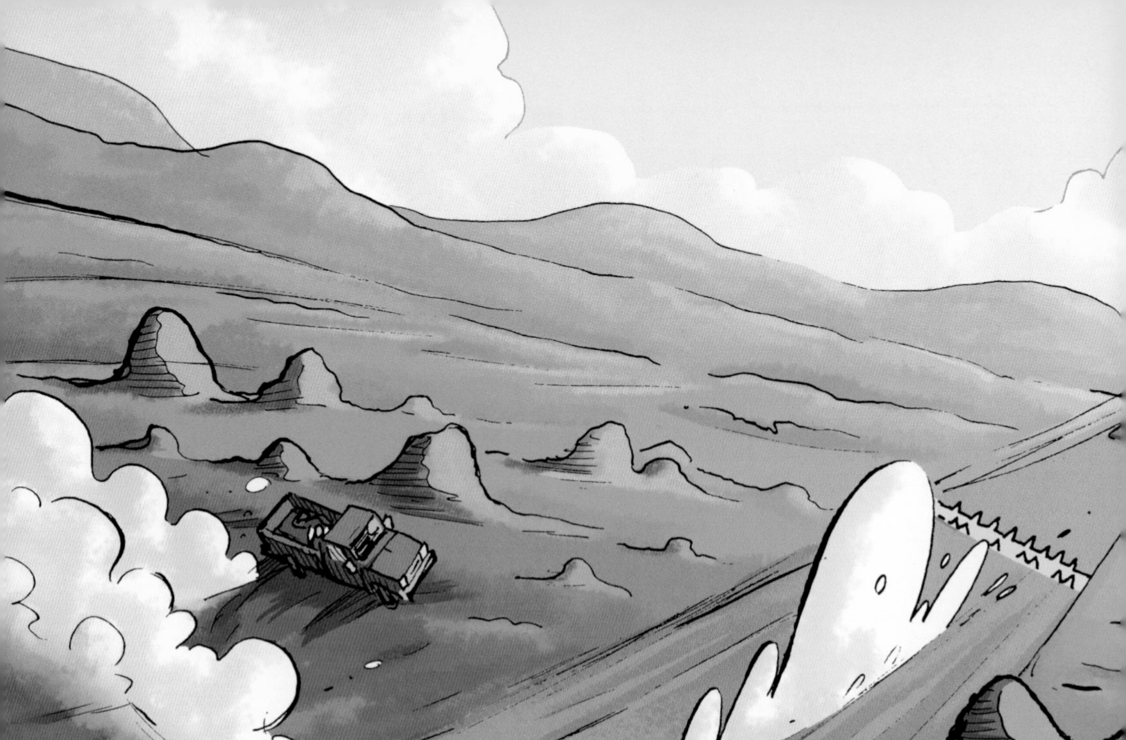
SKIIID!!

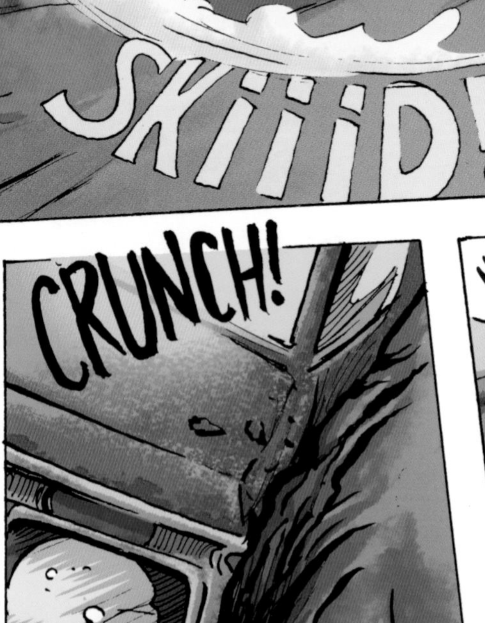
CRUNCH!

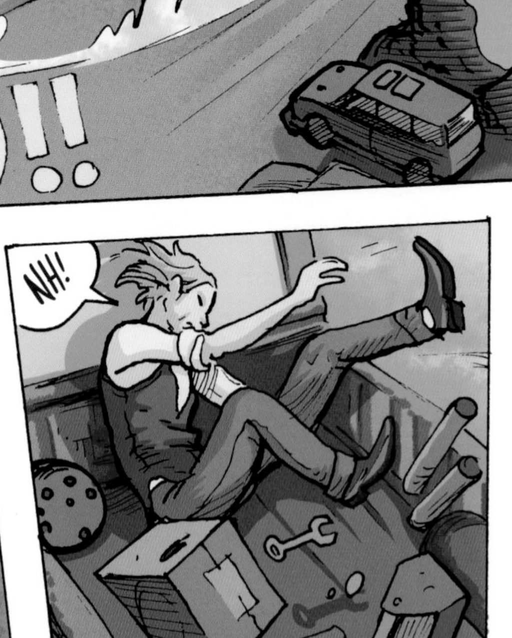
NH!

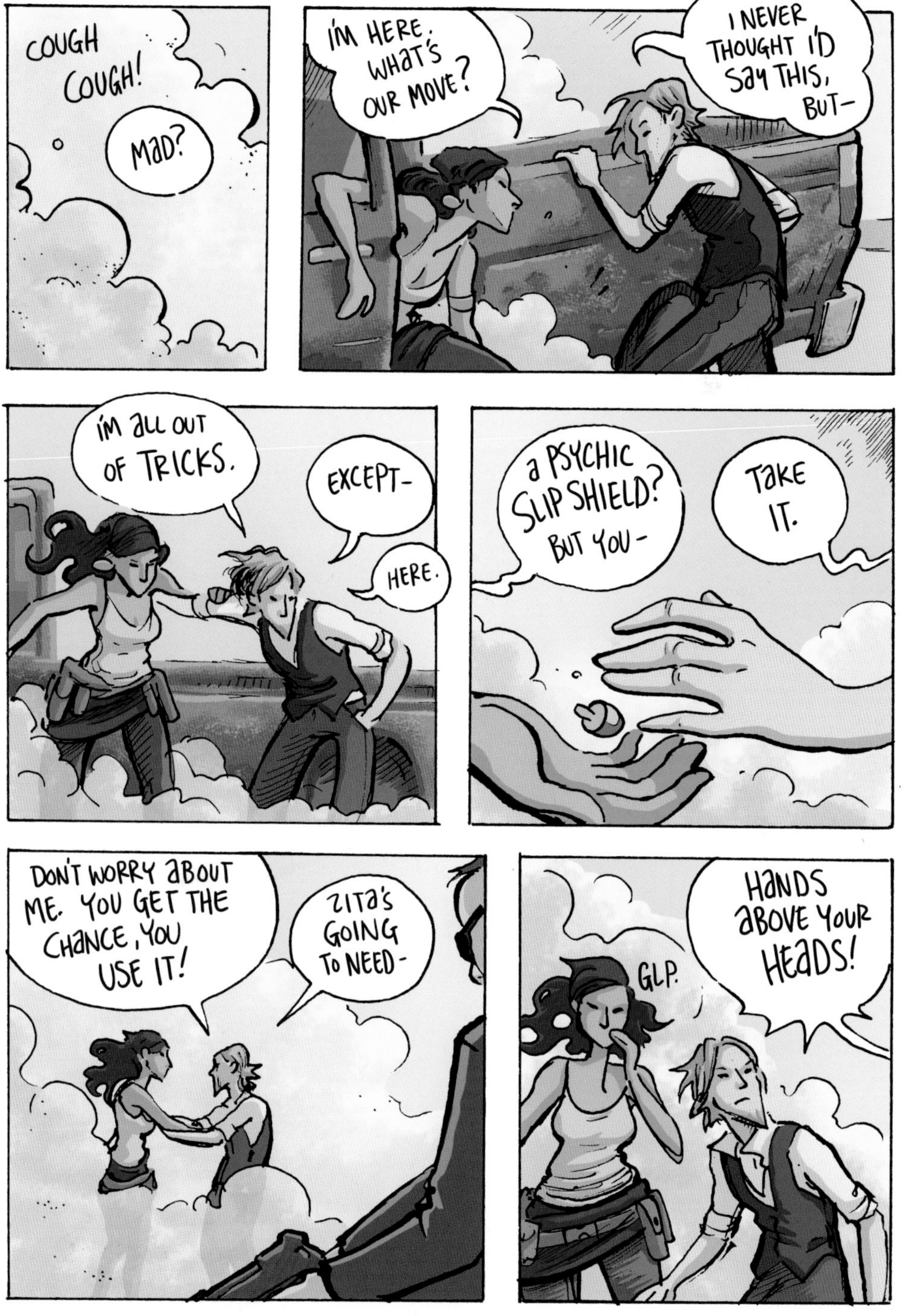
COUGH COUGH!
MAD?
I'M HERE. WHAT'S OUR MOVE?
I NEVER THOUGHT I'D SAY THIS, BUT-
I'M ALL OUT OF TRICKS.
EXCEPT-
HERE.
A PSYCHIC SLIP SHIELD? BUT YOU-
TAKE IT.
DON'T WORRY ABOUT ME. YOU GET THE CHANCE, YOU USE IT!
ZITA'S GOING TO NEED-
GLP.
HANDS ABOVE YOUR HEADS!

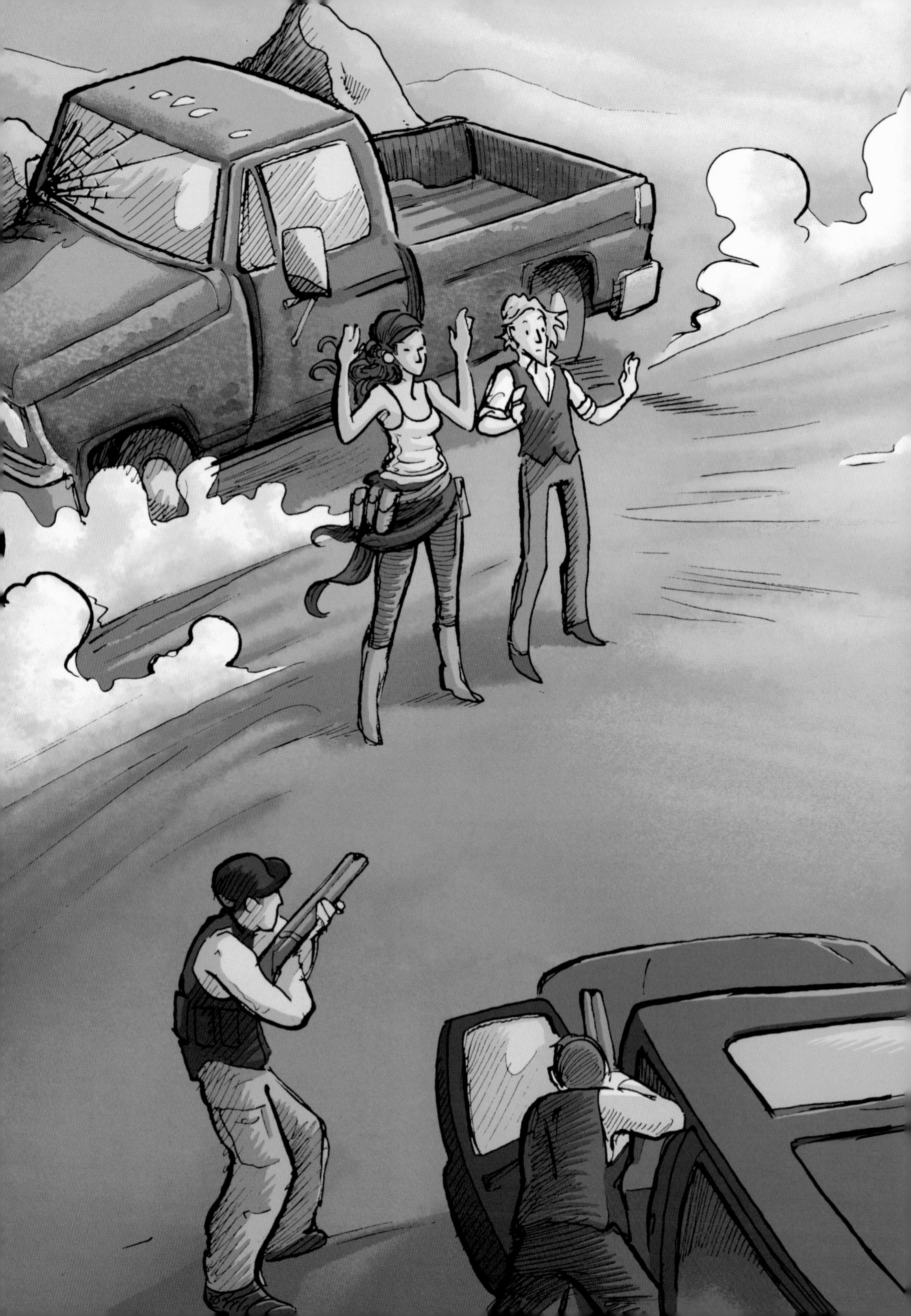

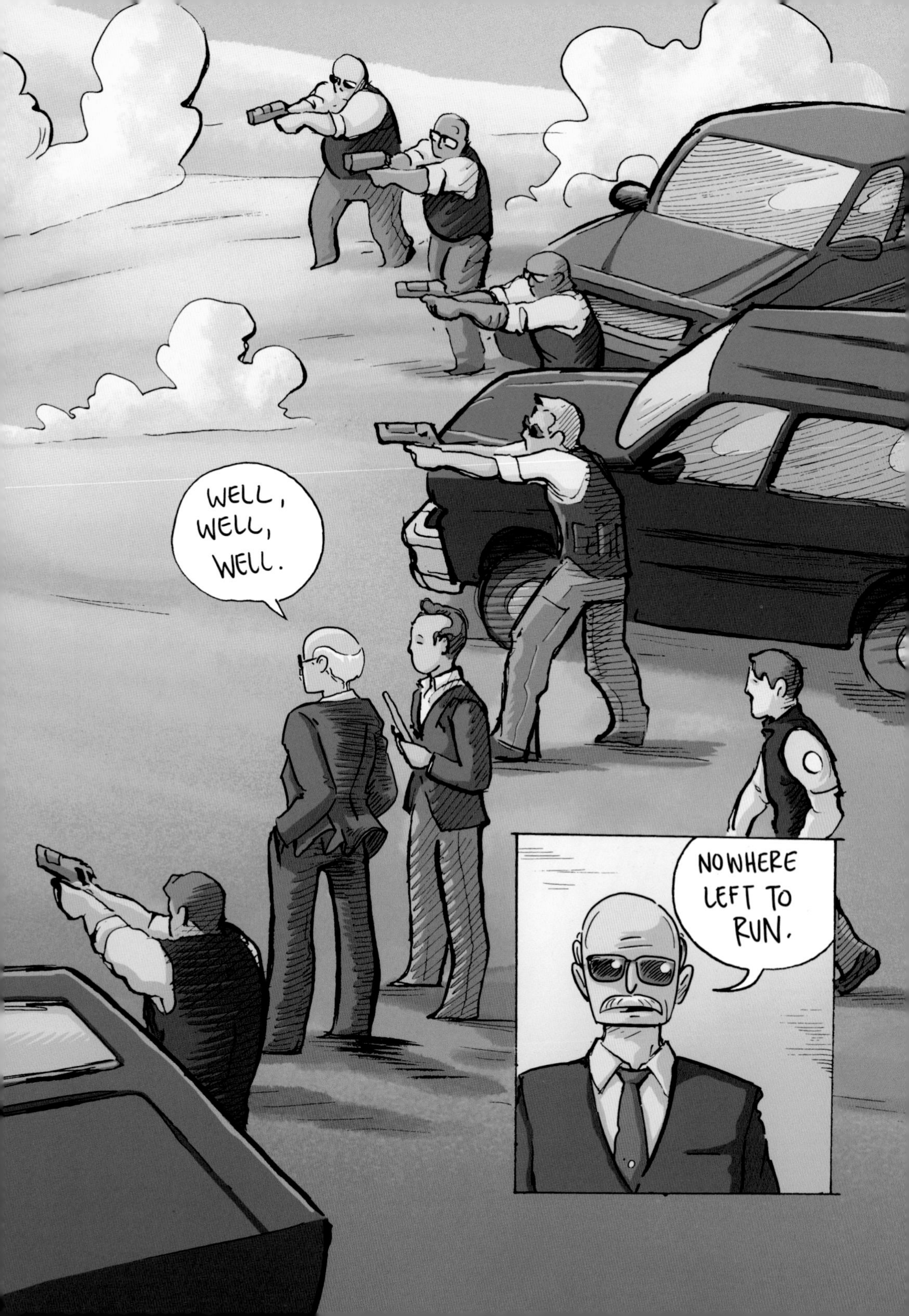
WELL, WELL, WELL.
NOWHERE LEFT TO RUN.

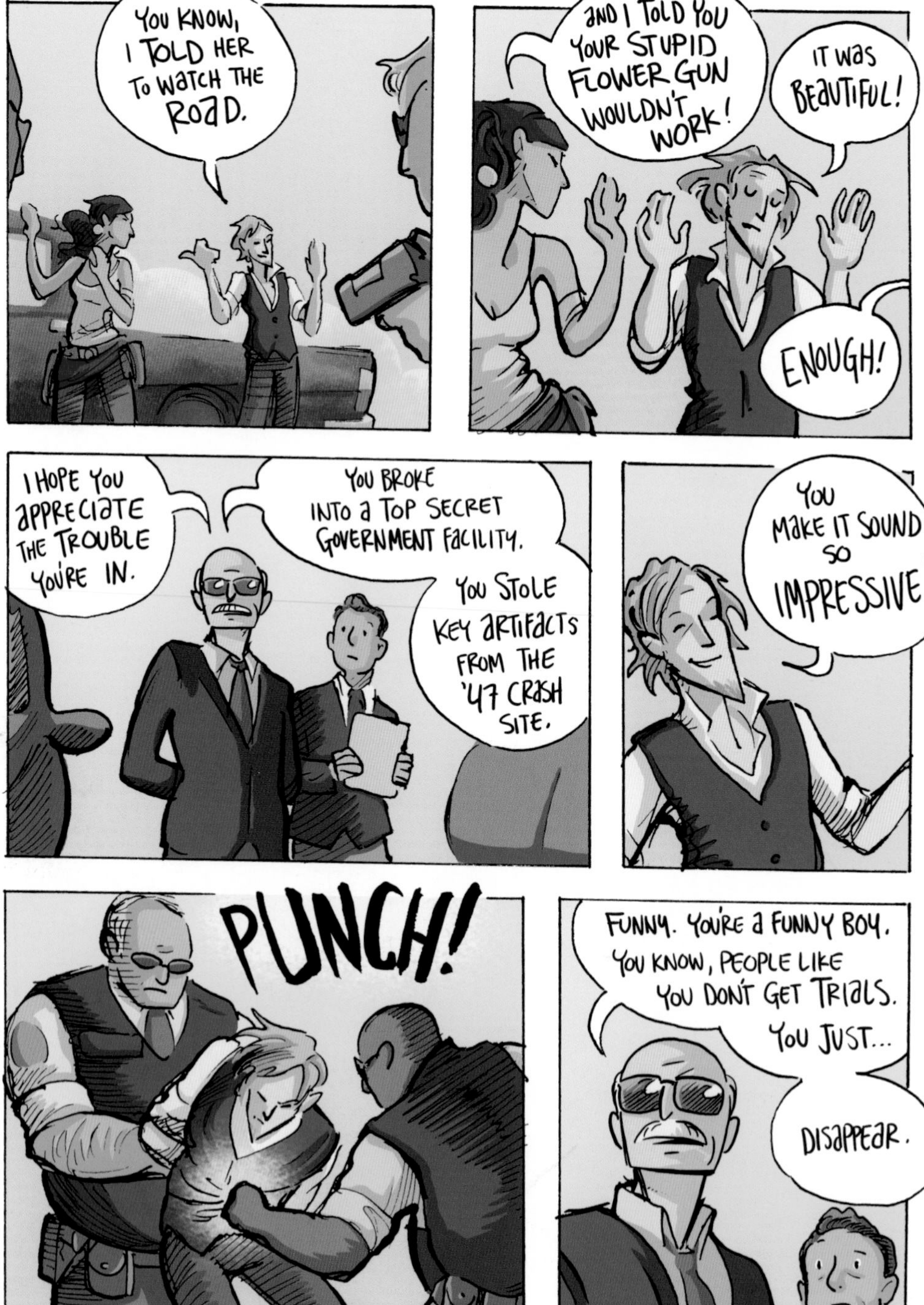
YOU KNOW, I TOLD HER TO WATCH THE ROAD.
AND I TOLD YOU YOUR STUPID FLOWER GUN WOULDN'T WORK!
IT WAS BEAUTIFUL!
ENOUGH!
I HOPE YOU APPRECIATE THE TROUBLE YOU'RE IN.
YOU BROKE INTO A TOP SECRET GOVERNMENT FACILITY.
YOU STOLE KEY ARTIFACTS FROM THE '47 CRASH SITE.
YOU MAKE IT SOUND SO IMPRESSIVE!
PUNCH!
FUNNY. YOU'RE A FUNNY BOY.
YOU KNOW, PEOPLE LIKE YOU DON'T GET TRIALS.
YOU JUST...
DISAPPEAR.

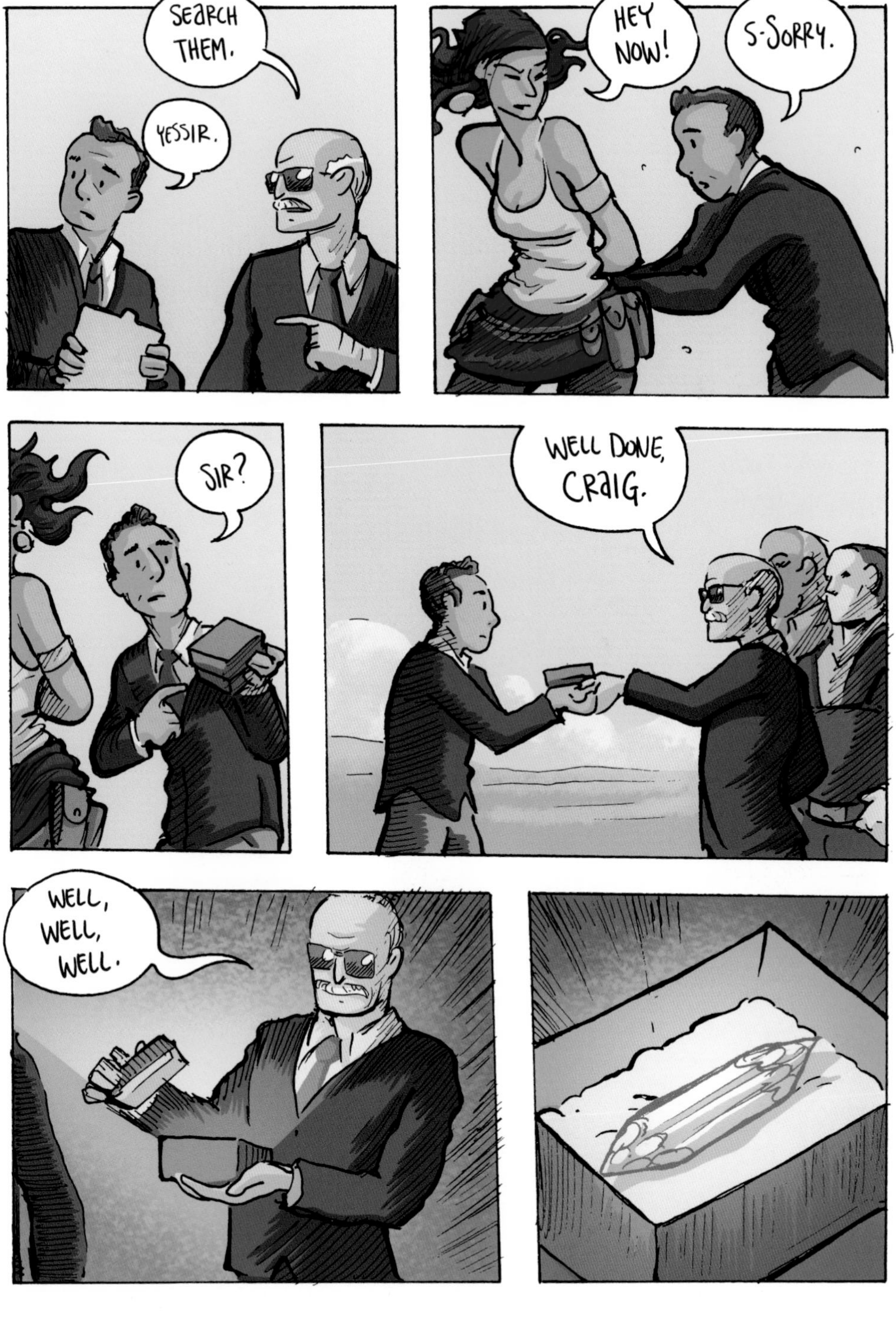
SEARCH THEM.
YESSIR.
HEY NOW!
S-SORRY.
SIR?
WELL DONE, CRAIG.
WELL, WELL, WELL.

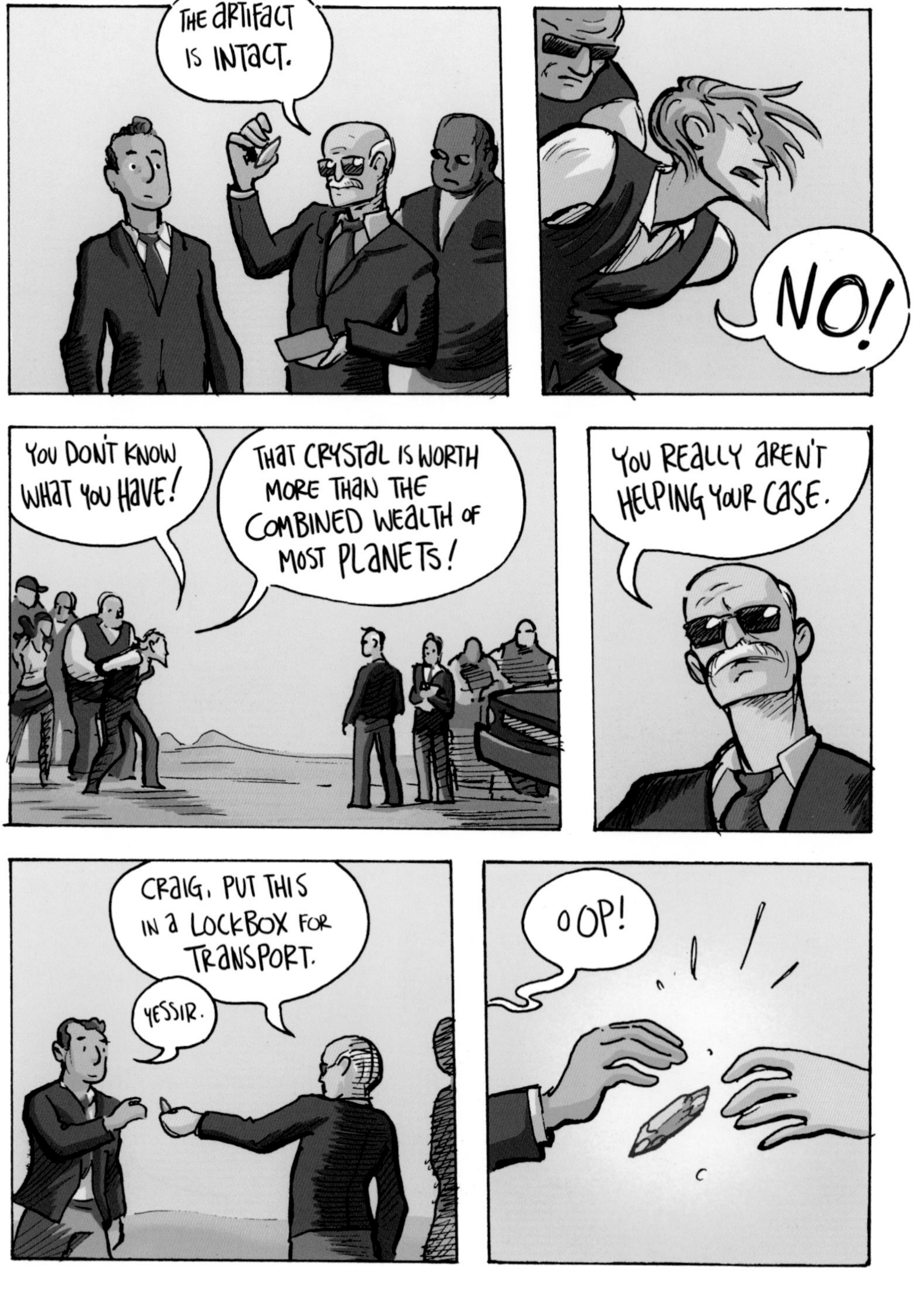
THE ARTIFACT IS INTACT.
NO!
YOU DON'T KNOW WHAT YOU HAVE!
THAT CRYSTAL IS WORTH MORE THAN THE COMBINED WEALTH OF MOST PLANETS!
YOU REALLY AREN'T HELPING YOUR CASE.
CRAIG, PUT THIS IN A LOCKBOX FOR TRANSPORT.
YESSIR.
OOP!

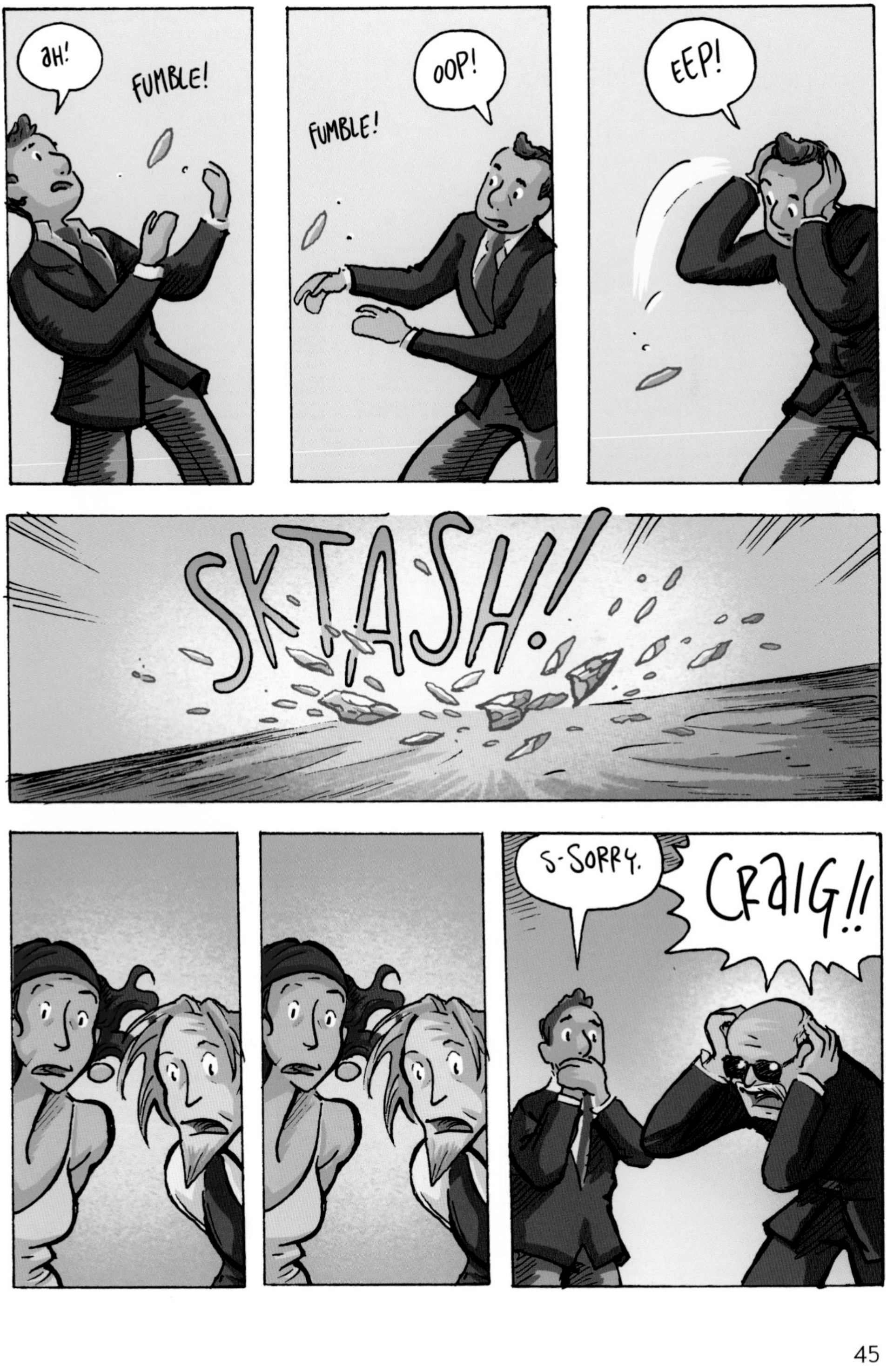
AH!
FUMBLE!
FUMBLE!
OOP!
EEP!
SKTASH!!
S-SORRY.
CRAIG!!

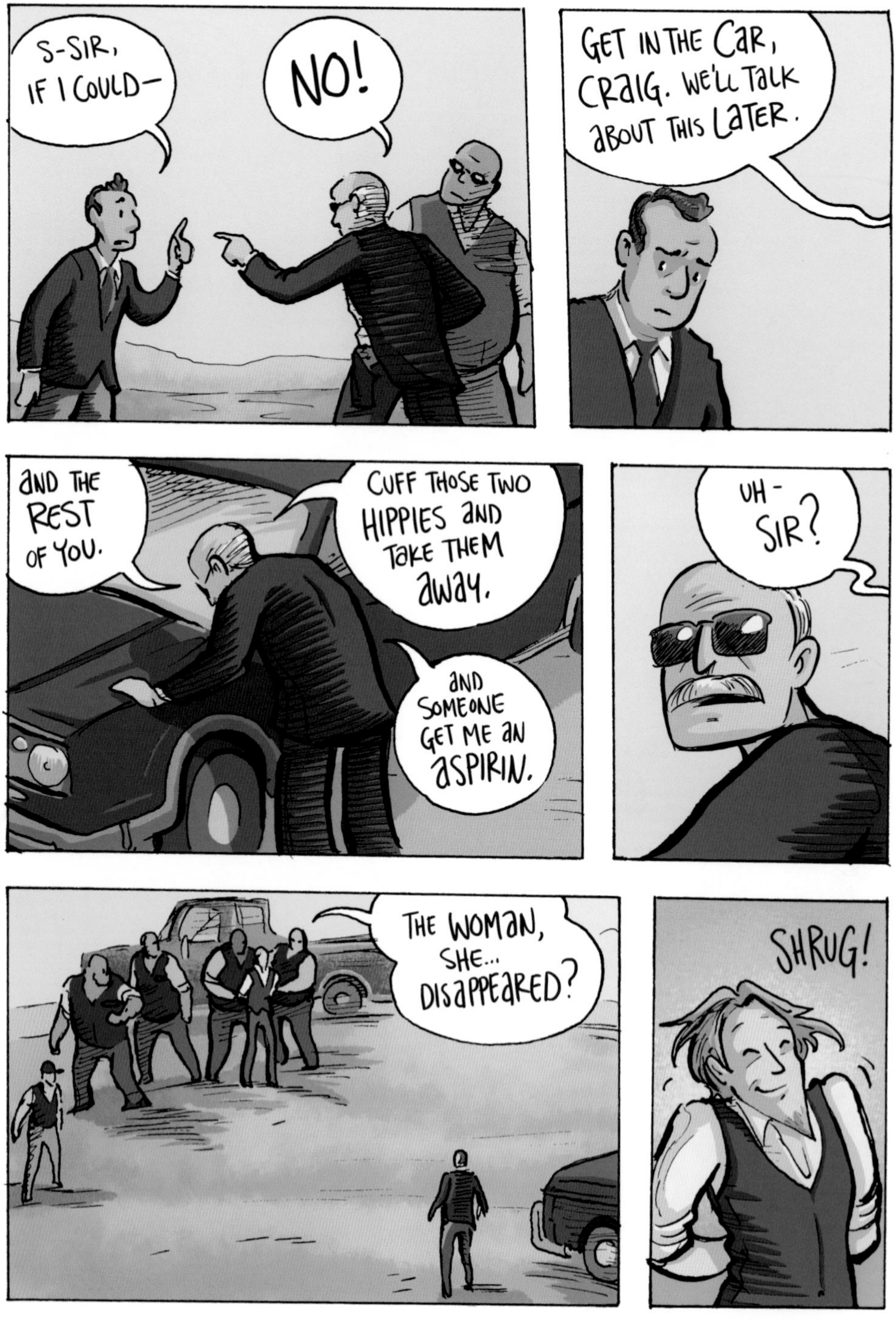
S-SIR, IF I COULD—
NO!
GET IN THE CAR, CRAIG. WE'LL TALK ABOUT THIS LATER.
AND THE REST OF YOU.
CUFF THOSE TWO HIPPIES AND TAKE THEM AWAY.
AND SOMEONE GET ME AN ASPIRIN.
UH - SIR?
THE WOMAN, SHE... DISAPPEARED?
SHRUG!

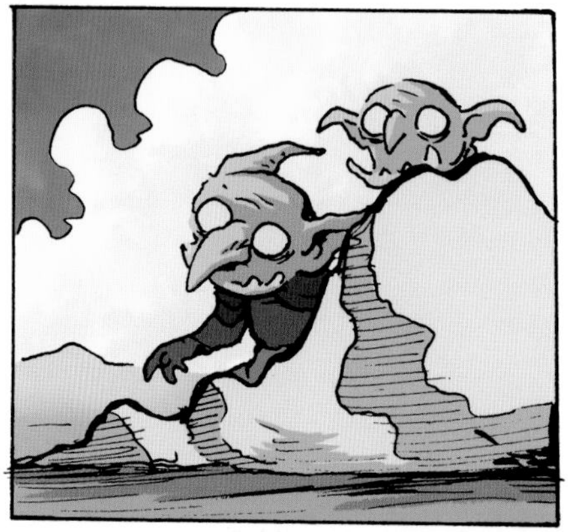
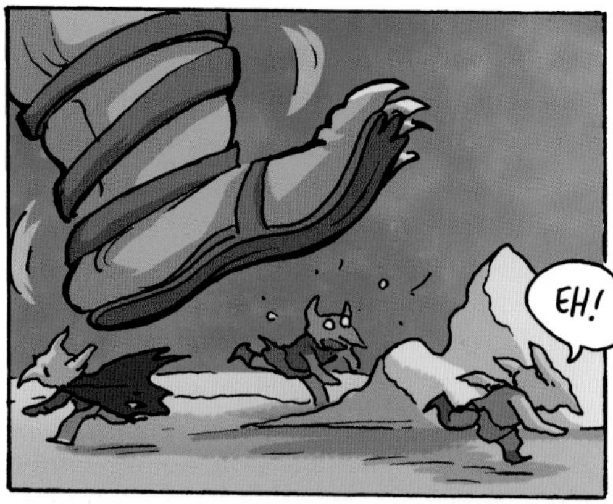
EH!
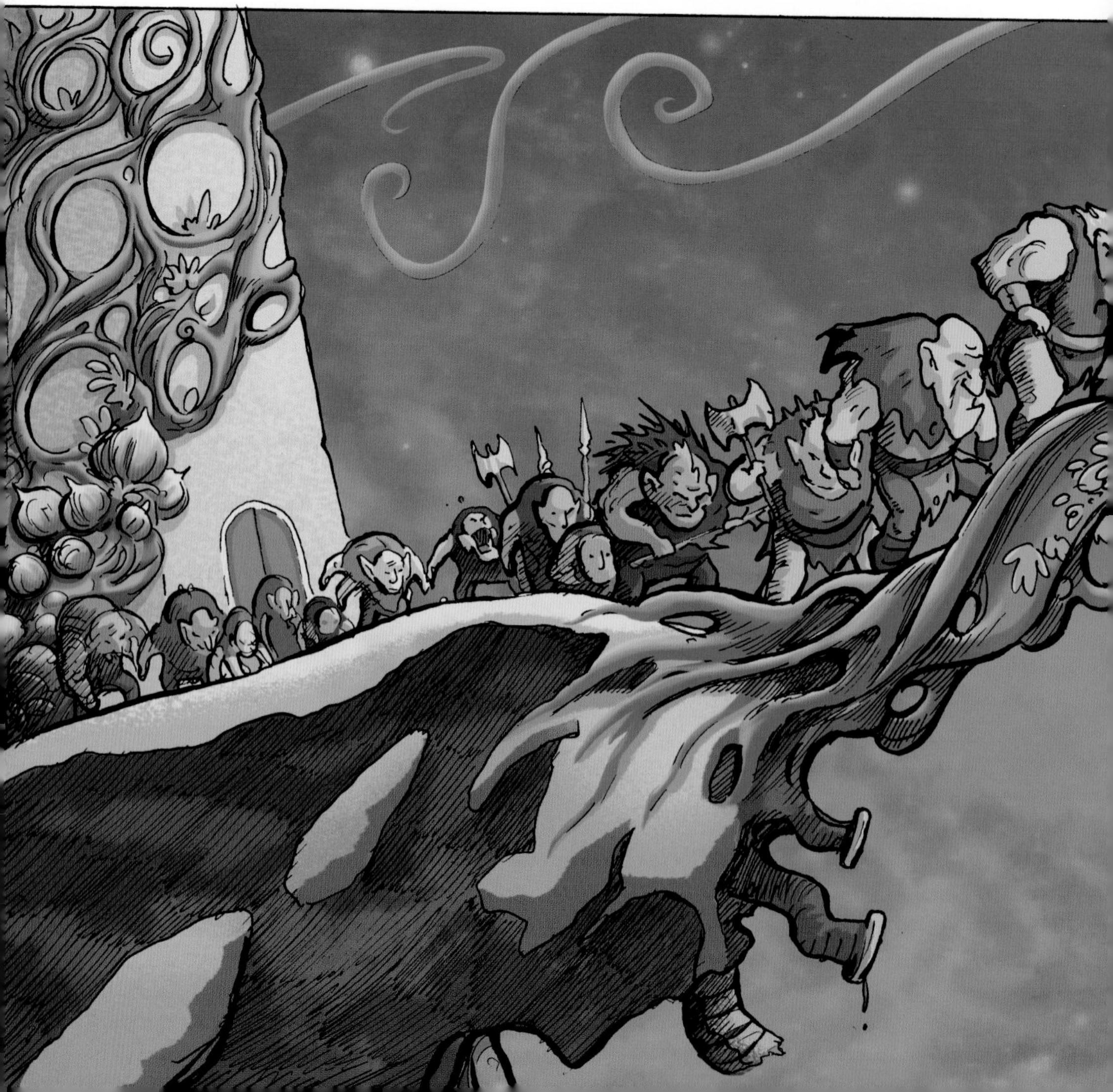

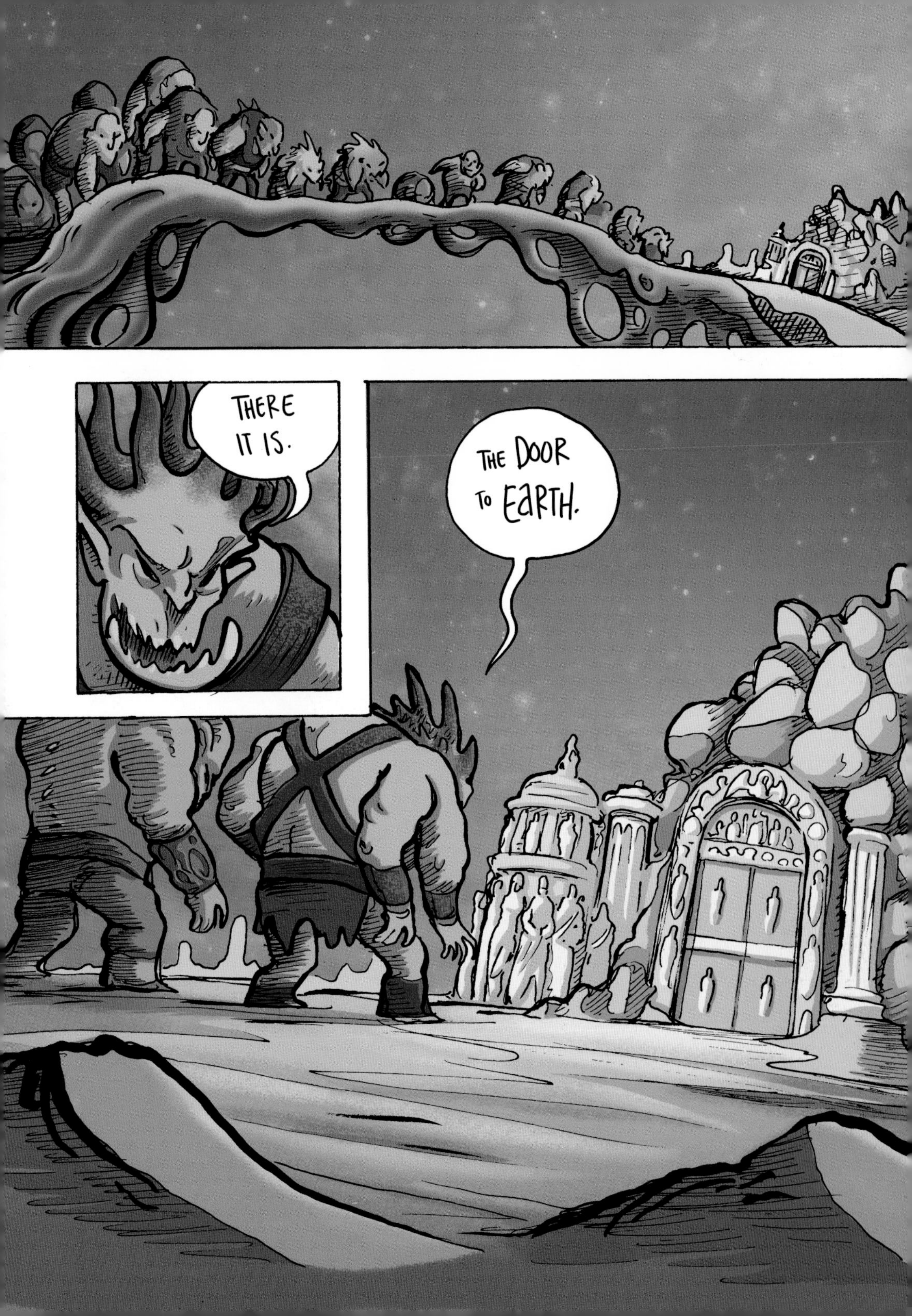
THERE IT IS.
THE DOOR TO EARTH.

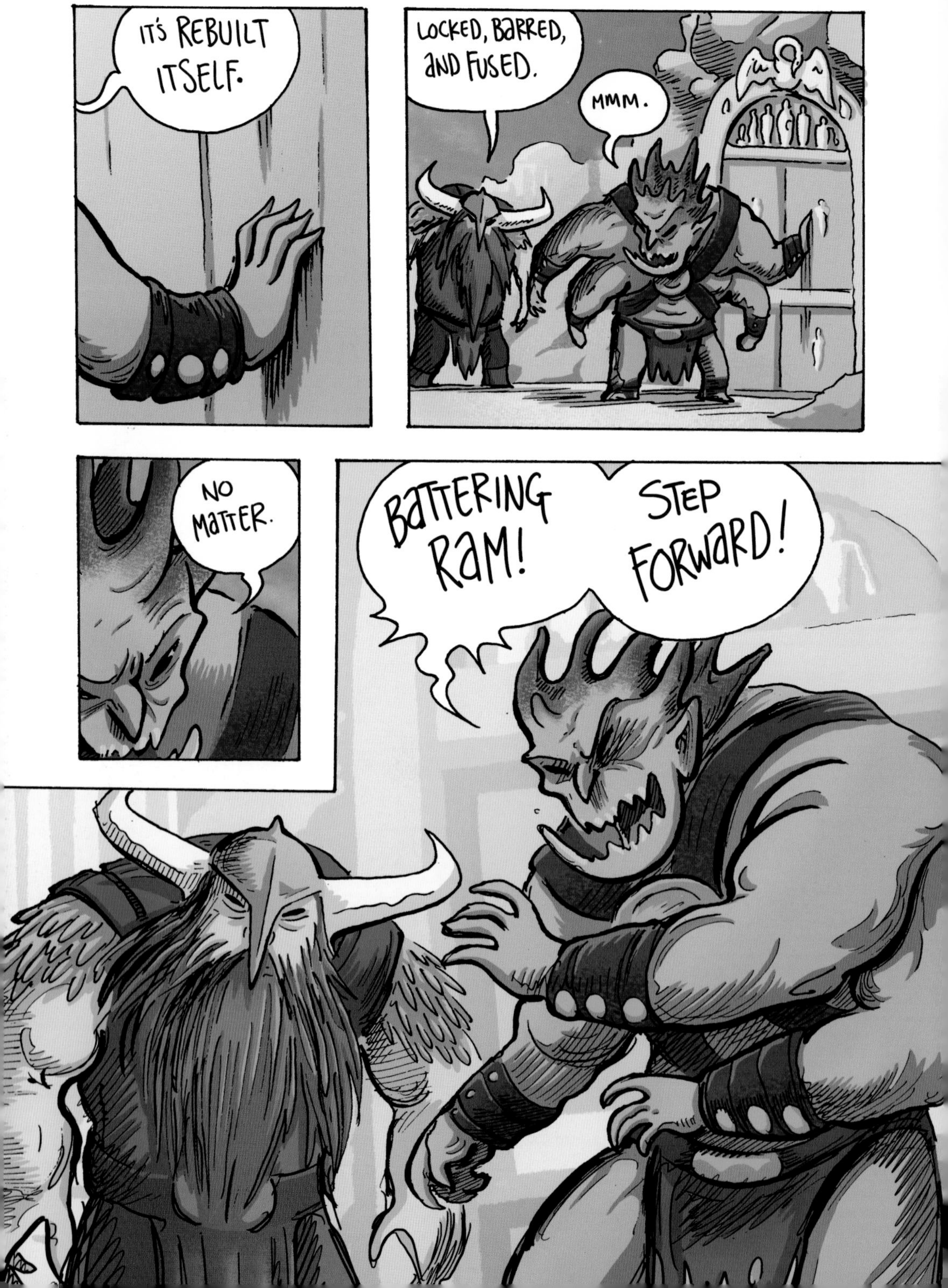
IT'S REBUILT ITSELF.
LOCKED, BARRED, AND FUSED.
MMM.
NO MATTER.
BATTERING RAM!
STEP FORWARD!

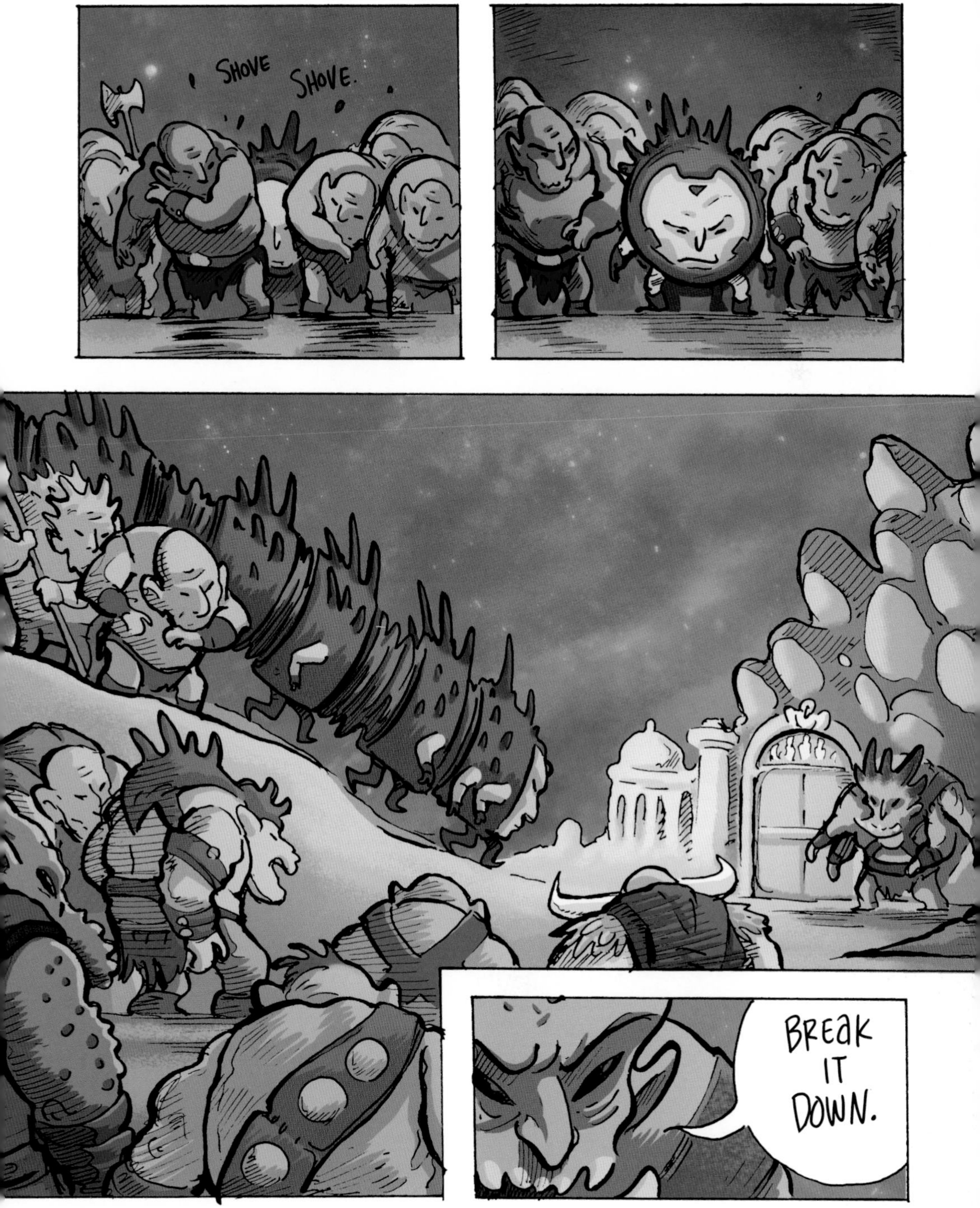
SHOVE
SHOVE.
BREAK IT DOWN.

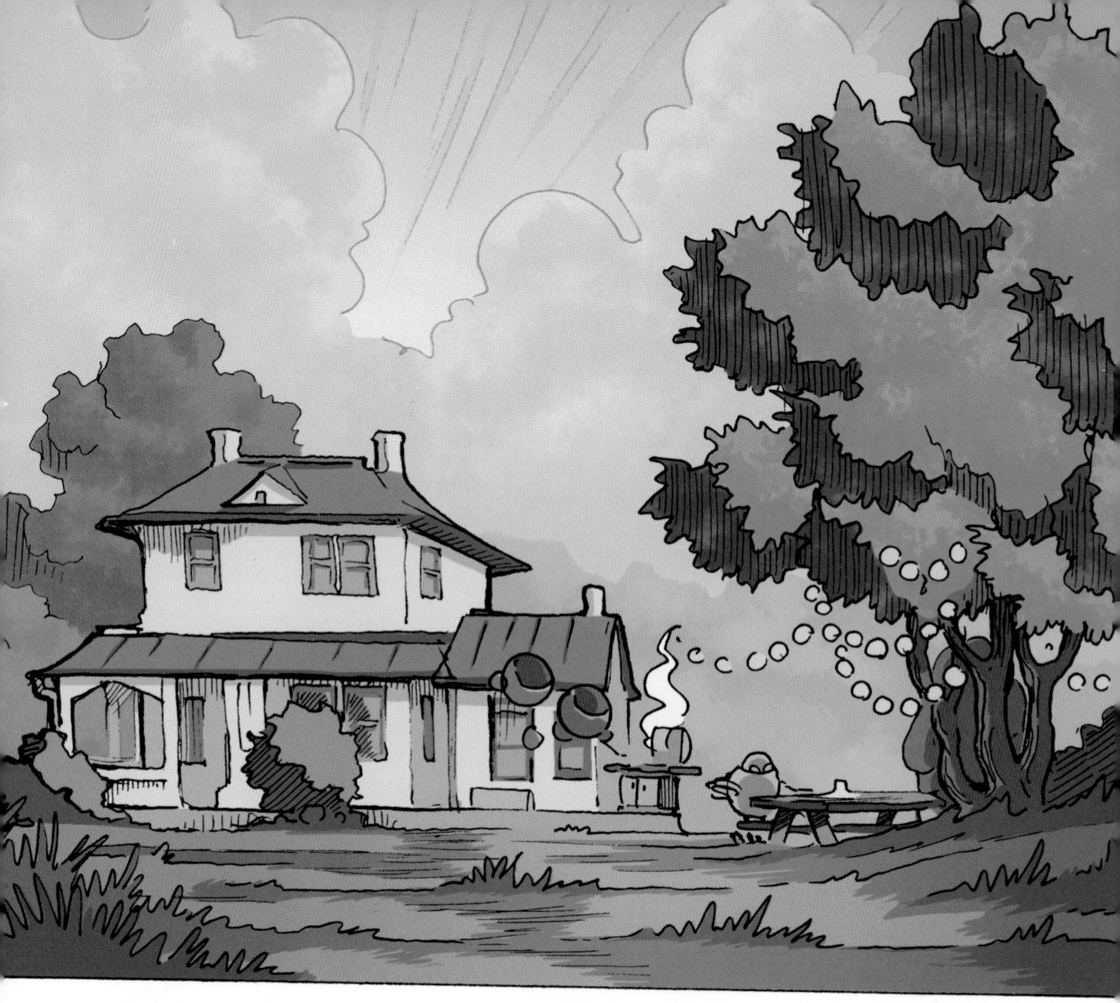

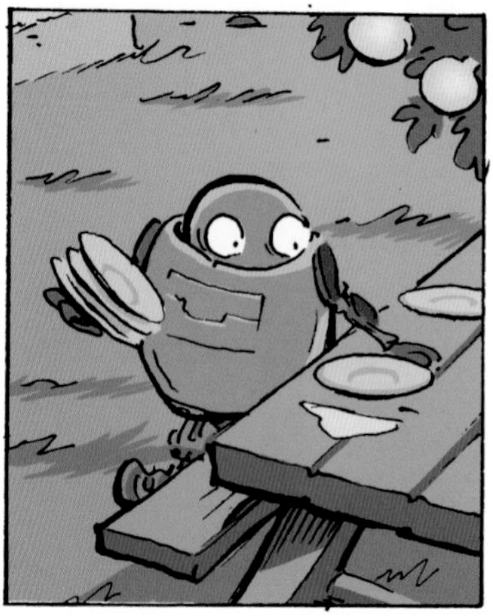

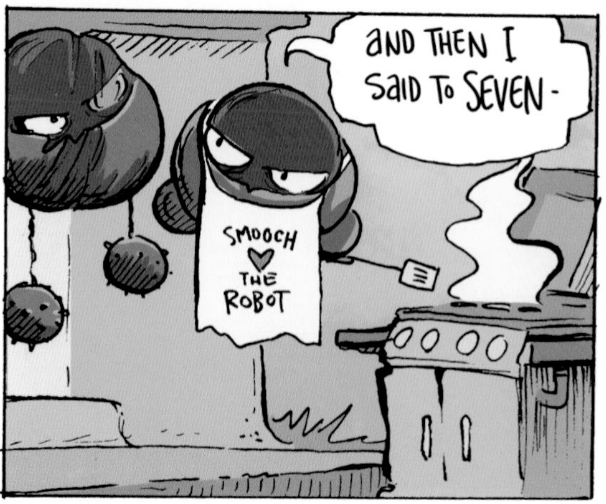
AND THEN I SAID TO SEVEN-
SMOOCH ♥ THE ROBOT

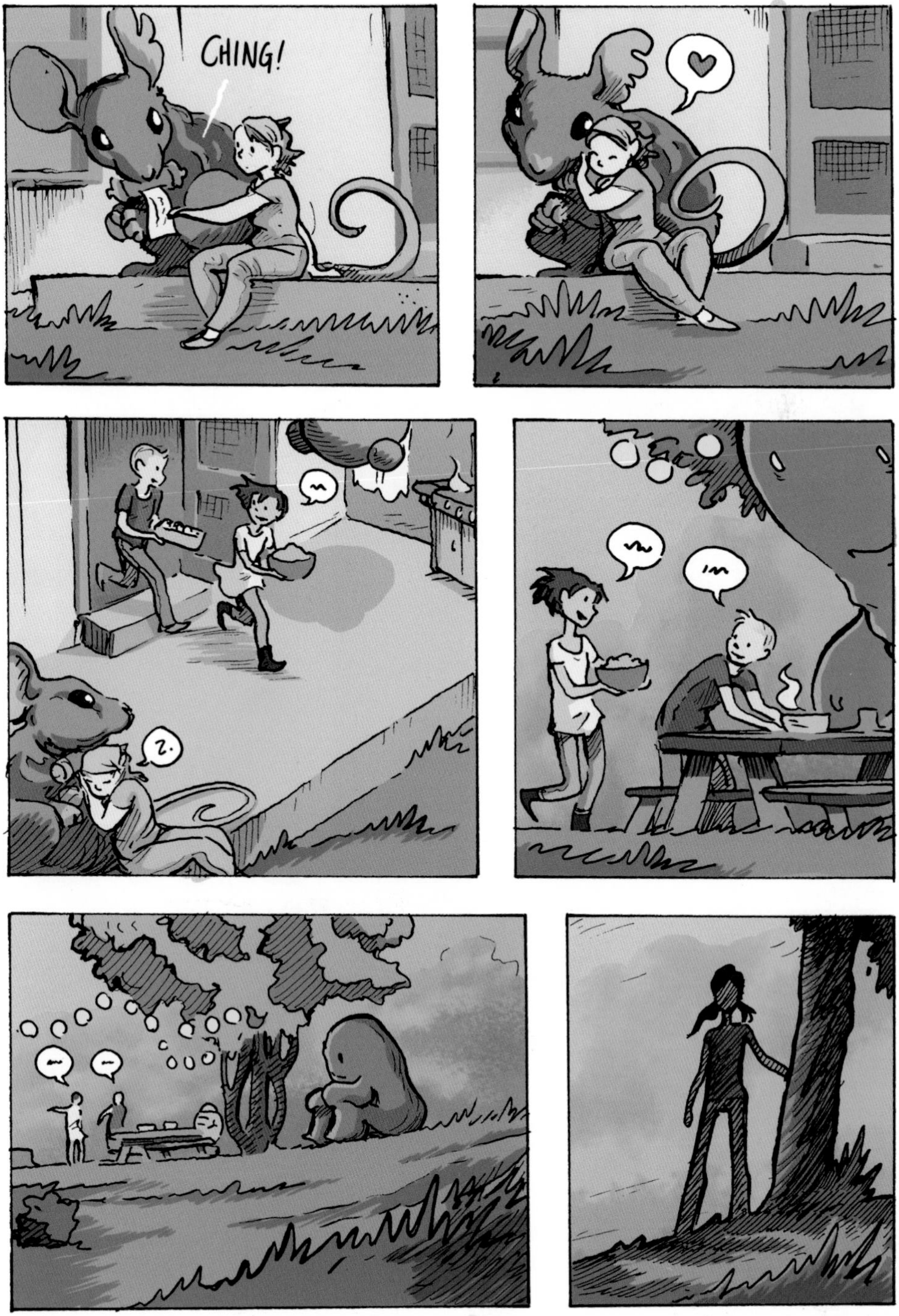
CHING!

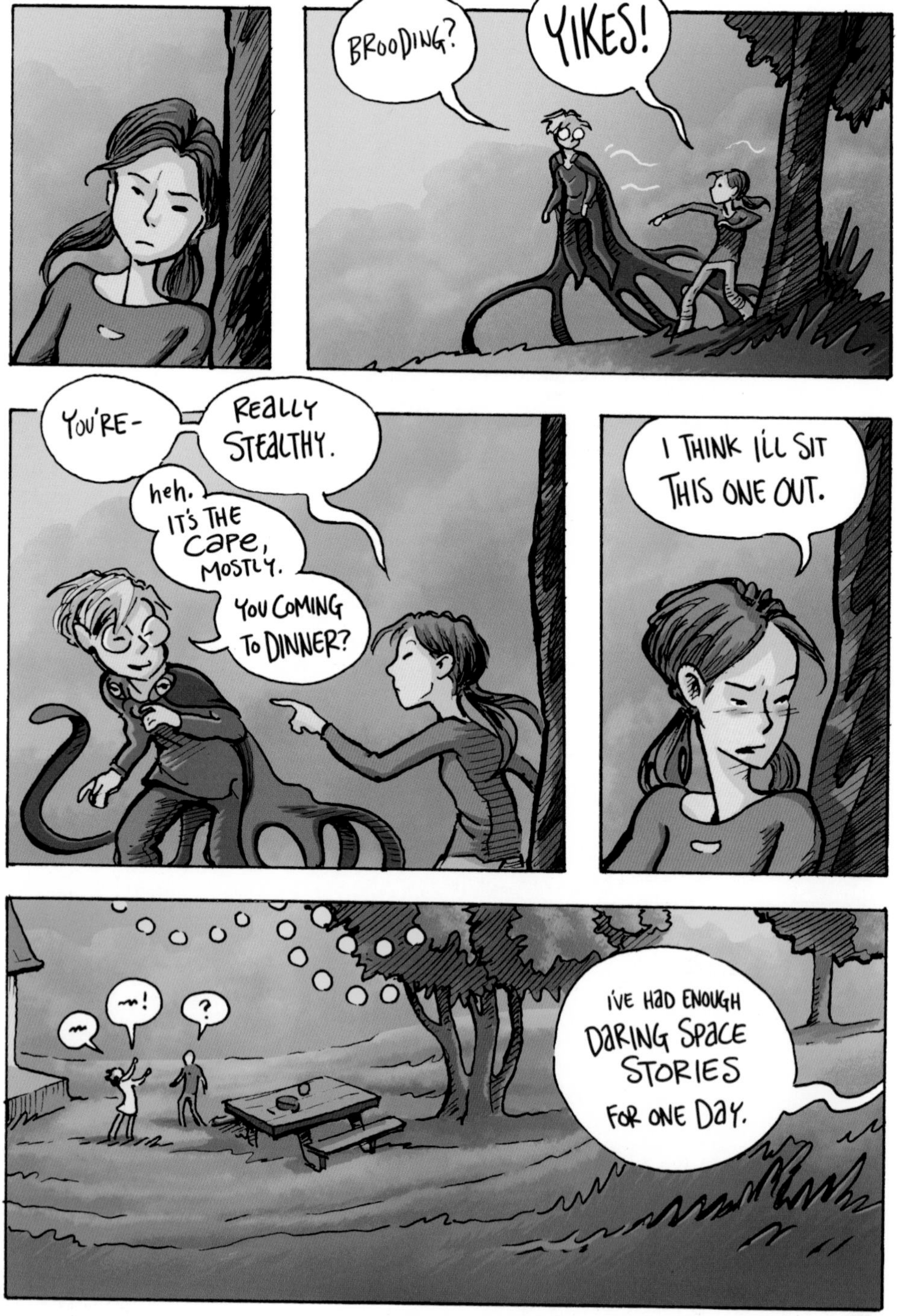
BROODING?
YIKES!
YOU'RE-
REALLY STEALTHY.
heh. IT'S THE cape, MOSTLY.
YOU COMING TO DINNER?
I THINK I'LL SIT THIS ONE OUT.
~!
?
I'VE HAD ENOUGH DARING SPACE STORIES FOR ONE DAY.

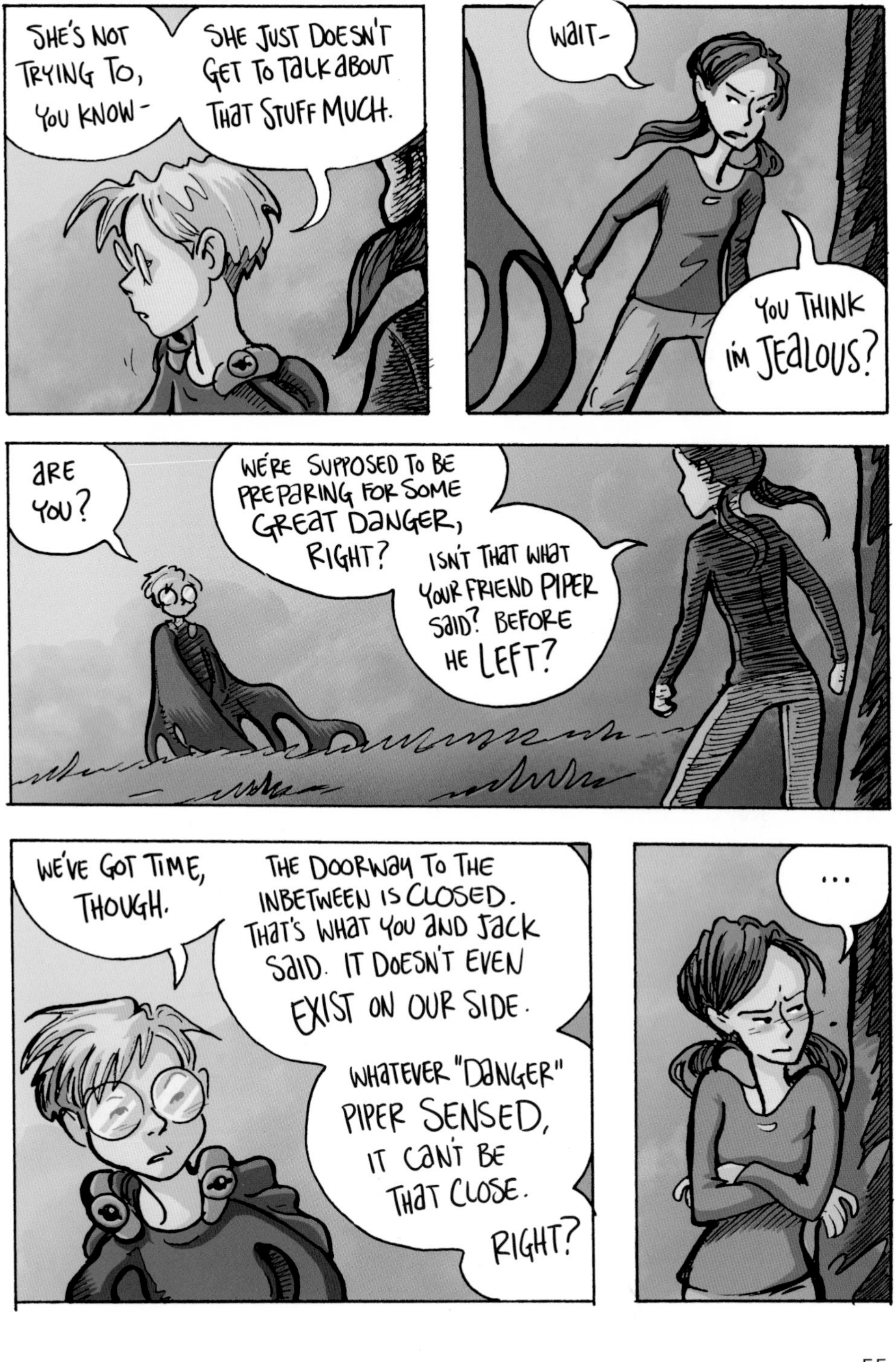
SHE'S NOT TRYING TO, YOU KNOW-
SHE JUST DOESN'T GET TO TALK ABOUT THAT STUFF MUCH.
WAIT-
YOU THINK I'M JEALOUS?
ARE YOU?
WE'RE SUPPOSED TO BE PREPARING FOR SOME GREAT DANGER, RIGHT?
ISN'T THAT WHAT YOUR FRIEND PIPER SAID? BEFORE HE LEFT?
WE'VE GOT TIME, THOUGH.
THE DOORWAY TO THE INBETWEEN IS CLOSED. THAT'S WHAT YOU AND JACK SAID. IT DOESN'T EVEN EXIST ON OUR SIDE.
WHATEVER "DANGER" PIPER SENSED, IT CAN'T BE THAT CLOSE.
RIGHT?
...

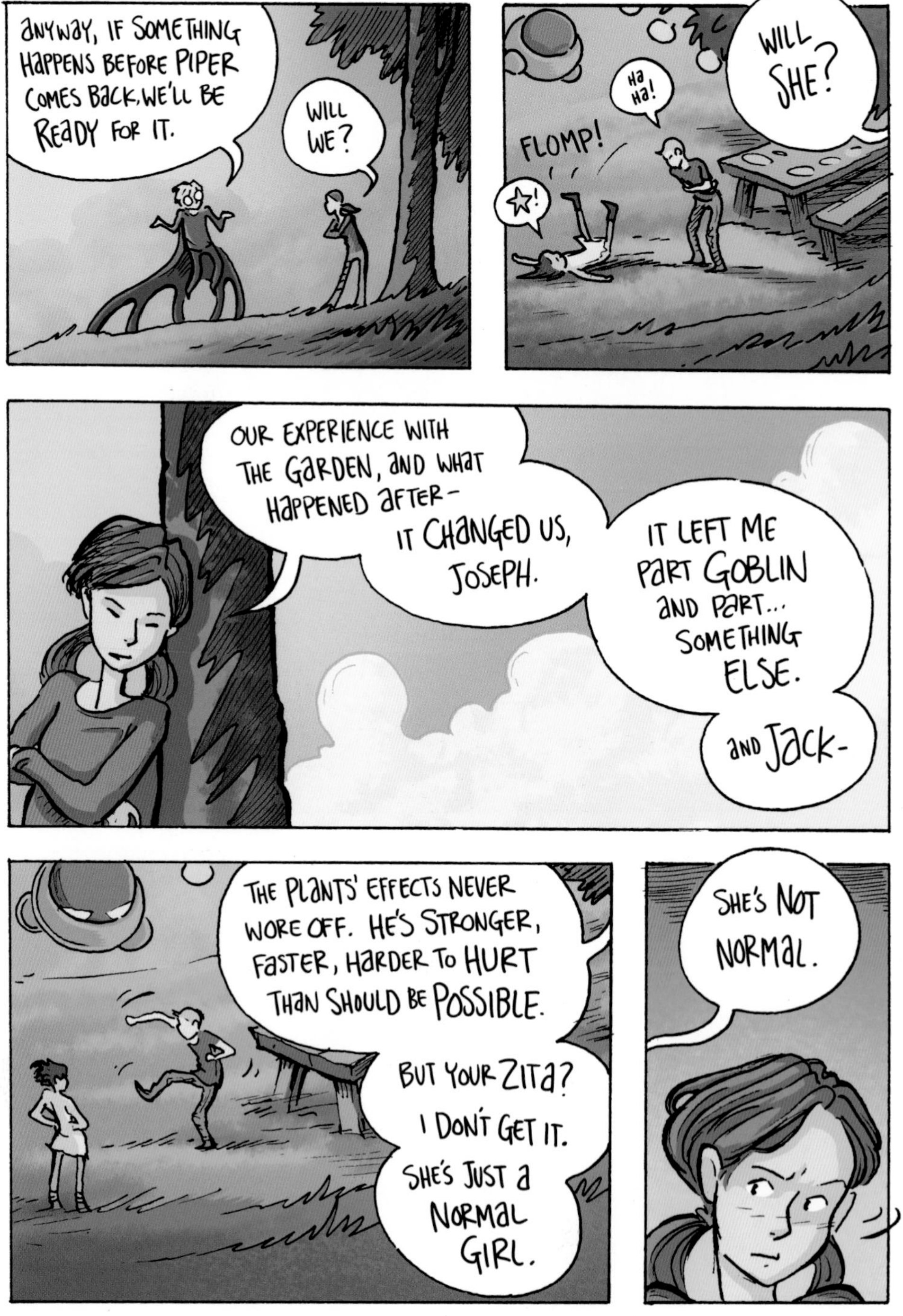
ANYWAY, IF SOMETHING HAPPENS BEFORE PIPER COMES BACK, WE'LL BE READY FOR IT.
WILL WE?
HA HA!
FLOMP!
WILL SHE?
OUR EXPERIENCE WITH THE GARDEN, AND WHAT HAPPENED AFTER-
IT CHANGED US, JOSEPH.
IT LEFT ME PART GOBLIN AND PART... SOMETHING ELSE.
AND JACK-
THE PLANTS' EFFECTS NEVER WORE OFF. HE'S STRONGER, FASTER, HARDER TO HURT THAN SHOULD BE POSSIBLE.
BUT YOUR ZITA?
I DON'T GET IT.
SHE'S JUST A NORMAL GIRL.
SHE'S NOT NORMAL.

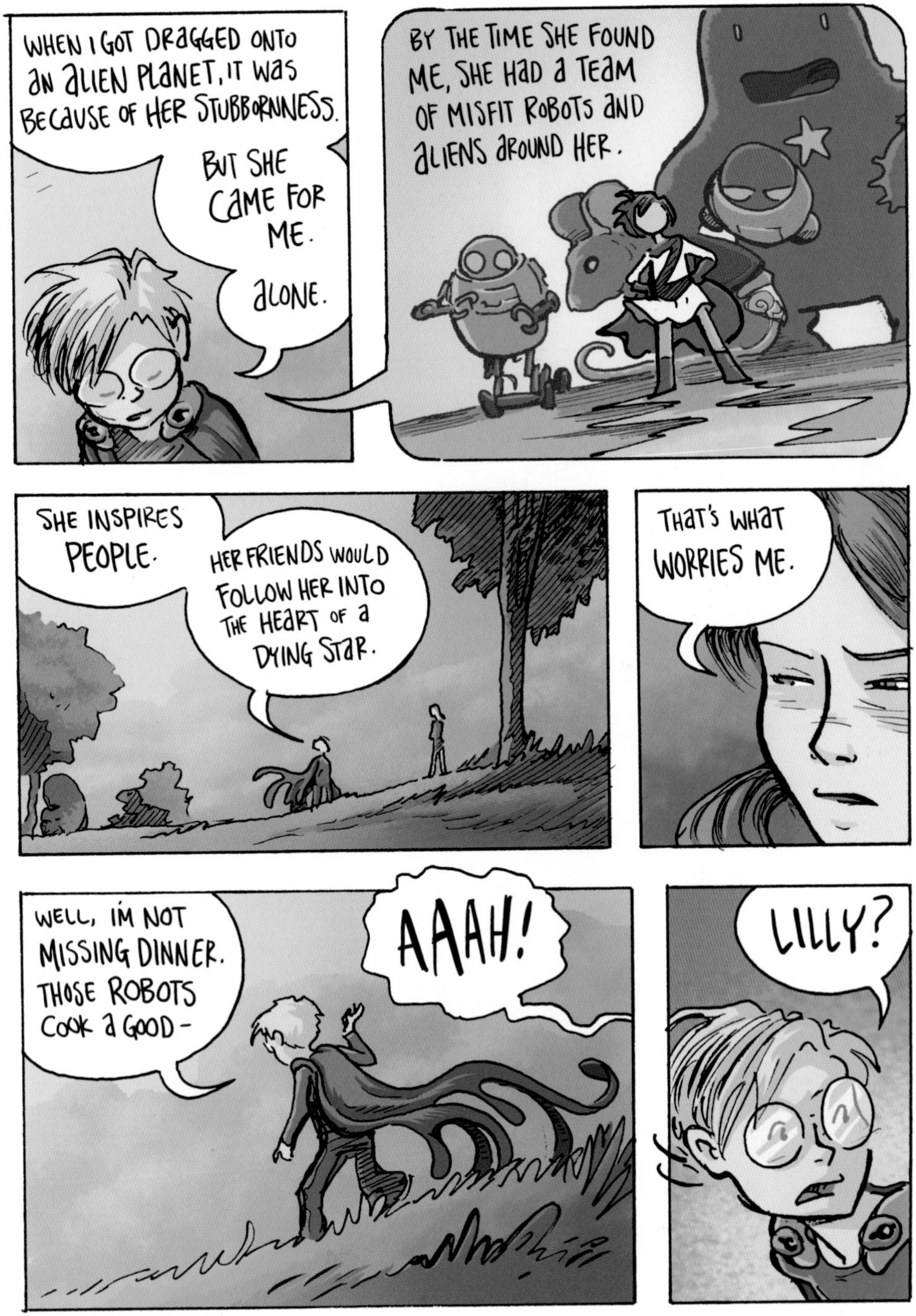
WHEN I GOT DRAGGED ONTO AN ALIEN PLANET, IT WAS BECAUSE OF HER STUBBORNNESS.
BUT SHE CAME FOR ME.
ALONE.
BY THE TIME SHE FOUND ME, SHE HAD A TEAM OF MISFIT ROBOTS AND ALIENS AROUND HER.
SHE INSPIRES PEOPLE.
HER FRIENDS WOULD FOLLOW HER INTO THE HEART OF A DYING STAR.
THAT'S WHAT WORRIES ME.
WELL, I'M NOT MISSING DINNER. THOSE ROBOTS COOK A GOOD-
AAAH!
LILLY?

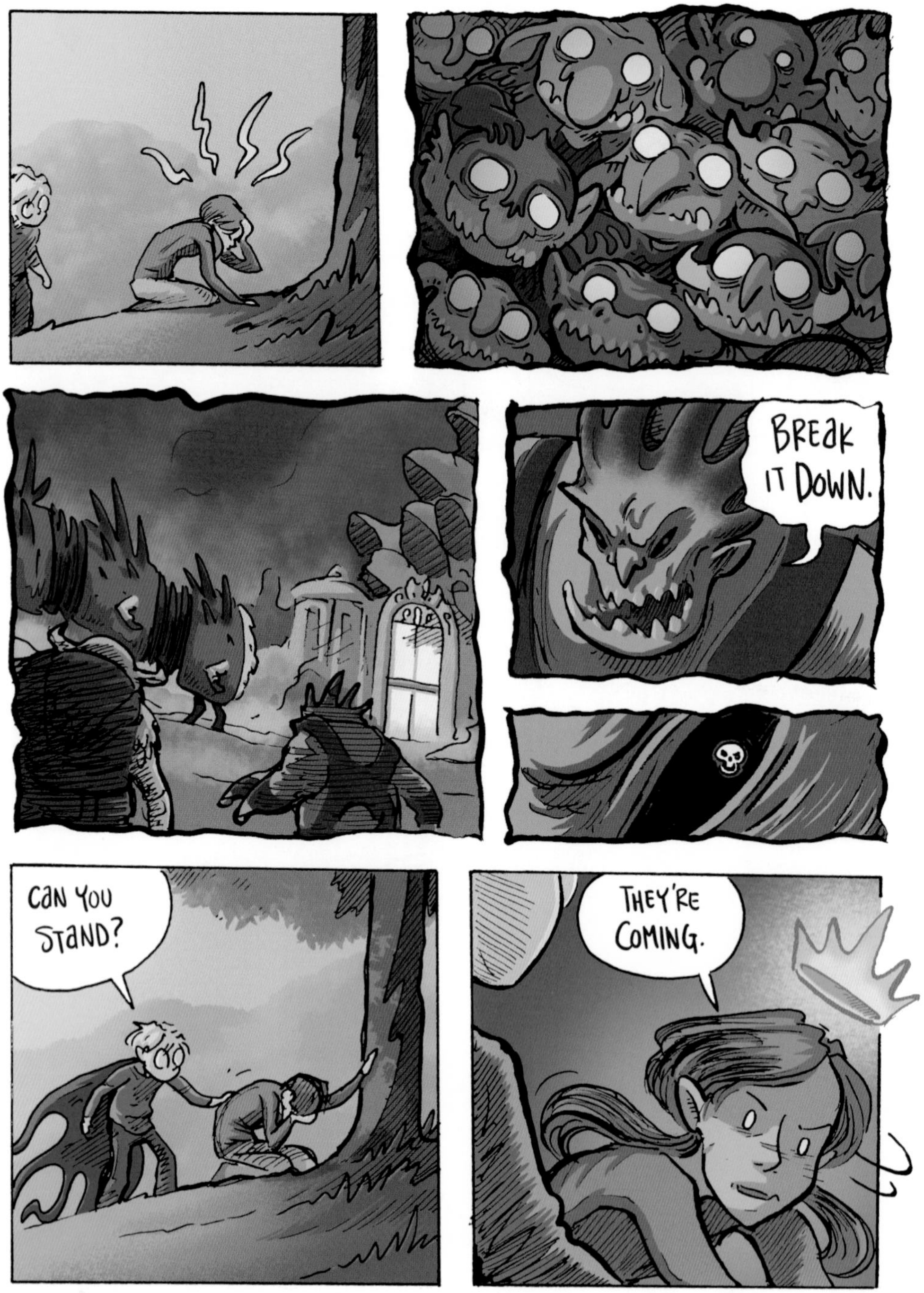
BREAK IT DOWN.
CAN YOU STAND?
THEY'RE COMING.

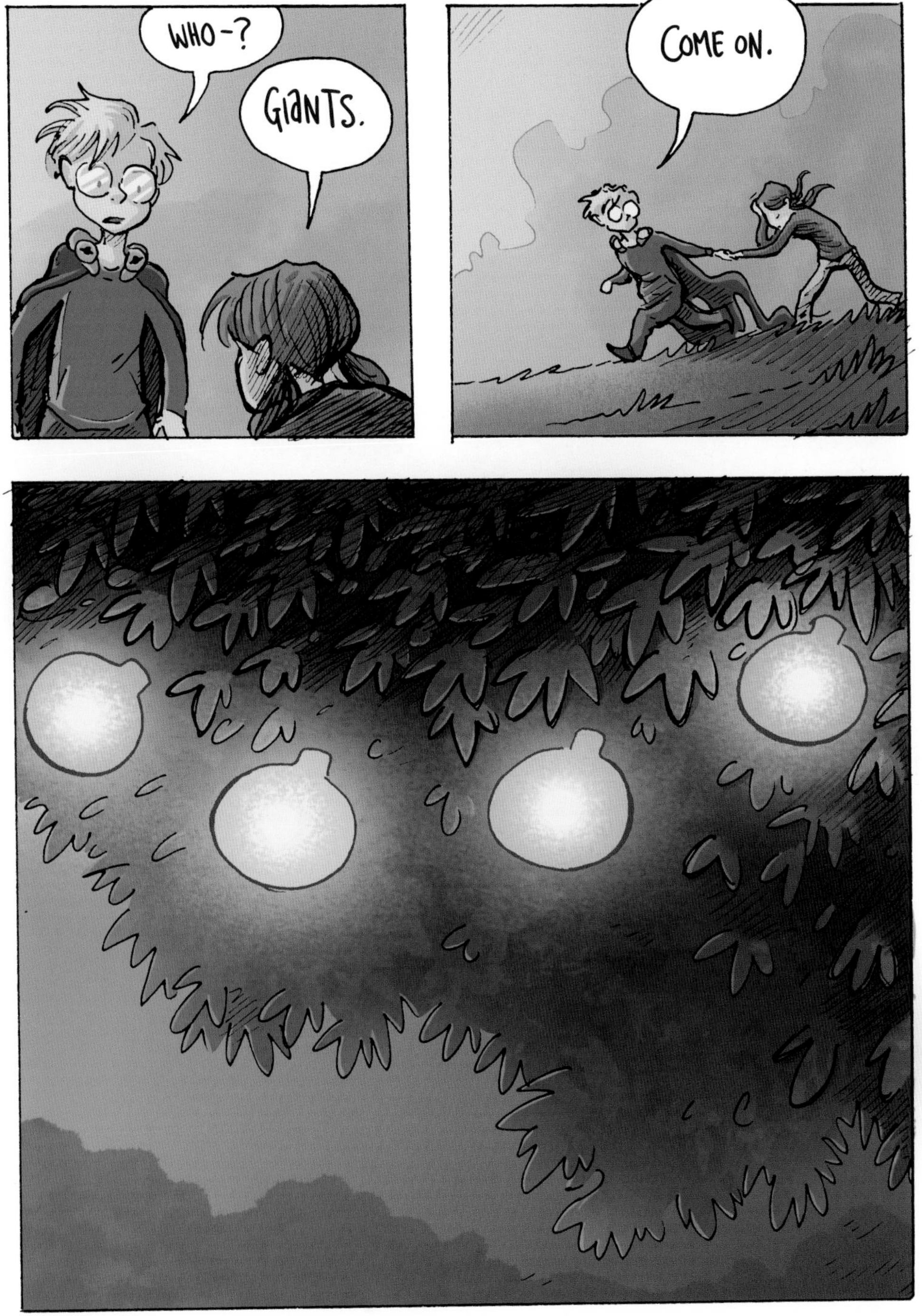
WHO-?
GIANTS.
COME ON.

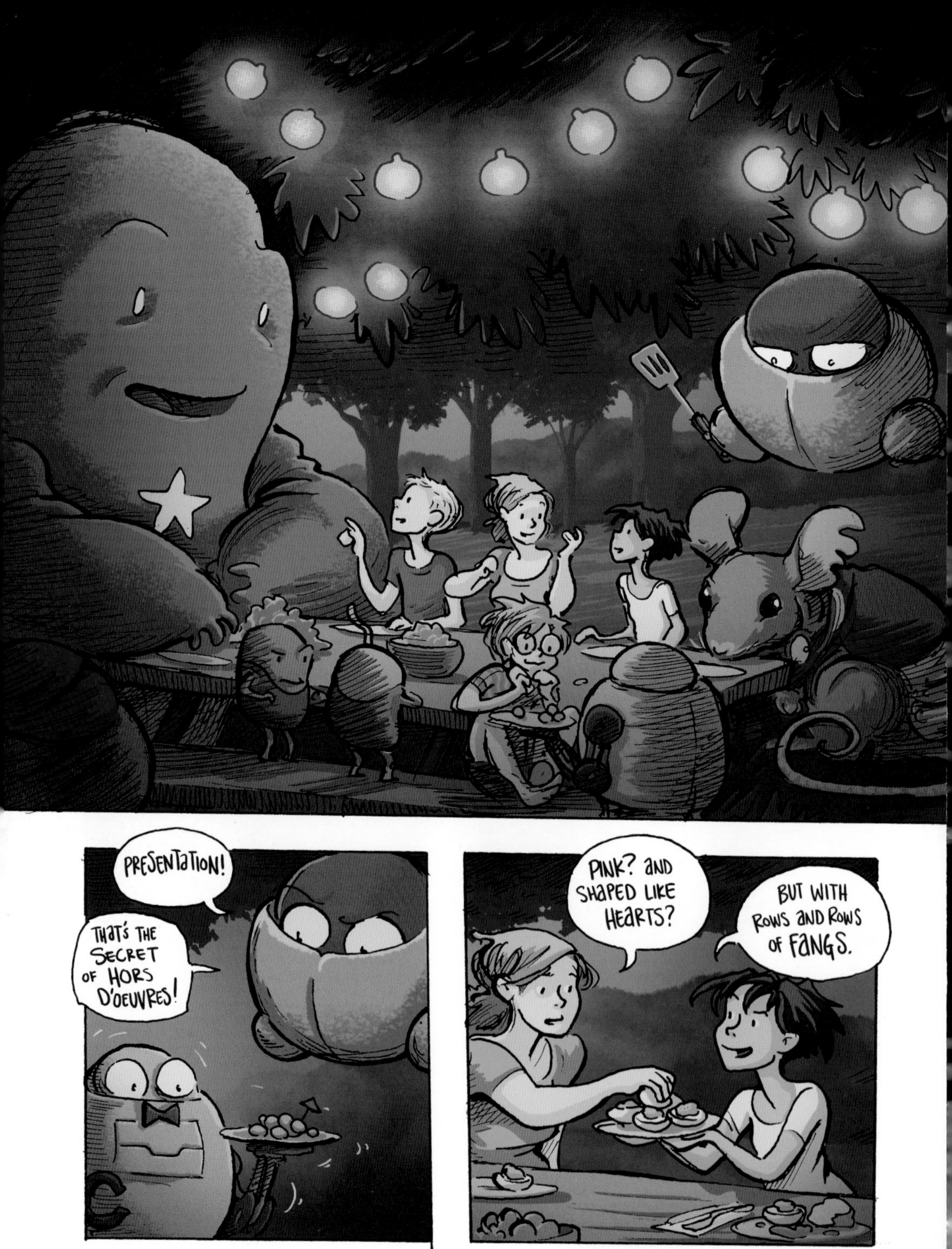
PRESENTATION!
THAT'S THE SECRET OF HORS D'OEUVRES!
PINK? AND SHAPED LIKE HEARTS?
BUT WITH ROWS AND ROWS OF FANGS.

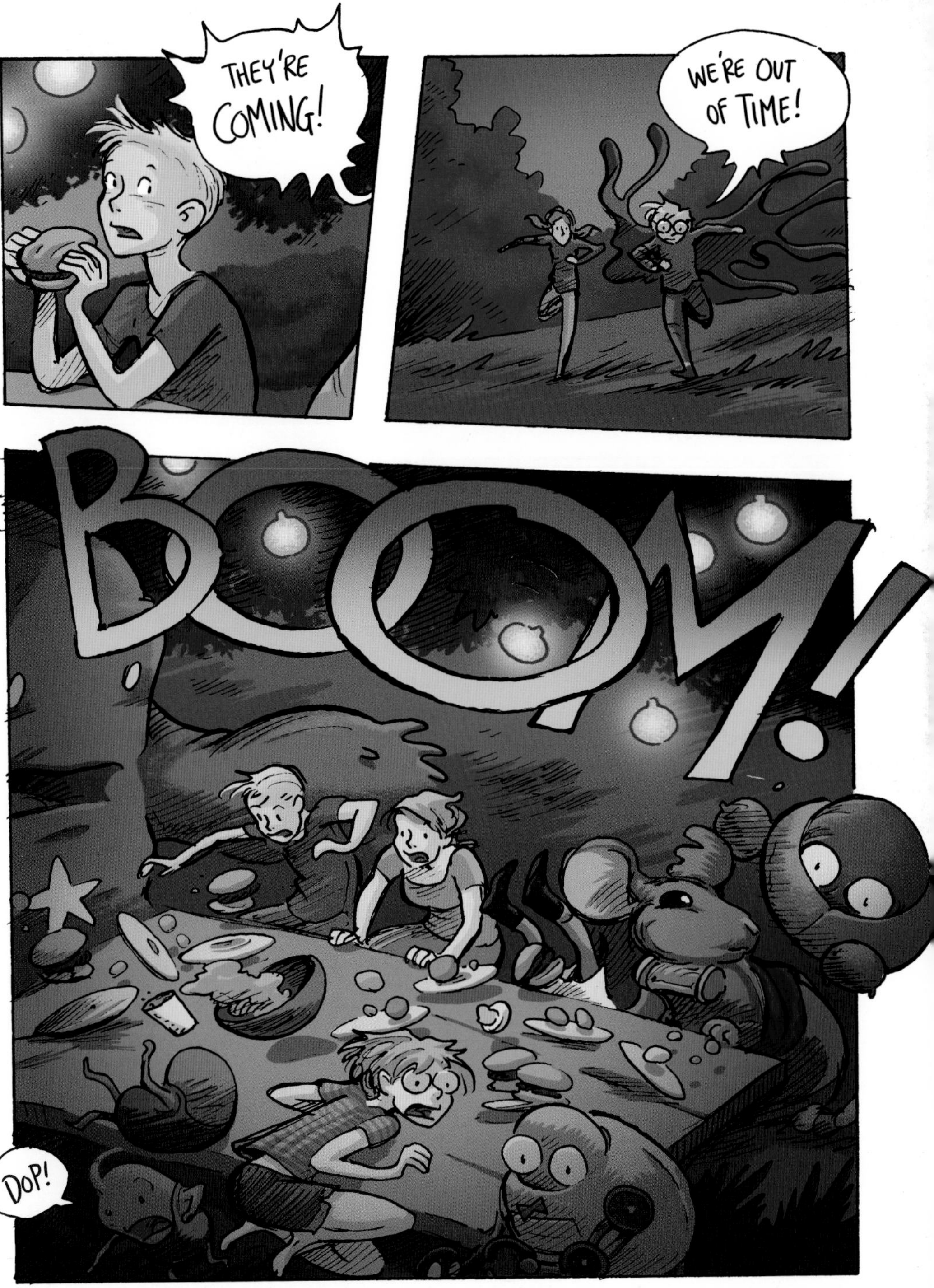
THEY'RE COMING!
WE'RE OUT OF TIME!
BOOM!
DOP!

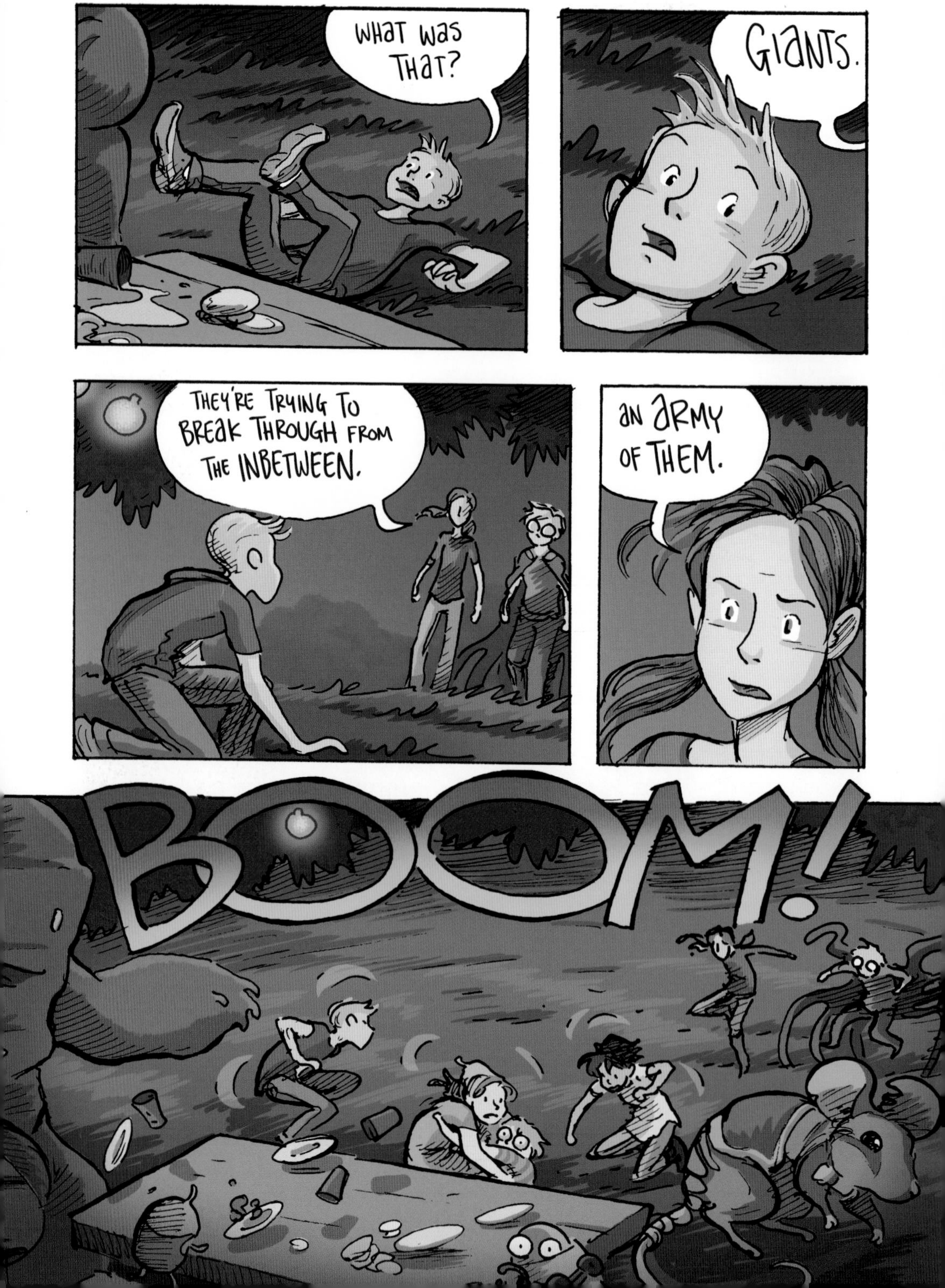
WHAT WAS THAT?
GIANTS.
THEY'RE TRYING TO BREAK THROUGH FROM THE INBETWEEN.
AN ARMY OF THEM.
BOOM!

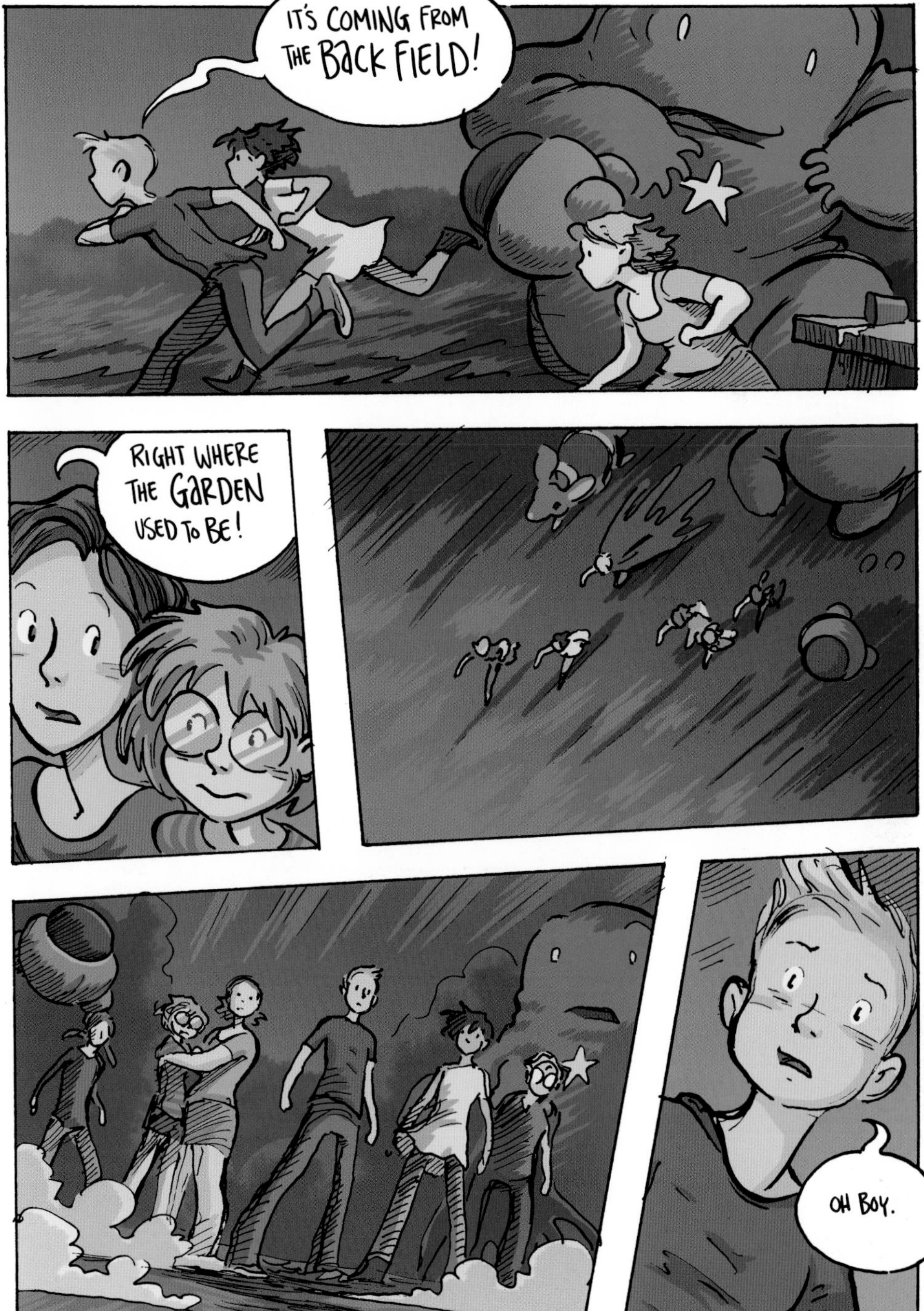
IT'S COMING FROM THE BACK FIELD!
RIGHT WHERE THE GARDEN USED TO BE!
OH BOY.

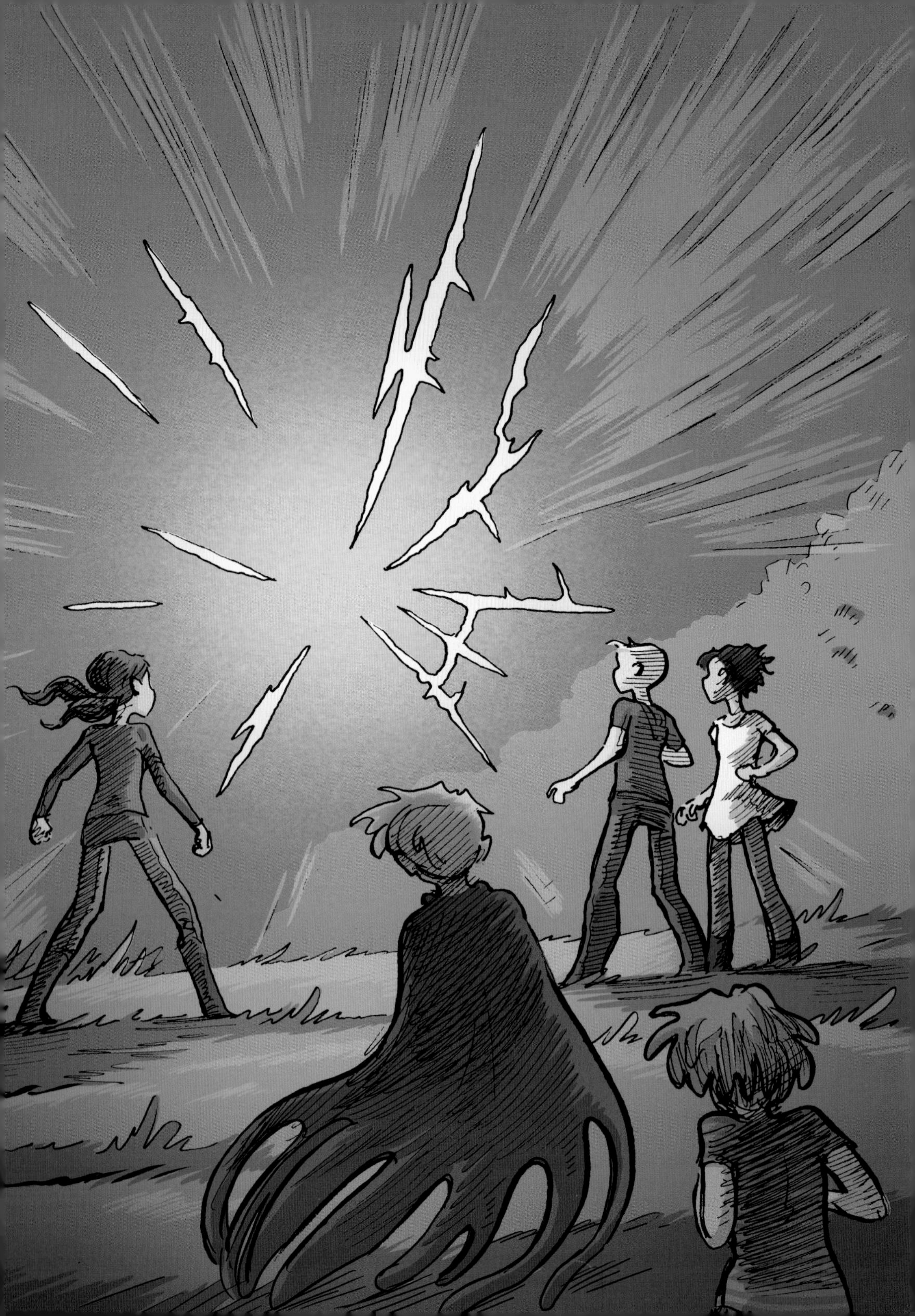

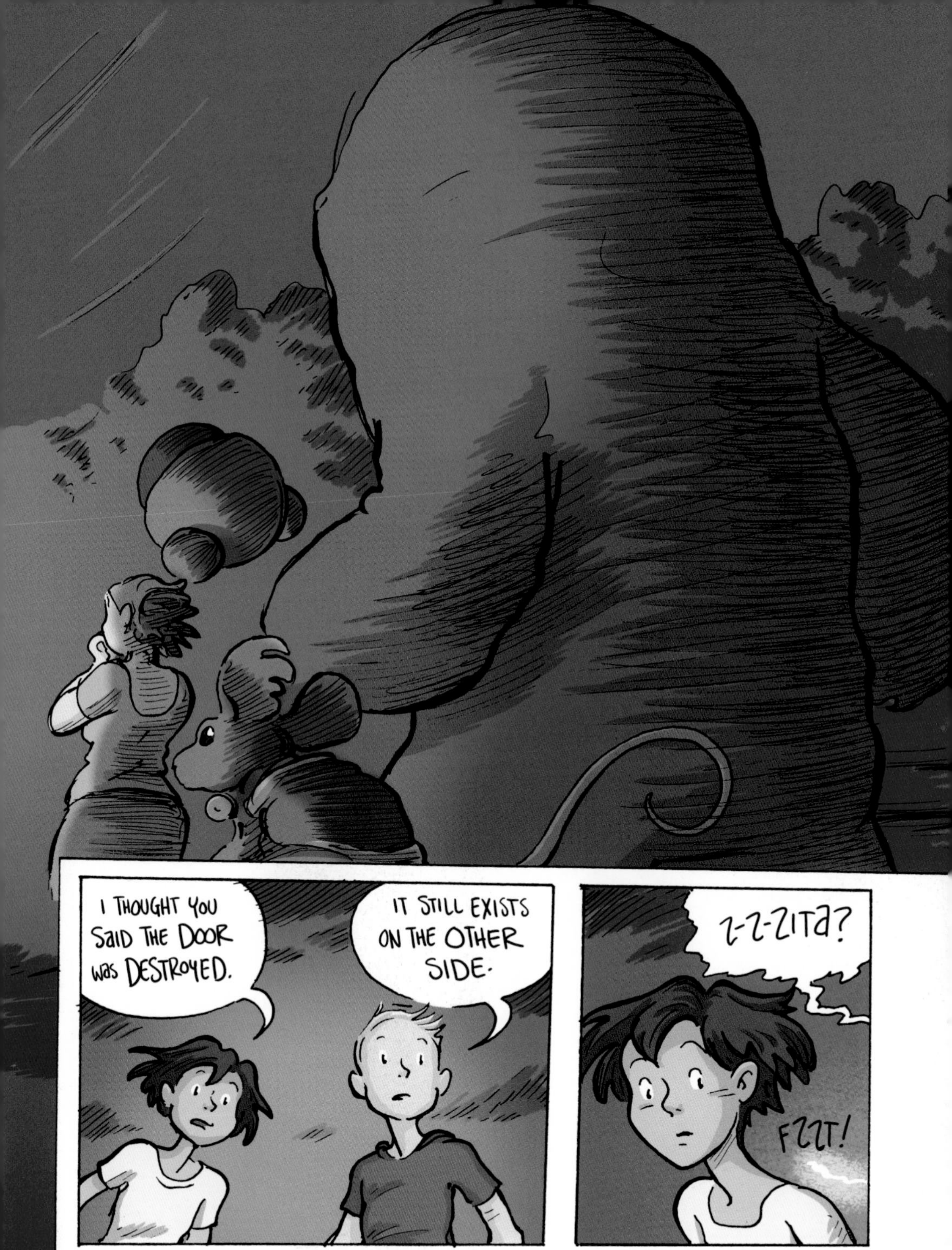
I THOUGHT YOU SAID THE DOOR WAS DESTROYED.
IT STILL EXISTS ON THE OTHER SIDE.
Z-Z-ZITA?
FZZT!

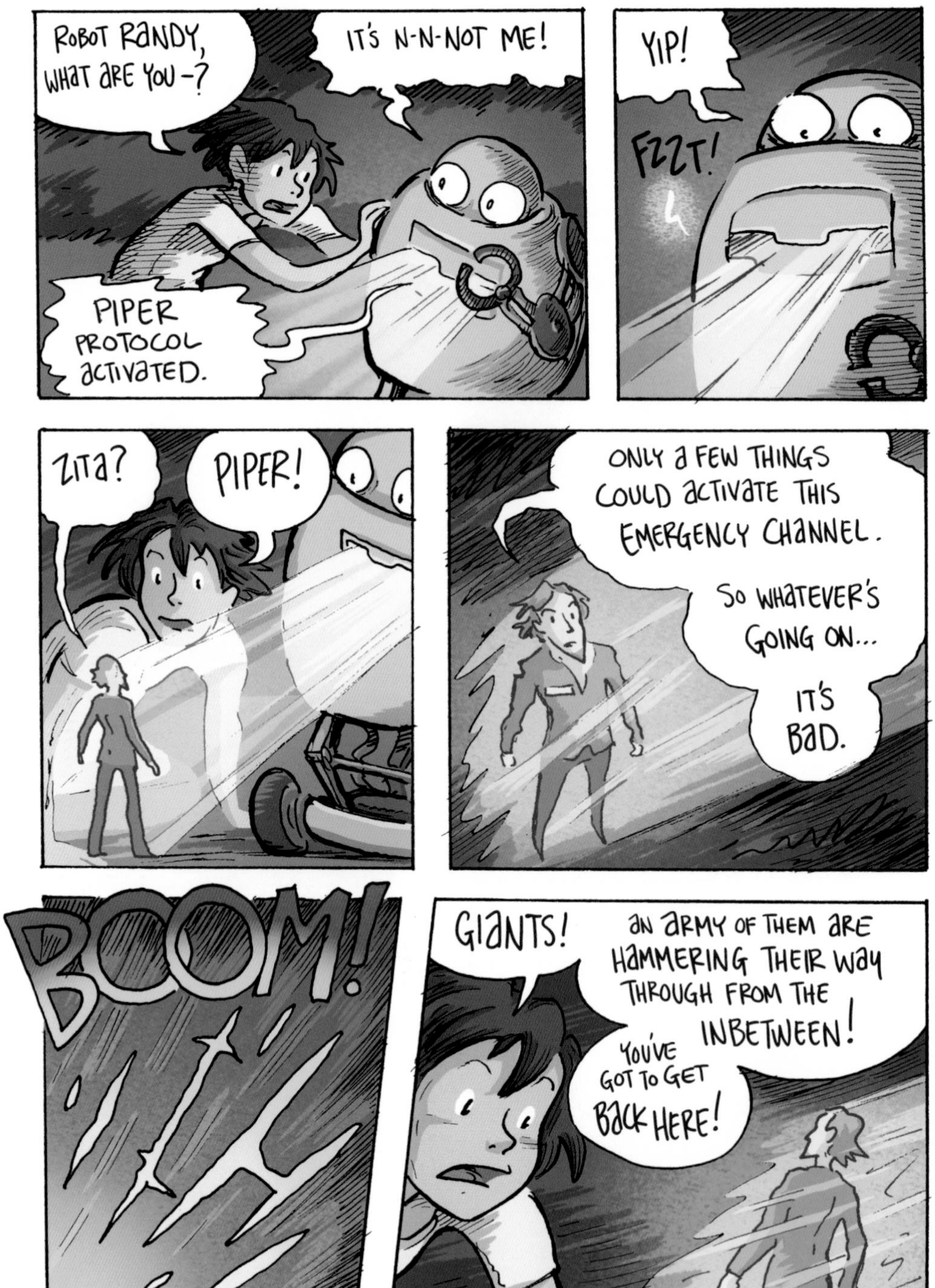

ROBOT RANDY, WHAT ARE YOU –?
IT'S N-N-NOT ME!
PIPER PROTOCOL ACTIVATED.
YIP!
FZZT!
ZITA?
PIPER!
ONLY A FEW THINGS COULD ACTIVATE THIS EMERGENCY CHANNEL.
SO WHATEVER'S GOING ON...
IT'S BAD.
BOOM!
GIANTS!
AN ARMY OF THEM ARE HAMMERING THEIR WAY THROUGH FROM THE INBETWEEN!
YOU'VE GOT TO GET BACK HERE!

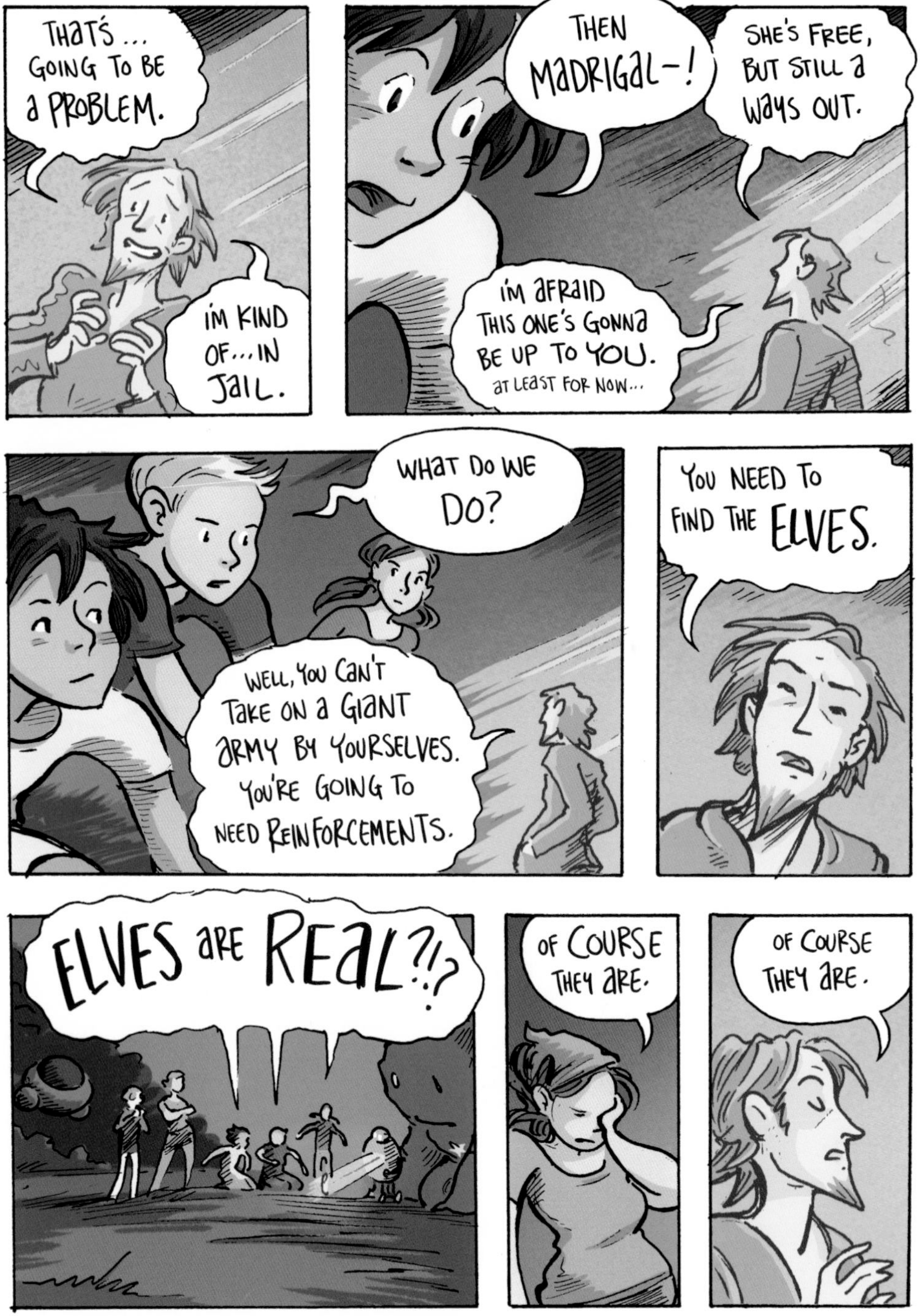

THAT'S ... GOING TO BE a PROBLEM.
I'M KIND OF... IN JaIL.
THEN MaDRIGaL-!
SHE'S FREE, BUT STILL a WaYS OUT.
I'M aFRaID THIS ONE'S GONNa BE UP TO YOU. aT LEaST FOR NOW...
WHaT DO WE DO?
WELL, YOU CaN'T TaKE ON a GIaNT aRMY BY YOURSELVES. YOU'RE GOING TO NEED REINFORCEMENTS.
YOU NEED TO FIND THE ELVES.
ELVES aRE REaL?!?
OF COURSE THEY aRE.
OF COURSE THEY aRE.

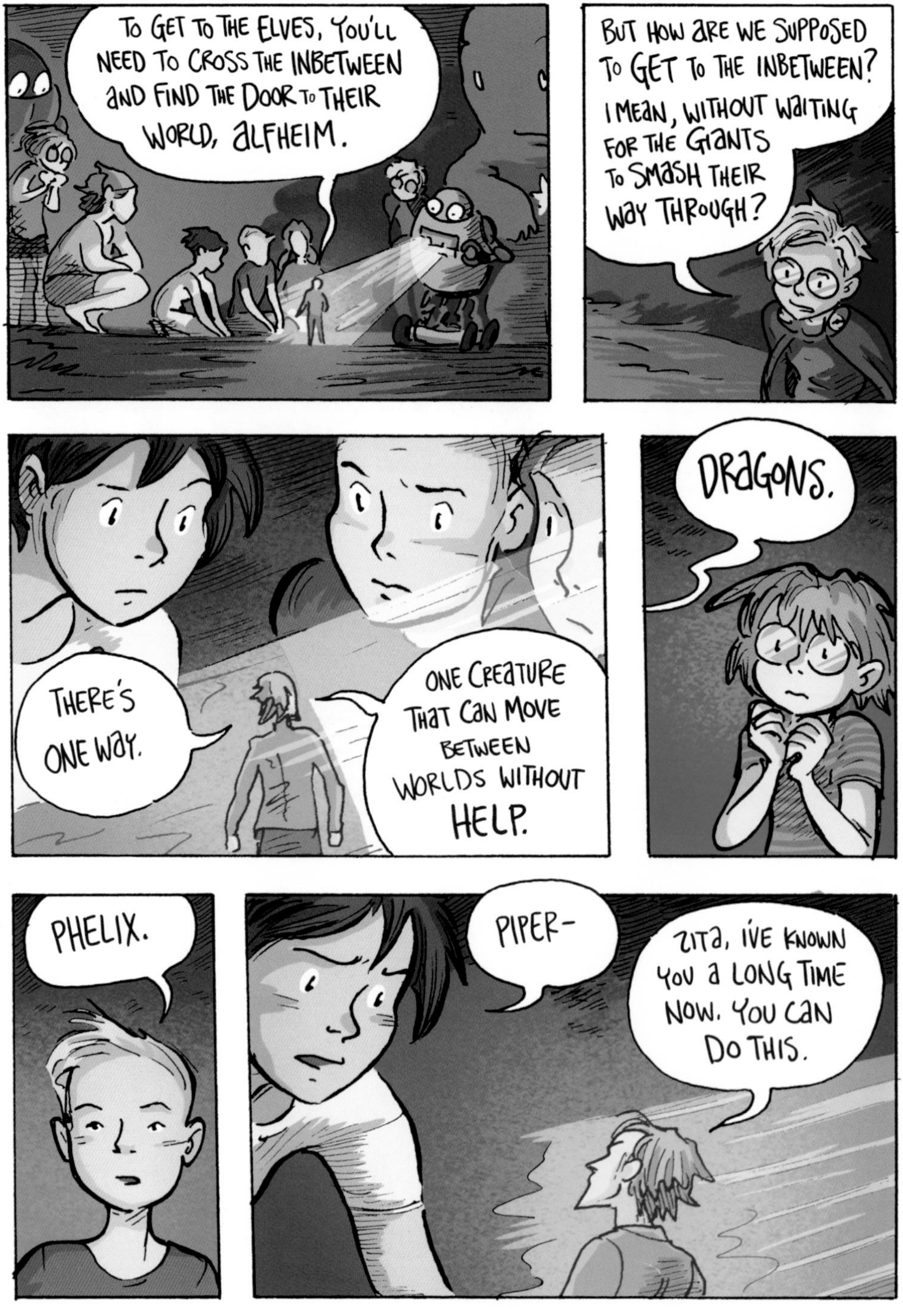
TO GET TO THE ELVES, YOU'LL NEED TO CROSS THE INBETWEEN AND FIND THE DOOR TO THEIR WORLD, ALFHEIM.
BUT HOW ARE WE SUPPOSED TO GET TO THE INBETWEEN? I MEAN, WITHOUT WAITING FOR THE GIANTS TO SMASH THEIR WAY THROUGH?
THERE'S ONE WAY.
ONE CREATURE THAT CAN MOVE BETWEEN WORLDS WITHOUT HELP.
DRAGONS.
PHELIX.
PIPER-
ZITA, I'VE KNOWN YOU A LONG TIME NOW. YOU CAN DO THIS.

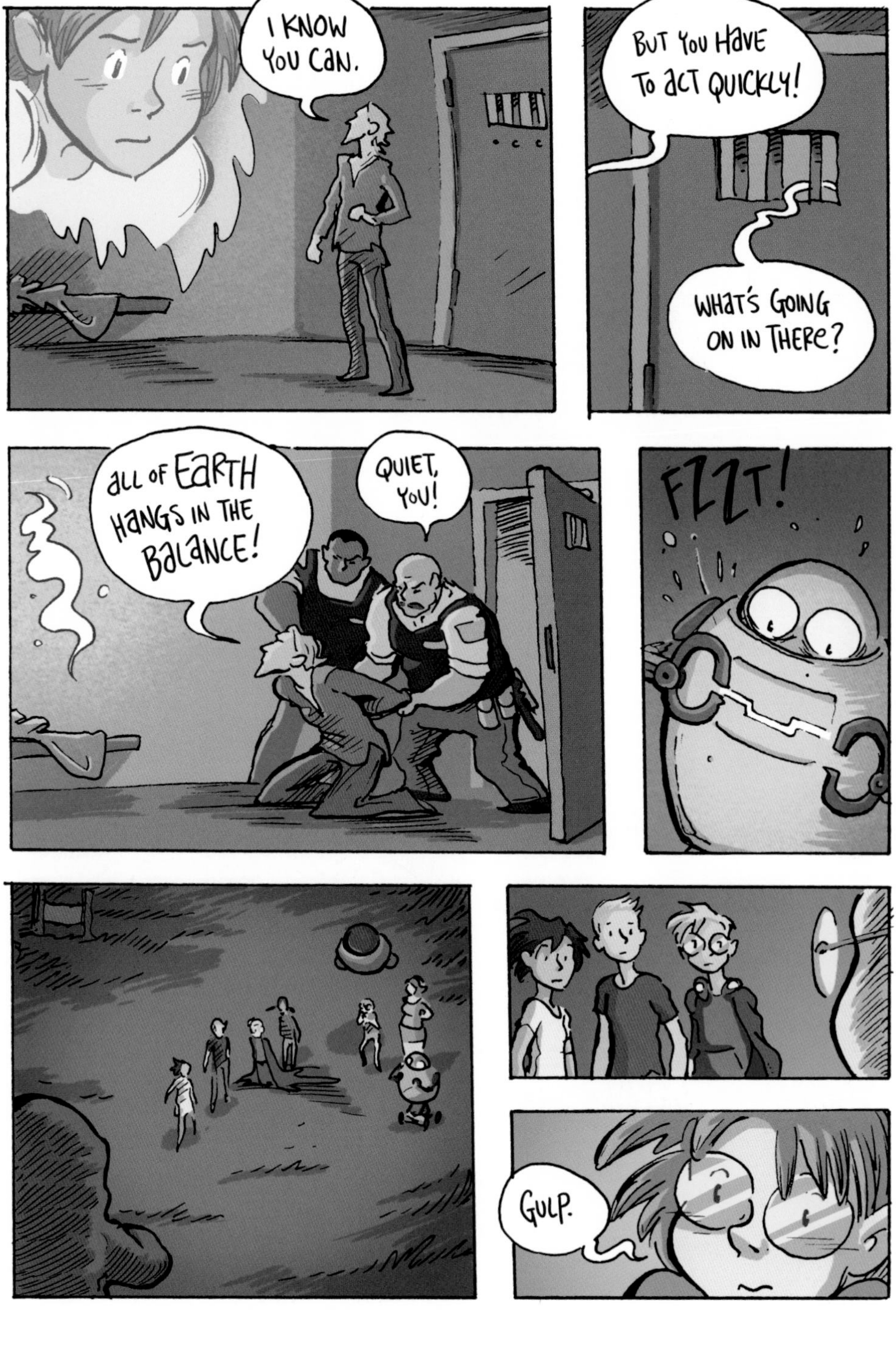
I KNOW YOU CAN.
BUT YOU HAVE TO ACT QUICKLY!
WHAT'S GOING ON IN THERE?
ALL OF EARTH HANGS IN THE BALANCE!
QUIET, YOU!
FZZT!
GULP.

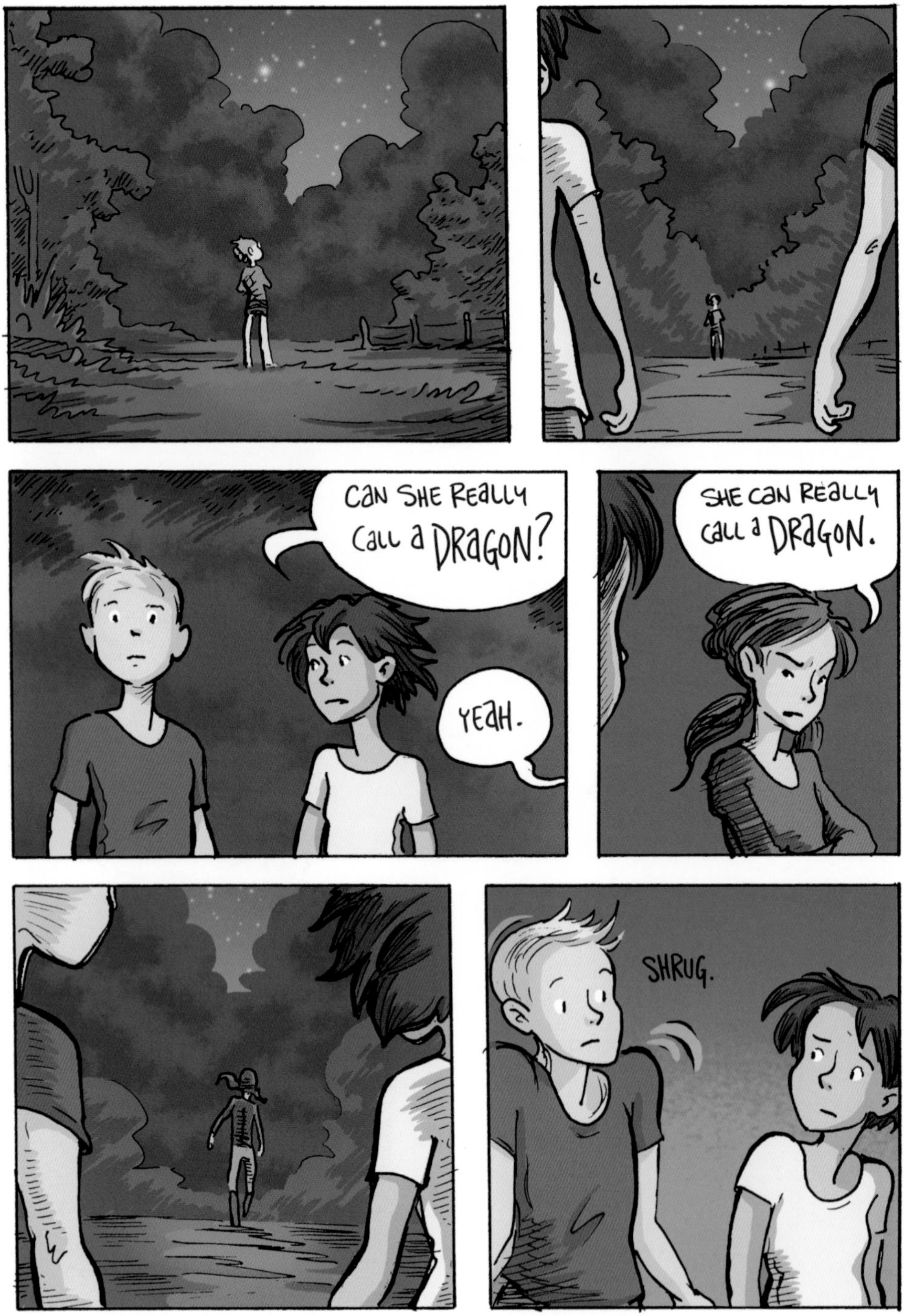
CAN SHE REALLY CALL A DRAGON?
YEAH.
SHE CAN REALLY CALL A DRAGON.
SHRUG.

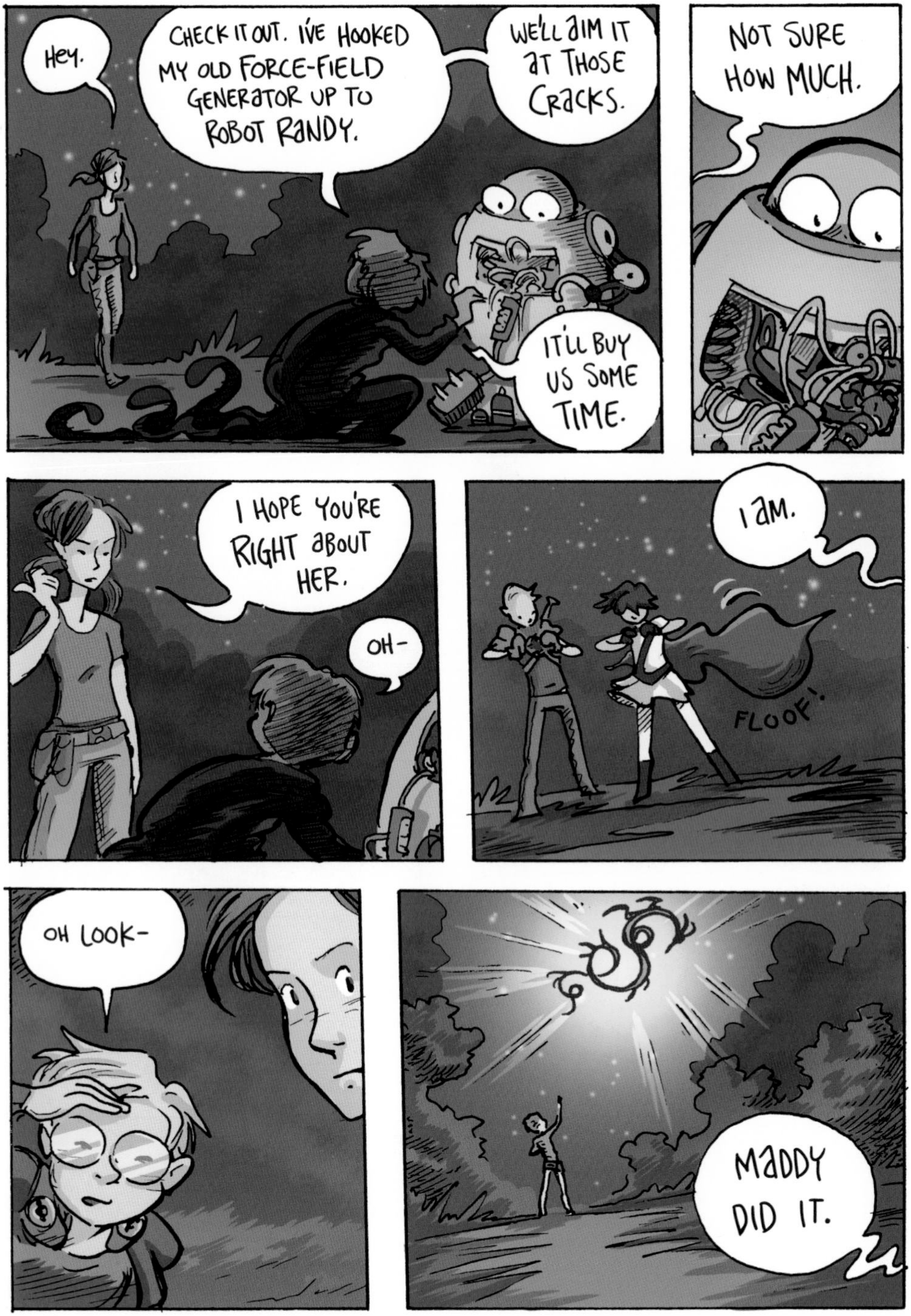
HEY.
CHECK IT OUT. I'VE HOOKED MY OLD FORCE-FIELD GENERATOR UP TO ROBOT RANDY.
WE'LL AIM IT AT THOSE CRACKS.
IT'LL BUY US SOME TIME.
NOT SURE HOW MUCH.
I HOPE YOU'RE RIGHT ABOUT HER.
OH-
I AM.
FLOOF!
OH LOOK-
MADDY DID IT.

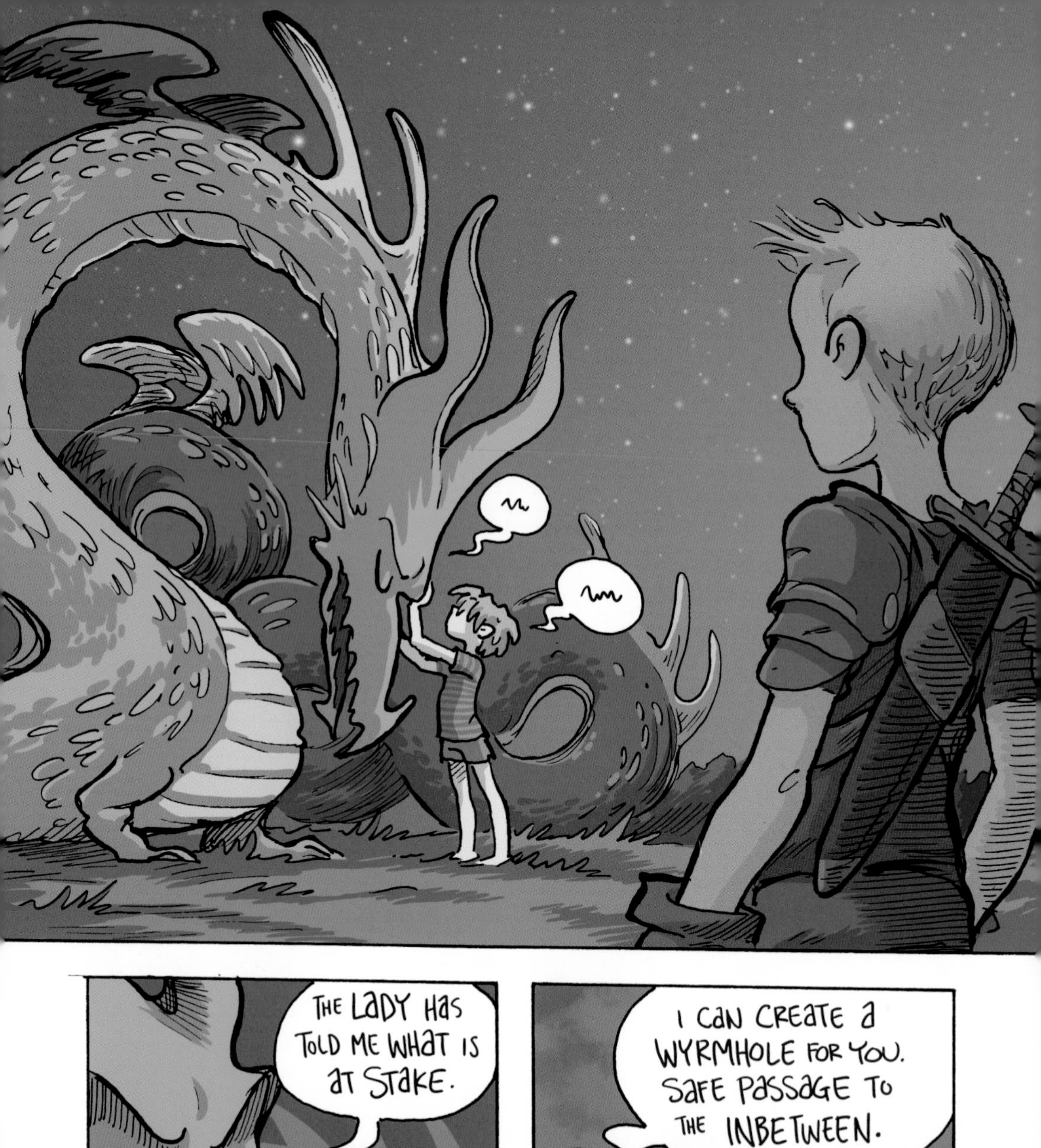

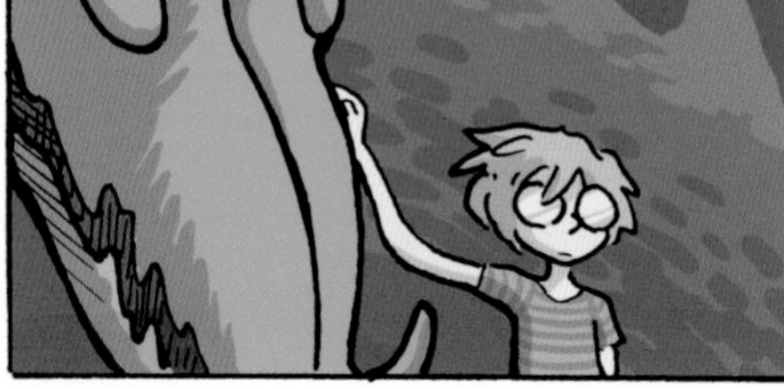
THE LADY HAS TOLD ME WHAT IS AT STAKE.

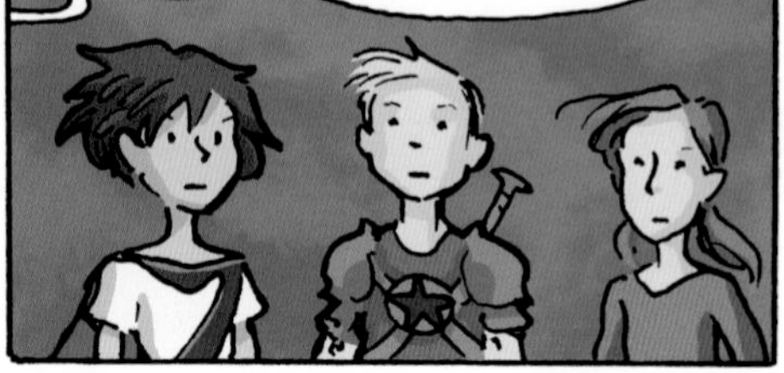
I CAN CREATE A WYRMHOLE FOR YOU. SAFE PASSAGE TO THE INBETWEEN.

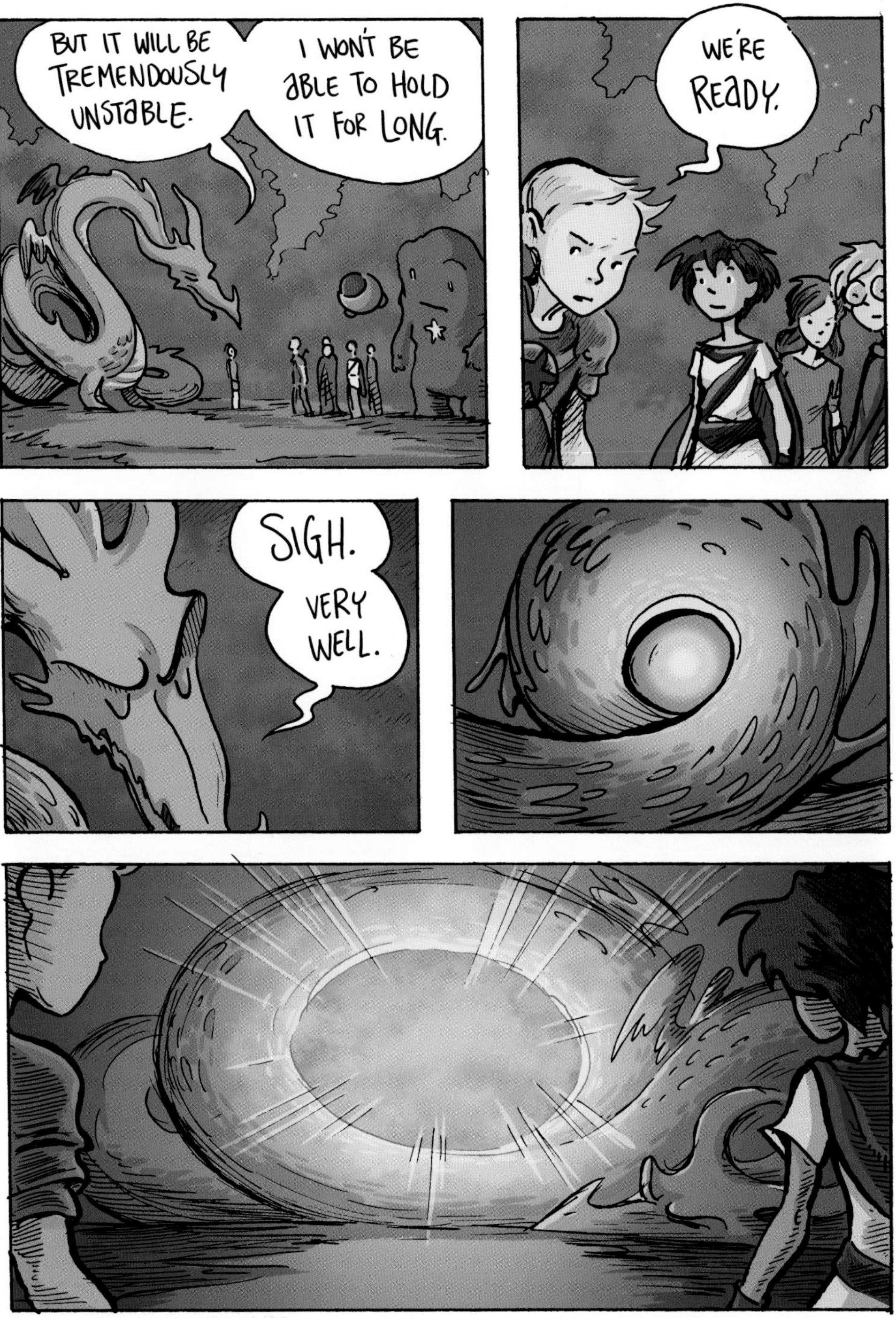
BUT IT WILL BE TREMENDOUSLY UNSTABLE.
I WON'T BE ABLE TO HOLD IT FOR LONG.
WE'RE READY.
SIGH.
VERY WELL.

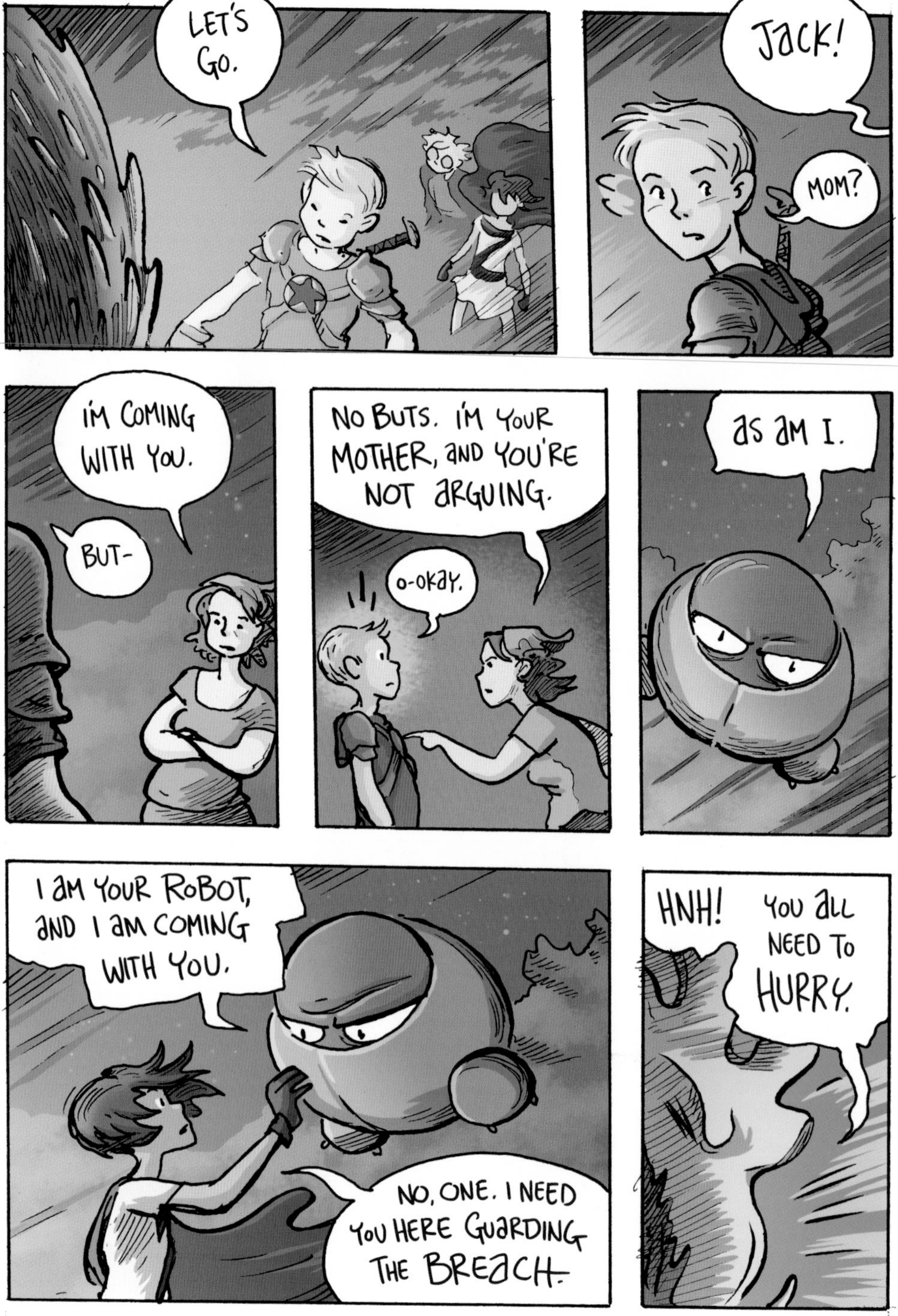
LET'S GO.
JACK!
MOM?
I'M COMING WITH YOU.
BUT-
NO BUTS. I'M YOUR MOTHER, AND YOU'RE NOT ARGUING.
O-OKAY.
AS AM I.
I AM YOUR ROBOT, AND I AM COMING WITH YOU.
NO, ONE. I NEED YOU HERE GUARDING THE BREACH.
HNH!
YOU ALL NEED TO HURRY.

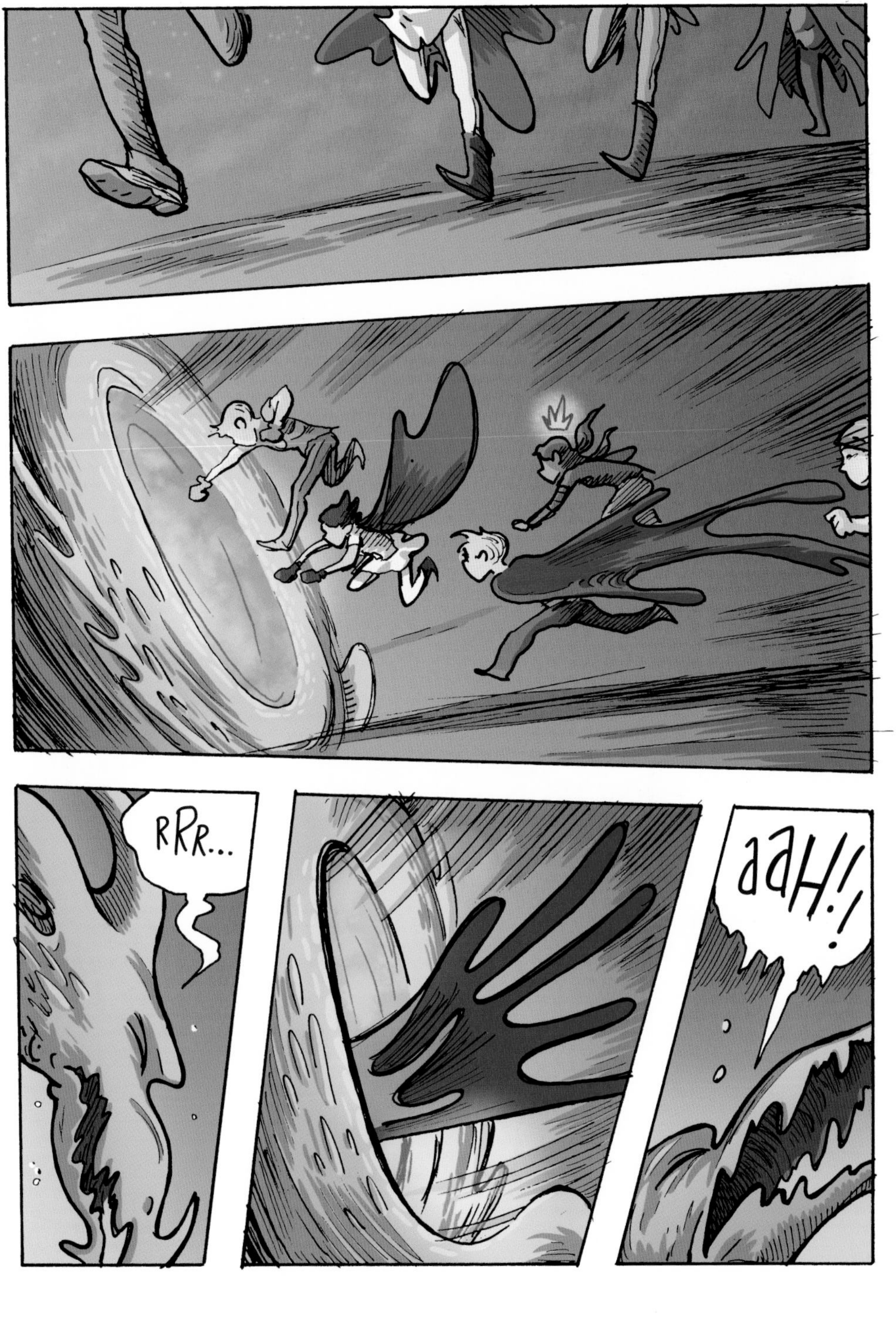
RRR...
aaH!!

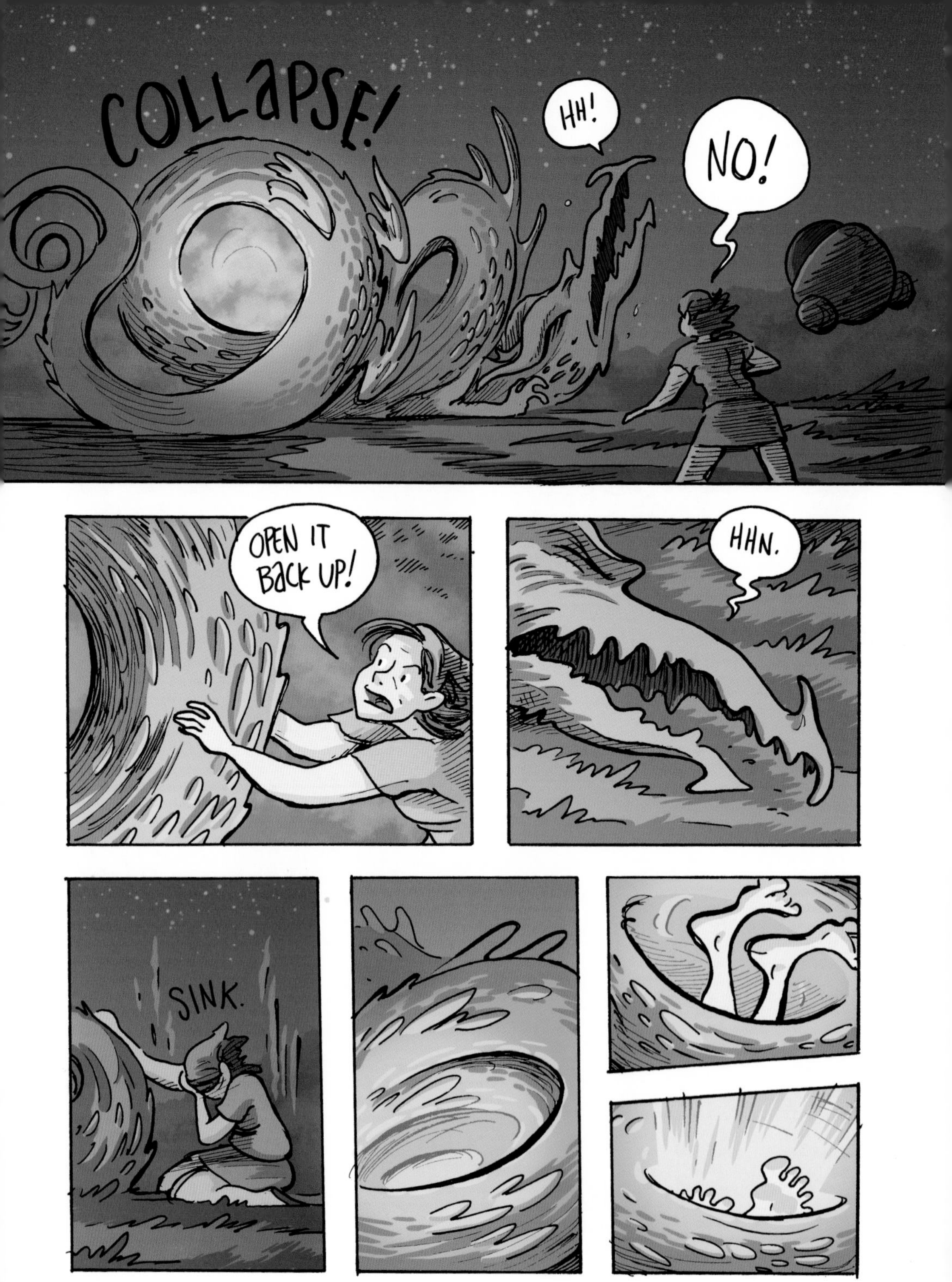
COLLAPSE!
HH!
NO!
OPEN IT BACK UP!
HHN.
SINK.

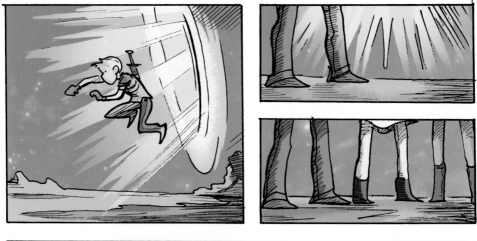

I GUESS WE'RE THE ONLY ONES WHO MADE IT THROUGH.

WE'LL MAKE IT WORK.

WE SHOULD START LOOKING—

GET DOWN!

aak!

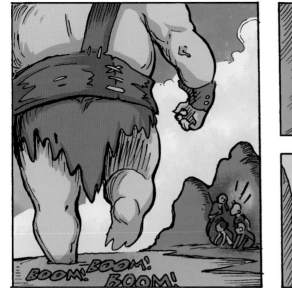

YIKES.

THERE'S MORE OF THEM THAN I EXPECTED.

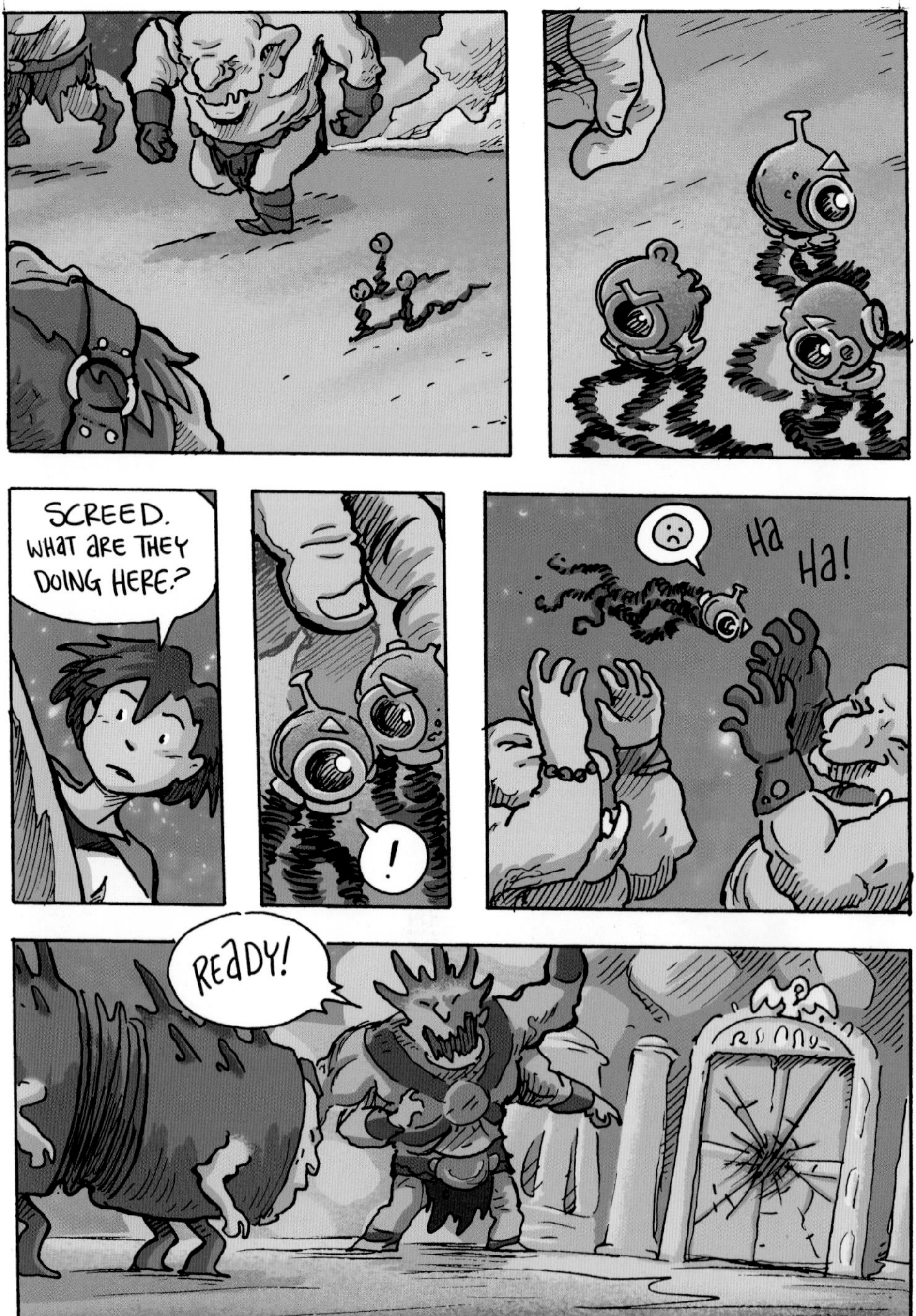
SCREED. WHAT ARE THEY DOING HERE?
!
HA HA!
READY!

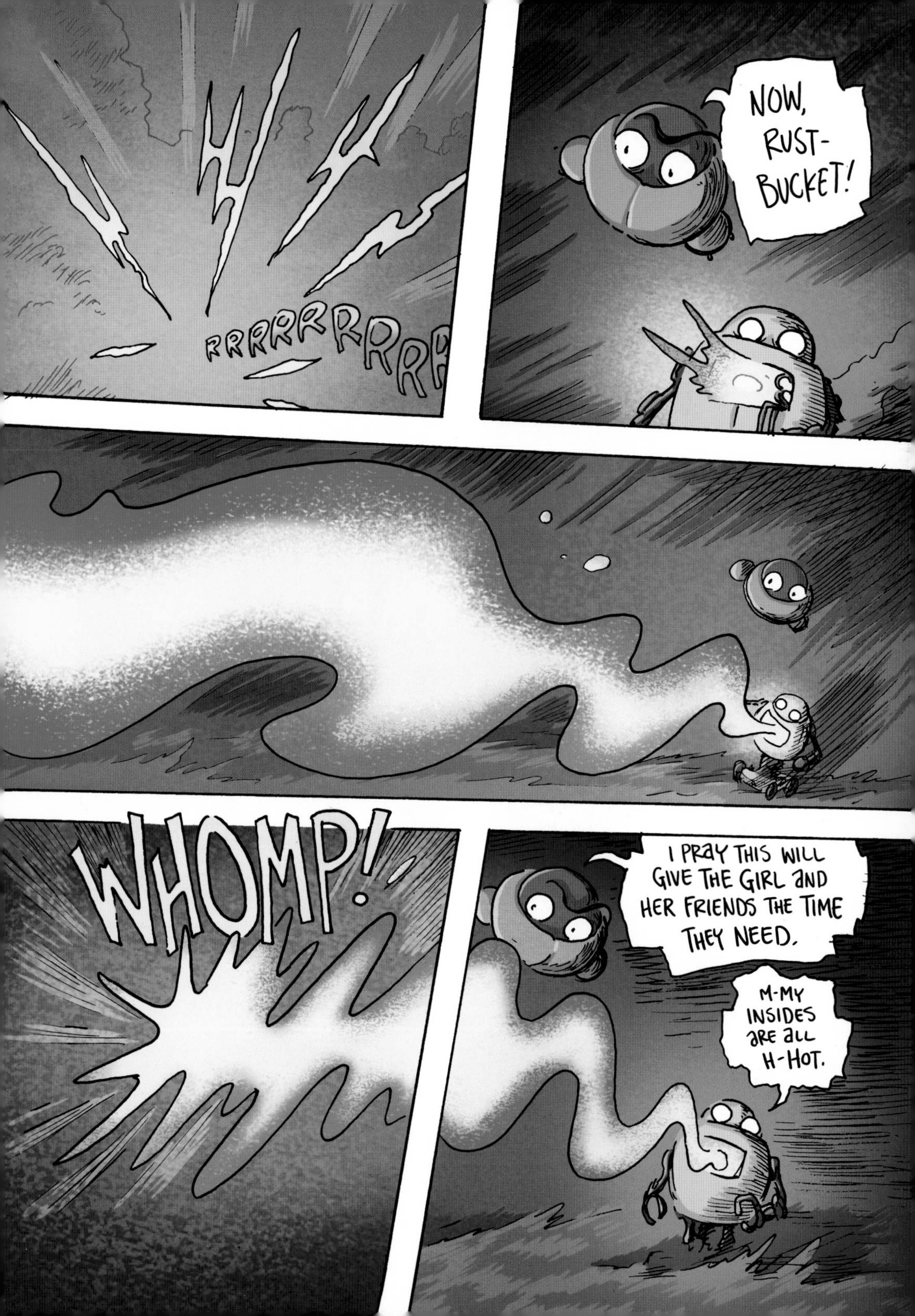
RRRRRRRRRR
NOW, RUST-BUCKET!
WHOMP!
I PRAY THIS WILL GIVE THE GIRL AND HER FRIENDS THE TIME THEY NEED.
M-MY INSIDES ARE ALL H-HOT.

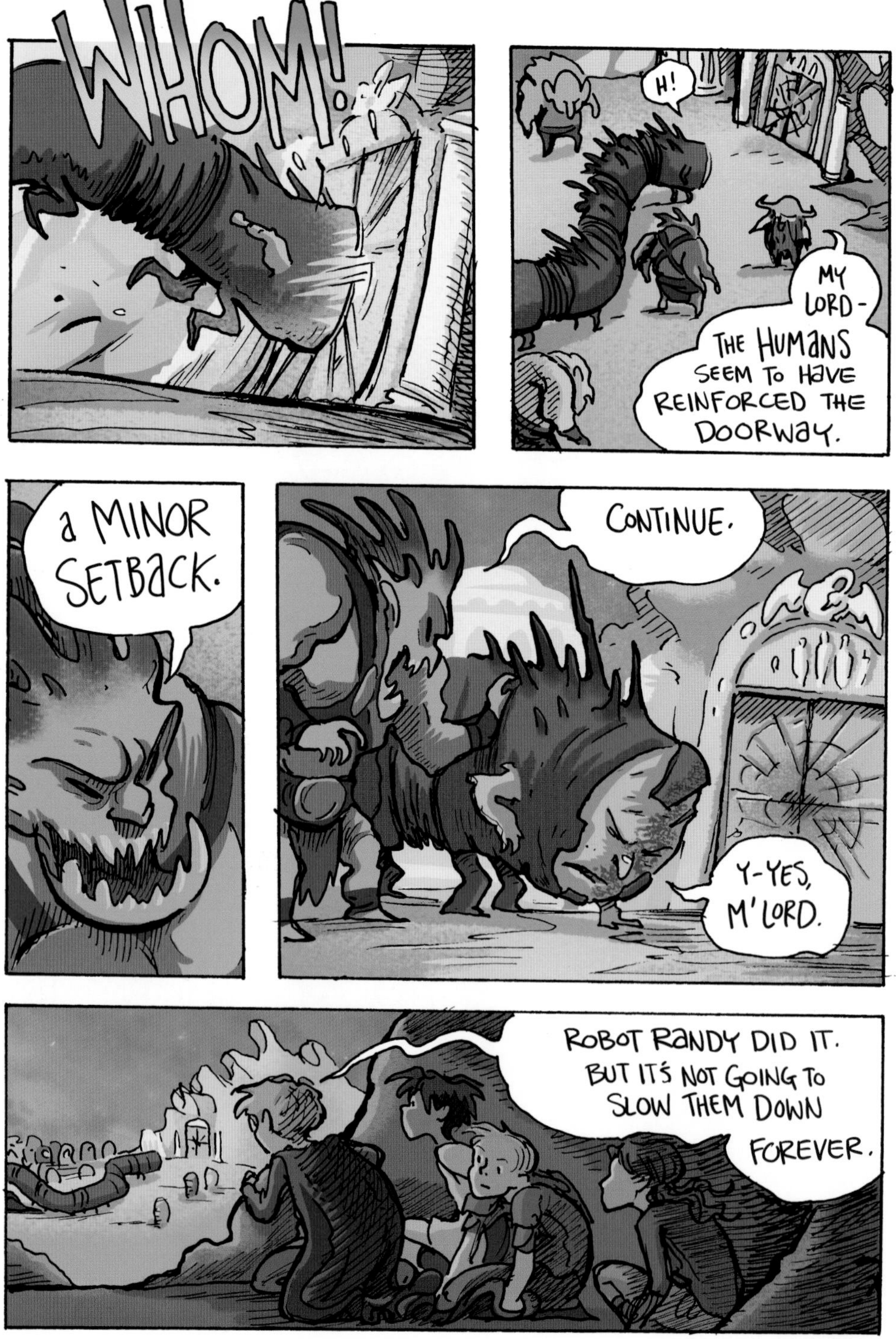
WHOM!
H!
MY LORD- THE HUMANS SEEM TO HAVE REINFORCED THE DOORWAY.
a MINOR SETBACK.
CONTINUE.
Y-YES, M'LORD.
ROBOT RANDY DID IT. BUT IT'S NOT GOING TO SLOW THEM DOWN FOREVER.

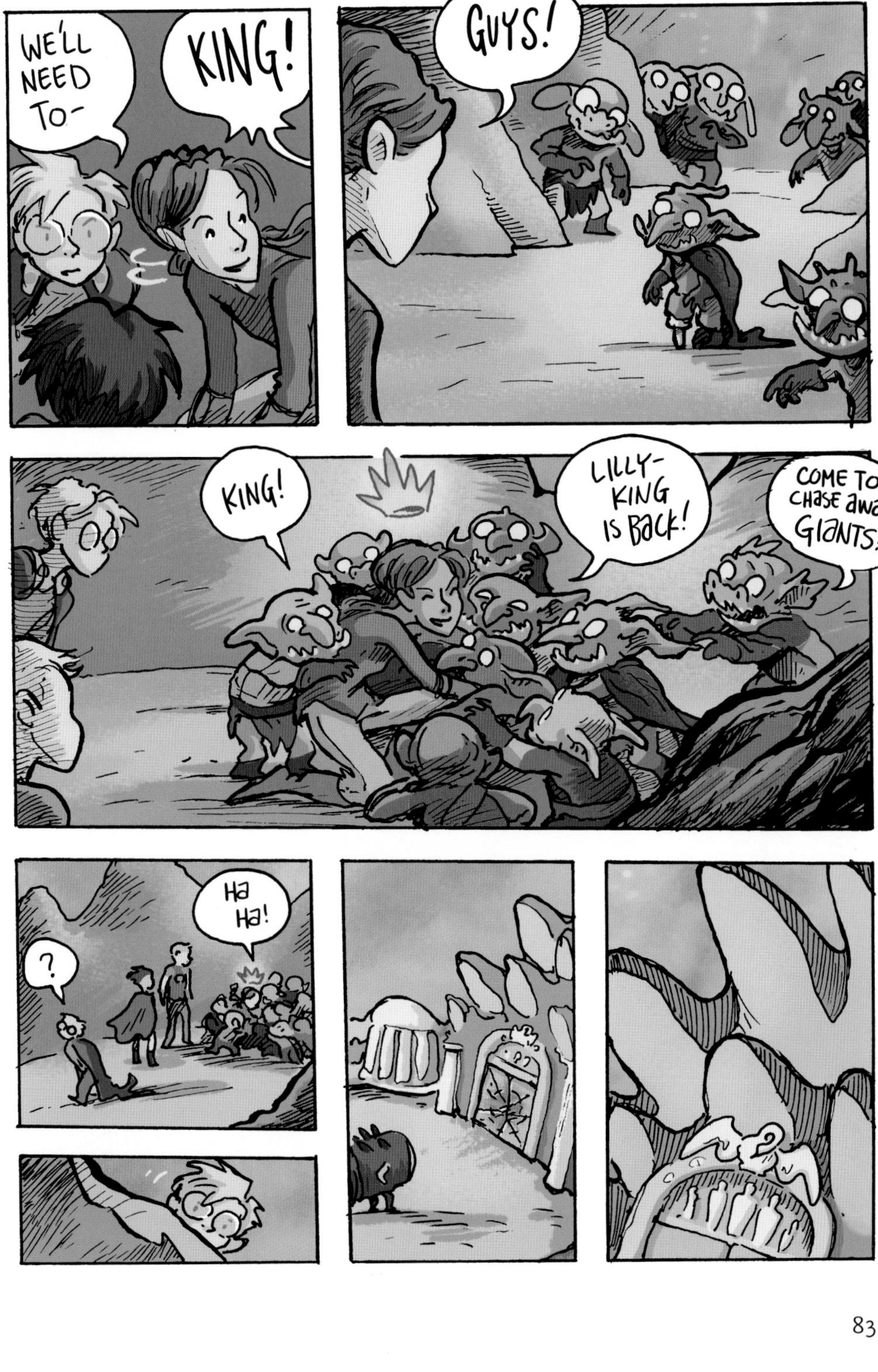
WE'LL NEED TO-
KING!
GUYS!
KING!
LILLY-KING IS BACK!
COME TO CHASE away GIANTS!
?
Ha Ha!

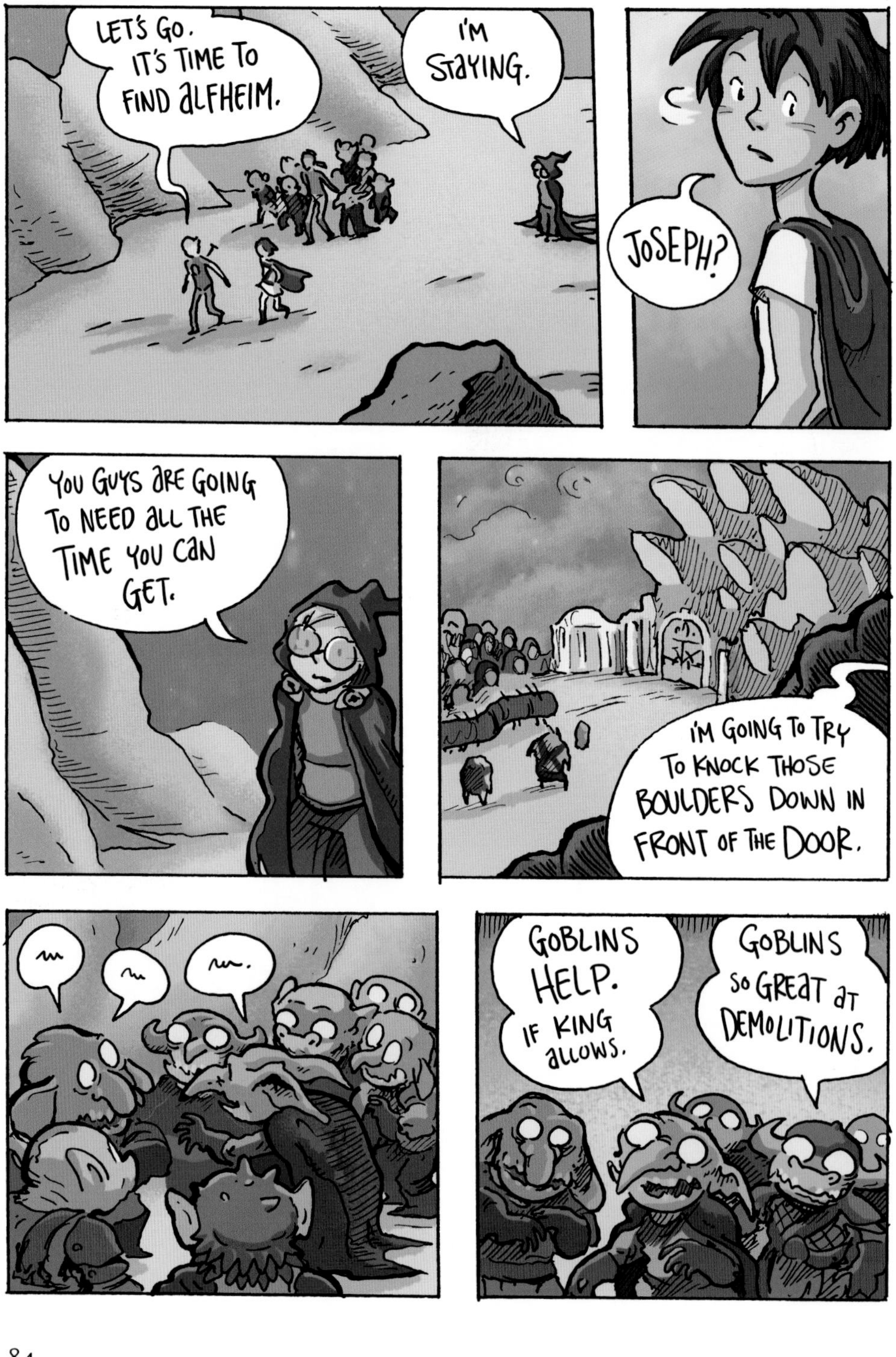
LET'S GO. IT'S TIME TO FIND ALFHEIM.
I'M STAYING.
JOSEPH?
YOU GUYS ARE GOING TO NEED ALL THE TIME YOU CAN GET.
I'M GOING TO TRY TO KNOCK THOSE BOULDERS DOWN IN FRONT OF THE DOOR.
GOBLINS HELP. IF KING ALLOWS.
GOBLINS SO GREAT AT DEMOLITIONS.

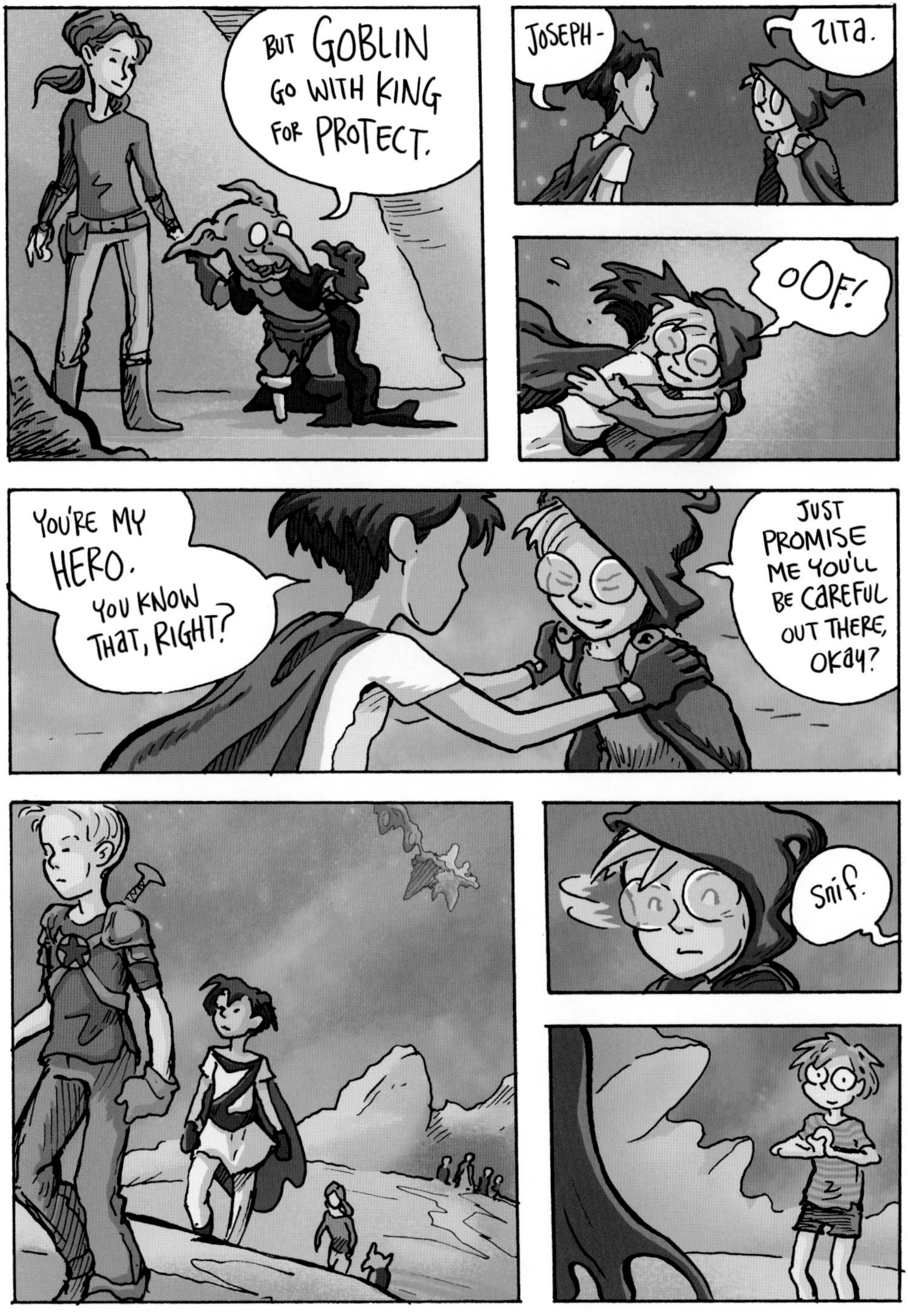
BUT GOBLIN GO WITH KING FOR PROTECT.
JOSEPH-
ZITA.
OOF!
YOU'RE MY HERO. YOU KNOW THAT, RIGHT?
JUST PROMISE ME YOU'LL BE CAREFUL OUT THERE, OKAY?
SNIF.

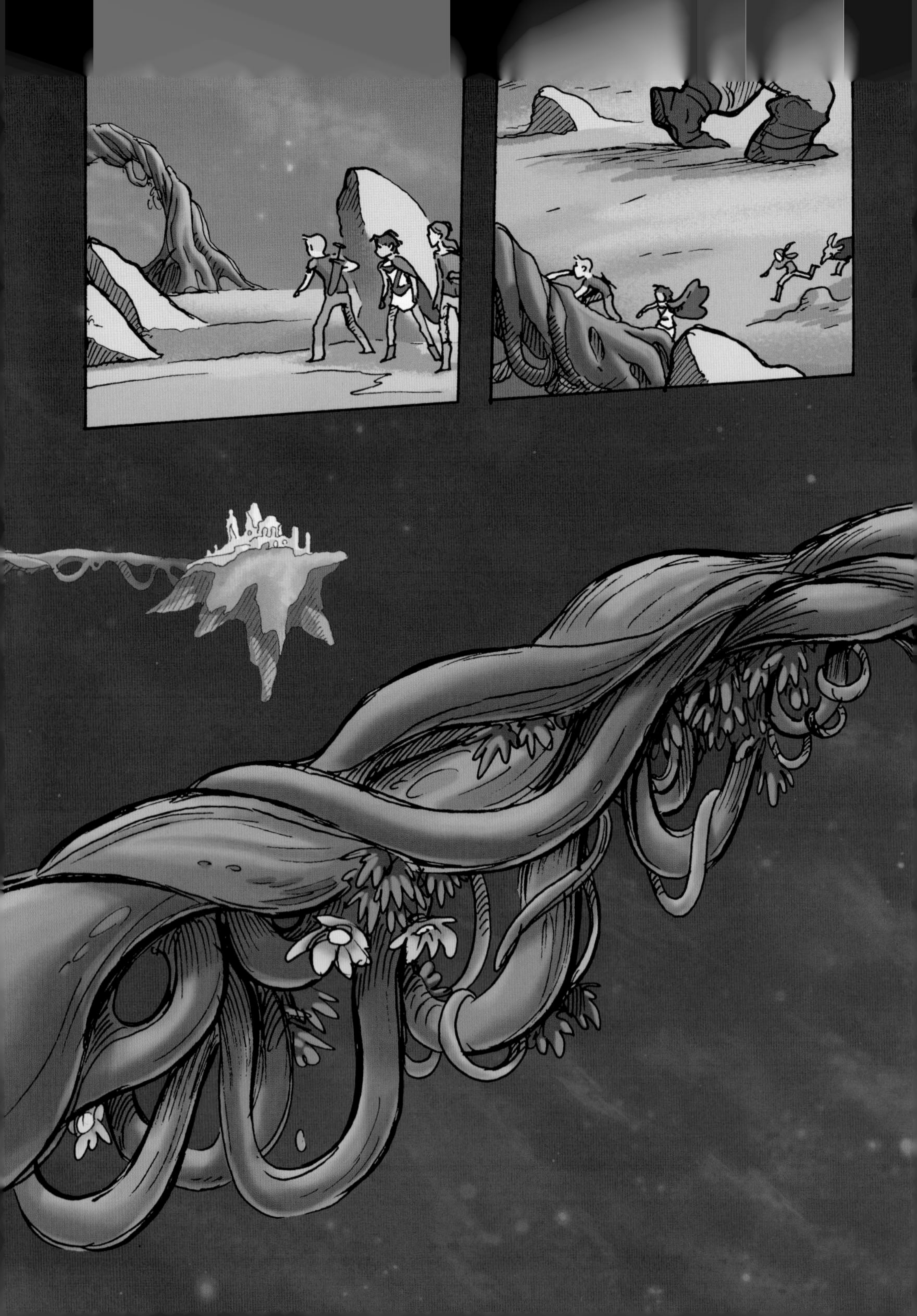

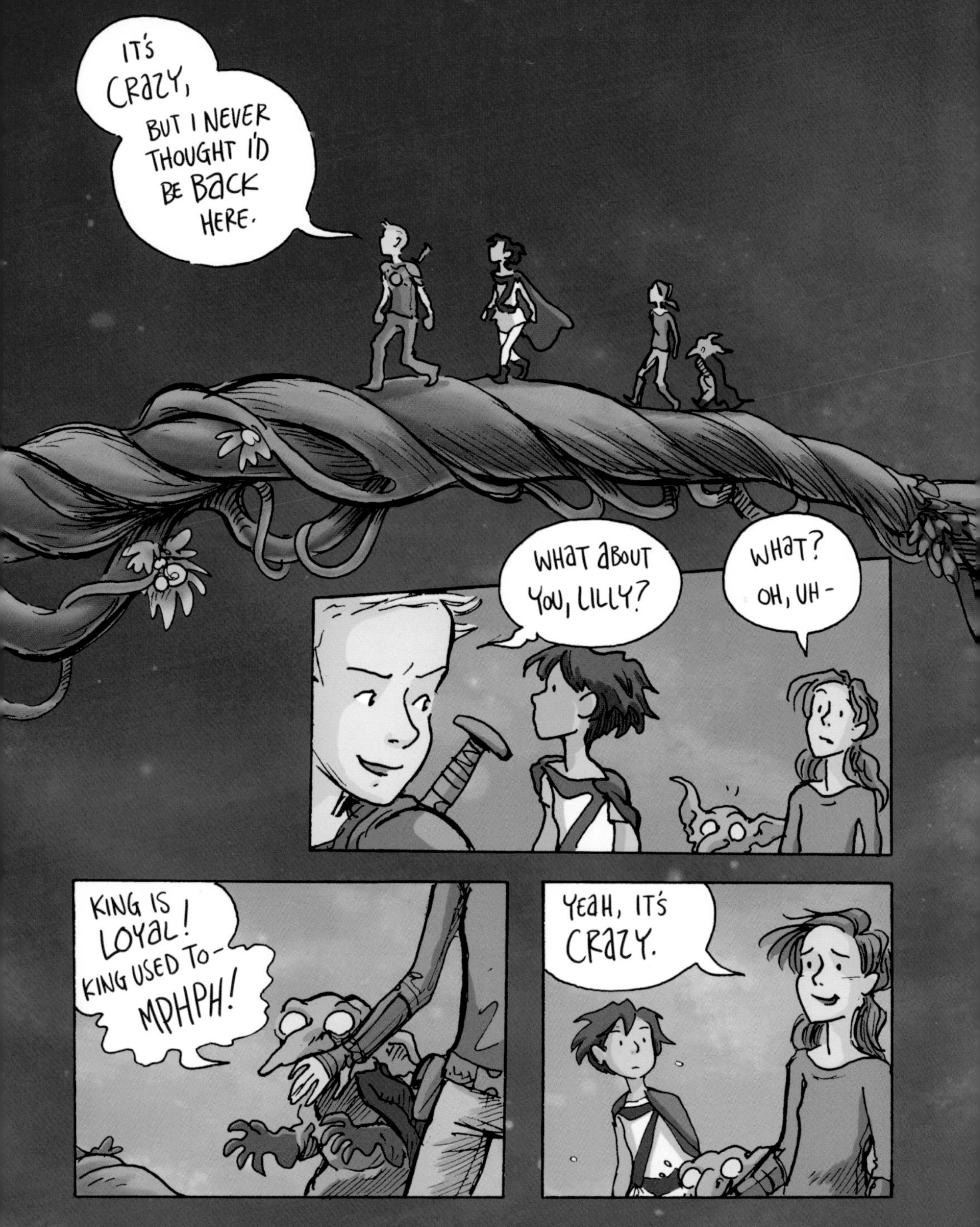
IT'S CRAZY, BUT I NEVER THOUGHT I'D BE BACK HERE.
WHAT ABOUT YOU, LILLY?
WHAT? OH, UH -
KING IS LOYAL! KING USED TO- MPHPH!
YEAH, IT'S CRAZY.

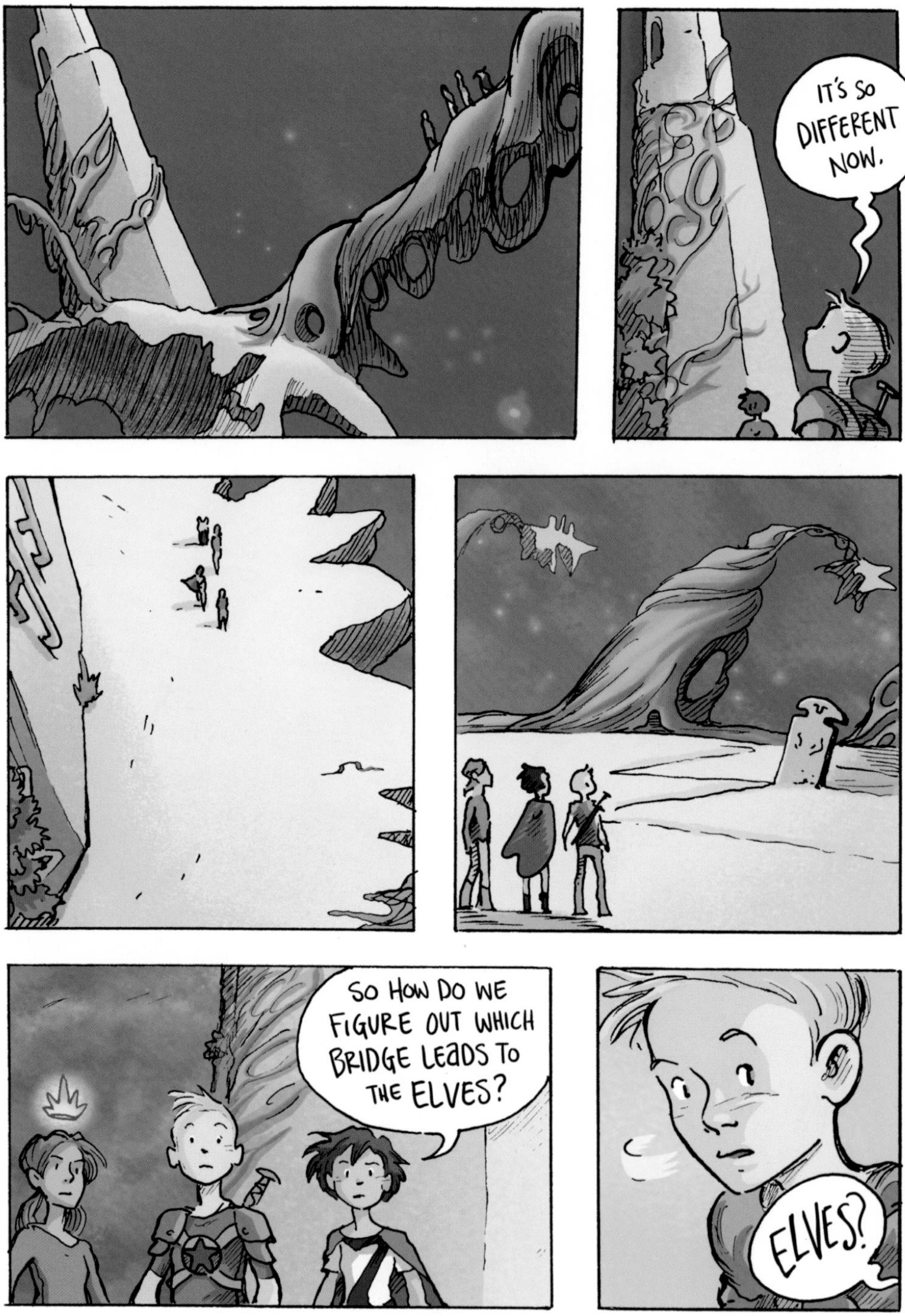
IT'S SO DIFFERENT NOW.
SO HOW DO WE FIGURE OUT WHICH BRIDGE LEADS TO THE ELVES?
ELVES?

WHY, IT'S THE HUMAN LAD!
WE WAS WONDERIN' ABOUCHOO!
TIG!
JERRY!
J-JER- D'YOU SEE WHAT I'M SEEIN'?
CAN IT BE? IZZAT-?!?
AAAAAAAAAHH!
I HAVEN'T SEEN YOU GUYS SINCE SCRIPTORIUS!
WE'VE BEEN FOLLERIN' YOUR CAREER!
FAMOUS HERO ZITA! WE ALWAYS KNOWED IT!

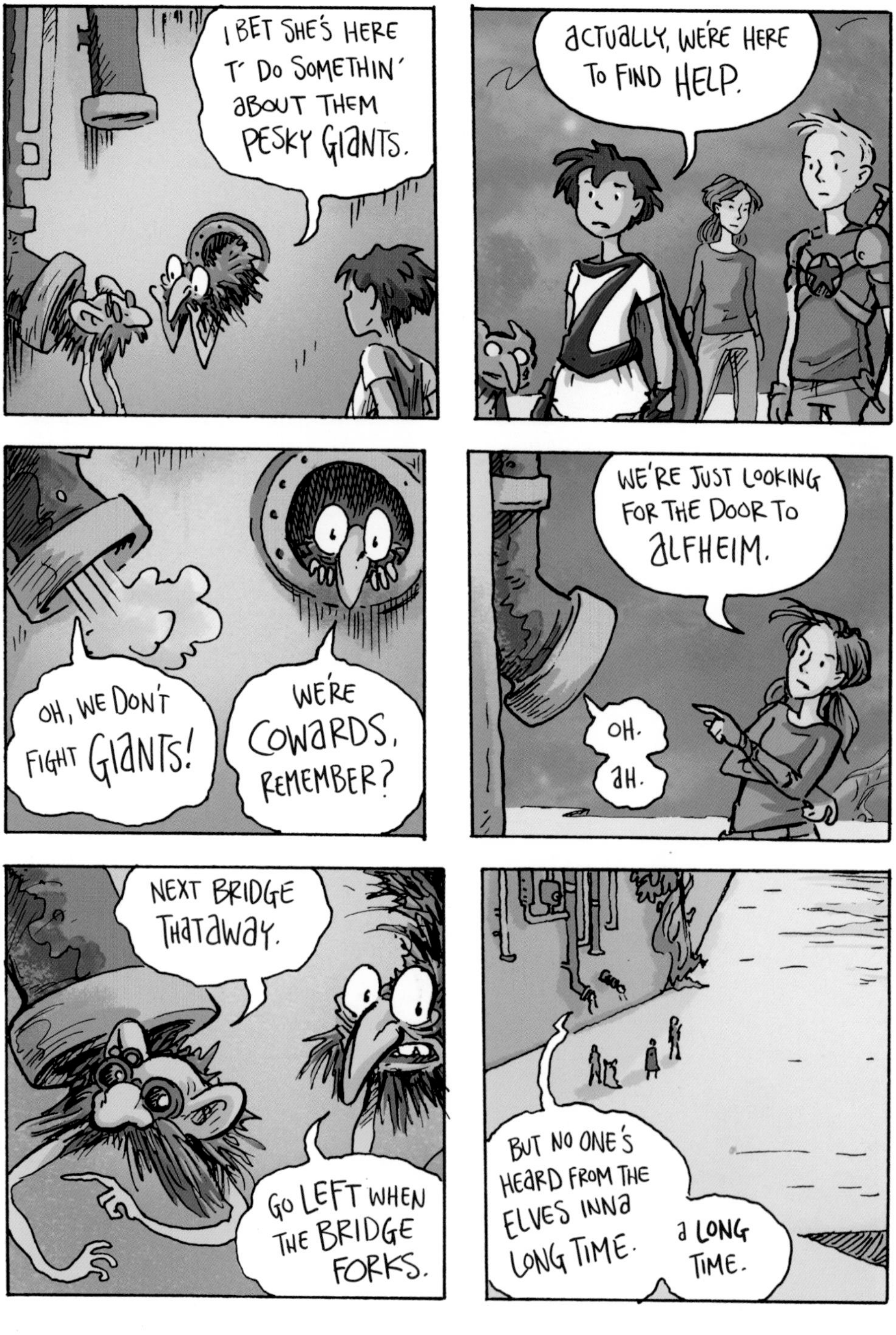
I BET SHE'S HERE T' DO SOMETHIN' ABOUT THEM PESKY GIANTS.
ACTUALLY, WE'RE HERE TO FIND HELP.
OH, WE DON'T FIGHT GIANTS!
WE'RE COWARDS, REMEMBER?
WE'RE JUST LOOKING FOR THE DOOR TO ALFHEIM.
OH.
AH.
NEXT BRIDGE THATAWAY.
GO LEFT WHEN THE BRIDGE FORKS.
BUT NO ONE'S HEARD FROM THE ELVES INNA LONG TIME.
A LONG TIME.

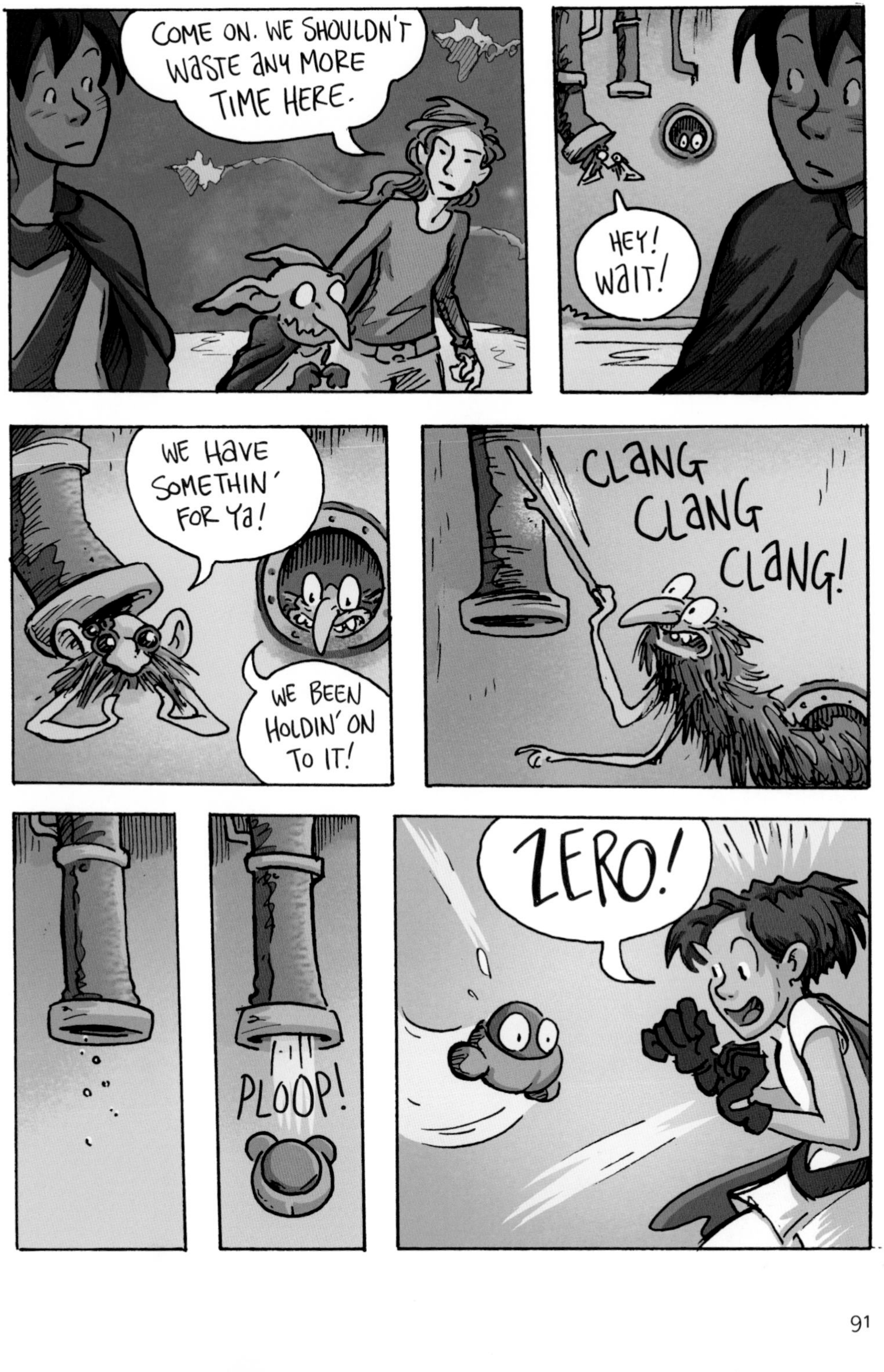

COME ON. WE SHOULDN'T WASTE ANY MORE TIME HERE.
HEY! WAIT!
WE HAVE SOMETHIN' FOR YA!
WE BEEN HOLDIN' ON TO IT!
CLANG CLANG CLANG!
PLOOP!
ZERO!

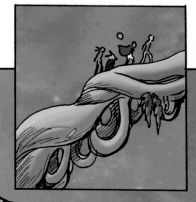

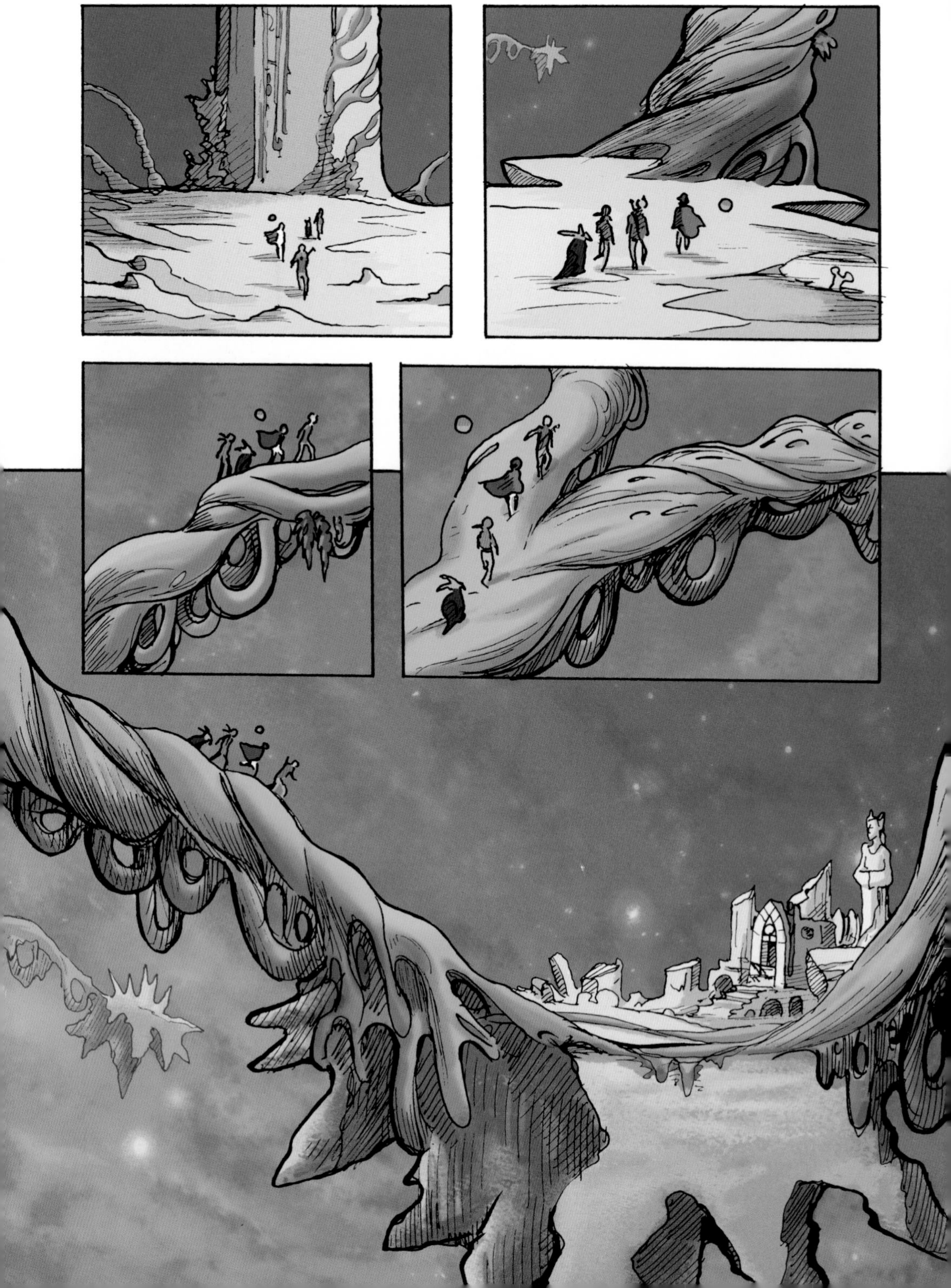

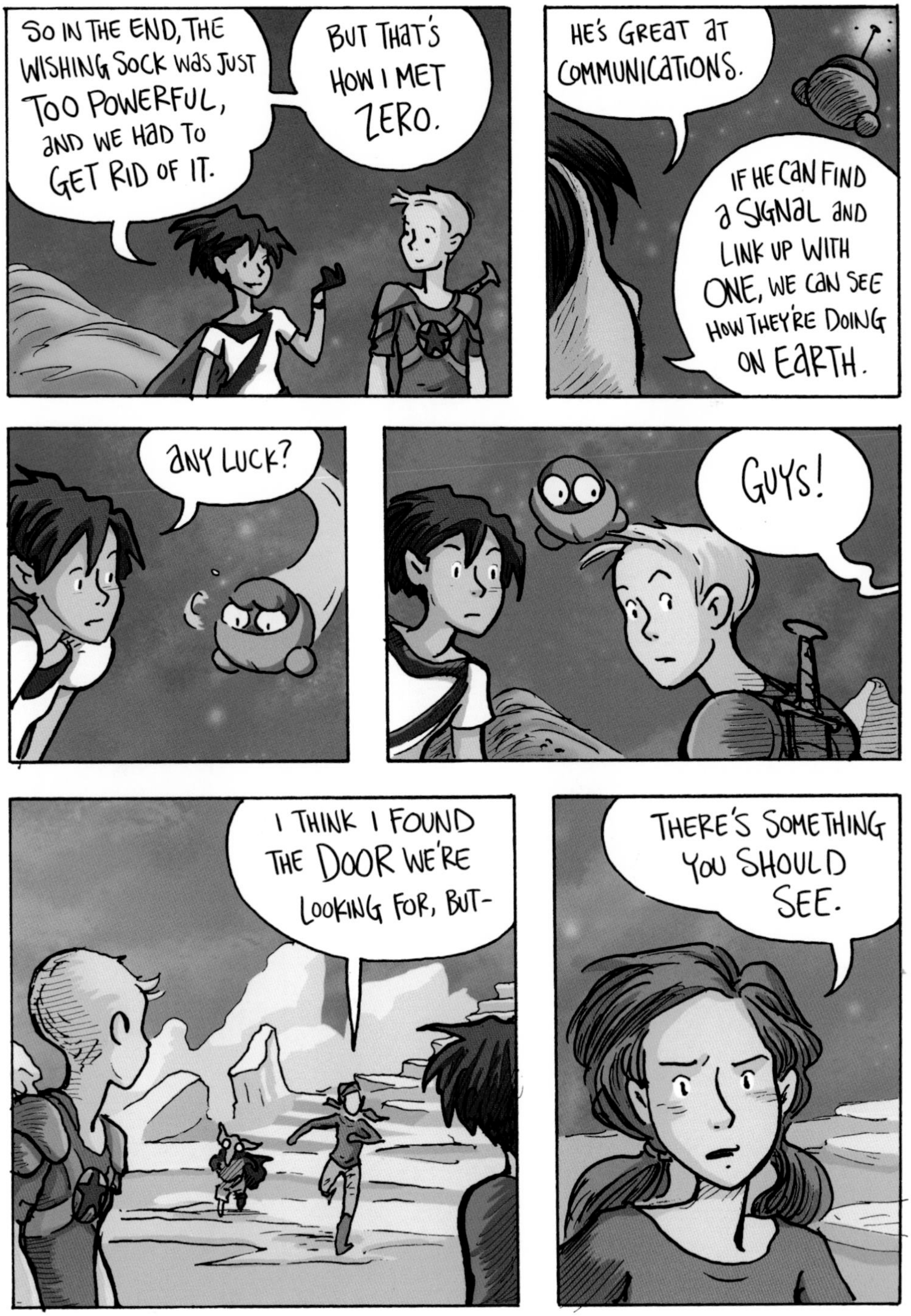

SO IN THE END, THE WISHING SOCK WAS JUST TOO POWERFUL, AND WE HAD TO GET RID OF IT.
BUT THAT'S HOW I MET ZERO.
HE'S GREAT AT COMMUNICATIONS.
IF HE CAN FIND A SIGNAL AND LINK UP WITH ONE, WE CAN SEE HOW THEY'RE DOING ON EARTH.
ANY LUCK?
GUYS!
I THINK I FOUND THE DOOR WE'RE LOOKING FOR, BUT-
THERE'S SOMETHING YOU SHOULD SEE.

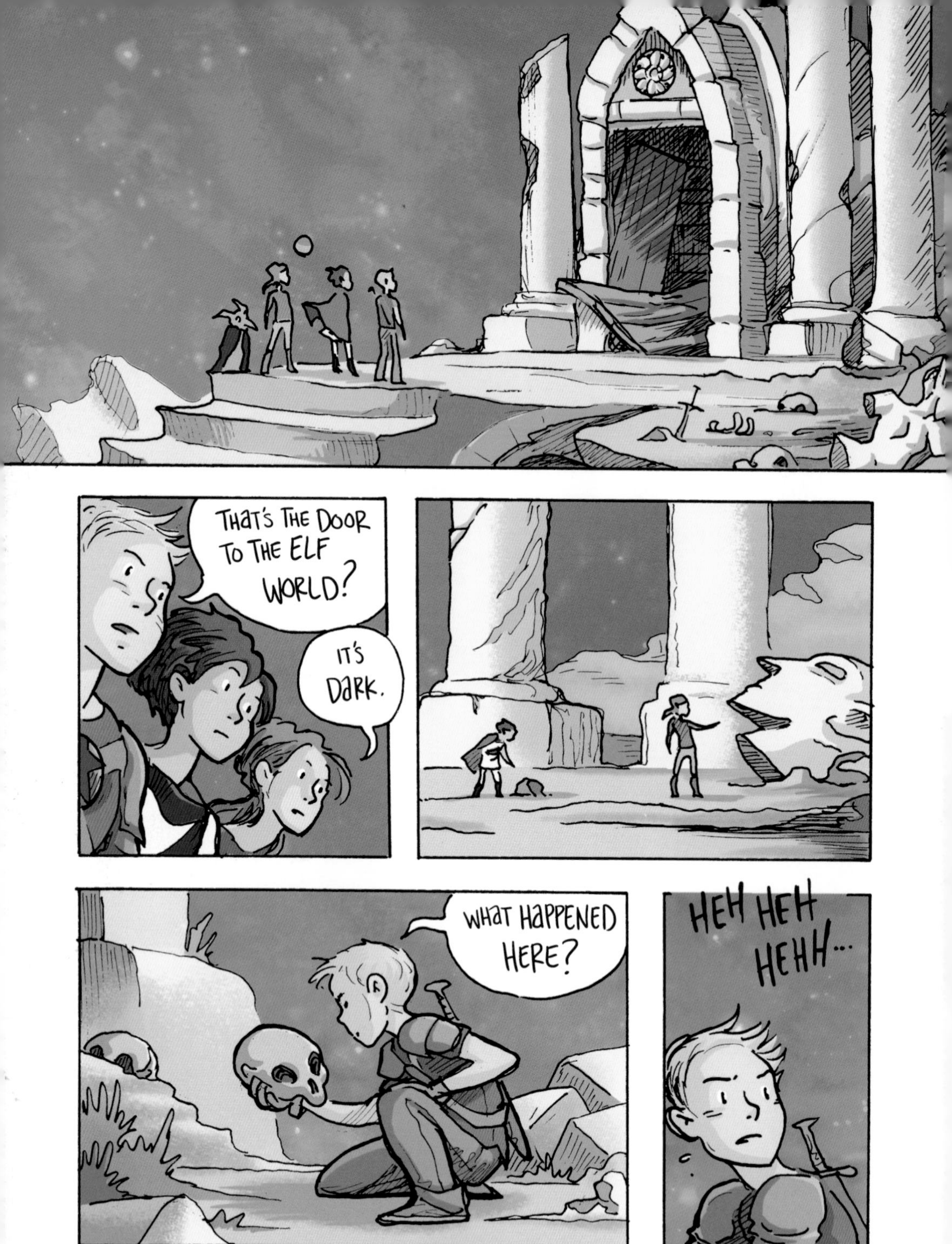
THAT'S THE DOOR TO THE ELF WORLD?
IT'S DARK.
WHAT HAPPENED HERE?
HEH HEH HEHH...

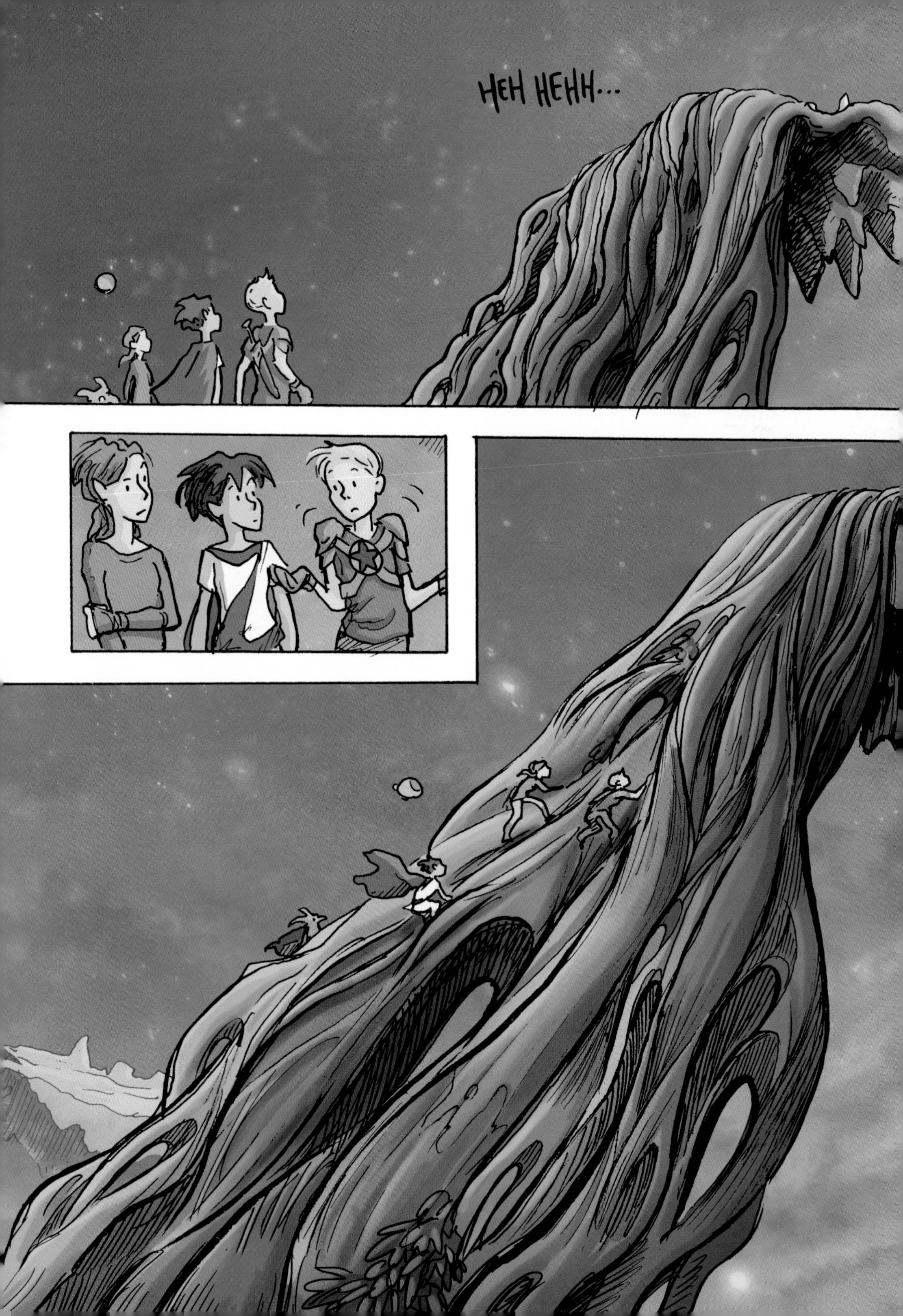
HEH HEHH...

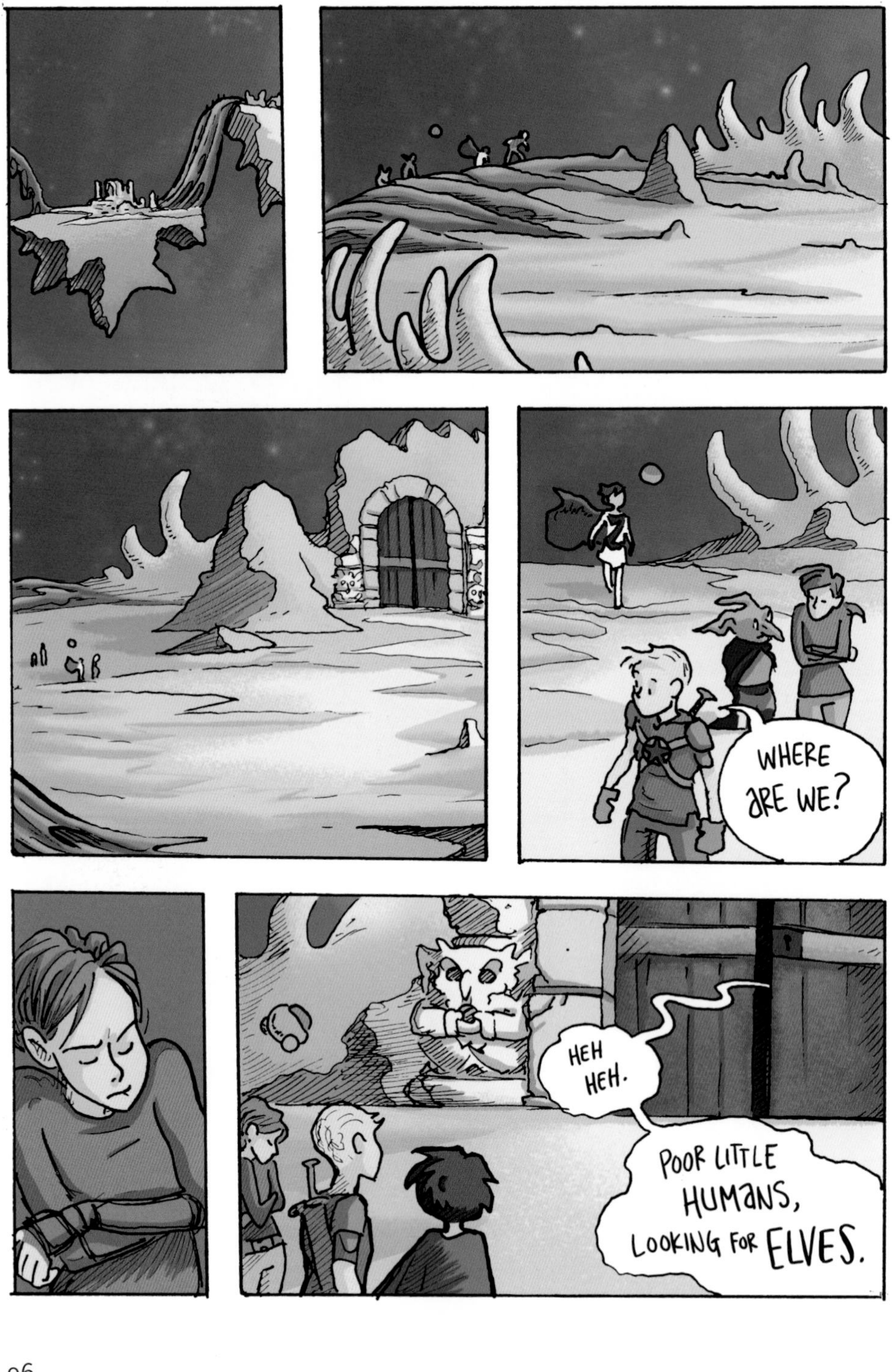
WHERE ARE WE?
HEH HEH.
POOR LITTLE HUMANS, LOOKING FOR ELVES.

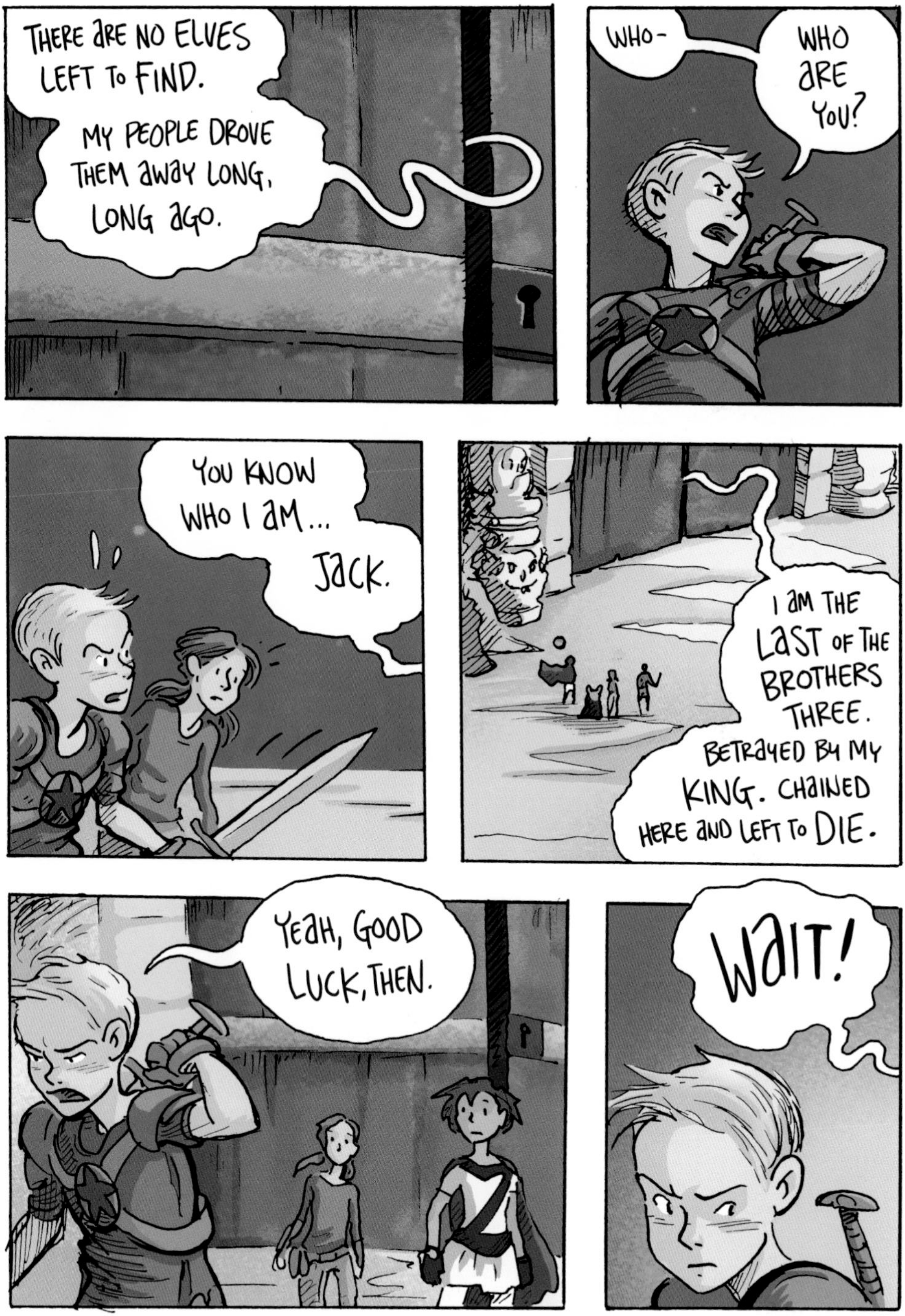
THERE ARE NO ELVES LEFT TO FIND.
MY PEOPLE DROVE THEM AWAY LONG, LONG AGO.
WHO-
WHO ARE YOU?
YOU KNOW WHO I AM...
JACK.
I AM THE LAST OF THE BROTHERS THREE.
BETRAYED BY MY KING. CHAINED HERE AND LEFT TO DIE.
YEAH, GOOD LUCK, THEN.
WAIT!

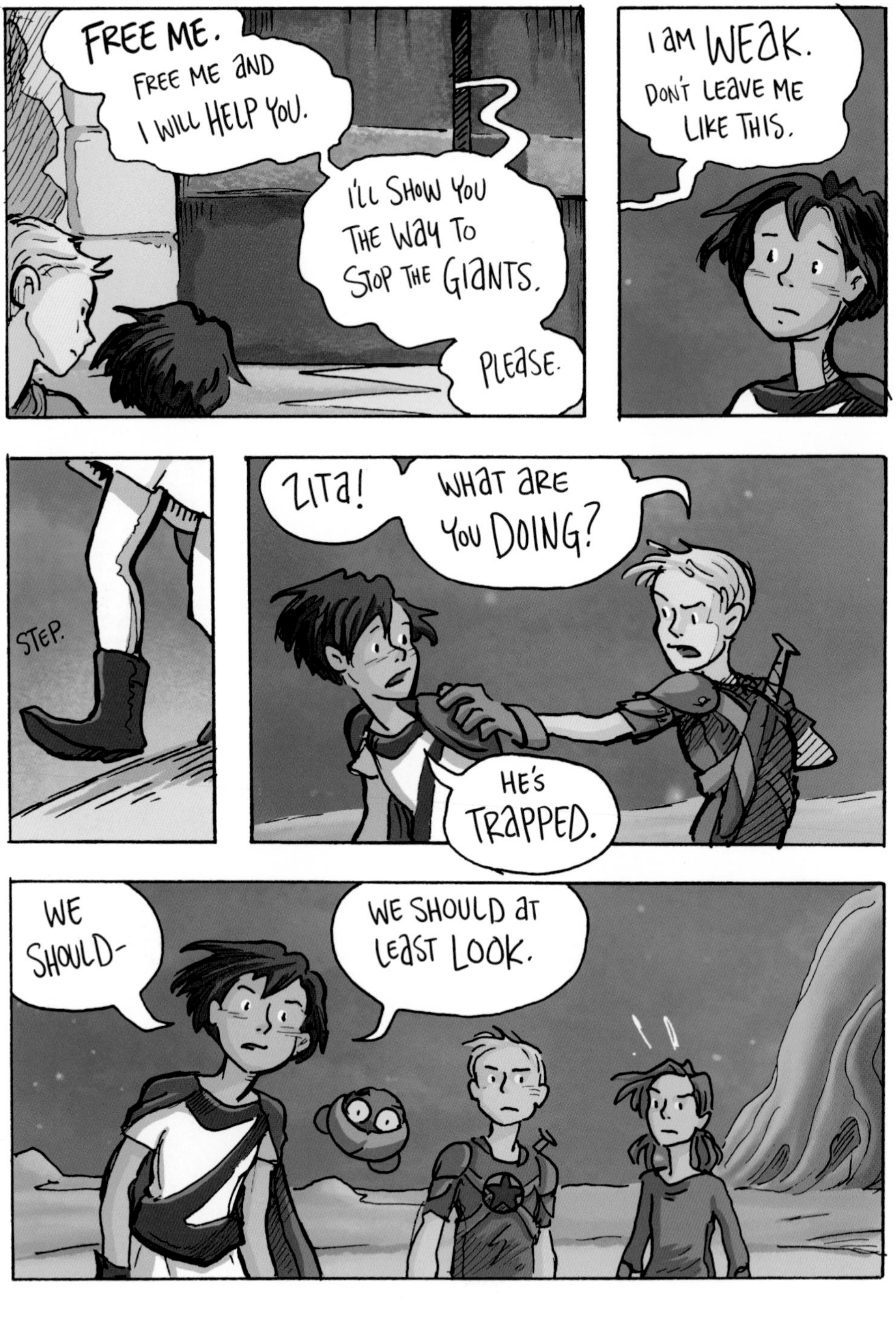
FREE ME. FREE ME AND I WILL HELP YOU.
I'LL SHOW YOU THE WAY TO STOP THE GIANTS.
PLEASE.
I AM WEAK. DON'T LEAVE ME LIKE THIS.
STEP.
ZITA!
WHAT ARE YOU DOING?
HE'S TRAPPED.
WE SHOULD-
WE SHOULD AT LEAST LOOK.

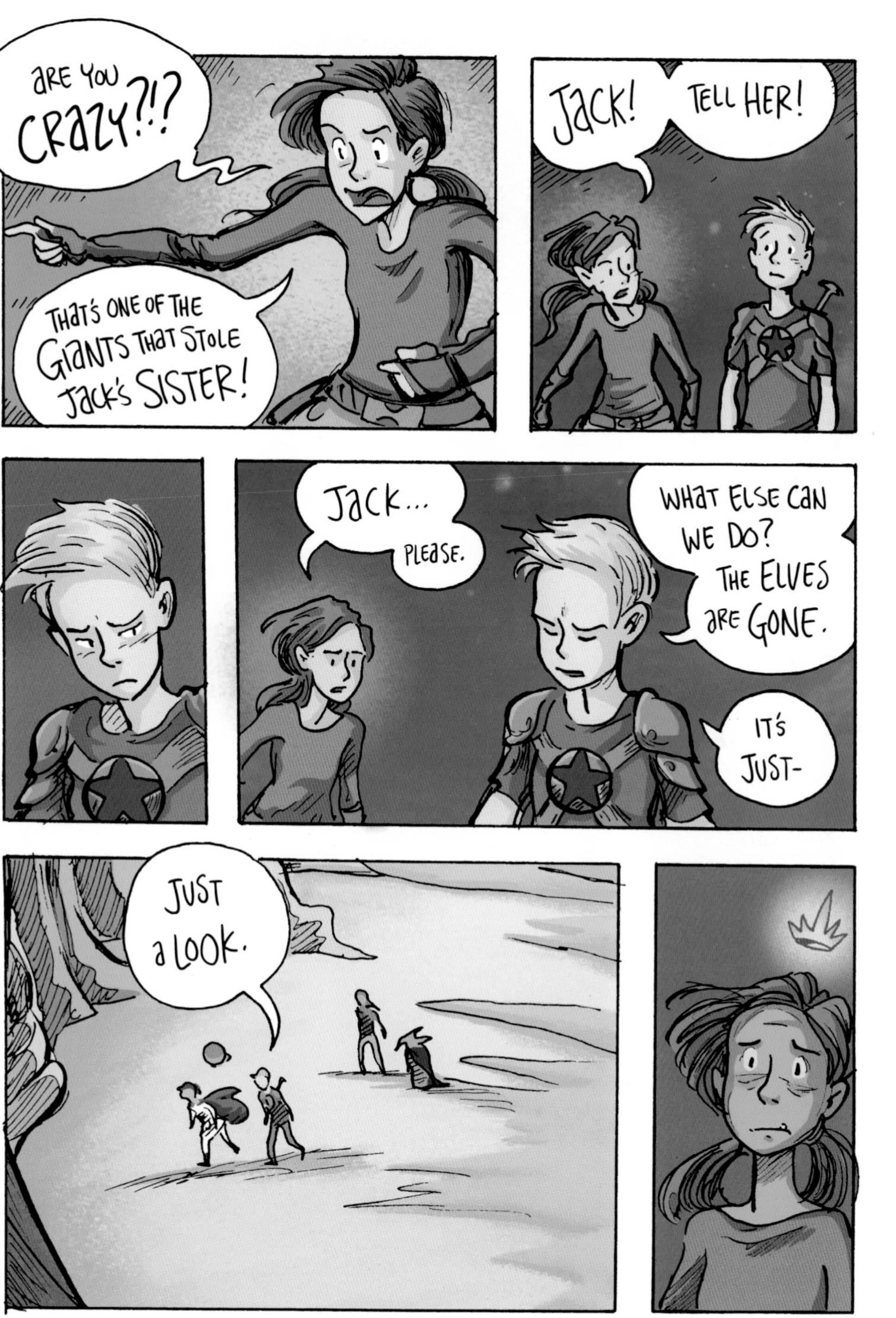

ARE YOU CRAZY?!?
THAT'S ONE OF THE GIANTS THAT STOLE JACK'S SISTER!
JACK!
TELL HER!
JACK...
PLEASE.
WHAT ELSE CAN WE DO? THE ELVES ARE GONE.
IT'S JUST-
JUST A LOOK.

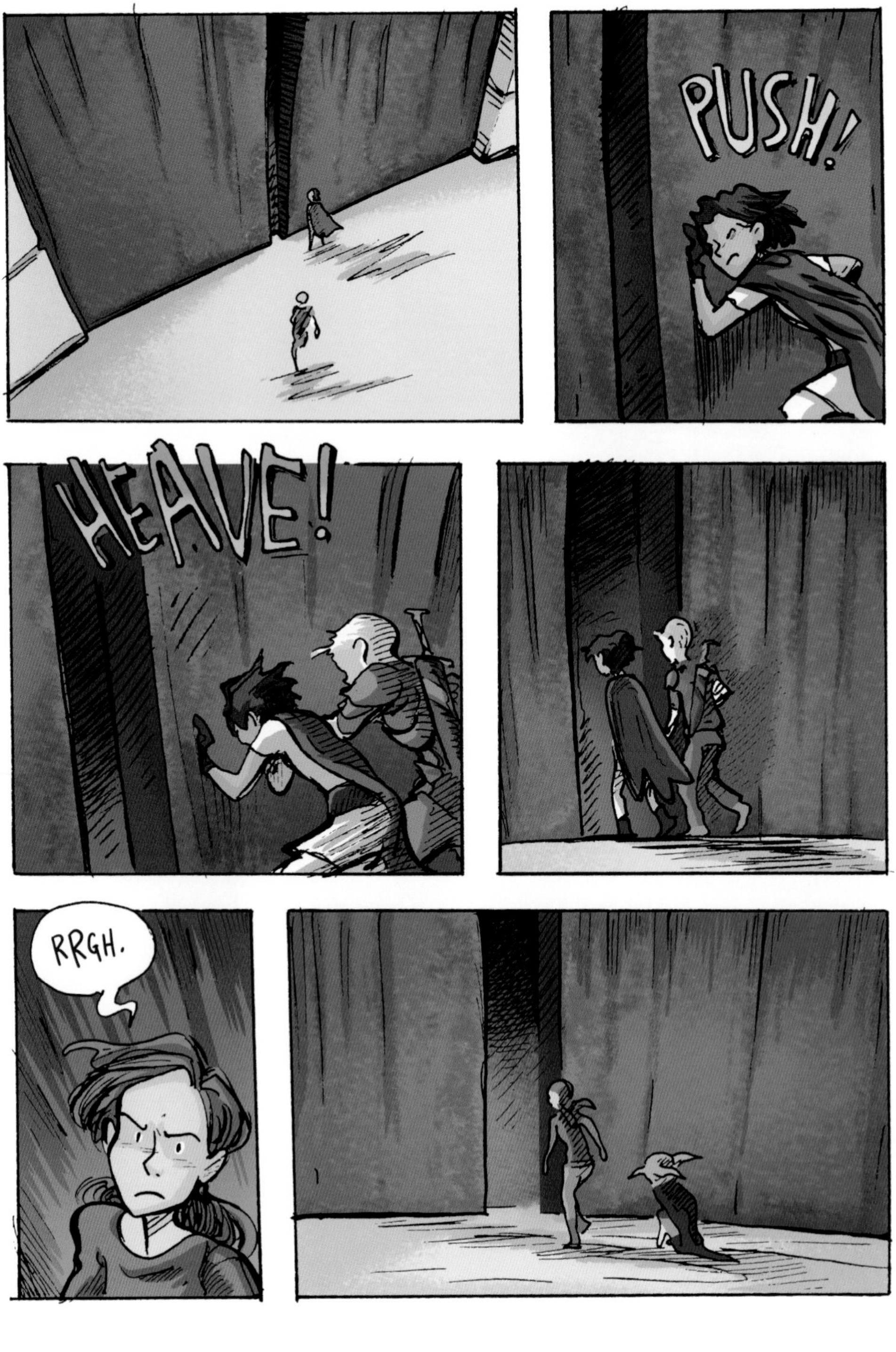
PUSH!
HEAVE!
RRGH.

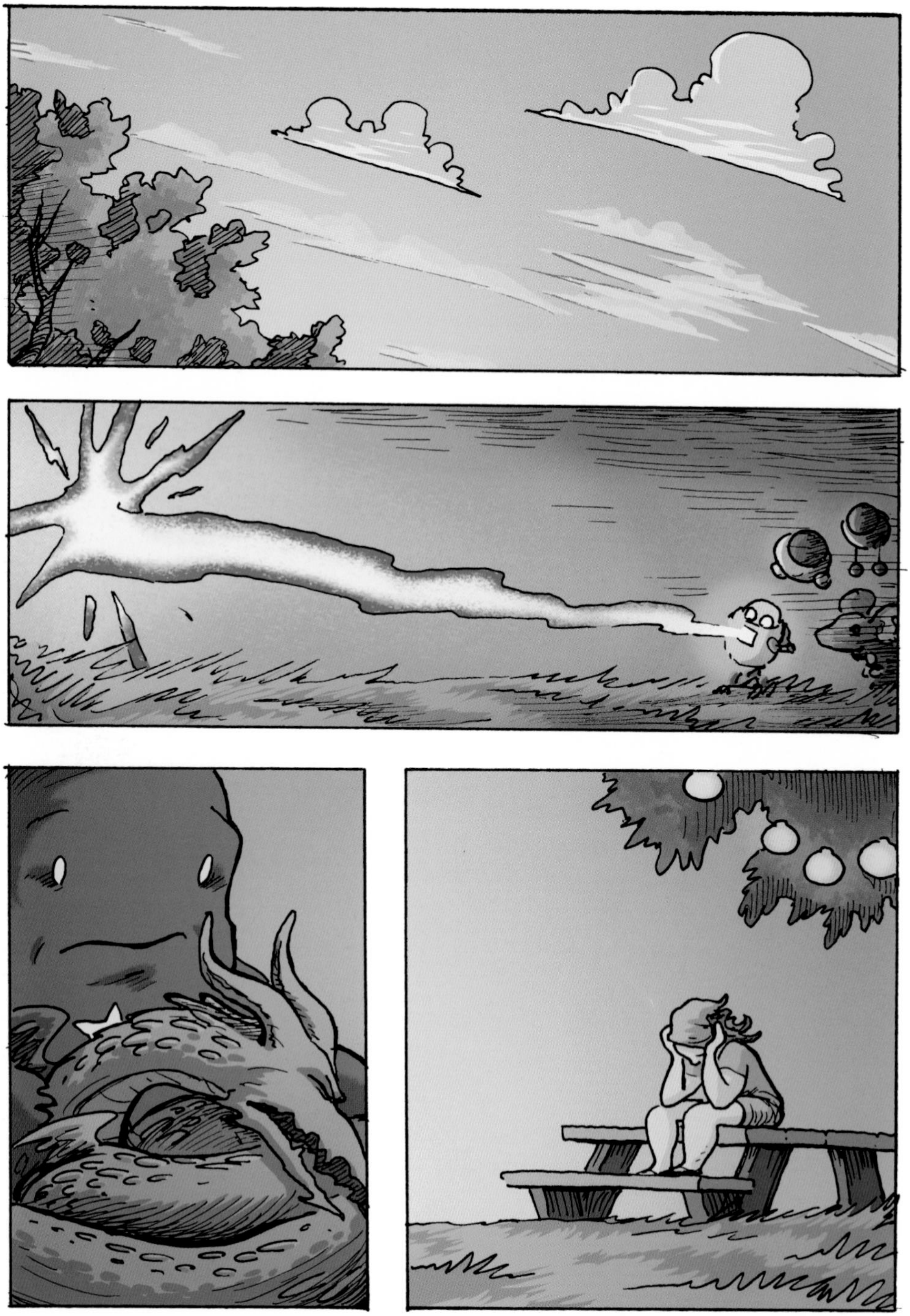

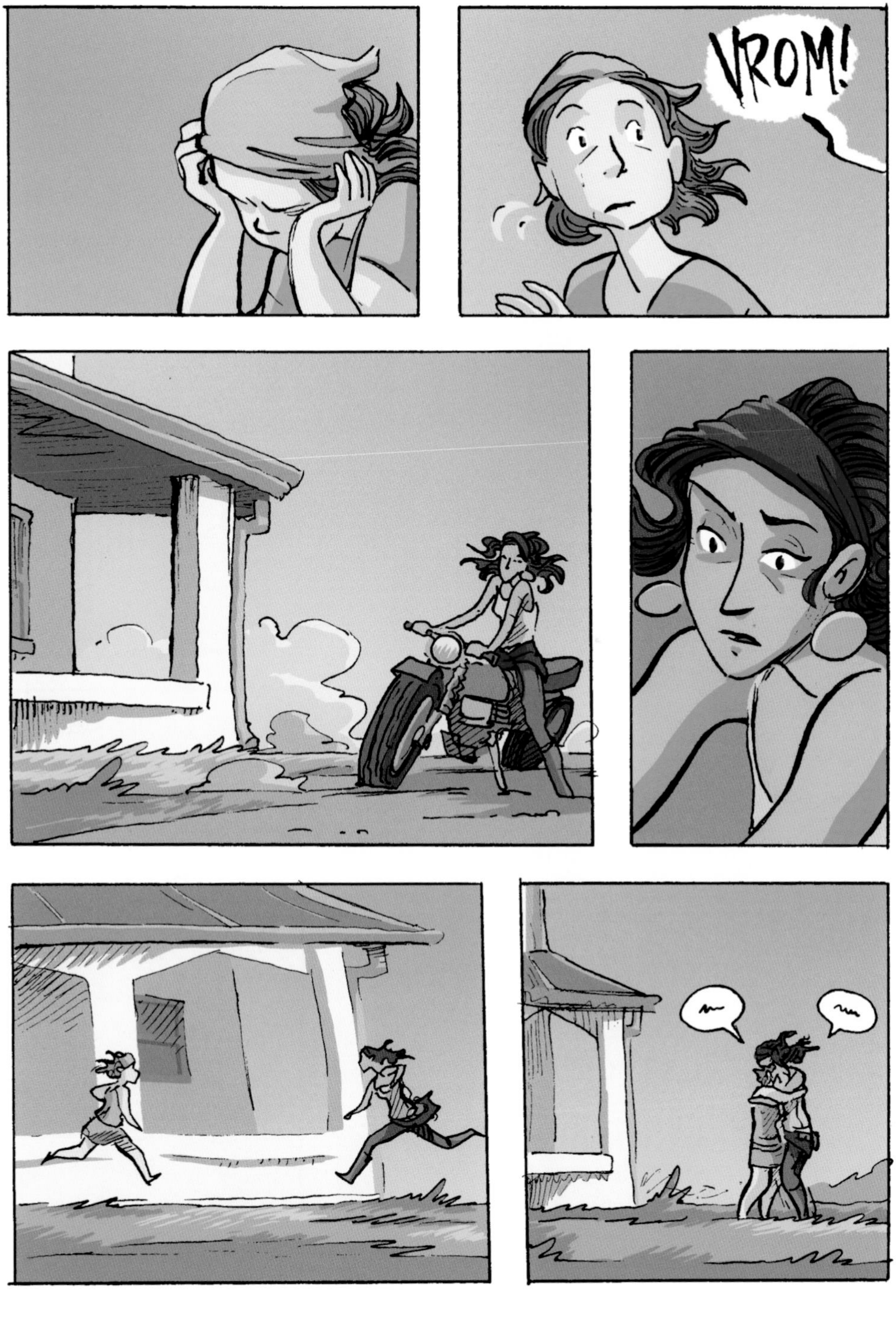
VROM!

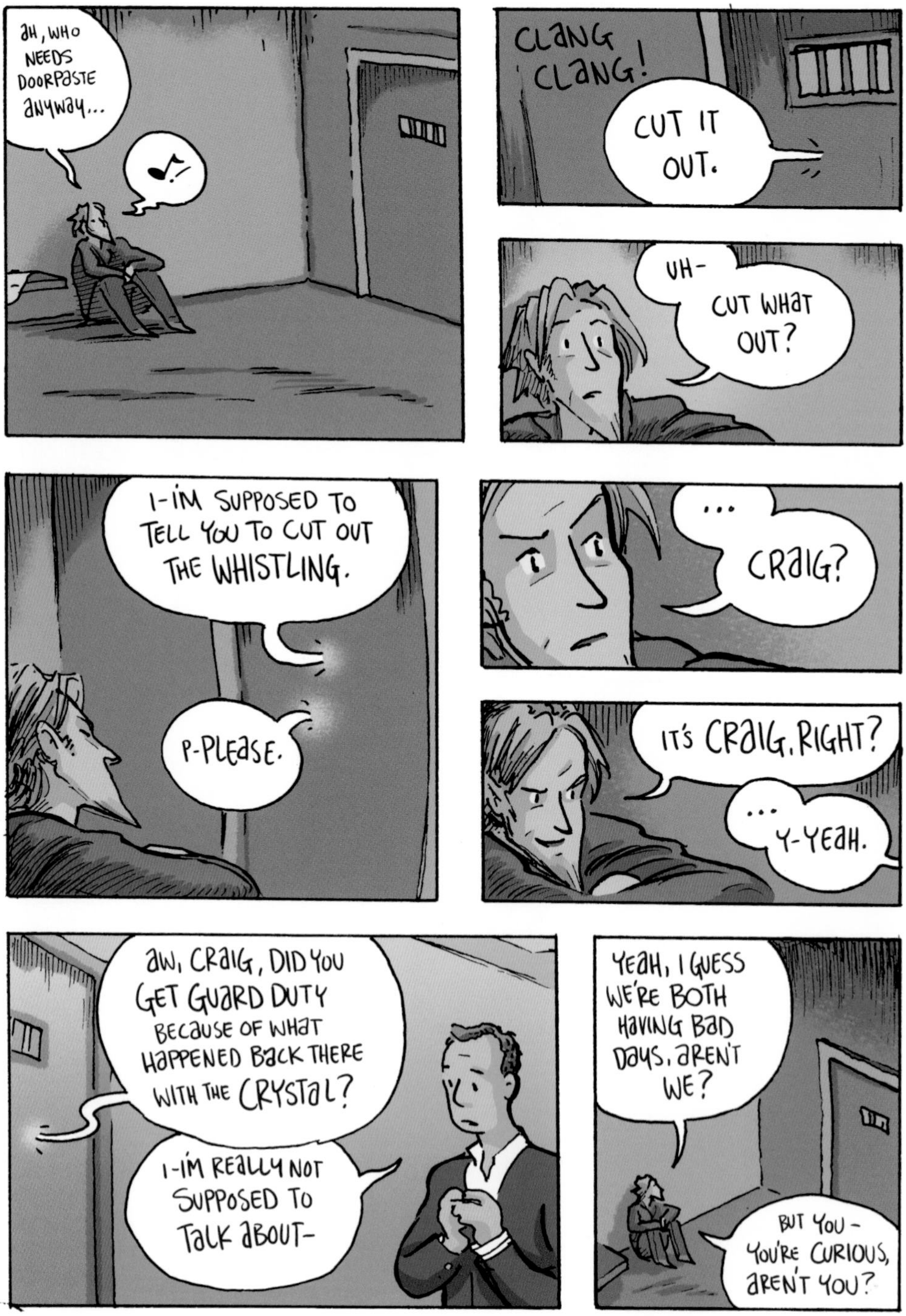
ah, who needs doorpaste anyway...
CLANG CLANG!
CUT IT OUT.
UH-
CUT WHAT OUT?
I-I'M SUPPOSED TO TELL YOU TO CUT OUT THE WHISTLING.
P-PLEASE.
...
CRAIG?
IT'S CRAIG, RIGHT?
...
Y-YEAH.
aw, CRAIG, DID YOU GET GUARD DUTY BECAUSE OF WHAT HAPPENED BACK THERE WITH THE CRYSTAL?
I-I'M REALLY NOT SUPPOSED TO TALK ABOUT-
YEAH, I GUESS WE'RE BOTH HAVING BAD DAYS, AREN'T WE?
BUT YOU - YOU'RE CURIOUS, AREN'T YOU?

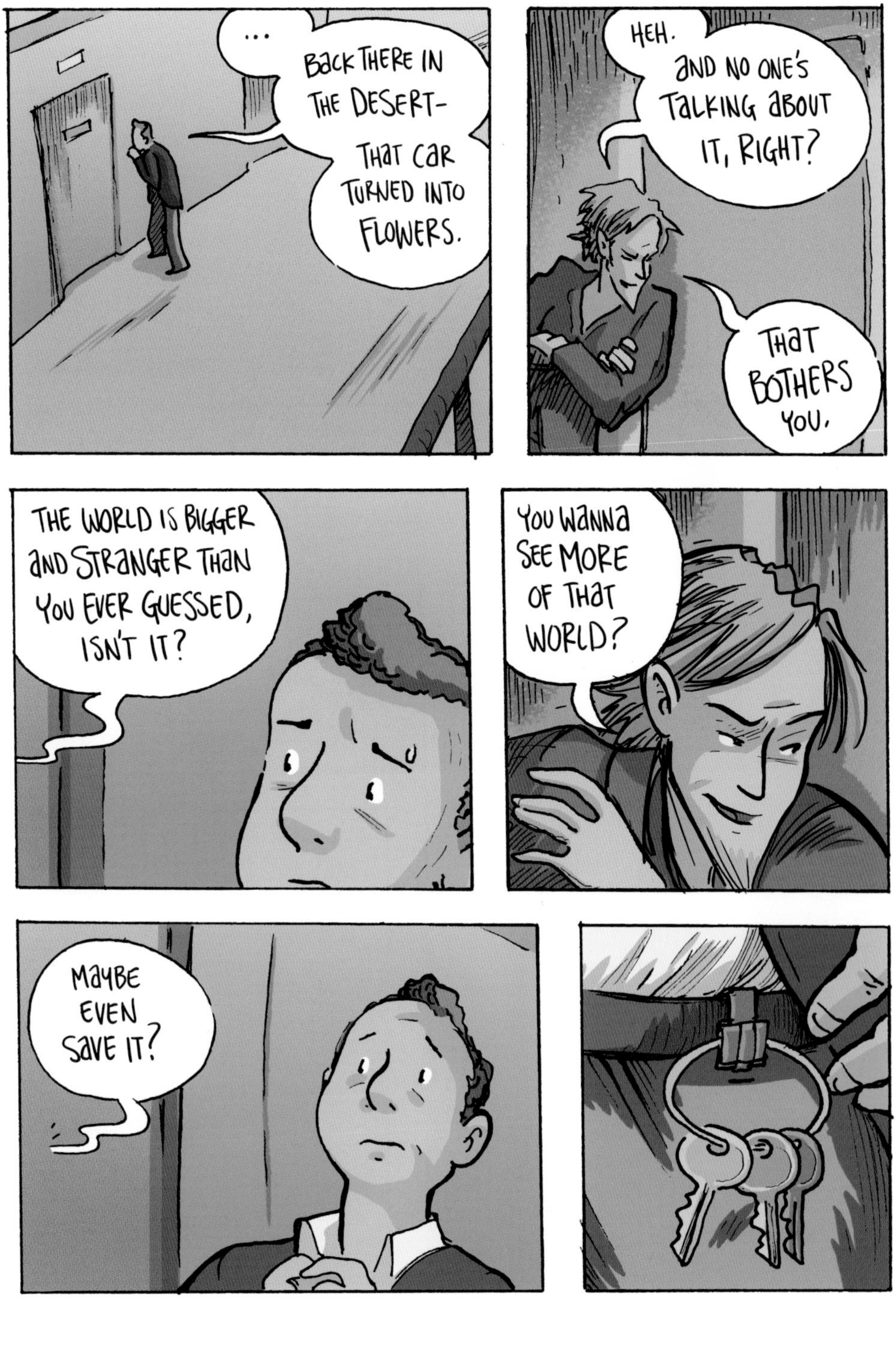
...
BACK THERE IN THE DESERT-
THAT CAR TURNED INTO FLOWERS.
HEH.
AND NO ONE'S TALKING ABOUT IT, RIGHT?
THAT BOTHERS YOU.
THE WORLD IS BIGGER AND STRANGER THAN YOU EVER GUESSED, ISN'T IT?
YOU WANNA SEE MORE OF THAT WORLD?
MAYBE EVEN SAVE IT?

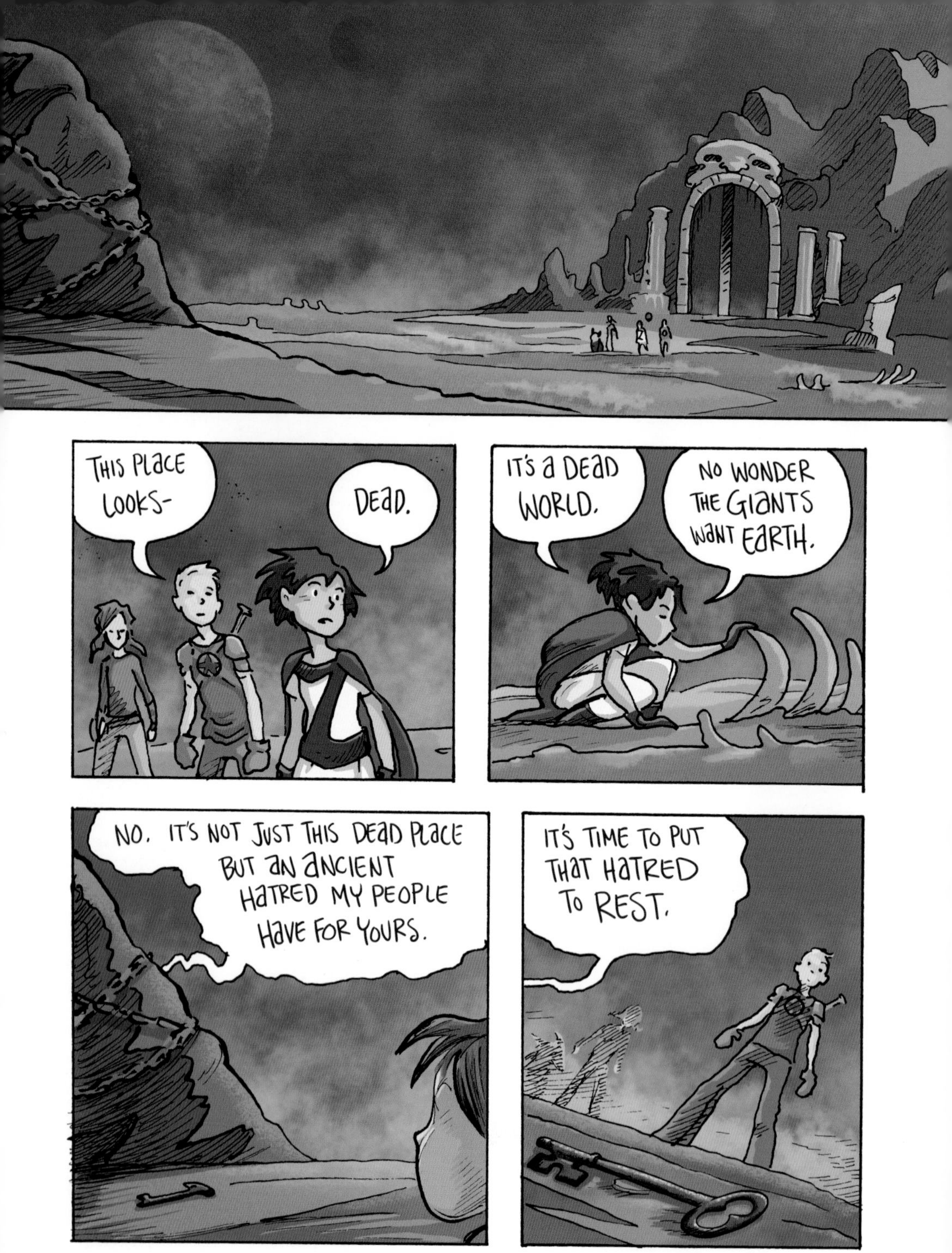
THIS PLACE LOOKS-
DEAD.
IT'S A DEAD WORLD.
NO WONDER THE GIANTS WANT EARTH.
NO. IT'S NOT JUST THIS DEAD PLACE BUT AN ANCIENT HATRED MY PEOPLE HAVE FOR YOURS.
IT'S TIME TO PUT THAT HATRED TO REST.

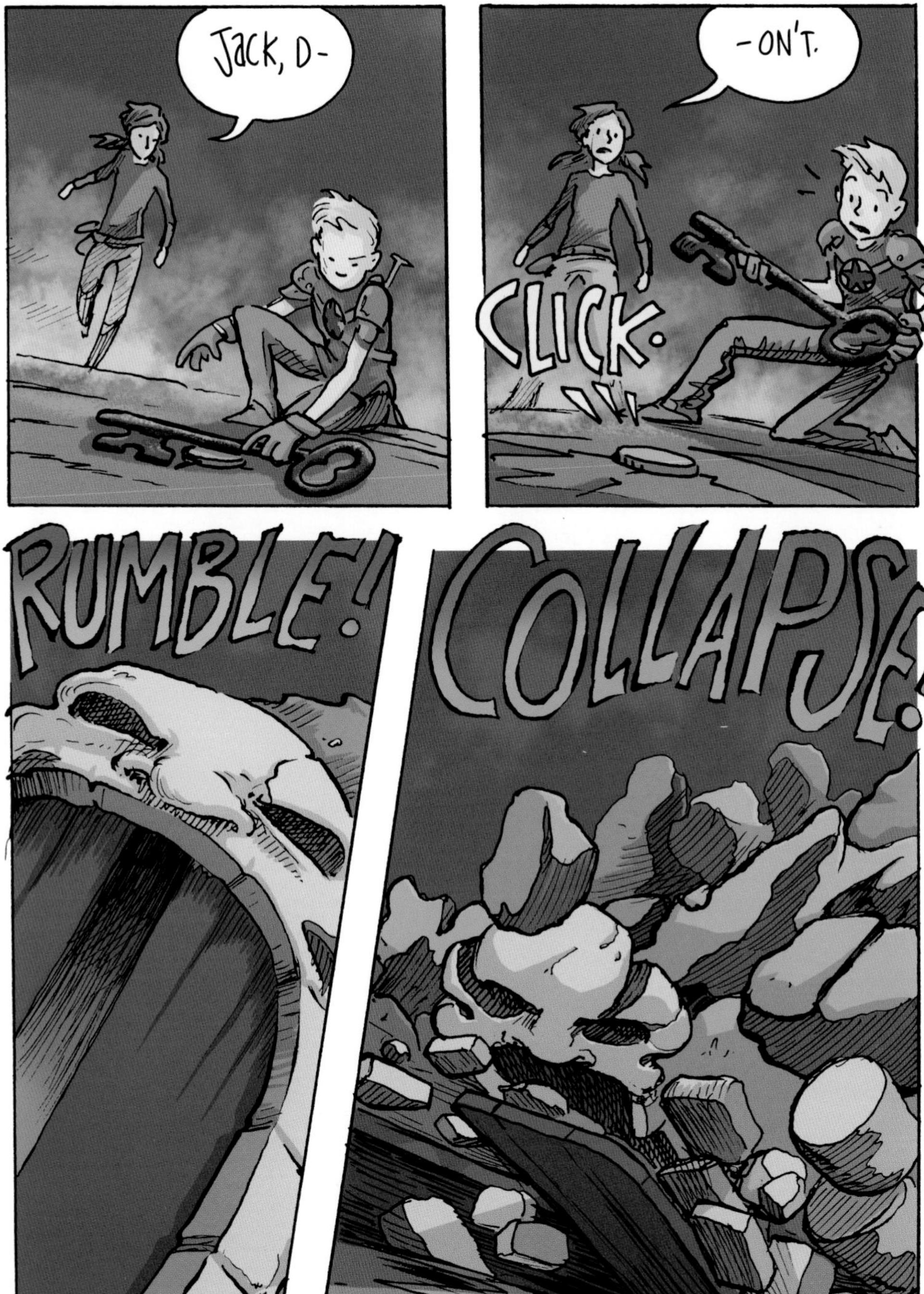
JACK, D-
-ON'T.
CLICK.
RUMBLE!
COLLAPSE!

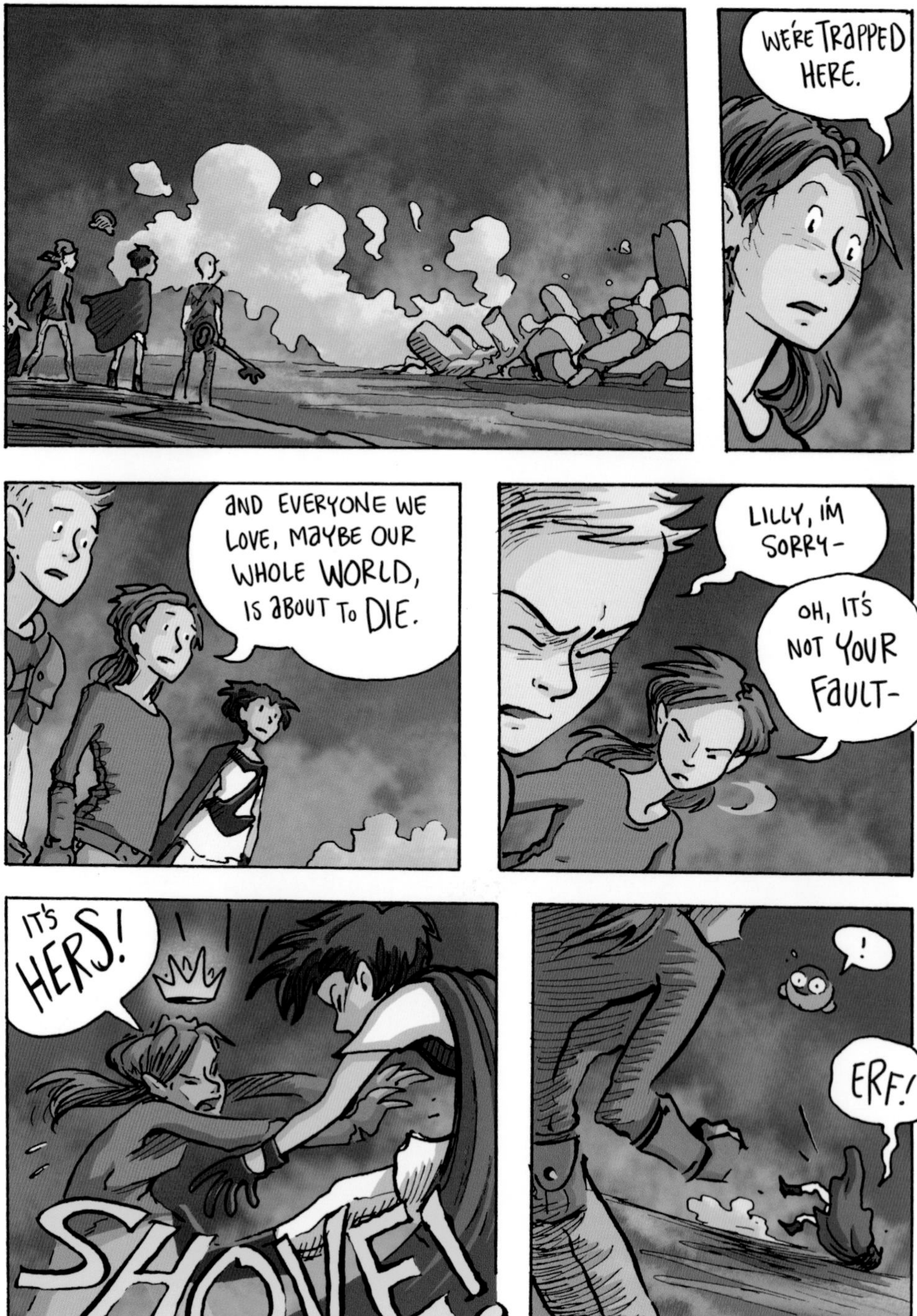
WE'RE TRAPPED HERE.
AND EVERYONE WE LOVE, MAYBE OUR WHOLE WORLD, IS ABOUT TO DIE.
LILLY, I'M SORRY-
OH, IT'S NOT YOUR FAULT-
IT'S HERS!
SHOVE!
!
ERF!

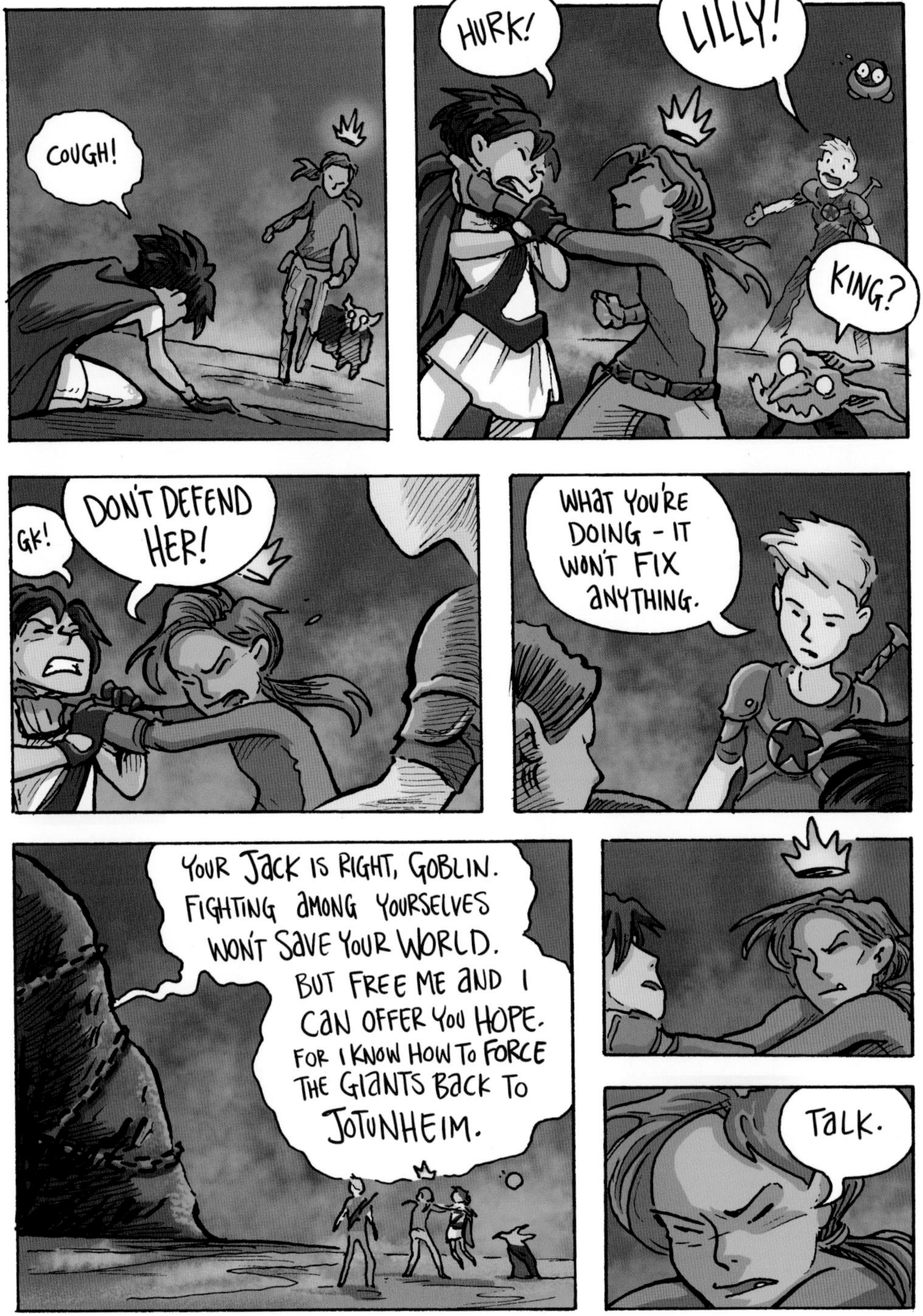
COUGH!
HURK!
LILLY!
KING?
GK!
DON'T DEFEND HER!
WHAT YOU'RE DOING - IT WON'T FIX ANYTHING.
YOUR JACK IS RIGHT, GOBLIN. FIGHTING AMONG YOURSELVES WON'T SAVE YOUR WORLD.
BUT FREE ME AND I CAN OFFER YOU HOPE.
FOR I KNOW HOW TO FORCE THE GIANTS BACK TO JOTUNHEIM.
TALK.

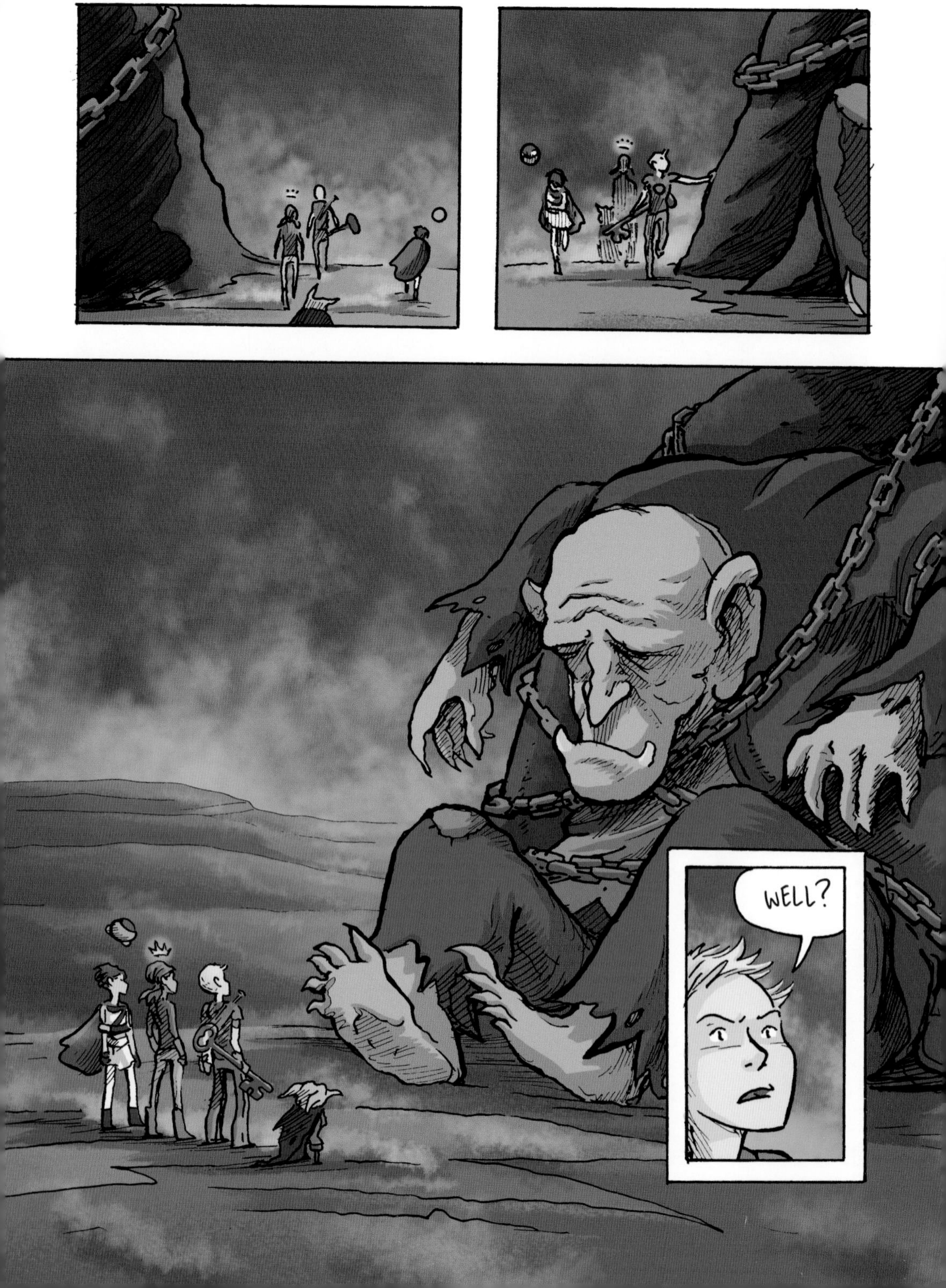
WELL?

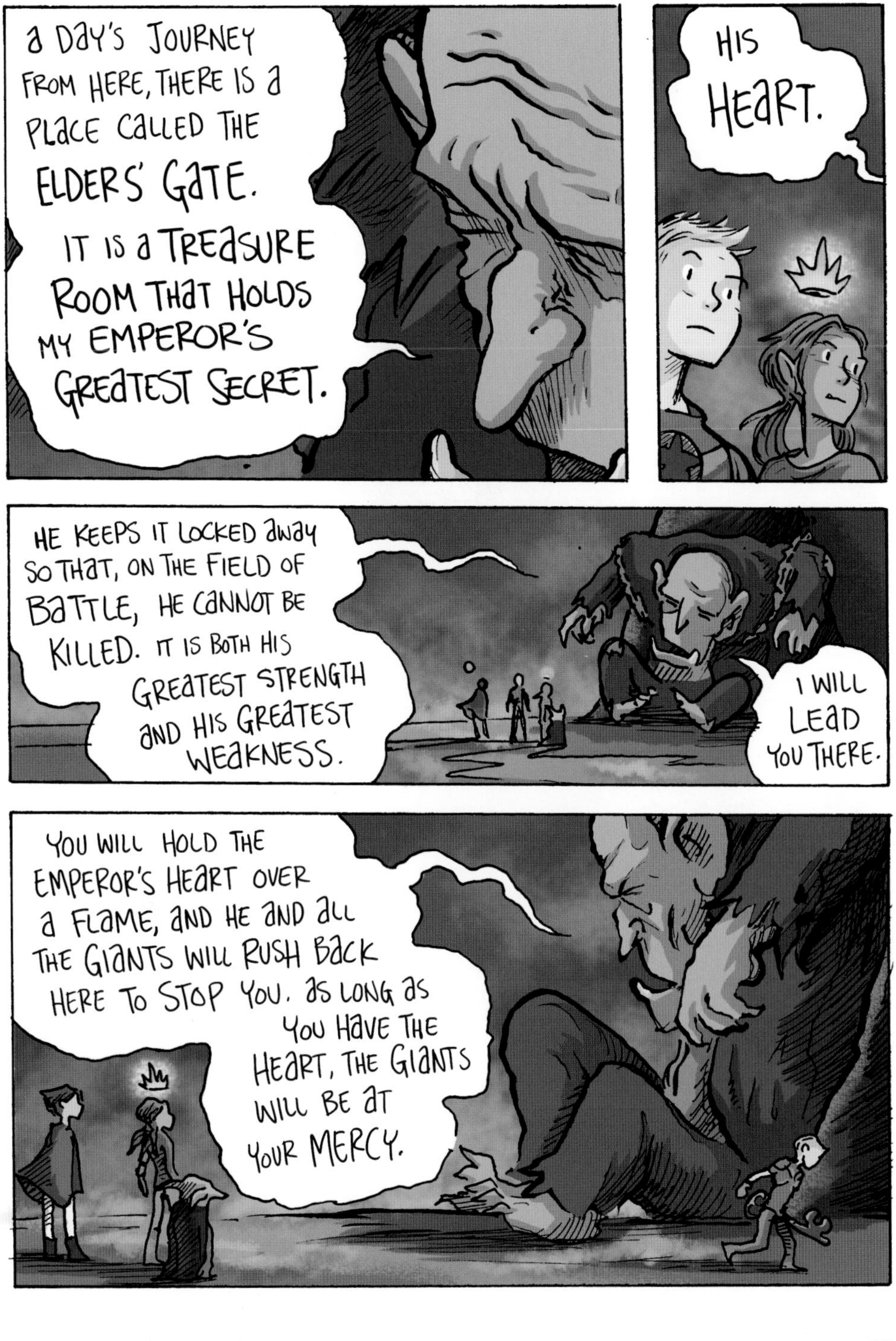
A DAY'S JOURNEY FROM HERE, THERE IS A PLACE CALLED THE ELDERS' GATE.
IT IS A TREASURE ROOM THAT HOLDS MY EMPEROR'S GREATEST SECRET.
HIS HEART.
HE KEEPS IT LOCKED AWAY SO THAT, ON THE FIELD OF BATTLE, HE CANNOT BE KILLED. IT IS BOTH HIS GREATEST STRENGTH AND HIS GREATEST WEAKNESS.
I WILL LEAD YOU THERE.
YOU WILL HOLD THE EMPEROR'S HEART OVER A FLAME, AND HE AND ALL THE GIANTS WILL RUSH BACK HERE TO STOP YOU. AS LONG AS YOU HAVE THE HEART, THE GIANTS WILL BE AT YOUR MERCY.

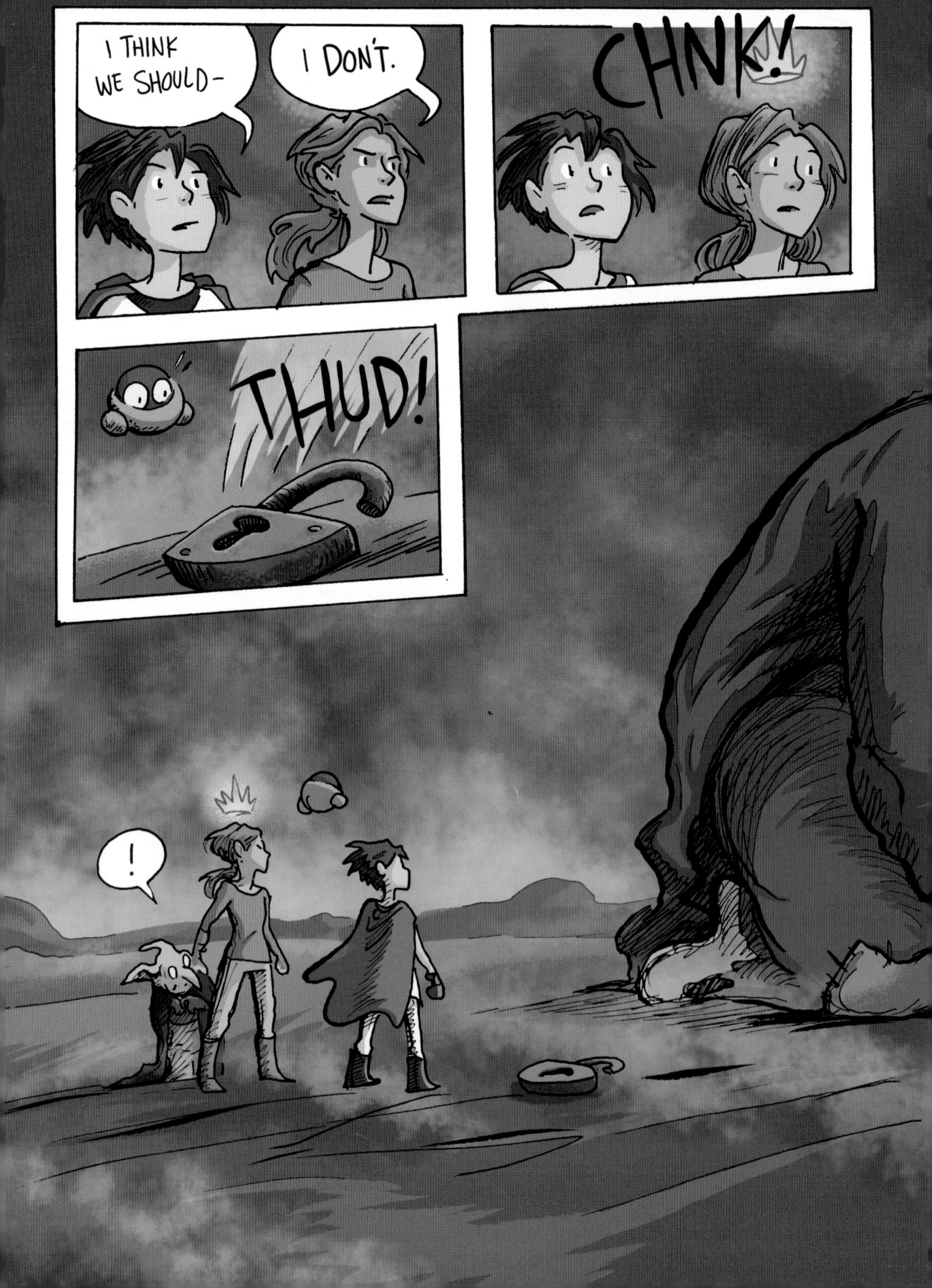
I THINK WE SHOULD-
I DON'T.
CHNK!
THUD!
!

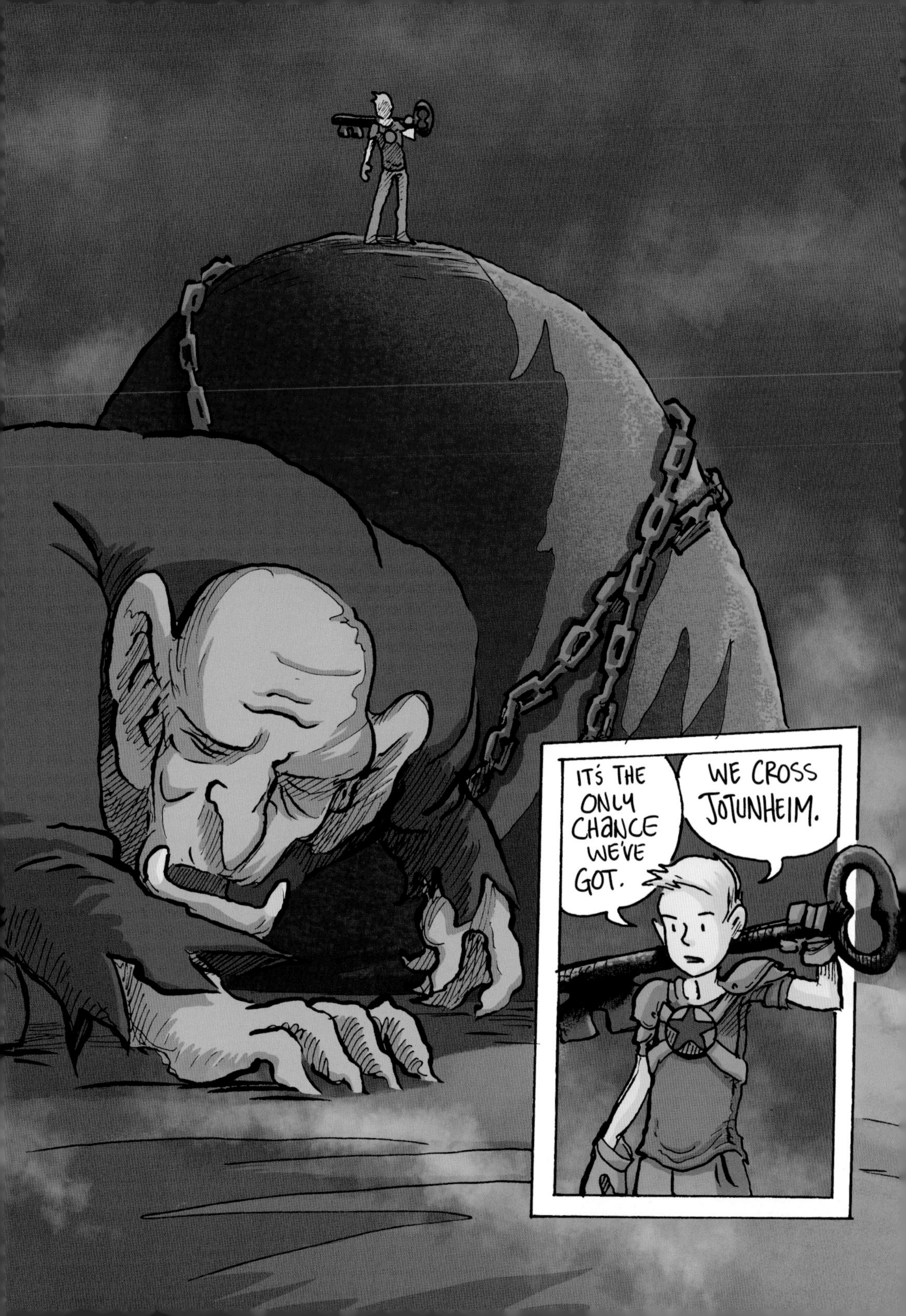

IT'S THE ONLY CHANCE WE'VE GOT.
WE CROSS JOTUNHEIM.

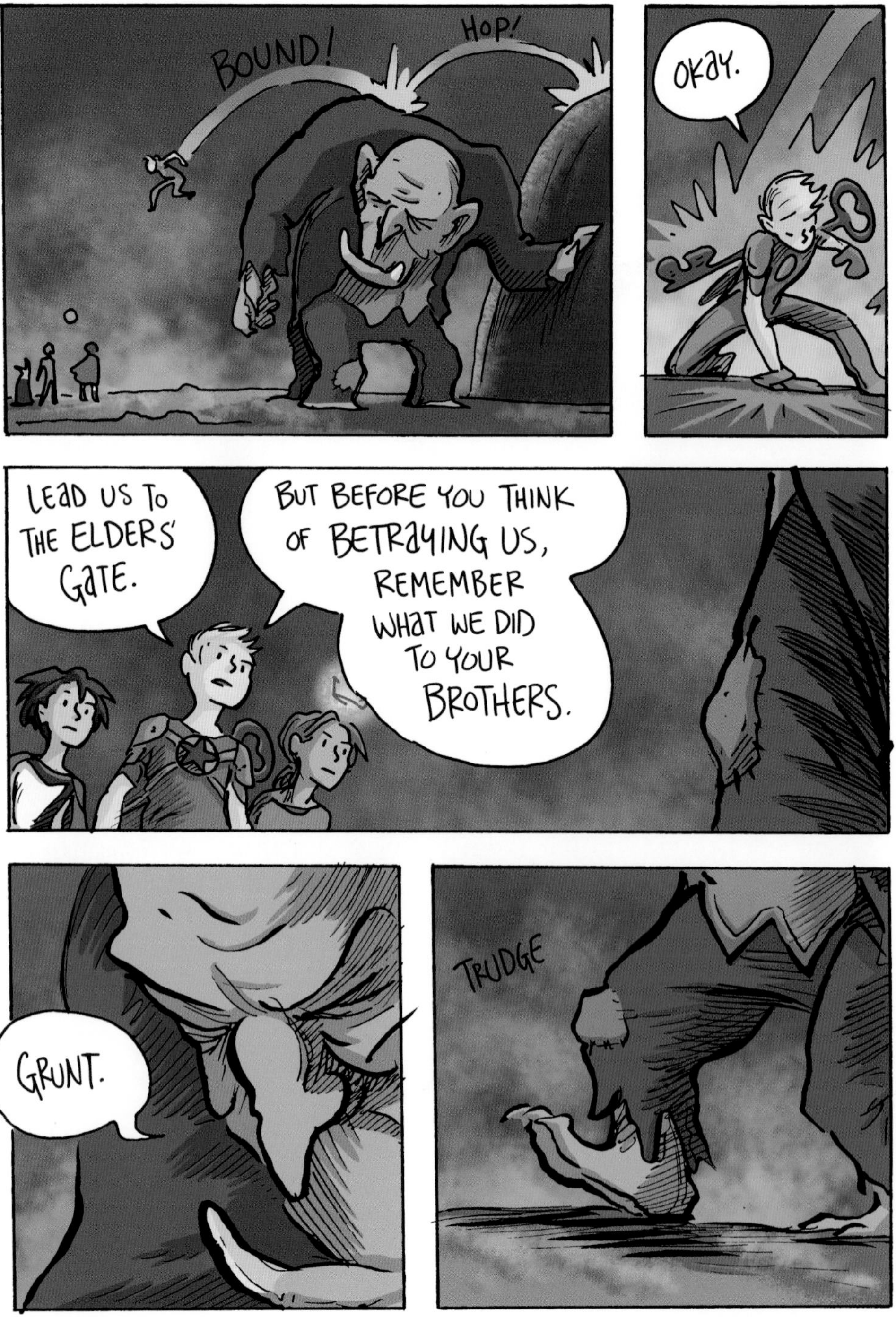
BOUND!
HOP!
OKAY.
LEAD US TO THE ELDERS' GATE.
BUT BEFORE YOU THINK OF BETRAYING US, REMEMBER WHAT WE DID TO YOUR BROTHERS.
GRUNT.
TRUDGE

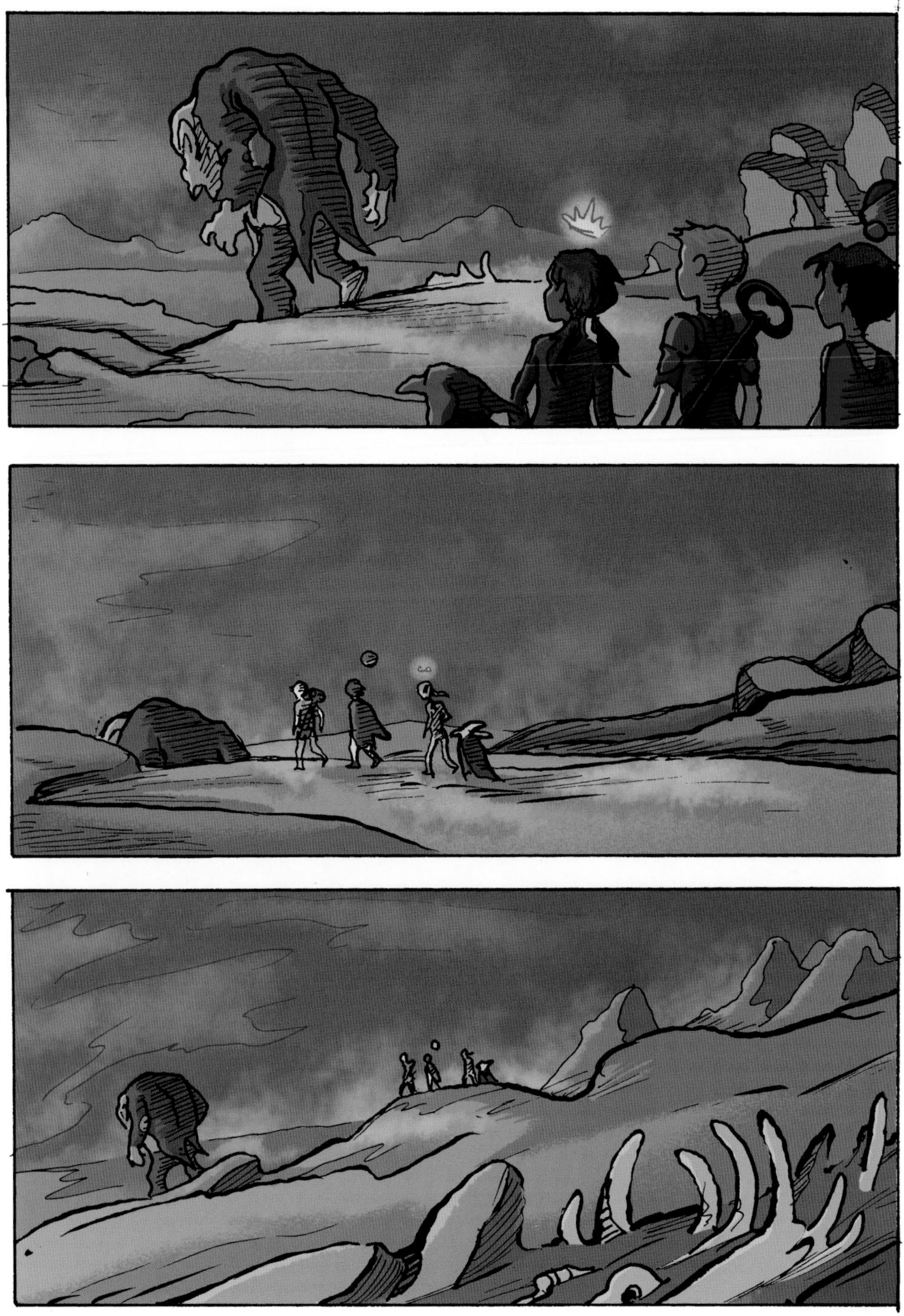

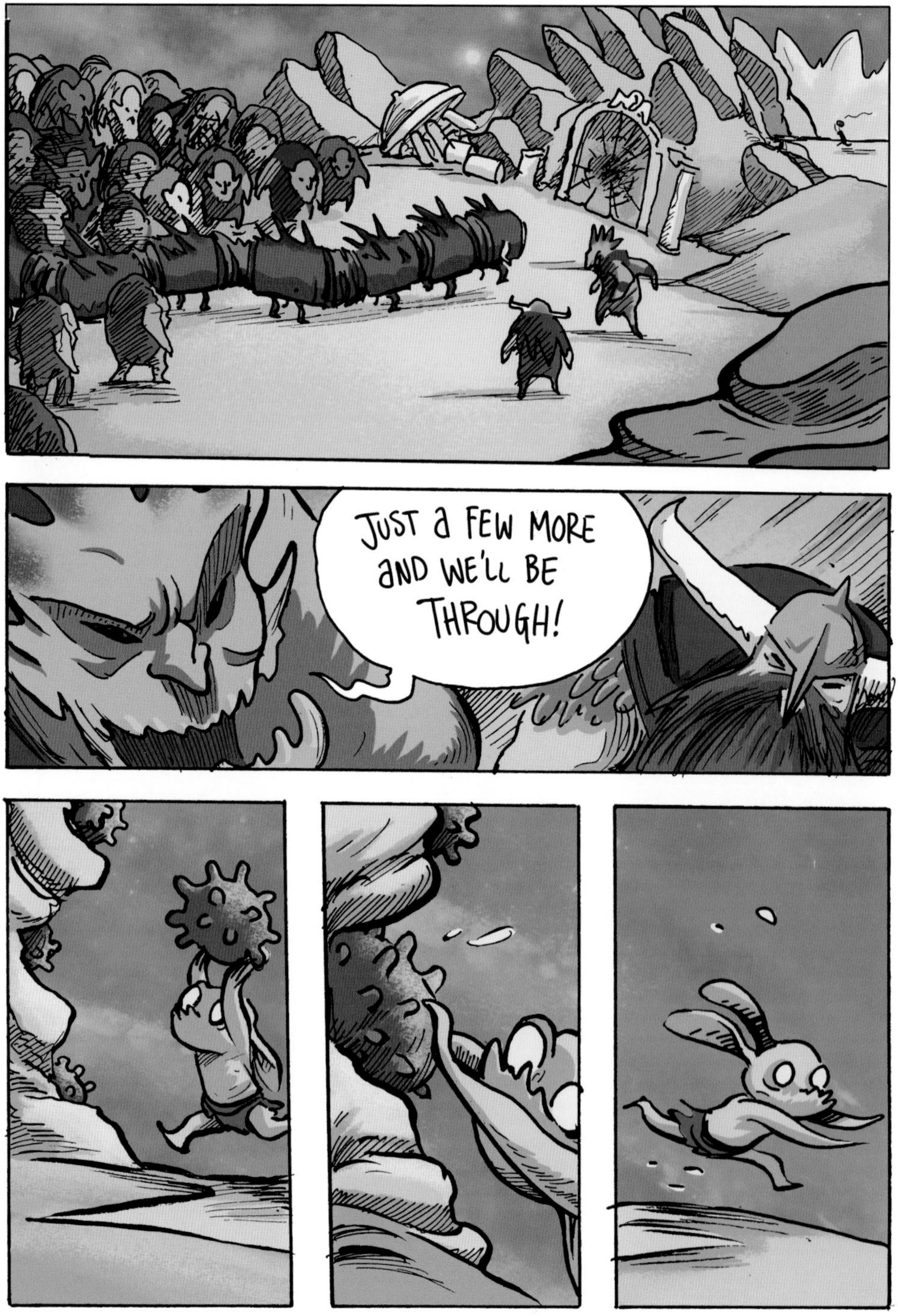
JUST a FEW MORE AND WE'LL BE THROUGH!

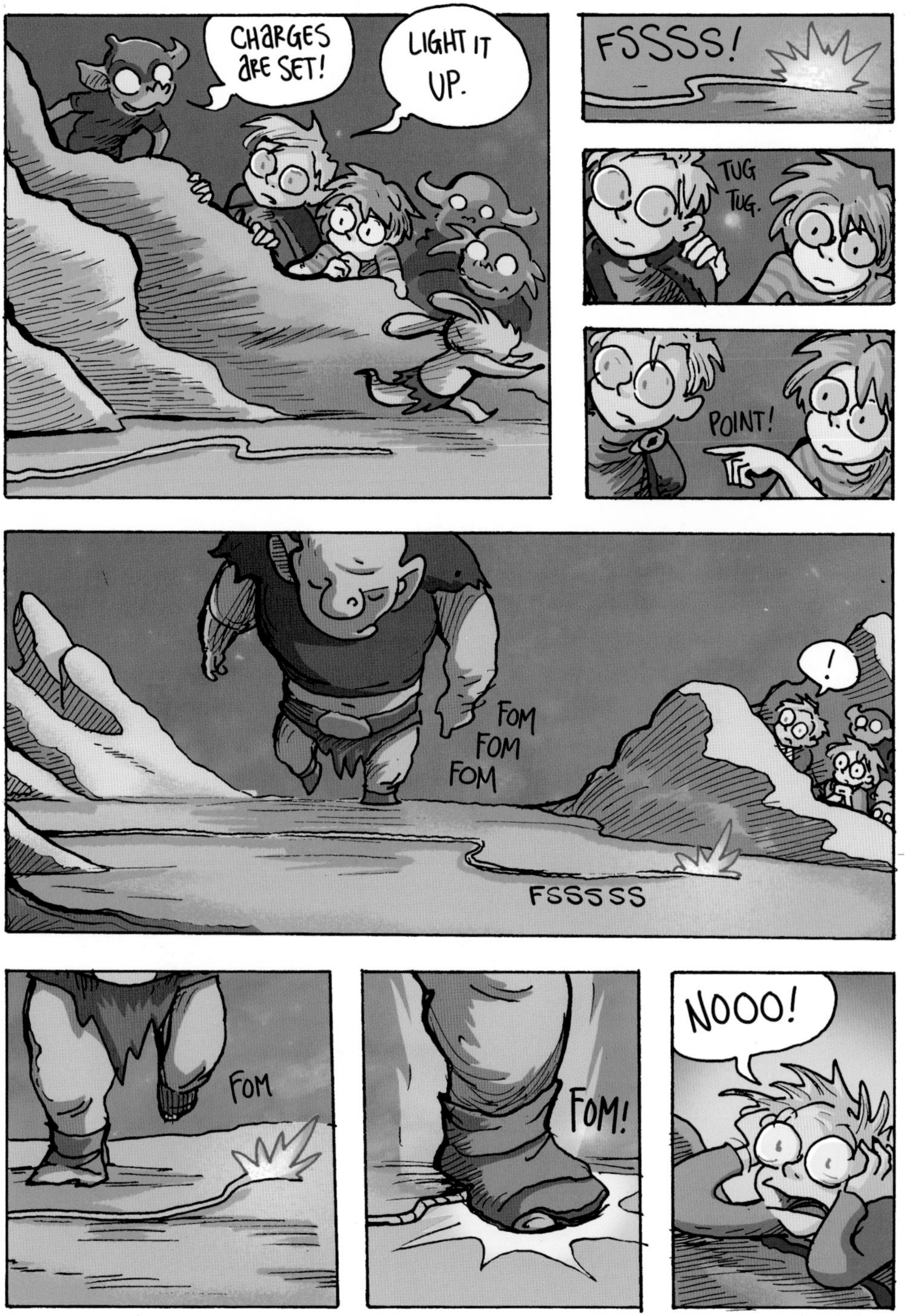

CHARGES ARE SET!
LIGHT IT UP.
FSSSS!
TUG TUG.
POINT!
!
FOM FOM FOM
FSSSSS
FOM
FOM!
NOOO!

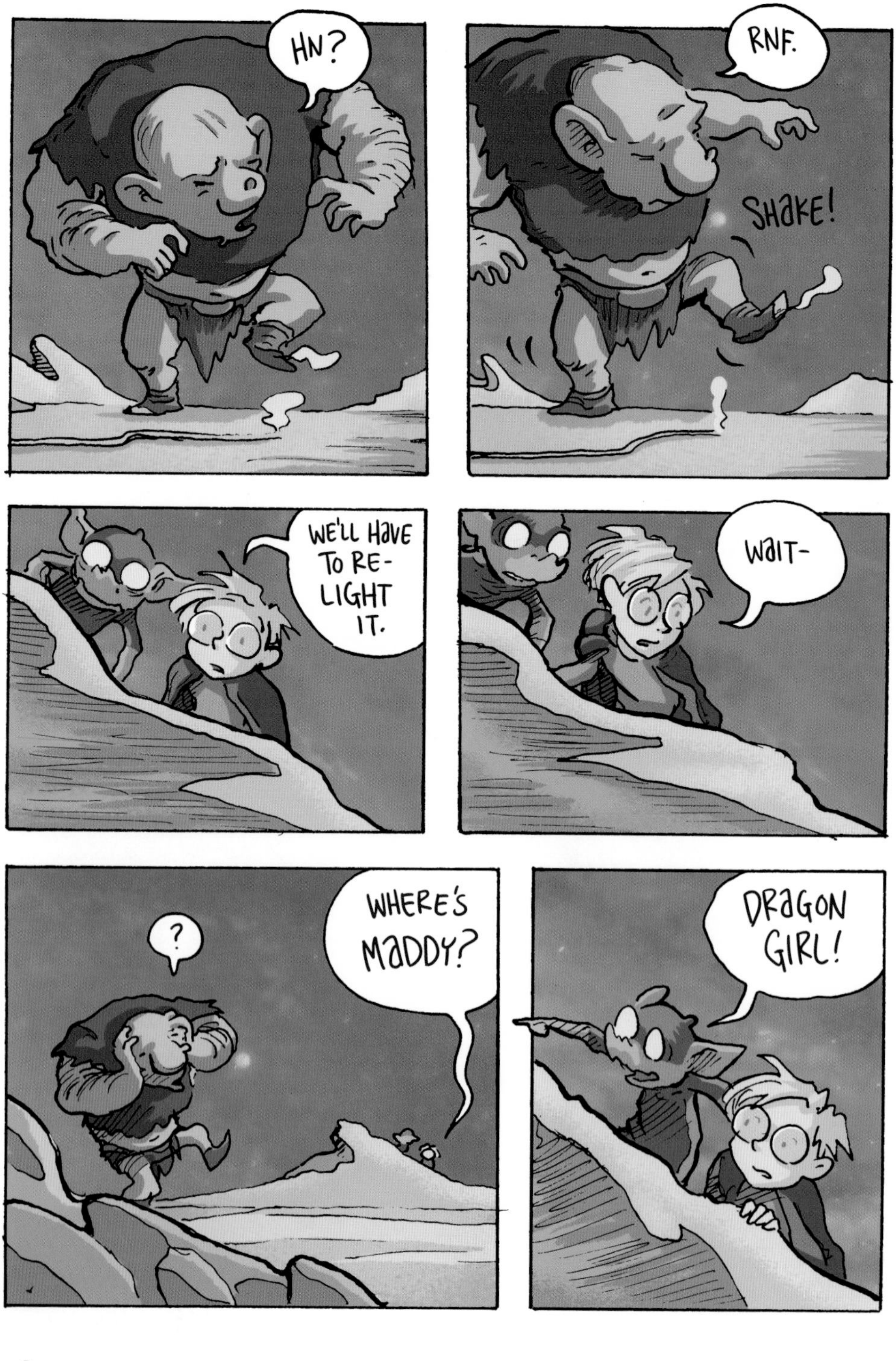
HN?
RNF.
SHAKE!
WE'LL HAVE TO RE-LIGHT IT.
WAIT-
?
WHERE'S MADDY?
DRAGON GIRL!

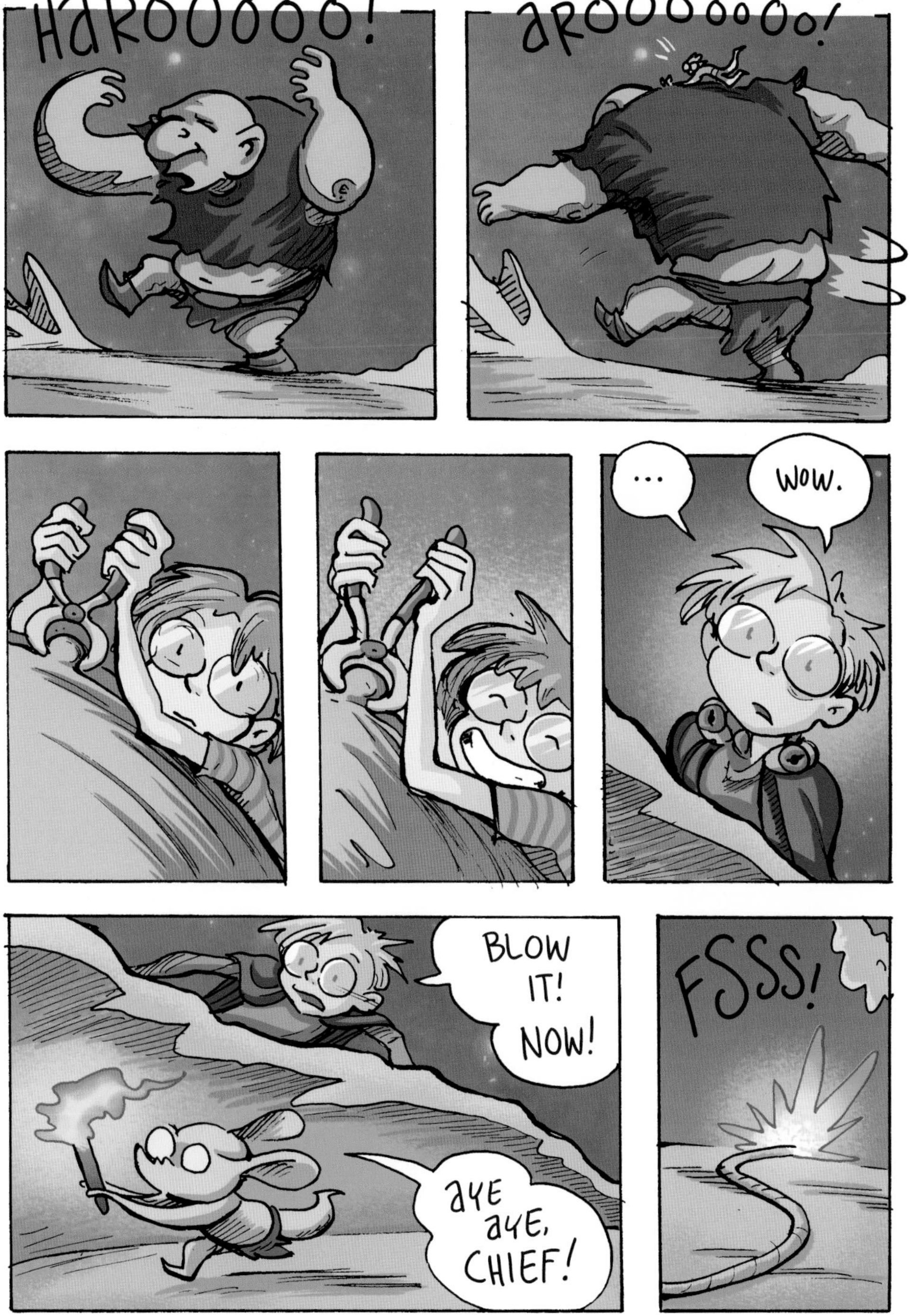
HAROOOOOO!
AROOOOOOOo!
...
WOW.
BLOW IT! NOW!
AYE AYE, CHIEF!
FSSS!

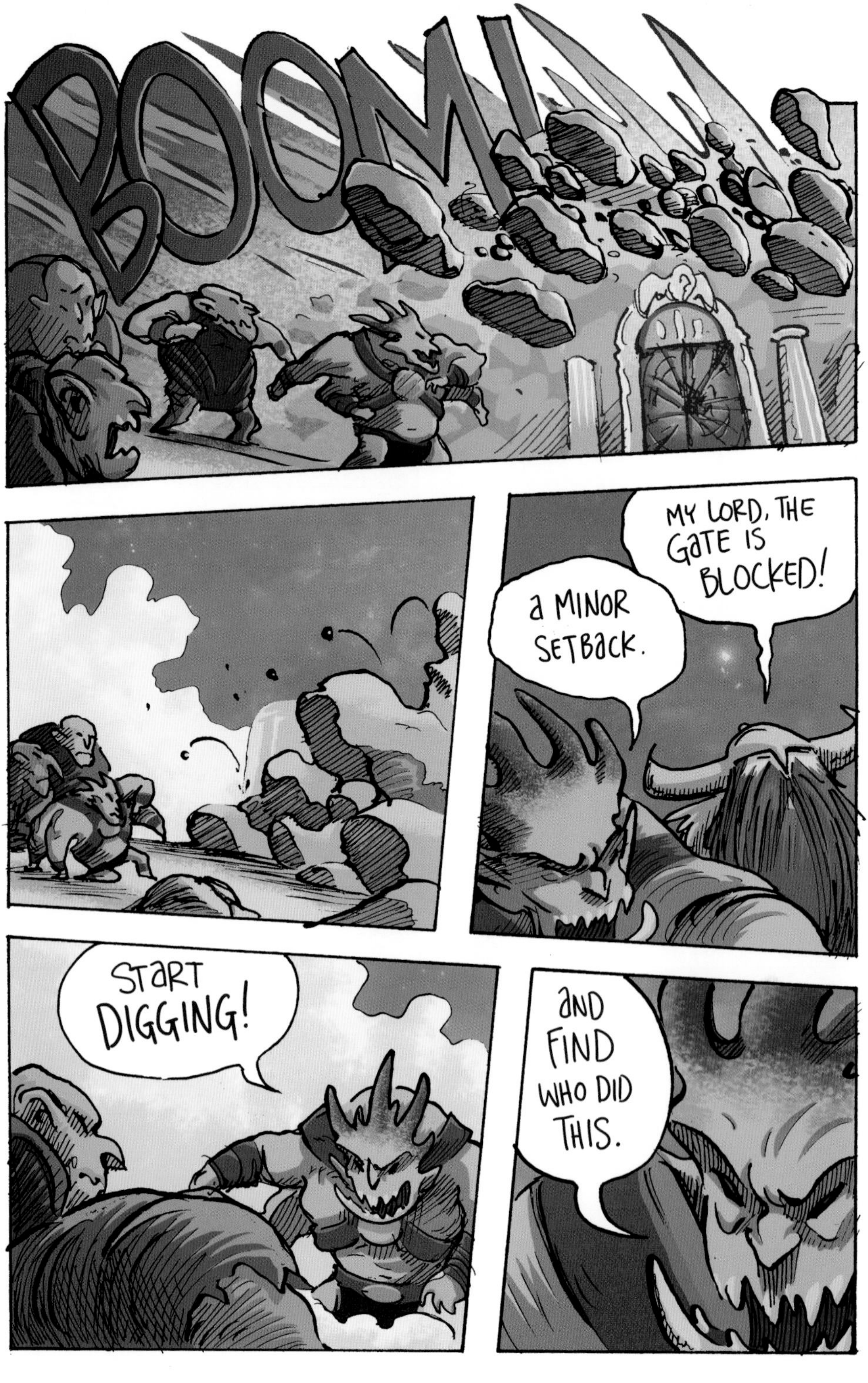
BOOM!
MY LORD, THE GATE IS BLOCKED!
A MINOR SETBACK.
START DIGGING!
AND FIND WHO DID THIS.

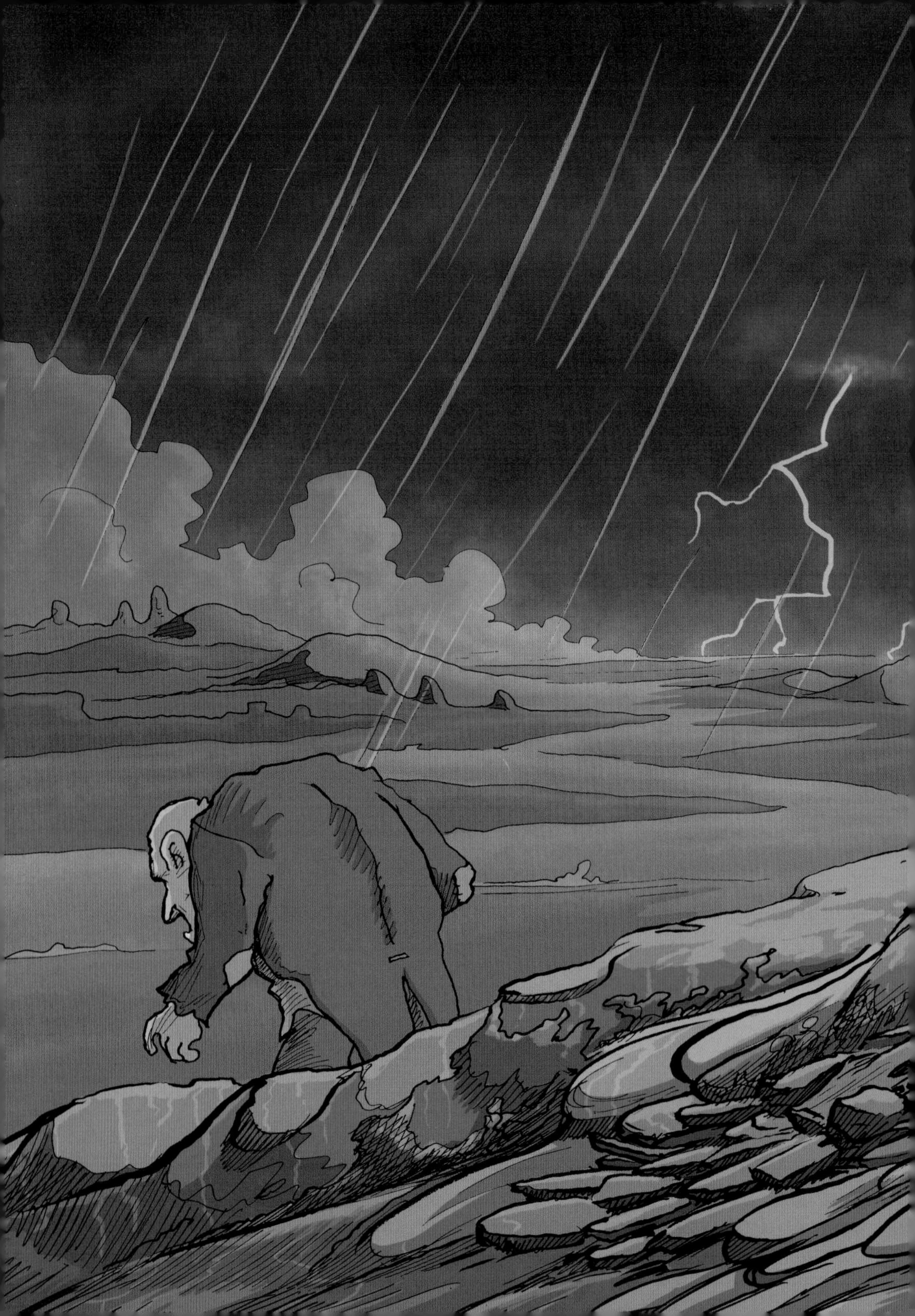

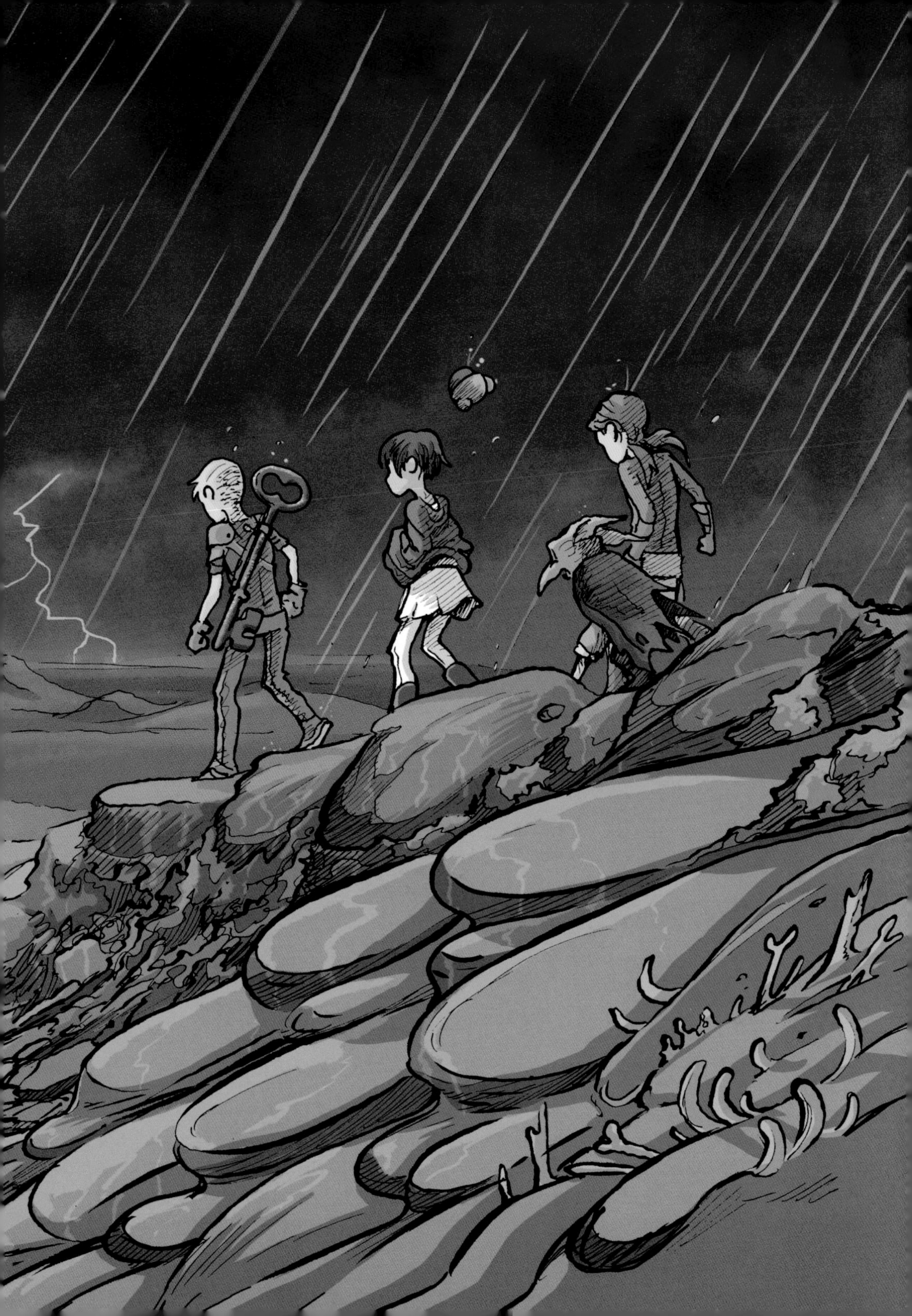

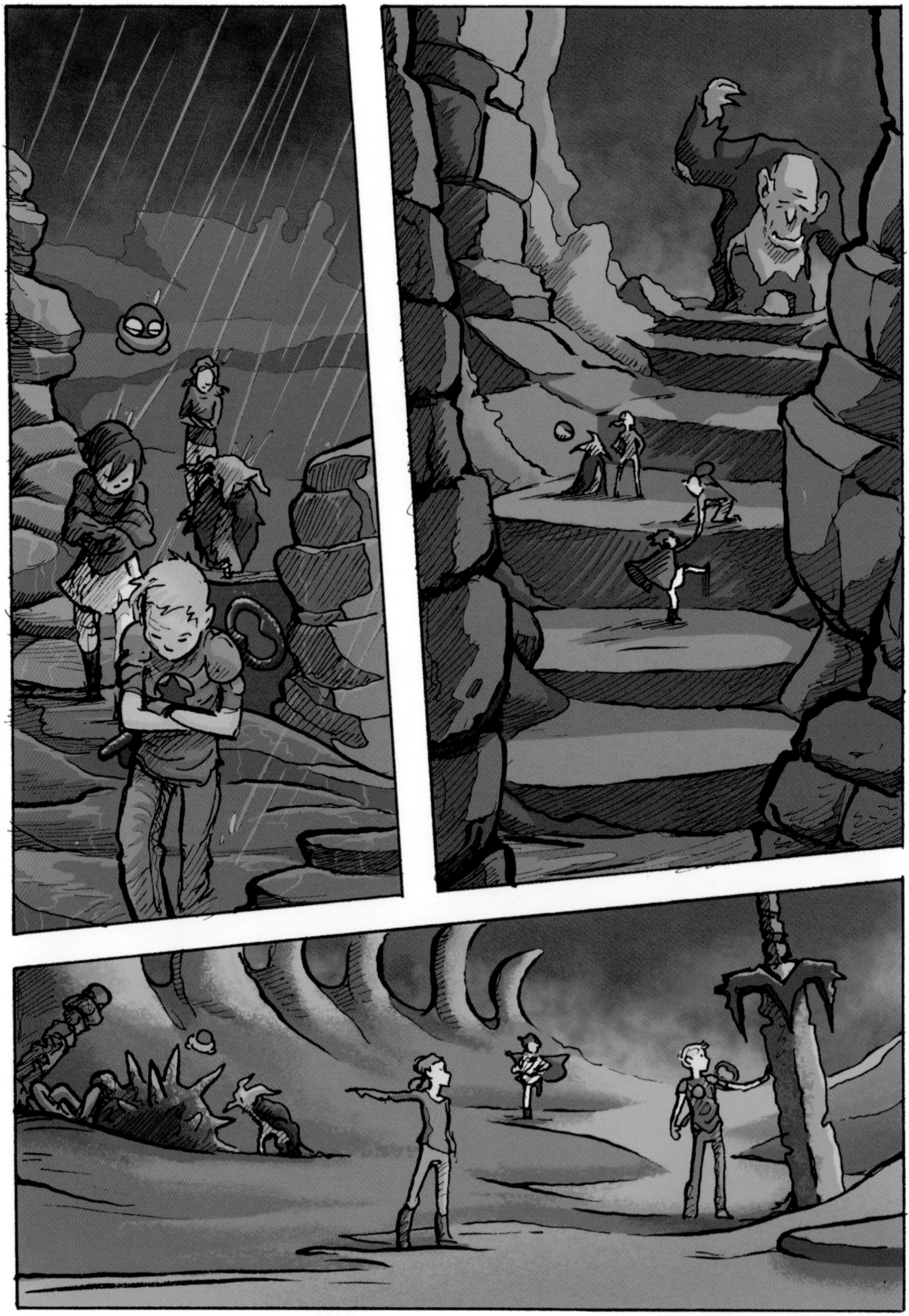

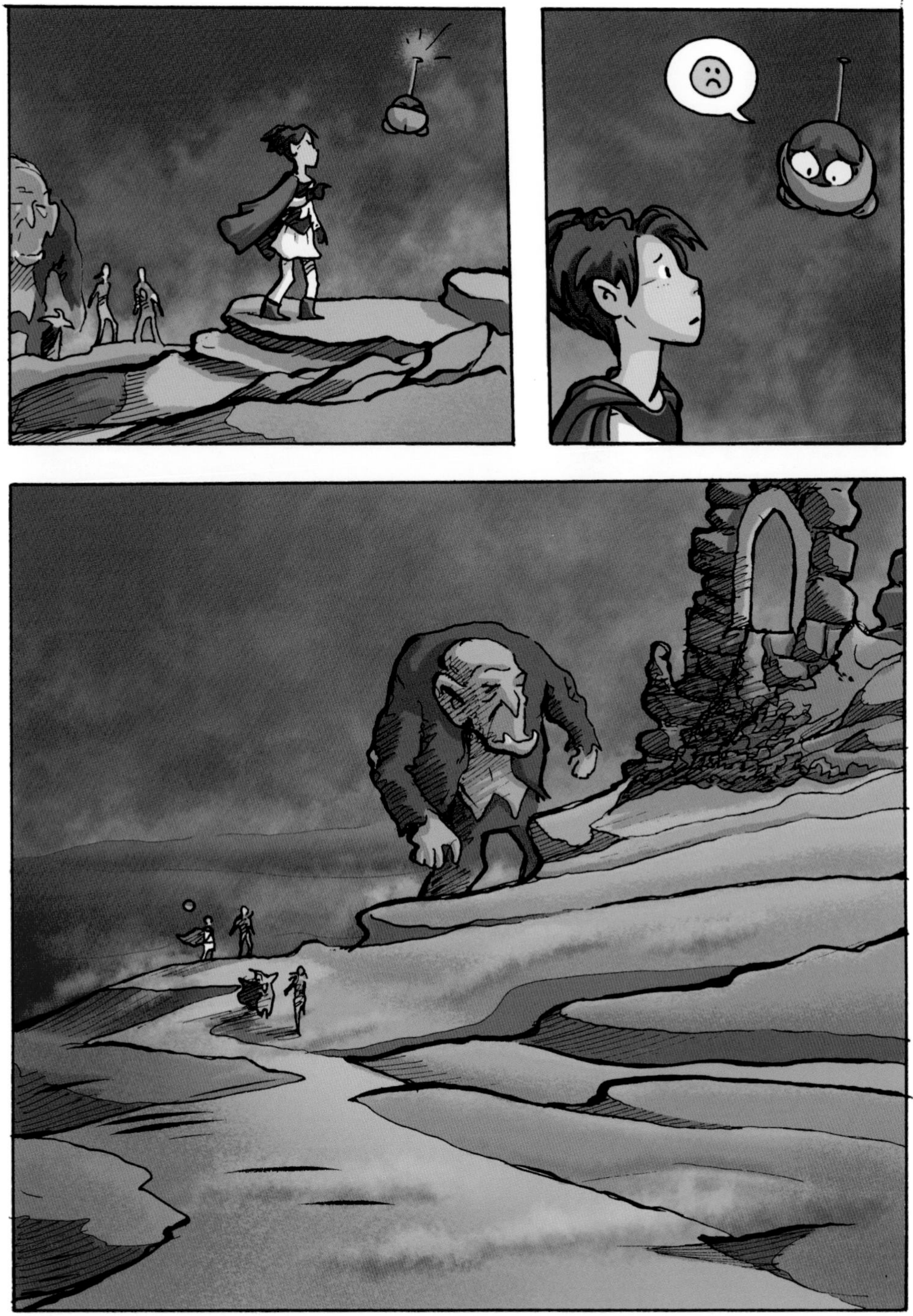

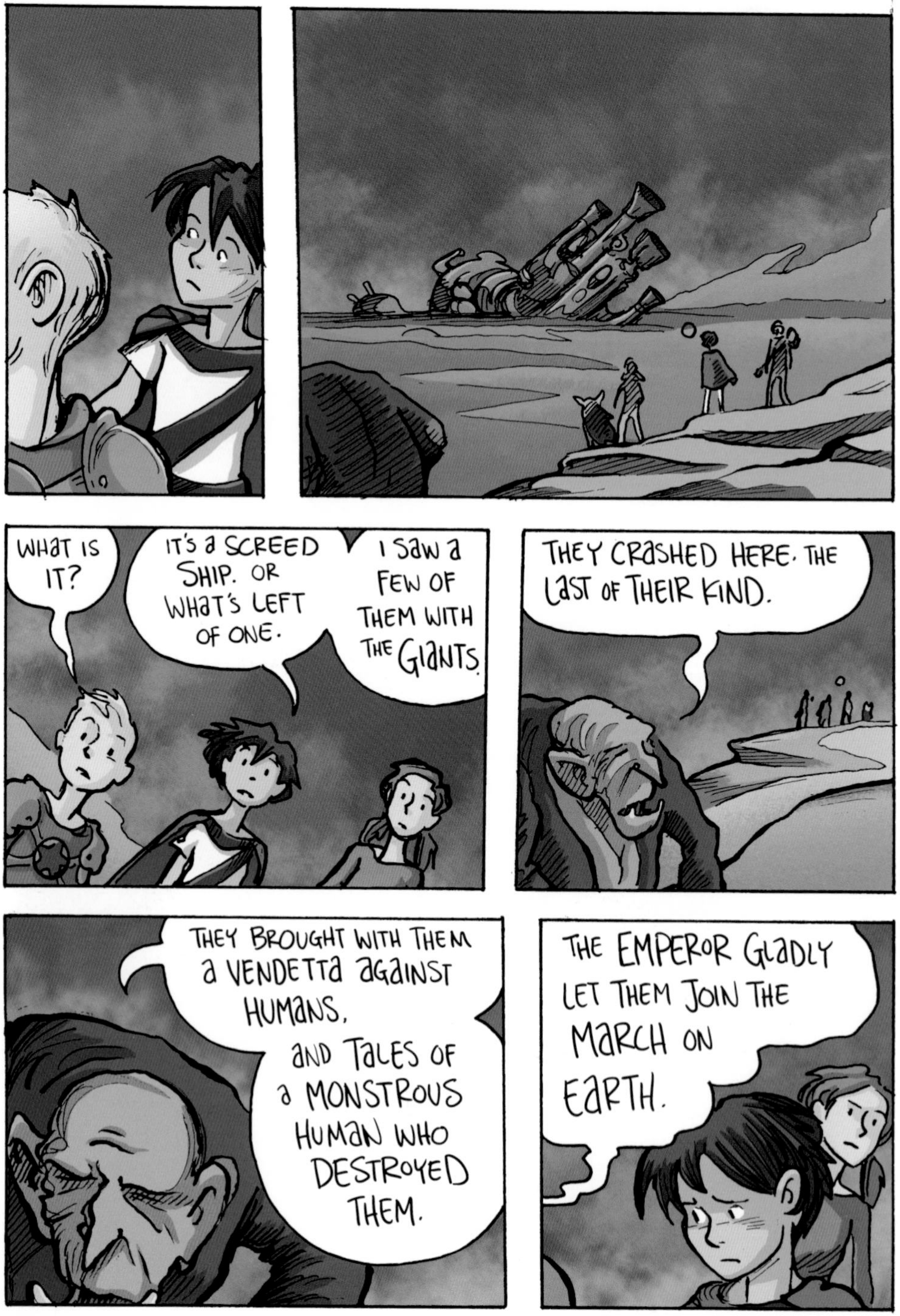
WHAT IS IT?
IT'S A SCREED SHIP. OR WHAT'S LEFT OF ONE.
I SAW A FEW OF THEM WITH THE GIANTS.
THEY CRASHED HERE. THE LAST OF THEIR KIND.
THEY BROUGHT WITH THEM A VENDETTA AGAINST HUMANS,
AND TALES OF A MONSTROUS HUMAN WHO DESTROYED THEM.
THE EMPEROR GLADLY LET THEM JOIN THE MARCH ON EARTH.

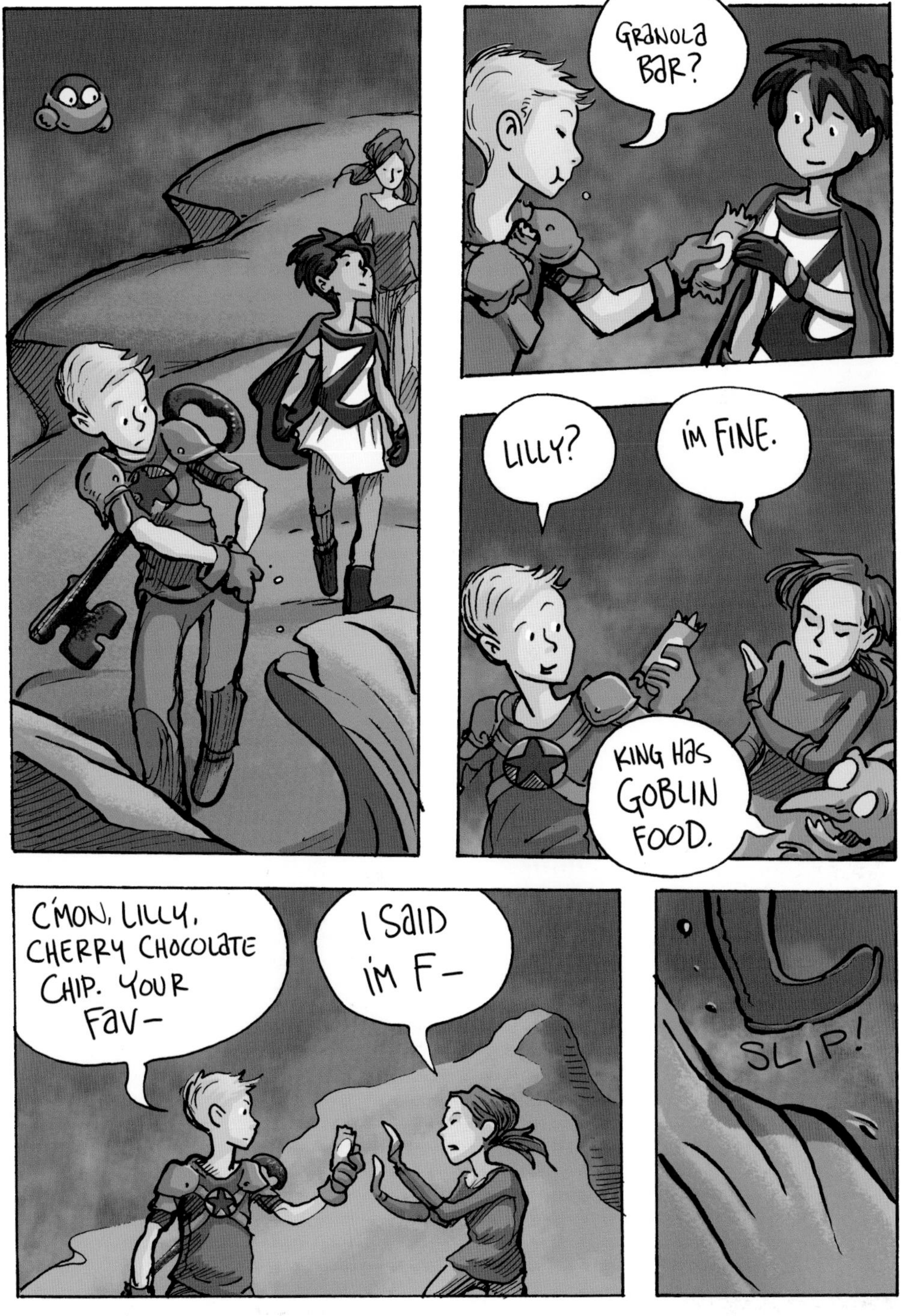
GRANOLA BAR?
LILLY?
I'M FINE.
KING HAS GOBLIN FOOD.
C'MON, LILLY. CHERRY CHOCOLATE CHIP. YOUR FAV–
I SAID I'M F–
SLIP!

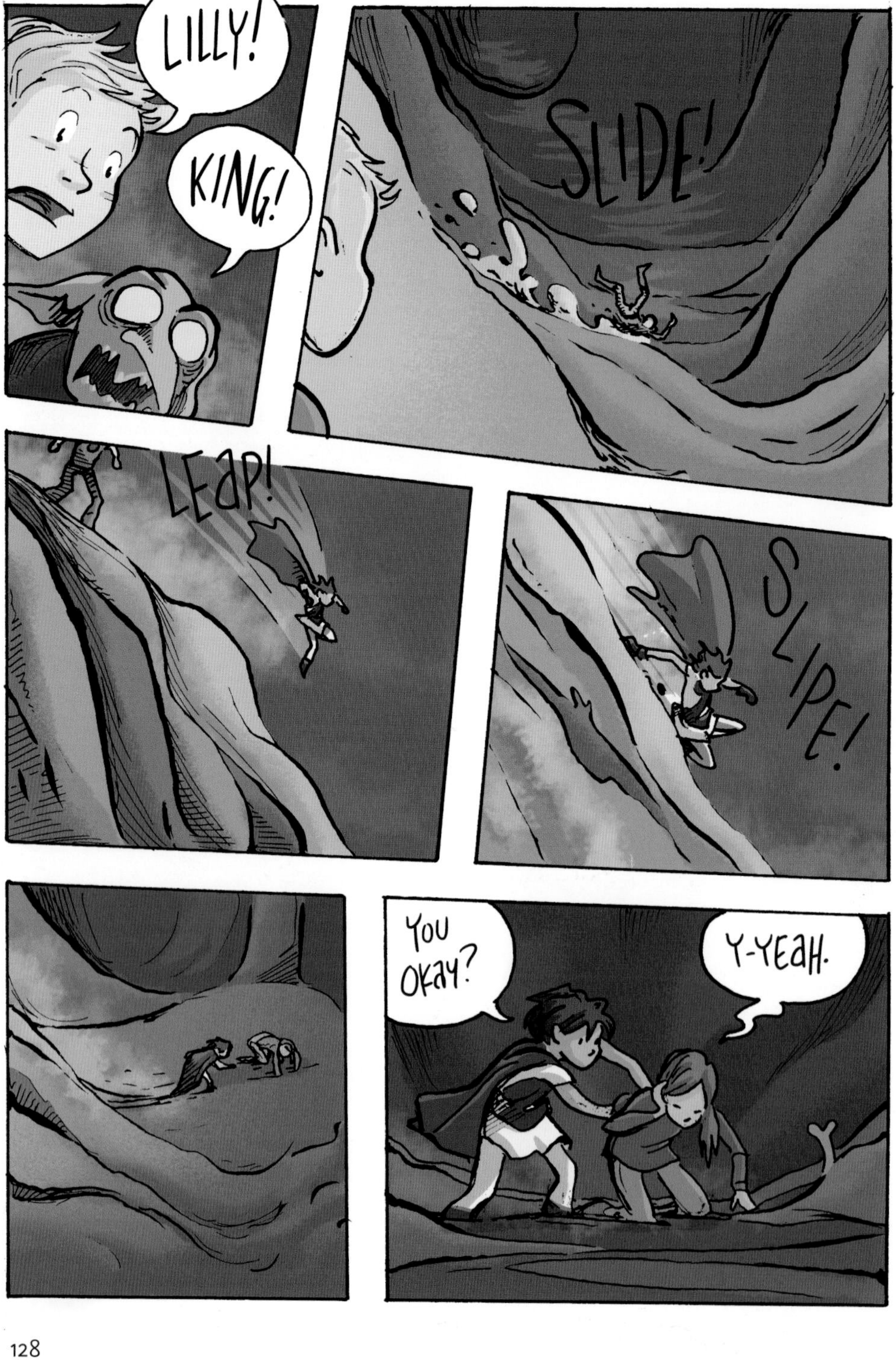
LILLY!
KING!
SLIDE!
LEAP!
SLIPE!
YOU OKAY?
Y-YEAH.

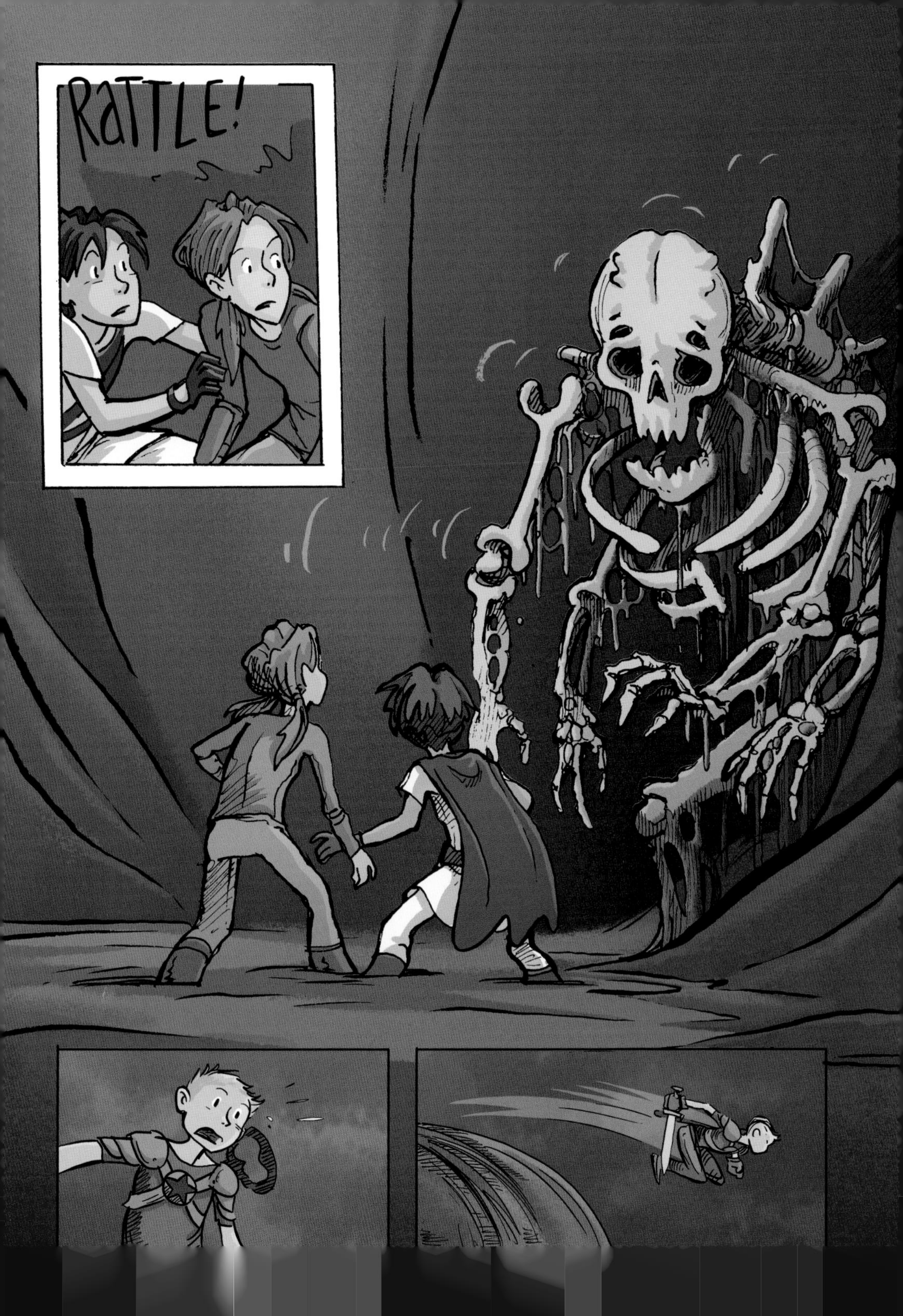
RATTLE!

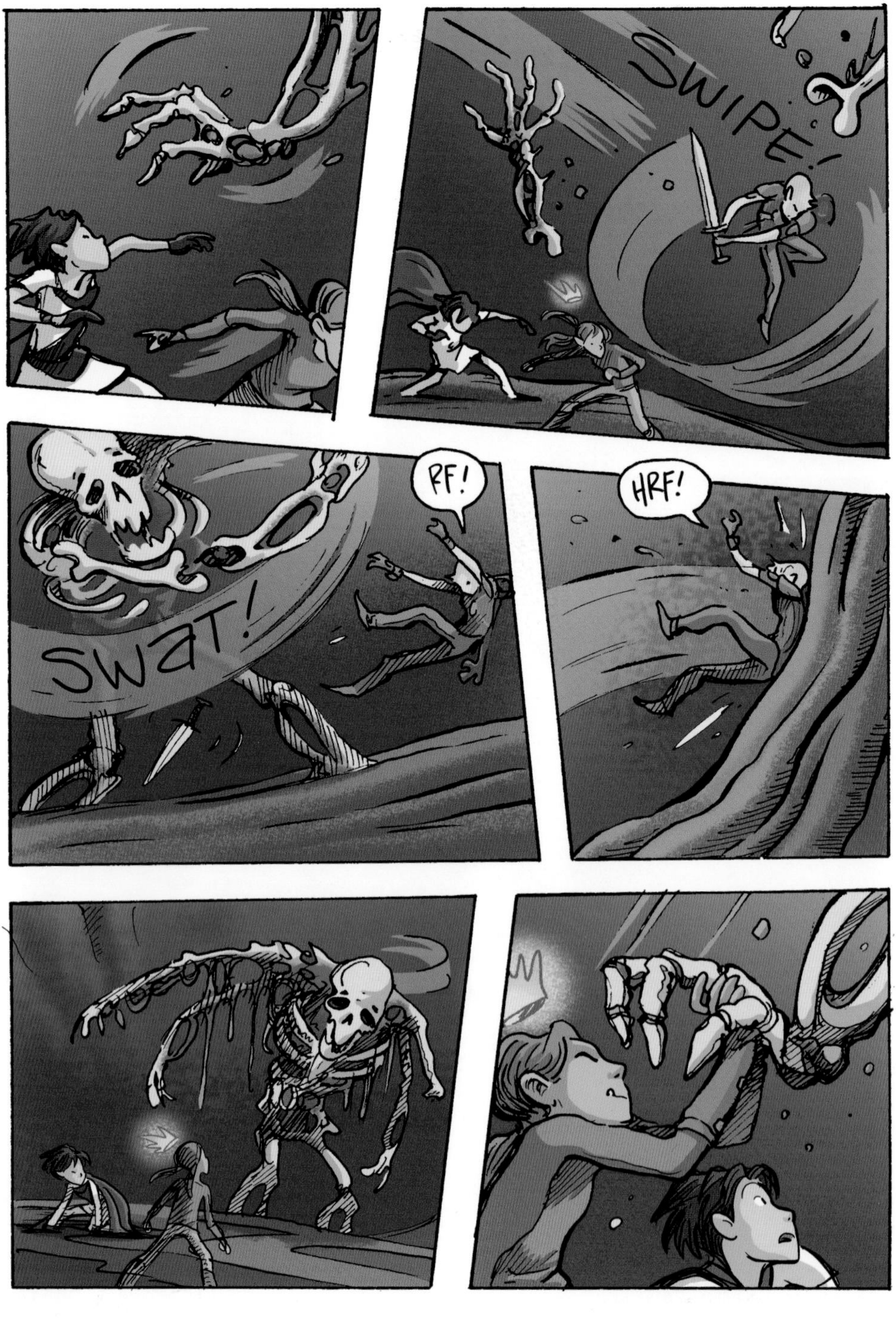
SWIPE!
RF!
SWAT!
HRF!

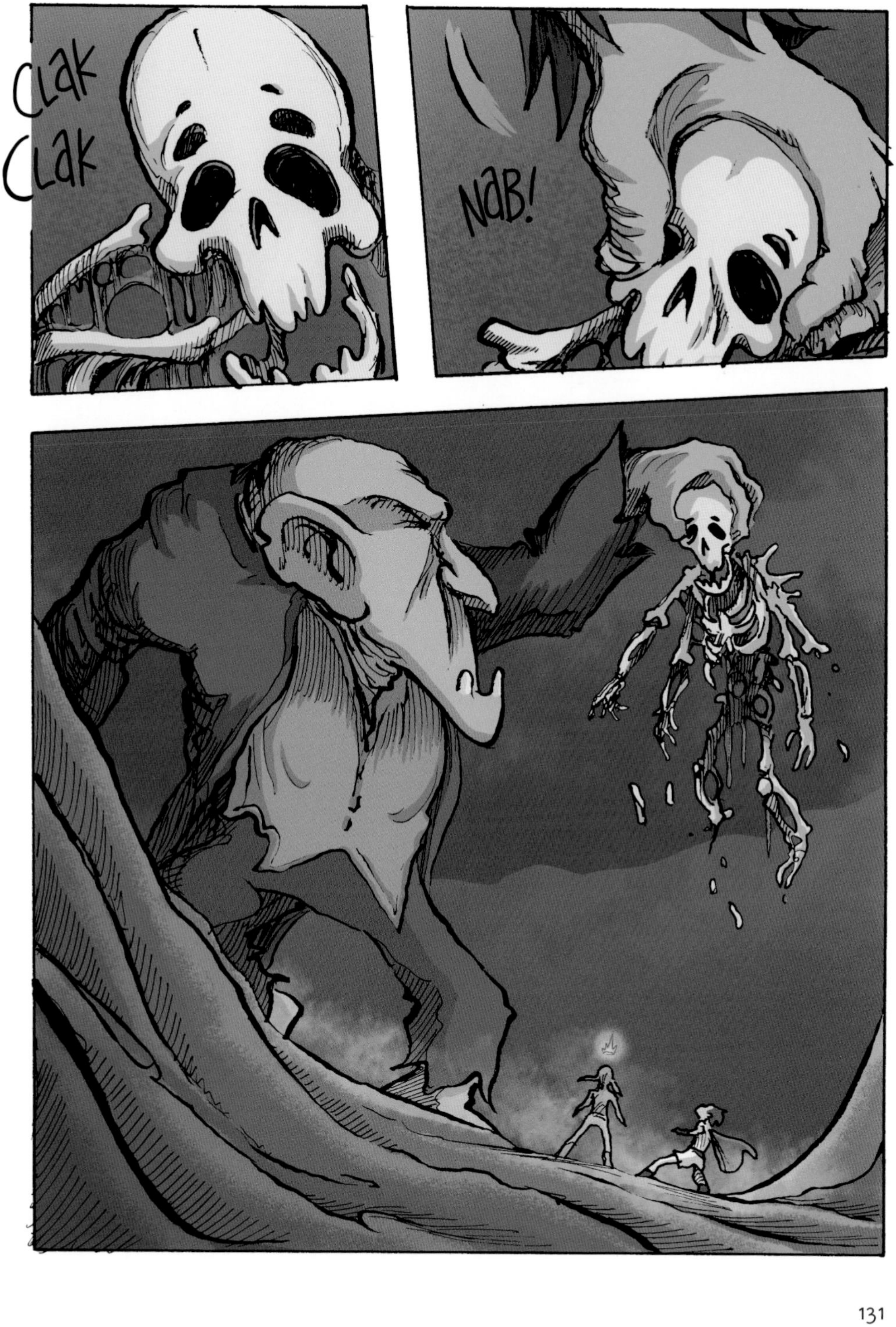
CLAK
CLAK
NAB!

SHAKE SHAKE

HEY!

TOSS!

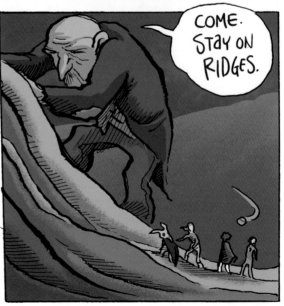

COME. STAY ON RIDGES.

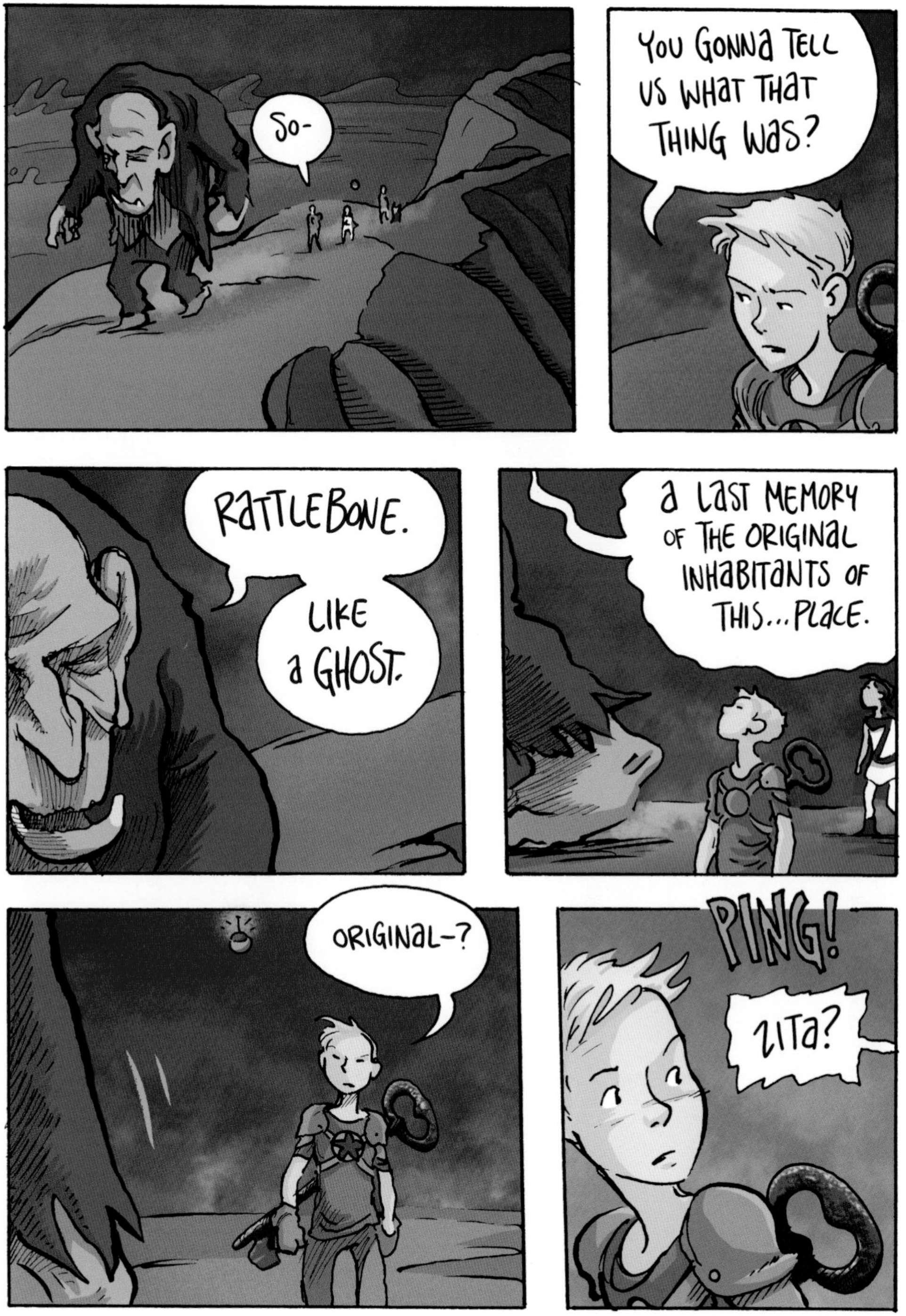
So-
YOU GONNA TELL US WHAT THAT THING WAS?
RATTLEBONE.
LIKE A GHOST.
A LAST MEMORY OF THE ORIGINAL INHABITANTS OF THIS...PLACE.
ORIGINAL-?
PING!
ZITA?

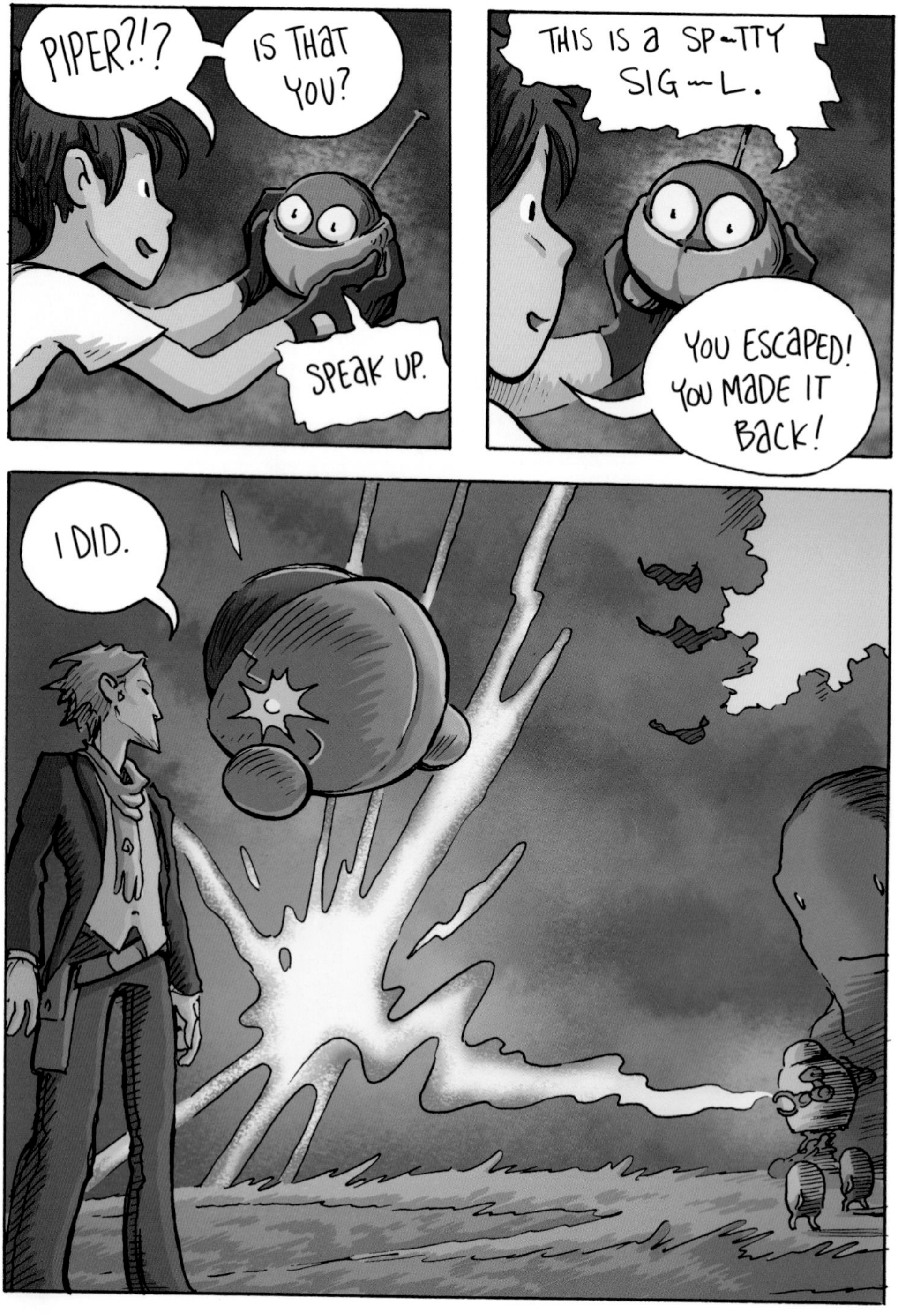
PIPER?!?
IS THAT YOU?
SPEAK UP.
THIS IS A SP--TTY SIG--L.
YOU ESCAPED! YOU MADE IT BACK!
I DID.

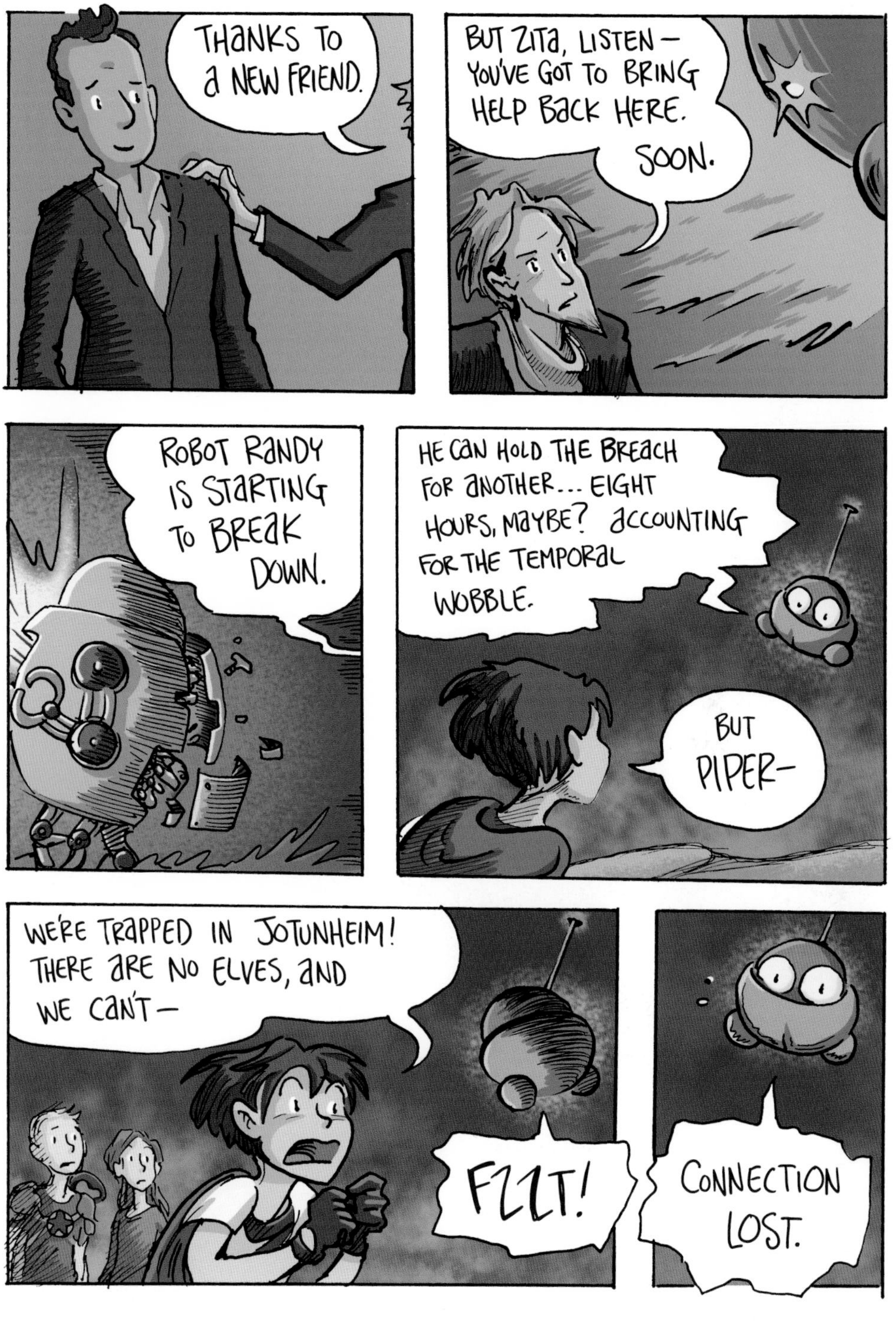
THANKS TO A NEW FRIEND.
BUT ZITA, LISTEN— YOU'VE GOT TO BRING HELP BACK HERE.
SOON.
ROBOT RANDY IS STARTING TO BREAK DOWN.
HE CAN HOLD THE BREACH FOR ANOTHER... EIGHT HOURS, MAYBE? ACCOUNTING FOR THE TEMPORAL WOBBLE.
BUT PIPER—
WE'RE TRAPPED IN JOTUNHEIM! THERE ARE NO ELVES, AND WE CAN'T—
FZZT!
CONNECTION LOST.

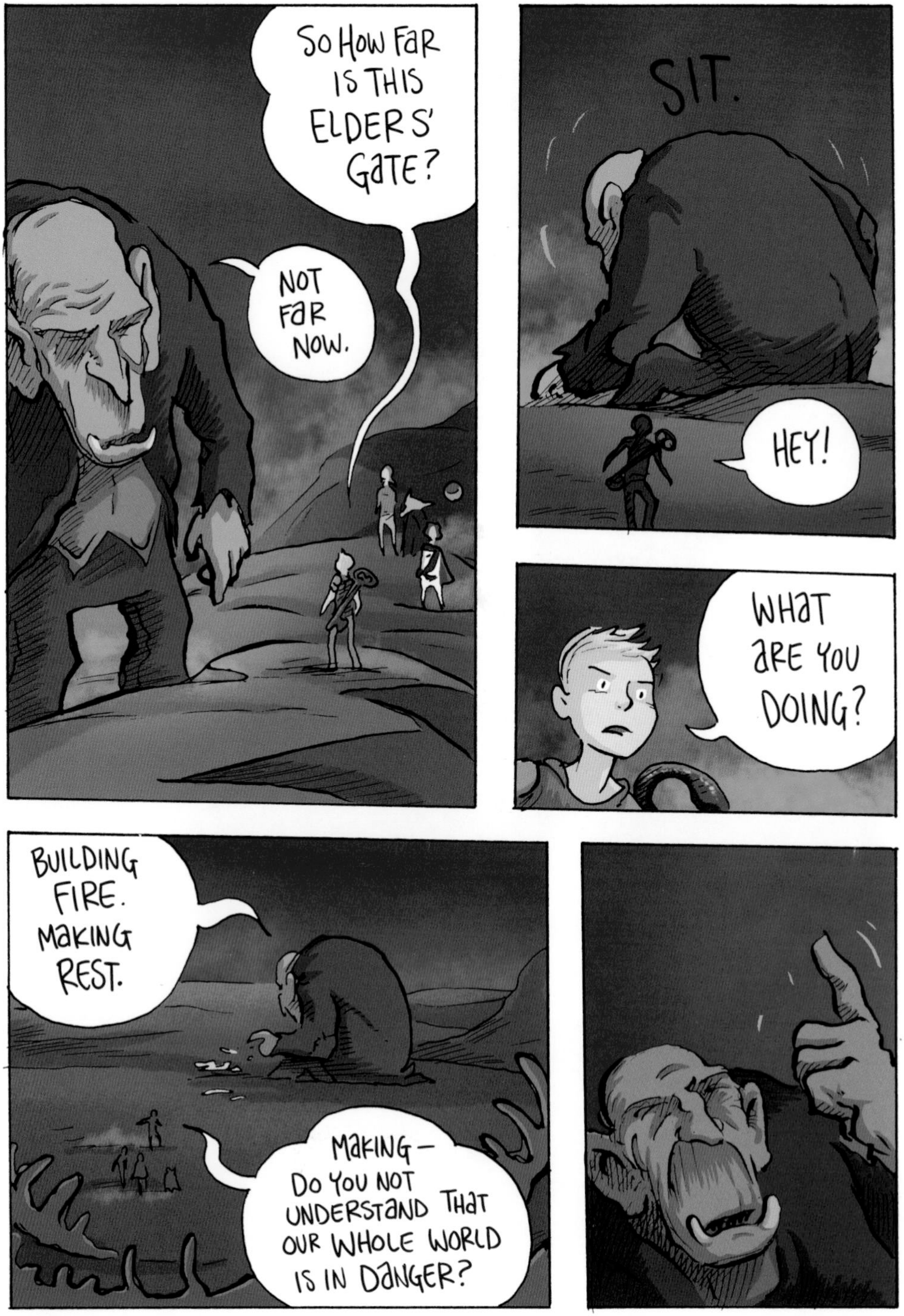

SO HOW FAR IS THIS ELDERS' GATE?
NOT FAR NOW.
SIT.
HEY!
WHAT ARE YOU DOING?
BUILDING FIRE. MAKING REST.
MAKING— DO YOU NOT UNDERSTAND THAT OUR WHOLE WORLD IS IN DANGER?

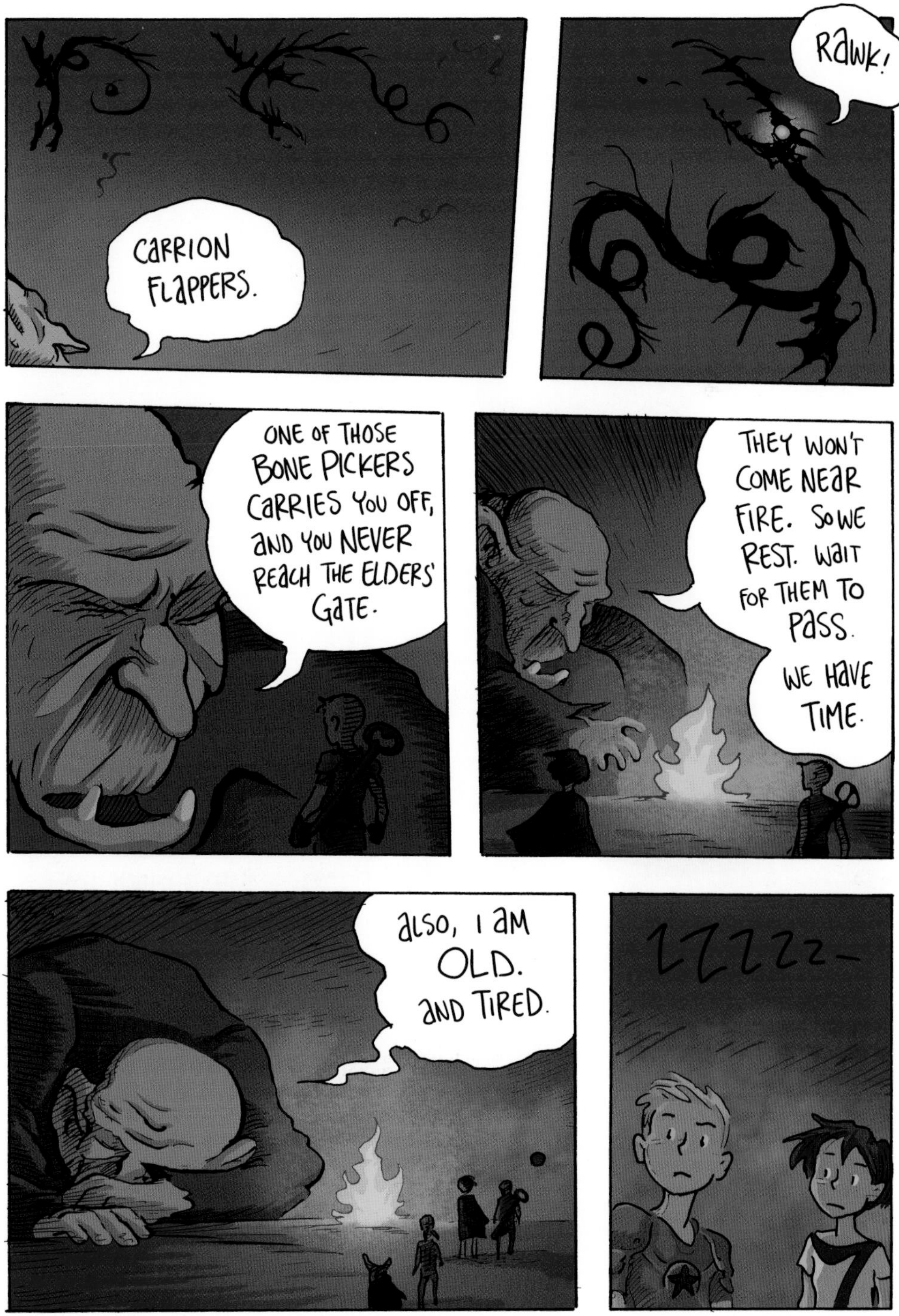
CARRION FLAPPERS.
RAWK!
ONE OF THOSE BONE PICKERS CARRIES YOU OFF, AND YOU NEVER REACH THE ELDERS' GATE.
THEY WON'T COME NEAR FIRE. SO WE REST. WAIT FOR THEM TO PASS.
WE HAVE TIME.
ALSO, I AM OLD. AND TIRED.
ZZZZZ—

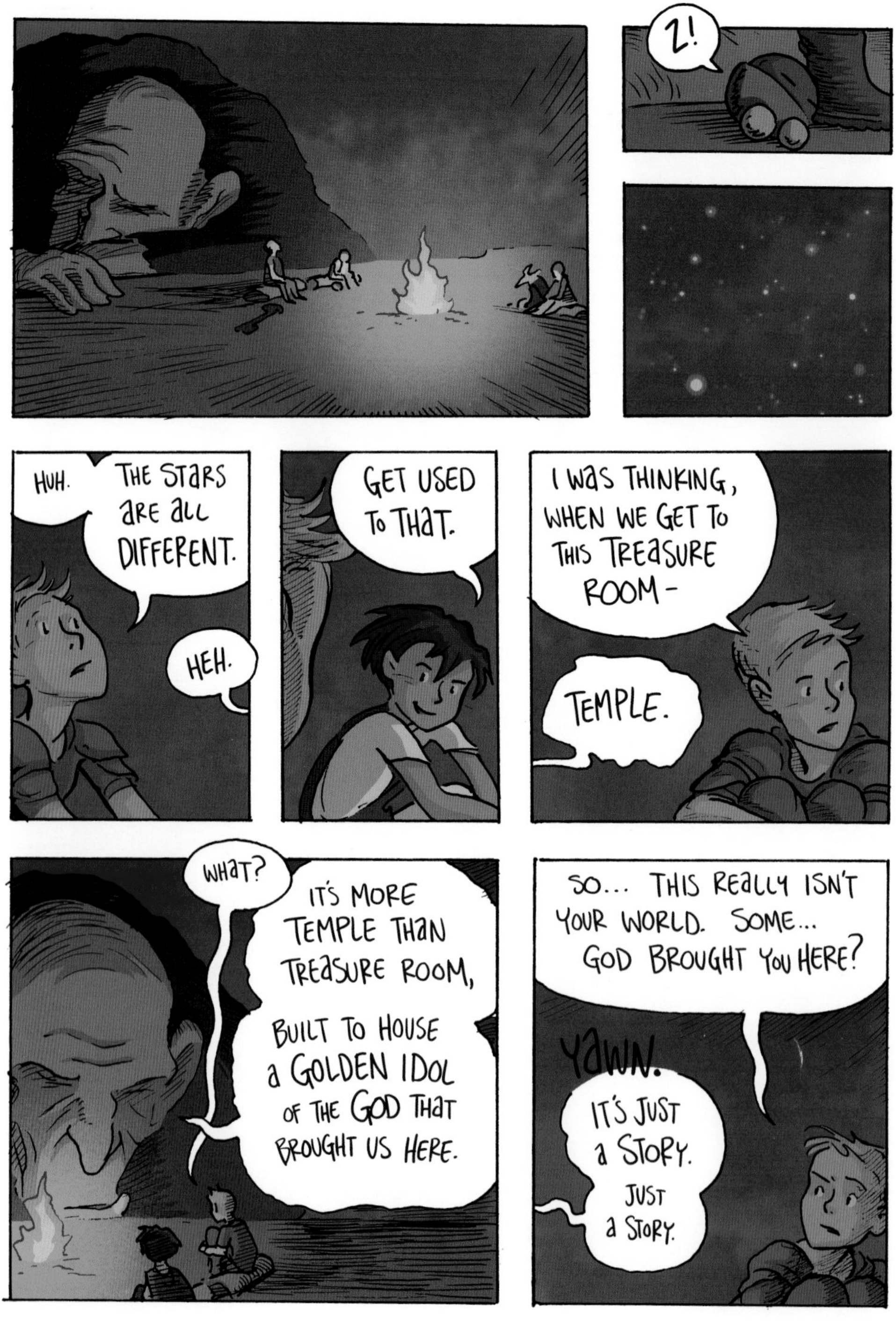
Z!
HUH.
THE STARS ARE ALL DIFFERENT.
HEH.
GET USED TO THAT.
I WAS THINKING, WHEN WE GET TO THIS TREASURE ROOM-
TEMPLE.
WHAT?
IT'S MORE TEMPLE THAN TREASURE ROOM,
BUILT TO HOUSE A GOLDEN IDOL OF THE GOD THAT BROUGHT US HERE.
SO... THIS REALLY ISN'T YOUR WORLD. SOME... GOD BROUGHT YOU HERE?
YAWN.
IT'S JUST A STORY.
JUST A STORY.

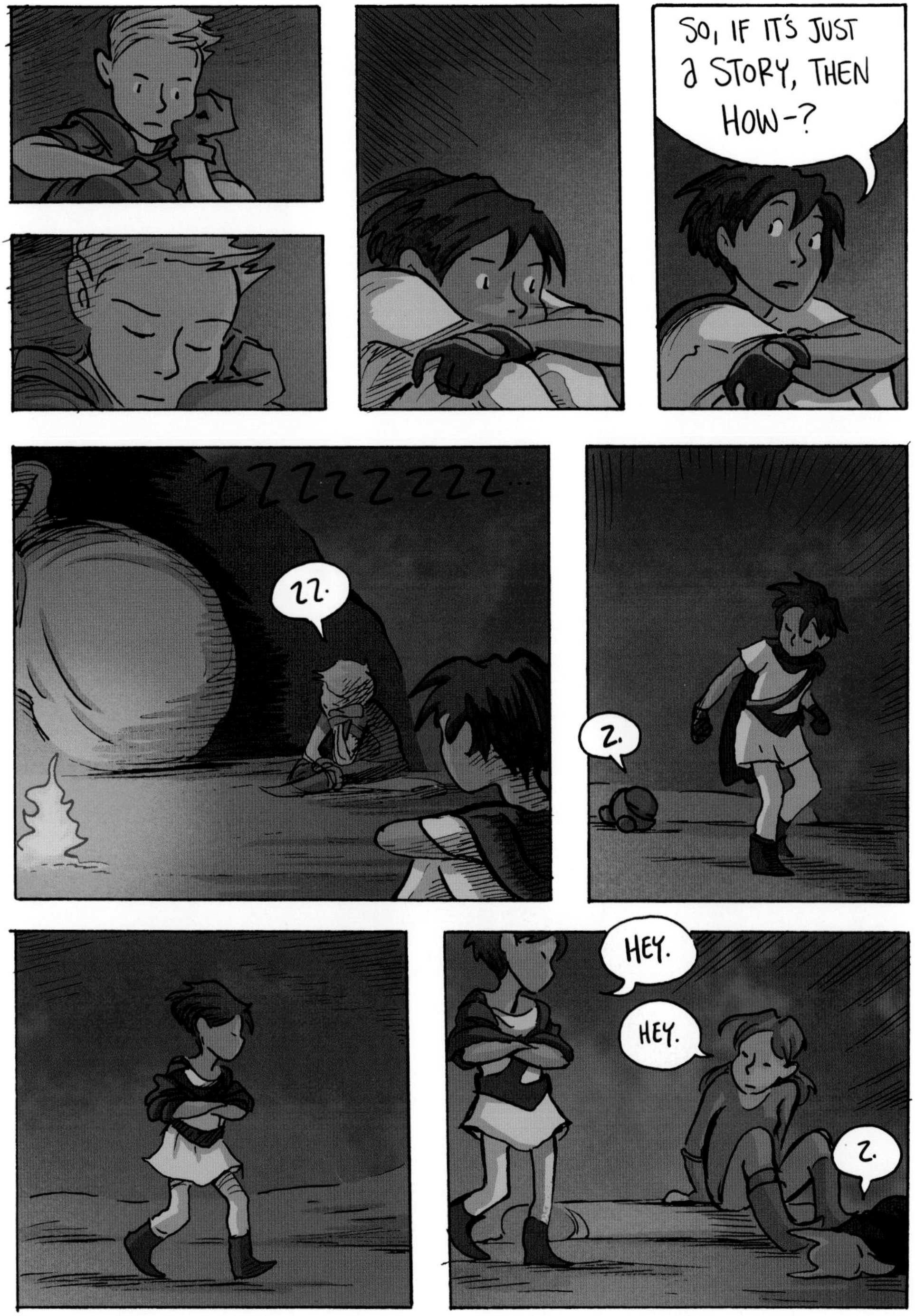

SO, IF IT'S JUST A STORY, THEN HOW-?
ZZZZZZZZZ...
ZZ.
Z.
HEY.
HEY.
Z.

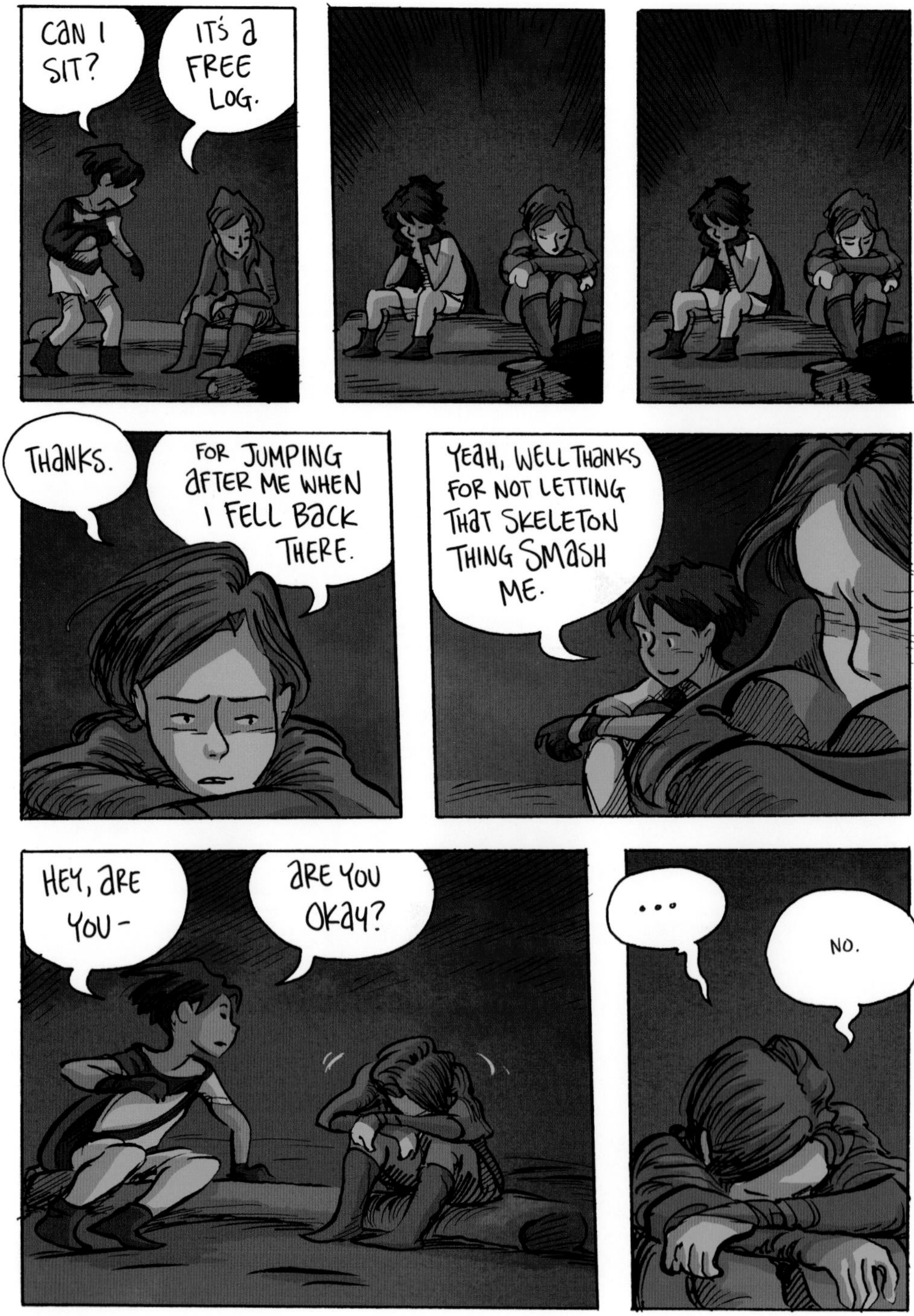
CAN I SIT?
IT'S A FREE LOG.
THANKS.
FOR JUMPING AFTER ME WHEN I FELL BACK THERE.
YEAH, WELL THANKS FOR NOT LETTING THAT SKELETON THING SMASH ME.
HEY, ARE YOU-
ARE YOU OKAY?
...
NO.

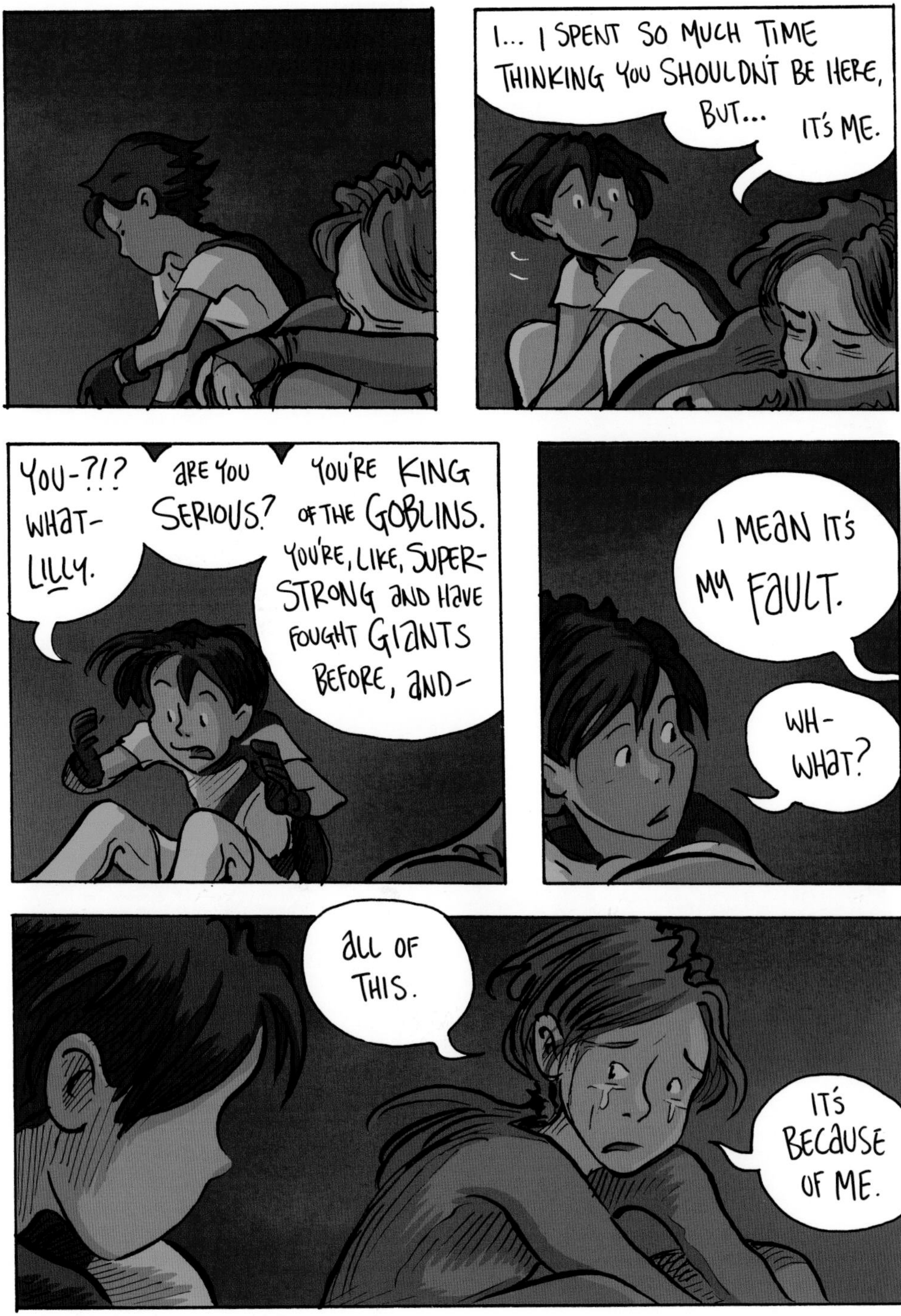
I... I SPENT SO MUCH TIME THINKING YOU SHOULDN'T BE HERE, BUT...
IT'S ME.
YOU-?!? WHAT- LILLY.
ARE YOU SERIOUS?
YOU'RE KING OF THE GOBLINS. YOU'RE, LIKE, SUPER-STRONG AND HAVE FOUGHT GIANTS BEFORE, AND-
I MEAN IT'S MY FAULT.
WH- WHAT?
ALL OF THIS.
IT'S BECAUSE OF ME.

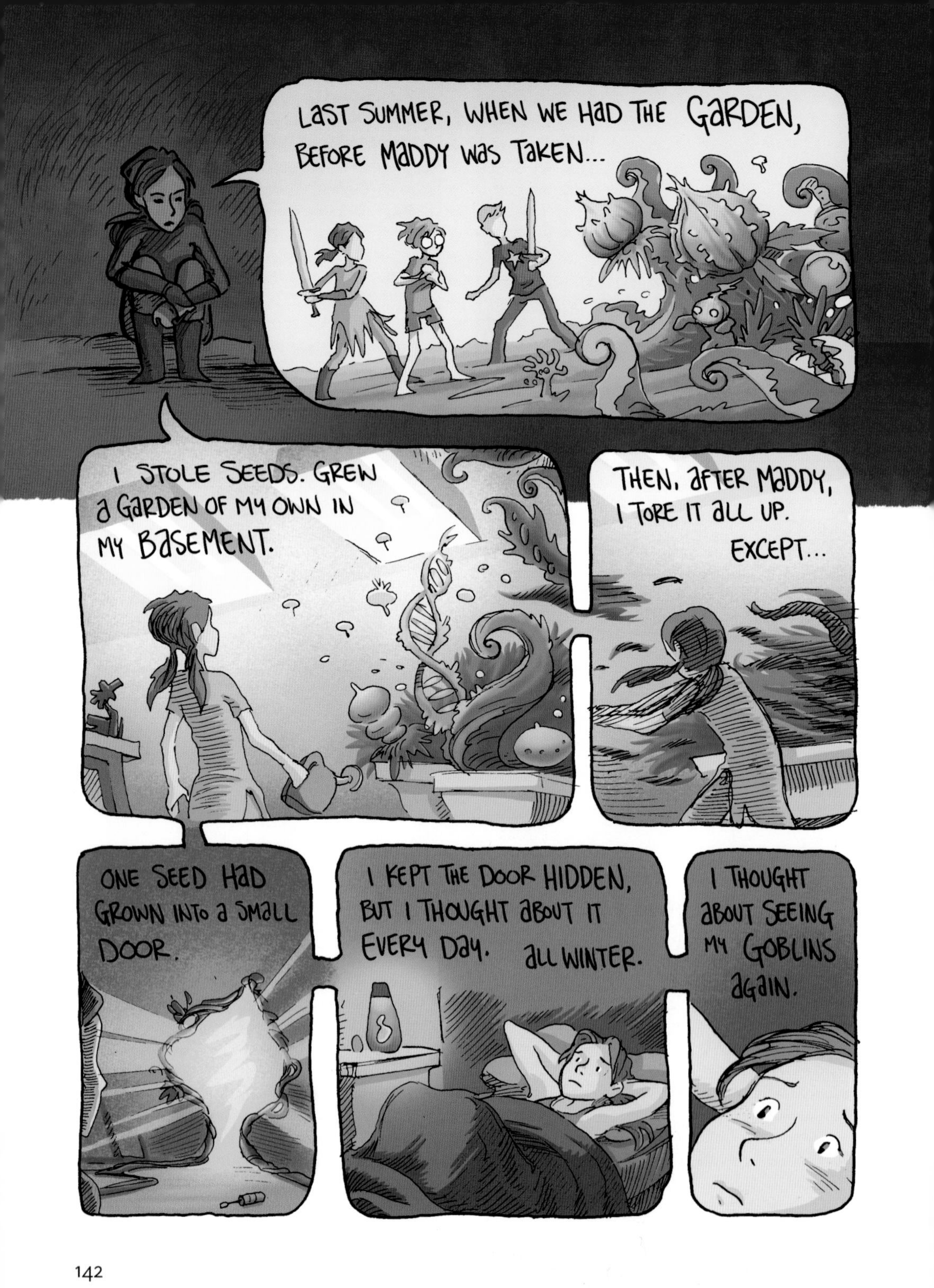

LAST SUMMER, WHEN WE HAD THE GARDEN, BEFORE MADDY WAS TAKEN...
I STOLE SEEDS. GREW A GARDEN OF MY OWN IN MY BASEMENT.
THEN, AFTER MADDY, I TORE IT ALL UP.
EXCEPT...
ONE SEED HAD GROWN INTO A SMALL DOOR.
I KEPT THE DOOR HIDDEN, BUT I THOUGHT ABOUT IT EVERY DAY.
ALL WINTER.
I THOUGHT ABOUT SEEING MY GOBLINS AGAIN.

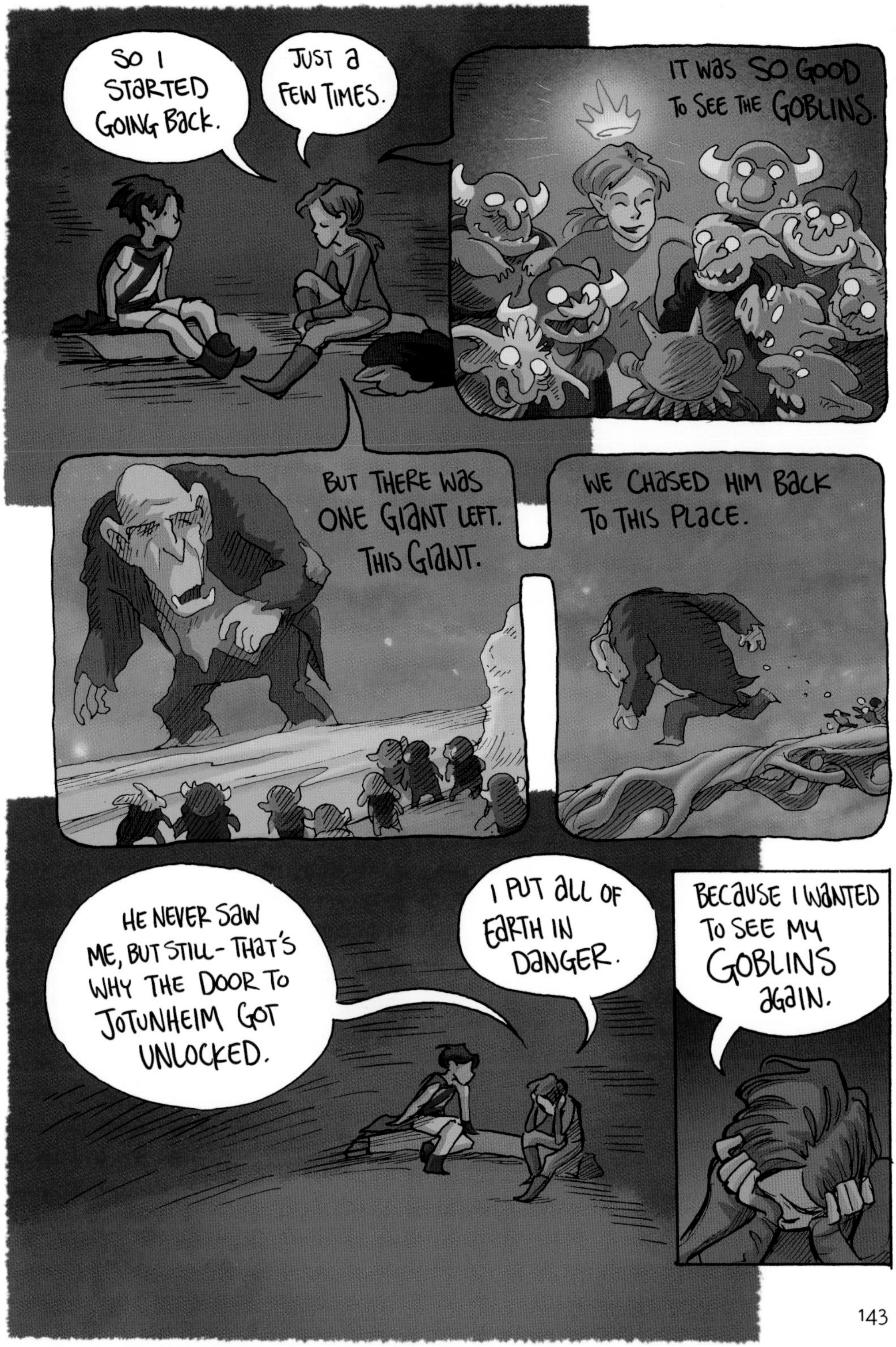
SO I STARTED GOING BACK.
JUST A FEW TIMES.
IT WAS SO GOOD TO SEE THE GOBLINS.
BUT THERE WAS ONE GIANT LEFT. THIS GIANT.
WE CHASED HIM BACK TO THIS PLACE.
HE NEVER SAW ME, BUT STILL- THAT'S WHY THE DOOR TO JOTUNHEIM GOT UNLOCKED.
I PUT ALL OF EARTH IN DANGER.
BECAUSE I WANTED TO SEE MY GOBLINS AGAIN.

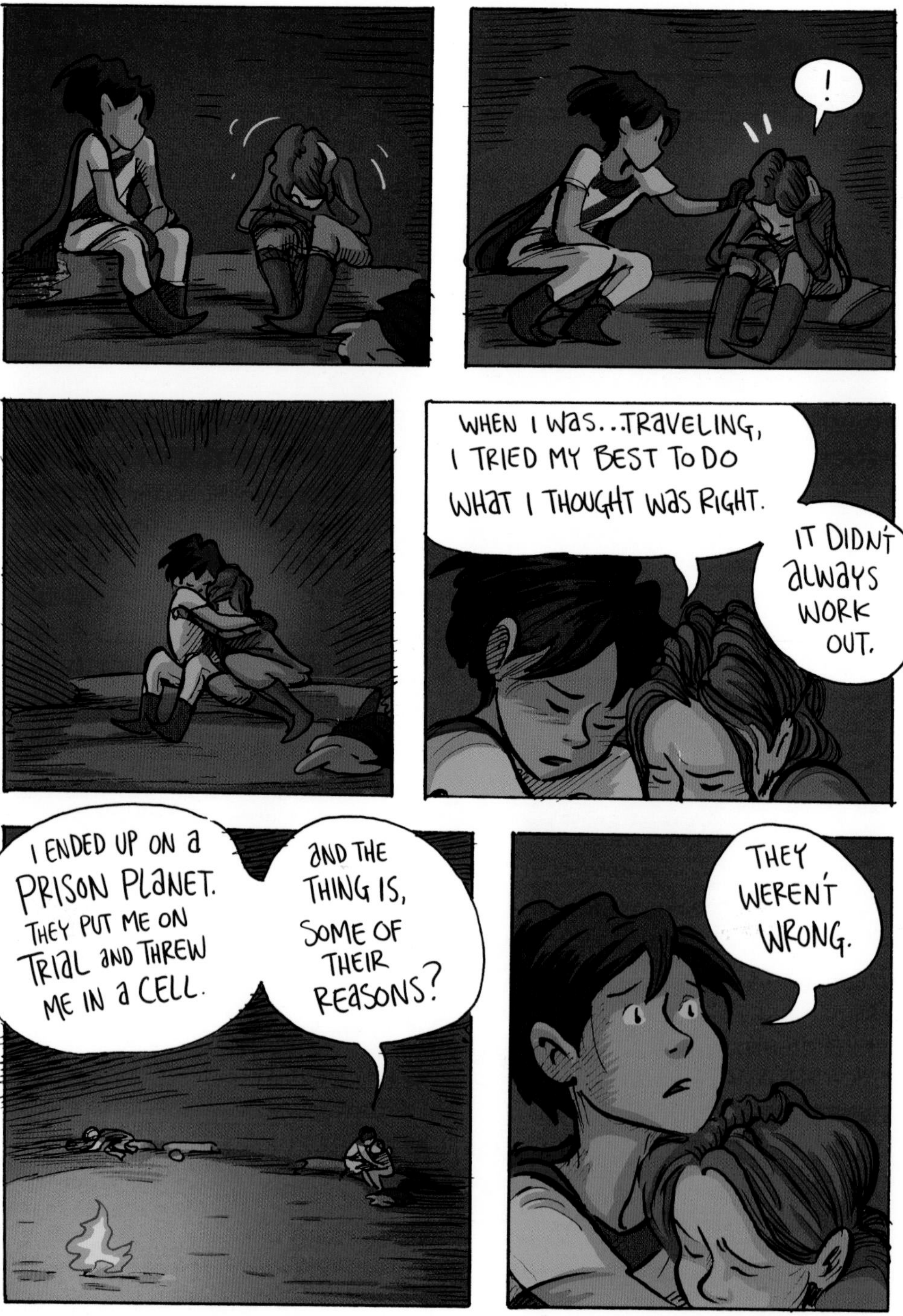
!
WHEN I WAS...TRAVELING, I TRIED MY BEST TO DO WHAT I THOUGHT WAS RIGHT.
IT DIDN'T ALWAYS WORK OUT.
I ENDED UP ON A PRISON PLANET. THEY PUT ME ON TRIAL AND THREW ME IN A CELL.
AND THE THING IS, SOME OF THEIR REASONS?
THEY WEREN'T WRONG.

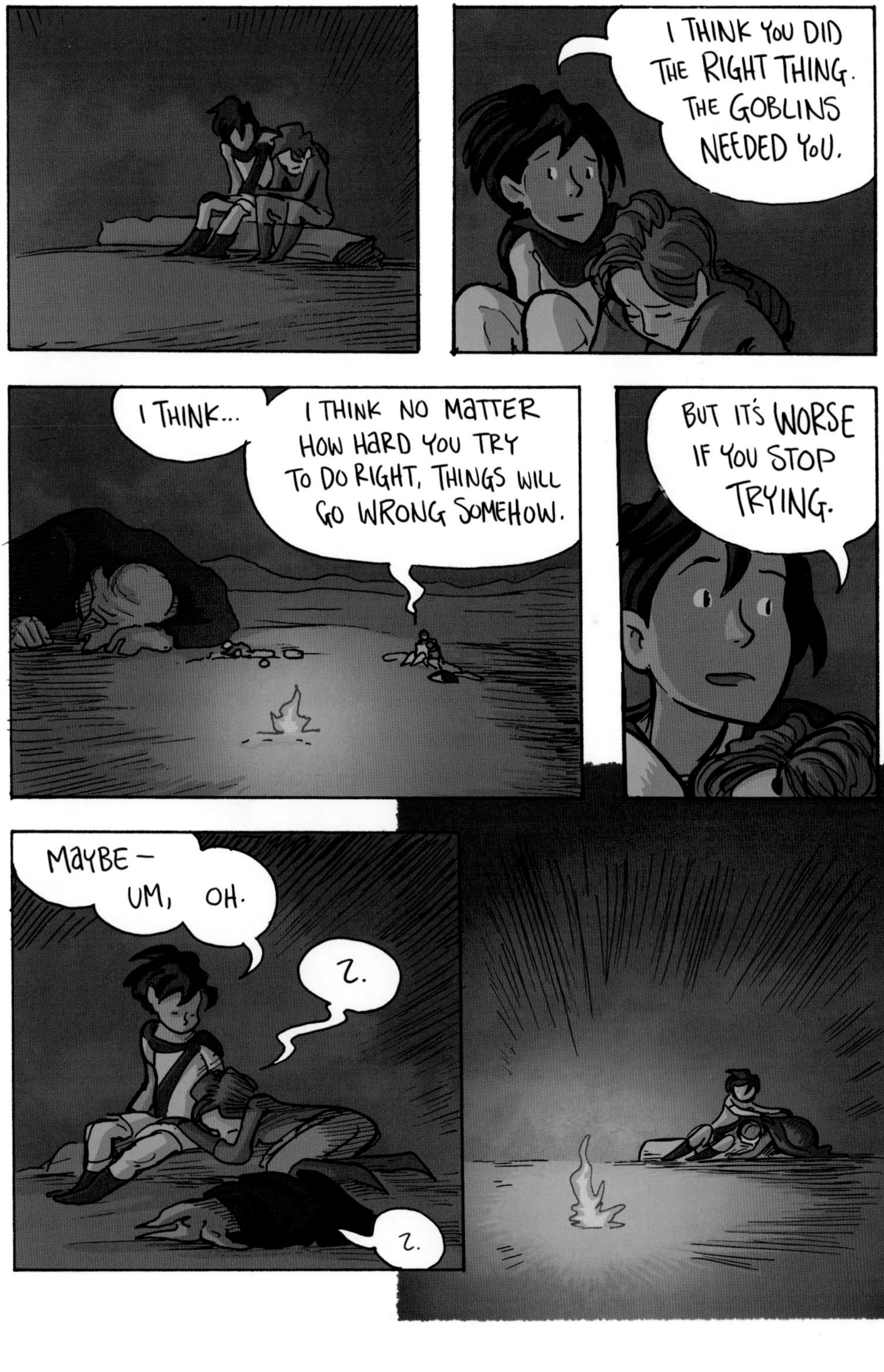
I THINK YOU DID THE RIGHT THING. THE GOBLINS NEEDED YOU.
I THINK...
I THINK NO MATTER HOW HARD YOU TRY TO DO RIGHT, THINGS WILL GO WRONG SOMEHOW.
BUT IT'S WORSE IF YOU STOP TRYING.
MAYBE— UM, OH.
Z.
Z.

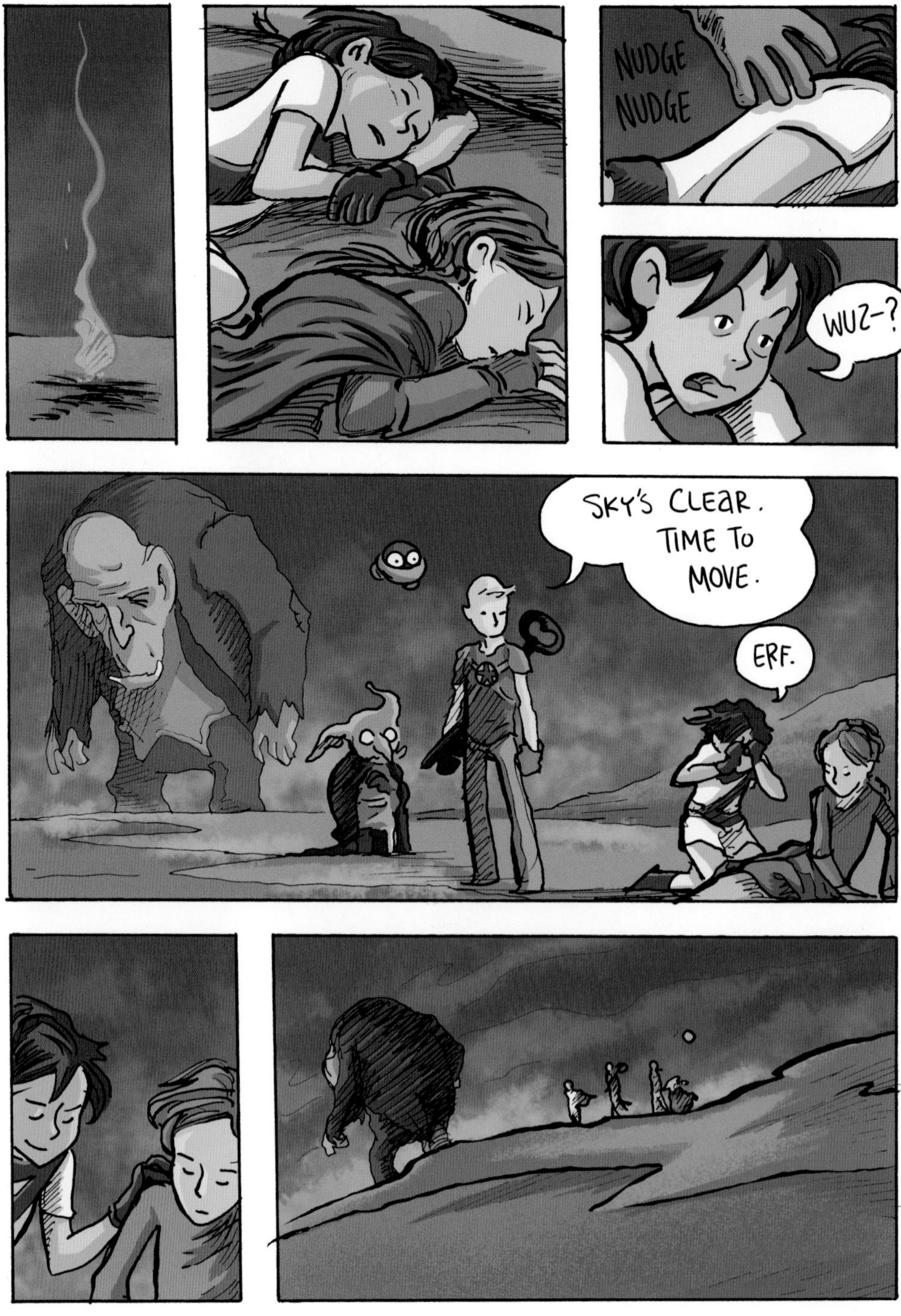
NUDGE
NUDGE
WUZ-?
SKY'S CLEAR. TIME TO MOVE.
ERF.

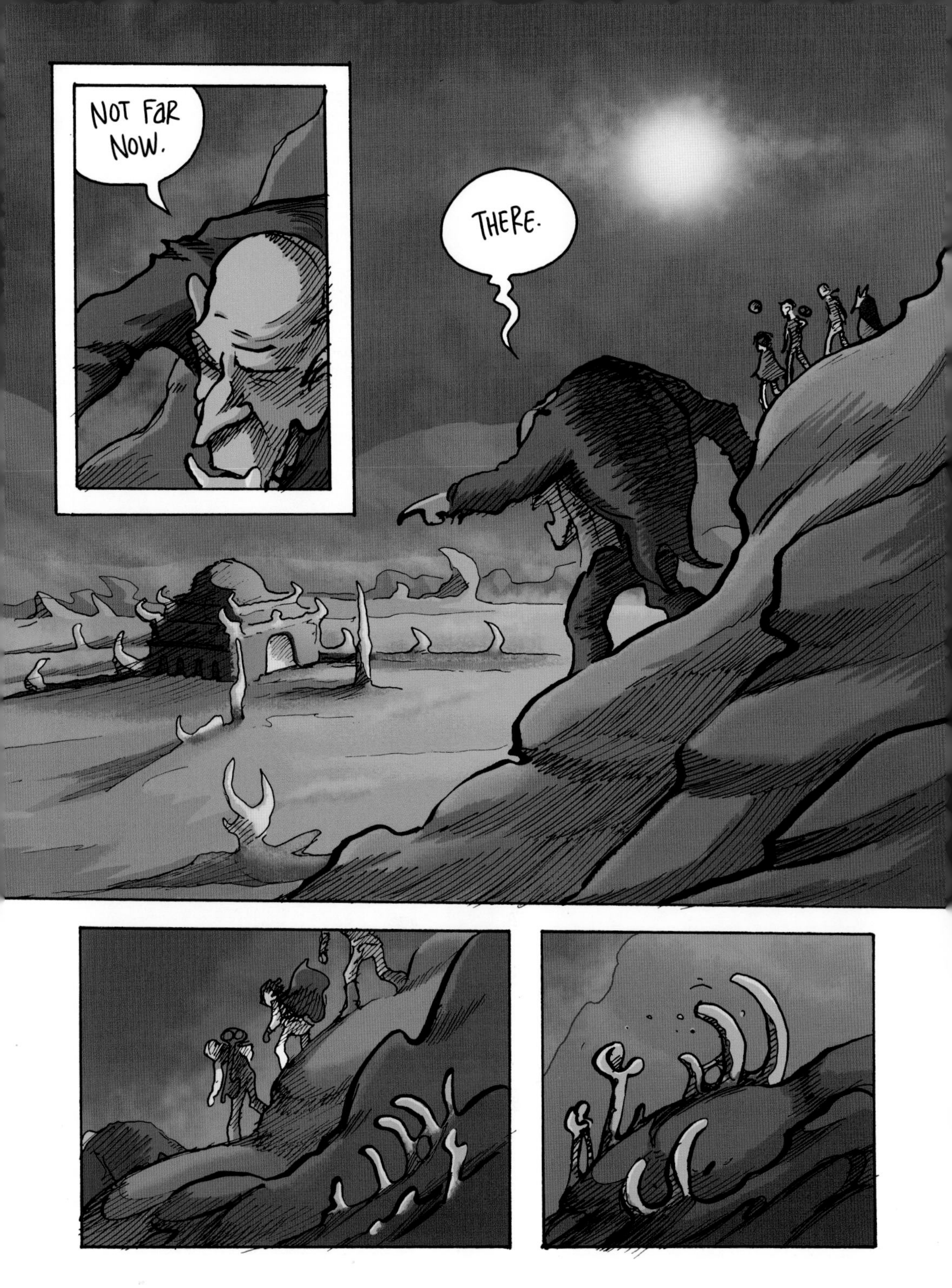
NOT FAR NOW.
THERE.

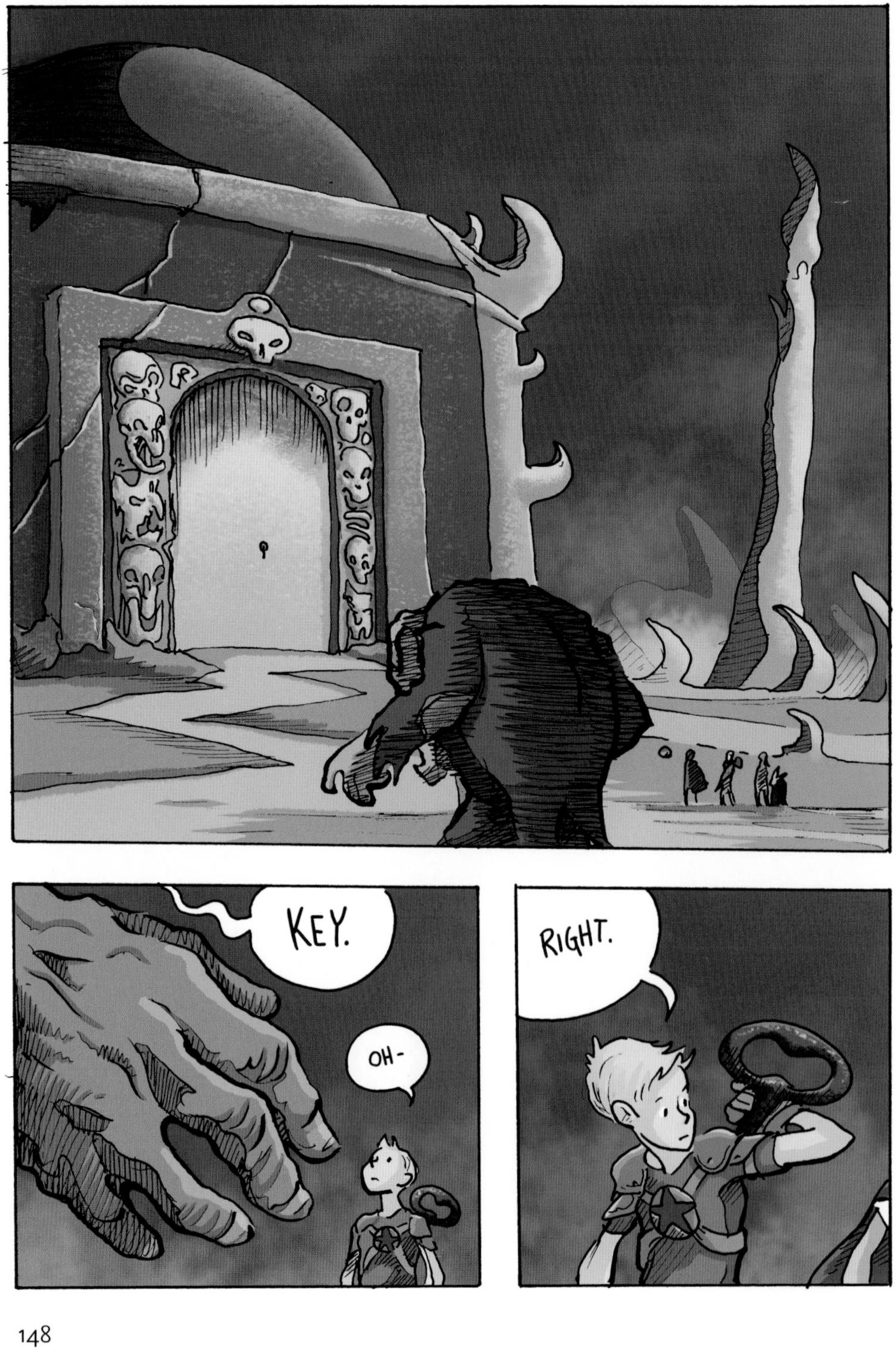
KEY.
OH-
RIGHT.

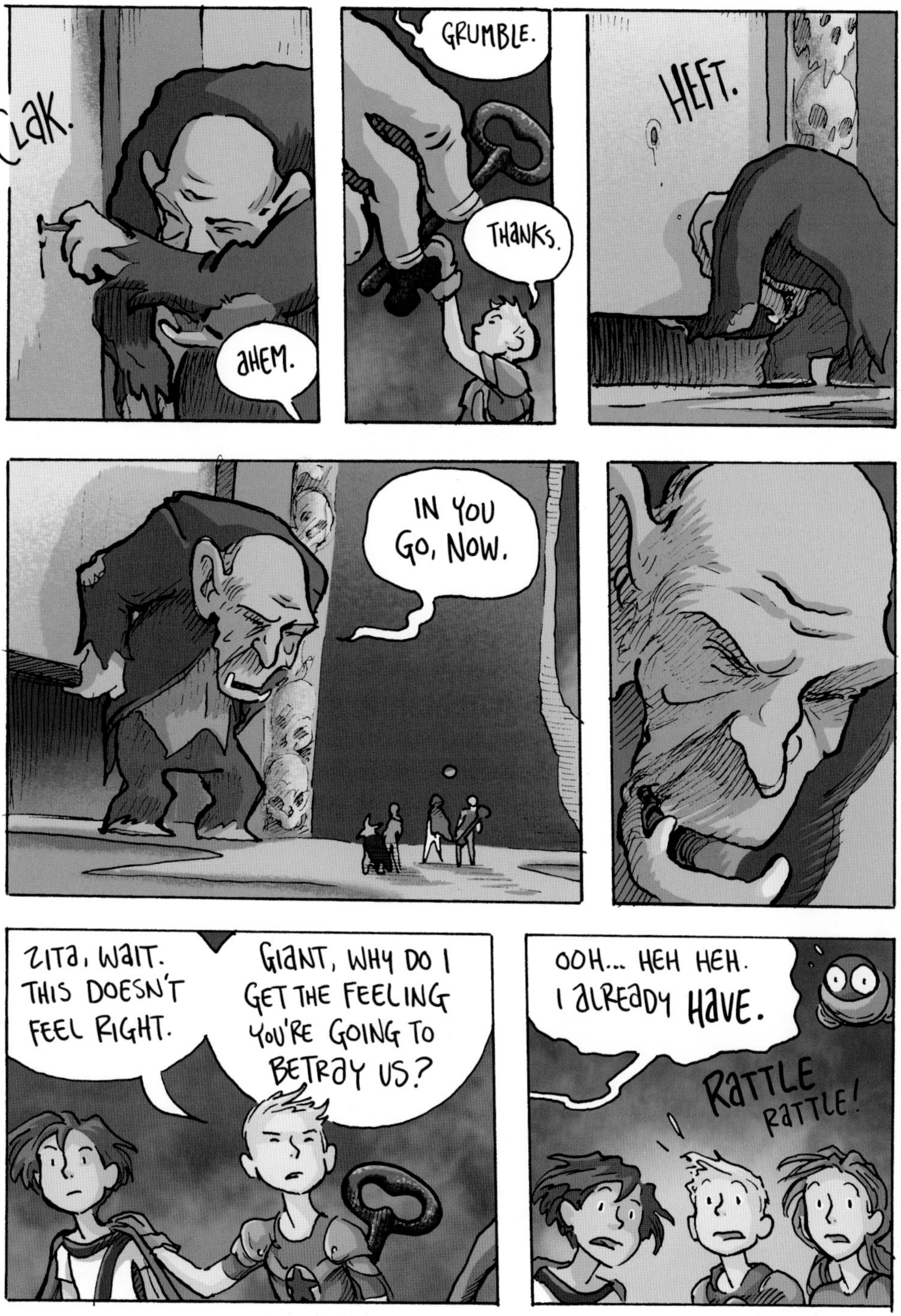

CLAK.
AHEM.
GRUMBLE.
THANKS.
HEFT.
IN YOU GO, NOW.
ZITA, WAIT. THIS DOESN'T FEEL RIGHT.
GIANT, WHY DO I GET THE FEELING YOU'RE GOING TO BETRAY US?
OOH... HEH HEH. I ALREADY HAVE.
RATTLE RATTLE!
!

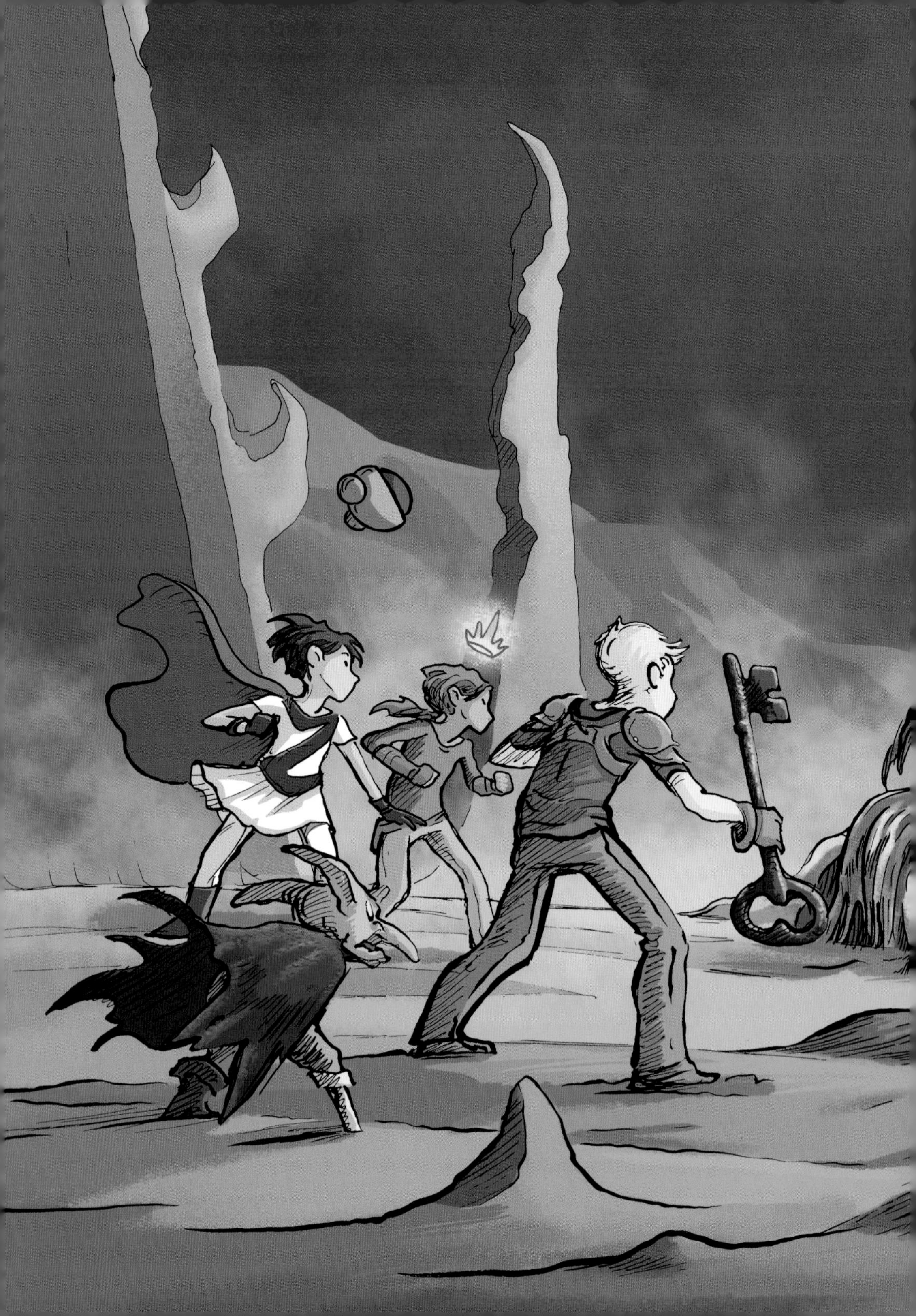

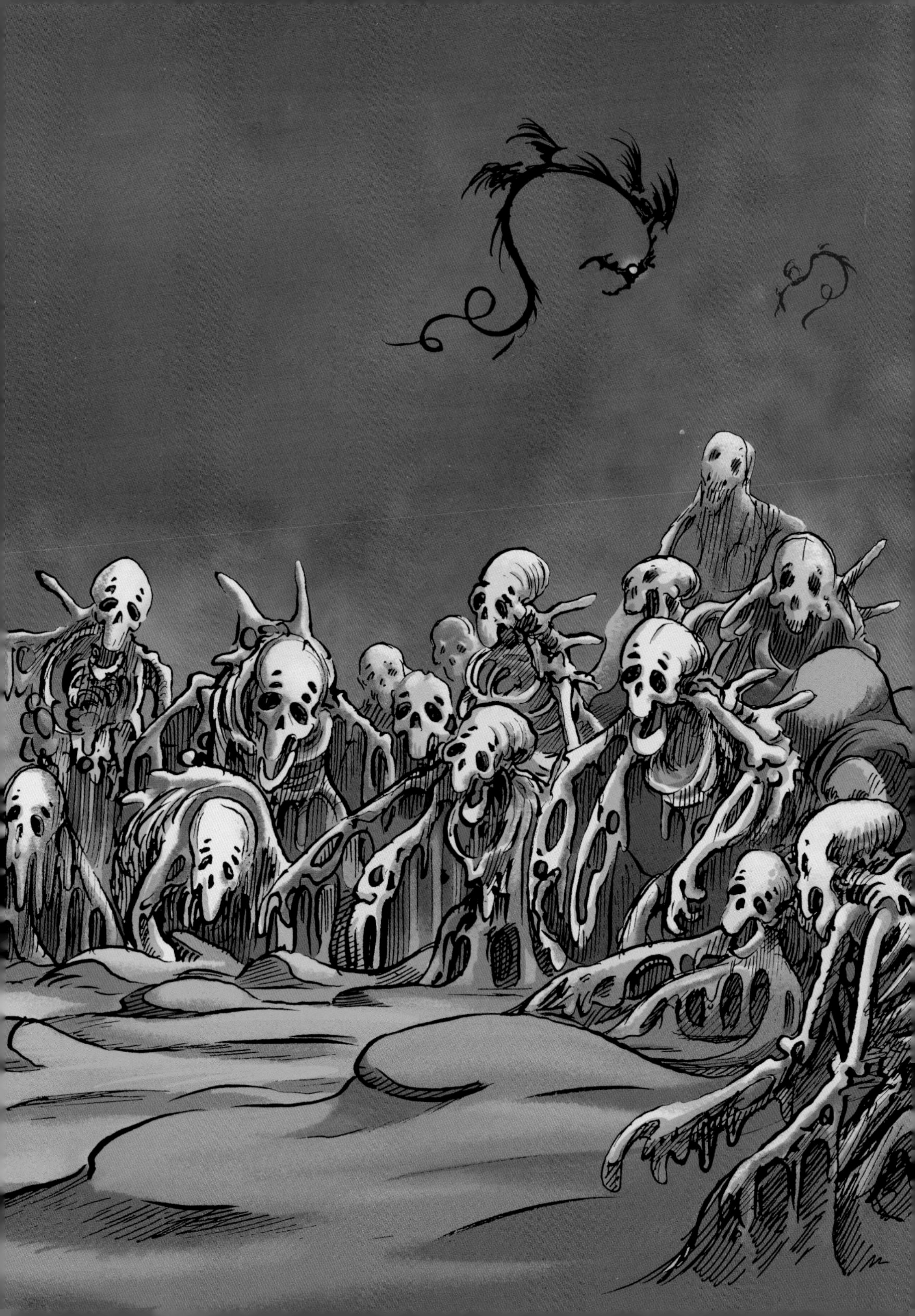

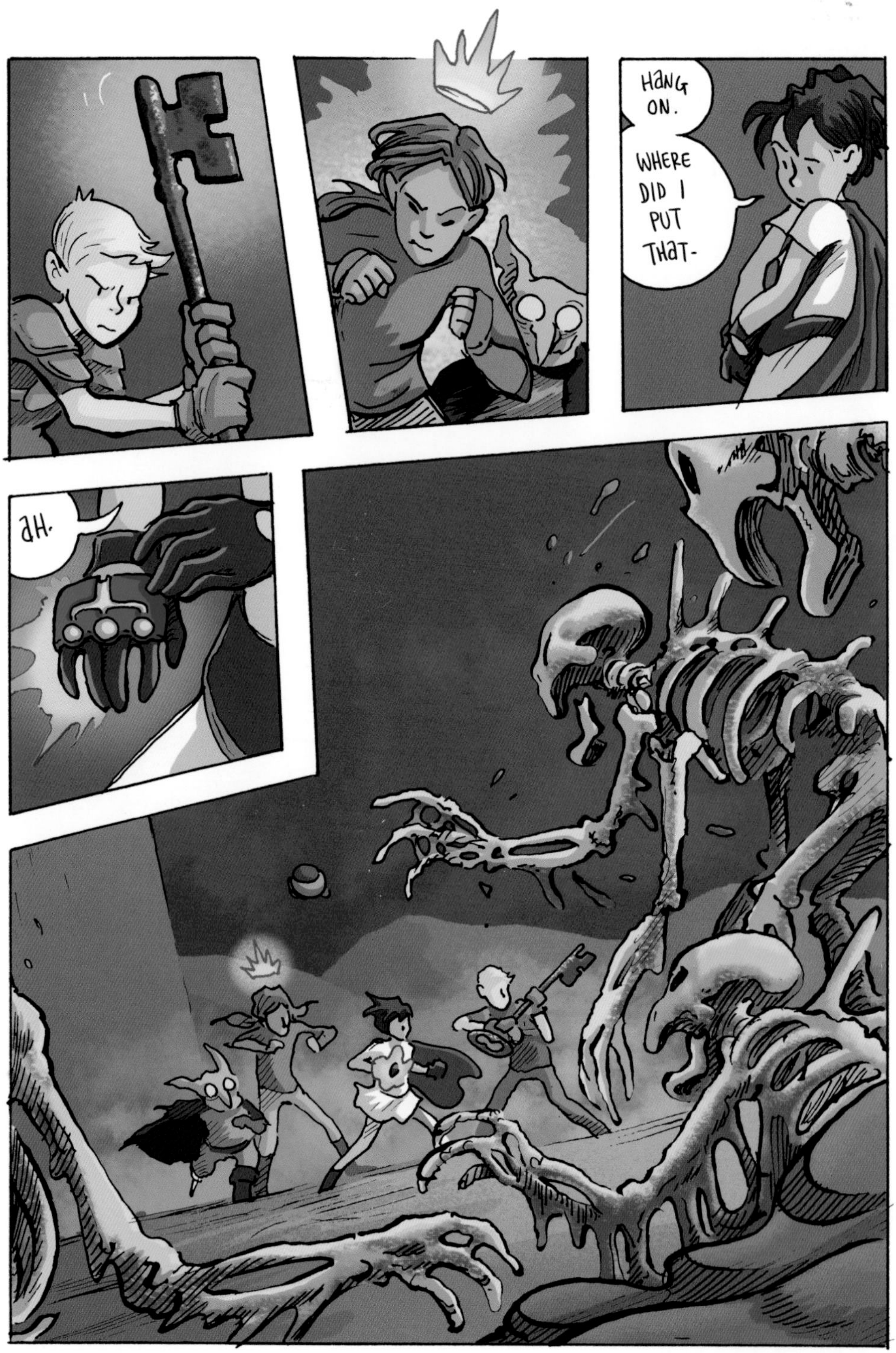
HANG ON.
WHERE DID I PUT THAT-
AH.

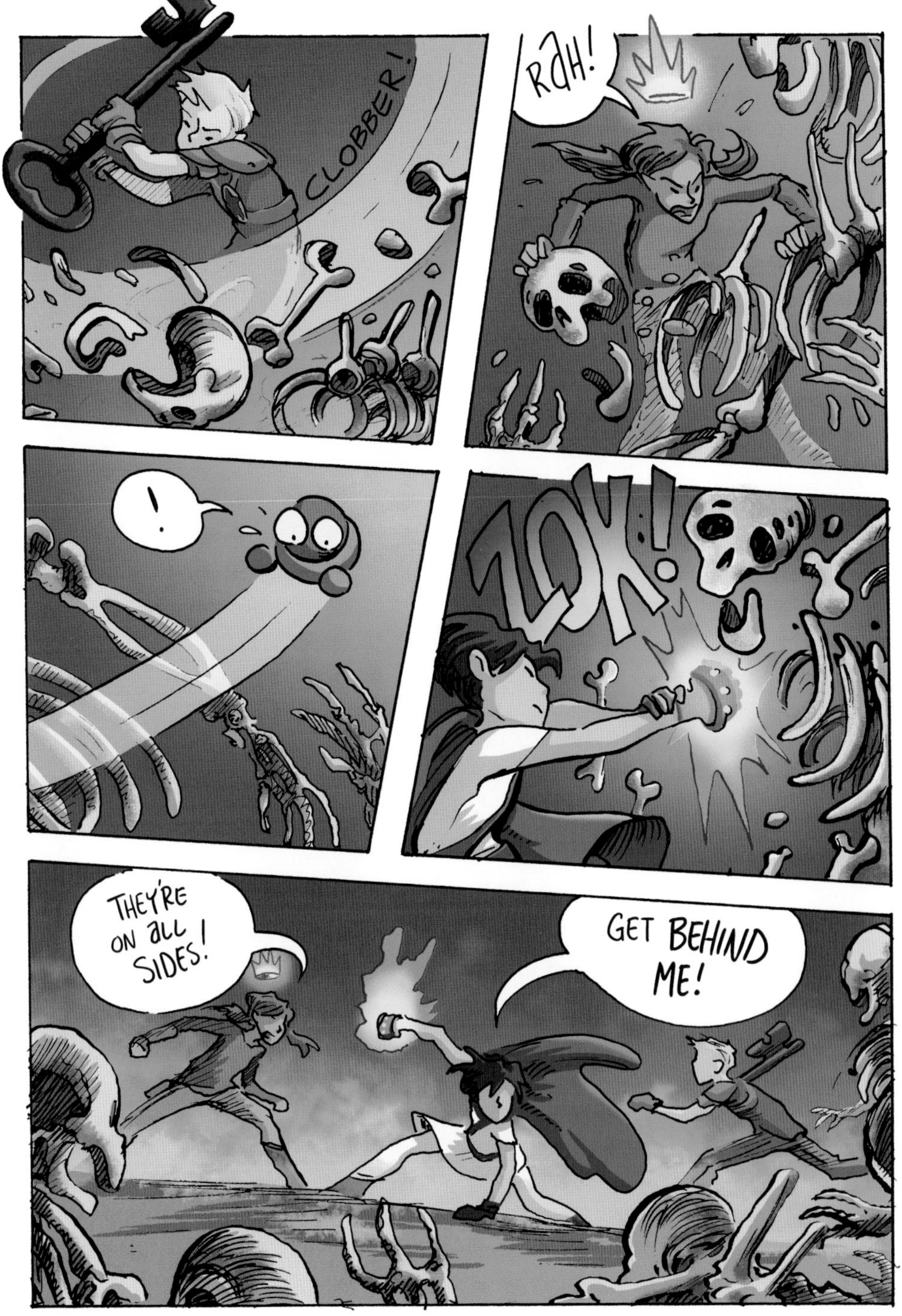
CLOBBER!
RAH!
!
ZOK!
THEY'RE ON ALL SIDES!
GET BEHIND ME!

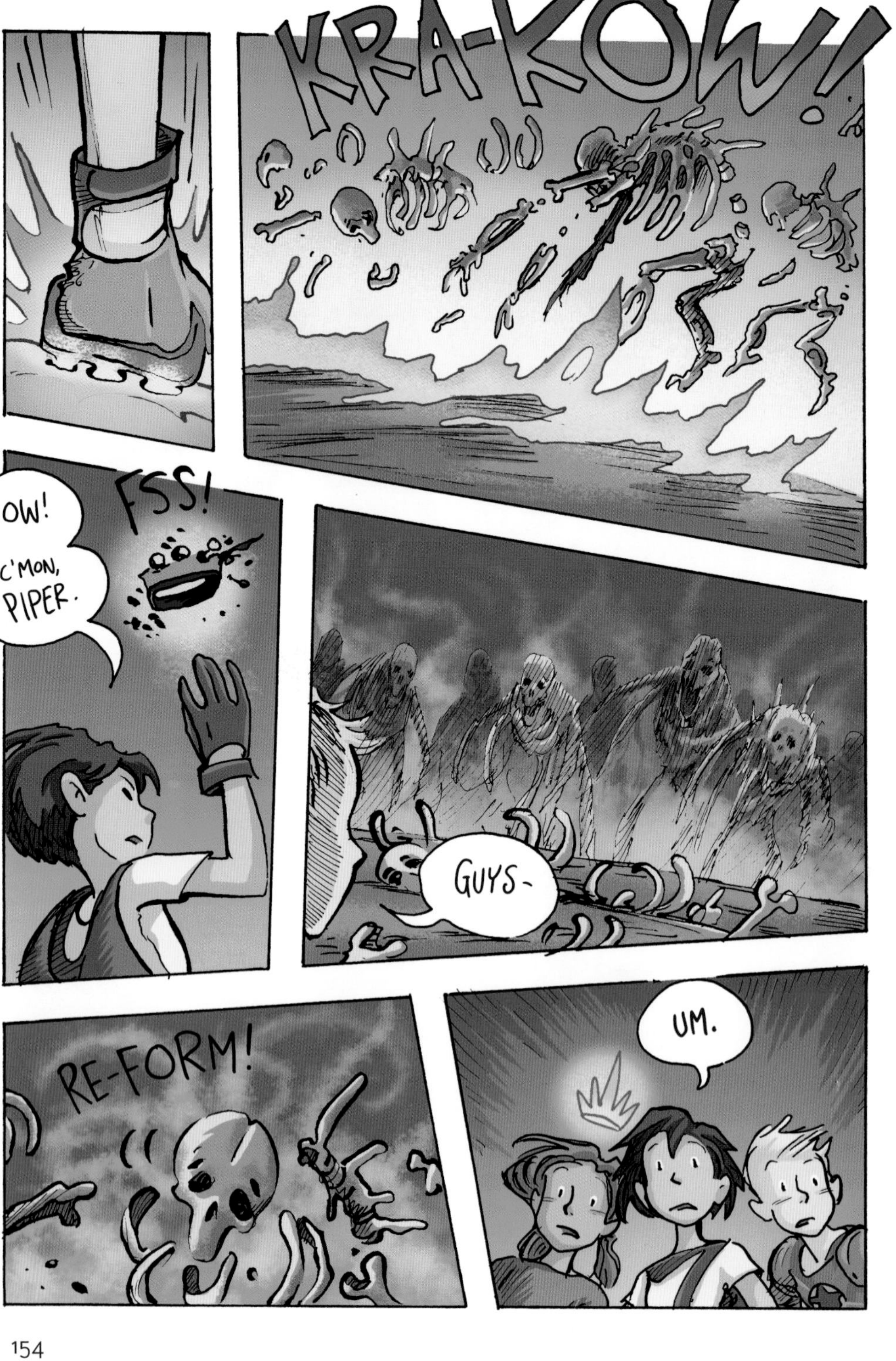
KRA-KOW!
FSS!
OW!
C'MON, PIPER.
GUYS-
RE-FORM!
UM.

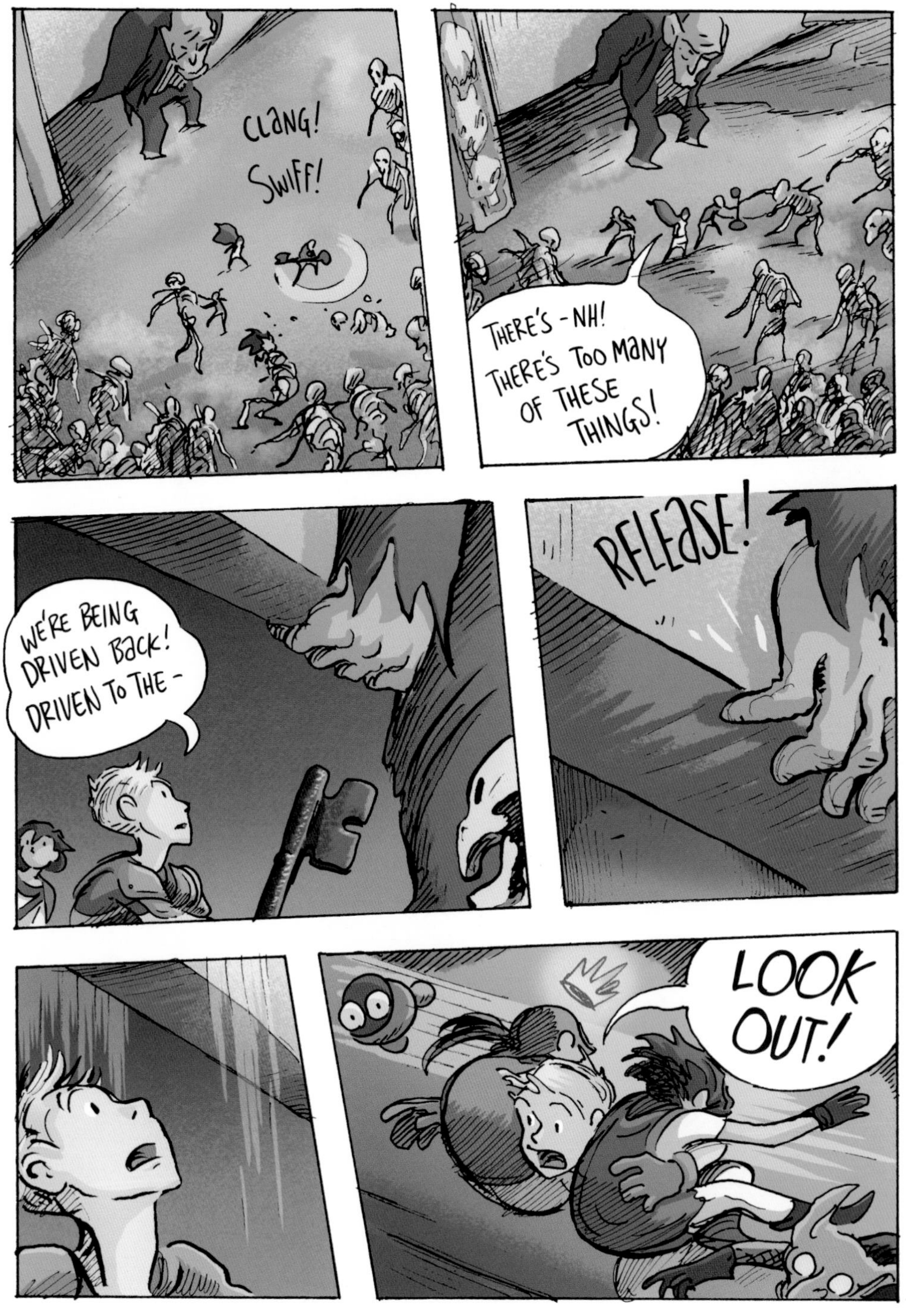
CLANG!
SWIFF!
THERE'S -NH! THERE'S TOO MANY OF THESE THINGS!
WE'RE BEING DRIVEN BACK! DRIVEN TO THE-
RELEASE!
LOOK OUT!

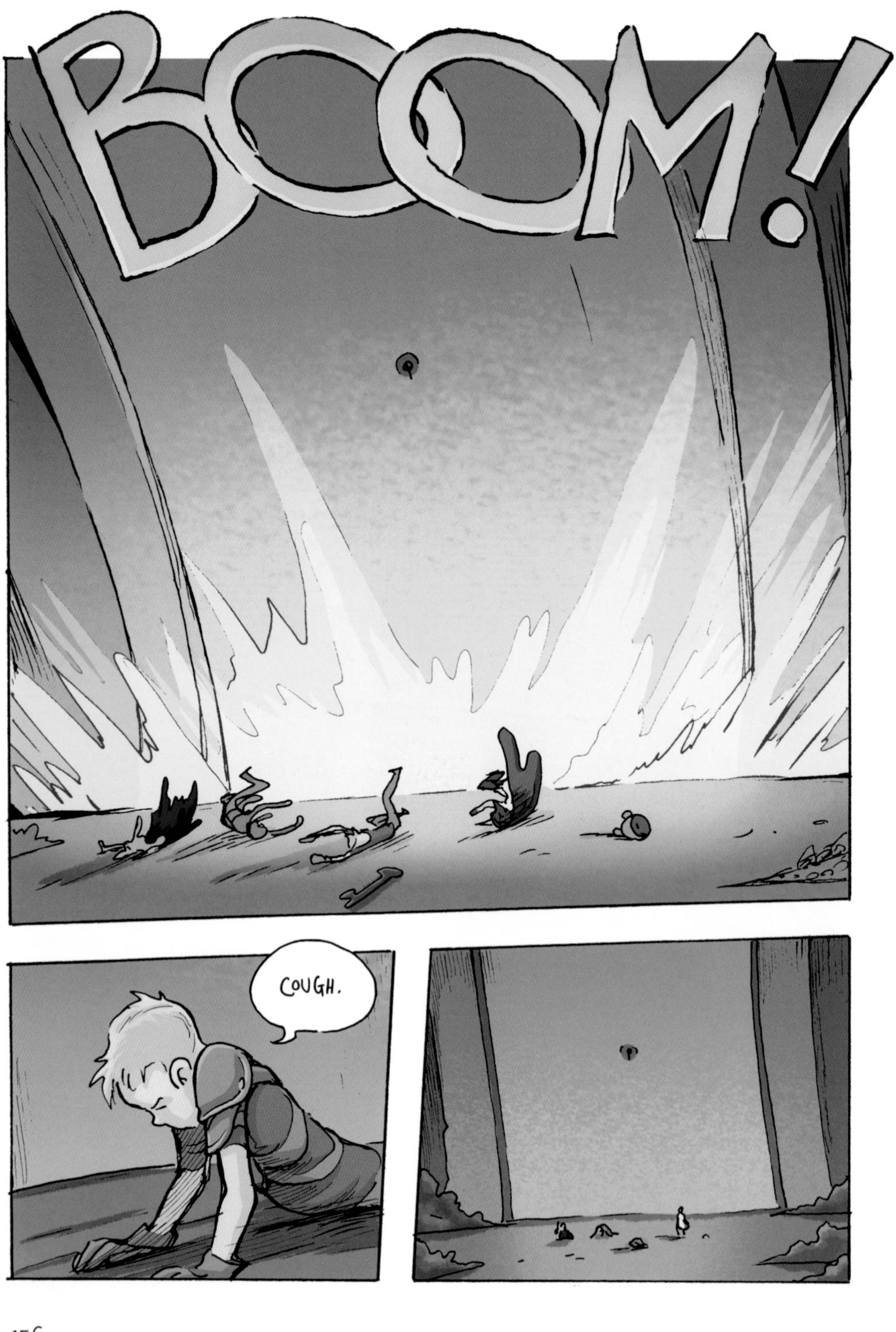
BOOM!
COUGH.

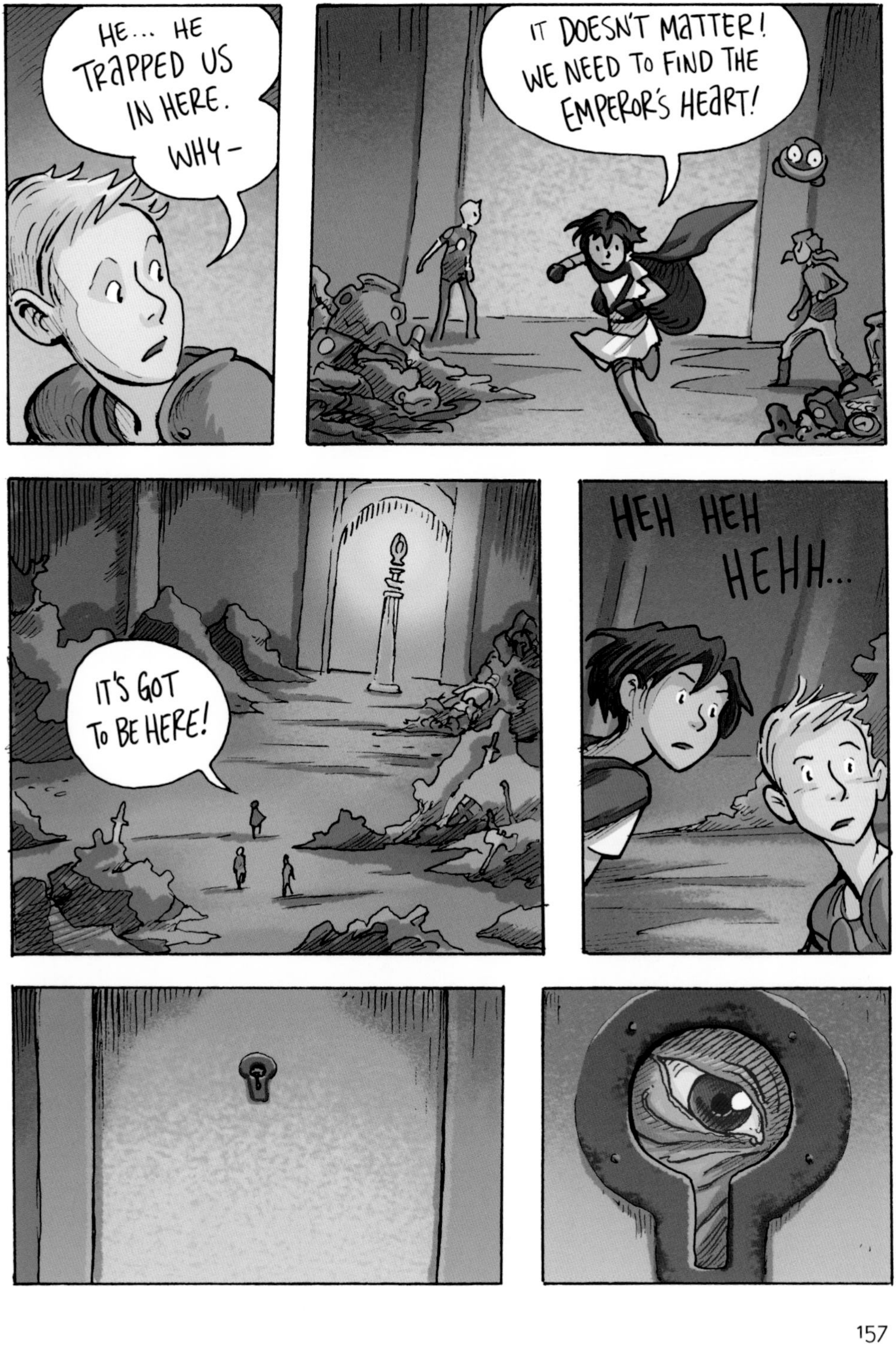
HE... HE TRAPPED US IN HERE.
WHY-
IT DOESN'T MATTER! WE NEED TO FIND THE EMPEROR'S HEART!
IT'S GOT TO BE HERE!
HEH HEH HEHH...

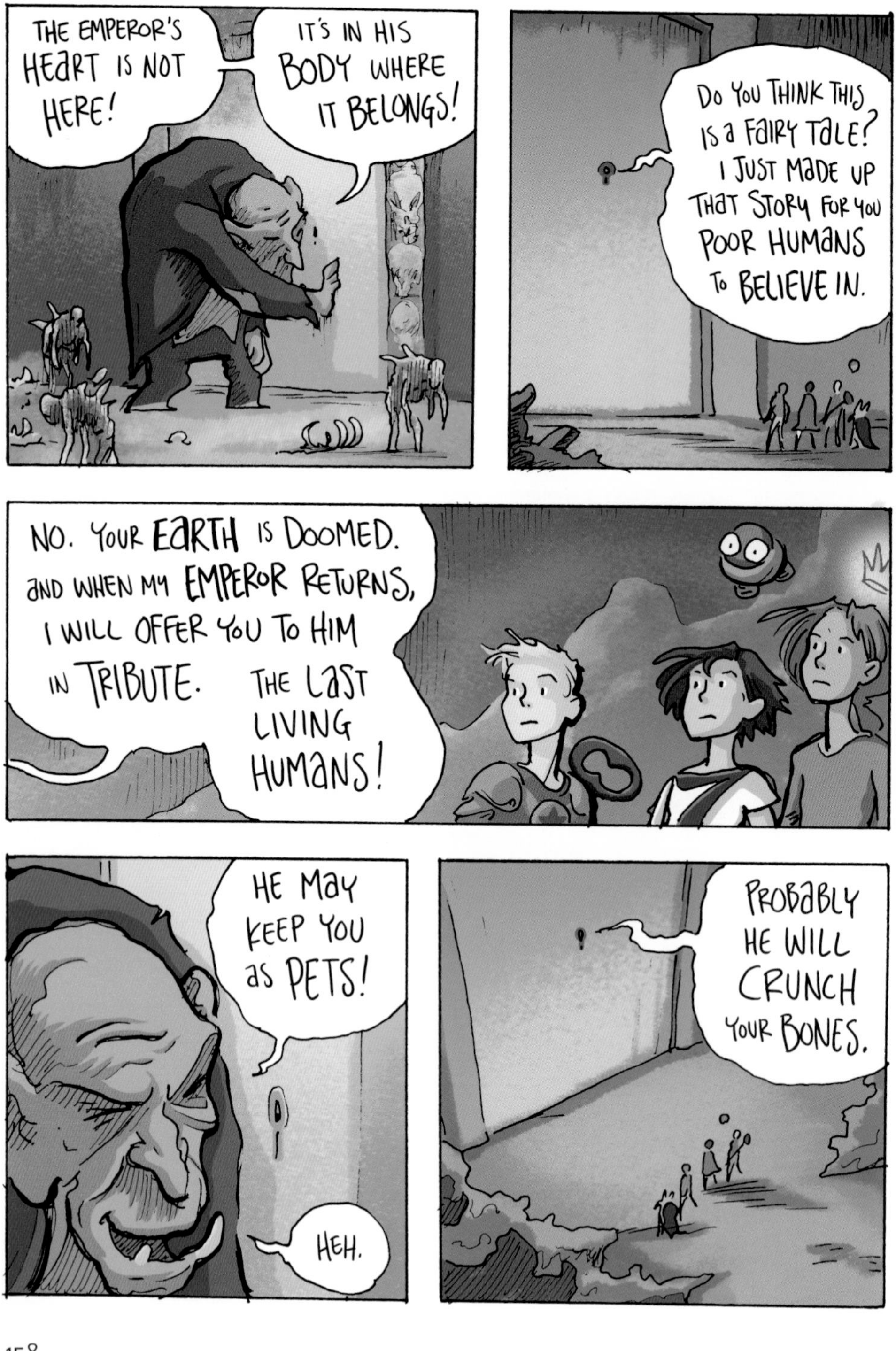
THE EMPEROR'S HEART IS NOT HERE!
IT'S IN HIS BODY WHERE IT BELONGS!
DO YOU THINK THIS IS A FAIRY TALE? I JUST MADE UP THAT STORY FOR YOU POOR HUMANS TO BELIEVE IN.
NO. YOUR EARTH IS DOOMED. AND WHEN MY EMPEROR RETURNS, I WILL OFFER YOU TO HIM IN TRIBUTE. THE LAST LIVING HUMANS!
HE MAY KEEP YOU AS PETS!
HEH.
PROBABLY HE WILL CRUNCH YOUR BONES.

WE'RE THROUGH.

EXCELLENT.

WHAT DO YOU SAY, OLD FRIEND?

SIGH.

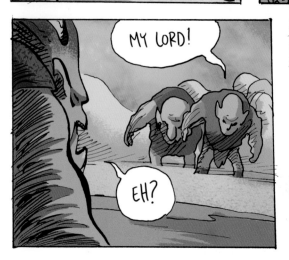

MY LORD!

EH?

WHAT IS IT?

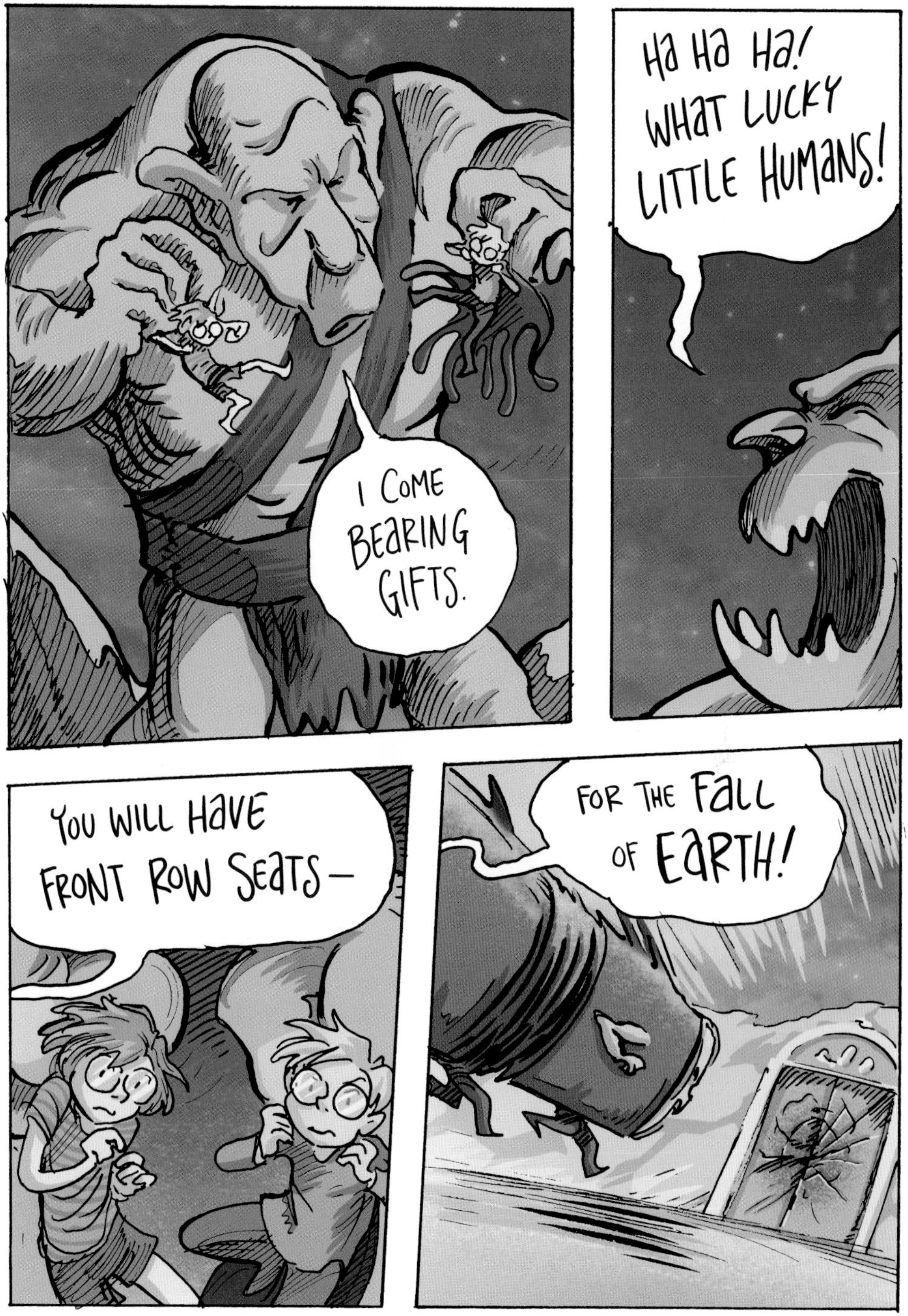
I COME BEARING GIFTS.
HA HA HA! WHAT LUCKY LITTLE HUMANS!
YOU WILL HAVE FRONT ROW SEATS—
FOR THE FALL OF EARTH!

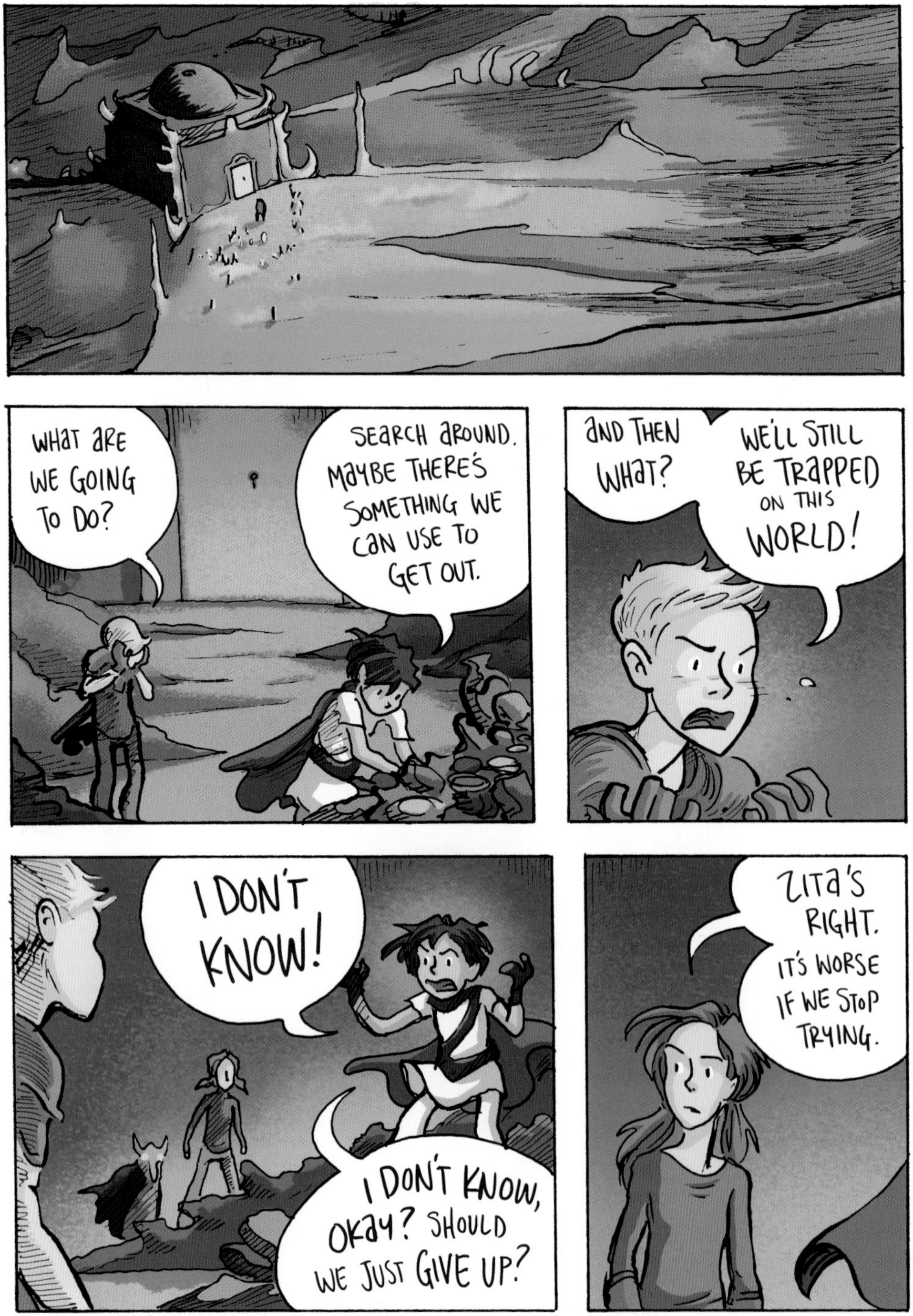
WHAT ARE WE GOING TO DO?
SEARCH AROUND. MAYBE THERE'S SOMETHING WE CAN USE TO GET OUT.
AND THEN WHAT?
WE'LL STILL BE TRAPPED ON THIS WORLD!
I DON'T KNOW!
I DON'T KNOW, OKAY? SHOULD WE JUST GIVE UP?
ZITA'S RIGHT. IT'S WORSE IF WE STOP TRYING.

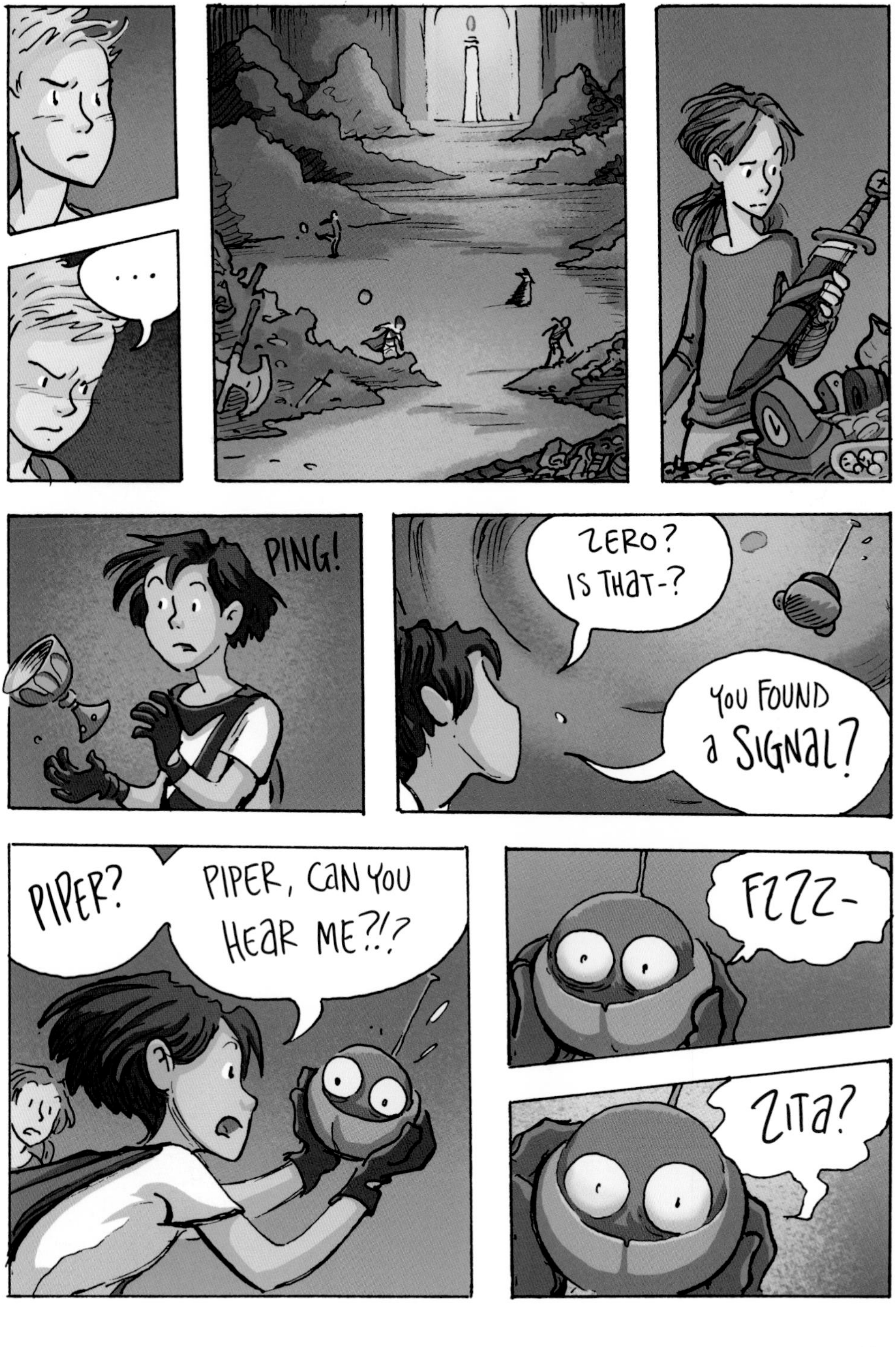
...
PING!
ZERO? IS THAT-?
YOU FOUND a SIGNAL?
PIPER?
PIPER, CaN YOU HEaR ME?!?
FZZZ-
ZITa?

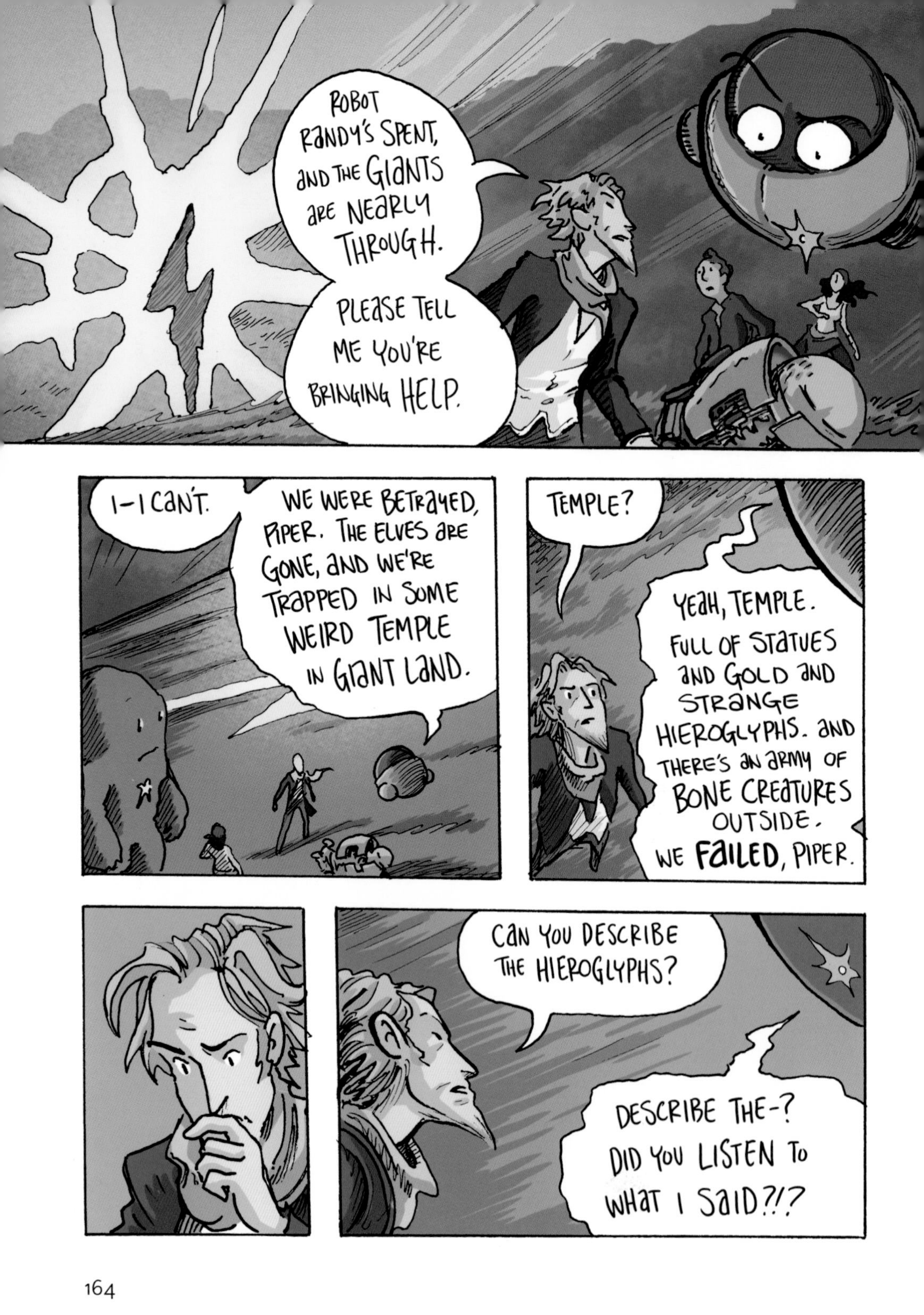
ROBOT RANDY'S SPENT, AND THE GIANTS ARE NEARLY THROUGH.
PLEASE TELL ME YOU'RE BRINGING HELP.
I-I CAN'T.
WE WERE BETRAYED, PIPER. THE ELVES ARE GONE, AND WE'RE TRAPPED IN SOME WEIRD TEMPLE IN GIANT LAND.
TEMPLE?
YEAH, TEMPLE.
FULL OF STATUES AND GOLD AND STRANGE HIEROGLYPHS. AND THERE'S AN ARMY OF BONE CREATURES OUTSIDE.
WE FAILED, PIPER.
CAN YOU DESCRIBE THE HIEROGLYPHS?
DESCRIBE THE-? DID YOU LISTEN TO WHAT I SAID?!?

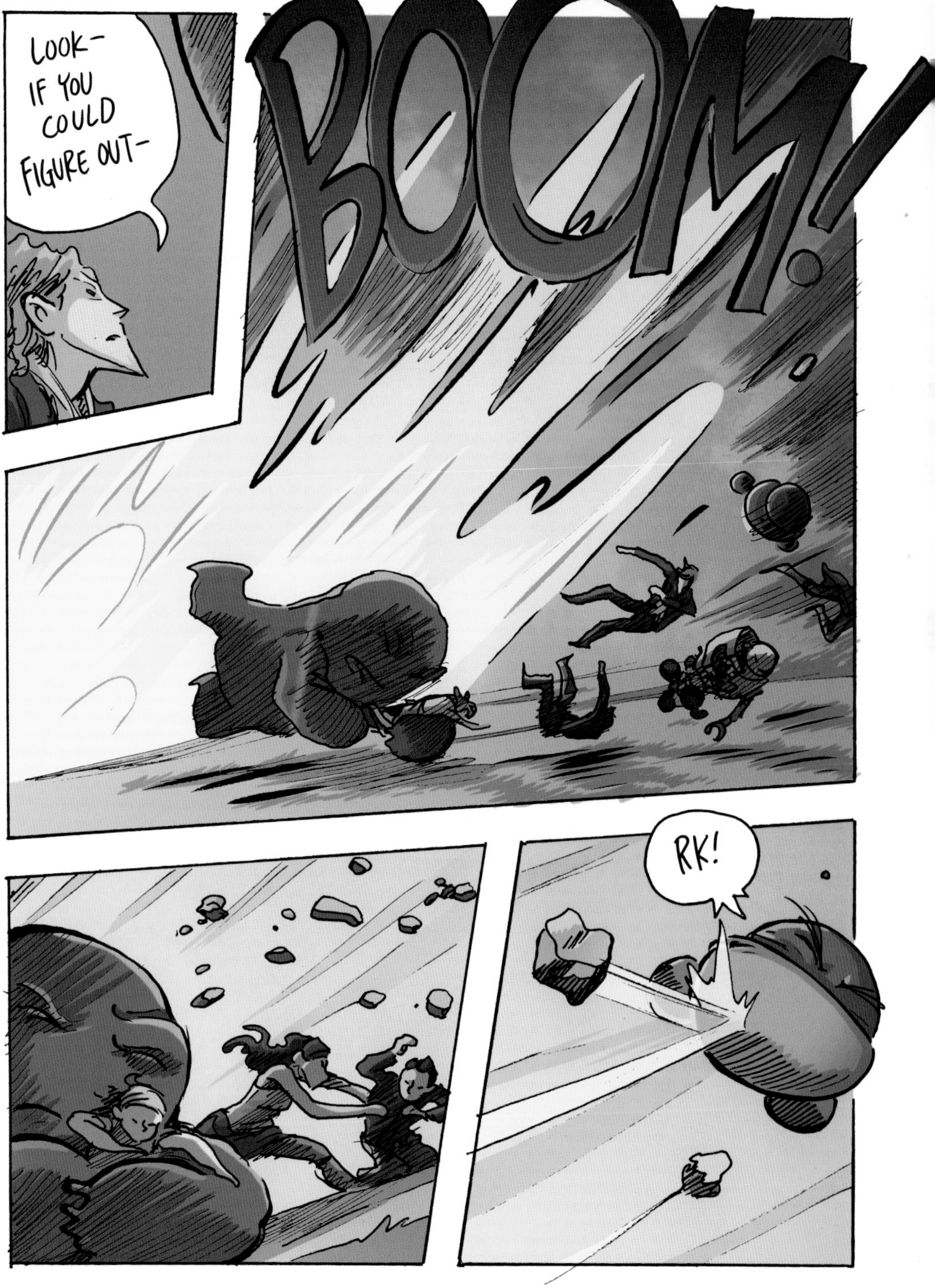
LOOK-
IF YOU
COULD
FIGURE OUT-
BOOM!
RK!

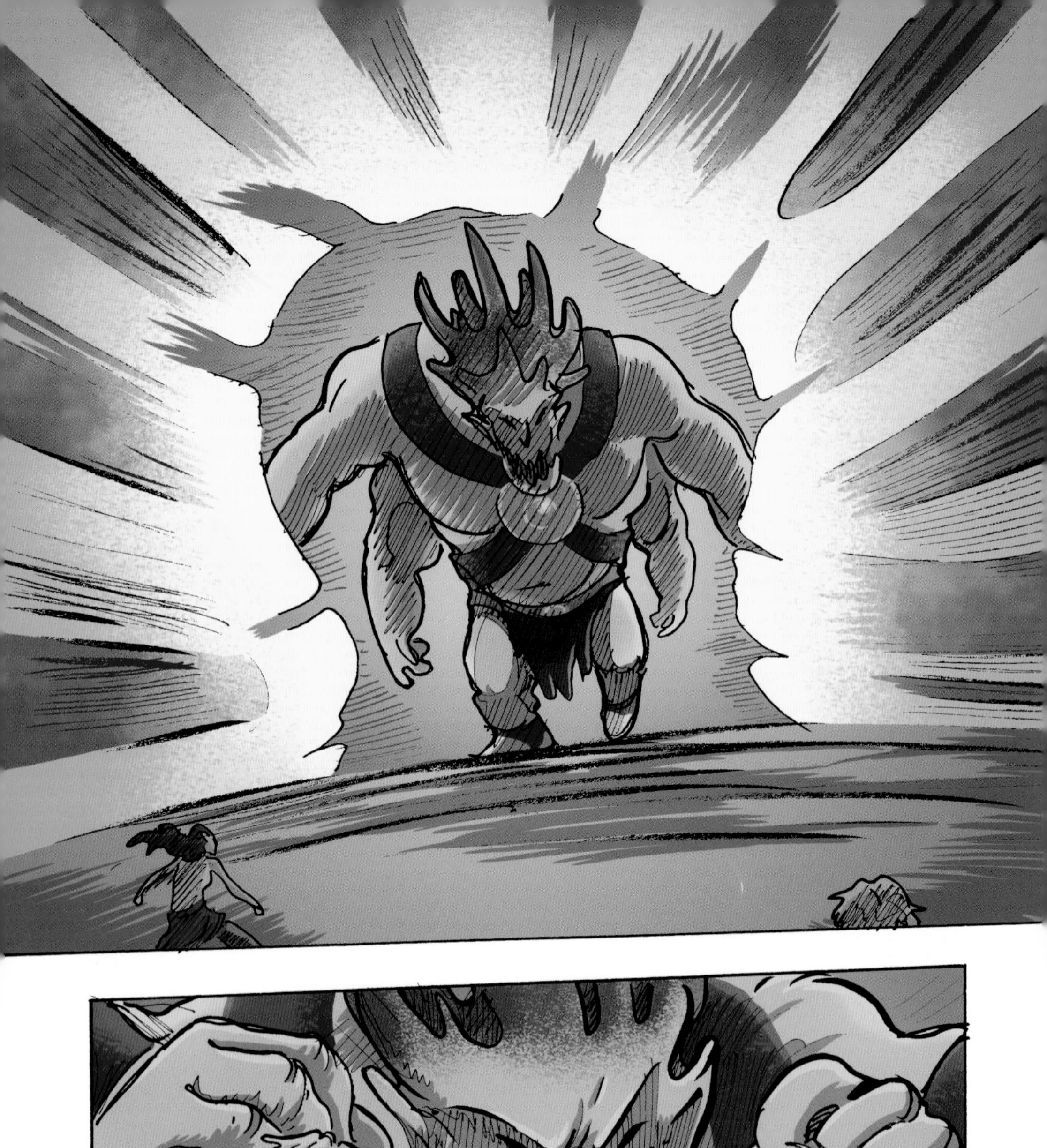

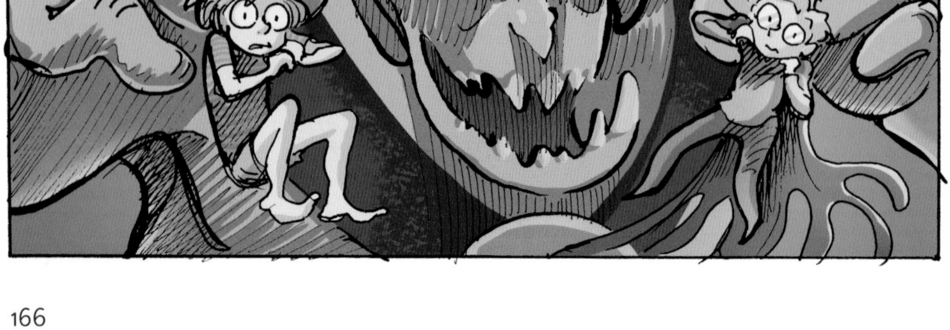

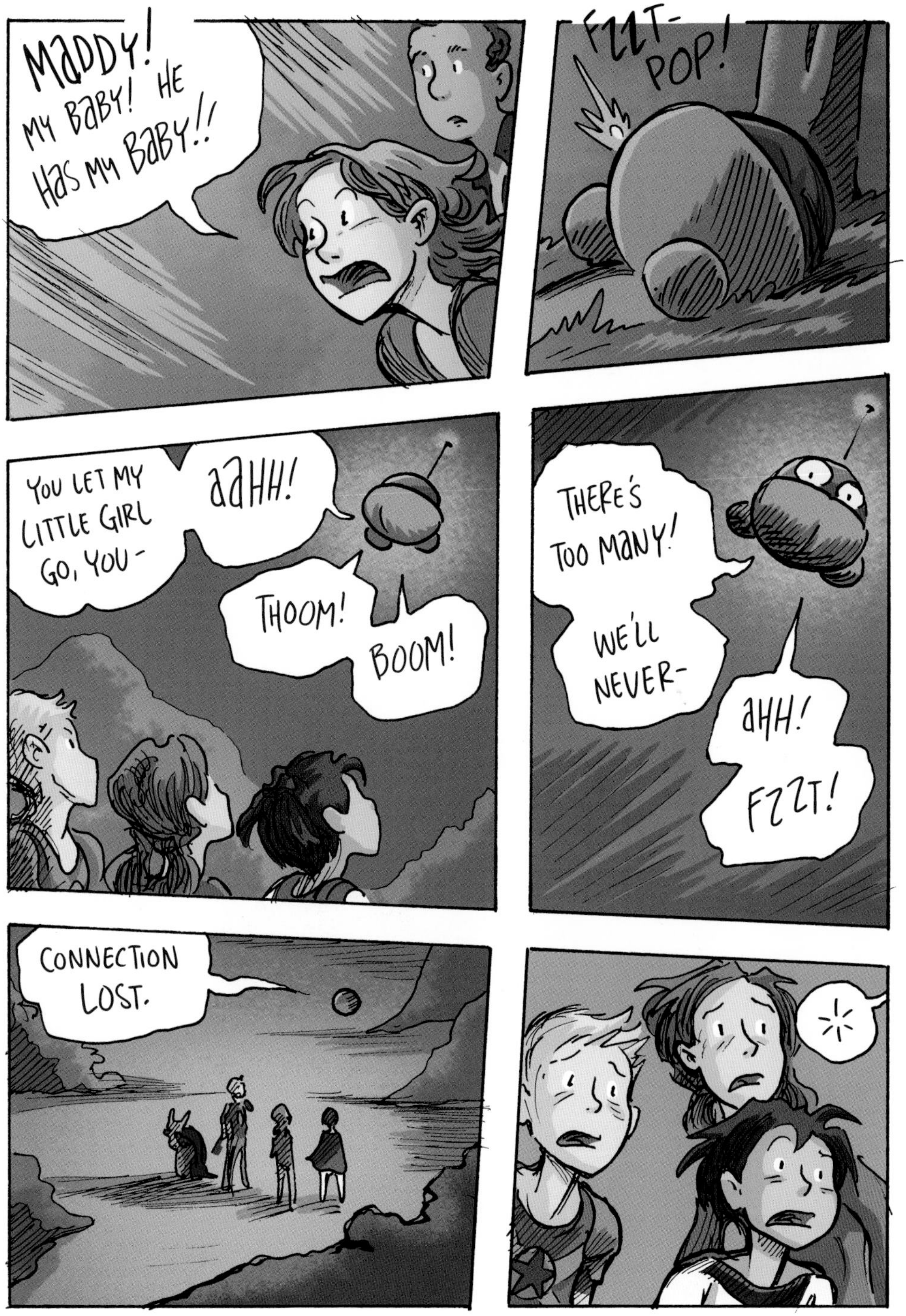
MADDY!
MY BABY! HE HAS MY BABY!!
FZZT-POP!
YOU LET MY LITTLE GIRL GO, YOU-
AAHH!
THOOM!
BOOM!
THERE'S TOO MANY!
WE'LL NEVER-
AHH!
FZZT!
CONNECTION LOST.
!

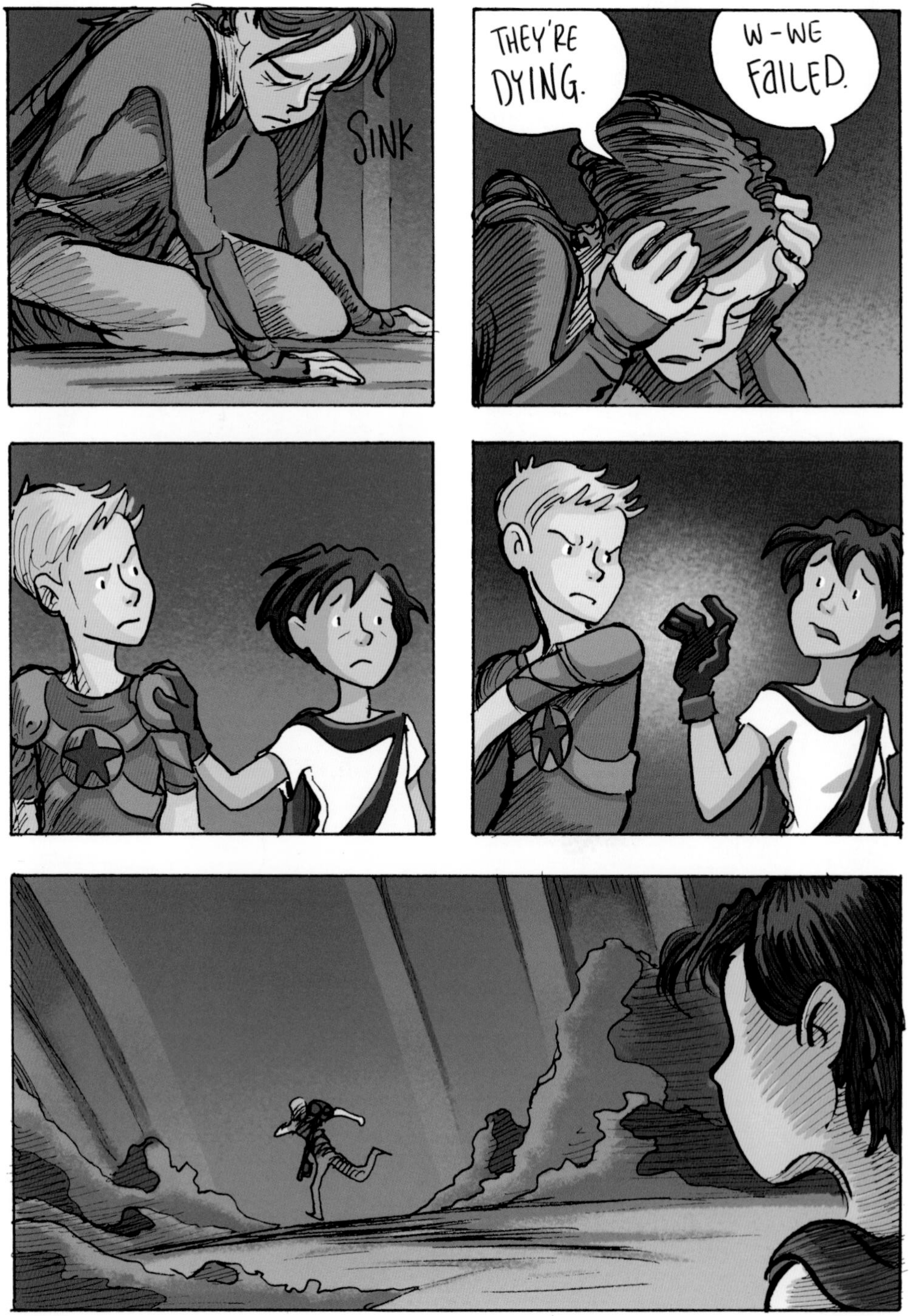
SINK
THEY'RE DYING.
W-WE FAILED.

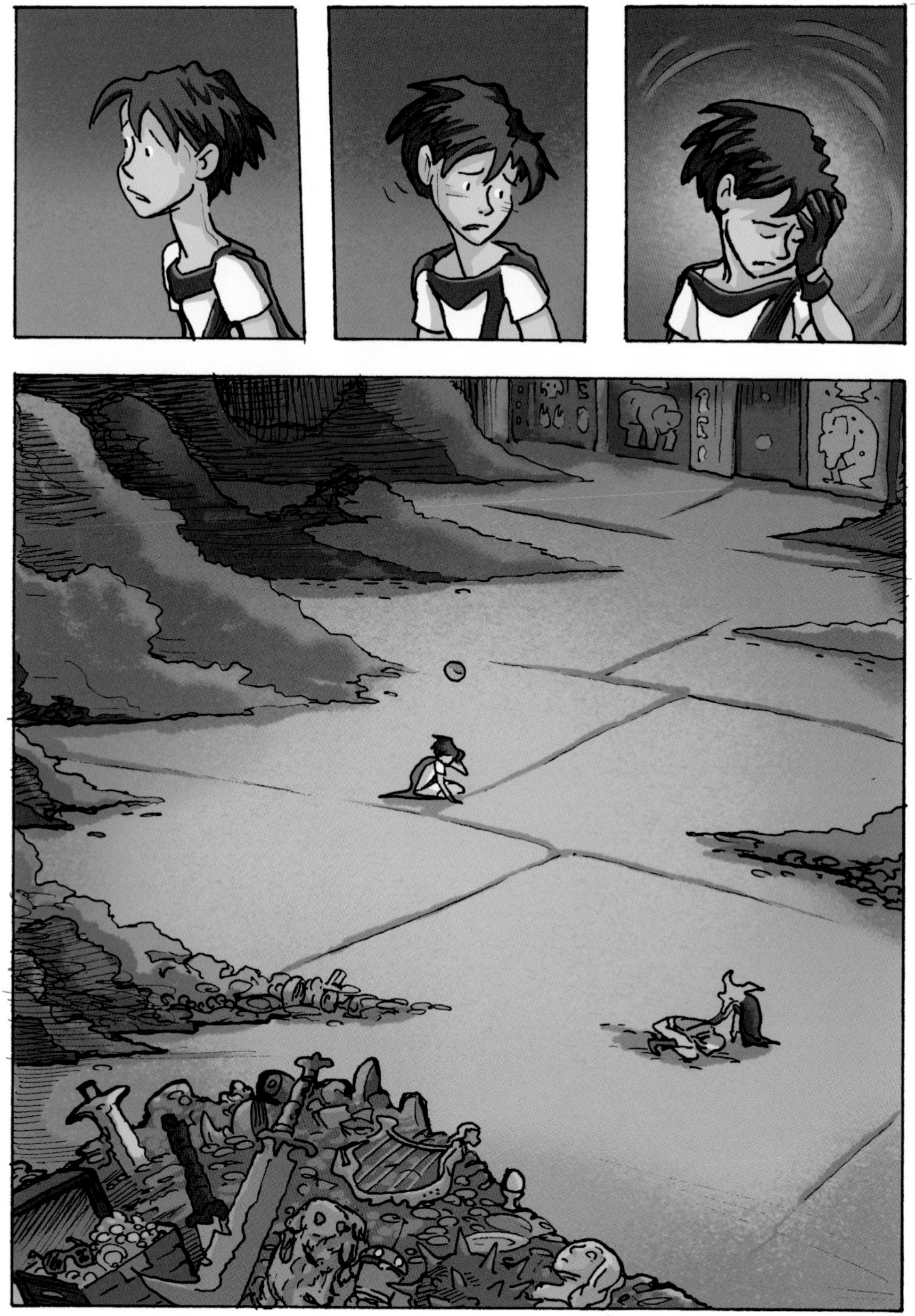

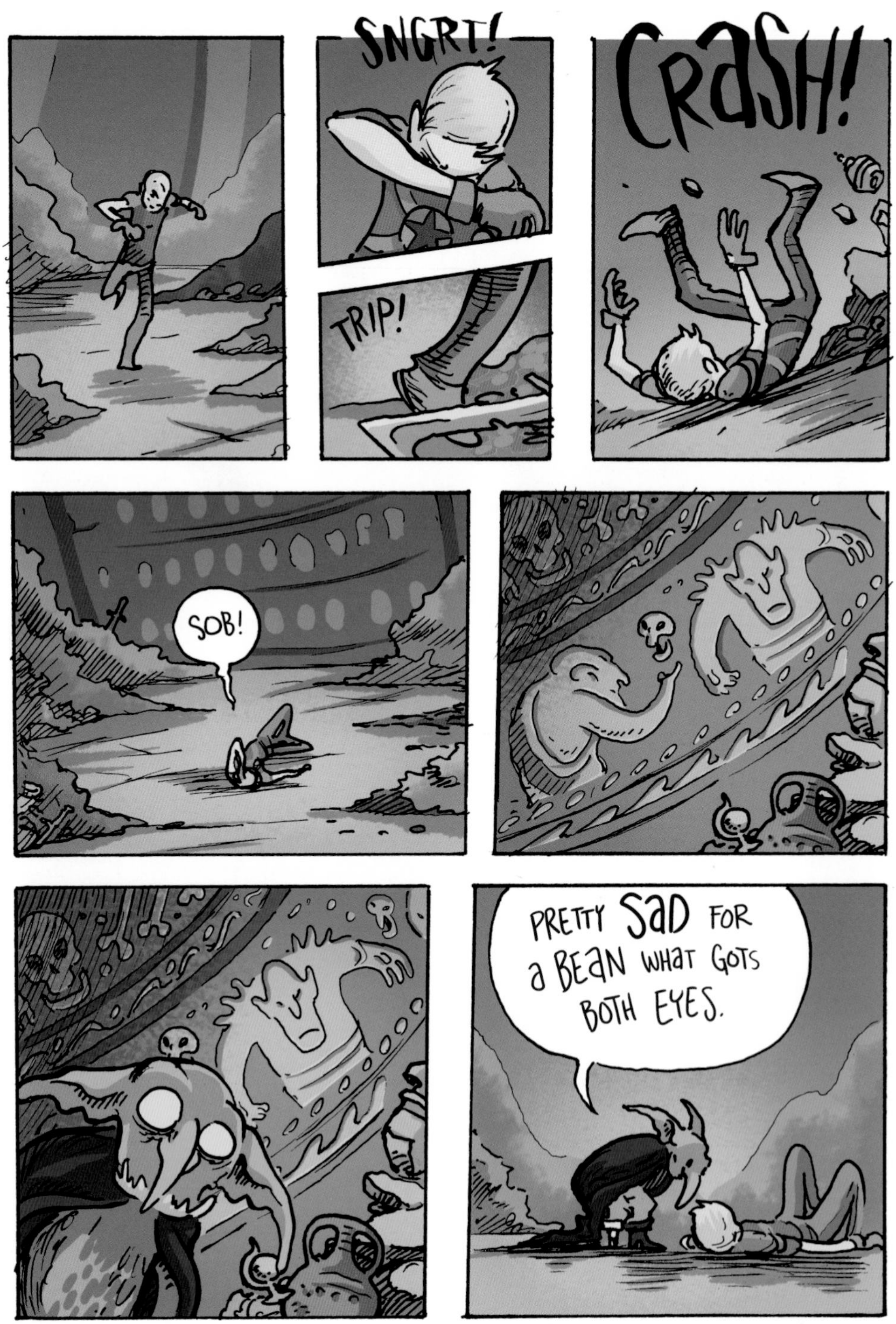
SNGRT!
TRIP!
CRASH!
SOB!
PRETTY SAD FOR a BEAN WHAT GOTS BOTH EYES.

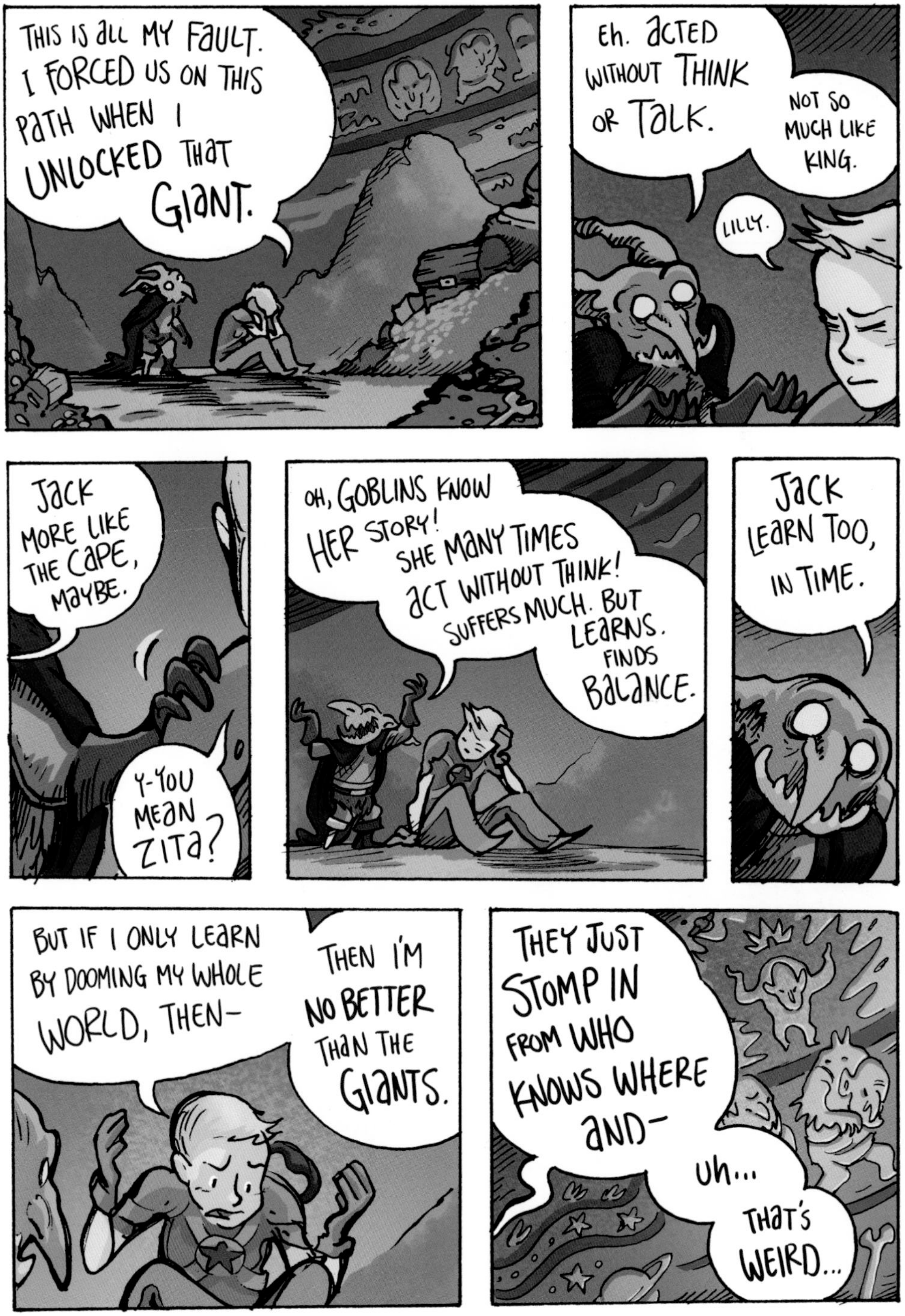
THIS IS ALL MY FAULT. I FORCED US ON THIS PATH WHEN I UNLOCKED THAT GIANT.
Eh. ACTED WITHOUT THINK OR TALK.
NOT SO MUCH LIKE KING.
LILLY.
JACK MORE LIKE THE CAPE, MAYBE.
Y-YOU MEAN ZITA?
OH, GOBLINS KNOW HER STORY!
SHE MANY TIMES ACT WITHOUT THINK!
SUFFERS MUCH. BUT LEARNS. FINDS BALANCE.
JACK LEARN TOO, IN TIME.
BUT IF I ONLY LEARN BY DOOMING MY WHOLE WORLD, THEN-
THEN I'M NO BETTER THAN THE GIANTS.
THEY JUST STOMP IN FROM WHO KNOWS WHERE AND-
UH...
THAT'S WEIRD...

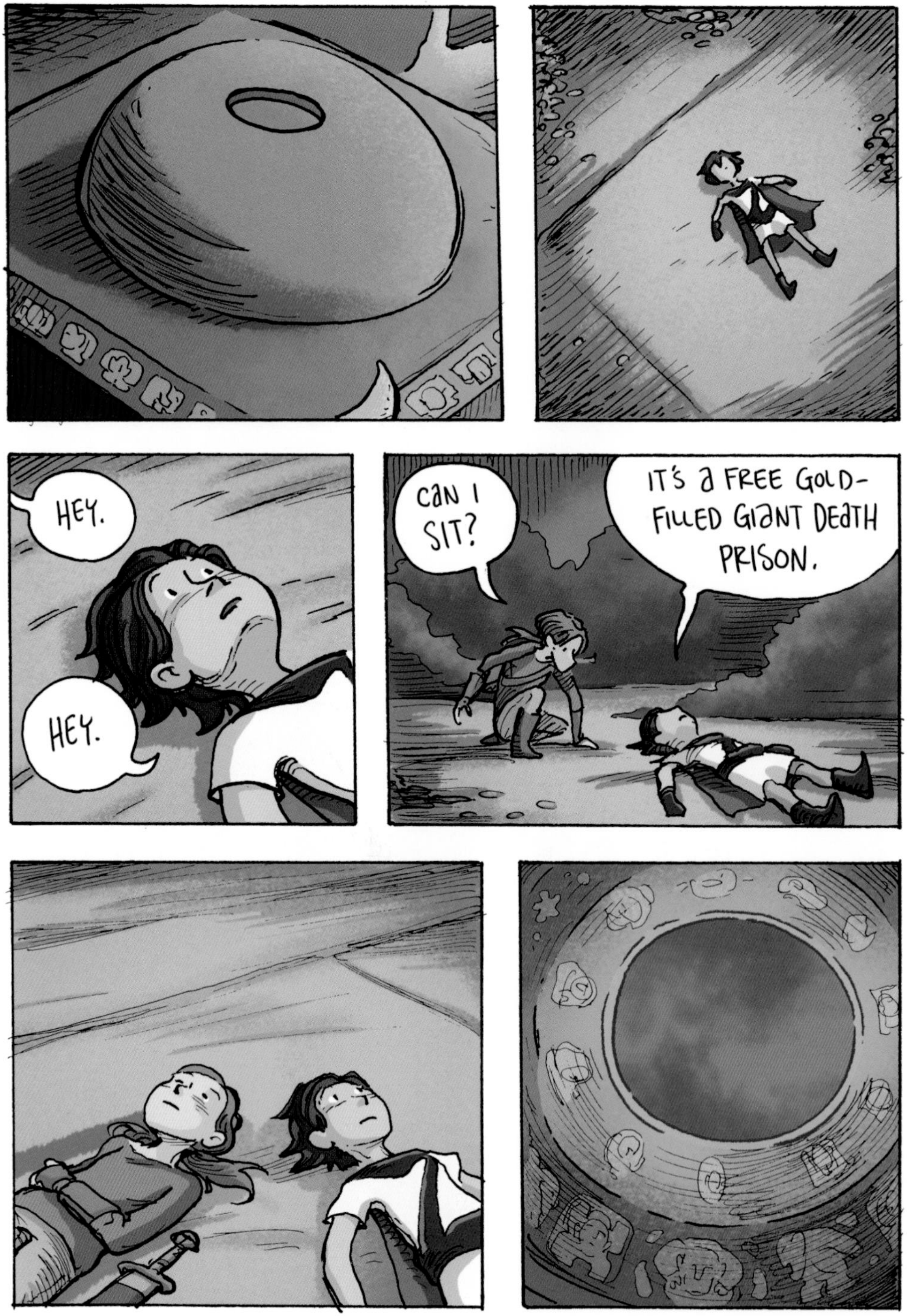
HEY.
HEY.
CAN I SIT?
IT'S A FREE GOLD-FILLED GIANT DEATH PRISON.

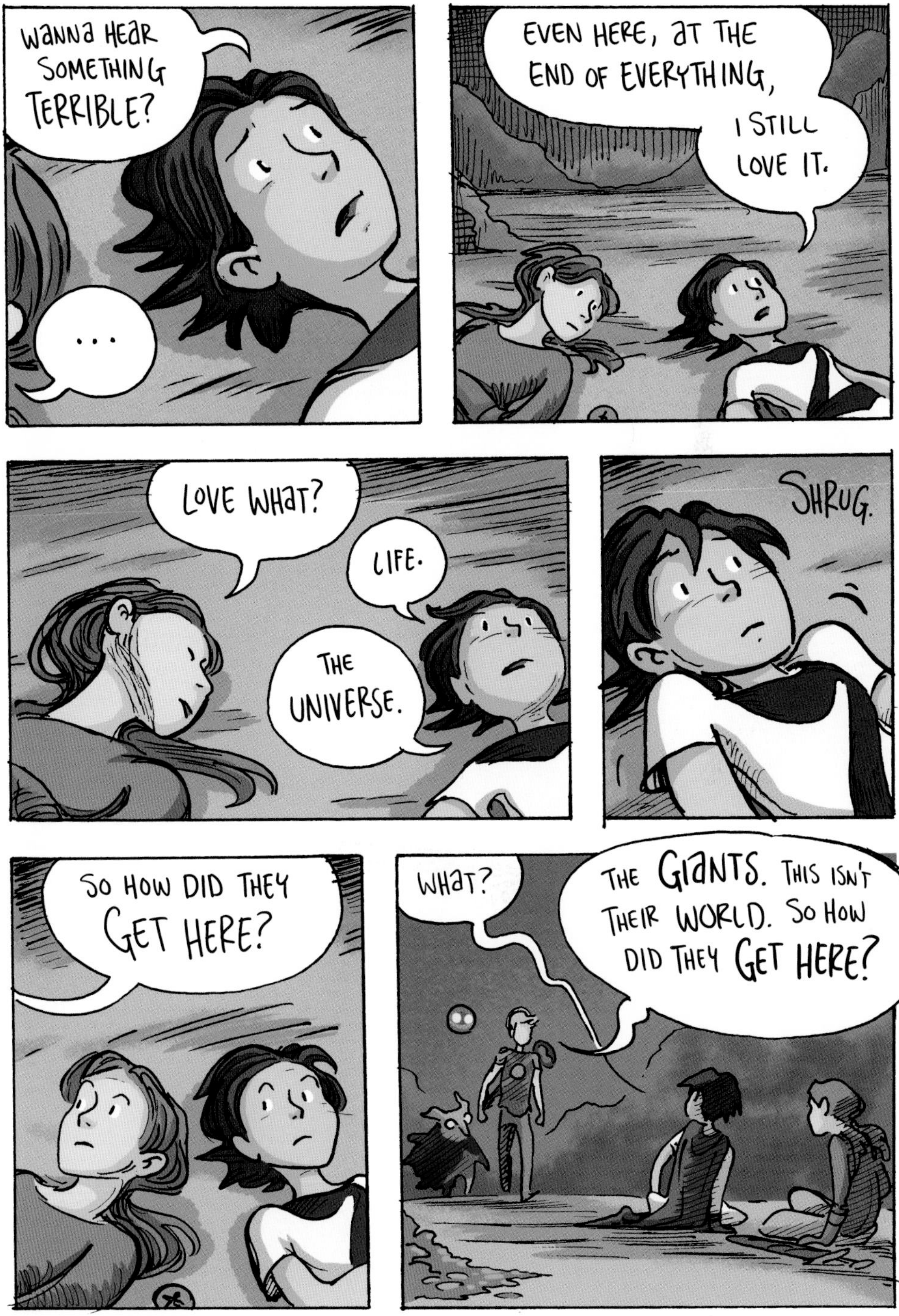
WANNA HEAR SOMETHING TERRIBLE?
...
EVEN HERE, AT THE END OF EVERYTHING,
I STILL LOVE IT.
LOVE WHAT?
LIFE.
THE UNIVERSE.
SHRUG.
SO HOW DID THEY GET HERE?
WHAT?
THE GIANTS. THIS ISN'T THEIR WORLD. SO HOW DID THEY GET HERE?

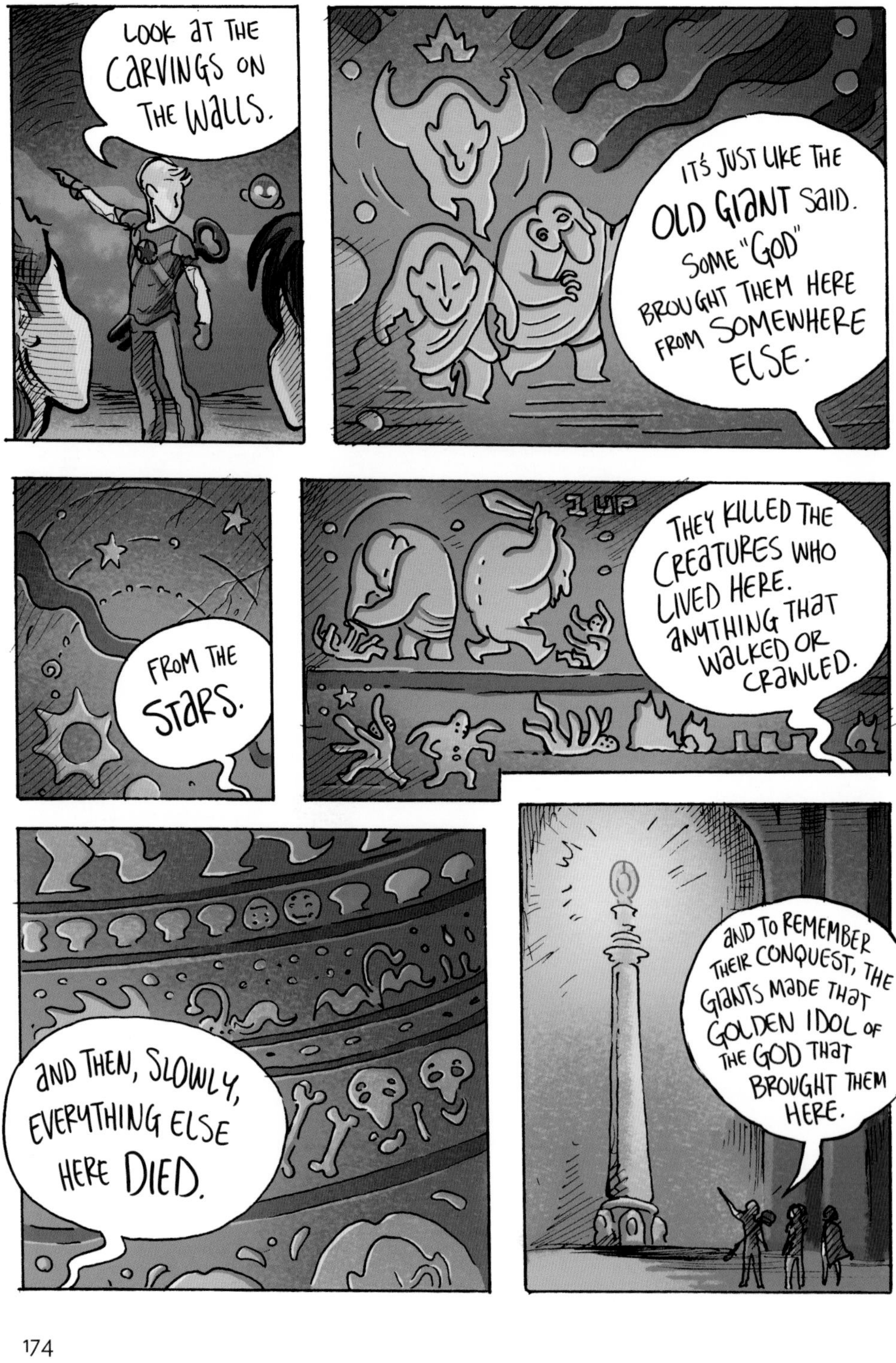

LOOK AT THE CARVINGS ON THE WALLS.
IT'S JUST LIKE THE OLD GIANT SAID. SOME "GOD" BROUGHT THEM HERE FROM SOMEWHERE ELSE.
FROM THE STARS.
1 UP
THEY KILLED THE CREATURES WHO LIVED HERE. ANYTHING THAT WALKED OR CRAWLED.
AND THEN, SLOWLY, EVERYTHING ELSE HERE DIED.
AND TO REMEMBER THEIR CONQUEST, THE GIANTS MADE THAT GOLDEN IDOL OF THE GOD THAT BROUGHT THEM HERE.

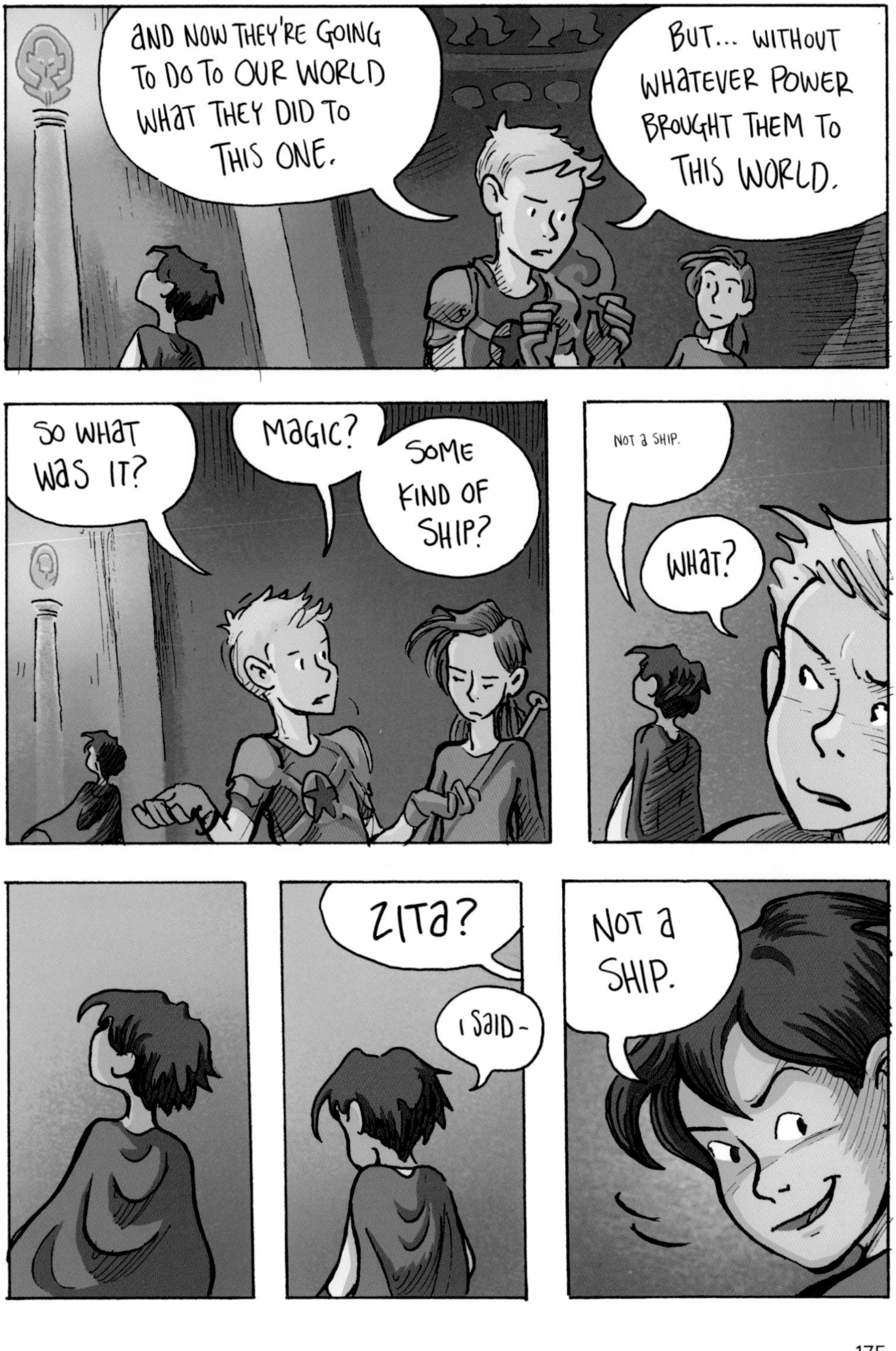
AND NOW THEY'RE GOING TO DO TO OUR WORLD WHAT THEY DID TO THIS ONE.
BUT... WITHOUT WHATEVER POWER BROUGHT THEM TO THIS WORLD.
SO WHAT WAS IT?
MAGIC?
SOME KIND OF SHIP?
NOT A SHIP.
WHAT?
ZITA?
I SAID-
NOT A SHIP.

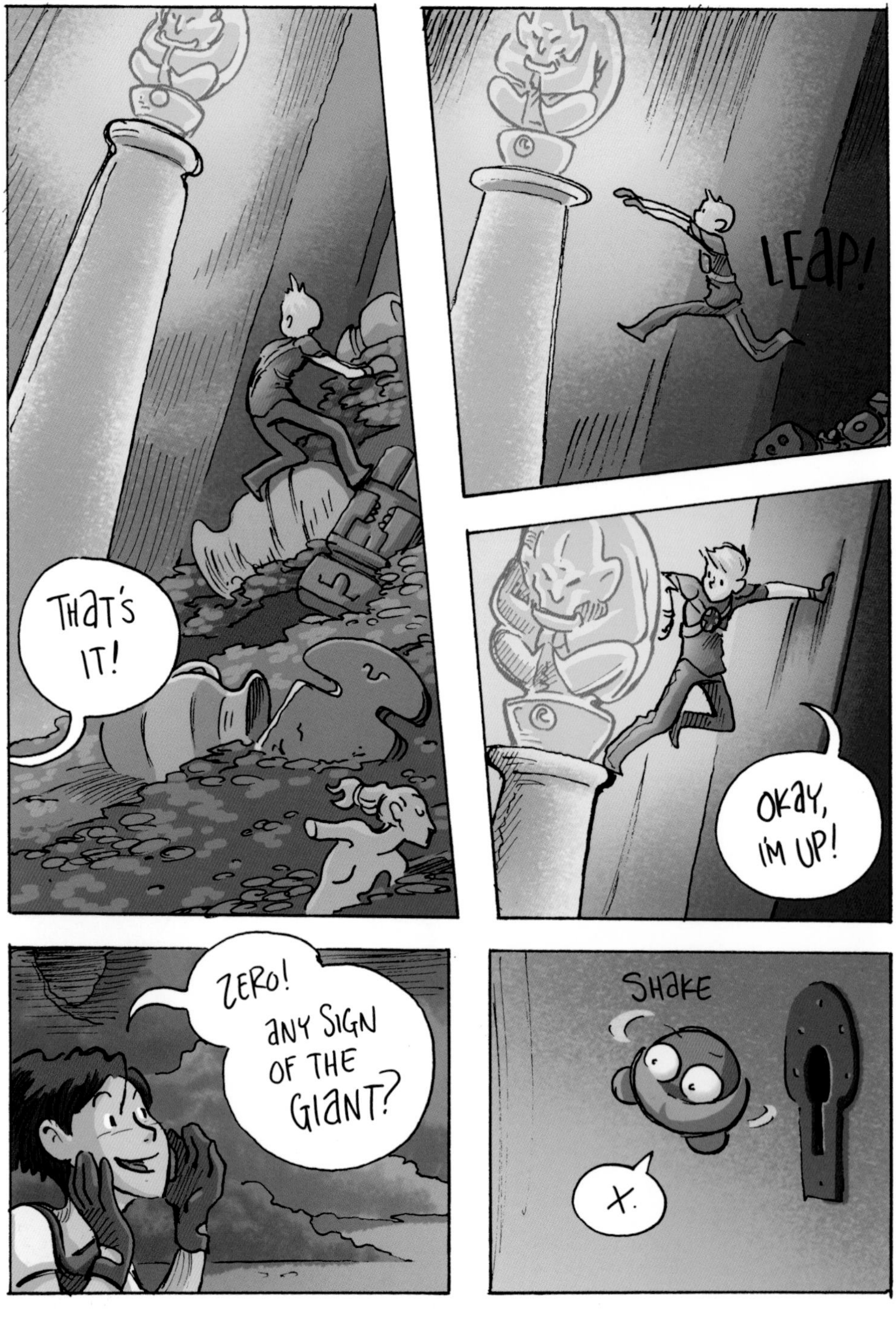
THAT'S IT!
LEAP!
OKAY, I'M UP!
ZERO! ANY SIGN OF THE GIANT?
SHAKE
X.

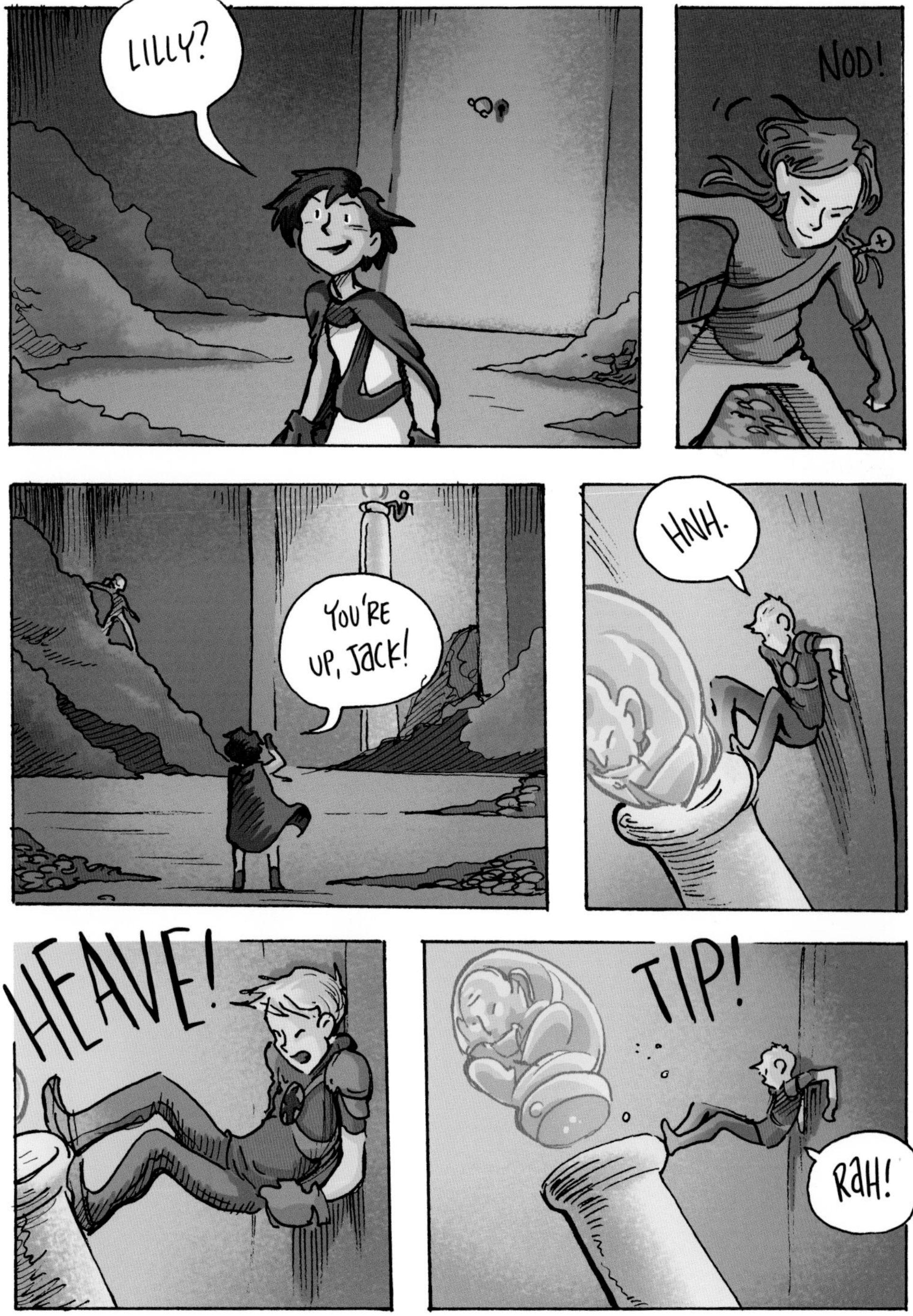
LILLY?
NOD!
YOU'RE UP, JACK!
HNH.
HEAVE!
TIP!
RAH!

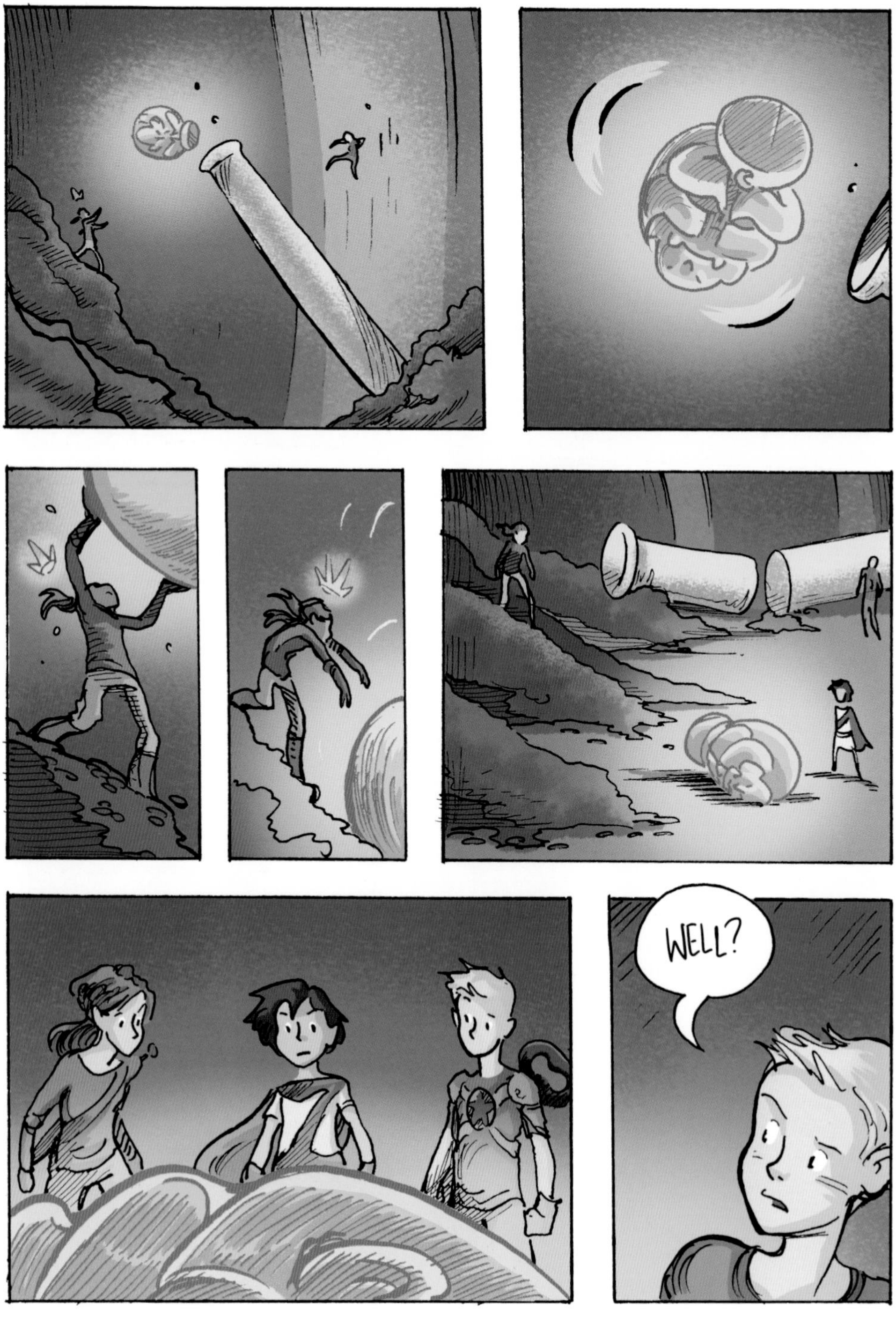
WELL?

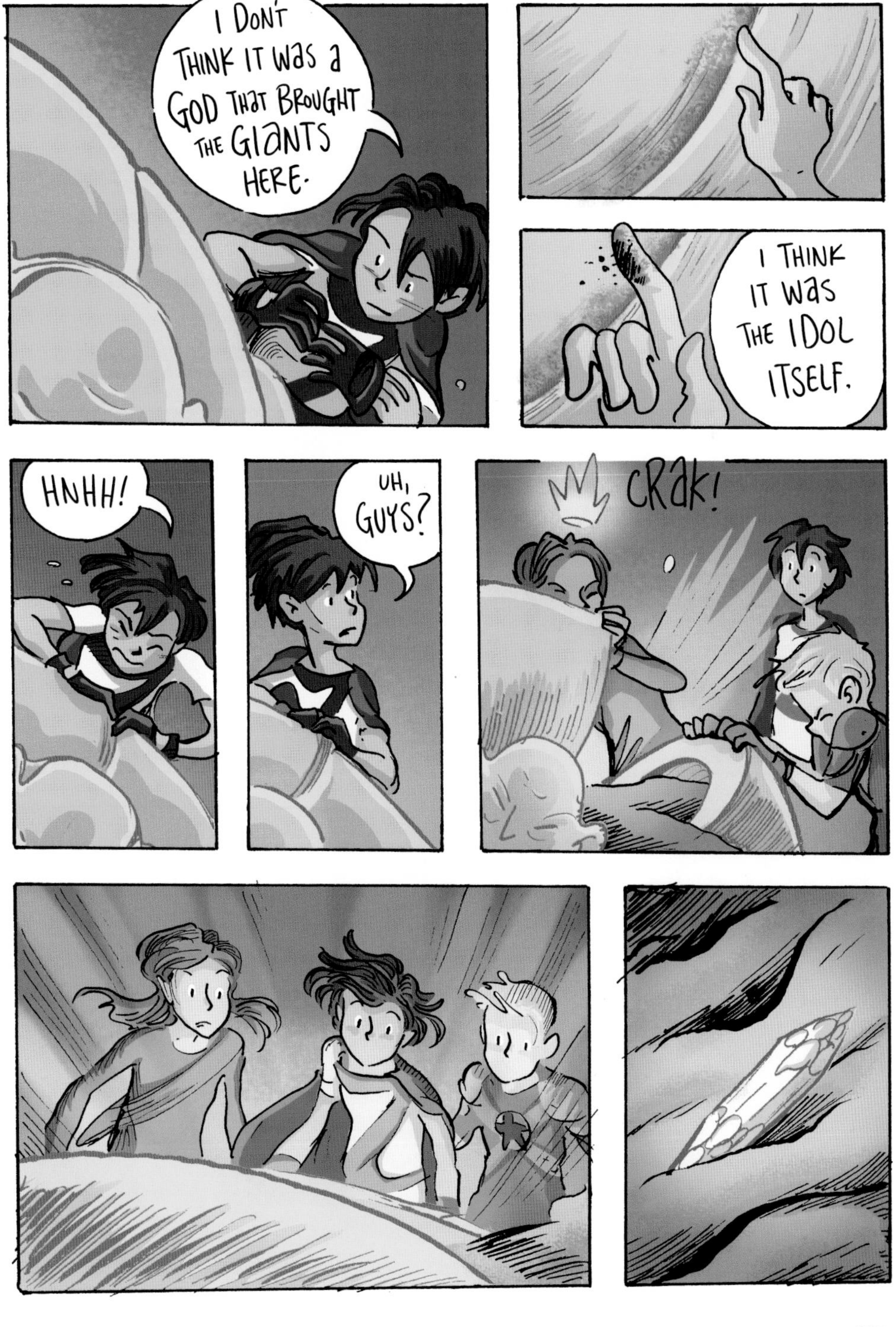
I DON'T THINK IT WAS A GOD THAT BROUGHT THE GIANTS HERE.
I THINK IT WAS THE IDOL ITSELF.
HNHH!
UH, GUYS?
CRAK!

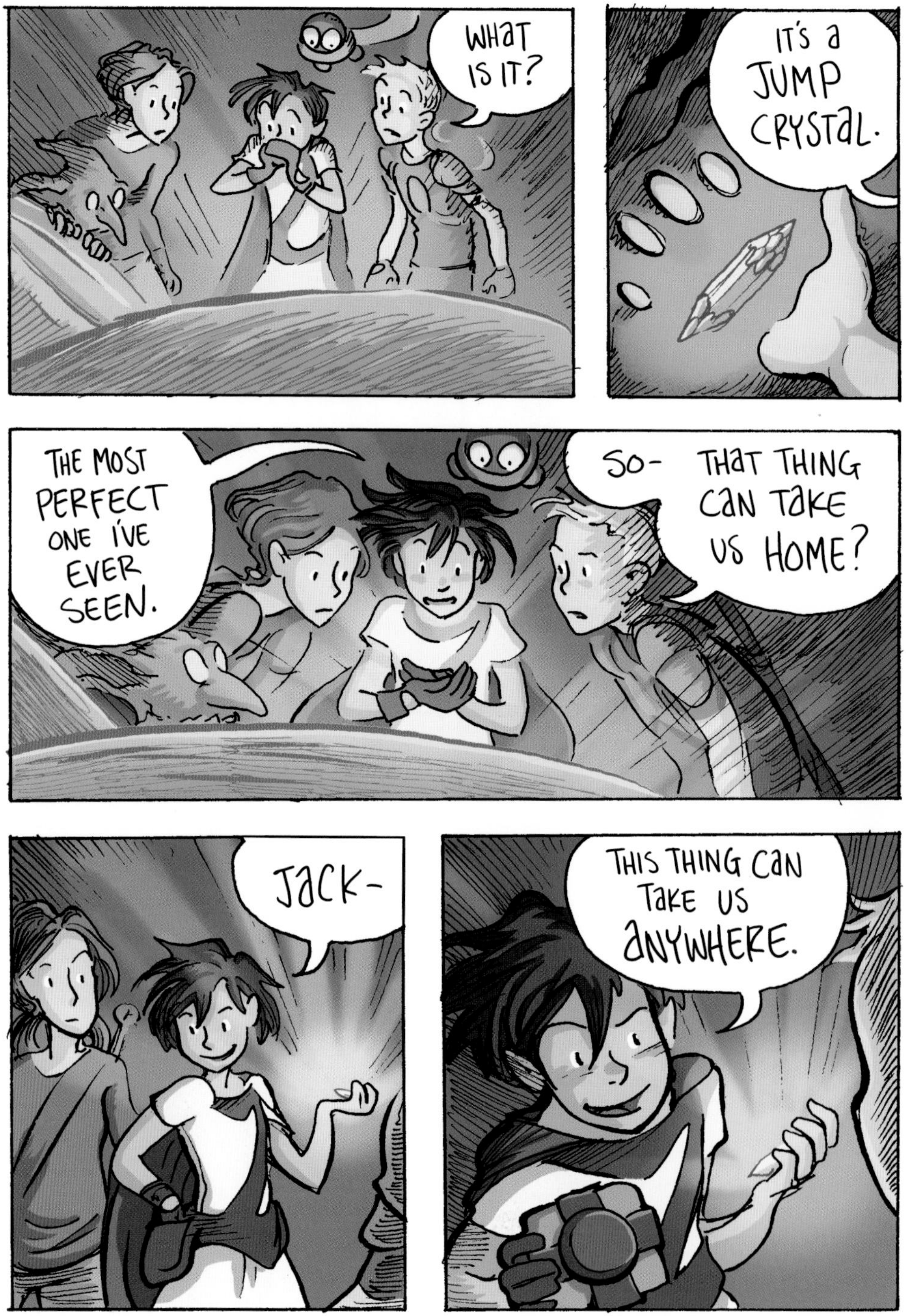
WHAT IS IT?
IT'S A JUMP CRYSTAL.
THE MOST PERFECT ONE I'VE EVER SEEN.
SO-
THAT THING CAN TAKE US HOME?
JACK-
THIS THING CAN TAKE US ANYWHERE.

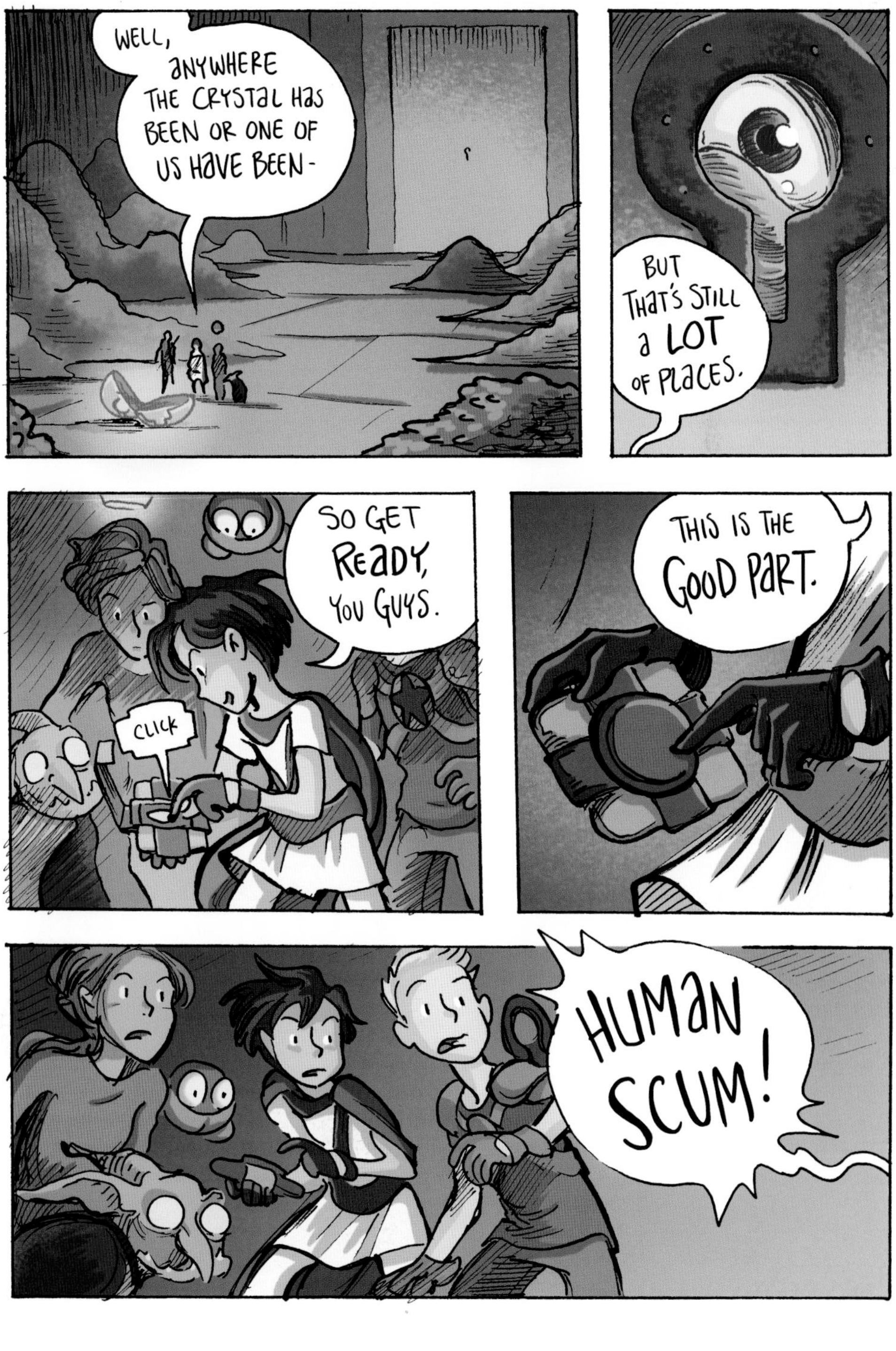
WELL, ANYWHERE THE CRYSTAL HAS BEEN OR ONE OF US HAVE BEEN-
BUT THAT'S STILL A LOT OF PLACES.
SO GET READY, YOU GUYS.
CLICK
THIS IS THE GOOD PART.
HUMAN SCUM!

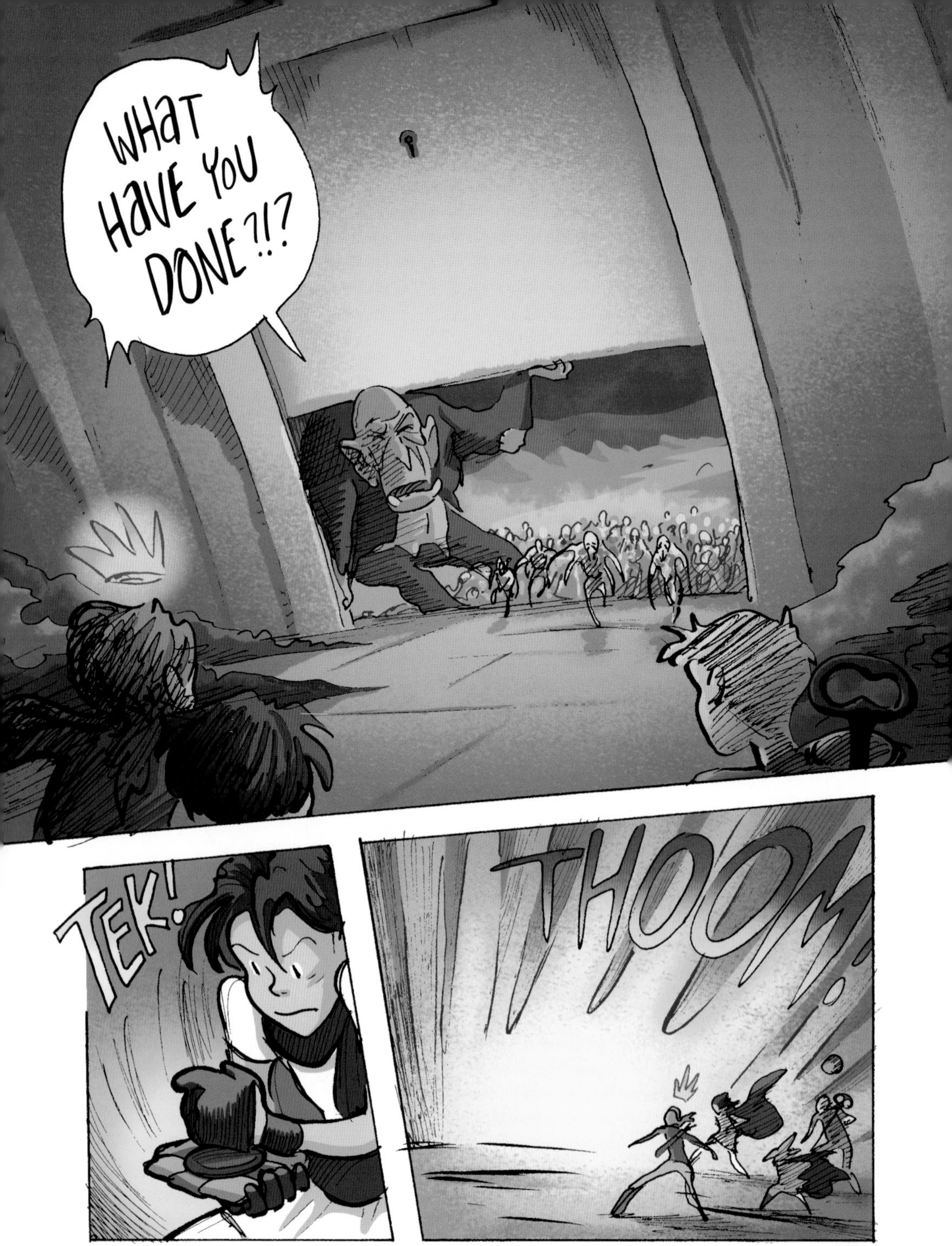
WHAT HAVE YOU DONE?!?
TEK!
THOOM!

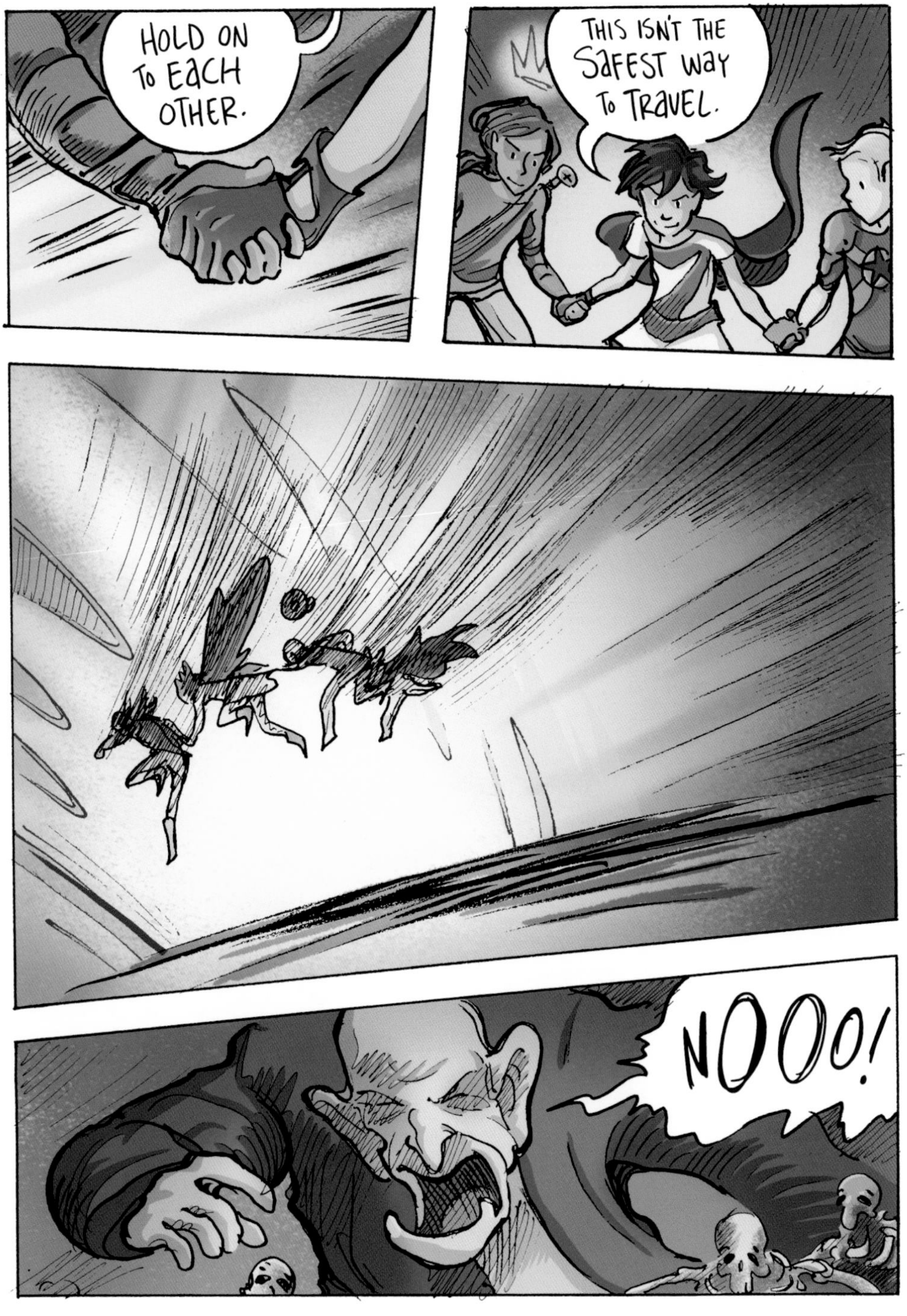
HOLD ON TO EACH OTHER.
THIS ISN'T THE SAFEST WAY TO TRAVEL.
NOOO!

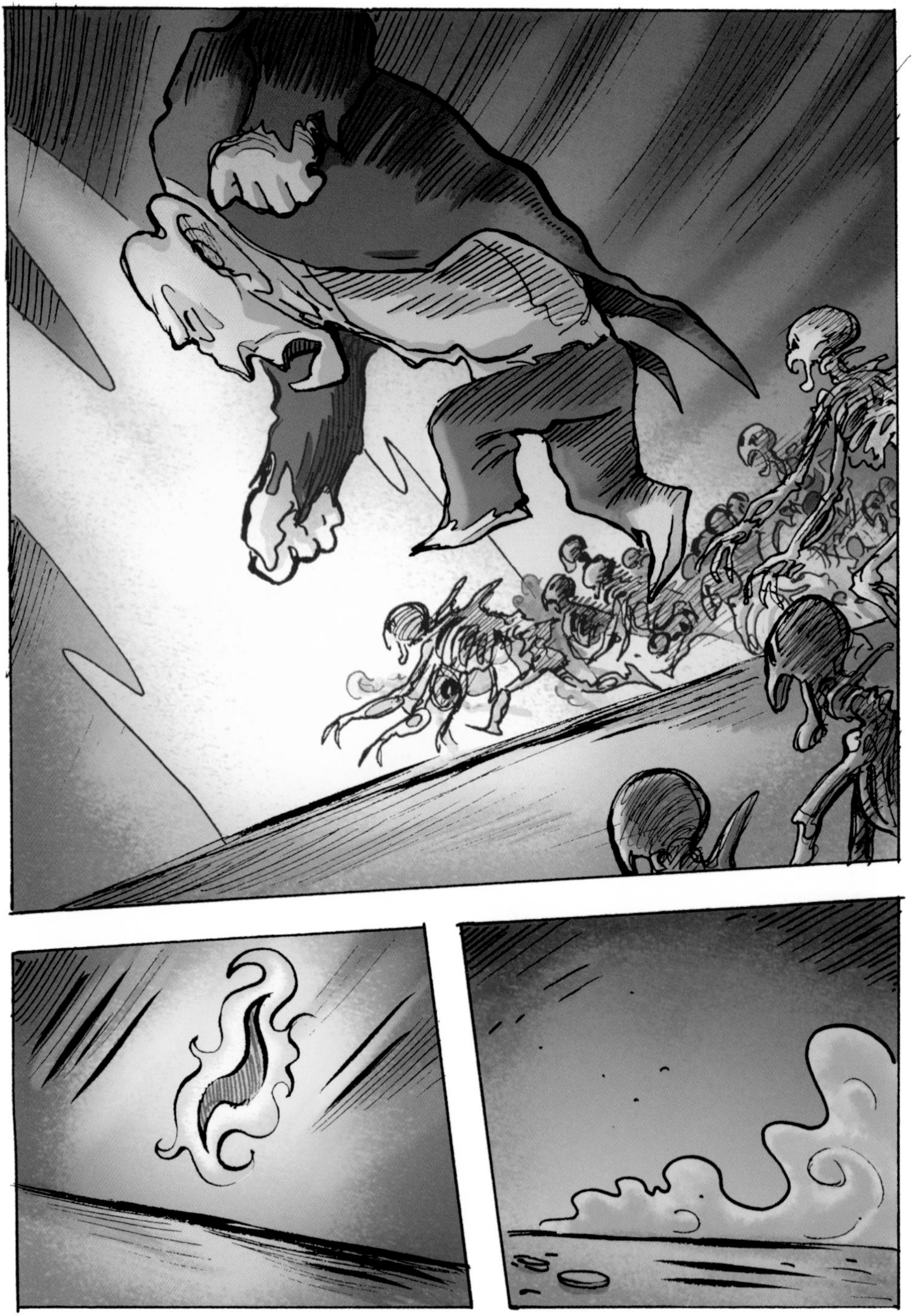

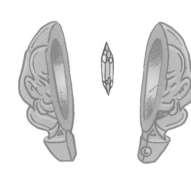

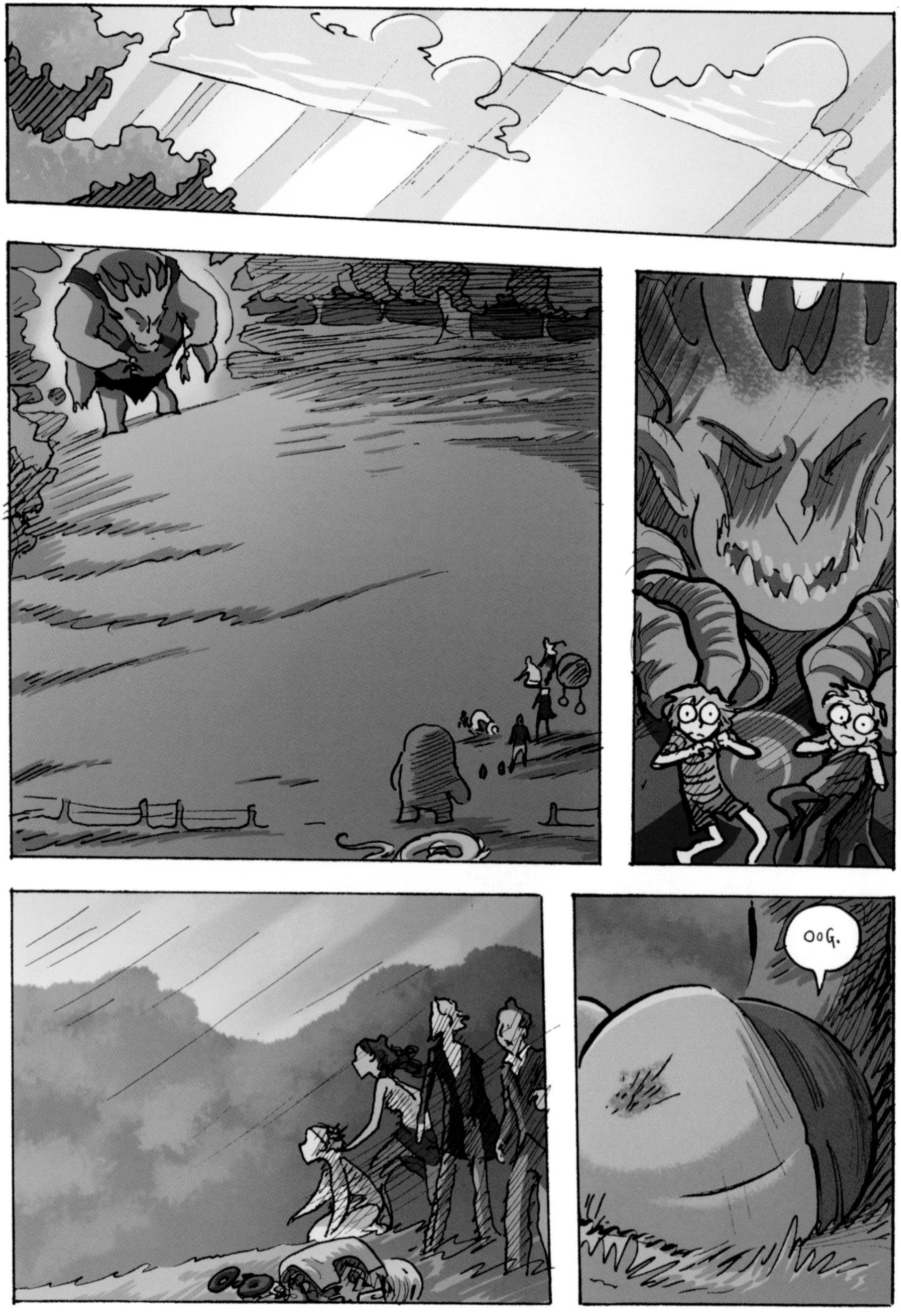
OOG.

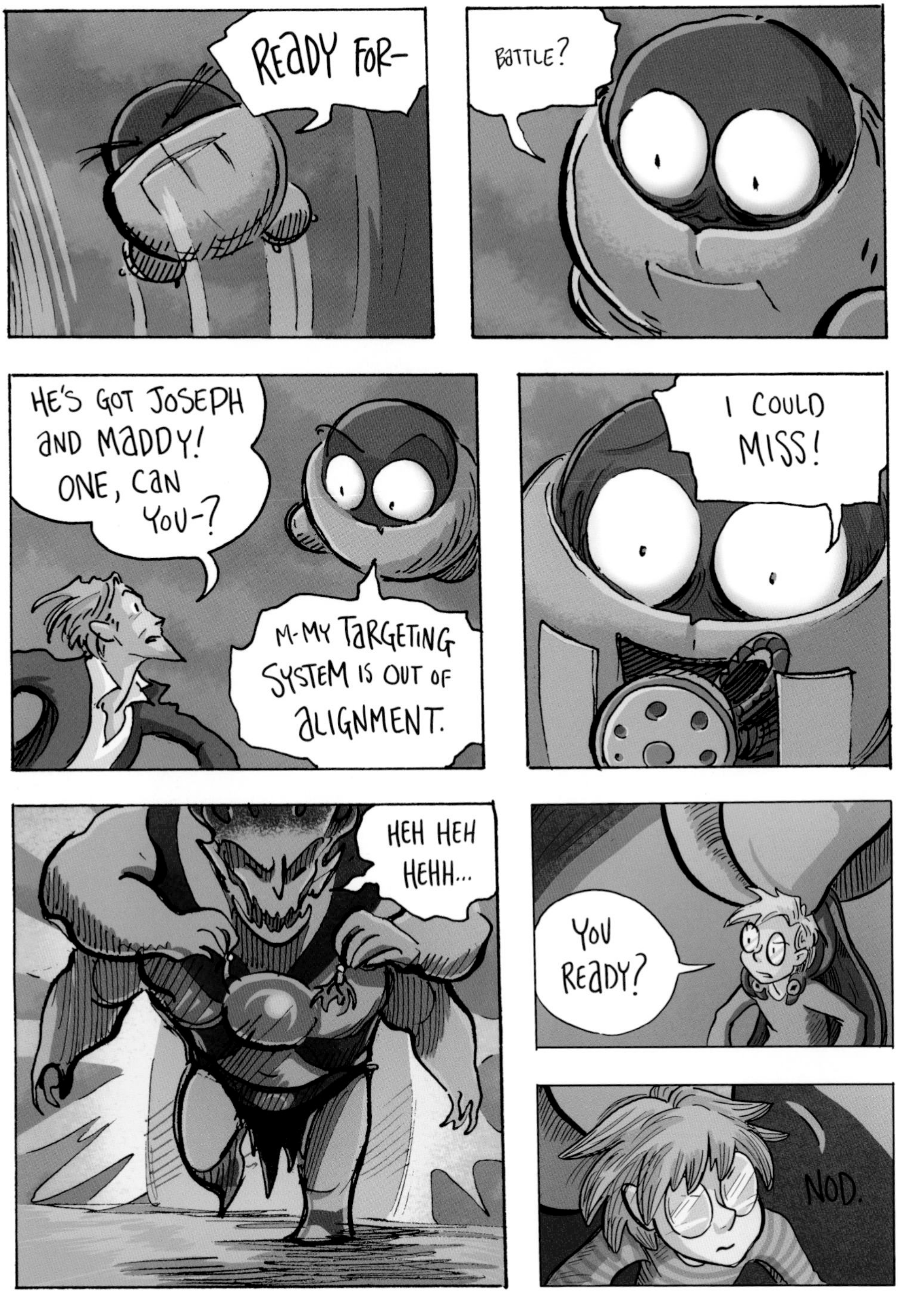
READY FOR-
BATTLE?
HE'S GOT JOSEPH AND MADDY! ONE, CAN YOU-?
M-MY TARGETING SYSTEM IS OUT OF ALIGNMENT.
I COULD MISS!
HEH HEH HEHH...
YOU READY?
NOD.

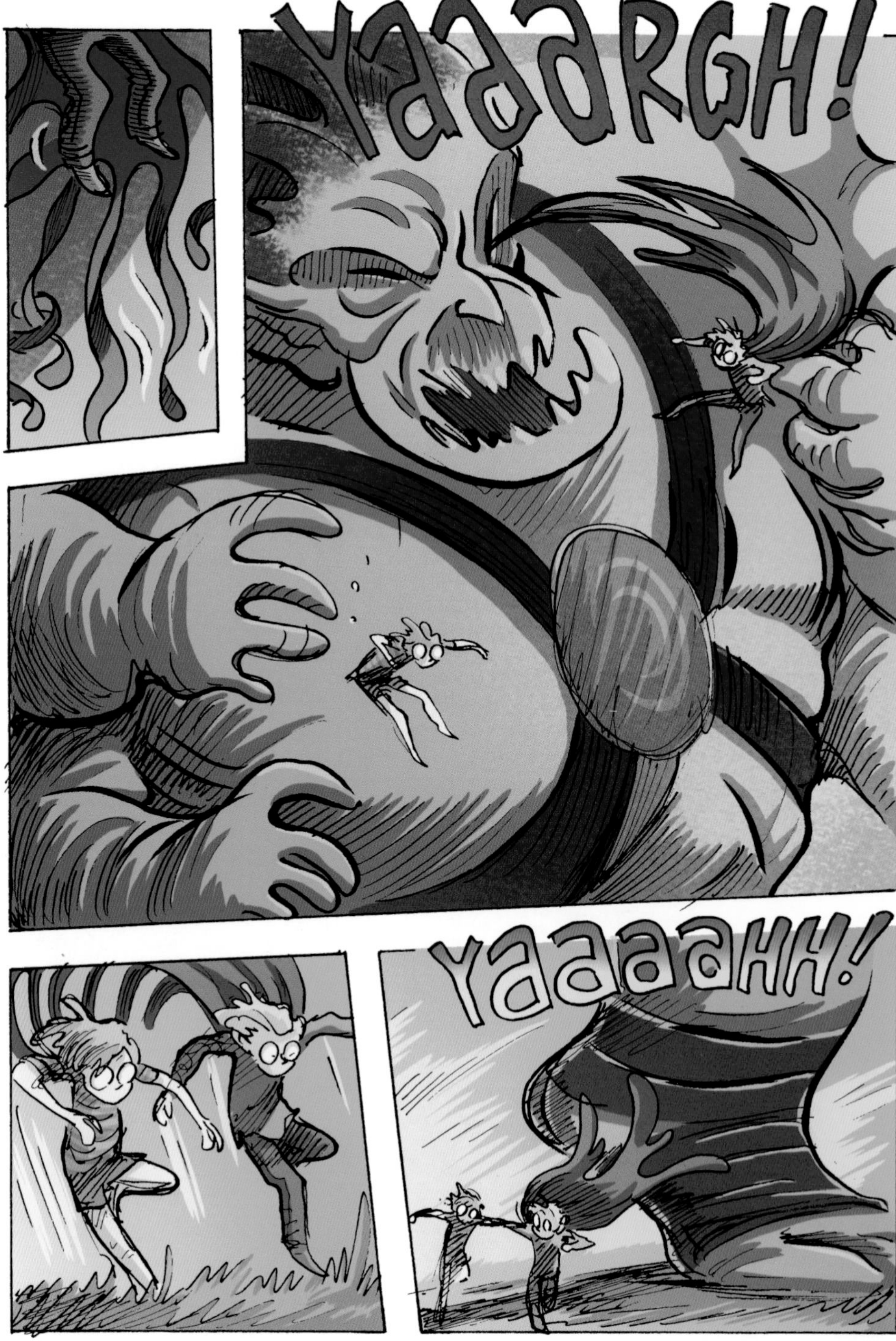
YAAARGH!
YAAAAAHH!

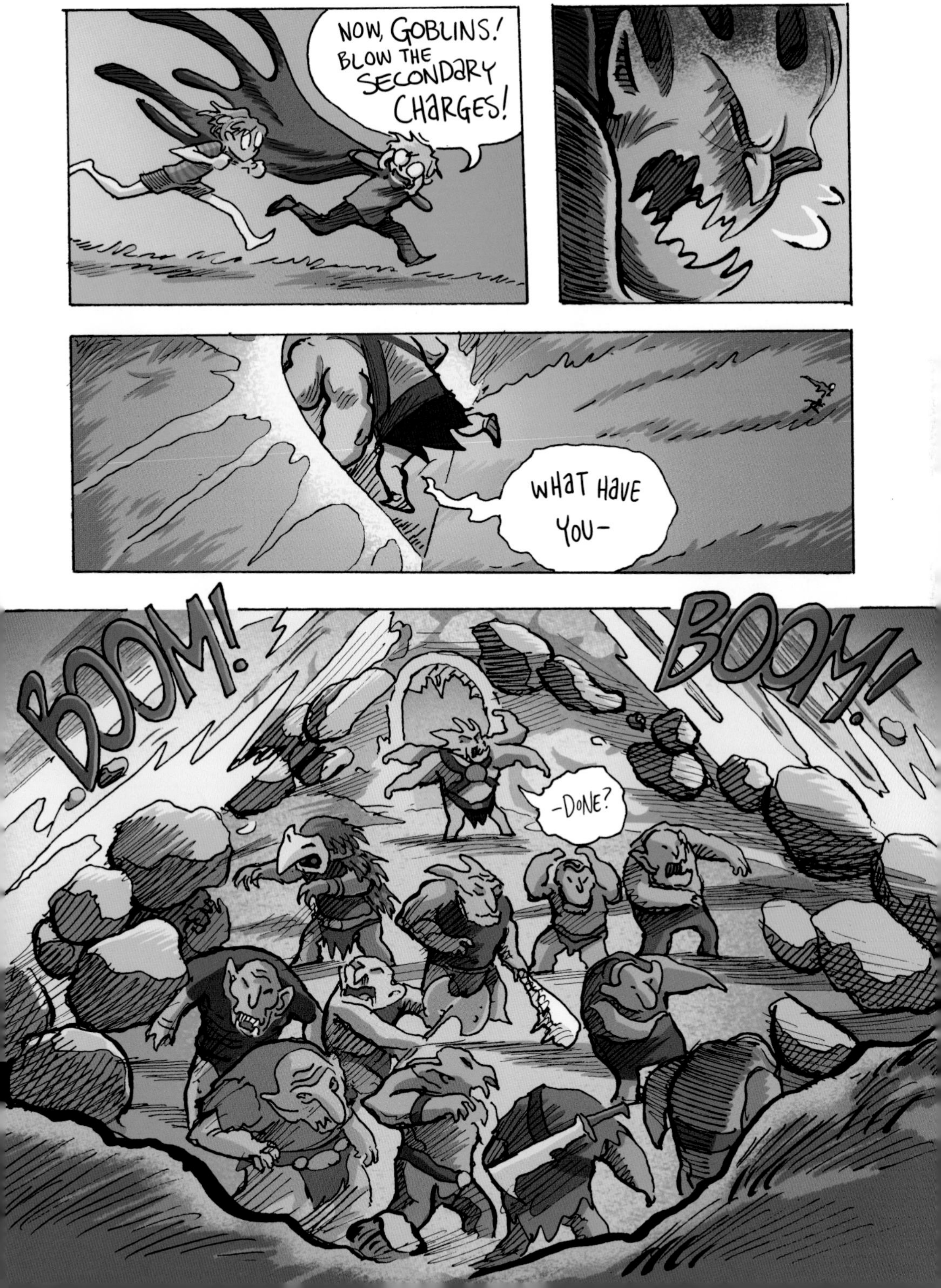
NOW, GOBLINS! BLOW THE SECONDARY CHARGES!
WHAT HAVE YOU-
BOOM!
BOOM!
-DONE?

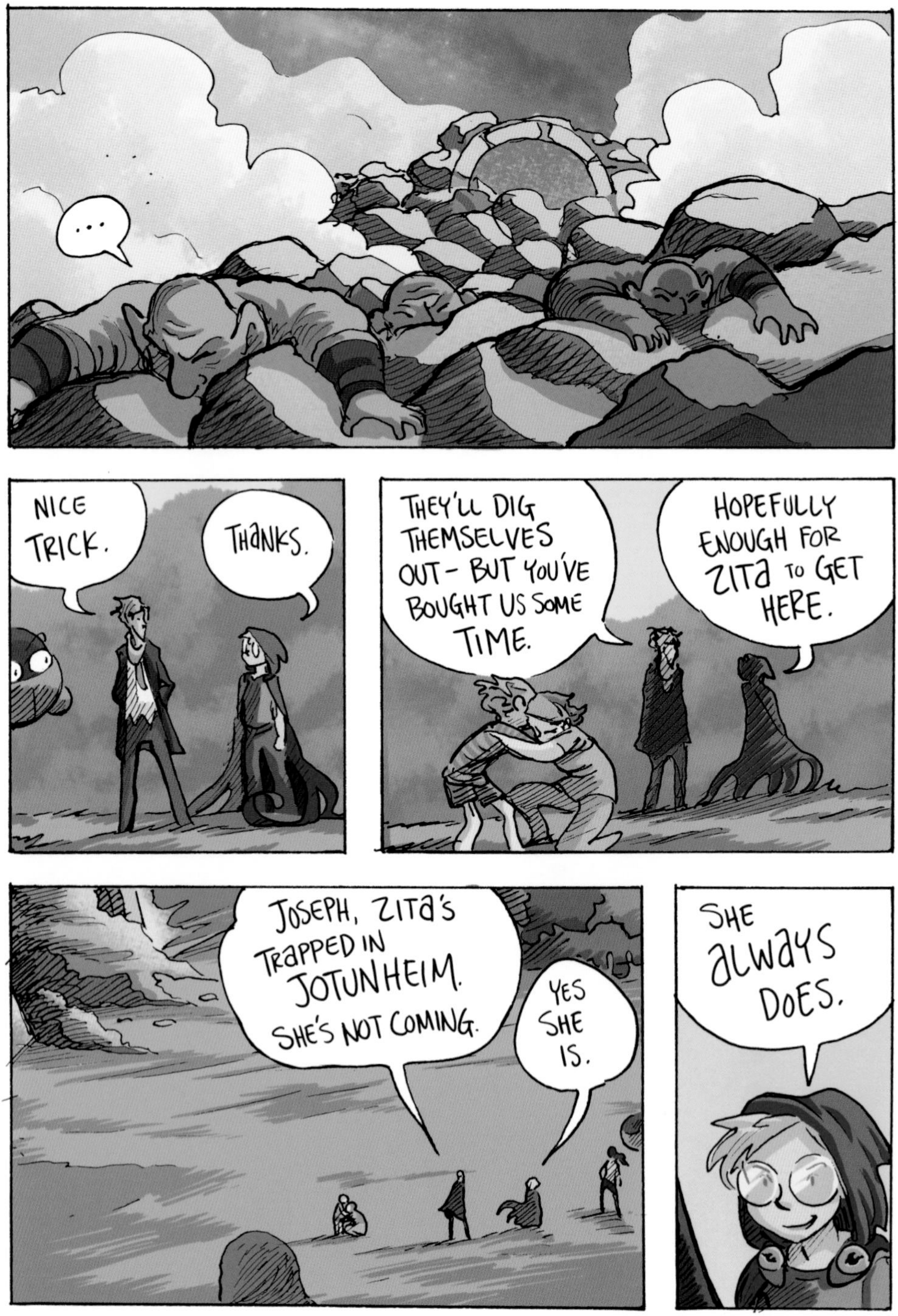
...
NICE TRICK.
THANKS.
THEY'LL DIG THEMSELVES OUT- BUT YOU'VE BOUGHT US SOME TIME.
HOPEFULLY ENOUGH FOR ZITA TO GET HERE.
JOSEPH, ZITA'S TRAPPED IN JOTUNHEIM. SHE'S NOT COMING.
YES SHE IS.
SHE ALWAYS DOES.

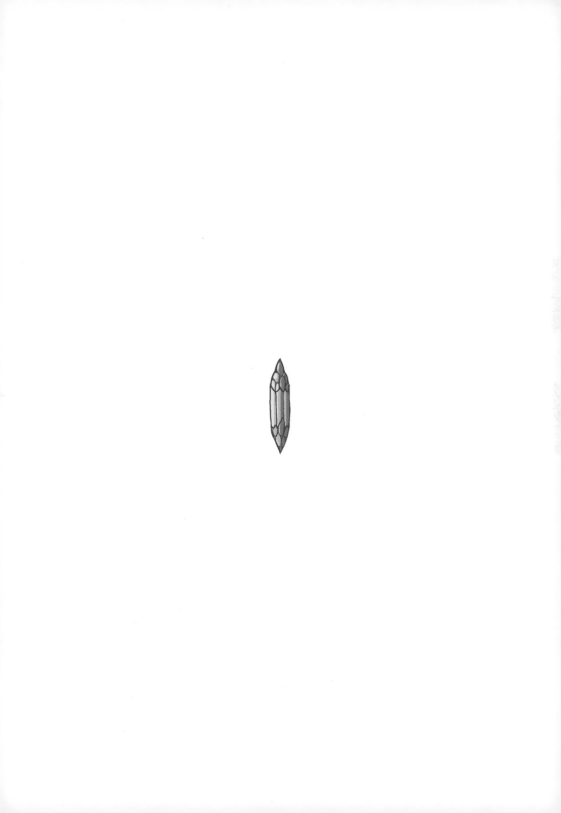

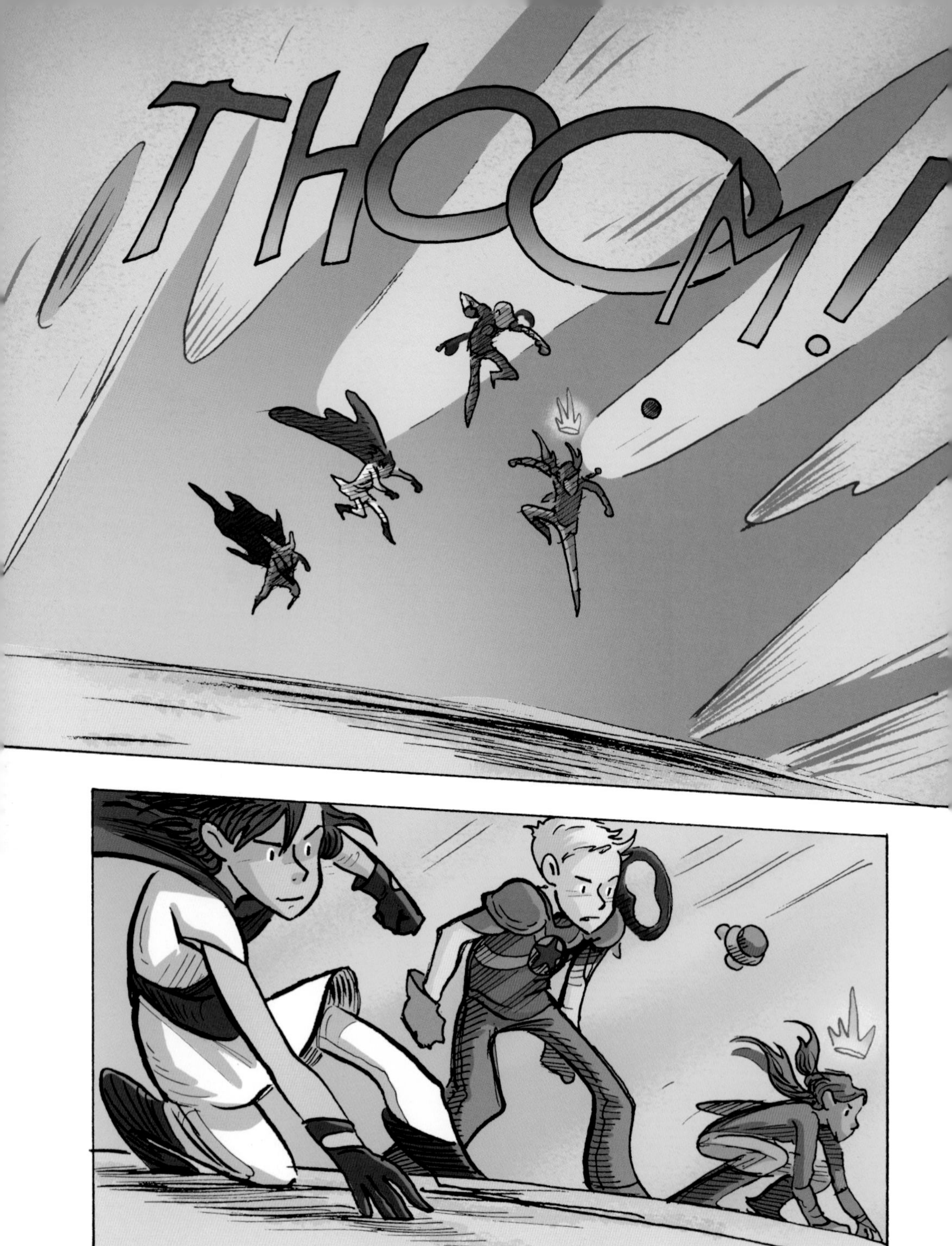
THOOM!

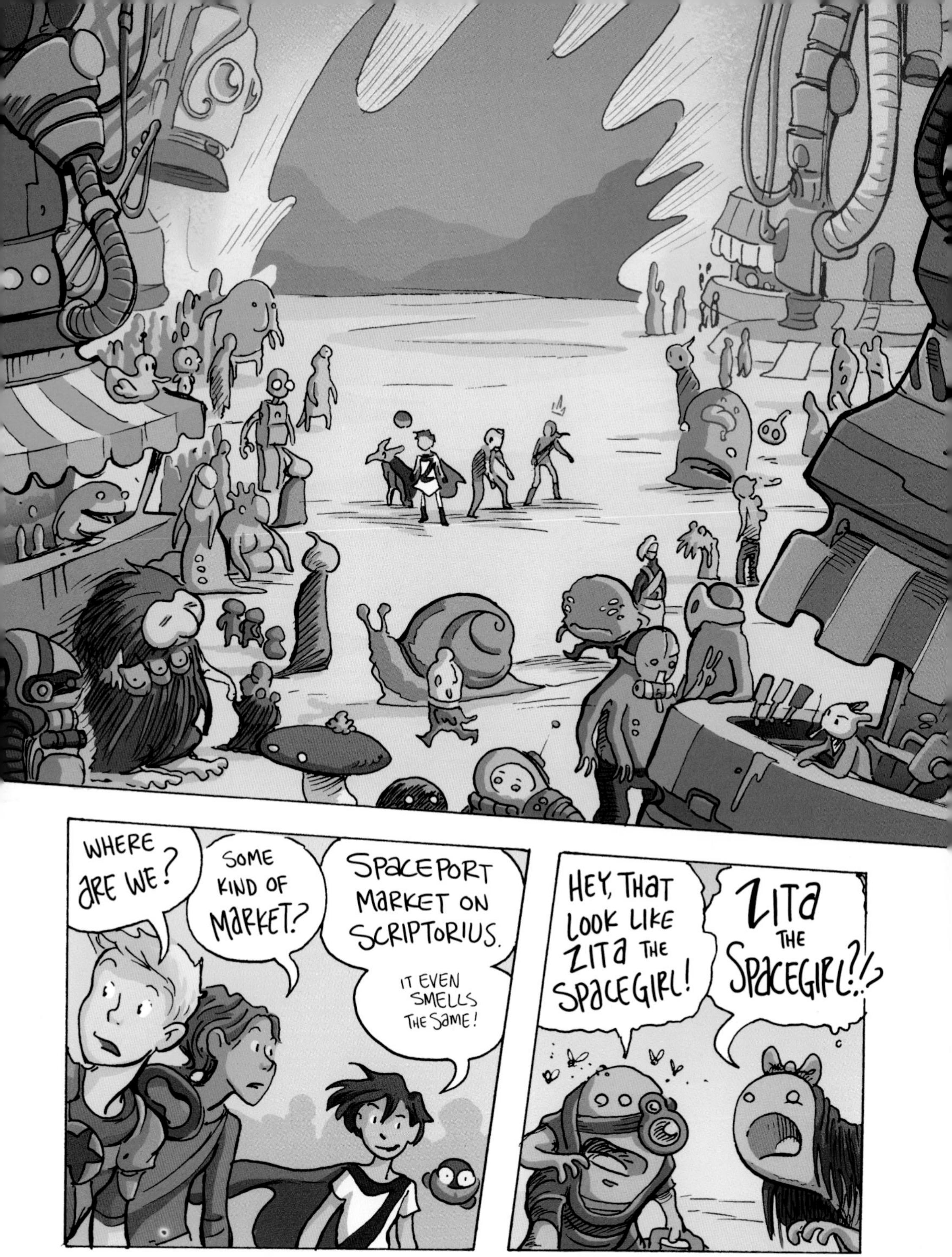
WHERE ARE WE?
SOME KIND OF MARKET?
SPACEPORT MARKET ON SCRIPTORIUS.
IT EVEN SMELLS THE SAME!
HEY, THAT LOOK LIKE ZITA THE SPACEGIRL!
ZITA THE SPACEGIRL?!!?

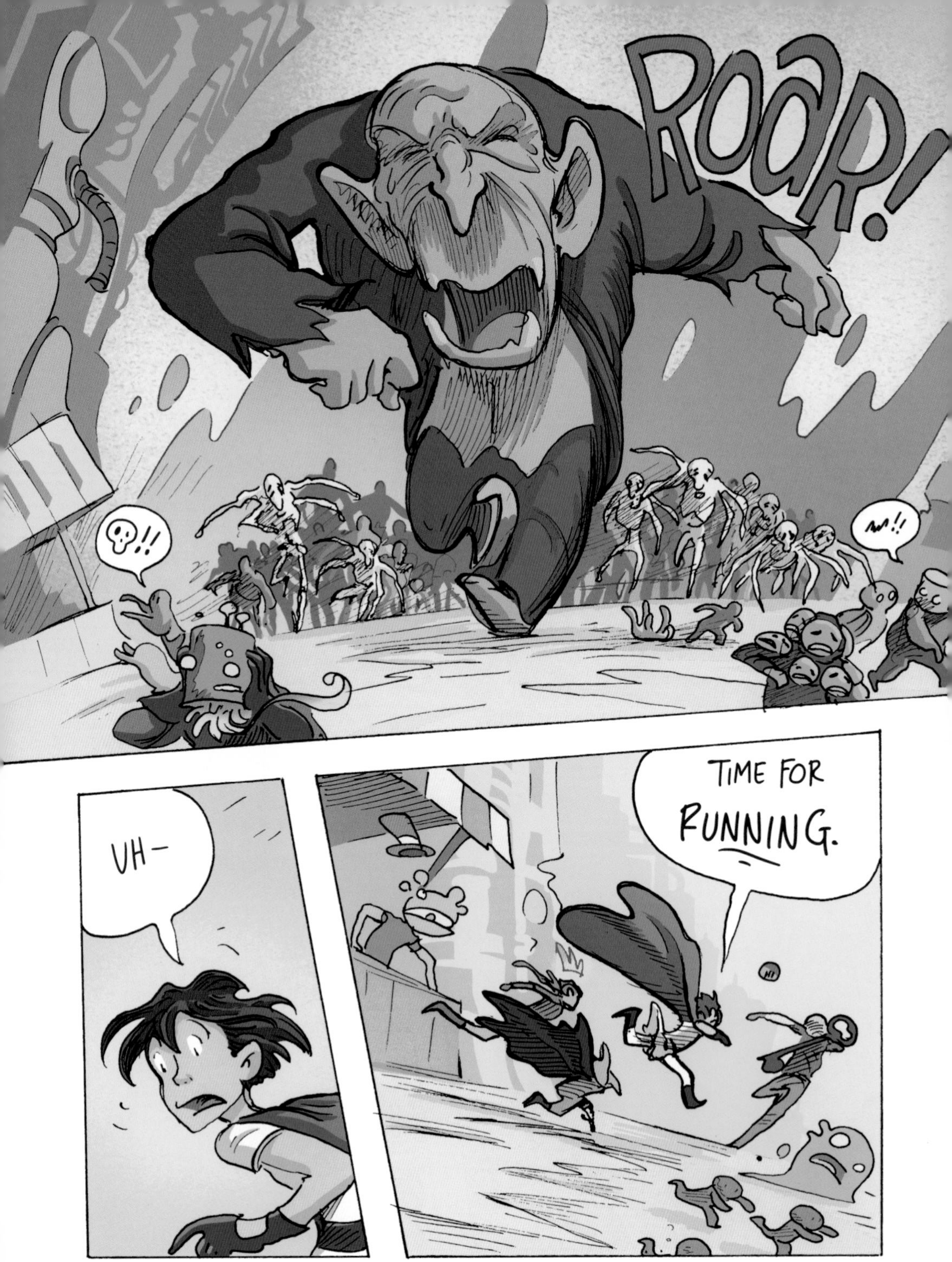
ROAR!
UH-
TIME FOR RUNNING.

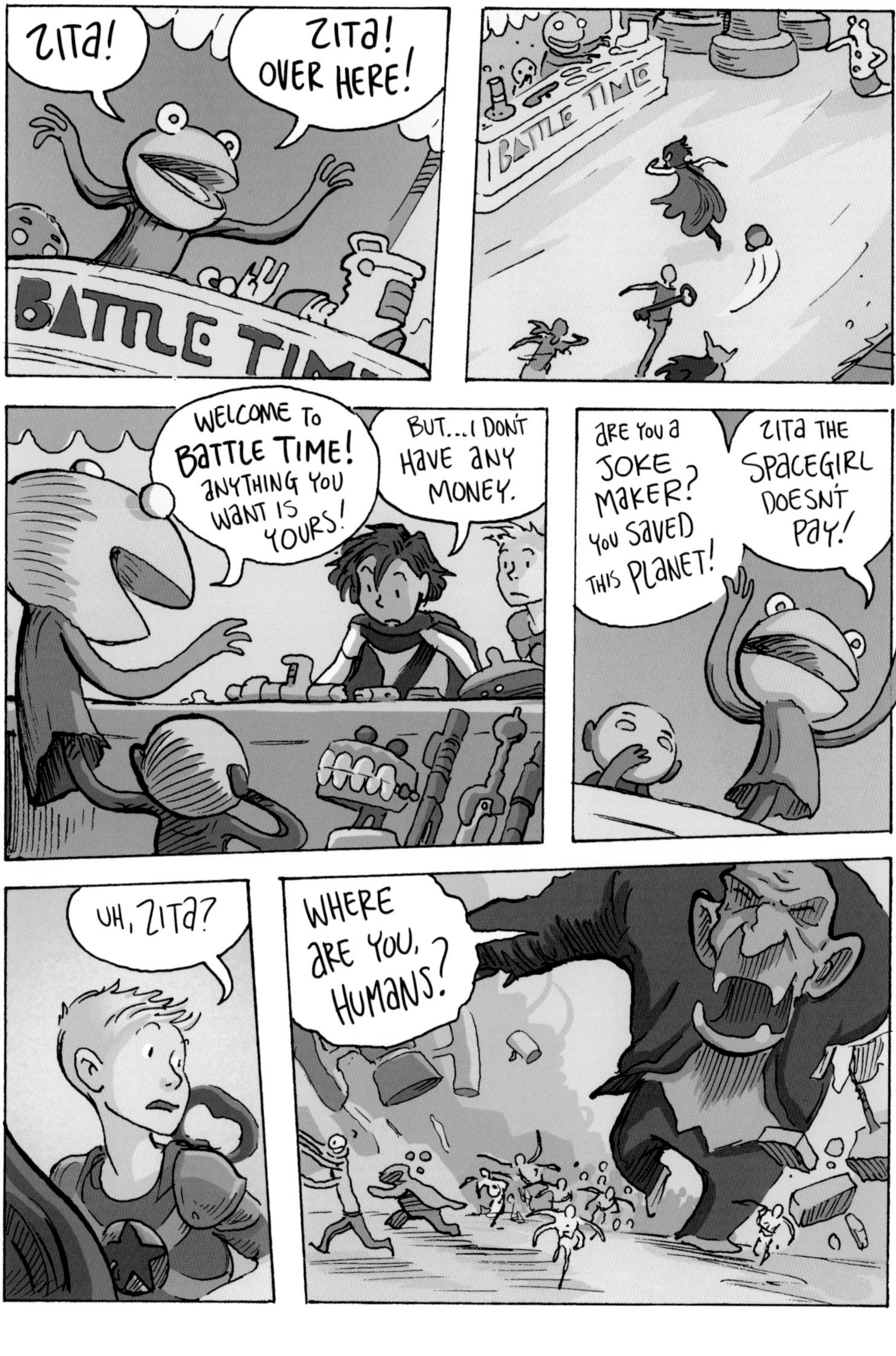
ZITA!
ZITA! OVER HERE!
BATTLE TIME
BATTLE TIME
WELCOME TO BATTLE TIME! ANYTHING YOU WANT IS YOURS!
BUT... I DON'T HAVE ANY MONEY.
ARE YOU A JOKE MAKER? YOU SAVED THIS PLANET!
ZITA THE SPACEGIRL DOESN'T PAY!
UH, ZITA?
WHERE ARE YOU, HUMANS?

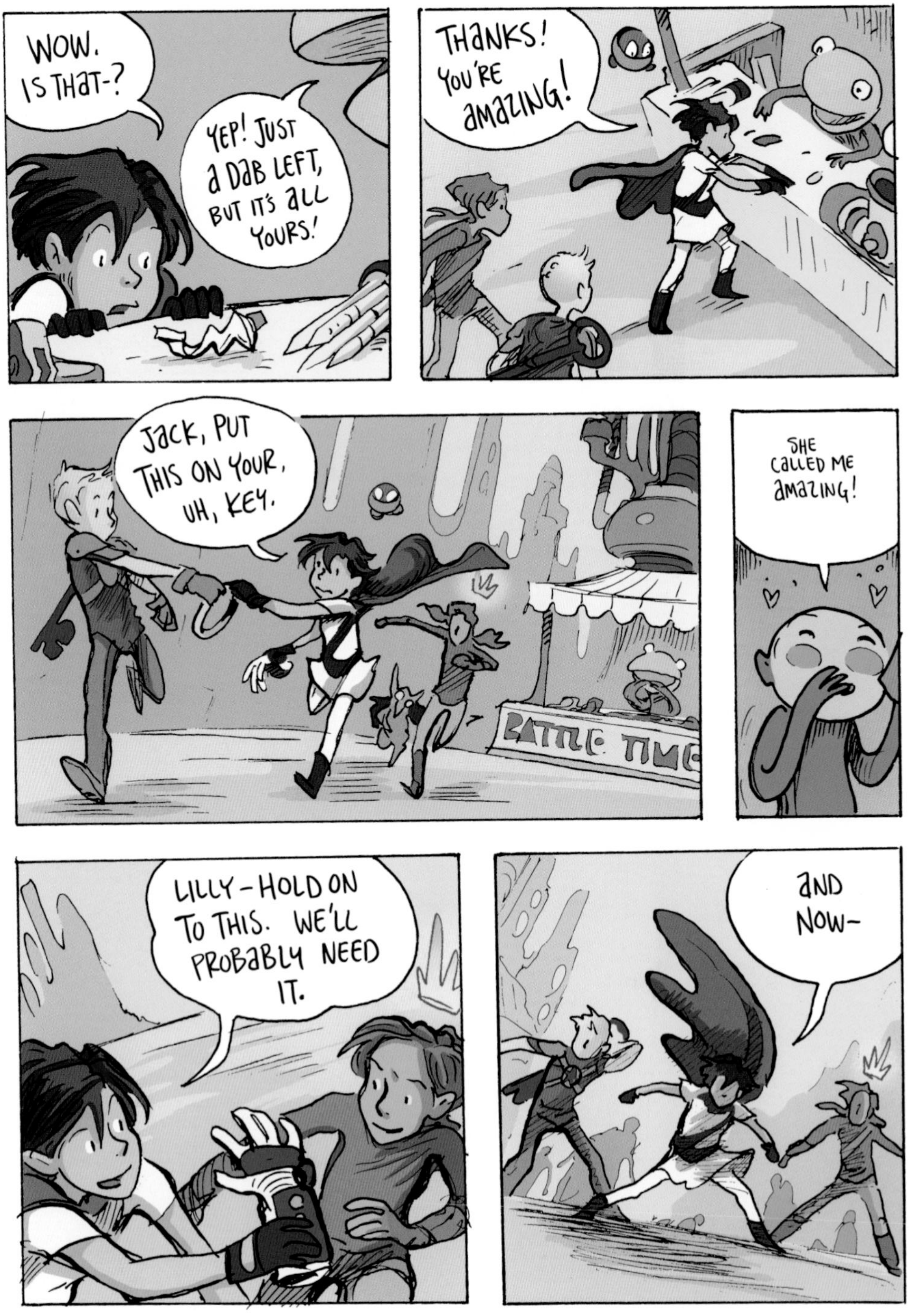
WOW. IS THAT-?
YEP! JUST A DAB LEFT, BUT IT'S ALL YOURS!
THANKS! YOU'RE AMAZING!
JACK, PUT THIS ON YOUR, UH, KEY.
BATTLE TIME
SHE CALLED ME AMAZING!
LILLY-HOLD ON TO THIS. WE'LL PROBABLY NEED IT.
AND NOW-

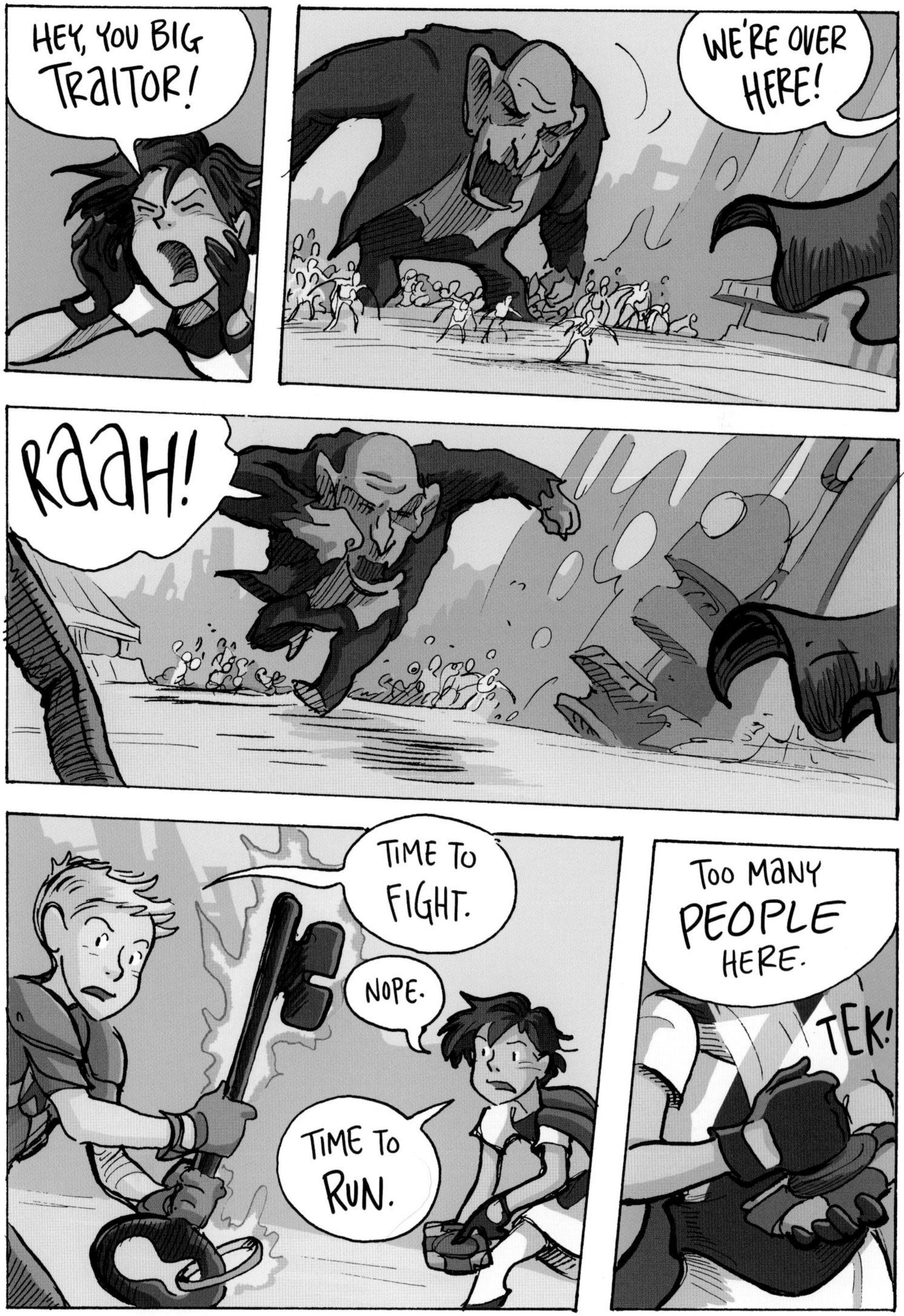
HEY, YOU BIG TRAITOR!
WE'RE OVER HERE!
RAAH!
TIME TO FIGHT.
NOPE.
TIME TO RUN.
TOO MANY PEOPLE HERE.
TEK!

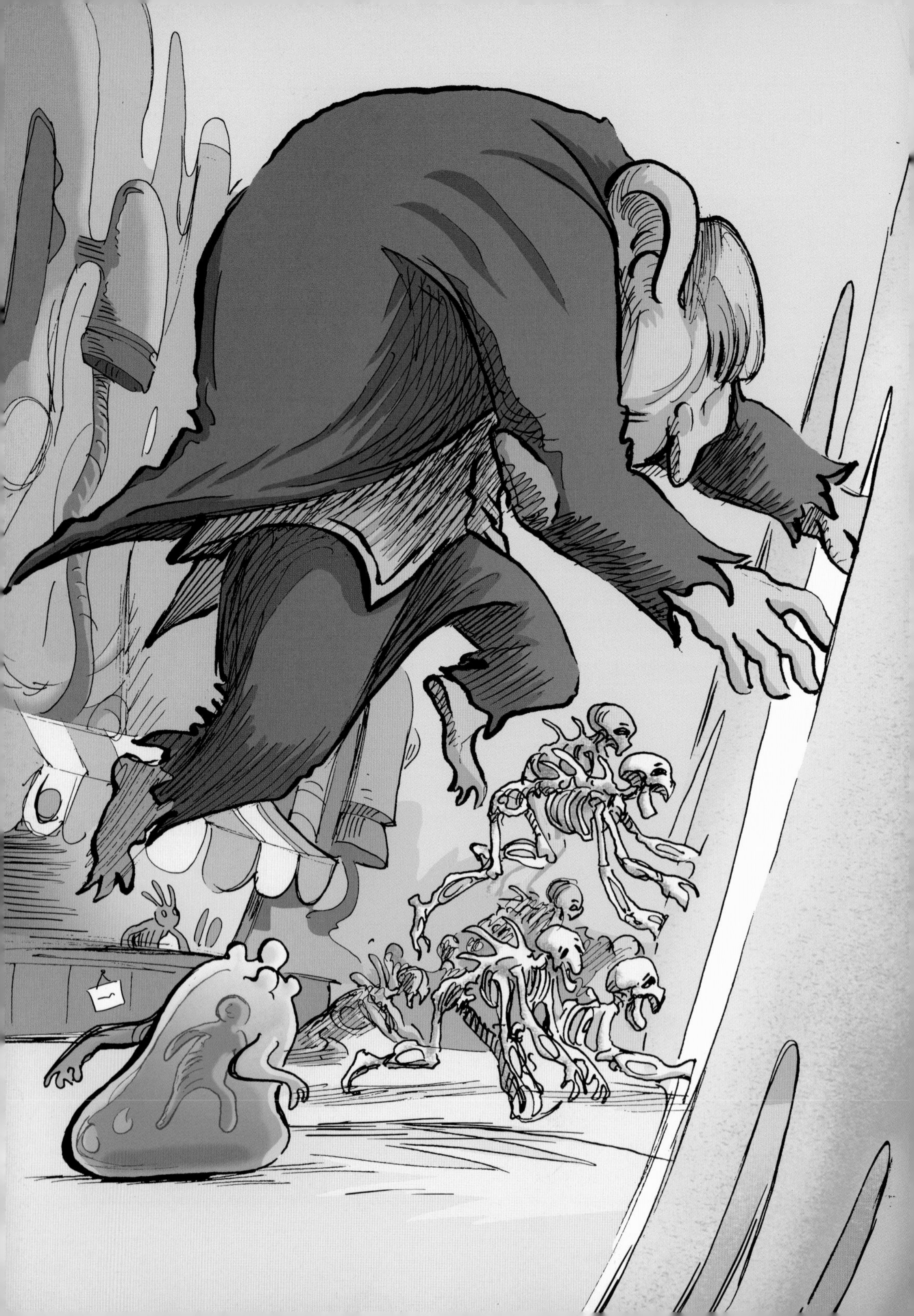

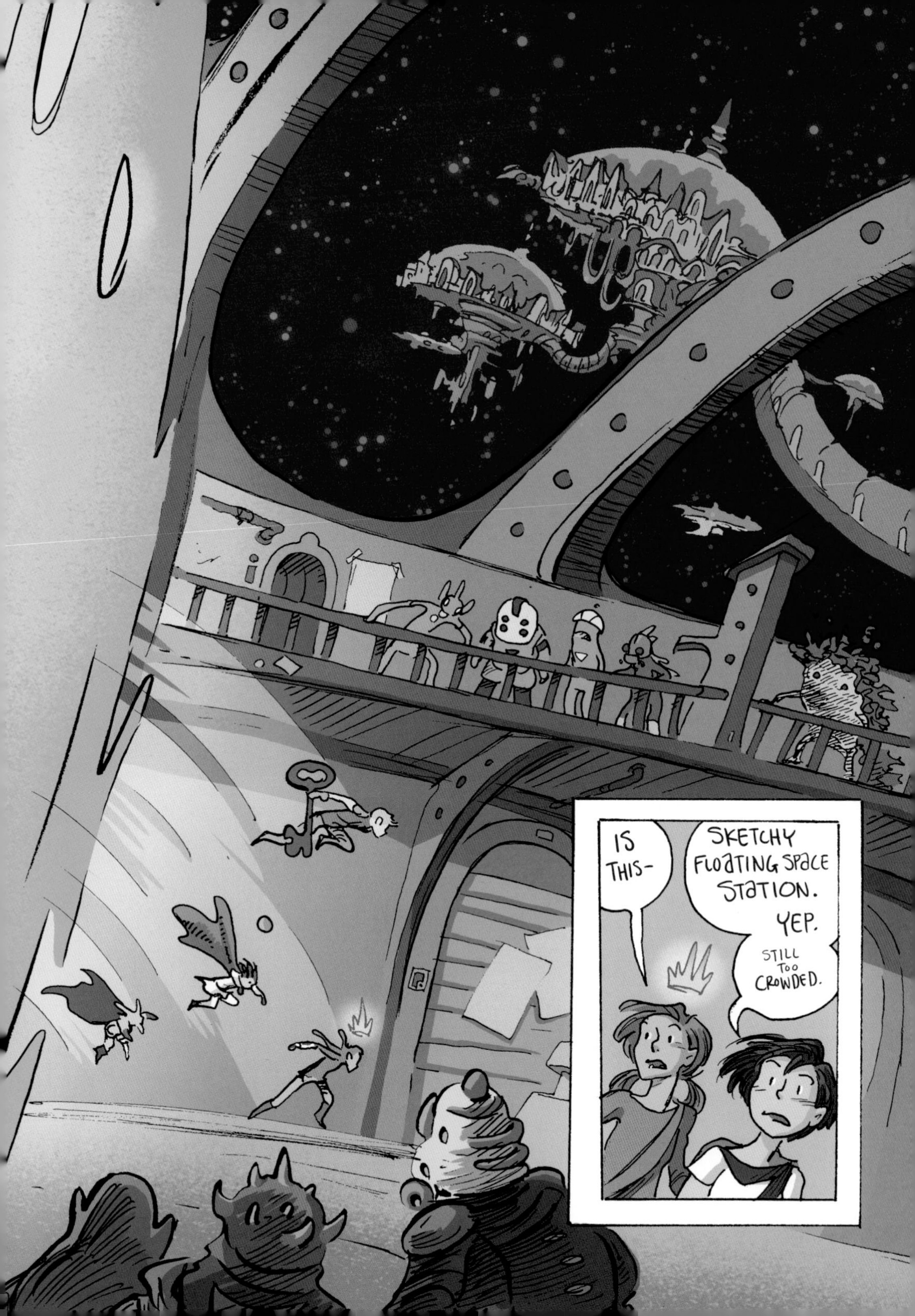
IS THIS-
SKETCHY FLOATING SPACE STATION.
YEP.
STILL TOO CROWDED.

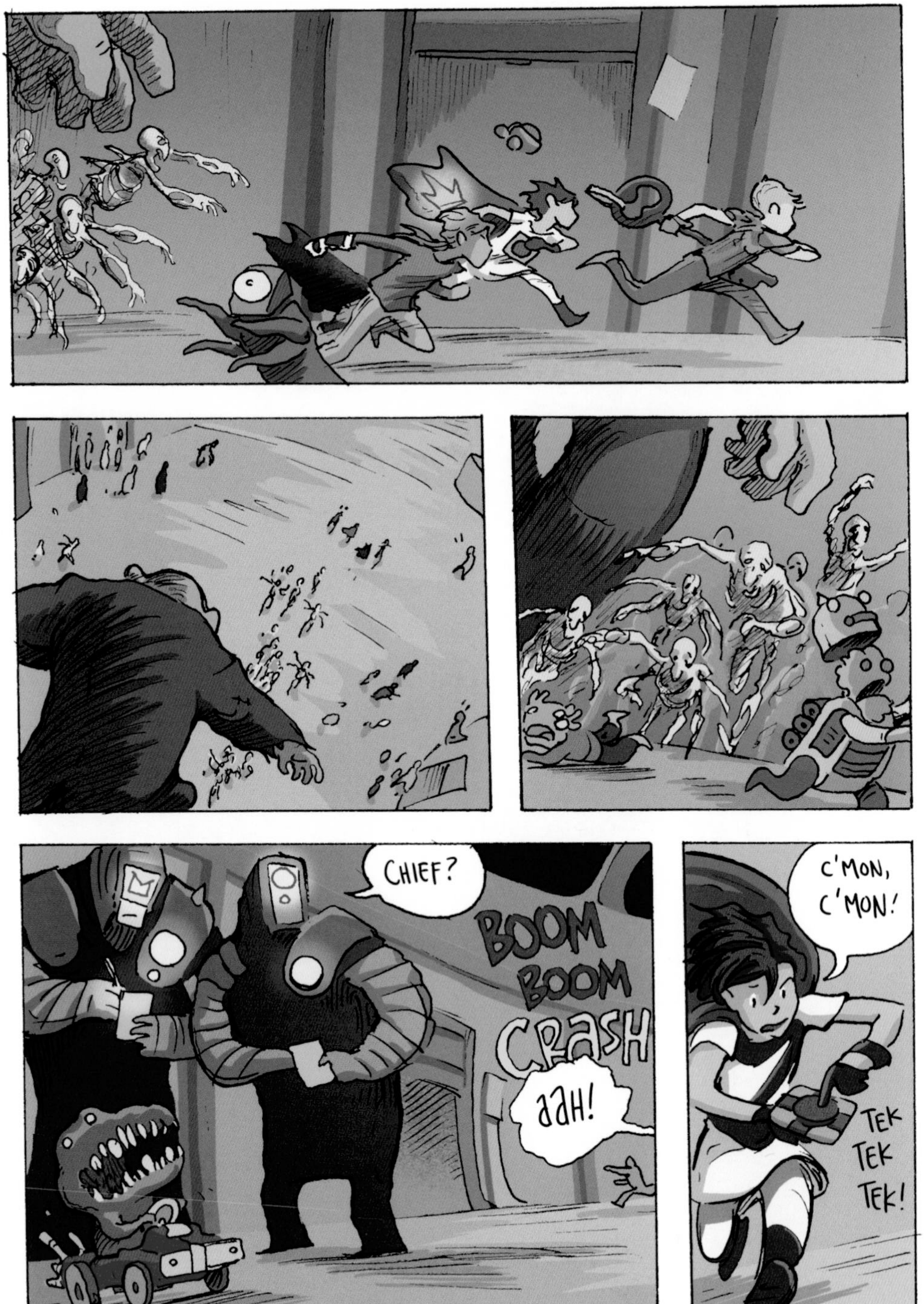
CHIEF?
BOOM BOOM CRASH
aah!
C'MON, C'MON!
TEK TEK TEK!

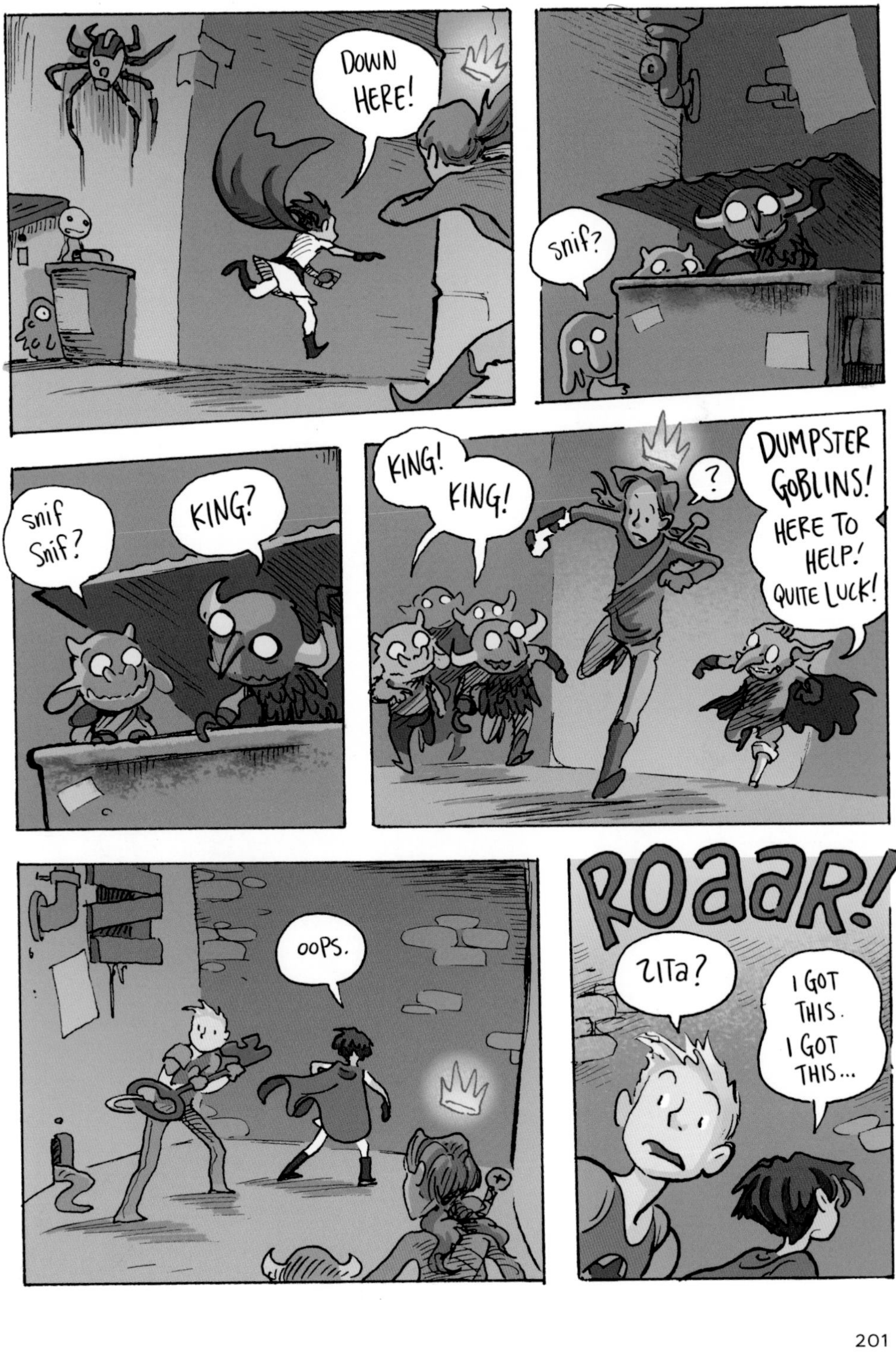

DOWN HERE!
snif?
snif Snif?
KING?
KING! KING!
?
DUMPSTER GOBLINS! HERE TO HELP! QUITE LUCK!
OOPS.
ROAAR!
ZITA?
I GOT THIS. I GOT THIS...

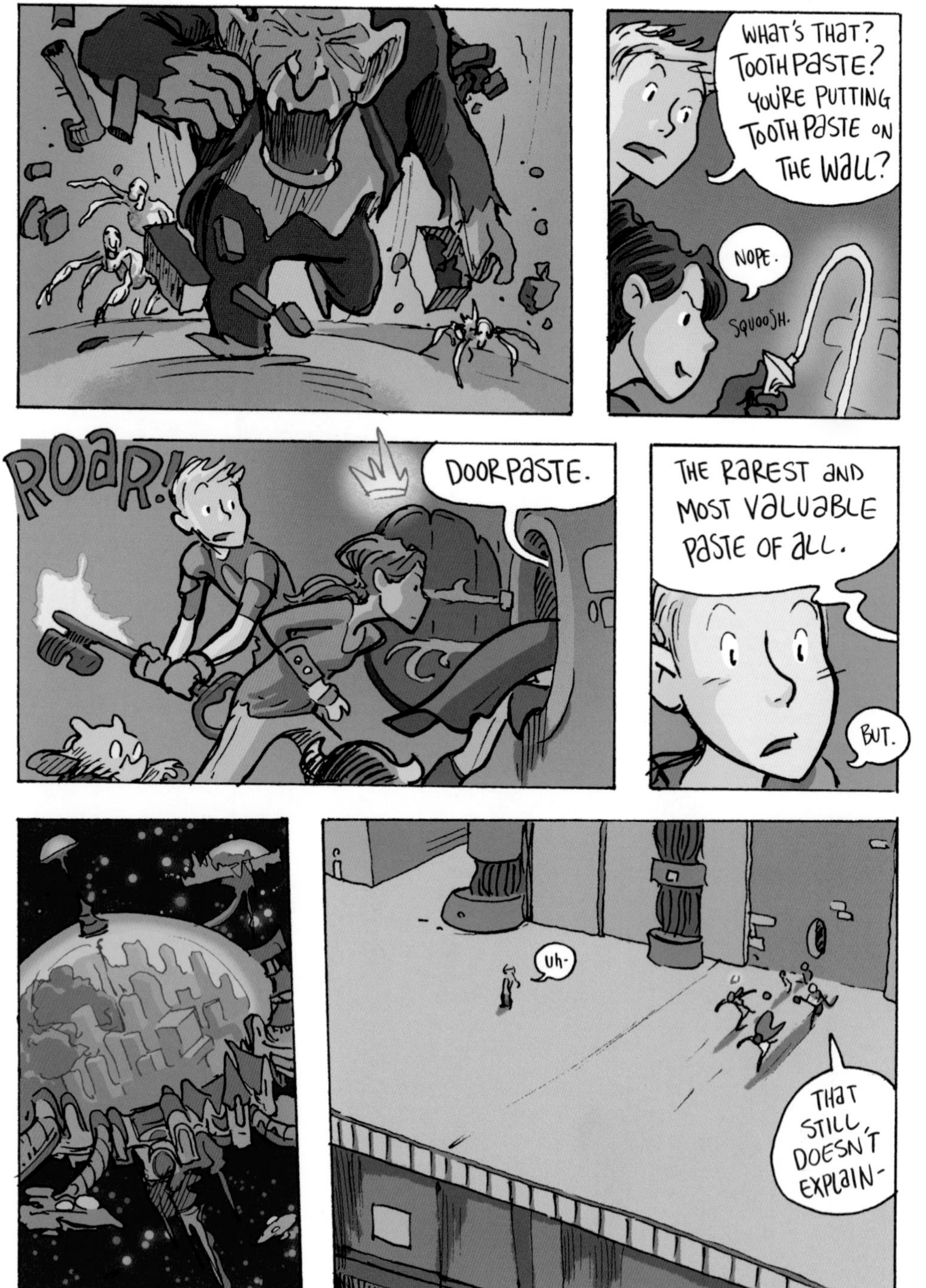
WHAT'S THAT? TOOTHPASTE? YOU'RE PUTTING TOOTHPASTE ON THE WALL?
NOPE.
SQUOOSH.
ROAR!
DOORPASTE.
THE RAREST AND MOST VALUABLE PASTE OF ALL.
BUT.
UH-
THAT STILL DOESN'T EXPLAIN-

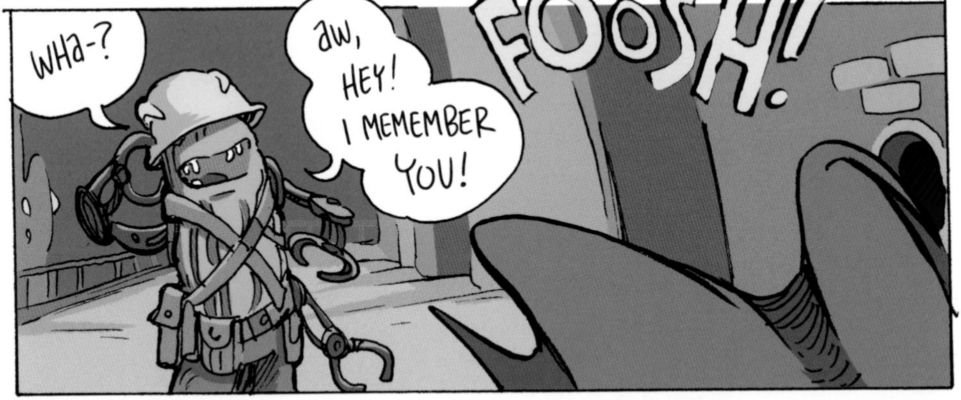
WHA-?
aw, HEY! I MEMEMBER YOU!
FOOSH!

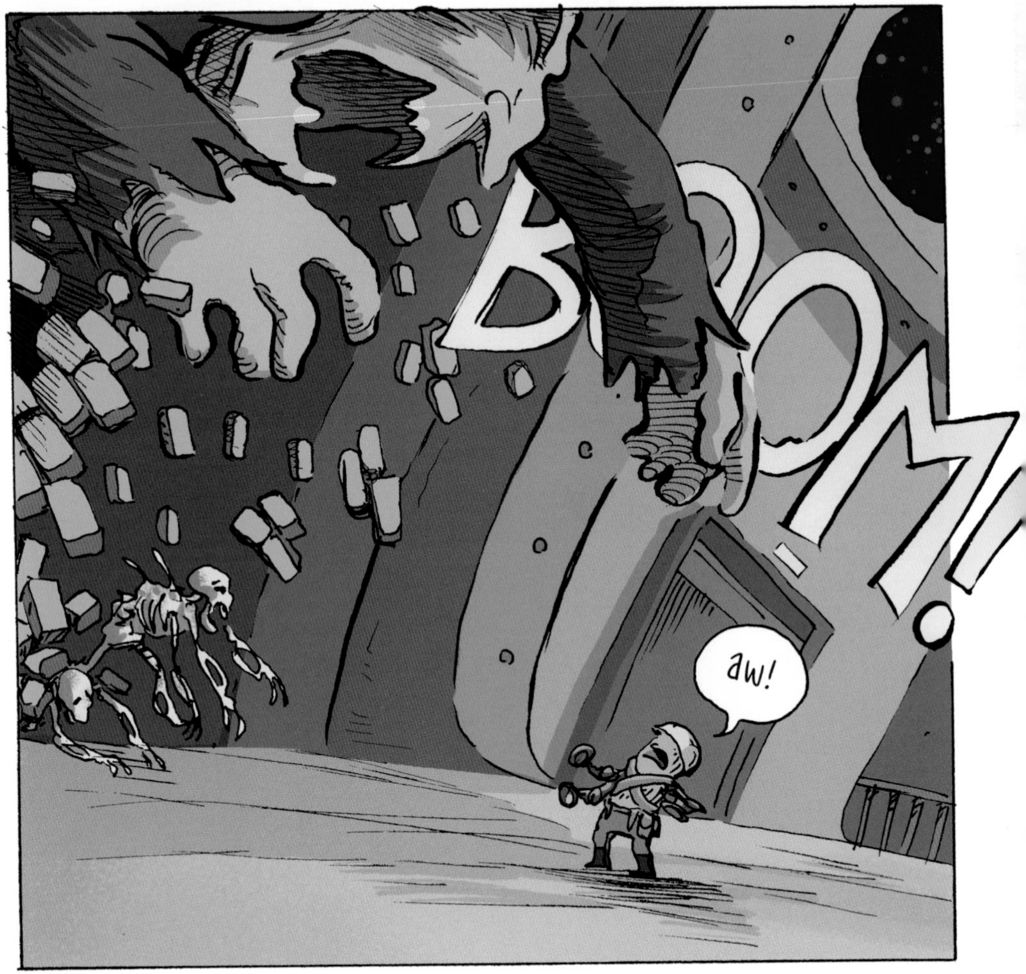
BOOM!!
aw!

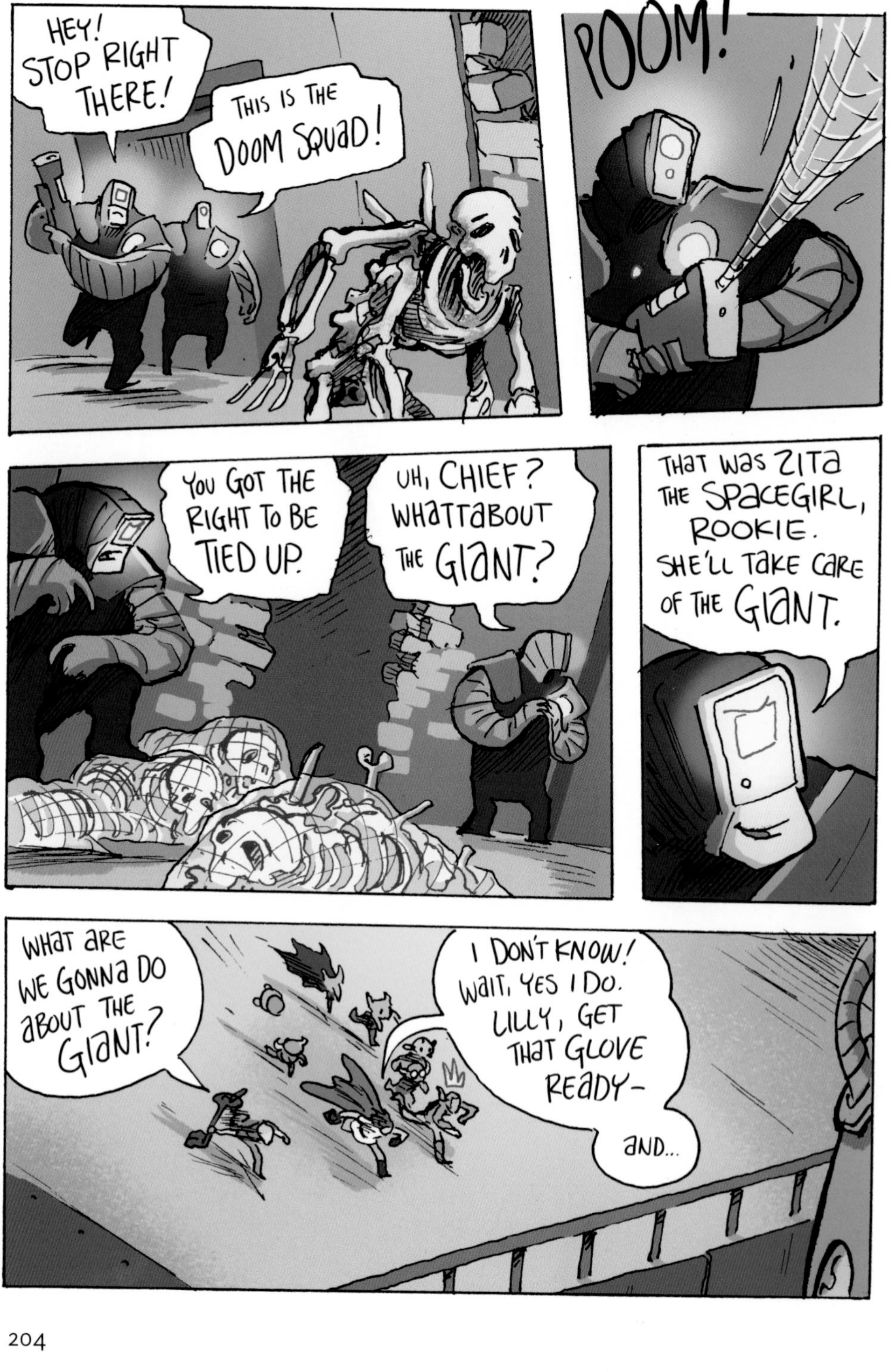
HEY! STOP RIGHT THERE!
THIS IS THE DOOM SQUAD!
POOM!
YOU GOT THE RIGHT TO BE TIED UP.
UH, CHIEF? WHATTABOUT THE GIANT?
THAT WAS ZITA THE SPACEGIRL, ROOKIE. SHE'LL TAKE CARE OF THE GIANT.
WHAT ARE WE GONNA DO ABOUT THE GIANT?
I DON'T KNOW! WAIT, YES I DO. LILLY, GET THAT GLOVE READY-
AND...

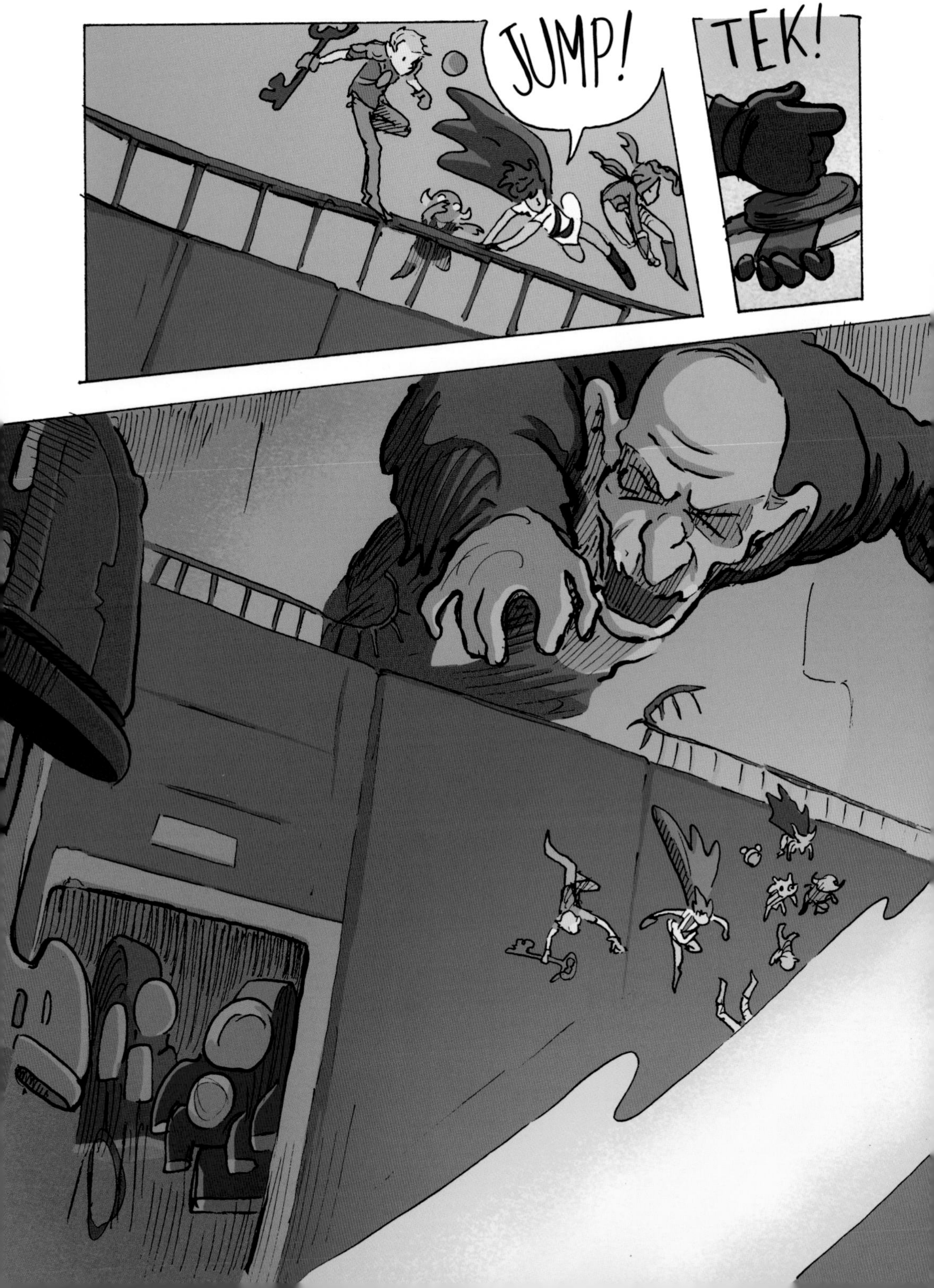

JUMP!
TEK!

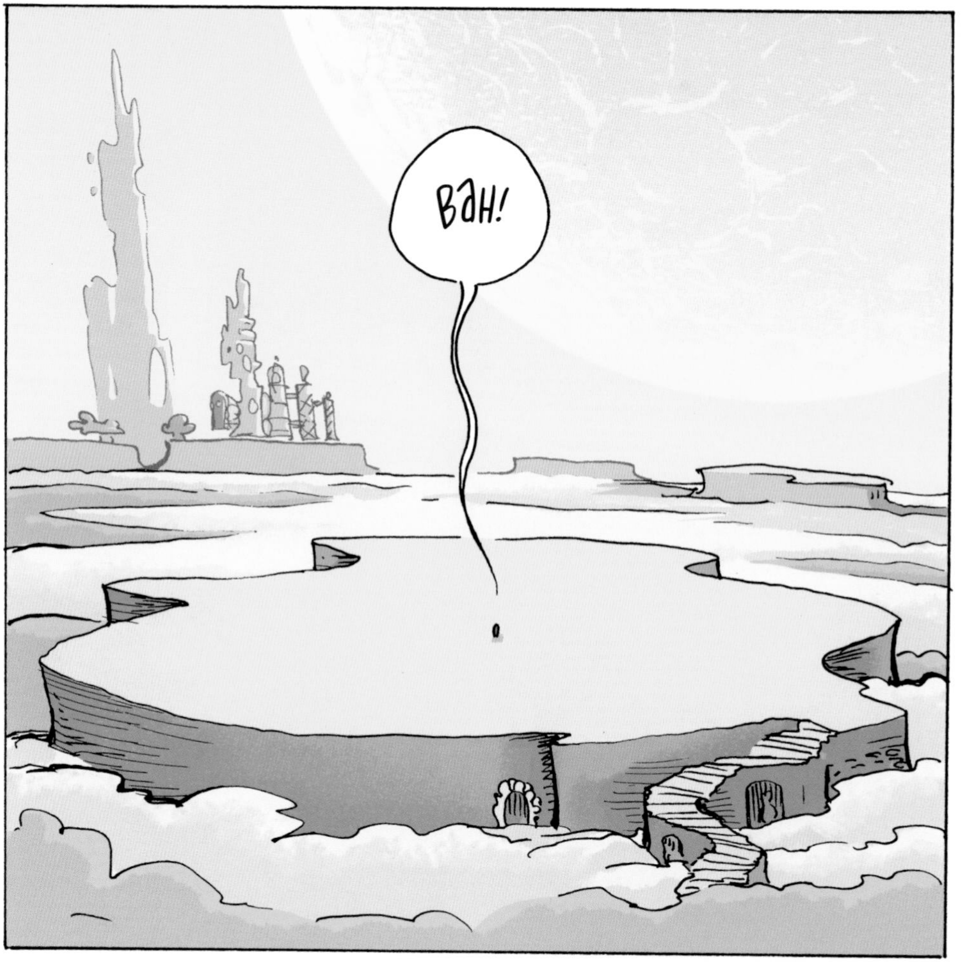
BAH!

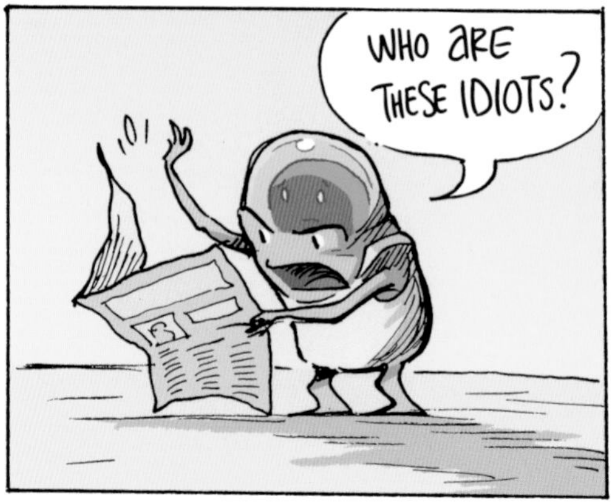
WHO ARE THESE IDIOTS?

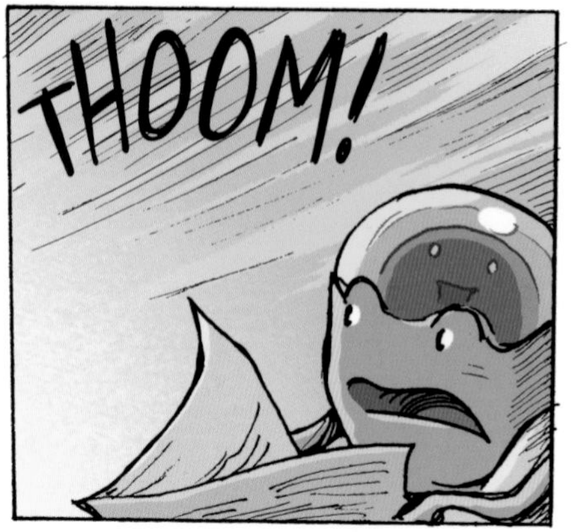
THOOM!

HEY!

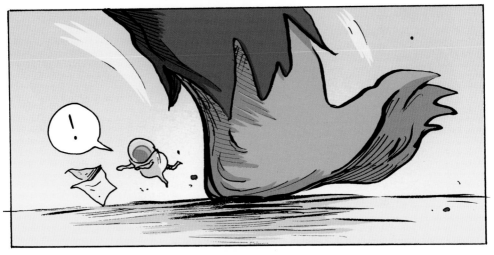

!

ADVENTURES! BAH!

WAIT FOR ME!

THOOM!

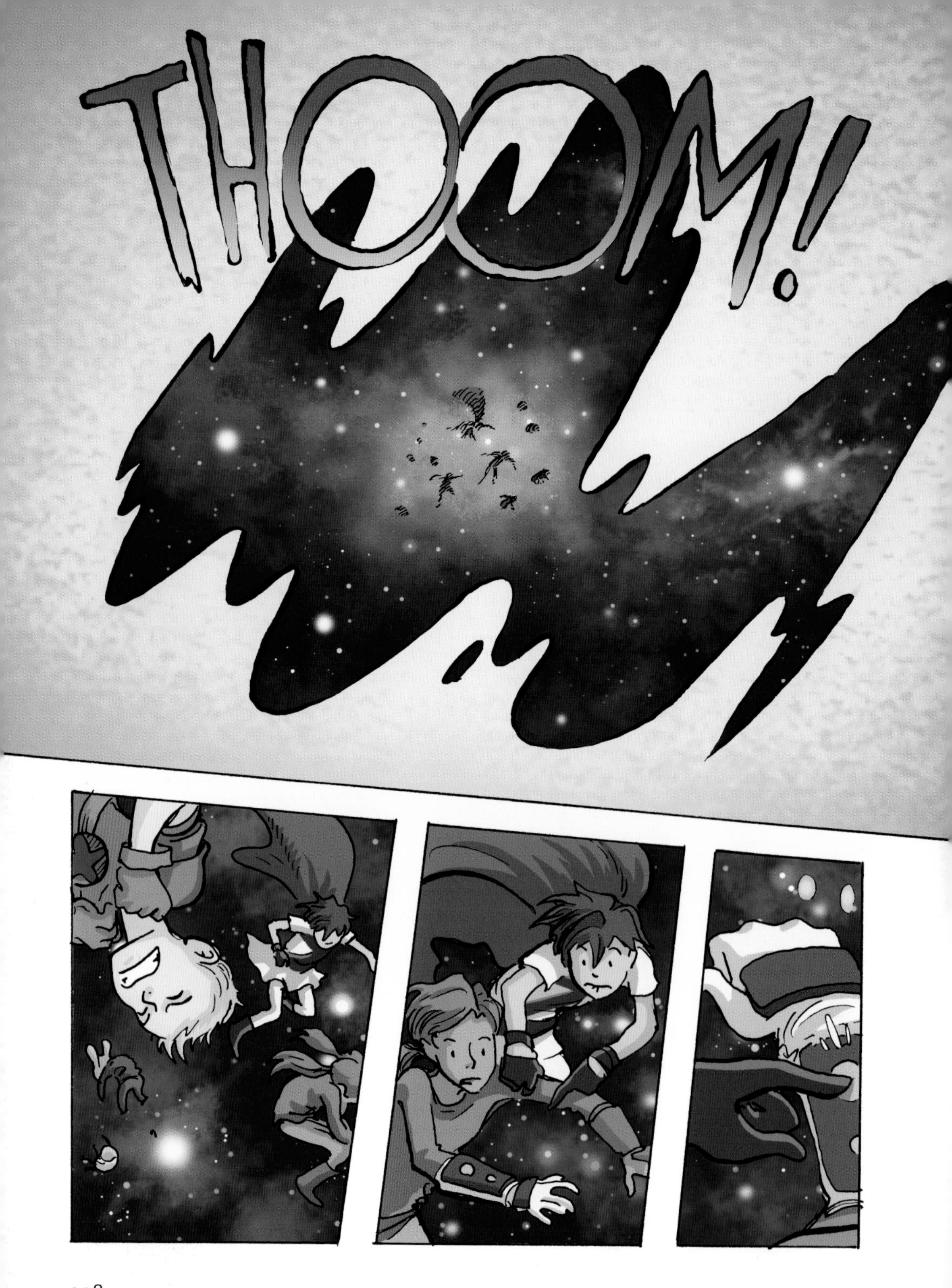
THOOM!

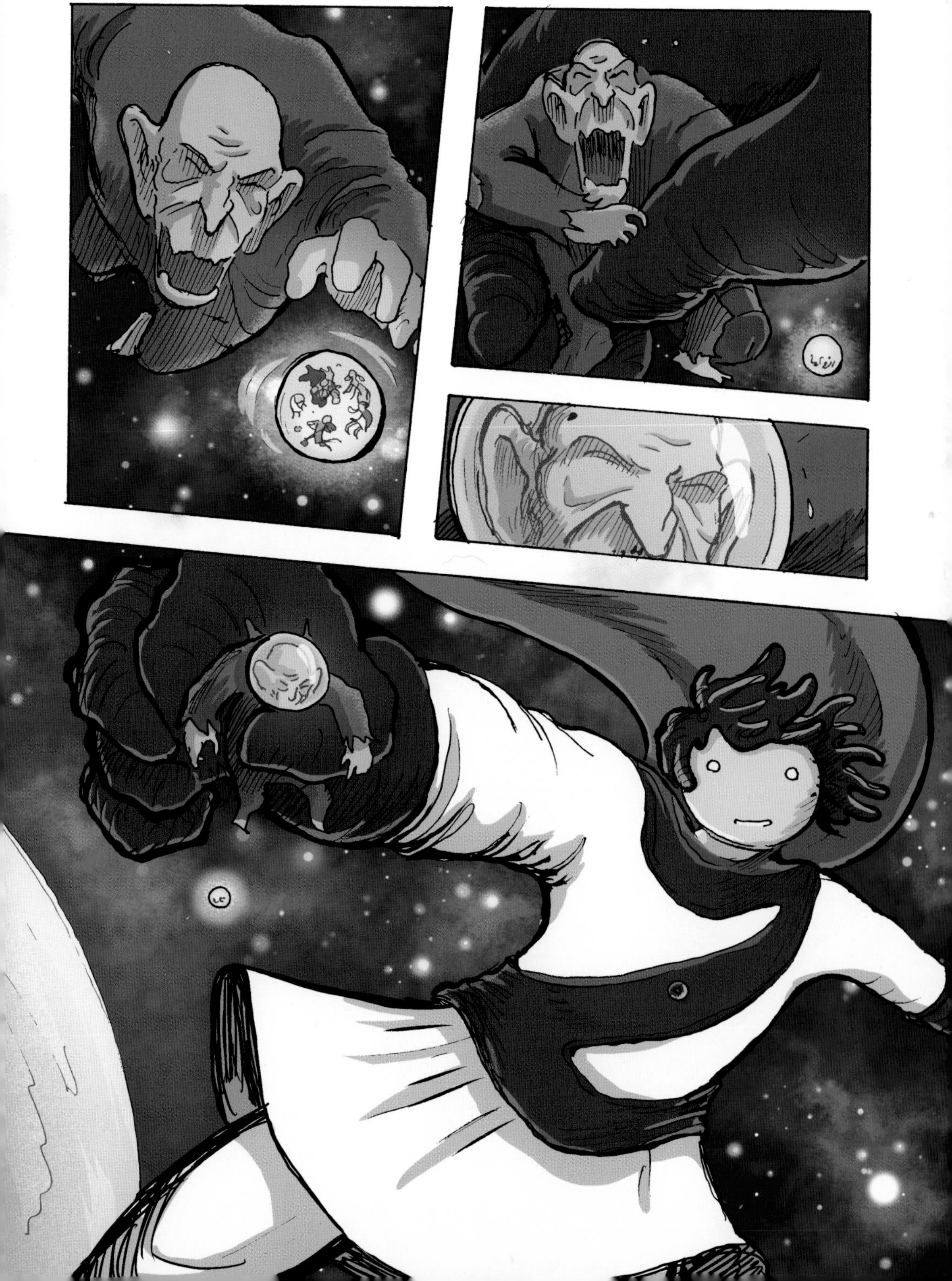

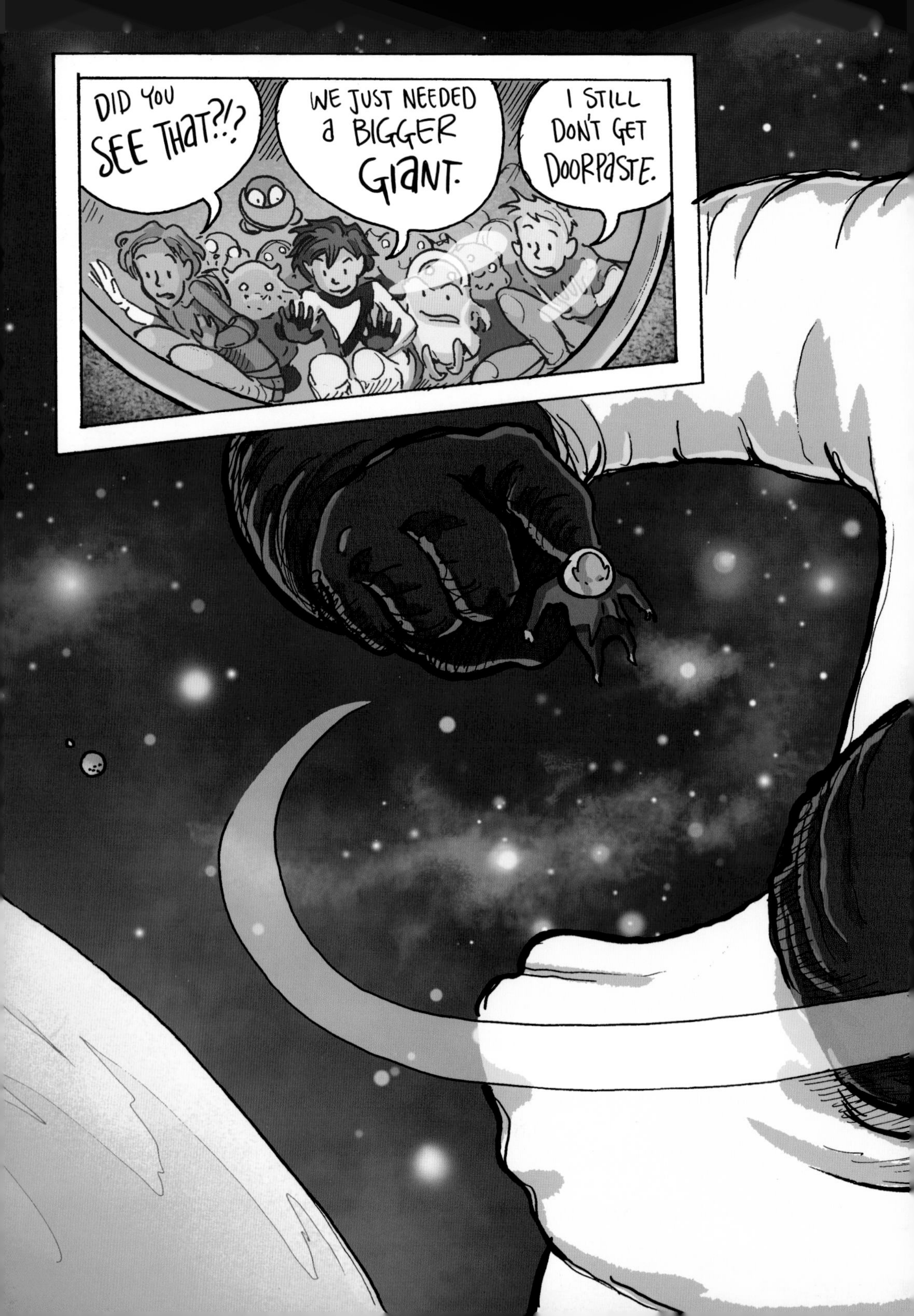
DID YOU SEE THAT?!?
WE JUST NEEDED a BIGGER GIANT.
I STILL DON'T GET DOORPASTE.

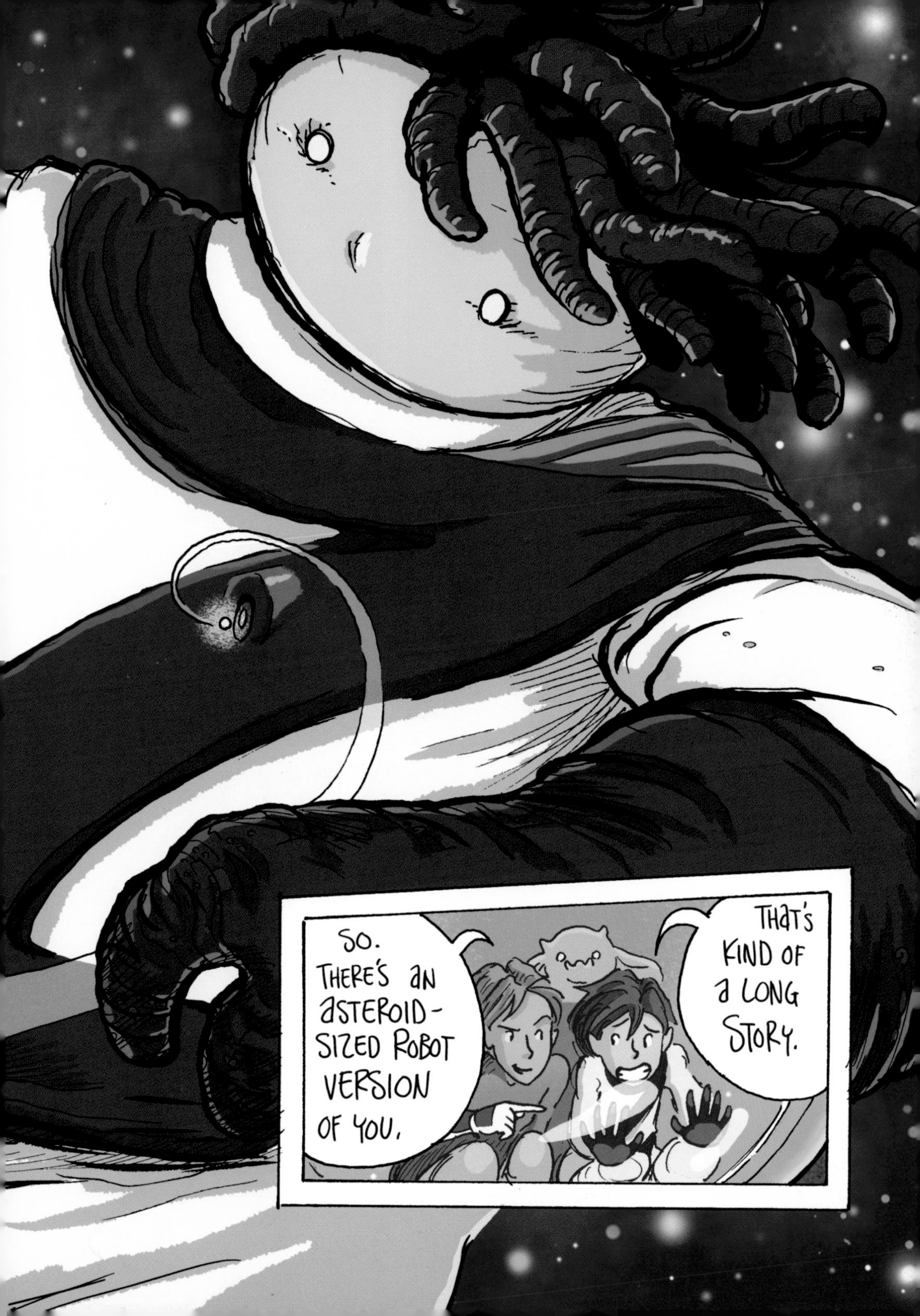
SO. THERE'S AN ASTEROID-SIZED ROBOT VERSION OF YOU.
THAT'S KIND OF A LONG STORY.

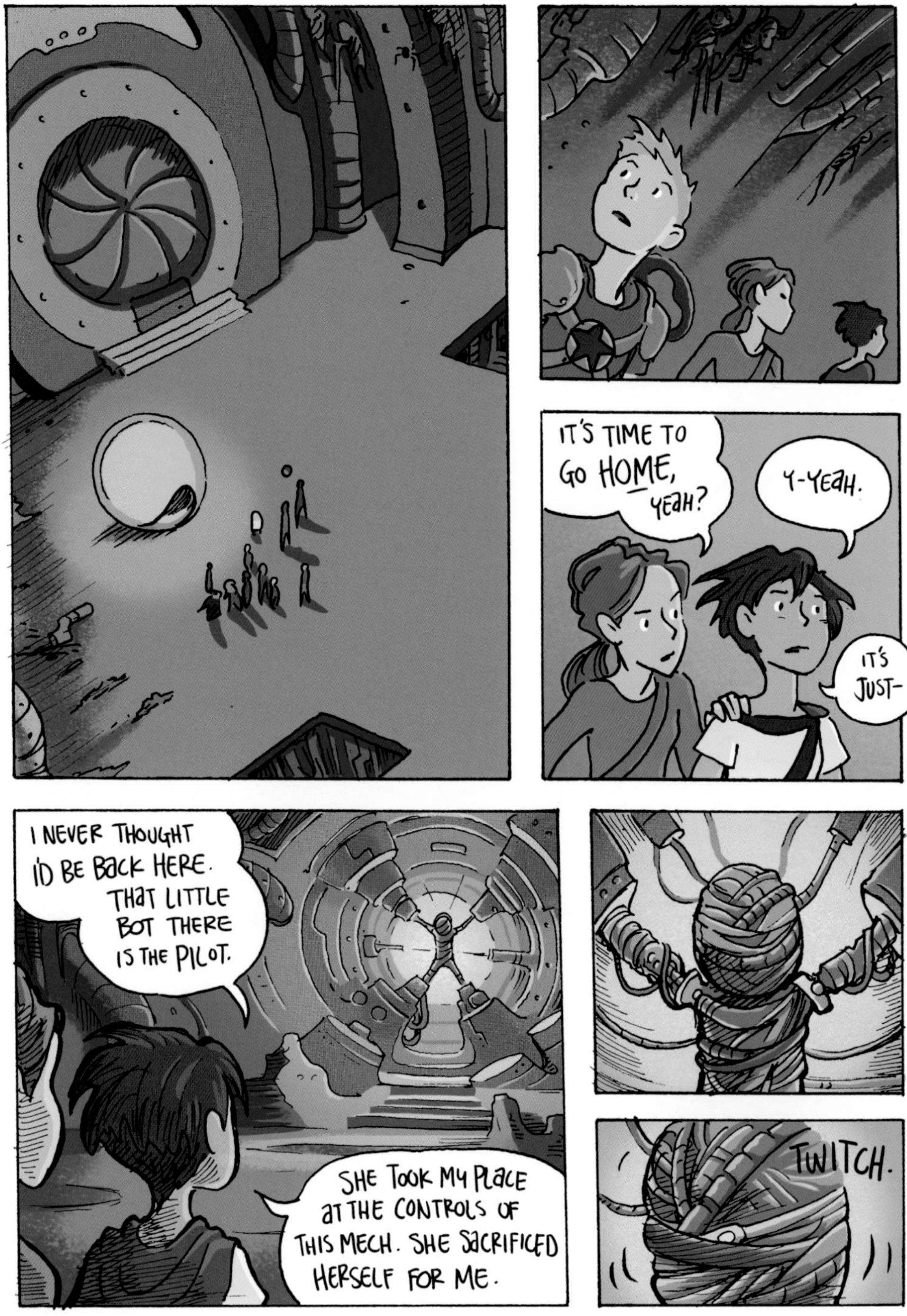
IT'S TIME TO GO HOME, YEAH?
Y-YEAH.
IT'S JUST-
I NEVER THOUGHT I'D BE BACK HERE. THAT LITTLE BOT THERE IS THE PILOT.
SHE TOOK MY PLACE AT THE CONTROLS OF THIS MECH. SHE SACRIFICED HERSELF FOR ME.
TWITCH.

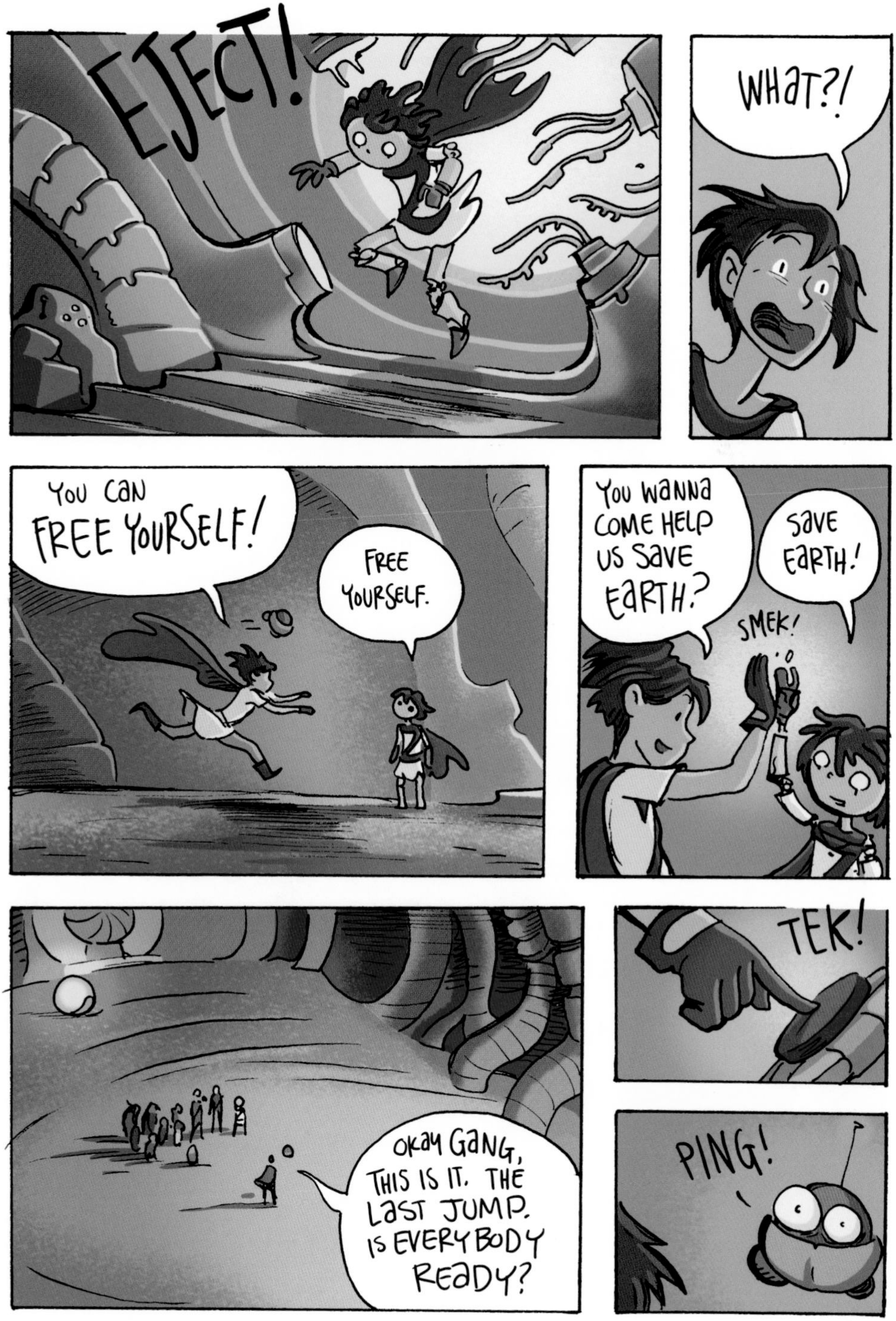
EJECT!
WHAT?!
YOU CAN FREE YOURSELF!
FREE YOURSELF.
YOU WANNA COME HELP US SAVE EARTH?
SAVE EARTH!
SMEK!
TEK!
OKAY GANG, THIS IS IT. THE LAST JUMP. IS EVERYBODY READY?
PING!

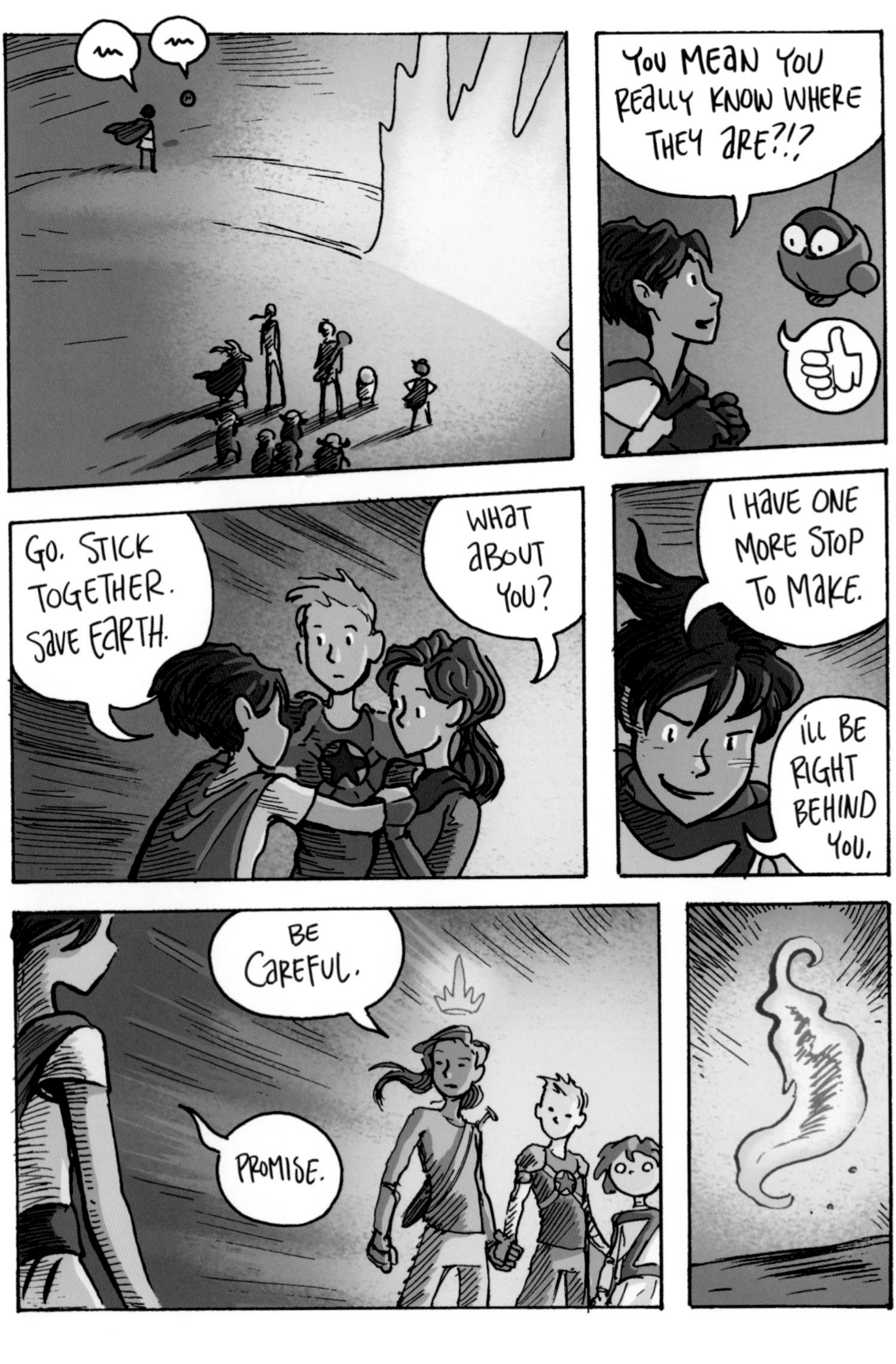
YOU MEAN YOU REALLY KNOW WHERE THEY ARE?!?
GO. STICK TOGETHER. SAVE EARTH.
WHAT ABOUT YOU?
I HAVE ONE MORE STOP TO MAKE.
I'LL BE RIGHT BEHIND YOU.
BE CAREFUL.
PROMISE.

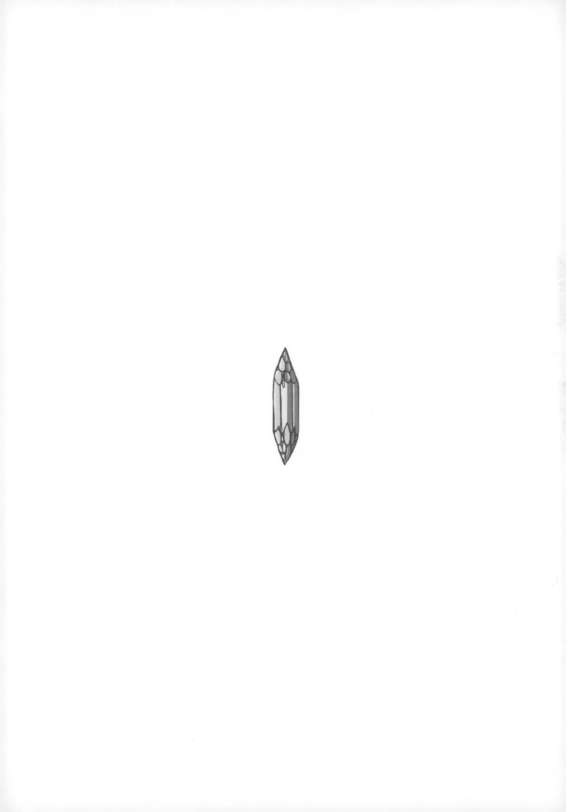

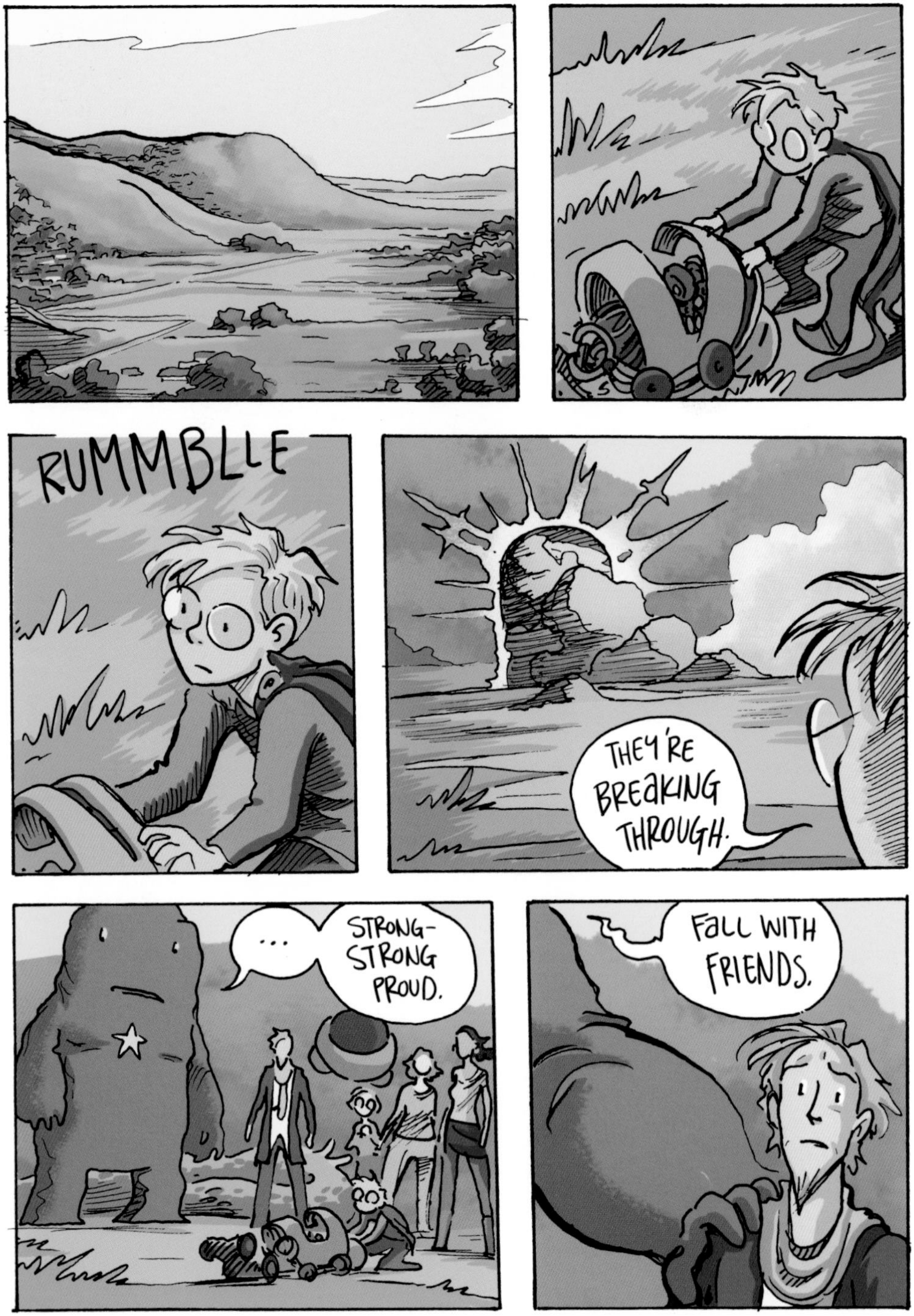
RUMMBLLE
THEY'RE BREAKING THROUGH.
...
STRONG-STRONG PROUD.
FALL WITH FRIENDS.

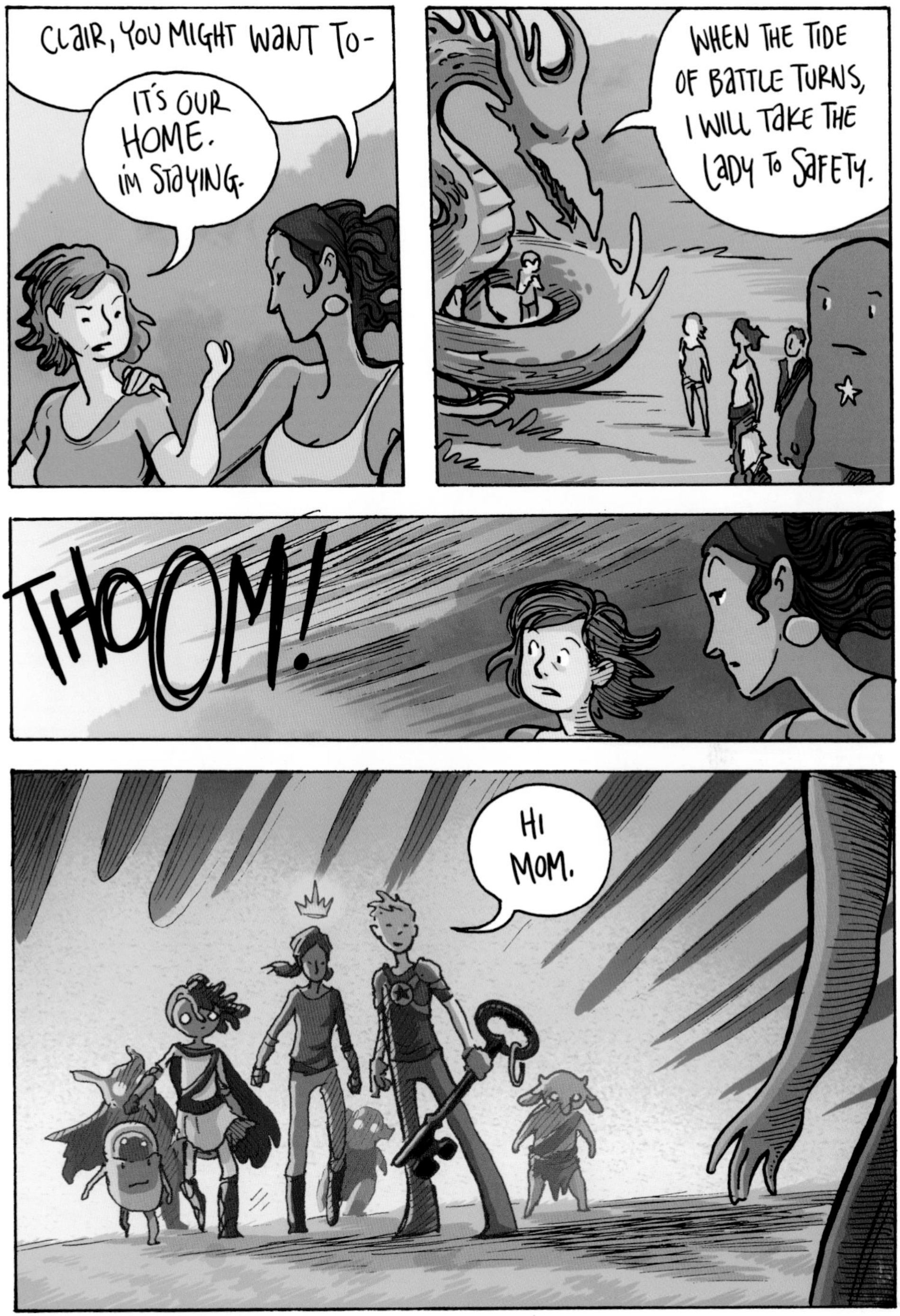
CLAIR, YOU MIGHT WANT TO-
IT'S OUR HOME. IM STAYING.
WHEN THE TIDE OF BATTLE TURNS, I WILL TAKE THE LADY TO SAFETY.
THOOM!
HI MOM.

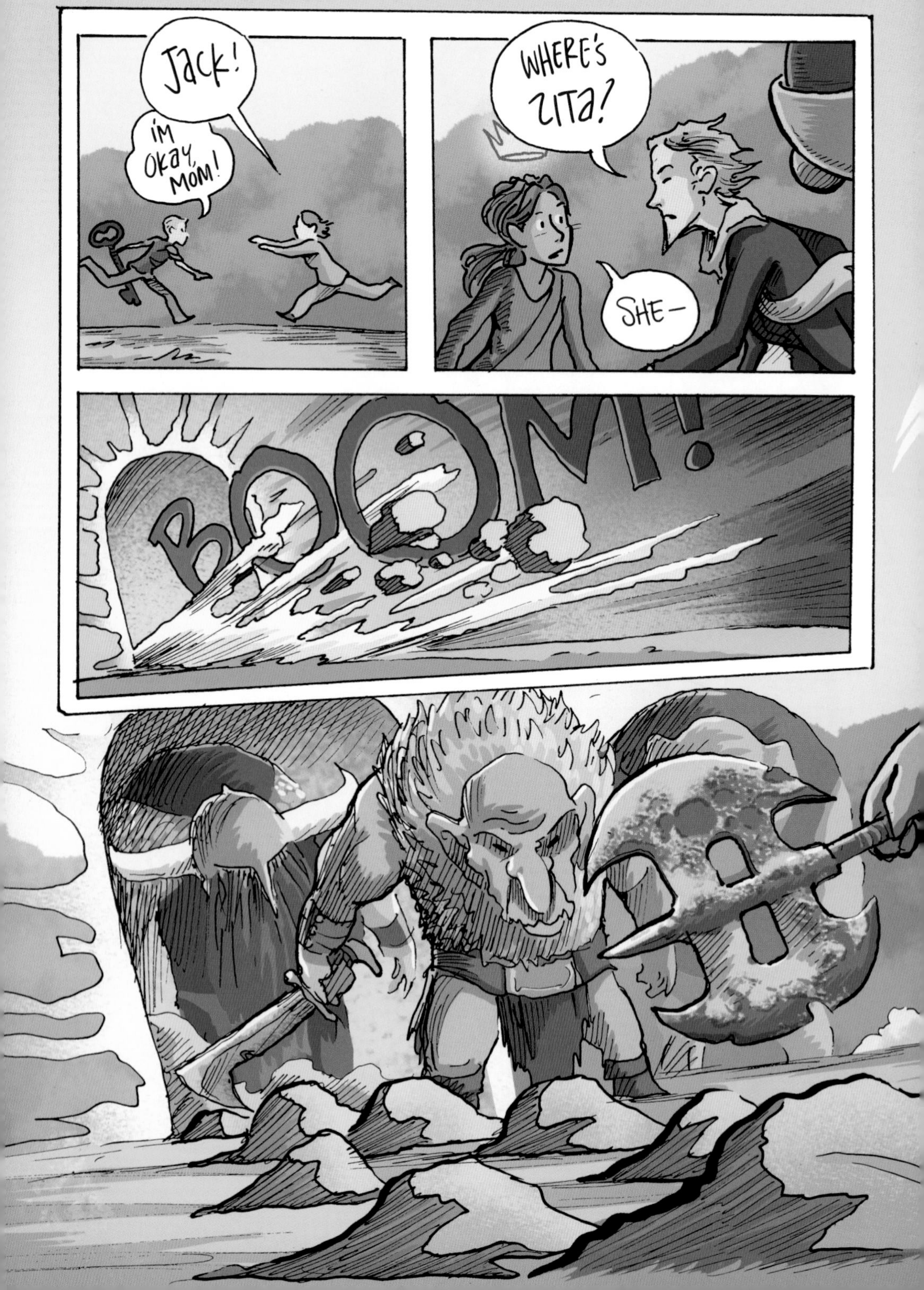
JACK!
I'M OKAY, MOM!
WHERE'S ZITA?
SHE–
BOOM!

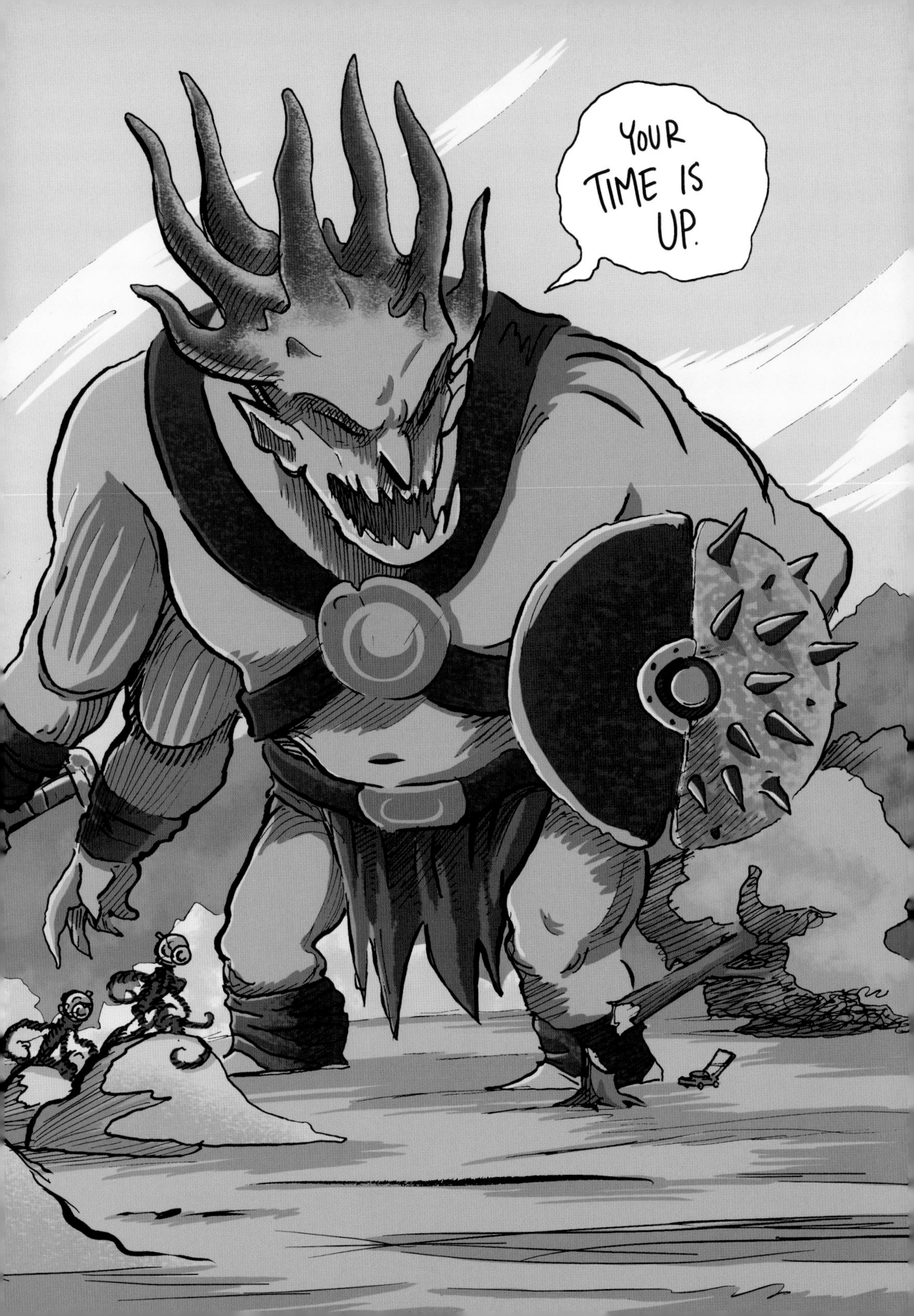
YOUR TIME IS UP.

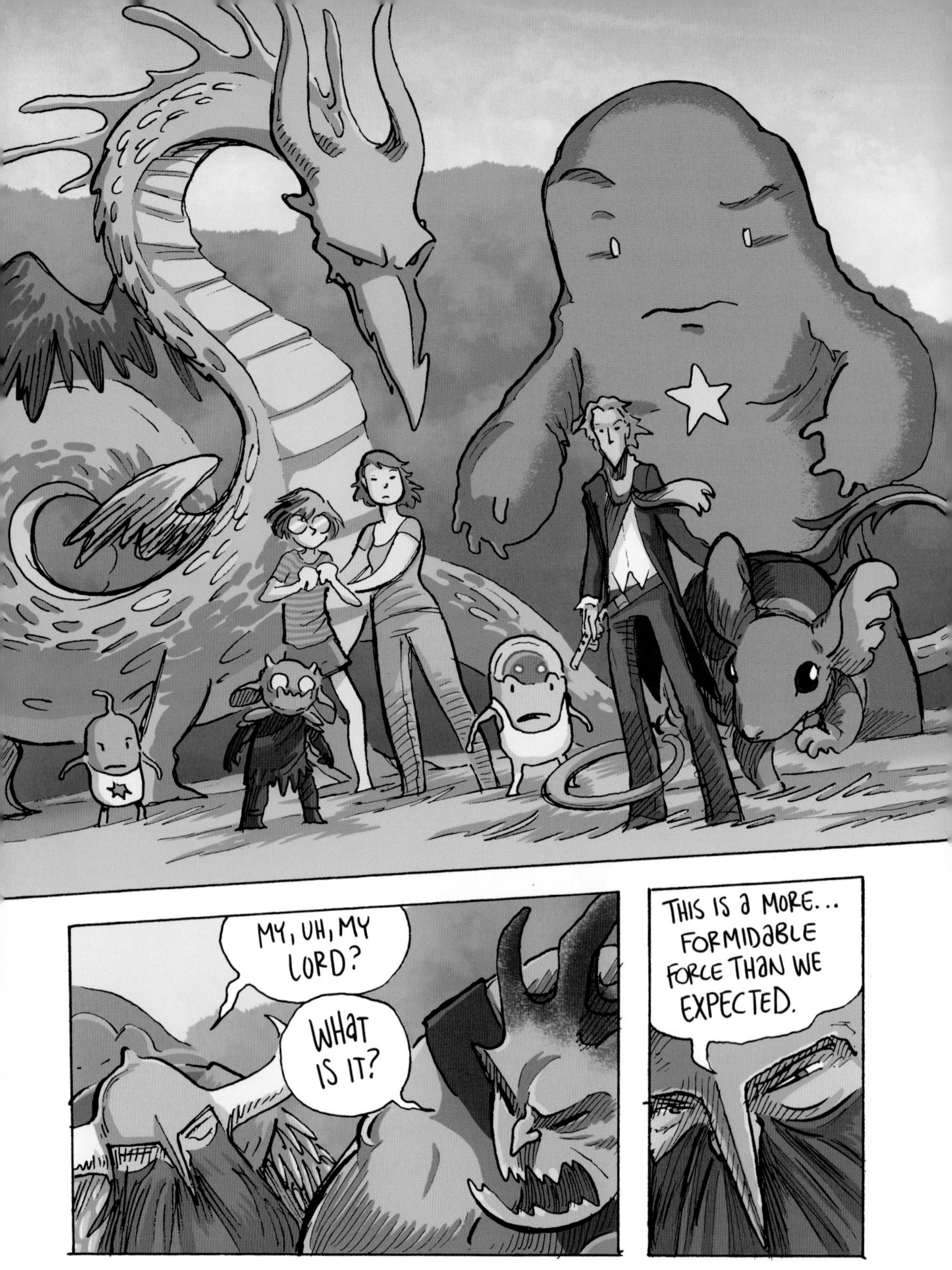
MY, UH, MY LORD?
WHAT IS IT?
THIS IS a MORE... FORMIDaBLE FORCE THaN WE EXPECTED.

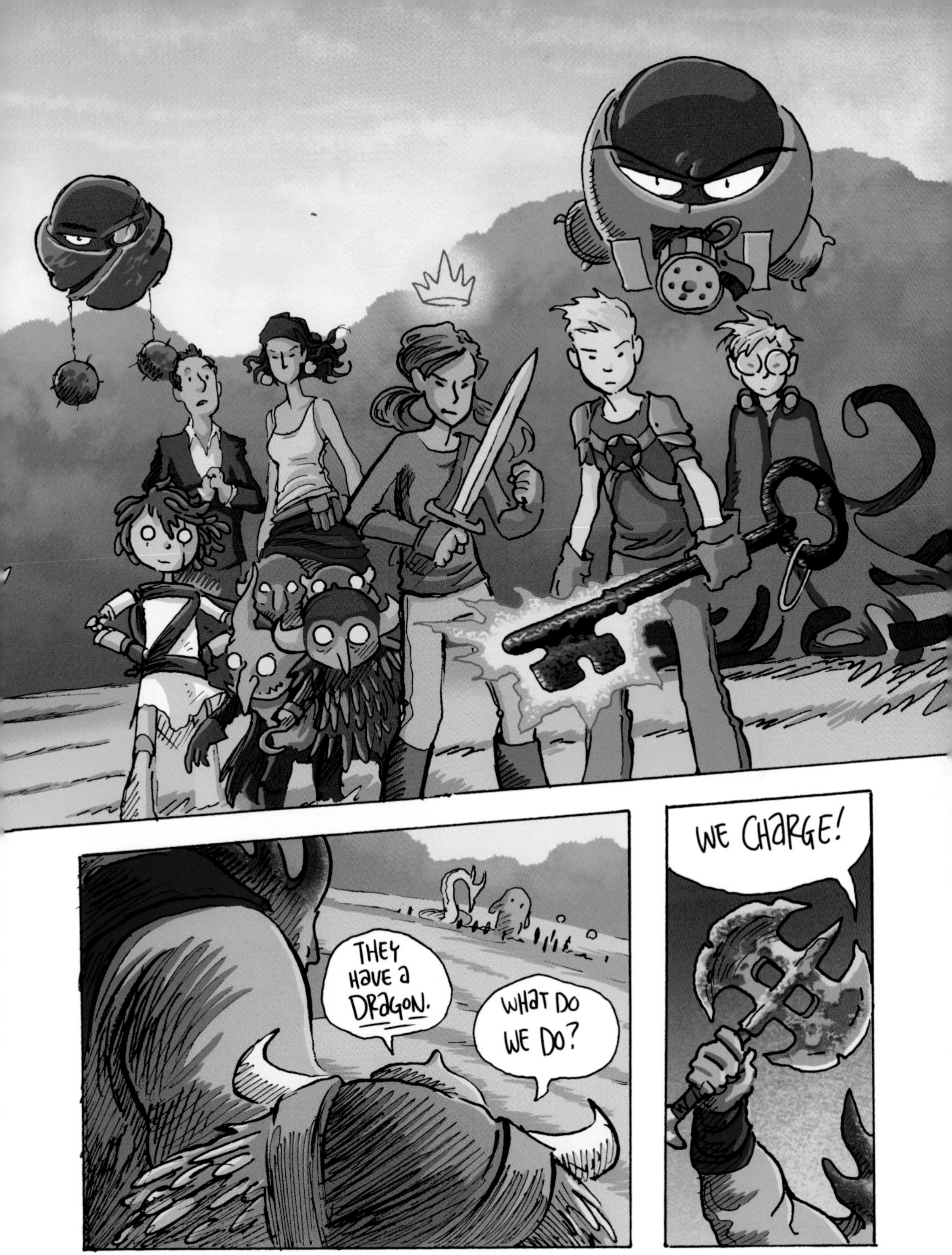
THEY HAVE A DRAGON.
WHAT DO WE DO?
WE CHARGE!

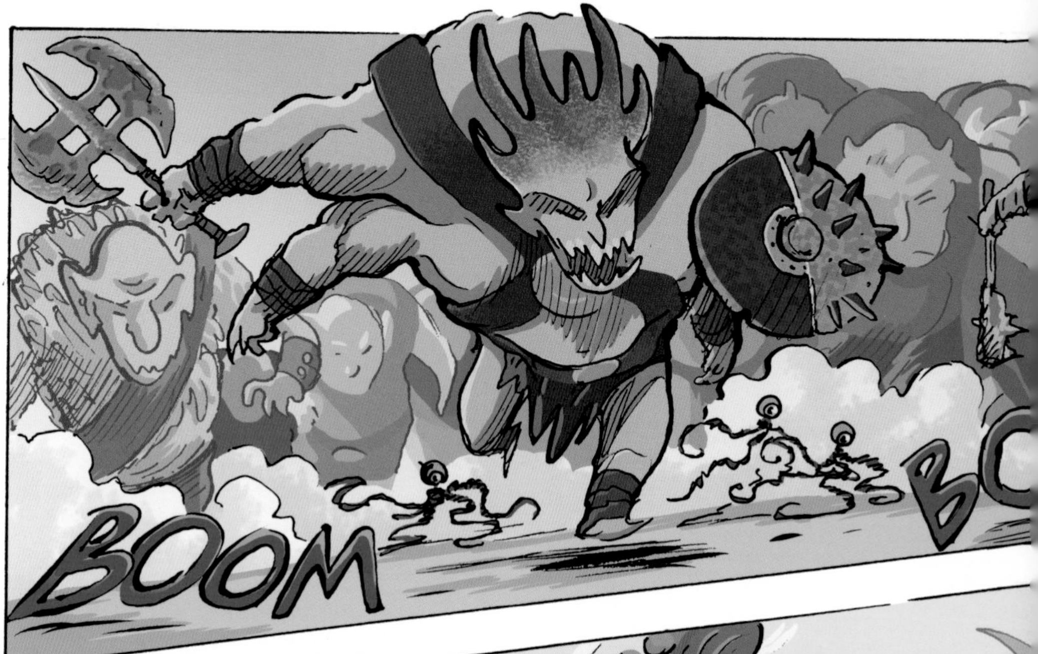
BOOM
BO

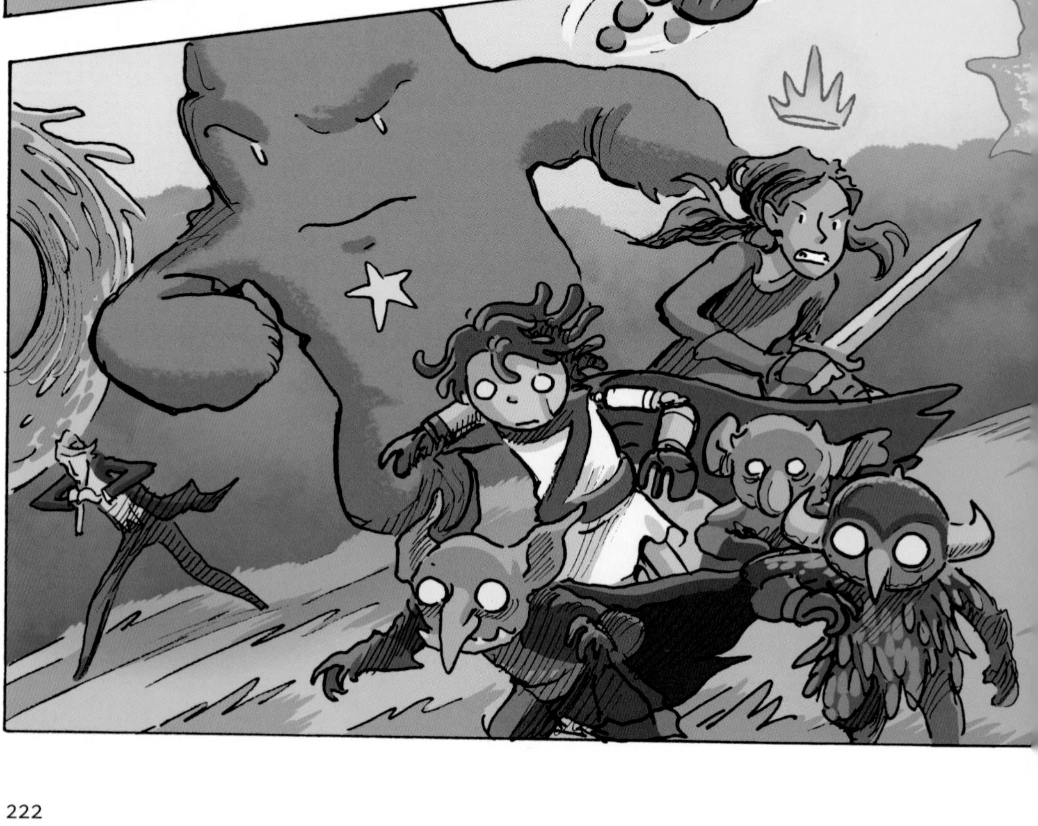

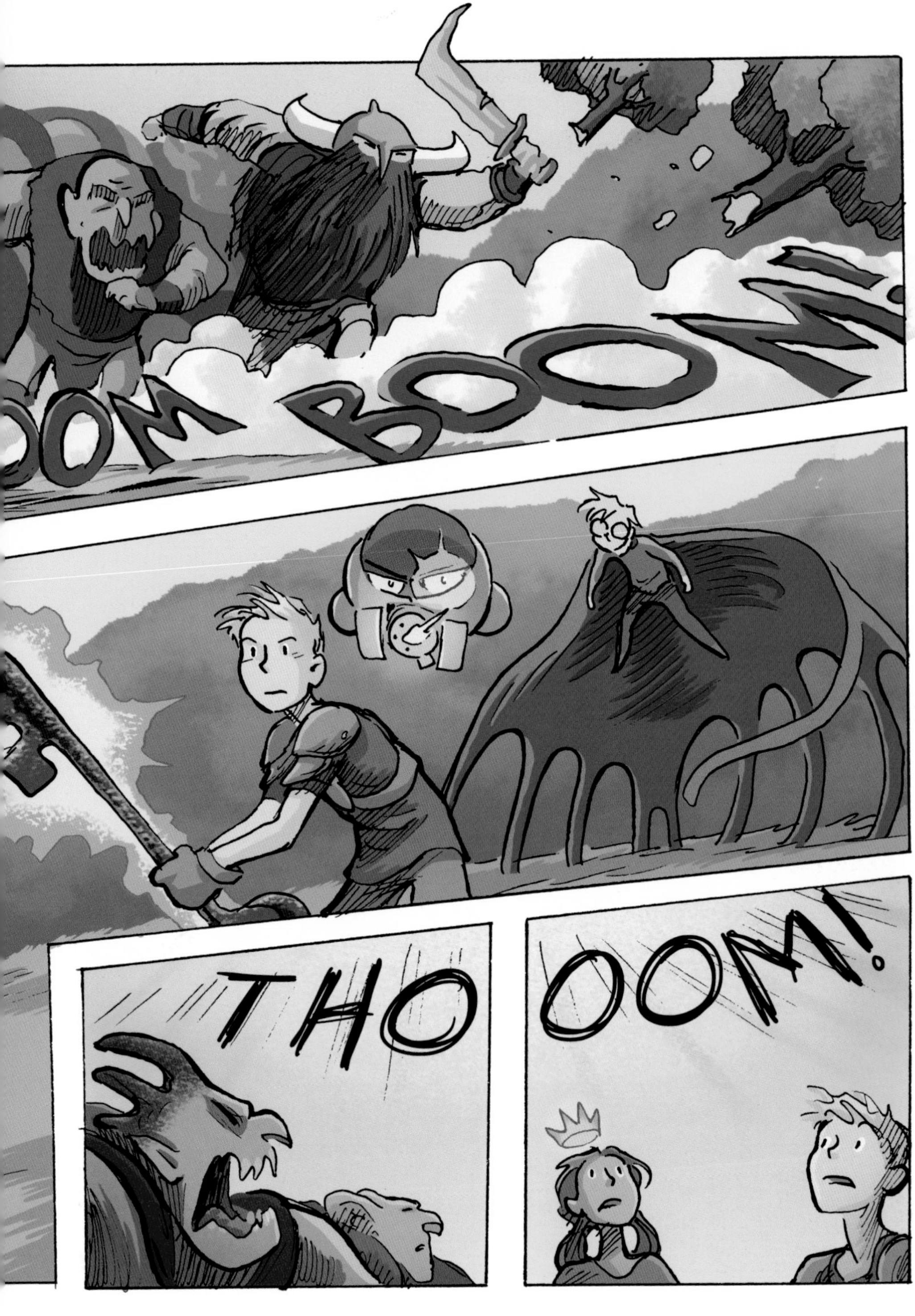

OOM BOOM!
THO
OOM!

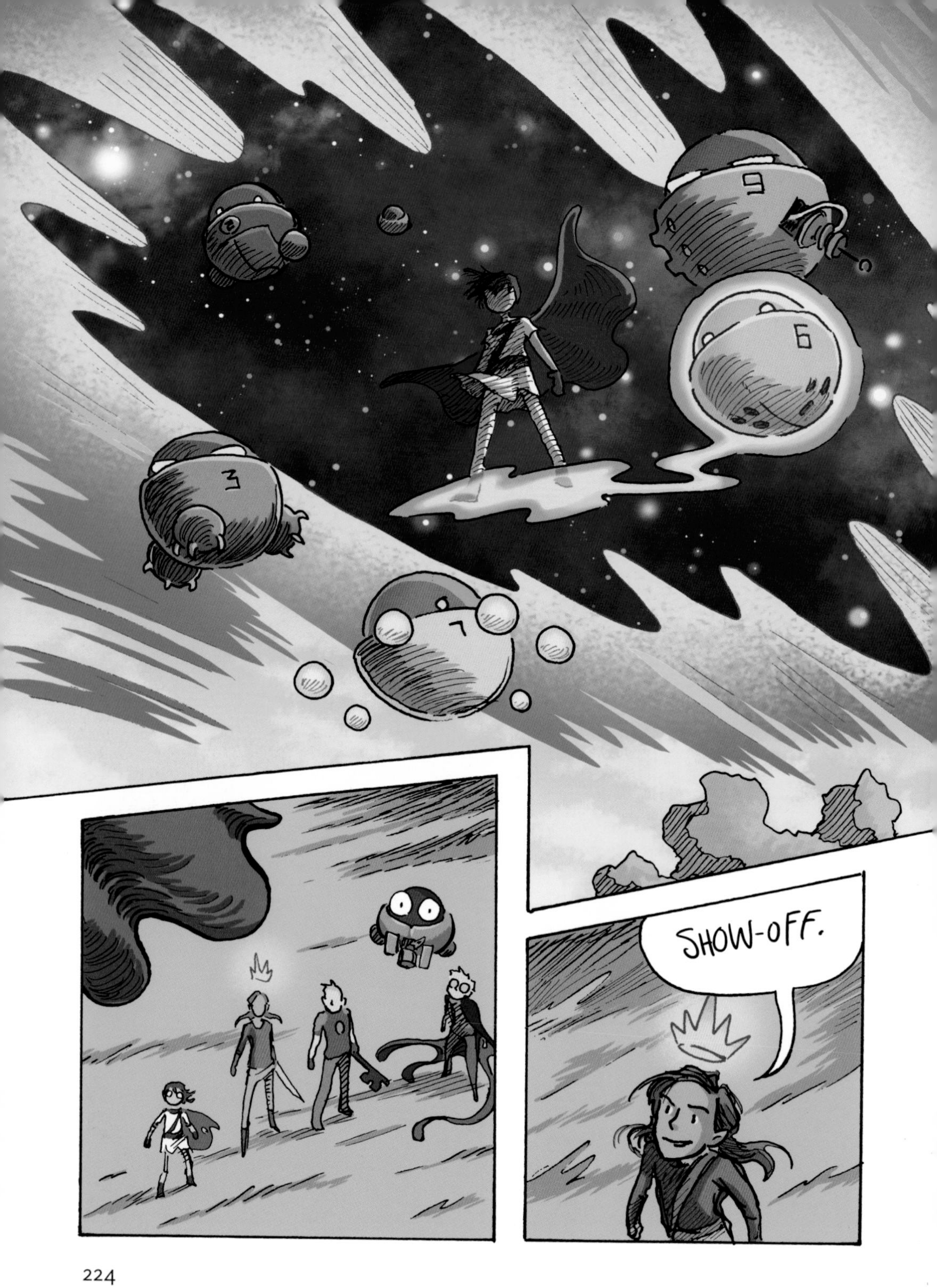
SHOW-OFF.

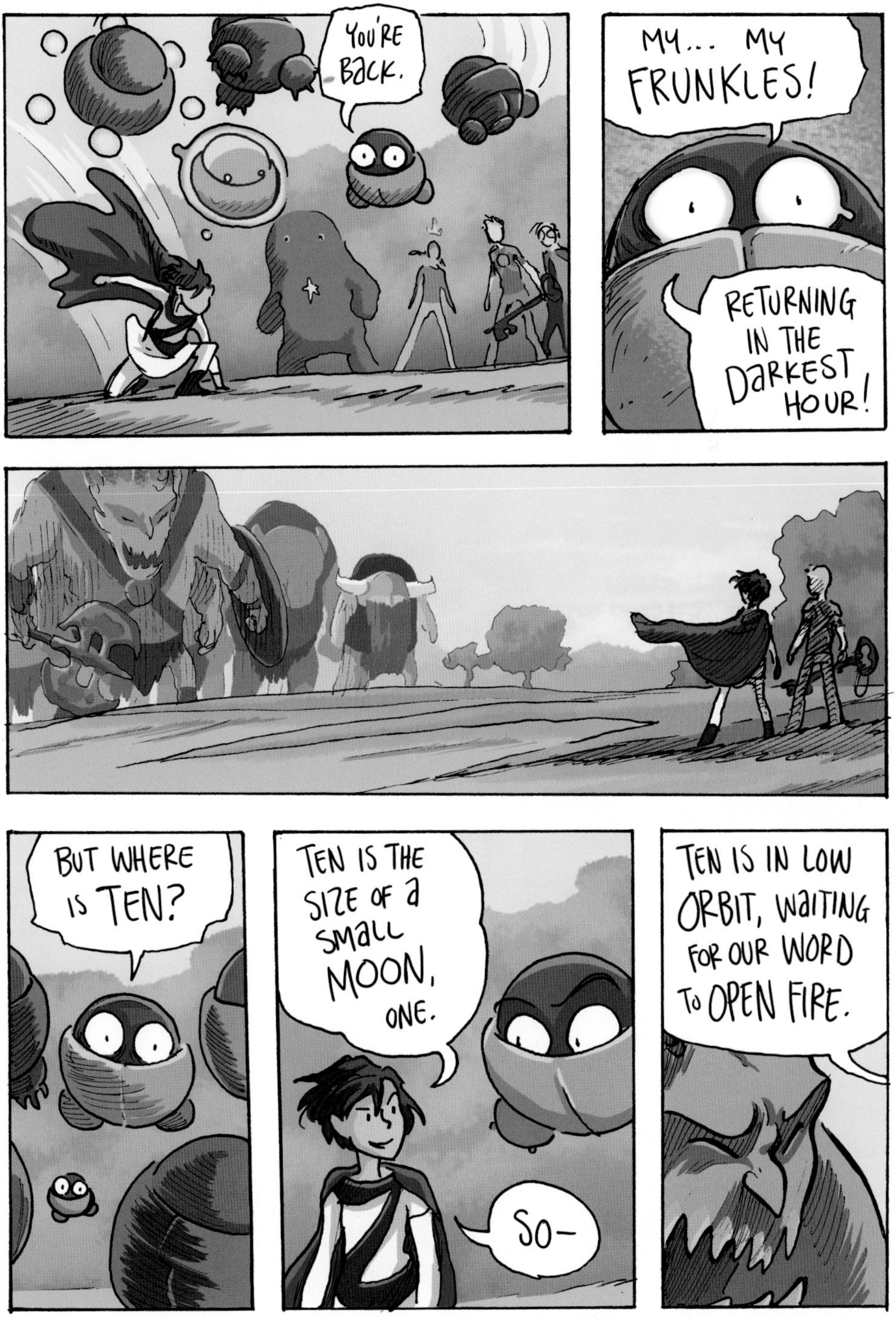
You're back.
My... my Frunkles!
Returning in the darkest hour!
But where is Ten?
Ten is the size of a small moon, one.
So-
Ten is in low orbit, waiting for our word to open fire.

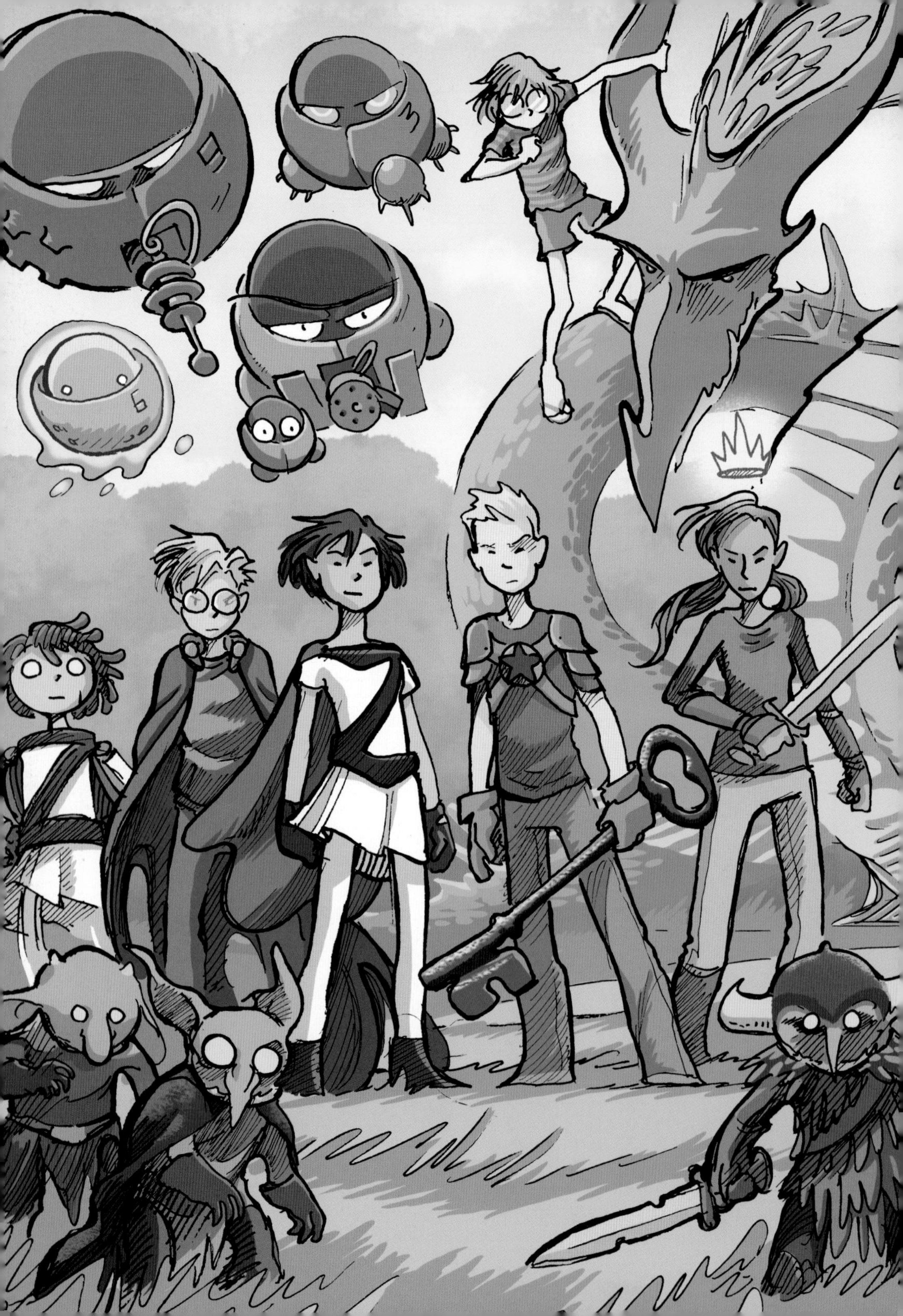

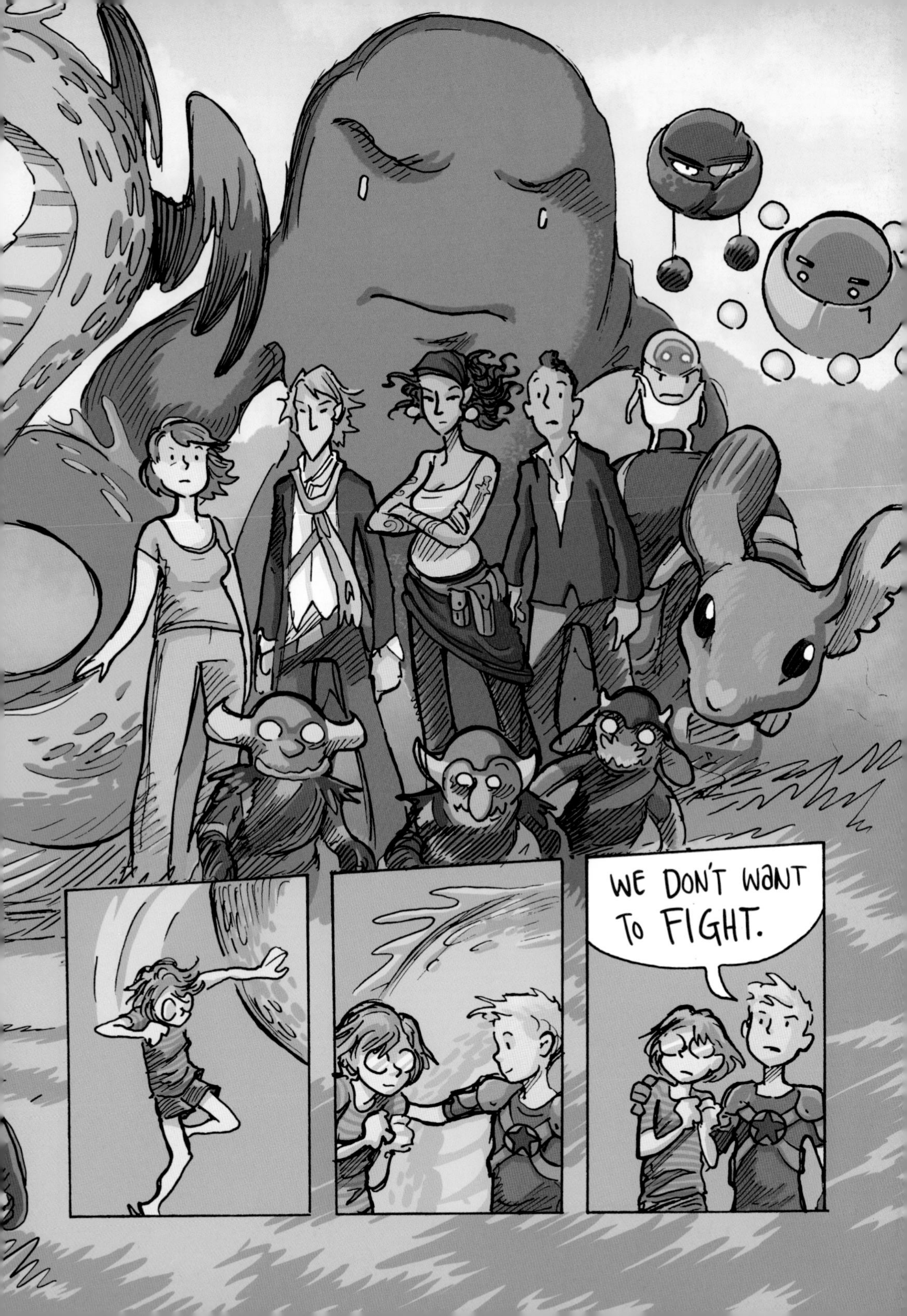
WE DON'T WANT TO FIGHT.

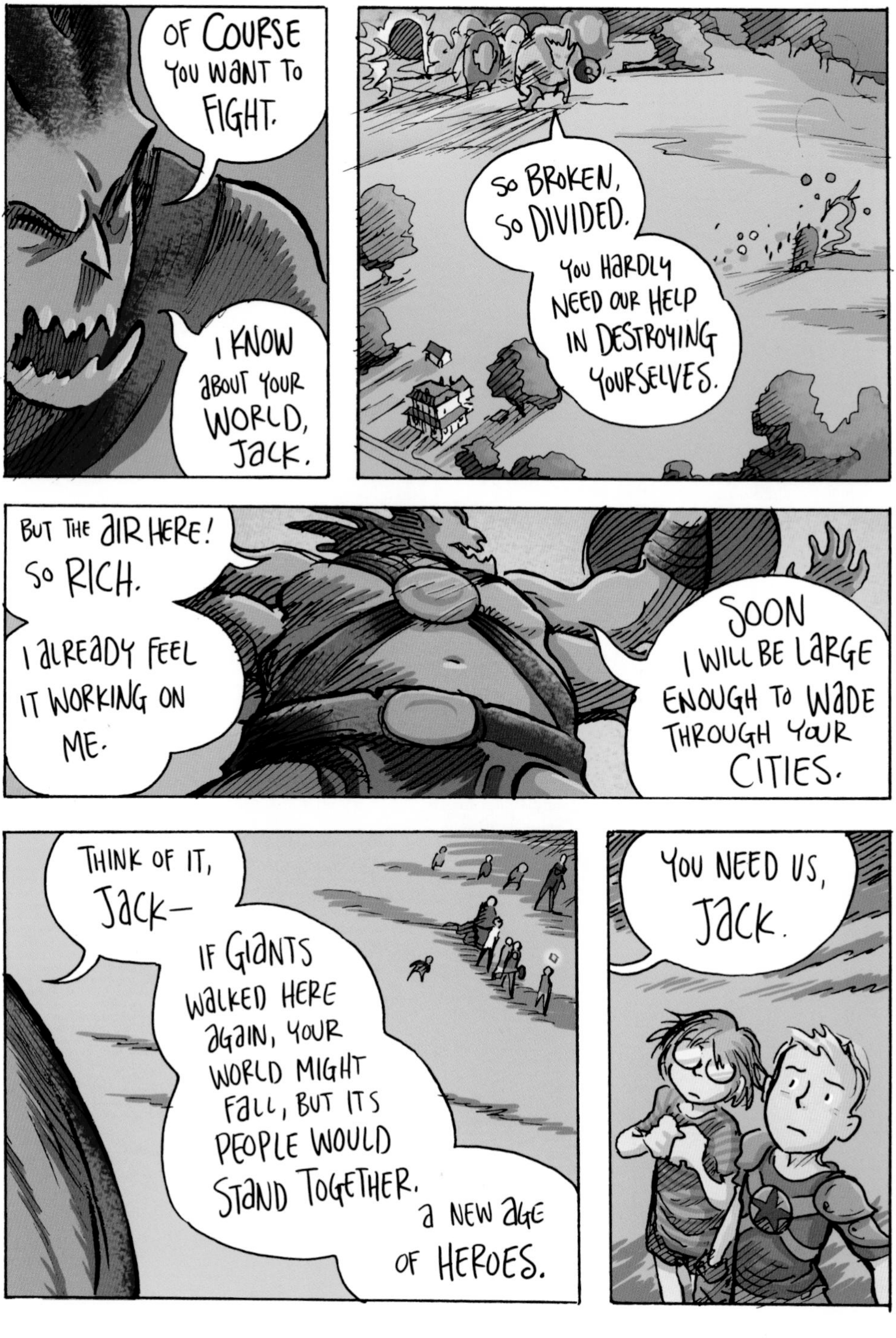
OF COURSE YOU WANT TO FIGHT.
I KNOW ABOUT YOUR WORLD, JACK.
SO BROKEN, SO DIVIDED.
YOU HARDLY NEED OUR HELP IN DESTROYING YOURSELVES.
BUT THE AIR HERE! SO RICH.
I ALREADY FEEL IT WORKING ON ME.
SOON I WILL BE LARGE ENOUGH TO WADE THROUGH YOUR CITIES.
THINK OF IT, JACK—
IF GIANTS WALKED HERE AGAIN, YOUR WORLD MIGHT FALL, BUT ITS PEOPLE WOULD STAND TOGETHER.
A NEW AGE OF HEROES.
YOU NEED US, JACK.

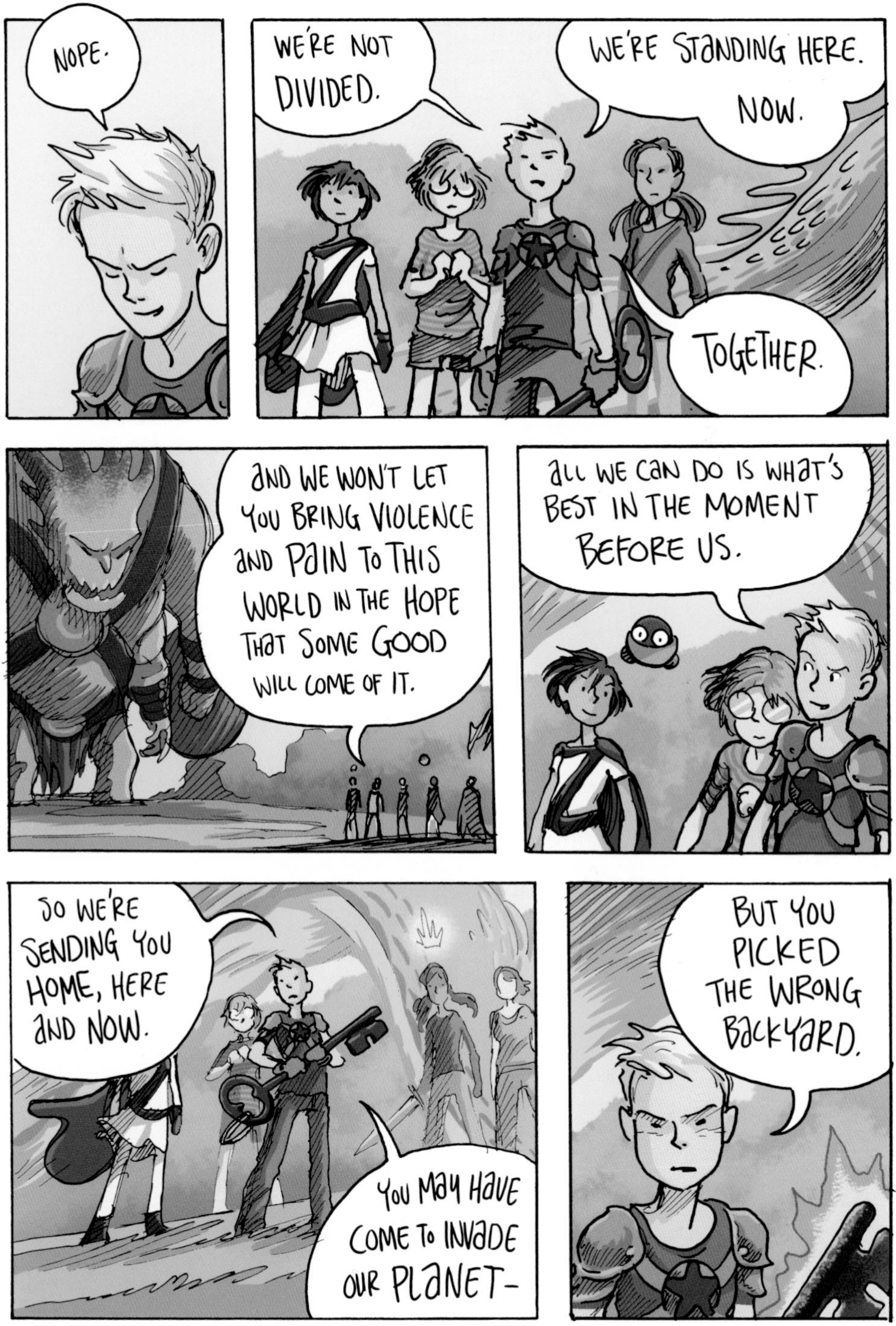
NOPE.
WE'RE NOT DIVIDED.
WE'RE STANDING HERE. NOW.
TOGETHER.
AND WE WON'T LET YOU BRING VIOLENCE AND PAIN TO THIS WORLD IN THE HOPE THAT SOME GOOD WILL COME OF IT.
ALL WE CAN DO IS WHAT'S BEST IN THE MOMENT BEFORE US.
SO WE'RE SENDING YOU HOME, HERE AND NOW.
YOU MAY HAVE COME TO INVADE OUR PLANET-
BUT YOU PICKED THE WRONG BACKYARD.

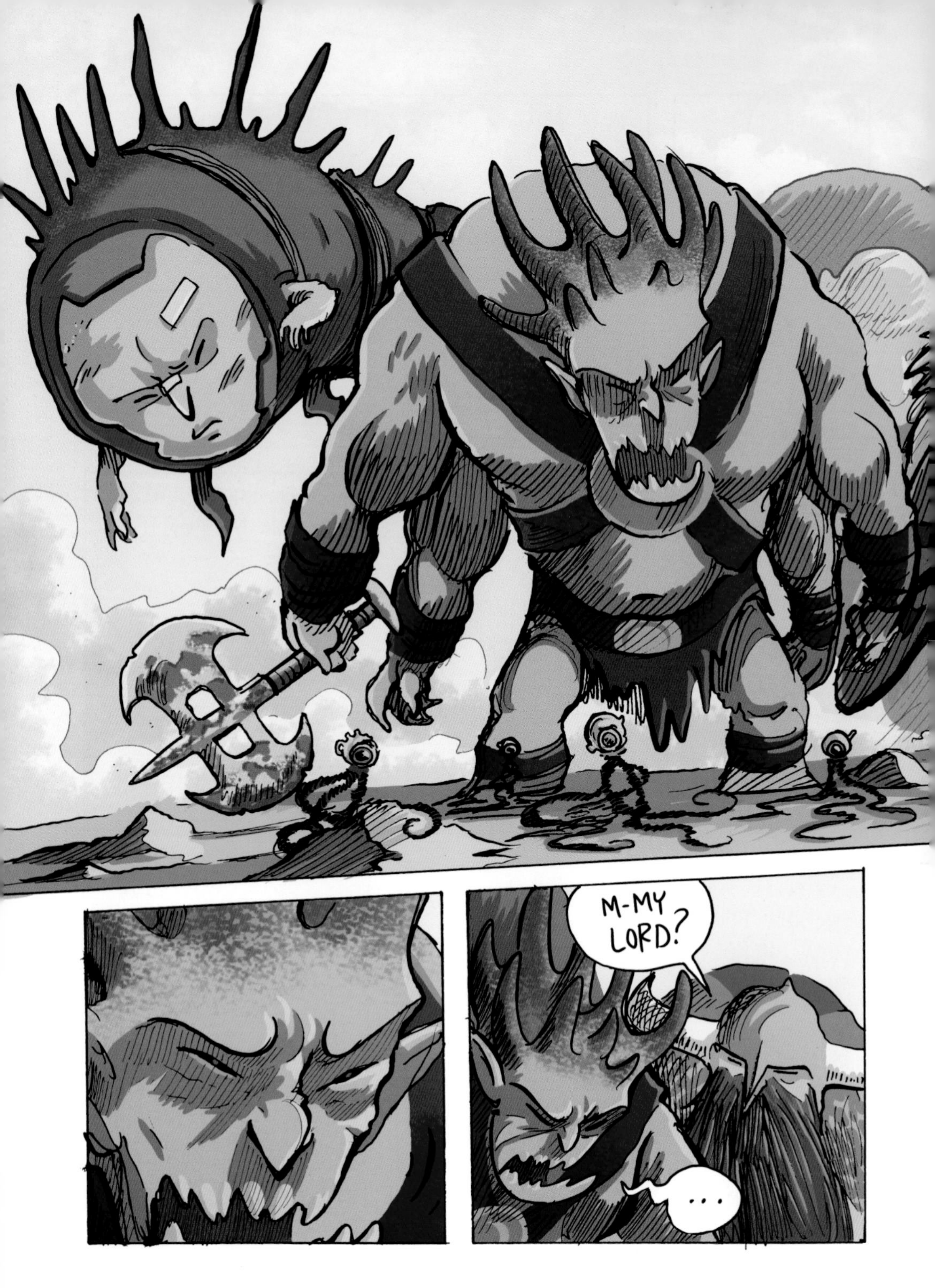
M-MY LORD?
...

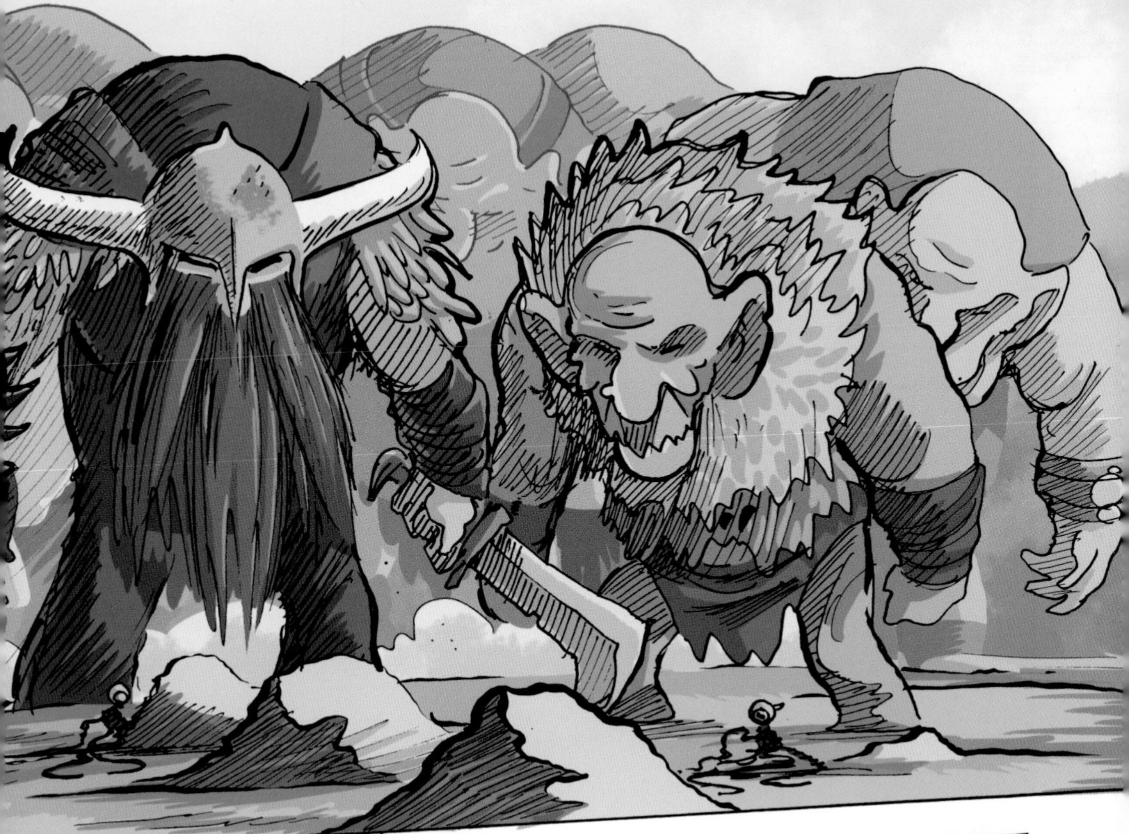

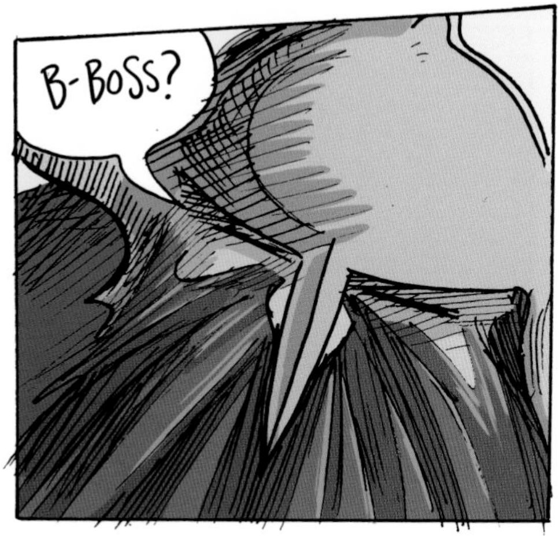
B-BOSS?

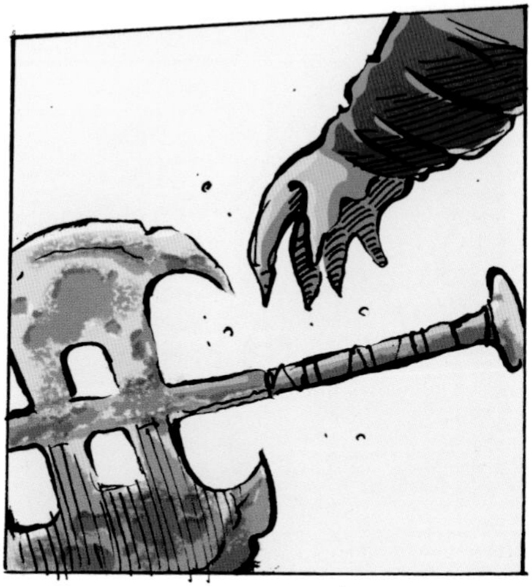

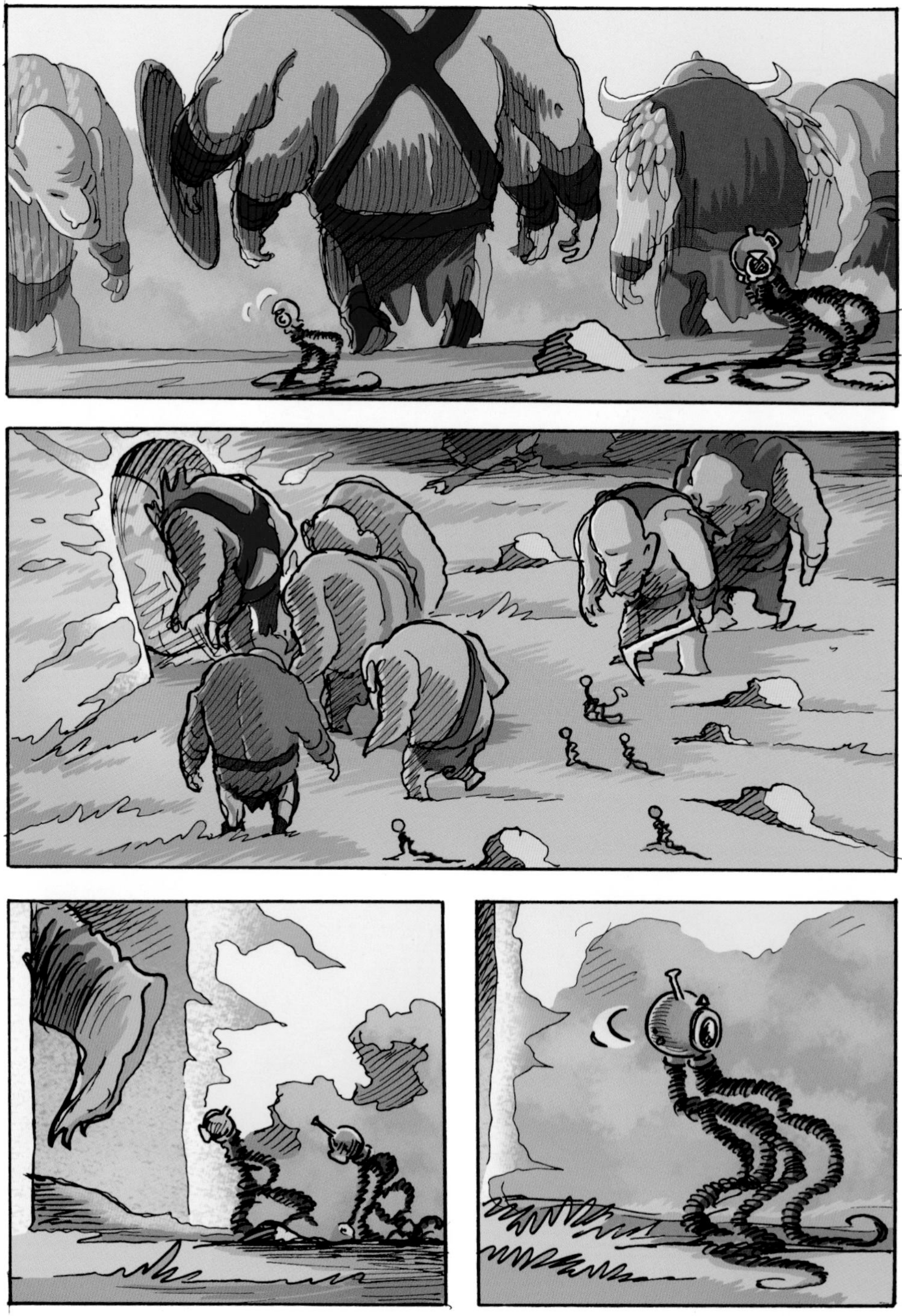

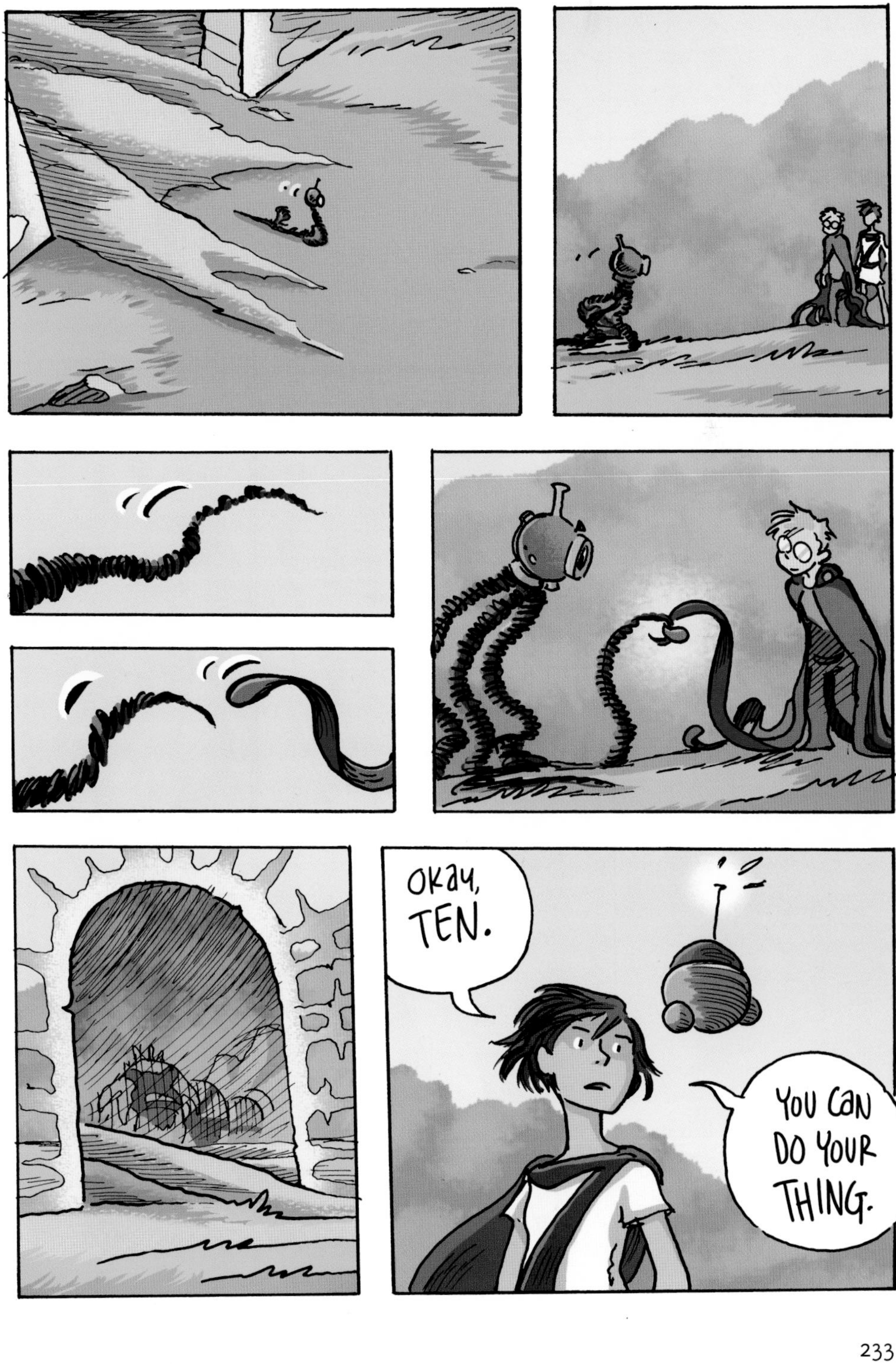
Okay, TEN.
YOU CAN DO YOUR THING.

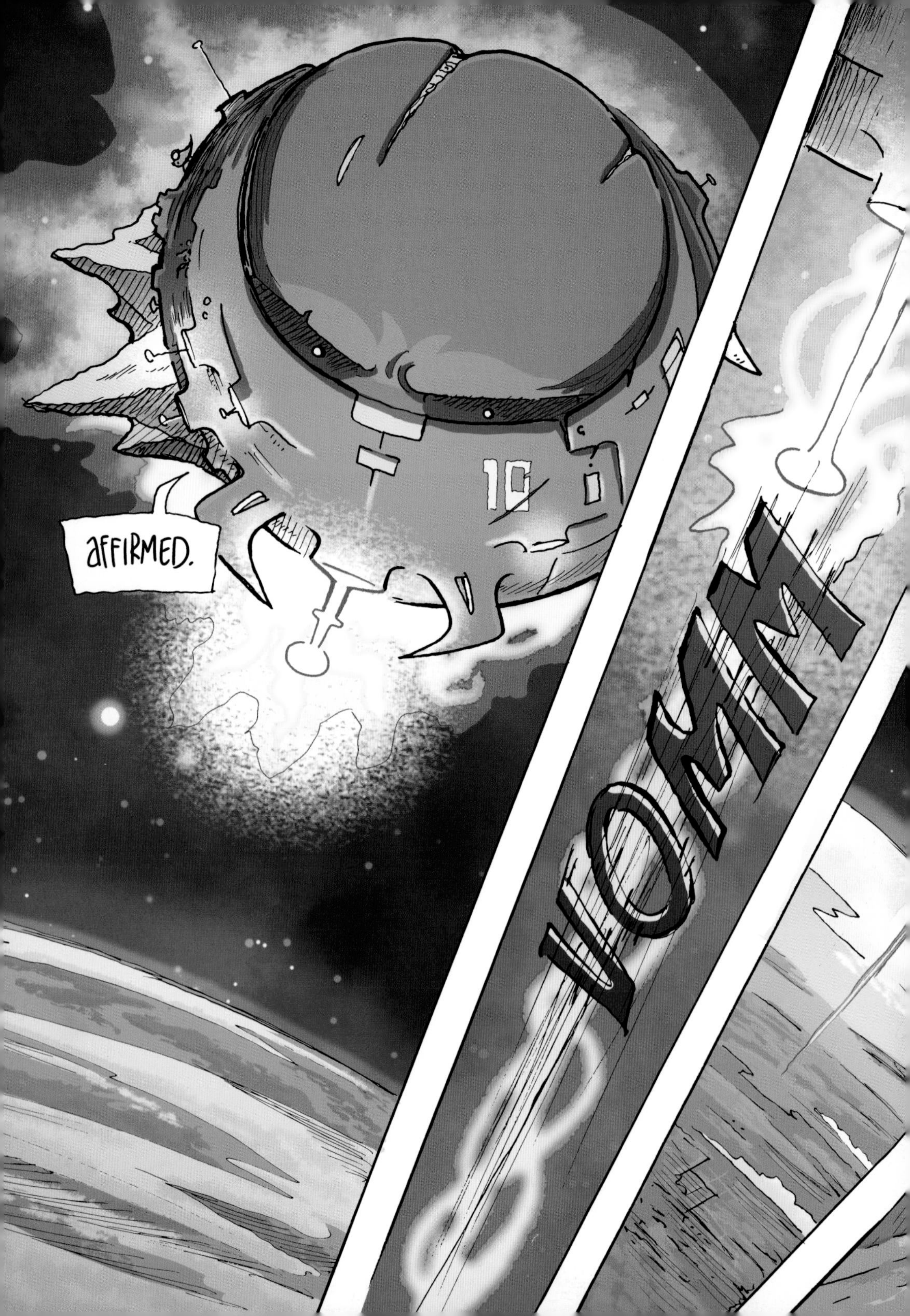
AFFIRMED.
VOMM

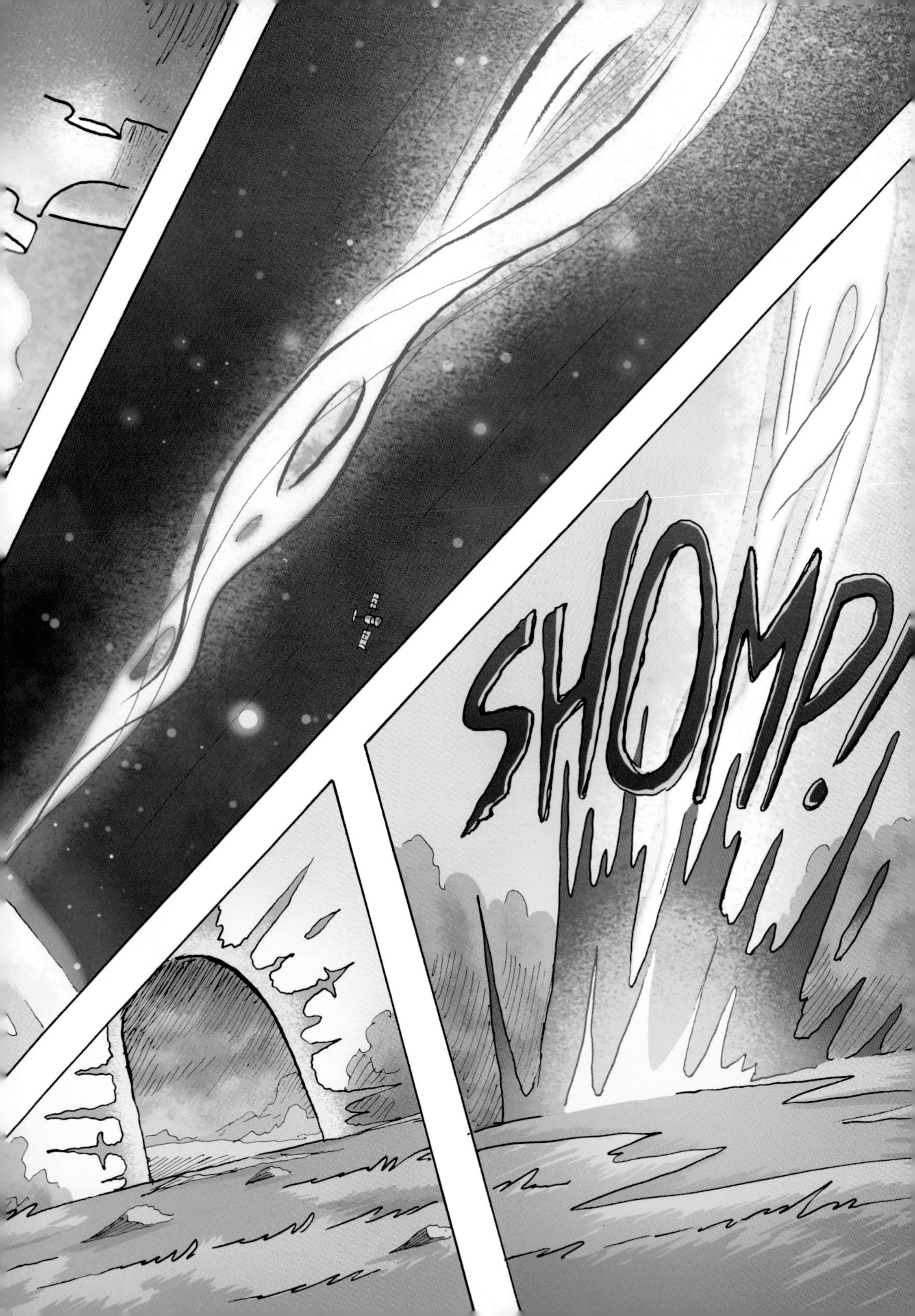
SHOMP!

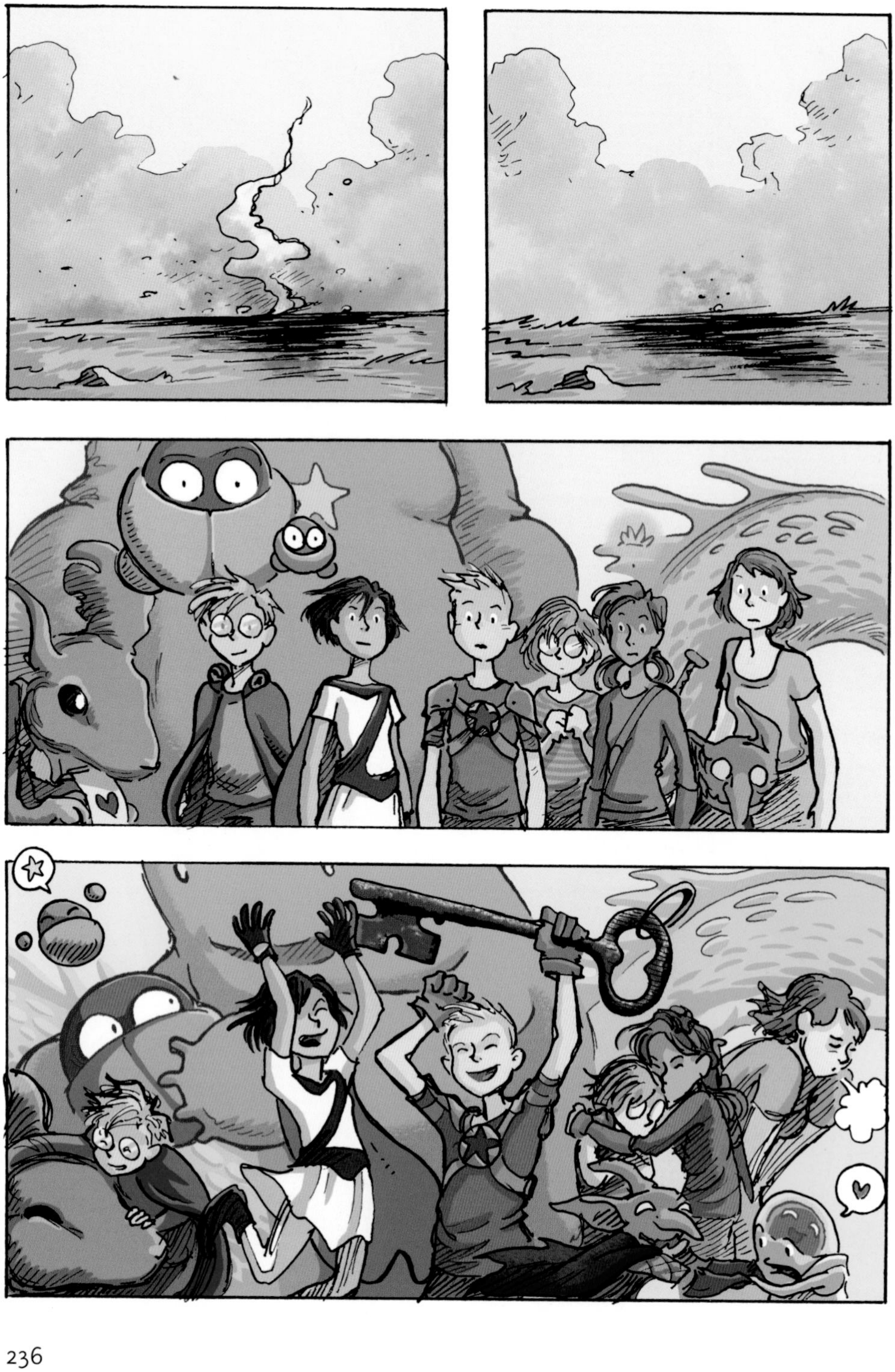

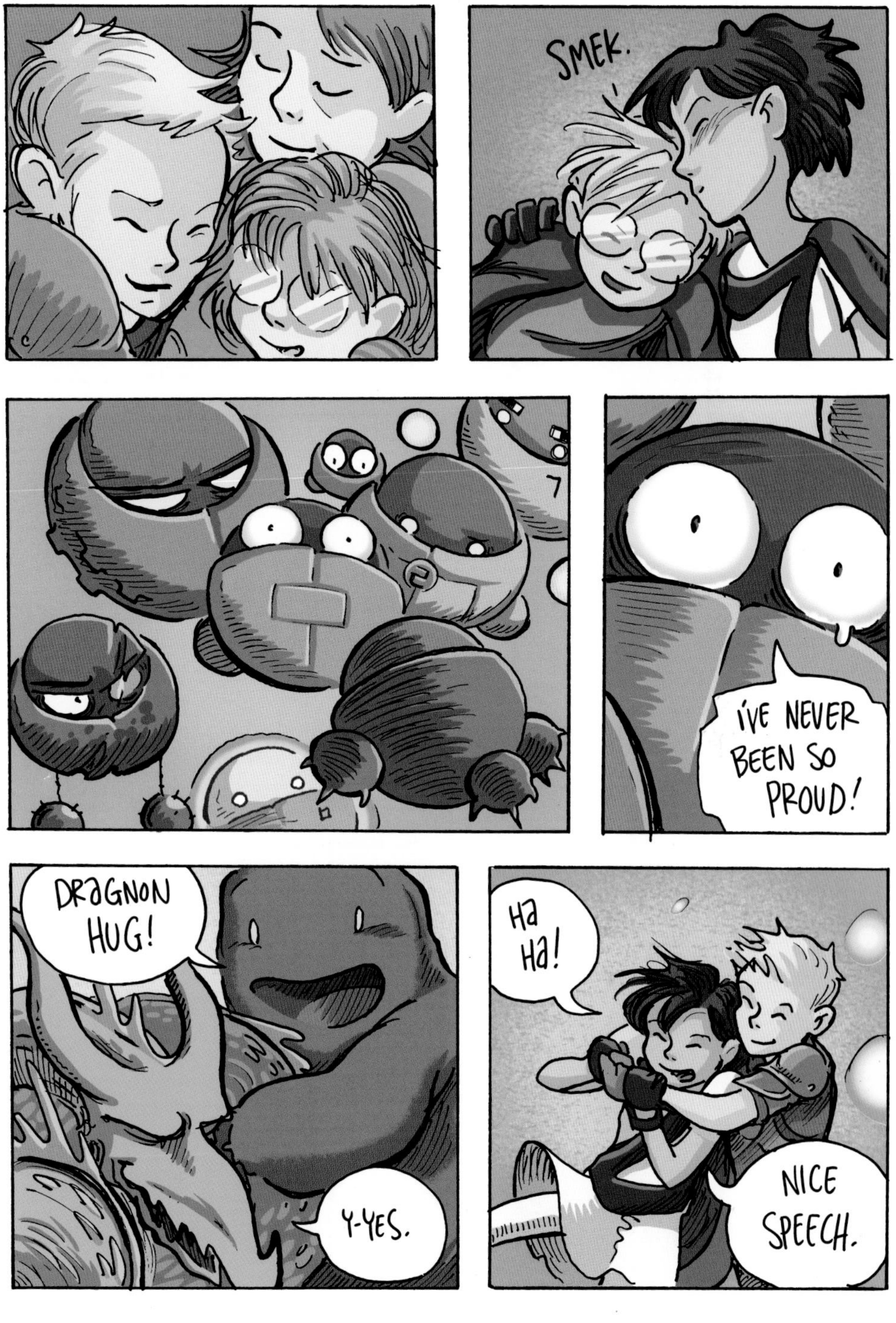
SMEK.
I'VE NEVER BEEN SO PROUD!
DRAGNON HUG!
Y-YES.
HA HA!
NICE SPEECH.

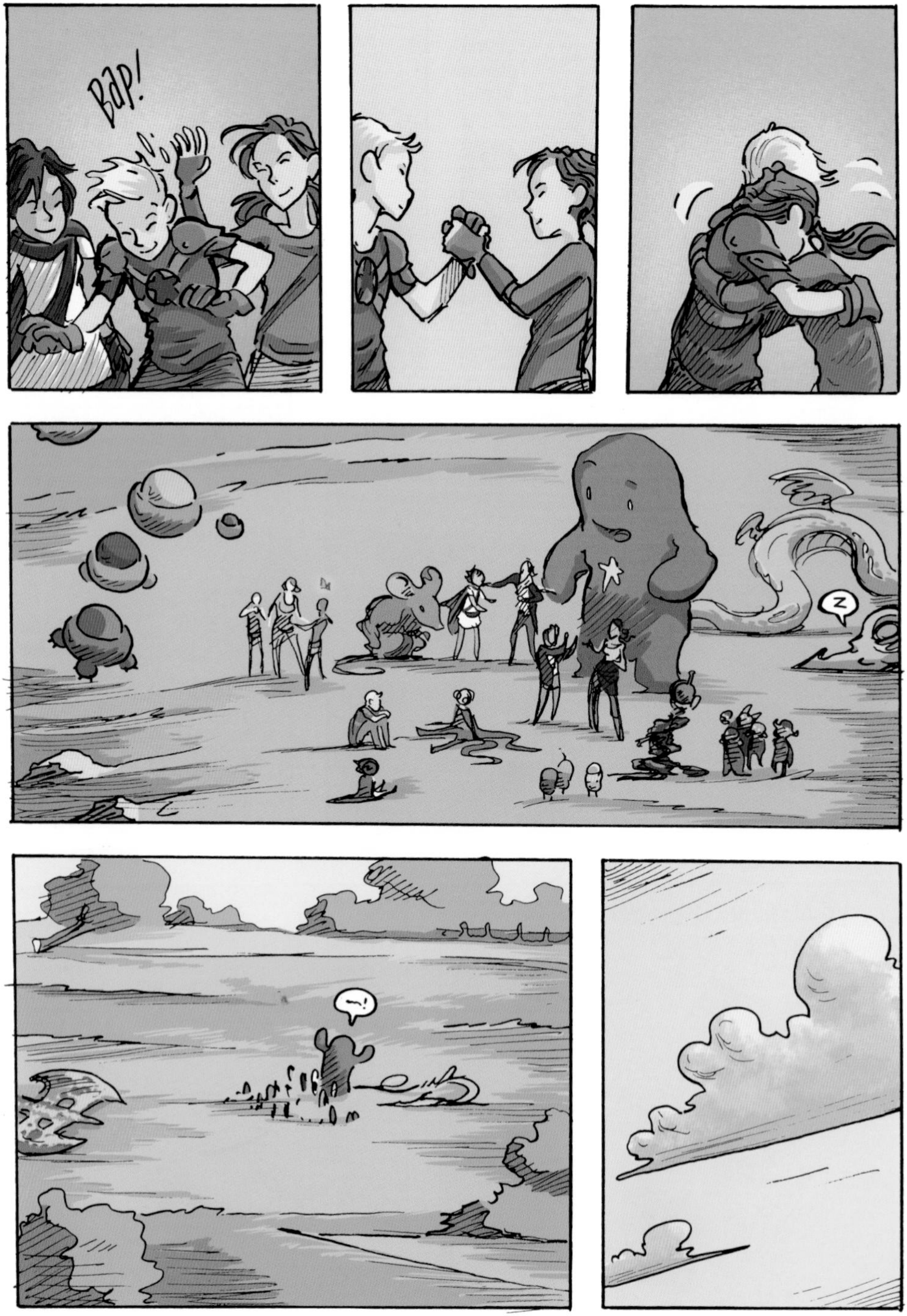
BAP!
Z
~!

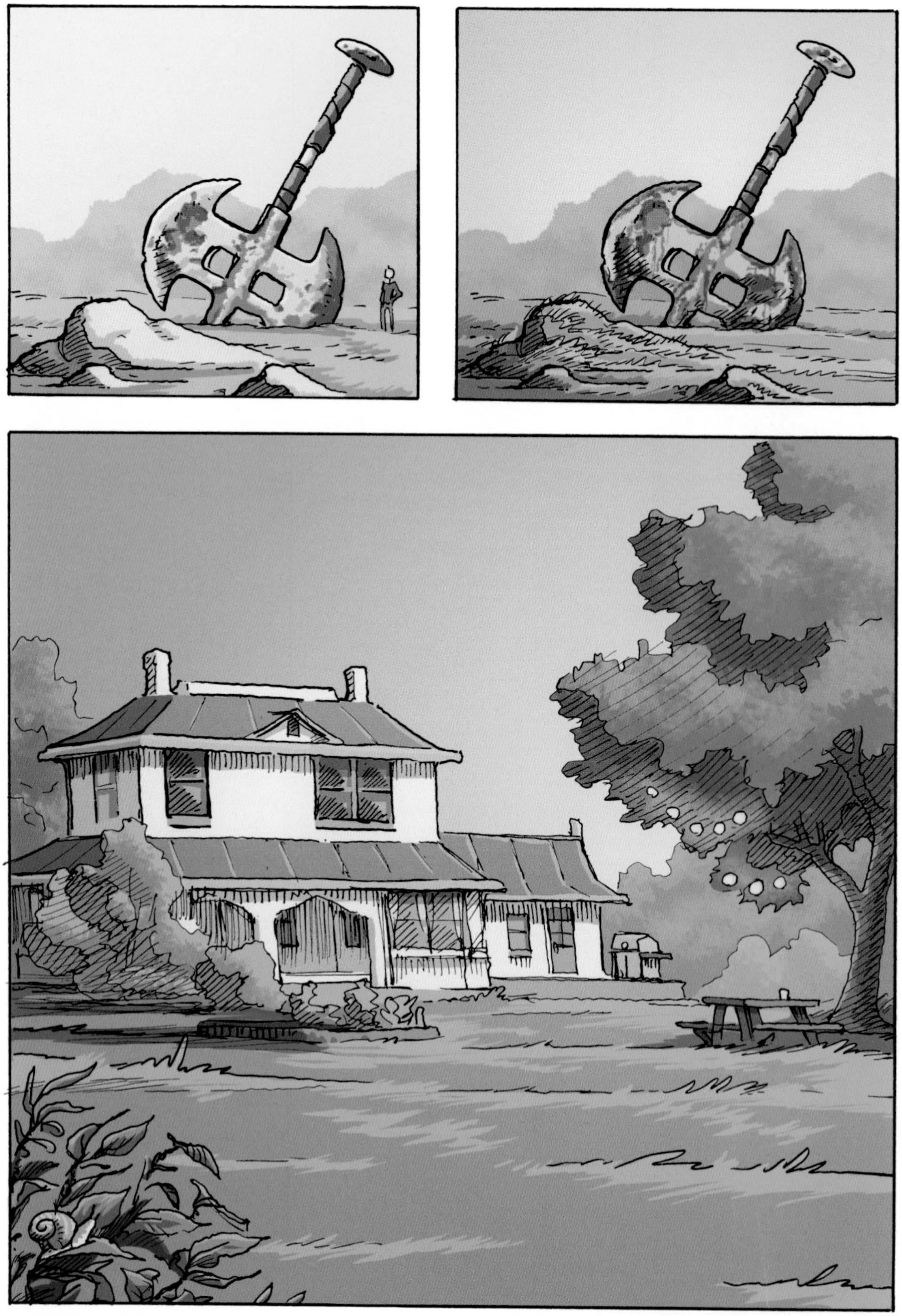

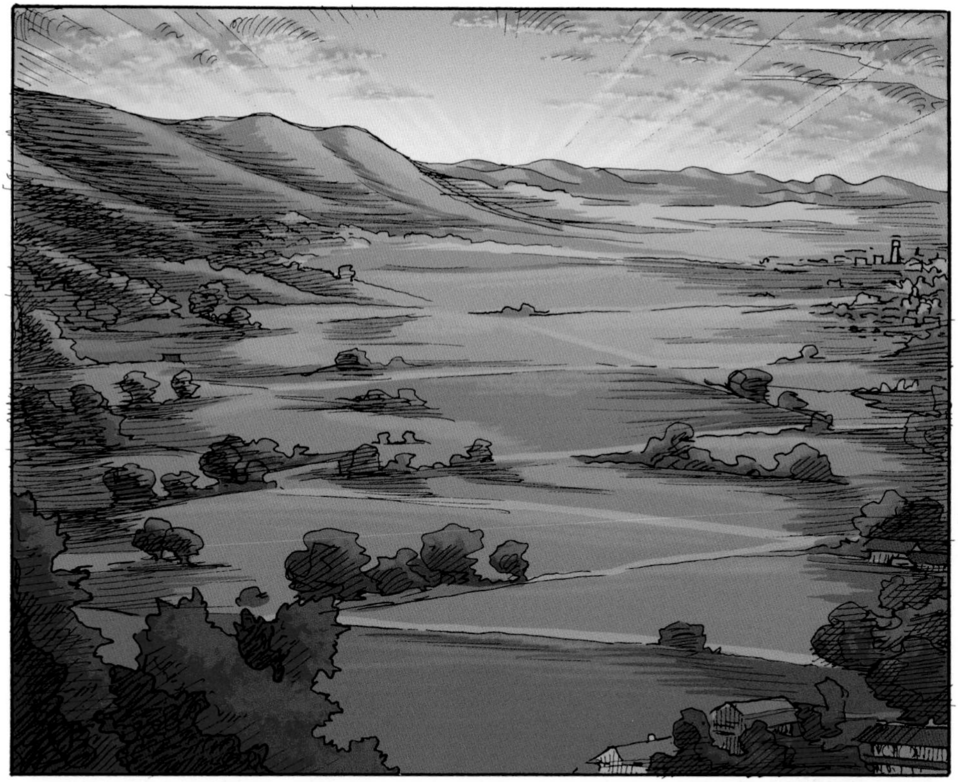

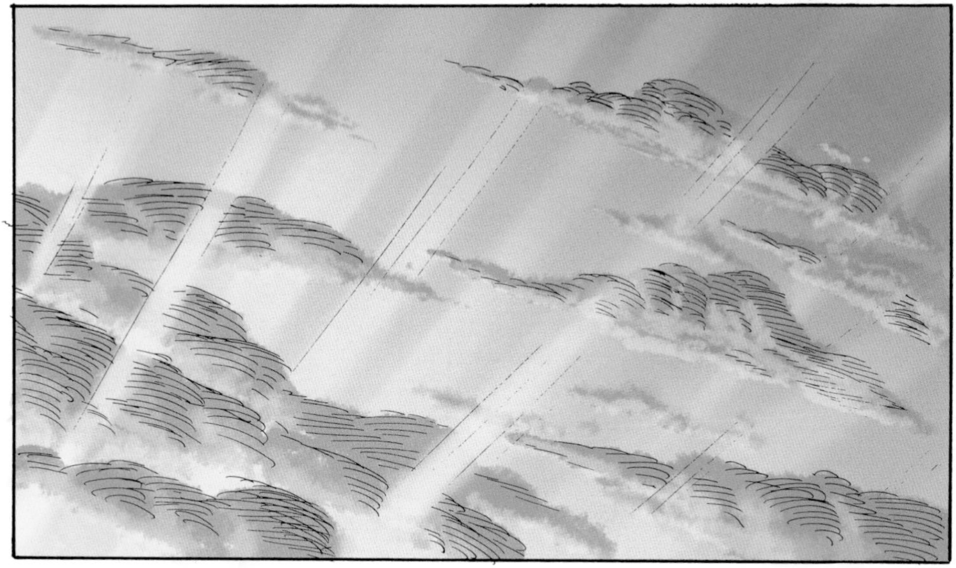

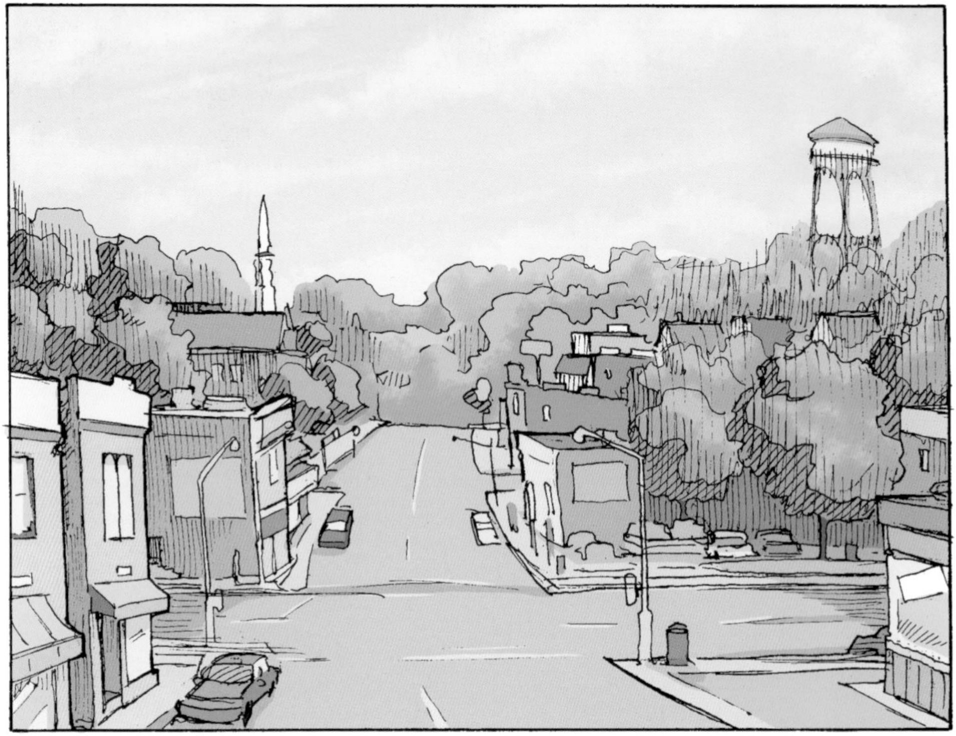

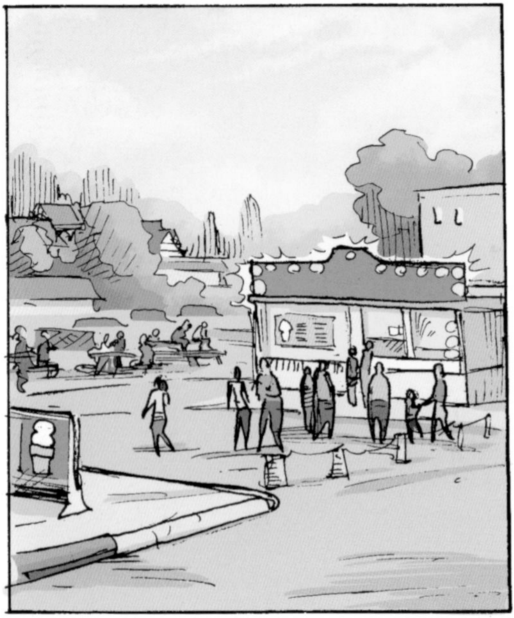

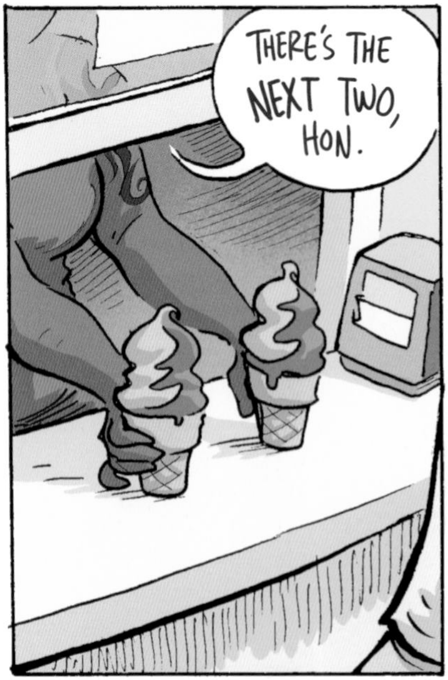
THERE'S THE NEXT TWO, HON.

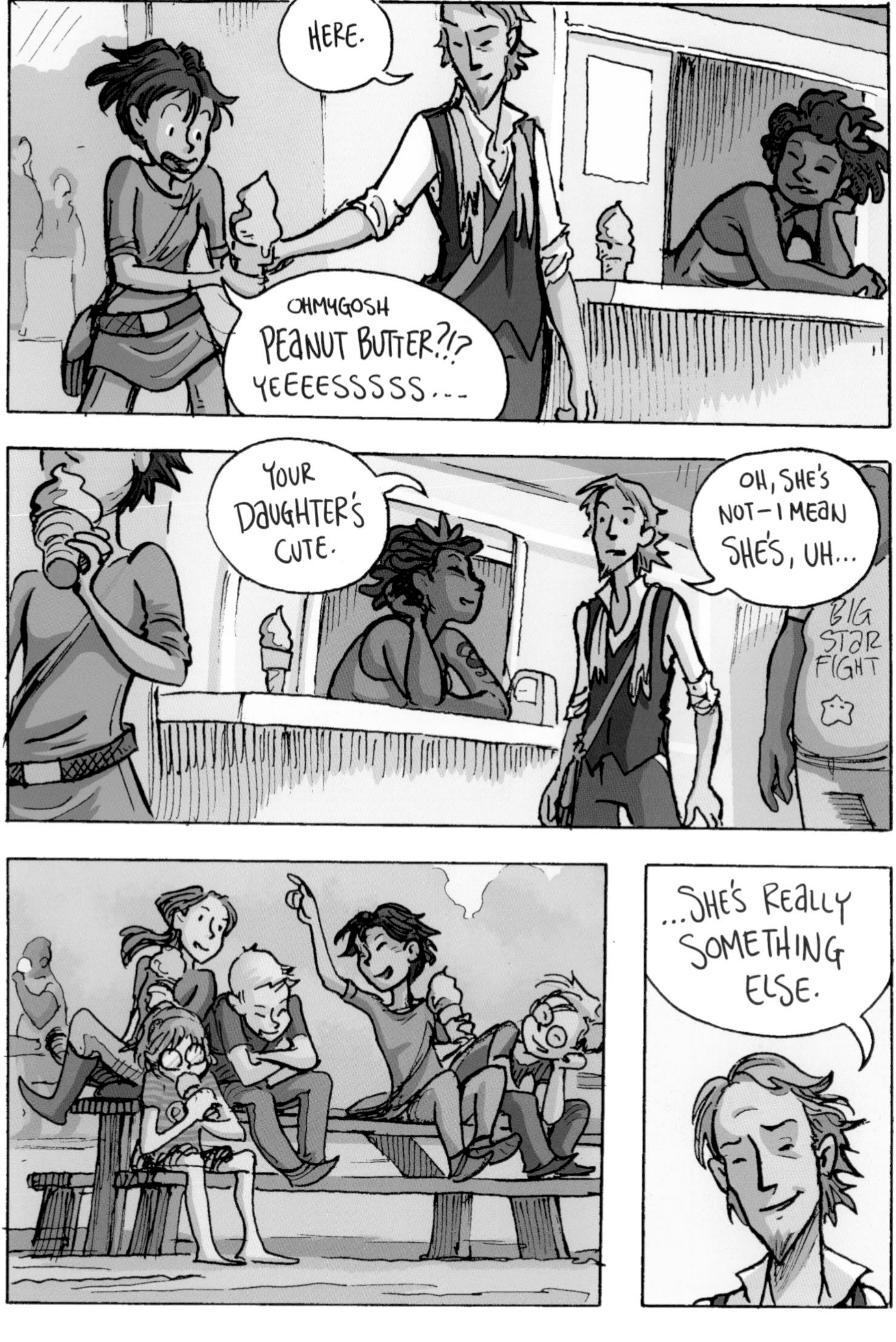
HERE.
OHMYGOSH PEANUT BUTTER?!? YEEEESSSSS...
YOUR DAUGHTER'S CUTE.
OH, SHE'S NOT—I MEAN SHE'S, UH...
BIG STAR FIGHT
...SHE'S REALLY SOMETHING ELSE.

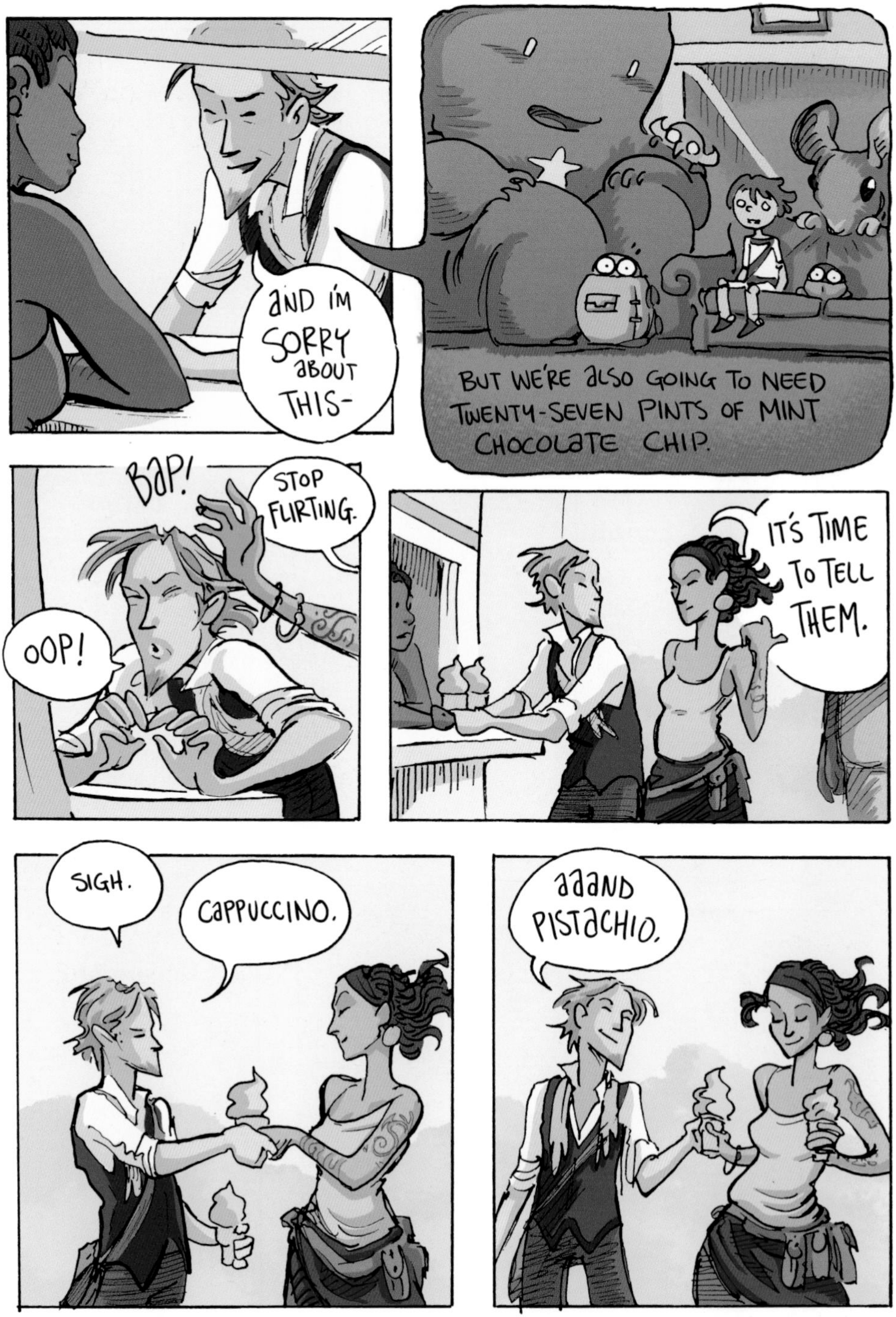
AND I'M SORRY ABOUT THIS-
BUT WE'RE ALSO GOING TO NEED TWENTY-SEVEN PINTS OF MINT CHOCOLATE CHIP.
BAP!
STOP FLIRTING.
OOP!
IT'S TIME TO TELL THEM.
SIGH.
CAPPUCCINO.
AAAND PISTACHIO.

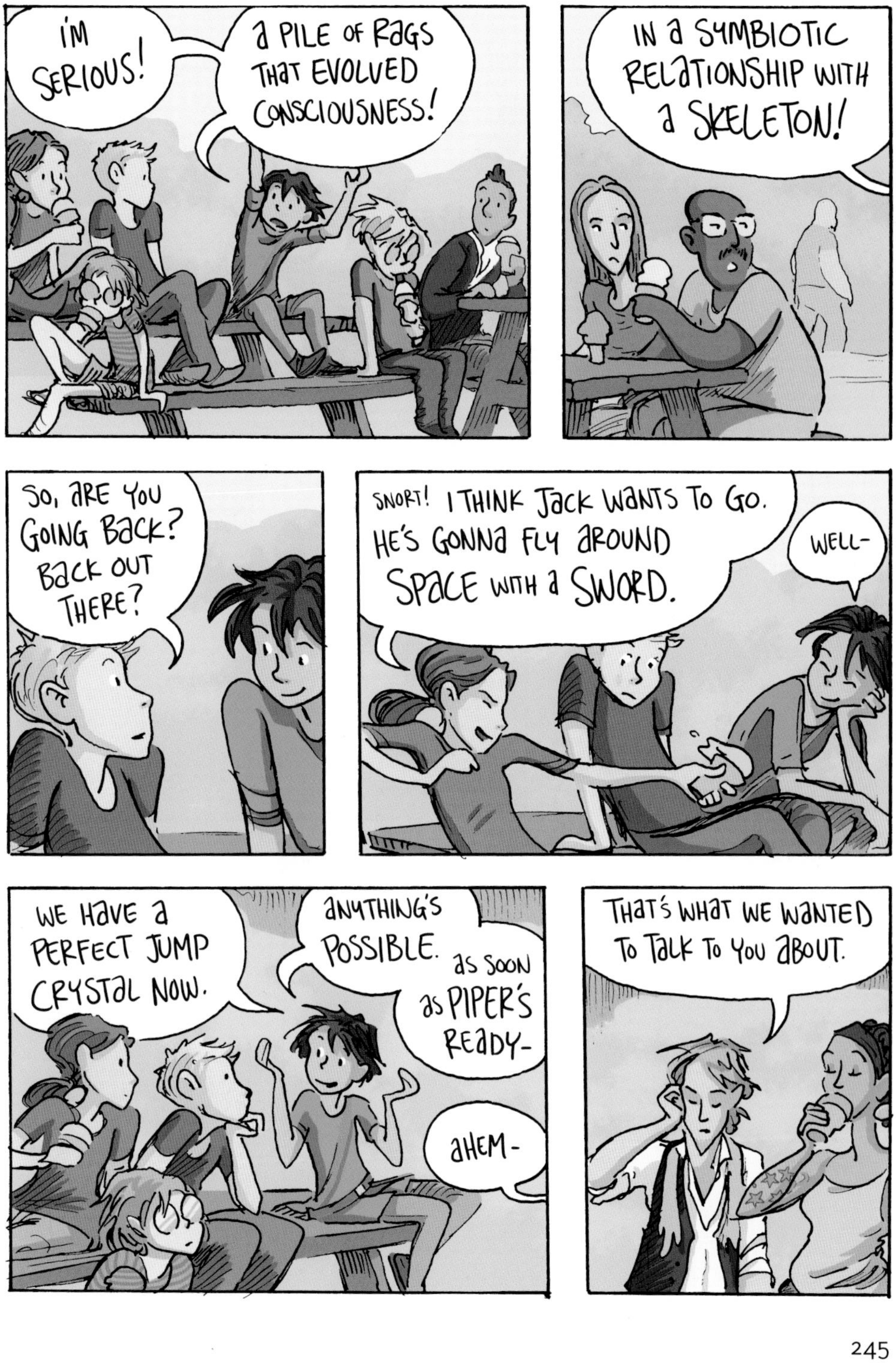
I'M SERIOUS!
A PILE OF RAGS THAT EVOLVED CONSCIOUSNESS!
IN A SYMBIOTIC RELATIONSHIP WITH A SKELETON!
SO, ARE YOU GOING BACK? BACK OUT THERE?
SNORT! I THINK JACK WANTS TO GO. HE'S GONNA FLY AROUND SPACE WITH A SWORD.
WELL-
WE HAVE A PERFECT JUMP CRYSTAL NOW.
ANYTHING'S POSSIBLE.
AS SOON AS PIPER'S READY-
AHEM-
THAT'S WHAT WE WANTED TO TALK TO YOU ABOUT.

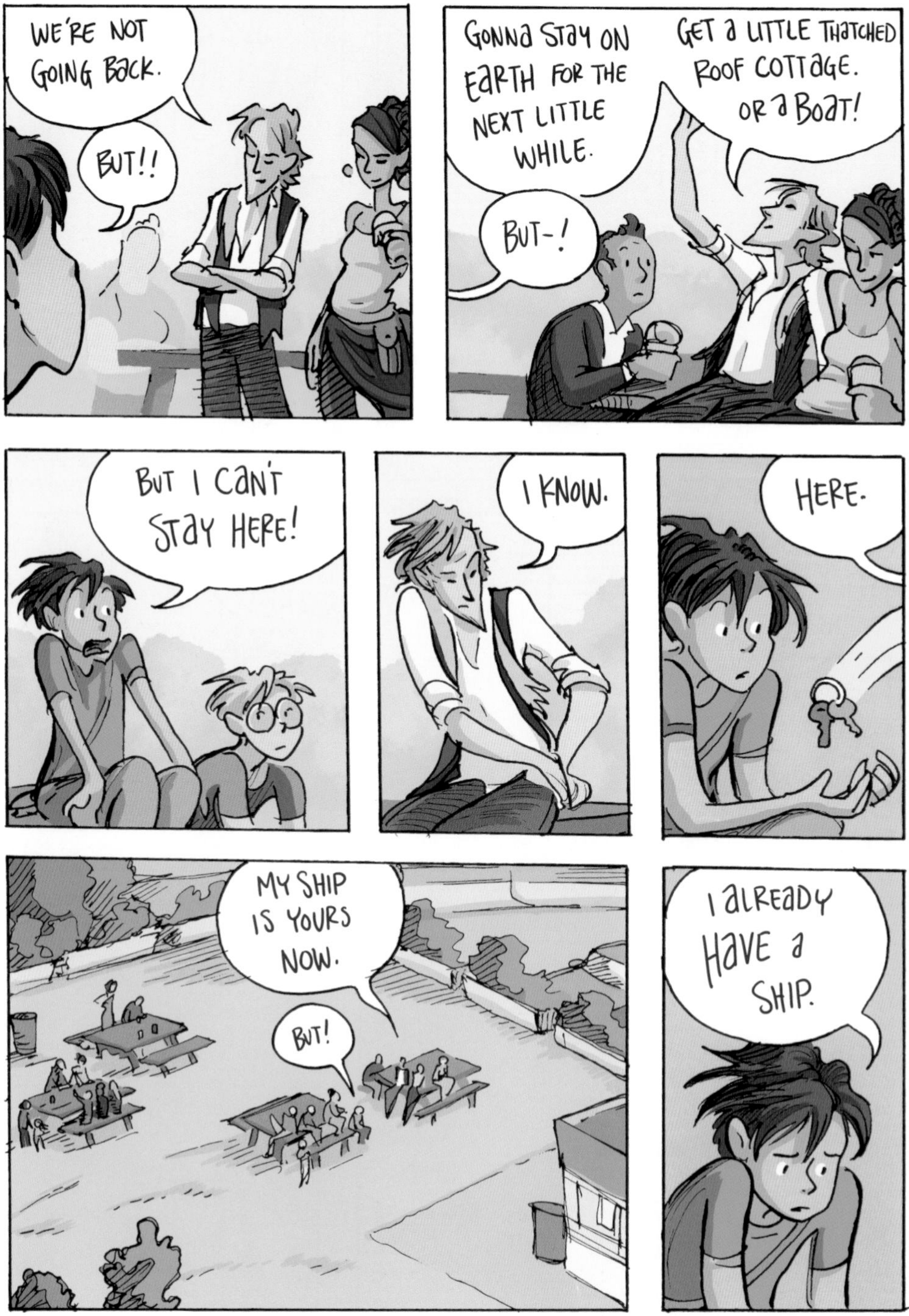
WE'RE NOT GOING BACK.
BUT!!
GONNA STAY ON EARTH FOR THE NEXT LITTLE WHILE.
GET A LITTLE THATCHED ROOF COTTAGE. OR A BOAT!
BUT-!
BUT I CAN'T STAY HERE!
I KNOW.
HERE.
MY SHIP IS YOURS NOW.
BUT!
I ALREADY HAVE A SHIP.

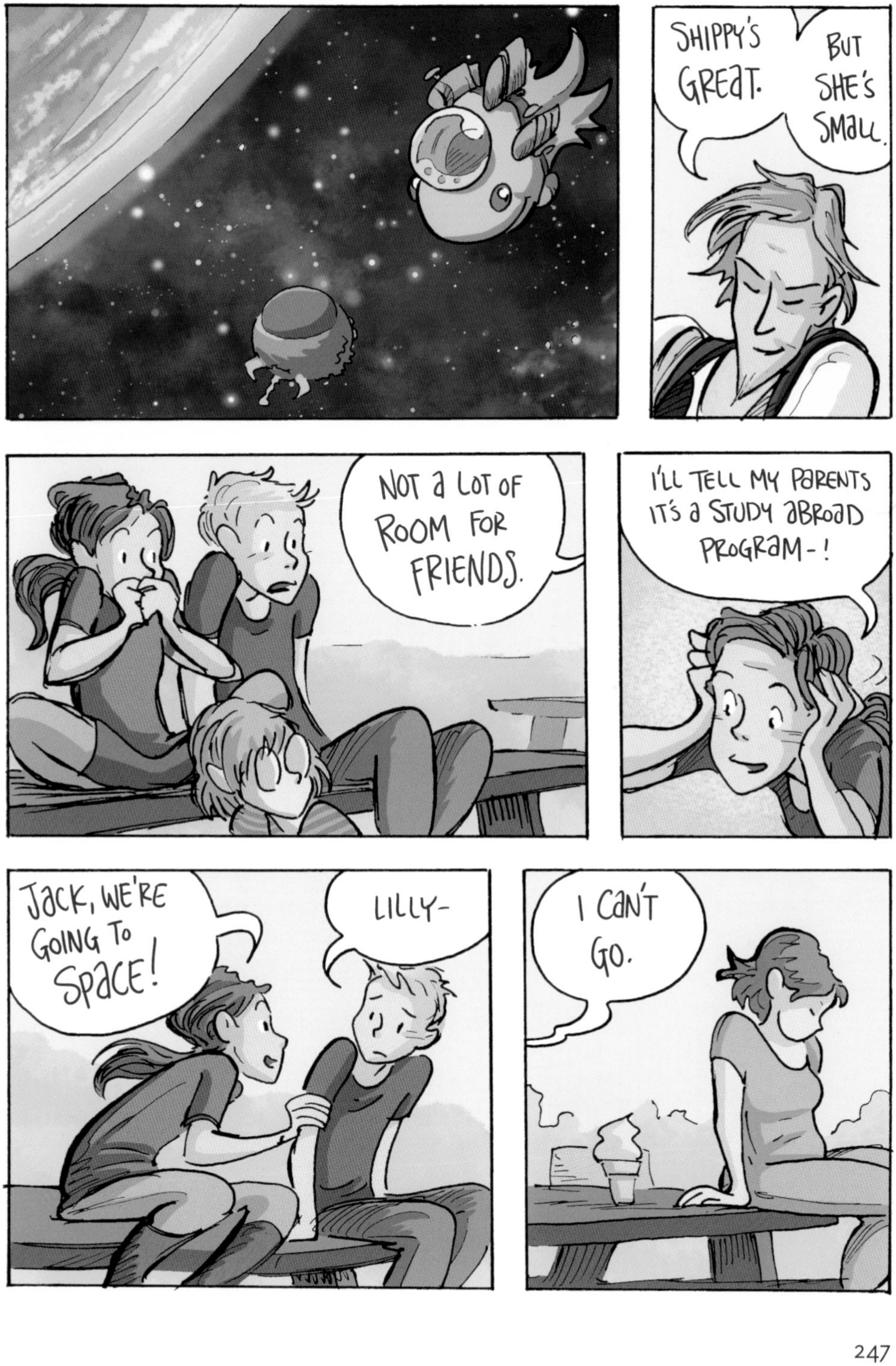
SHIPPY'S GREAT.
BUT SHE'S SMALL.
NOT A LOT OF ROOM FOR FRIENDS.
I'LL TELL MY PARENTS IT'S A STUDY ABROAD PROGRAM-!
JACK, WE'RE GOING TO SPACE!
LILLY-
I CAN'T GO.

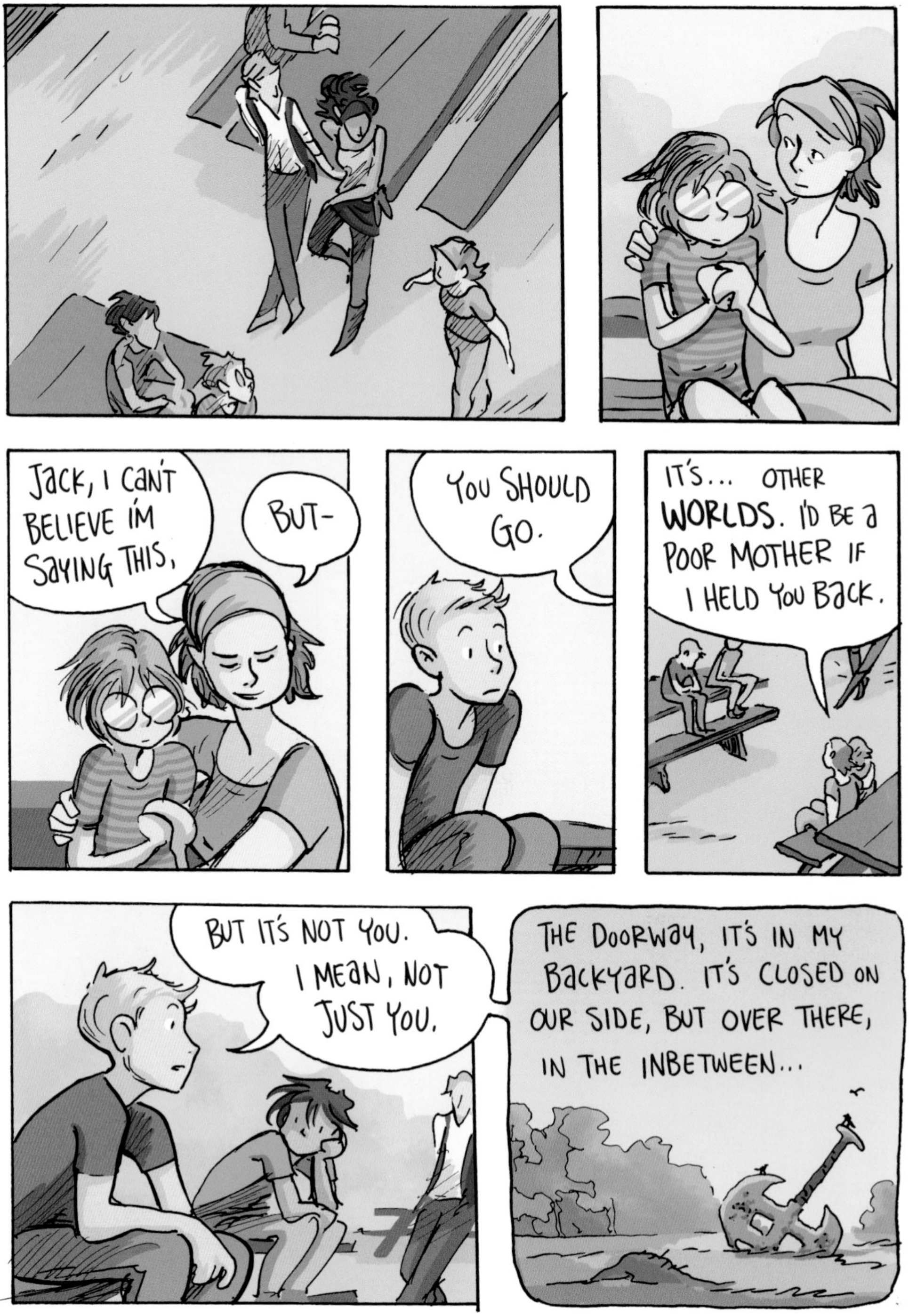
JACK, I CAN'T BELIEVE I'M SAYING THIS,
BUT-
YOU SHOULD GO.
IT'S... OTHER WORLDS. I'D BE A POOR MOTHER IF I HELD YOU BACK.
BUT IT'S NOT YOU. I MEAN, NOT JUST YOU.
THE DOORWAY, IT'S IN MY BACKYARD. IT'S CLOSED ON OUR SIDE, BUT OVER THERE, IN THE INBETWEEN...

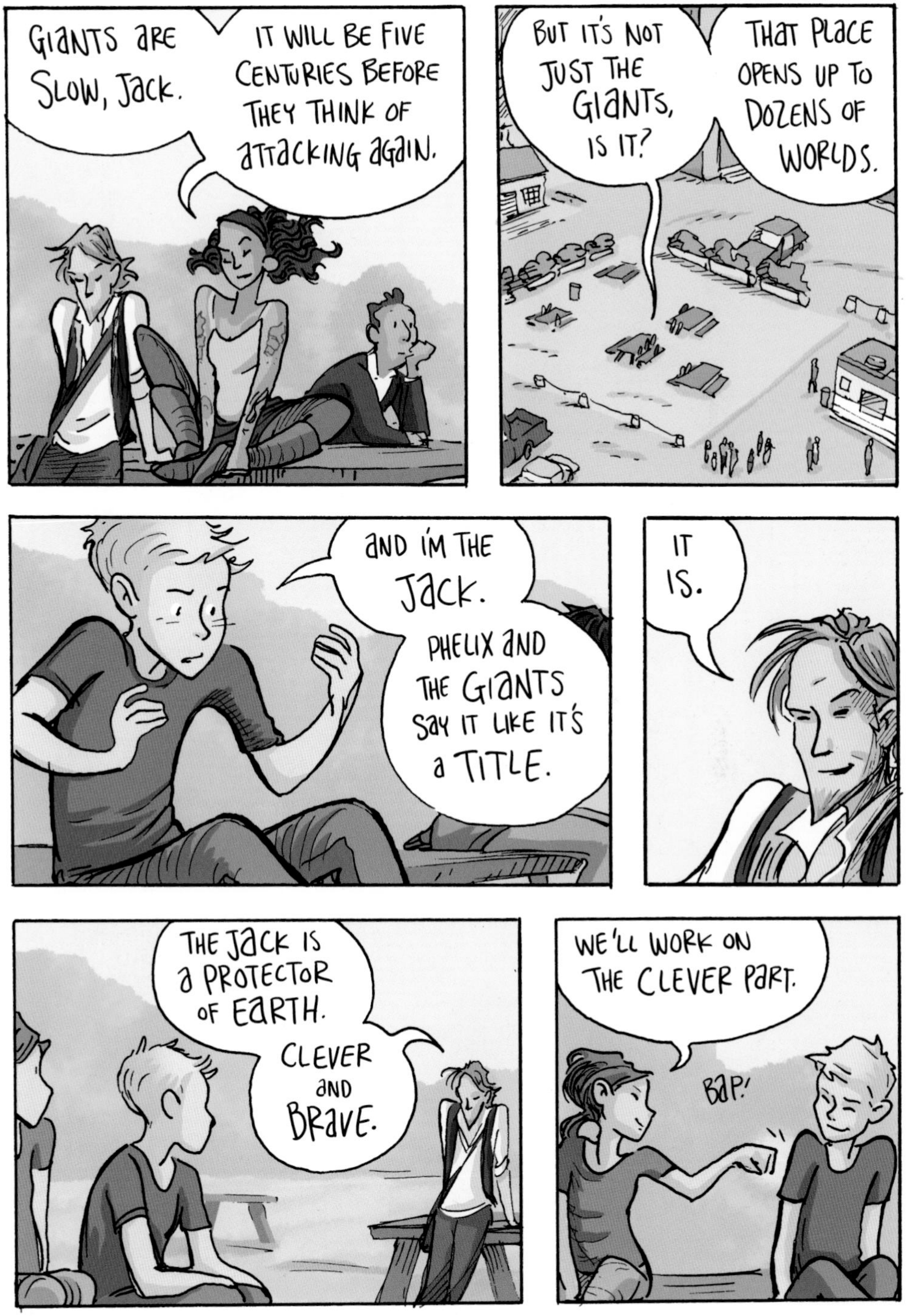
GIANTS ARE SLOW, JACK.
IT WILL BE FIVE CENTURIES BEFORE THEY THINK OF ATTACKING AGAIN.
BUT IT'S NOT JUST THE GIANTS, IS IT?
THAT PLACE OPENS UP TO DOZENS OF WORLDS.
AND I'M THE JACK.
PHELIX AND THE GIANTS SAY IT LIKE IT'S A TITLE.
IT IS.
THE JACK IS A PROTECTOR OF EARTH.
CLEVER AND BRAVE.
WE'LL WORK ON THE CLEVER PART.
BAP!

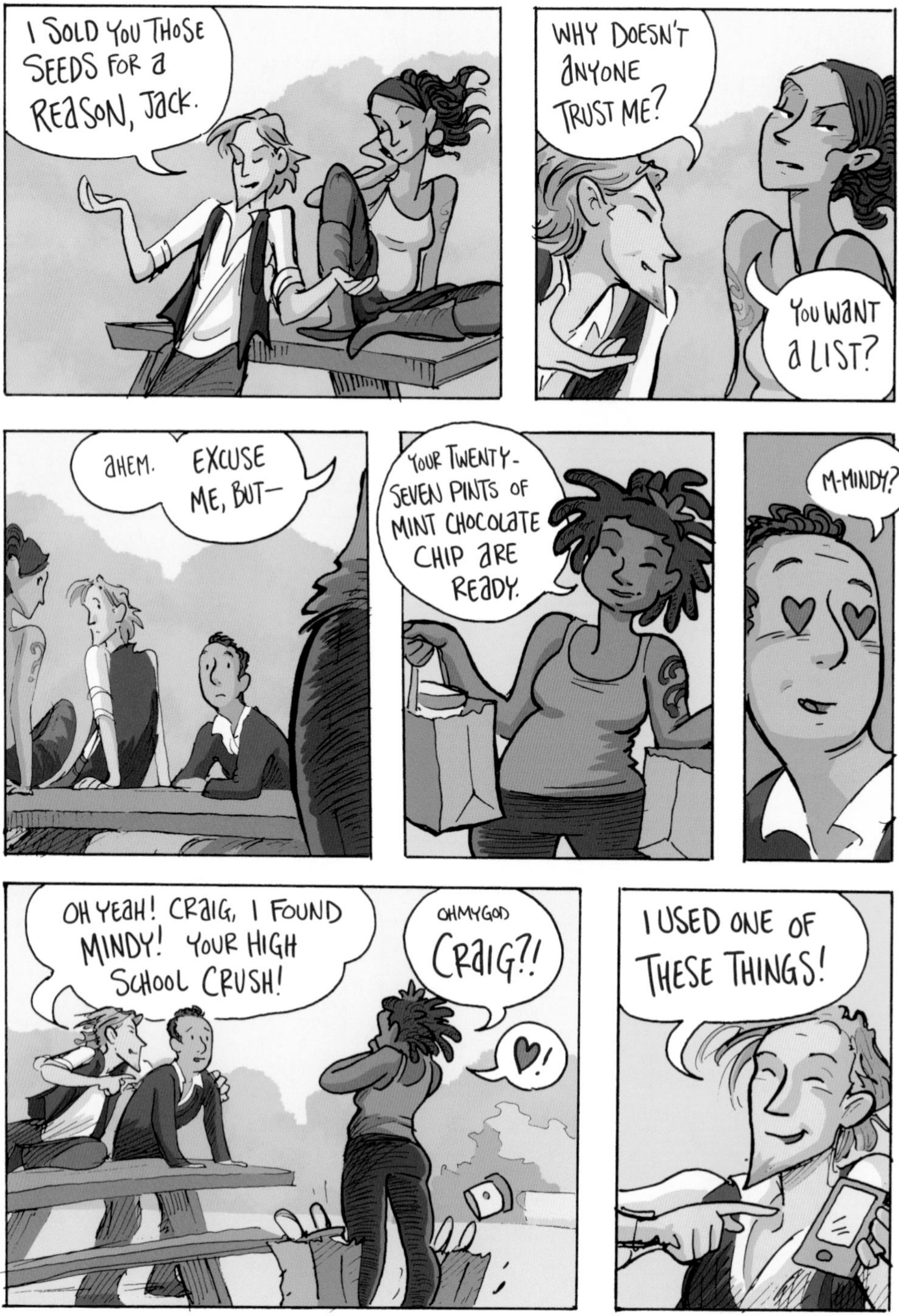
I SOLD YOU THOSE SEEDS FOR a REaSON, JaCK.
WHY DOESN'T aNYONE TRUST ME?
YOU WaNT a LIST?
aHEM.
EXCUSE ME, BUT—
YOUR TWENTY-SEVEN PINTS OF MINT CHOCOLaTE CHIP aRE READY.
M-MINDY?
OH YEaH! CRaIG, I FOUND MINDY! YOUR HIGH SCHOOL CRUSH!
OHMYGOD
CRaIG?!
!
I USED ONE OF THESE THINGS!

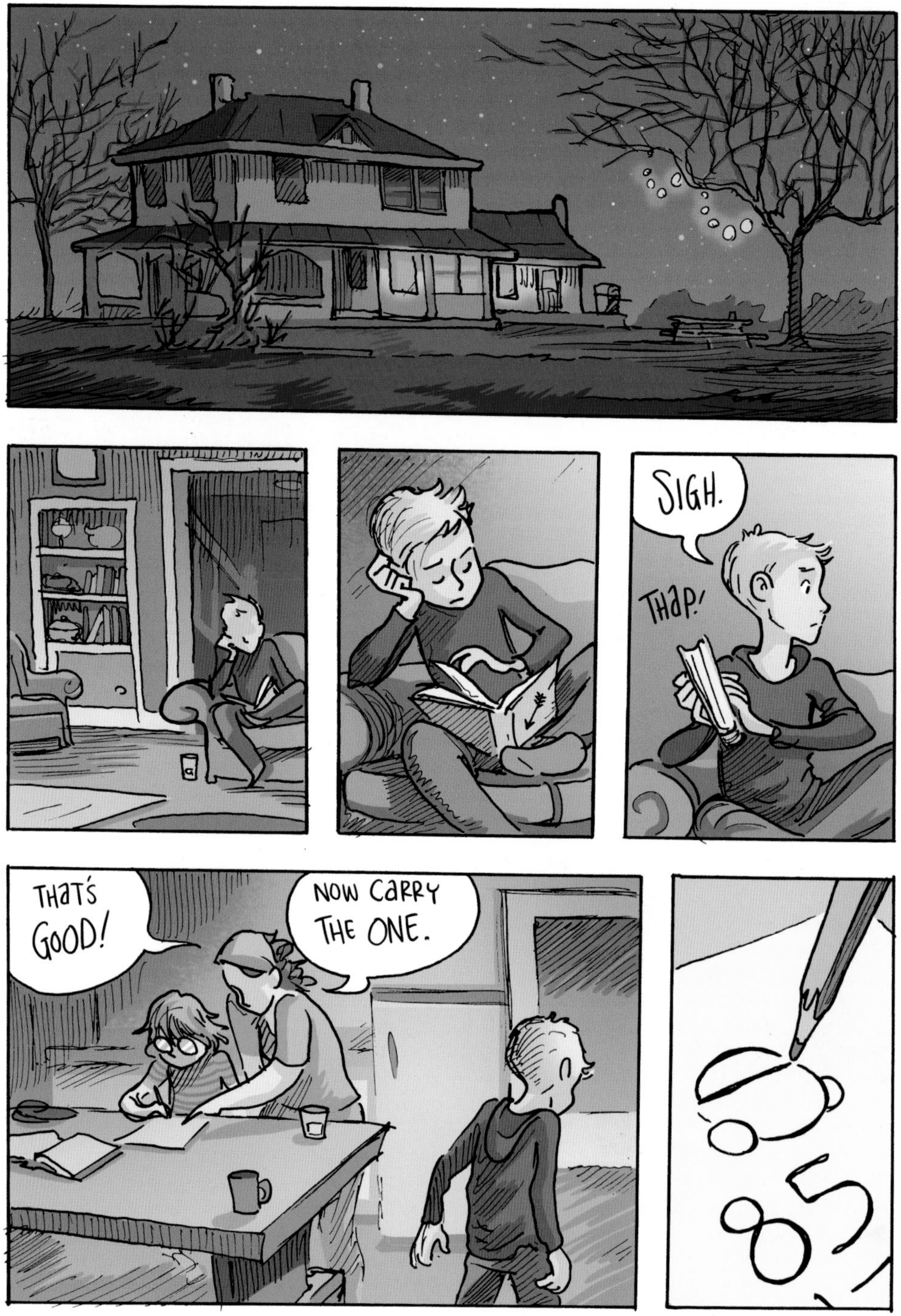
SIGH.
THAP!
THAT'S GOOD!
NOW CARRY THE ONE.

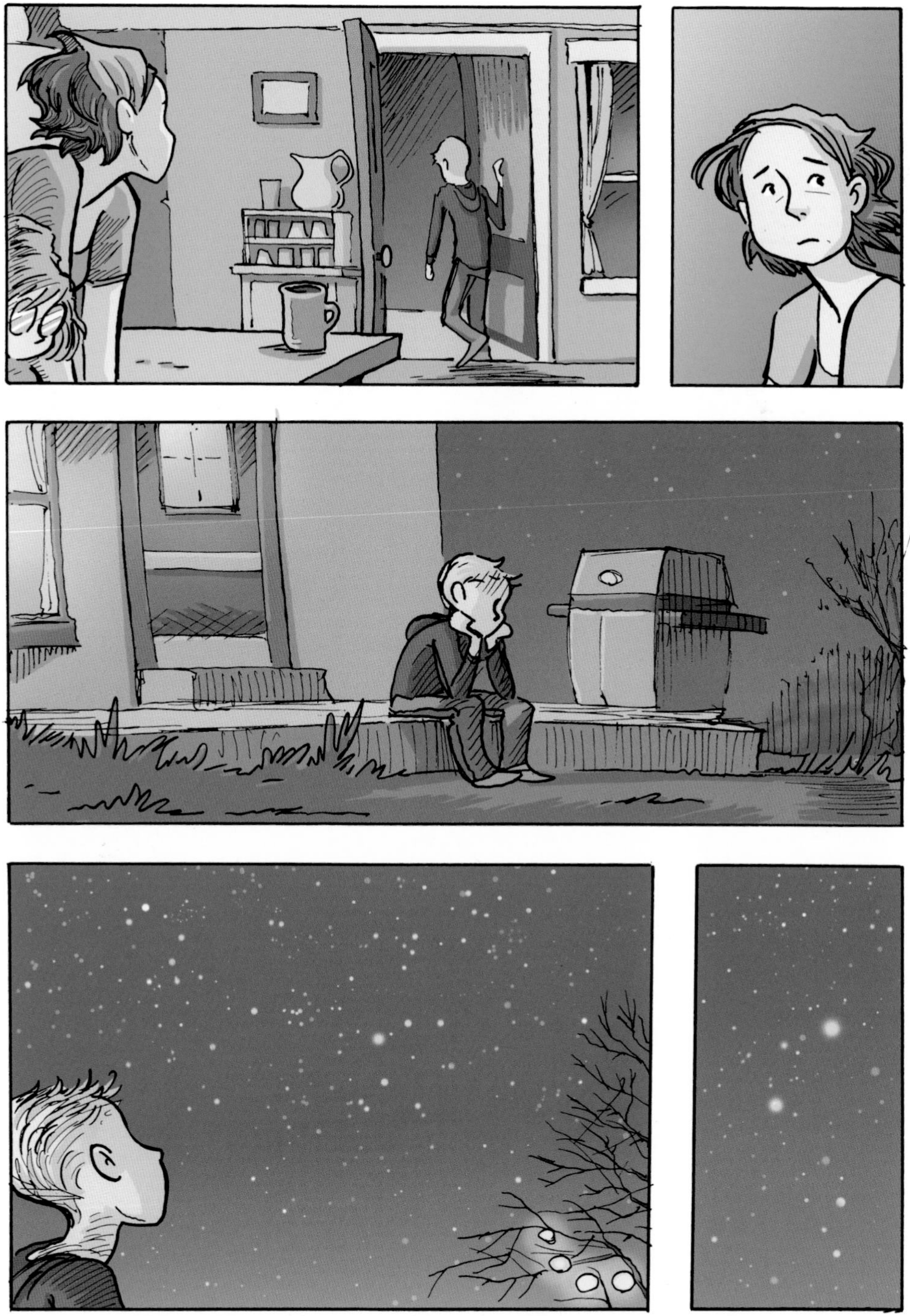

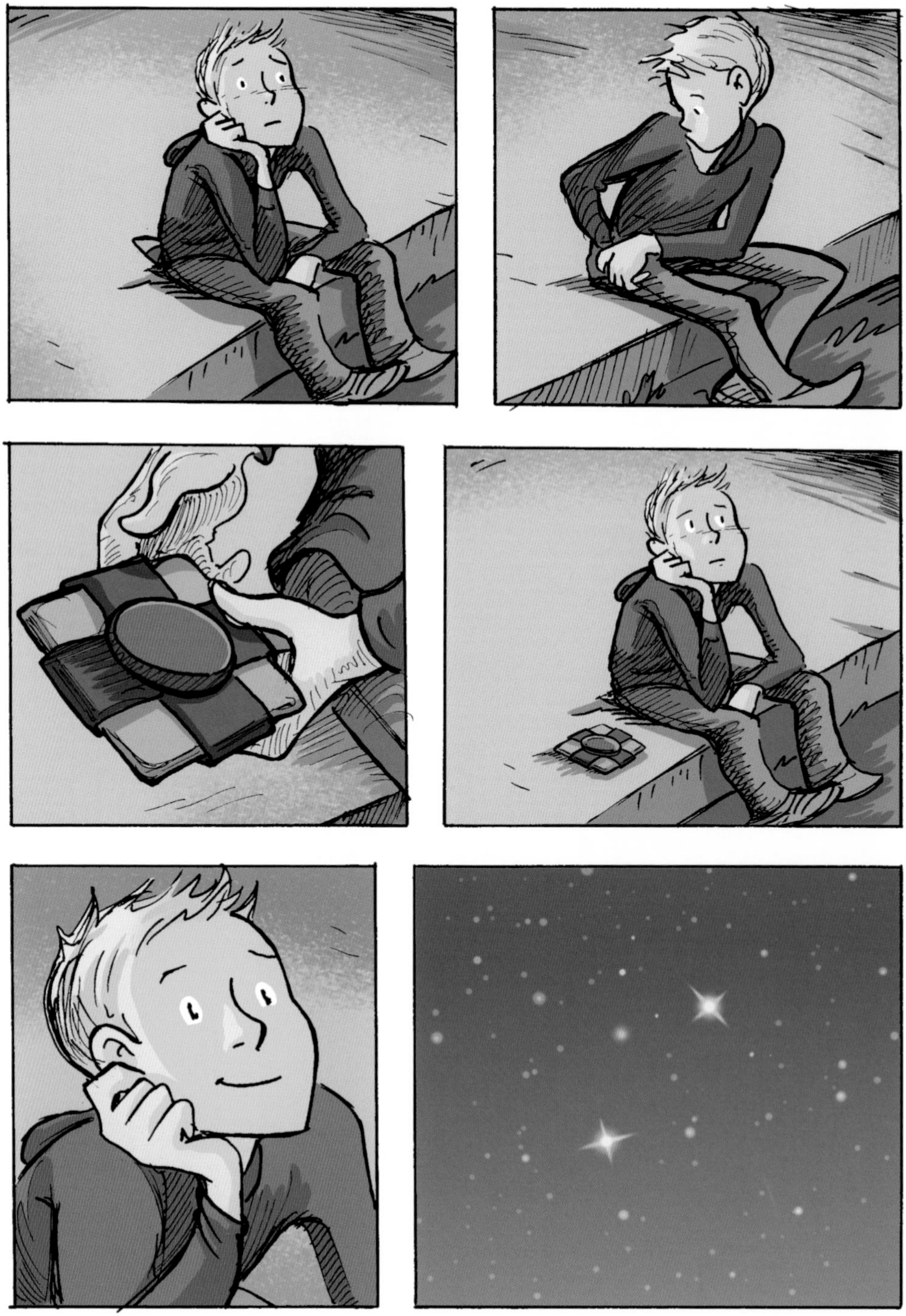

THE
END

THE ORIGIN AND EVOLUTION OF MIGHTY JACK

As best I can remember, I started working on the beginnings of the story that would become *Mighty Jack* in 2006. That's right, I started working on Jack's story *ten years* before the first book was released. Some stories arrive all in a rush; others grow more slowly. I think this story needed a decade to develop.

At that time, my family lived in a tiny little box of a house just a stone's throw from the Shenandoah River. I remember I had just moved my drawing board out of our gloomy, cinderblock basement and into a sunny upstairs room with a window that looked right out over our garden. My wife had planted the garden, and in the steamy Virginia summer it had grown into a scrappy, tangled beast of a thing. I was doing mostly freelance design work at the time, but the garden was where my eyes turned when I daydreamed.

Ten years!

Ten years of development means that the story went through a lot of changes, particularly in its visual development and character design. (Maddy, for instance, started out as a pig-tailed six-year-old!) Of course, throughout those ten years I was also developing the stories of a certain spacegirl, often in the very same notebooks. Looking back, the intersection of those stories' worlds seems inevitable.

Here, then, on the following pages, is a look at how the characters, creatures, and world of Mighty Jack, and the world of Zita the Spacegirl, have changed through the years . . .

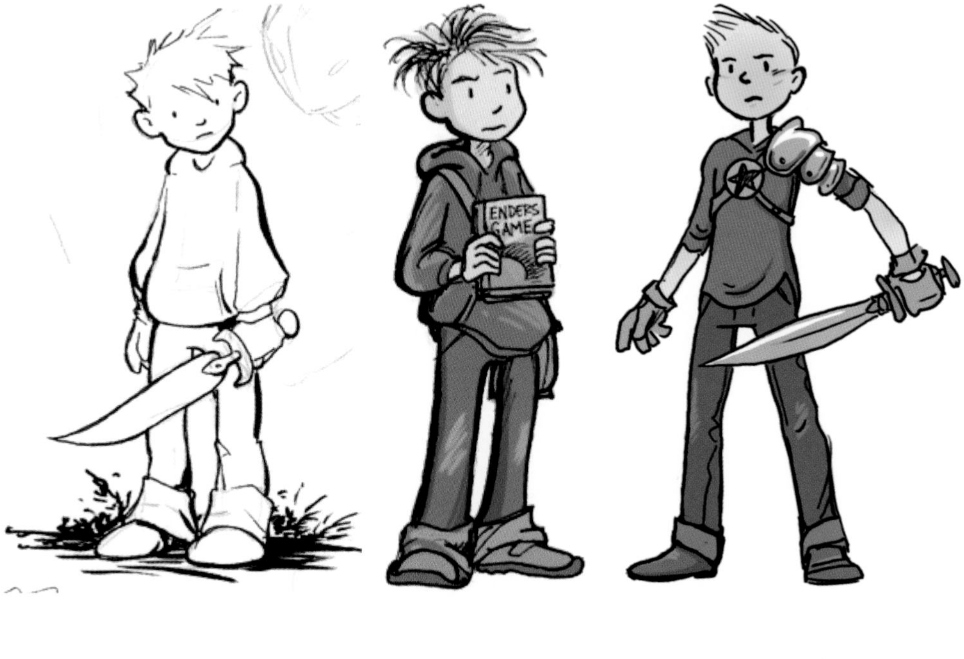
ENDERS
GAME

VEGGIE
THAT BRINGS
TURNIPS

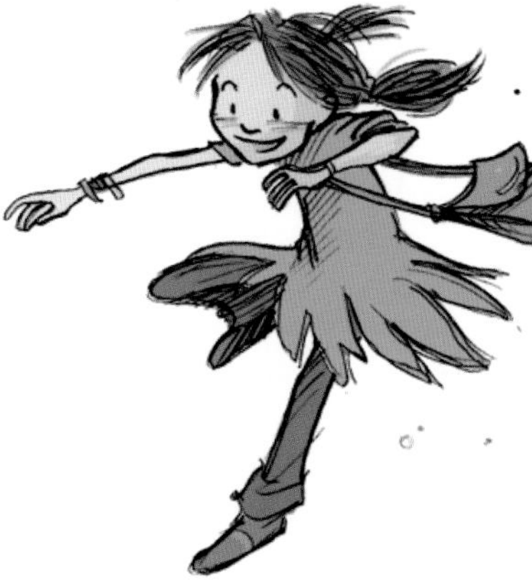

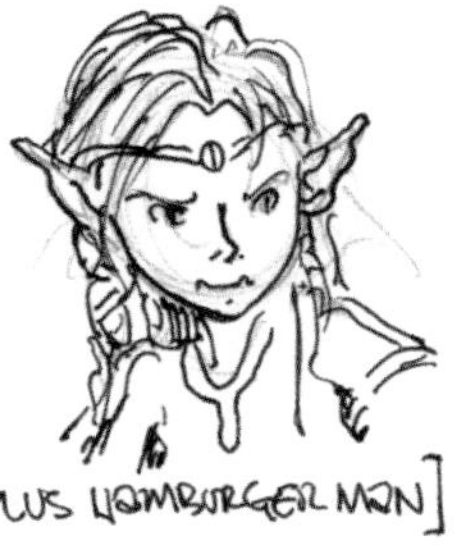
[PLUS HAMBURGER MAN]

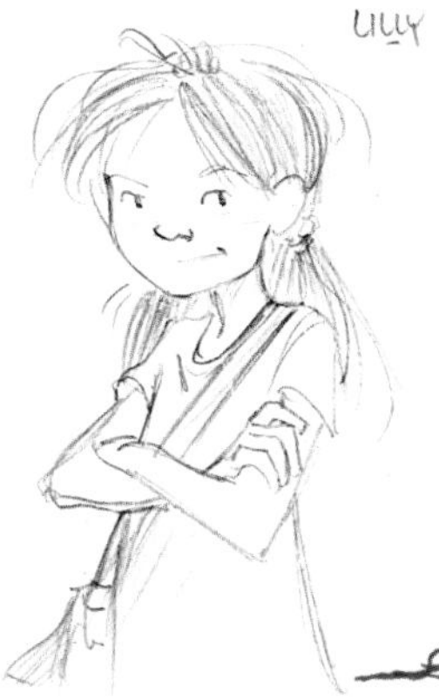
LILLY

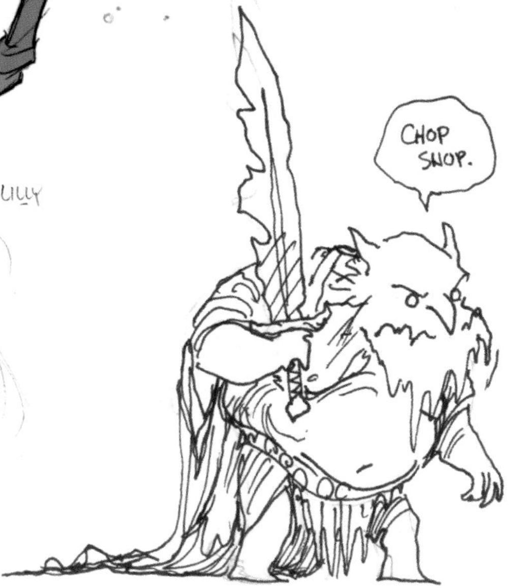
CHOP SNOP.

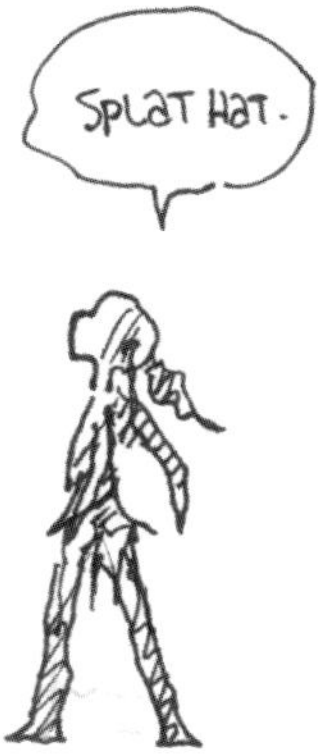
SPLAT HAT.

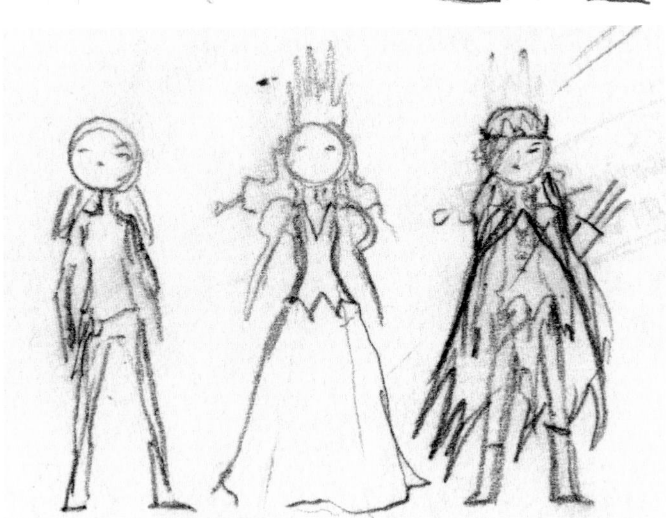

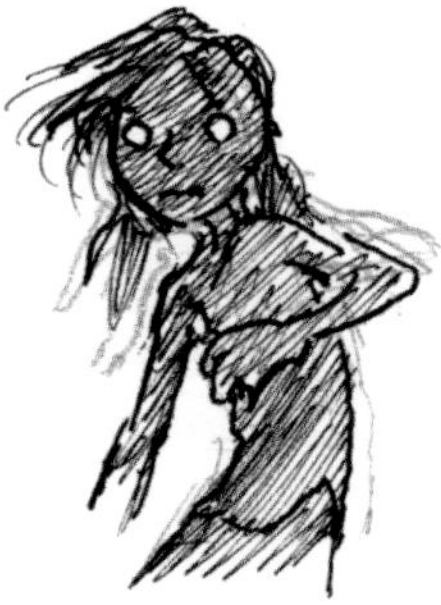

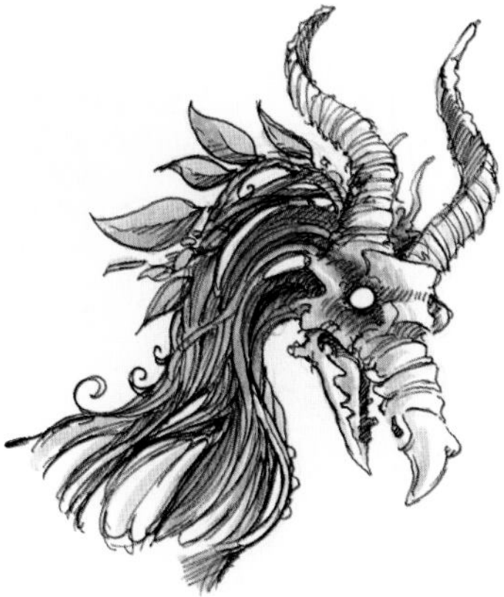

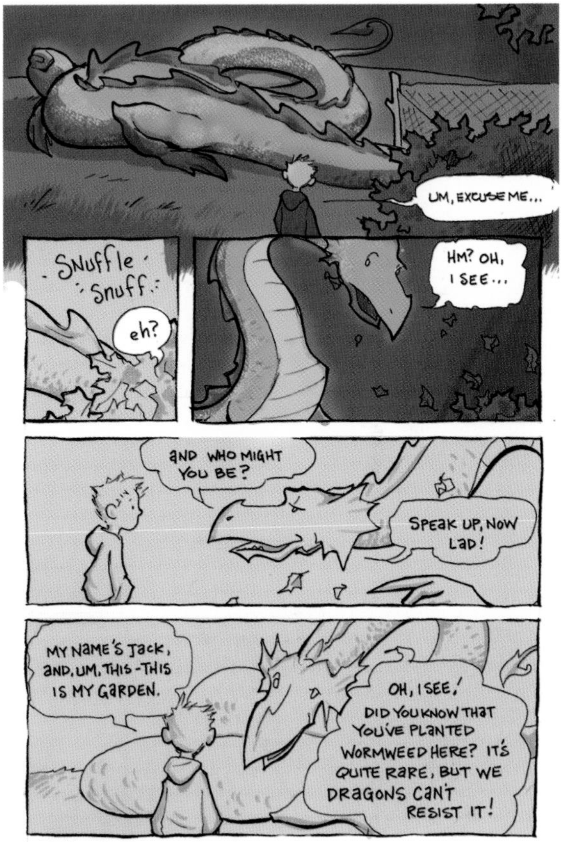

UM, EXCUSE ME...
SNuffle Snuff
eh?
HM? OH, I SEE...
and WHO MIGHT YOU BE?
SPeak UP, NOW Lad!
MY NAME'S Jack, and, UM, THIS-THIS IS MY GaRDEN.
OH, I SEE! DID YOU KNOW THAT YOU'VE PLANTED WORMWEED HERE? IT'S QUITE RaRE, BUT WE DRaGONS CaN'T RESIST IT!

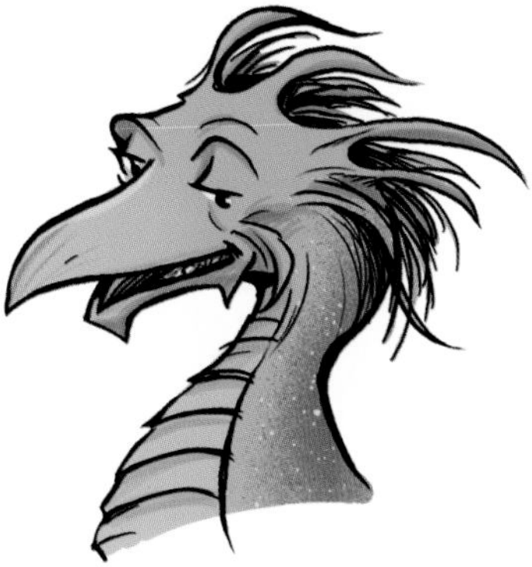

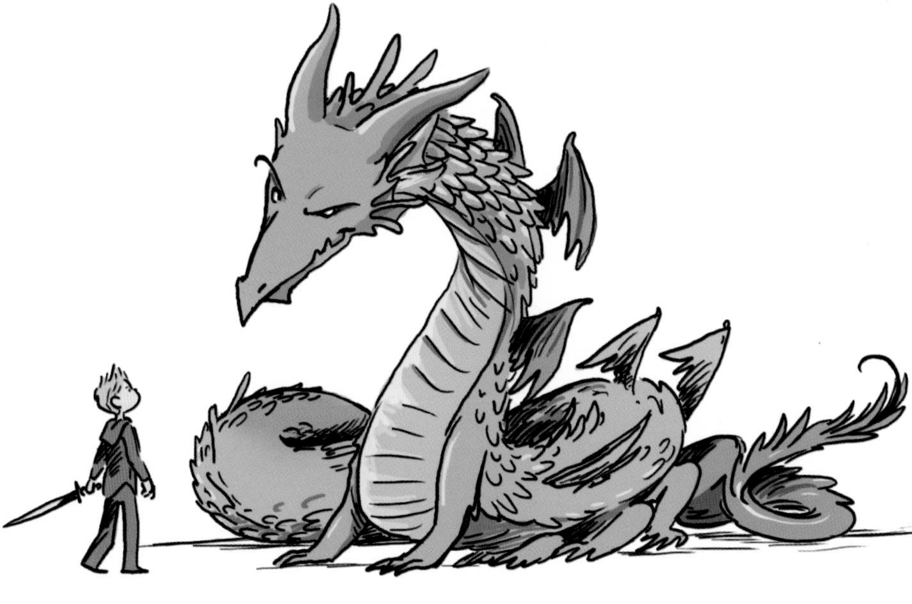

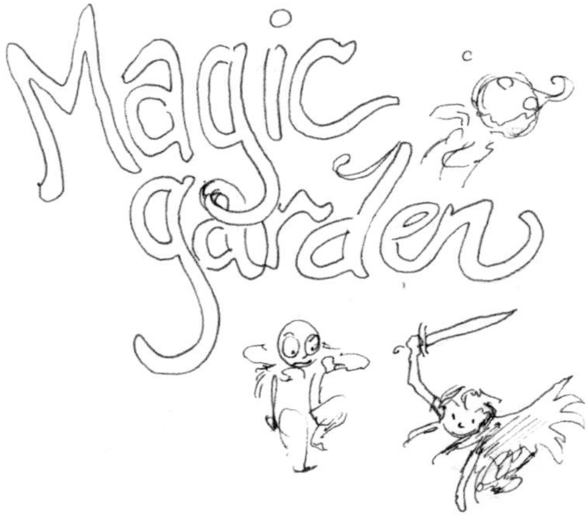
Magic garden

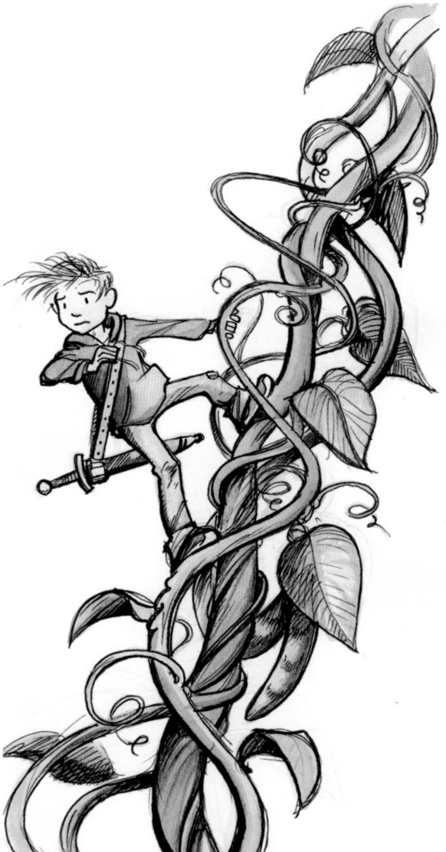

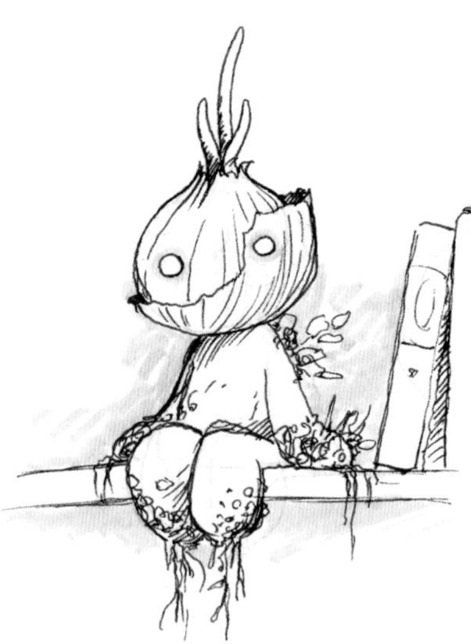

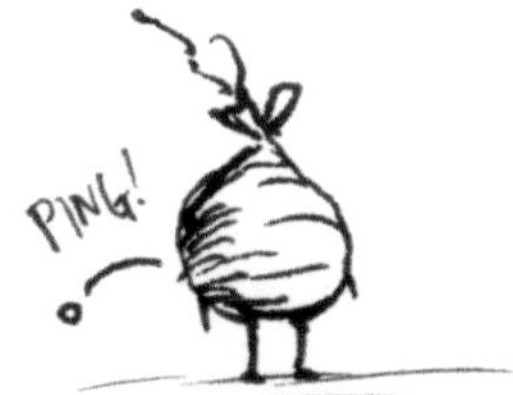
PING!

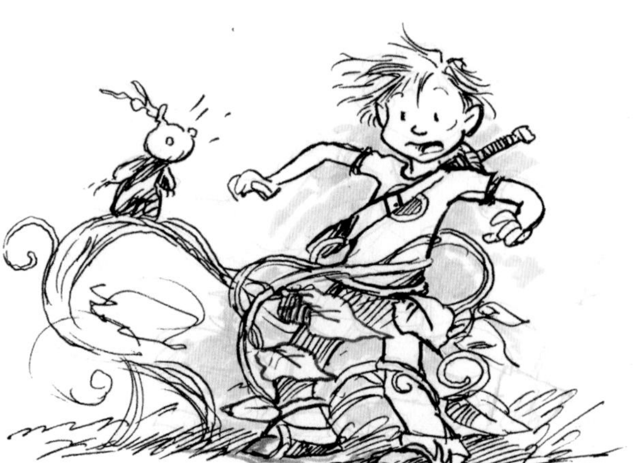

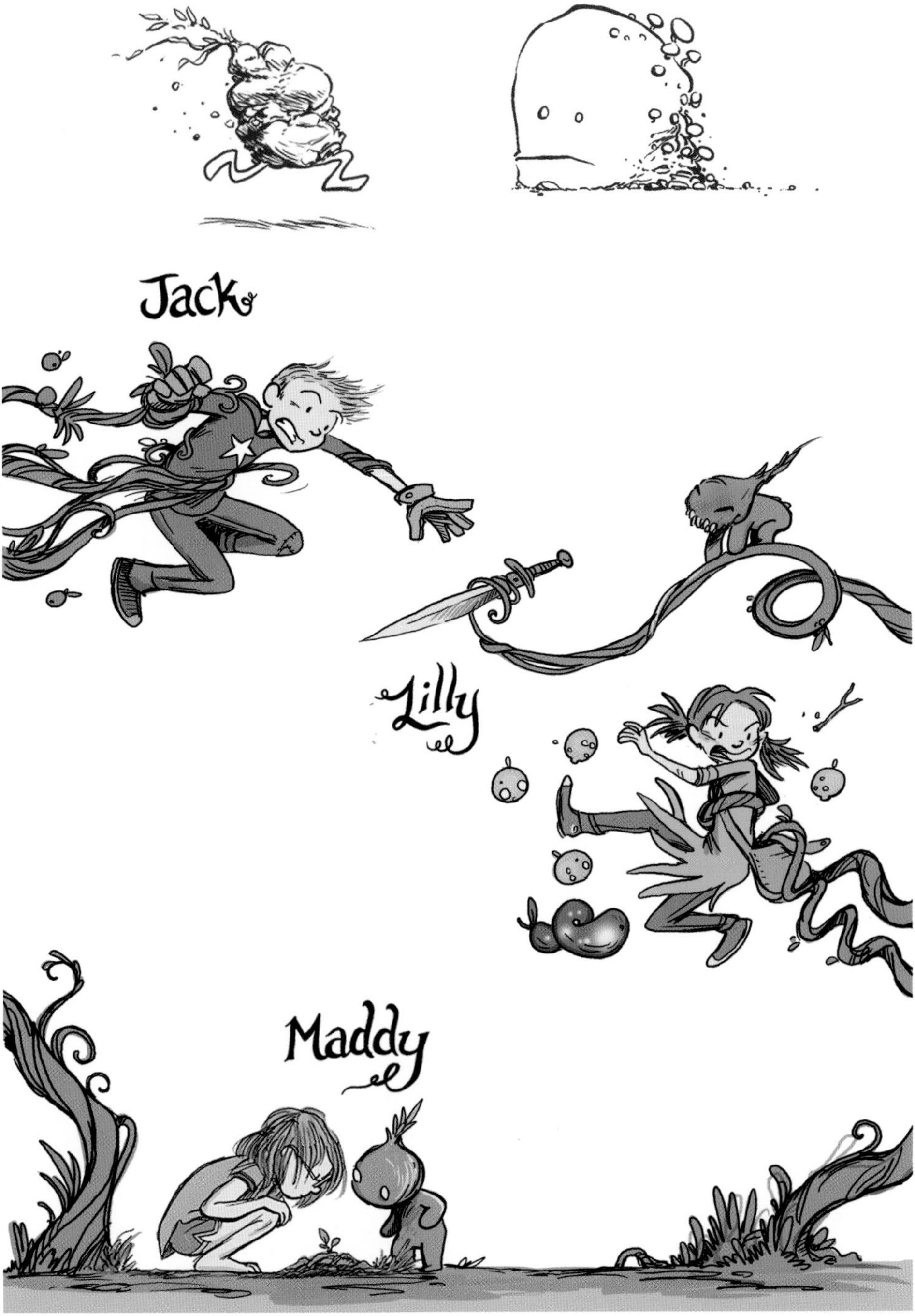
Jack
Lilly
Maddy

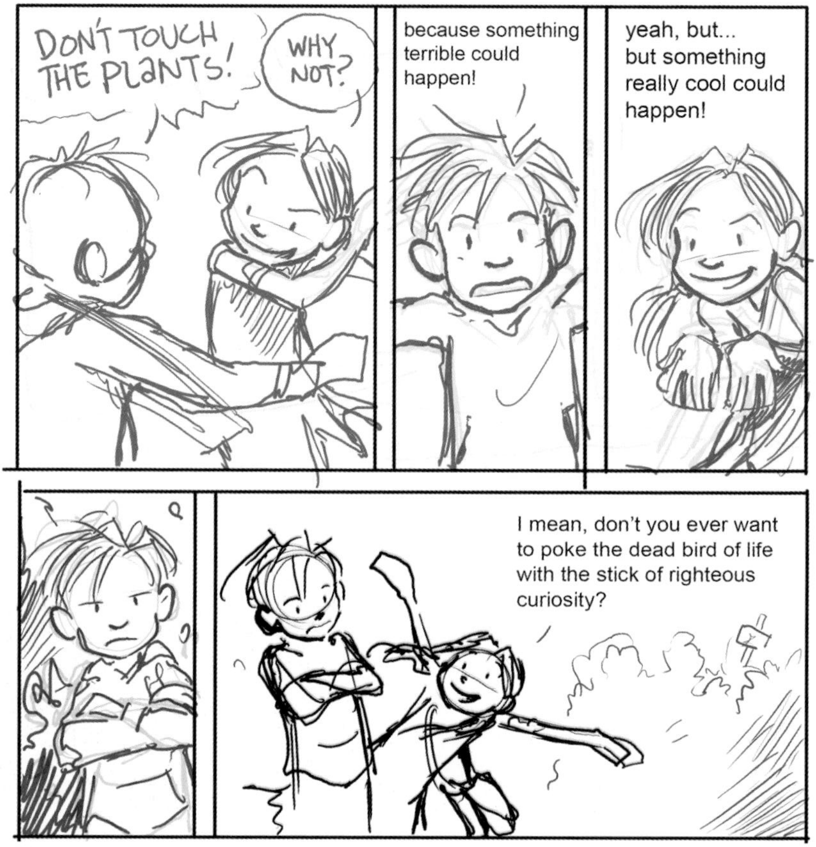
DON'T TOUCH THE PLANTS!
WHY NOT?
because something terrible could happen!
yeah, but... but something really cool could happen!
I mean, don't you ever want to poke the dead bird of life with the stick of righteous curiosity?

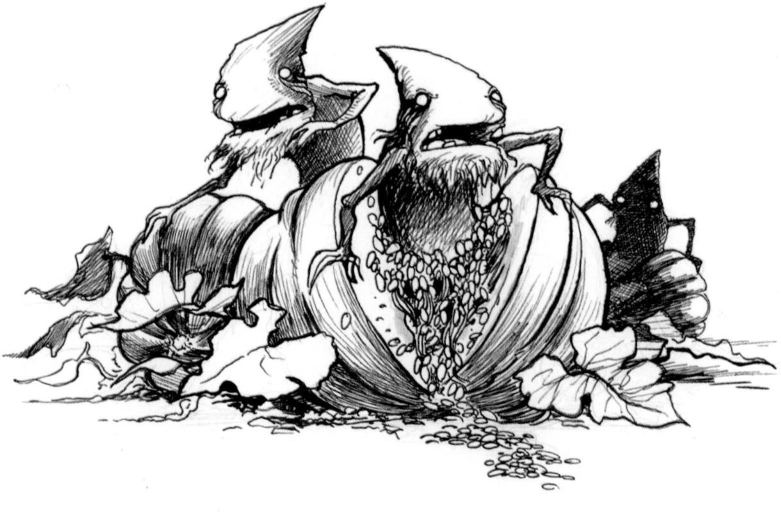

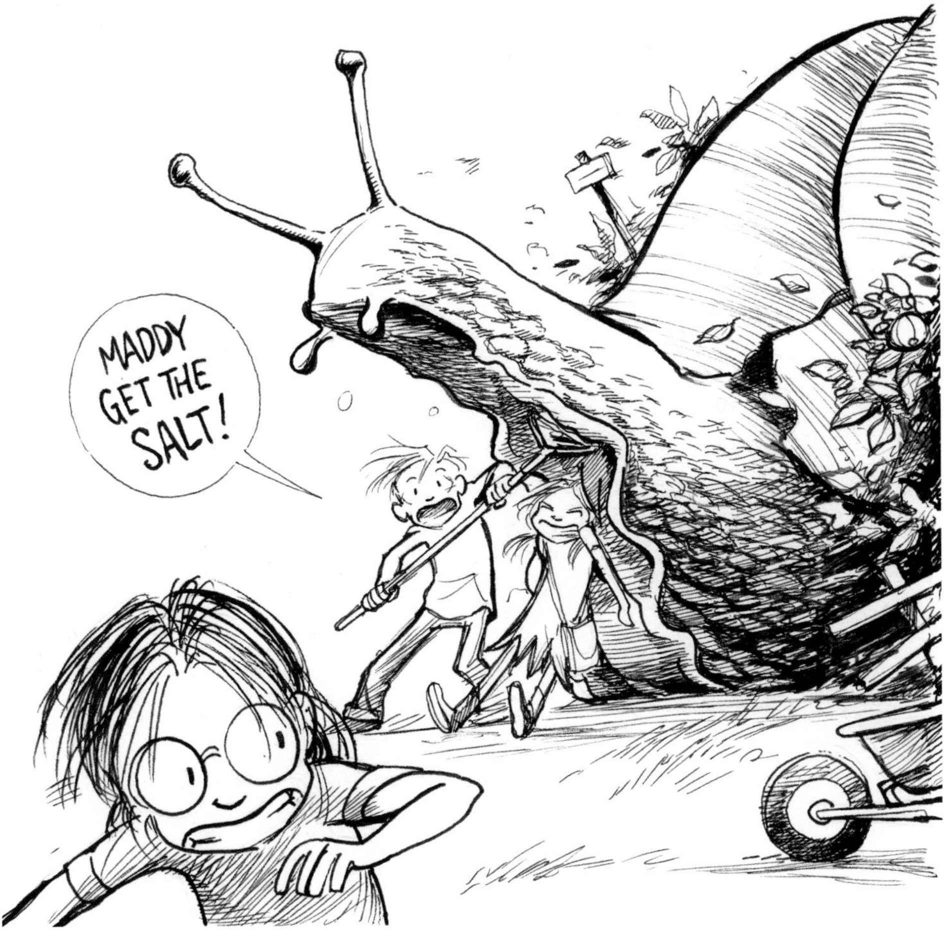
MADDY GET THE SALT!

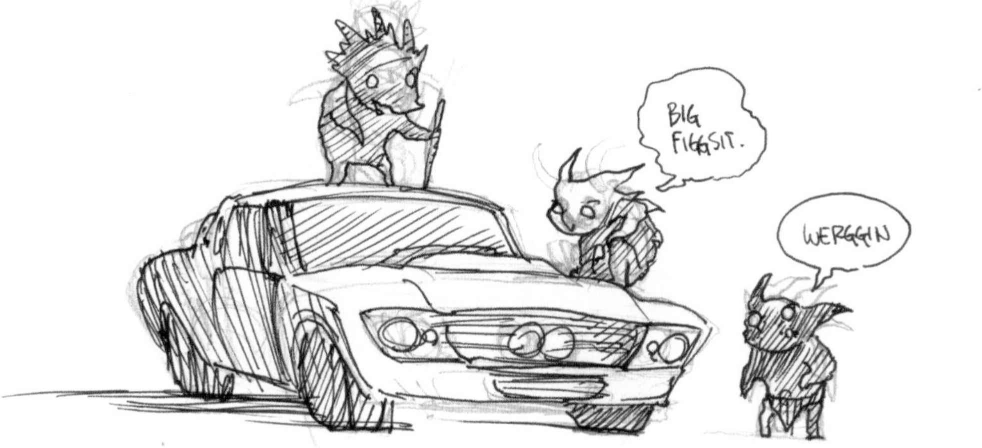
BIG FIGGSIT.
WERGGIN

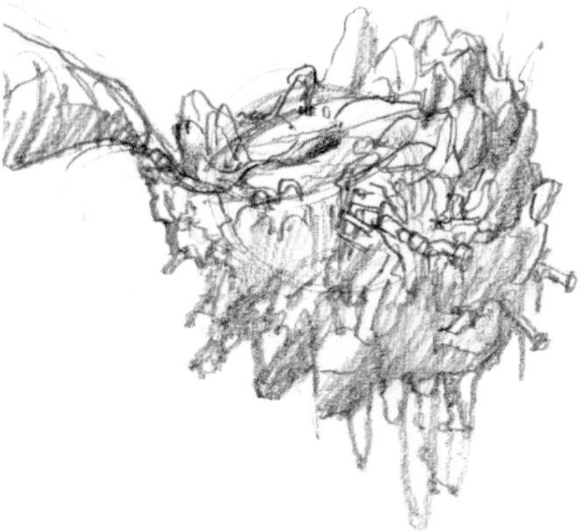

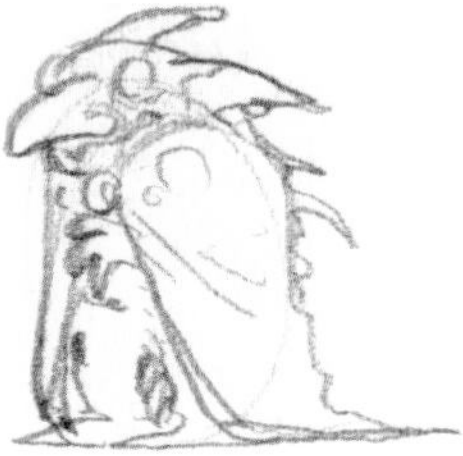

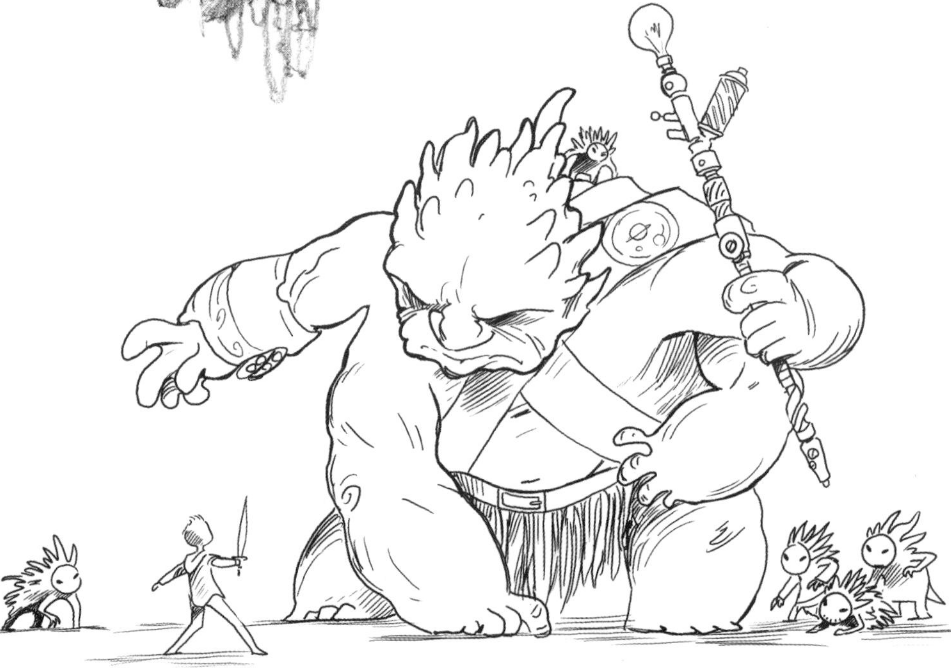

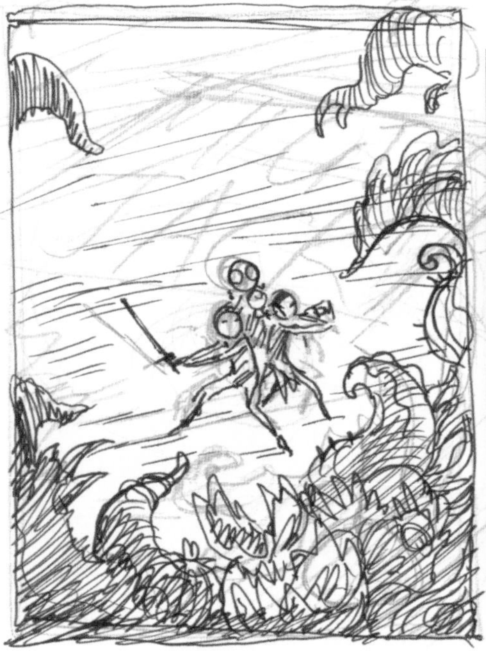

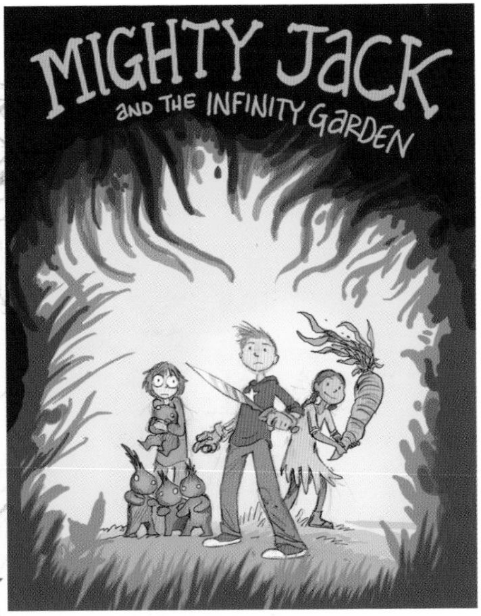
MIGHTY JACK
and THE INFINITY GARDEN

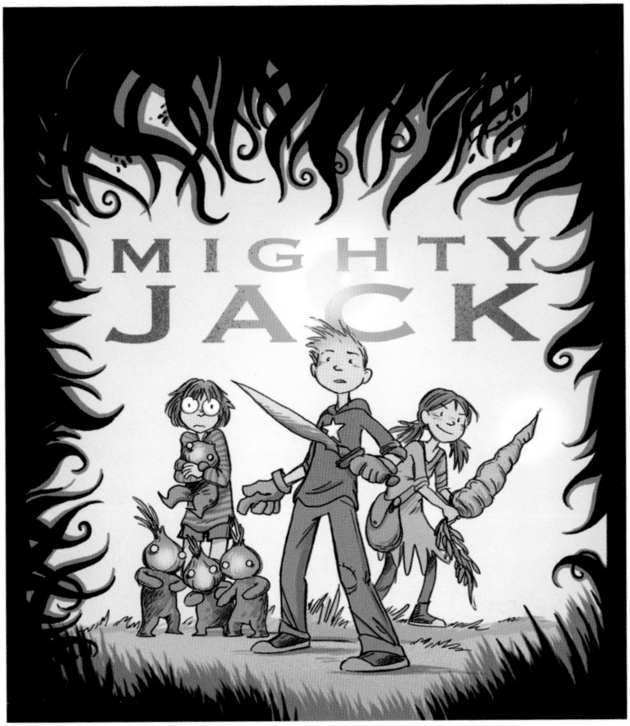
MIGHTY
JACK

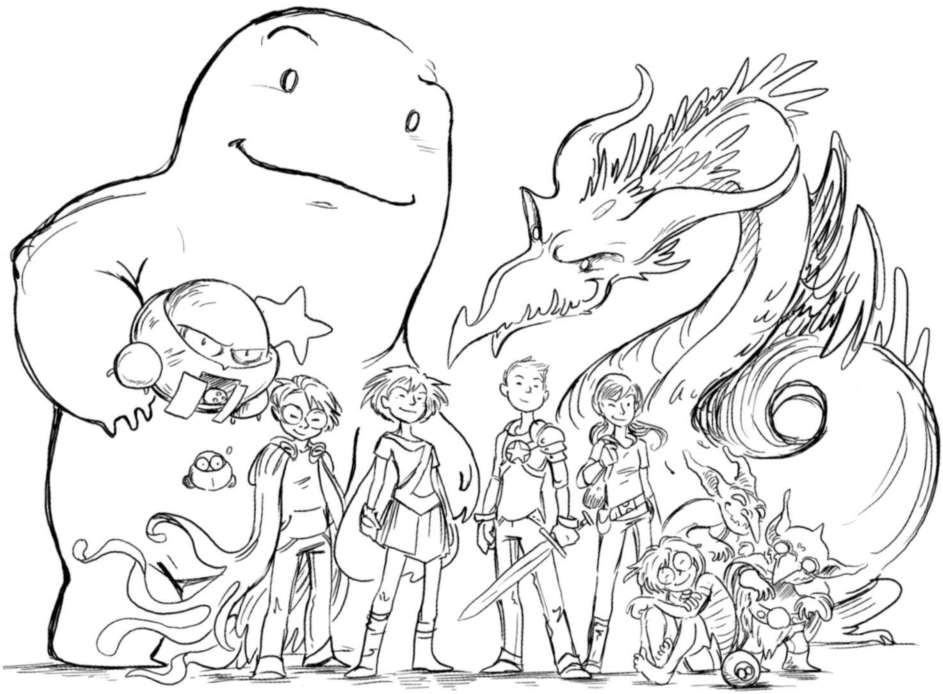

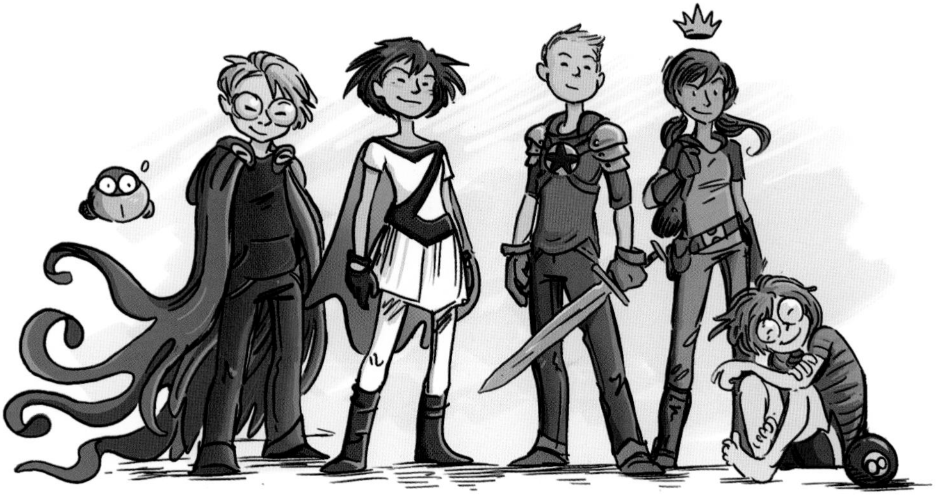

ACKNOWLEDGMENTS

It feels like I worked on this book all over the world.

I began drawing the layouts during a surprise blizzard that trapped me, for one perfect, silent day, in a little cabin outside of Portland, Maine. (Thanks, Julia Colvin and Deanne Gouzie!)

I drew a couple of the early pages, surrounded by some of my Very Best Artist Friends, in a lodge outside of Juneau, Alaska. (Thanks Pat Race and co.!)

I drew more of the early pages in my own little studio, next to the rambly farmhouse in the Shenandoah Valley that I call home. (Thanks, dear Anna! And Angelica and Zita and Julia and Ronia and Ida and Pepper! [Pepper's the dog.])

But I drew the bulk of the pages for this book in the village of Gravagna Montale, way up in the Apennine Mountains in Italy. I have tremendous gratitude for all the people of the village who showed me such kindness and interest, particularly Teresa, Sara, Carla, "Galileo," Paulo, Other Paulo, and Mafalda.

Thanks to everyone who read the first inks, particularly Andy O'Neill, who pointed out some places where the action was hard to follow. Oh, and another big thank-you to my daughter Zita, because she gave me some very good advice about the ending.

And, of course, thanks to my agent, Judy Hansen, my publisher, Mark Seigel, and my lovely editor, Calista Brill. Oh, and big bonus thanks to my interim editor, Rachel Stark, and a sage nod of the head to my copyeditor, Kat Kopit, who's been watching over my work since the first Zita book.

And, lastly, thanks to cousins Flavia and Ida Bertolini, keepers of the bright yellow house in Gravagna, whose peaceful veranda I'm sitting on right now as I write these acknowledgments.

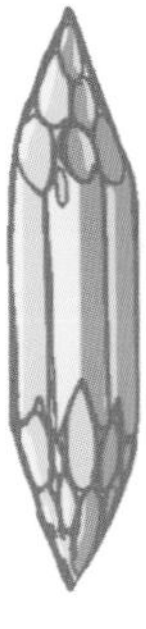
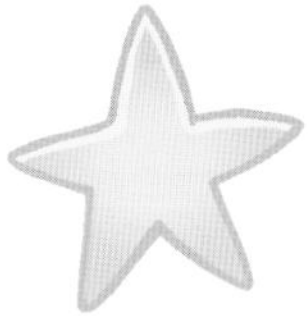
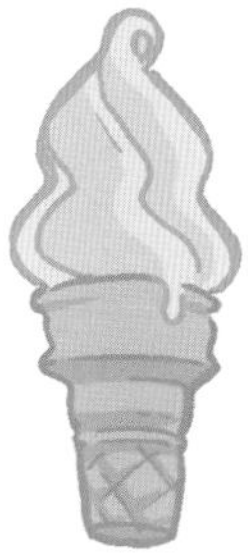

First Second

Copyright © 2019 by Ben Hatke
Published by First Second
First Second is an imprint of Roaring Brook Press,
a division of Holtzbrinck Publishing
Holdings Limited Partnership
120 Broadway, New York, NY 10271

Don't miss your next favorite book from First Second!
For the latest updates go to firstsecondnewsletter.com and sign up for our enewsletter.

Library of Congress Control Number: 2018953659

Hardcover ISBN: 978-1-250-19172-4
Paperback ISBN: 978-1-250-19173-1

Our books may be purchased in bulk for promotional, educational, or business use. Please contact your
local bookseller or the Macmillan Corporate and Premium Sales Department at (800) 221-7945 ext. 5442
or by email at MacmillanSpecialMarkets@macmillan.com.

First edition, 2019
Edited by Calista Brill and Rachel Stark
Book design by Andrew Arnold and Joyana McDiarmid
Colors by Alex Campbell and Hilary Sycamore of Sky Blue Ink
Printed in China by Toppan Leefung Printing Ltd.,
Dongguan City, Guangdong Province

Penciled in light blue or light red colored pencils (Crayola or Giotto Supermina). Inked on laser printer paper with Sakura
Pigma Microns and Pentel Pocket Brush Pens. Colored digitally in Photoshop.

Hardcover: 10 9 8 7 6 5 4 3
Paperback: 10 9 8 7